Glittering Images
Glamorous Powers

BY THE SAME AUTHOR

Ultimate Prizes

Scandalous Risks

Mystical Paths

Glittering Images
Glamorous Powers

Susan Howatch

Diamond Books
An Imprint of HarperCollins Publishers,
77–85 Fulham Palace Road
Hammersmith, London W6 8JB

This Diamond Books Omnibus edition first published 1994

Glittering Images © Leaftree Ltd 1987
Glamorous Powers © Leaftree Ltd 1988
Extracts from *The Bishoprick Papers, Letters of Herbert Hensley Henson, More Letters
of Herbert Hensley Henson* and *Spiritual Counsels and Letters of Baron Friedrich von
Hügel* printed by kind permission of SPCK.

ISBN 0 261 66282-1

Printed and bound in Great Britain by
BPC Hazell Books Ltd
A member of
The British Printing Company Ltd

Glittering Images

FOR BARBARA,
in memory of our conversations
about the two Herberts.

PART ONE

THE MYSTERY

'The deeper we get into reality,
the more numerous will be
the questions we cannot answer.'
Spiritual Counsels and Letters of
Baron Friedrich von Hügel
ed. DOUGLAS V. STEERE

ONE

'A bishop, I remind myself, is not quite as other men.'
                                    HERBERT HENSLEY HENSON
                                    Bishop of Durham 1920–1939
                                    The Bishoprick Papers

I

My ordeal began one summer afternoon when I received a telephone call from the Archbishop of Canterbury. It was a hot day, and beyond the window the quadrangle of Laud's shimmered in the hazy light. Term had ended; the resulting peace provided an atmosphere conducive to work, and when the telephone rang it was with reluctance that I reached for the receiver.

A voice announced itself as Lambeth Palace and proclaimed that His Grace wished to speak to Dr Ashworth on a matter of extreme urgency. Apparently the Archbishop was still infecting his chaplains with his love of melodrama.

'My dear Charles!' Dr Lang's voice, always sonorous, now achieved a pitch of theatrical splendour. He was a member of that generation which regards the telephone as at worst a demonic intruder and at best a thespian challenge, and when I inquired diplomatically about his health I was treated to a dramatic discourse on the more tedious aspects of senectitude. The Archbishop, on that first day of July in 1937, was in his seventy-third year and as fit as an ecclesiastical grandee has a right to expect, but in common with all men he hated the manifestations of old age.

'. . . however enough of my tiresome little ailments,' he concluded as I added the finishing touches to the mitre I had sketched on my memo-pad. 'Charles, I'm preaching at Ely next Sunday, and because I'm most anxious that we should meet I've arranged to spend the night in Cambridge at the house of my old friend the Master of Laud's. I shall come to your rooms after Evensong, but let me stress that I wish my visit to be entirely private. I have a commission which I wish to entrust to you, and the commission,' said the Archbishop, milking the situation of every ounce of drama by allowing his voice to sink to a whisper, 'is very delicate indeed.'

9

I wondered if he imagined he could arrive at my rooms without being recognized. Archbishops hardly find it easy to travel incognito, and an archbishop who had recently played a leading part in the abdication of one king and the coronation of another was hardly the most anonymous of clerics.

I said politely, 'Of course I'd be glad to help you in any way I can, Your Grace.'

'Then I'll see you on Sunday evening. Thank you, Charles,' said Dr Lang, and after giving me a brisk blessing he terminated the call. I was left staring at the mitre I had sketched, but gradually I became aware that my gaze had shifted to the last words I had written before the interruption.

'Modalism appealed to the Church's desire for monotheism, but in the second half of the fourth century it was propounded that the modalist God metamorphosed himself to meet – '

The impact of Modalism on the doctrine of the Trinity seemed a long way from the machinations of Dr Lang.

I found I had lost interest in my new book.

My ordeal had begun.

II

'My commission,' said the Archbishop with a reverence calculated to underline the importance of the subject, 'concerns the Bishop of Starbridge. Have you met him?'

'Only briefly. He preached in Cambridge Cathedral during Advent last year.'

We had achieved the private meeting in my rooms, and I had offered the Archbishop a cup of his favourite tea; one of my London friends, visiting Cambridge the previous day, had brought the tea directly from Fortnum's. Dr Lang, formally attired in his archiepiscopal clothes, was now sipping from one of my best china cups as he sat in my most comfortable armchair while I, wearing my cassock beneath my doctoral gown, was busy repressing the urge for a whisky. My cigarettes had been hidden. I had even left the windows wide open all day to banish any hint of smoke.

Lang took another sip of tea. He was a man whose features cast themselves without effort into an autocratic expression, and as I glanced at him I was reminded of the story which had circulated the Church of England after he had displayed his portrait by Orpen to a group of bishops. Lang had mused: 'I feel I must object when the critics say the painting makes me look pompous, proud and prelatical!' Whereupon Dr Henson, the caustic Bishop of Durham, had inquired: 'And may I ask to which of these epithets Your Grace takes exception?' The Archbishop was not without his enemies in the Church, and as I remembered Henson of Durham my thoughts turned to Jardine of Starbridge who, so Lang now informed me, was the subject of the mysterious commission.

'Before I explain further, Charles, answer me this: what did you Cambridge theologians think of Jardine's speech in the House of Lords ten days ago?'

That was an easy question to answer. During the debate on Mr A. P. Herbert's Marriage Bill, which advocated extending the grounds for divorce, Dr Jardine had attacked the Archbishop in a speech which had tossed a fireball into the tinderbox of the Church of England.

'We were all horrified, Your Grace.'

'Of course he's a brilliant speaker,' said Lang, careful to go through the motions of exercising Christian charity by giving credit where credit was due. 'Technically the speech was a masterpiece.'

'But a deplorable masterpiece.'

Lang was satisfied. He must have been confident of my support, but it was over ten years since I had been his chaplain and like all prudent statesmen he no doubt felt it unwise to take loyalty too readily for granted. 'Jardine's attack was quite inexcusable,' he said, sufficiently reassured to indulge in the luxury of indignation. 'After all, I was in the most unenviable position. I couldn't condone any relaxation of the divorce law; that would have been morally repugnant to me. On the other hand if I had openly opposed all change there would have been much damaging criticism of the Church. Caught between the Scylla of my moral inclinations and the Charybdis of my political duty,' declared the Archbishop, unable to resist a grandiloquent flourish, 'I had no choice but to adopt a position of neutrality.'

'I do see the difficulty, Your Grace.'

'Of course you do! So do all reasonable churchmen! Yet the Bishop of Starbridge has the insufferable insolence not only to accuse me of "sitting on the fence" – what a vulgar phrase! – but to advocate that multiple grounds for divorce are compatible with Christian teaching! No doubt one shouldn't expect too much of someone who's clearly very far from being a gentleman, but Jardine has behaved with gross disloyalty to me personally and with gross indifference to the welfare of the Church.'

The snobbery was unattractive. Lang might long since have acquired the manner of an English aristocrat, but he came from the Scottish middle classes and no doubt he himself had once been regarded as an 'arriviste'. Perhaps he thought this gave him a license to be virulent on the subject of class but I thought the virulence underlined not Jardine's social origins but his own.

Meanwhile he had discarded all grandiloquence in order to deliver himself of the bluntest of perorations. 'In my opinion,' he said, 'Jardine's no longer merely an embarrassment. He's become a dangerous liability, and I've decided that the time has come when I must take action to guard against a disaster.'

I wondered if malice had combined with old age to produce irrationality. 'I agree he's controversial, Your Grace, but –'

'Controversial! My dear Charles, what you and the general public have seen so far is just the tip of the iceberg – you should hear what goes on at our bishops' meetings! Jardine's views on marriage, divorce and – heaven help us – contraception have been notorious for some time in episcopal circles, and my greatest fear now is that if he continues to parade his questionable views on family life, some unscrupulous newshound from Fleet Street will eventually put Jardine's own domestic situation under the microscope.'

'You're surely not implying –'

'No, no.' Lang's voice was suddenly very smooth. 'No, of course I'm not implying any fatal error, but Jardine's domestic situation is unusual and could well be exploited by a press-baron with an axe to grind.' He paused before adding, 'I have enemies in Fleet Street, Charles. Since the Abdication there are powerful people who would like nothing better than to see me humiliated and the Church put to shame.'

The speech was florid but for the first time I felt he was not motivated solely by malice. His words reflected an undeniable political reality.

I heard myself say, 'And where do I come in, Your Grace?'

'I want you to go down to Starbridge,' said the Archbishop without hesitation, 'and make sure that Jardine hasn't commited some potentially disastrous indiscretion – because if he has, I want all evidence of it destroyed.'

III

Lang was talking in calculated euphemisms; he was anxious not to blacken the Bishop's reputation too deeply in the presence of a junior member of the Church's hierarchy, but at the same time he wished to signal to me that where Jardine was concerned almost any nightmare was feasible. Jardine was not suspected of a 'fatal error'; that meant adultery, a moral failure which would render a bishop, or indeed any clergyman, unfit for office. On the other hand Lang was raising the possibility that Jardine had committed a 'potentially disastrous indiscretion', a phrase which could mean anything from an unwise comment on the Virgin Birth to holding hands with a twenty-year-old blonde.

'How much do you know about him?' Lang added before I could speculate further.

'Just the outlines of his career. I know nothing about his private life.'

'He's married to an exceedingly feather-brained little lady who must now, I suppose, be in her early fifties. Jardine himself is fifty-eight. Both of them look younger than their years.' Lang made this good fortune sound like a breach of taste, and I sensed that his envy of Jardine's youthfulness was mingling with his dislike.

'Any children?' I said, pouring him some more tea.

'None living.' He took a sip from his replenished cup before adding, 'Ten years ago soon after Jardine became Dean of Radbury, a young woman called Miss Lyle Christie was engaged by him to be Mrs Jardine's companion. Poor feather-brained little Mrs Jardine couldn't cope with her new responsibilities as the Dean's wife, and all was the most inappropriate confusion.'

'And did Miss Lyle Christie bring order out of chaos?'

'Miss Christie. We're not dealing here with a double-barrelled name – the misguided parents gave her the name Lyle instead of a decent Christian name such as Jane or Mary. Yes,' said Lang, setting aside his teacup, 'Miss Christie's been keeping her employers' household in admirable order ever since her arrival. However although this innocent little *ménage à trois* would normally be unremarkable, there are three aspects of the situation which – after ten years – can and do cause unfortunate comment. The first is that Miss Christie is a good-looking woman; the second is that she shows no inclination to marry, and the third is that Jardine himself has what might be charitably described as a healthy interest in the opposite sex.' Lang, whose own good looks had ensured a steady stream of feminine admirers throughout his long bachelor's life, gazed out of the window at this point in order to appear non-committal. As a Christian he was obliged to approve of a healthy sexual interest which led to marriage, but I knew he found a more pervasive carnal preoccupation with women distasteful.

'In other words,' I said, easing him around the awkward subject of Jardine's attitude to the ladies, 'you're afraid that if the press start delving into Jardine's private life they may make some embarrassing deductions about Miss Christie. But with all due respect, Your Grace, why should this worry you? Even the gutter press aren't above the laws of libel, and they'd never print salacious allegations without written evidence to back them up.'

'That's exactly why I'm so worried.' Lang shed all affectation at last to reveal the canny Scot who still lurked behind his English façade. 'Jardine keeps a journal. Supposing some newshound bribes the servants and gets his hands on it?'

'But surely this is a journal of spiritual progress, not an outpouring of girlish chatter?'

'Spiritual progress can encompass confession.'

'Yes, but –'

'Let me make my position quite clear. I doubt that any blatantly indiscreet written evidence exists. What I'm much more concerned about is the possibility of an innocent document being quoted out of context and distorted. You know how unscrupulous the gutter press can be.'

In the pause which followed I found I was again sharing his view of an unpalatable but undeniable reality for I could see that Jardine's private life, no matter how innocent, might well prove to be the Church's Achilles heel in its current uneasy relationship with Fleet Street. A new king might have been crowned but the memory of the previous king still aroused much sympathy, and Lang's speech criticizing Edward VIII for abandoning his duty in order to marry a divorced woman had been widely resented for its priggishness. In these circumstances the last thing Lang needed, as he strove to regain the ground he had lost, was a scandal about a sexually alert bishop who lived in a questionable *ménage à trois*.

'Well, Charles? Are you going to help me?'

The ringmaster was cracking his whip, but in fact no whip was needed. I was loyal to my Church and despite a considerable ambivalence I was loyal to my Archbishop. 'Of course I'll help you, Your Grace,' I said without hesitation, and the die was cast.

IV

'How do I start?' I said, surveying my new role of archiepiscopal spy and at once confronting the depths of my inexperience.

Lang was immediately soothing. 'Once you're safely established at the Bishop's palace I'm sure it won't take you long to decide whether I do in fact have cause for anxiety.'

'But how on earth do I establish myself at the palace?'

'That's simple. I'll telephone Jardine and ask him to put you up for a couple of nights. He's not going to refuse me, particularly when I tell him you wish to visit the Cathedral library in order to do some research for your new book. Have you ever been to the Cathedral library at Starbridge? The chief glory, as you probably know, is that early manuscript of St Anselm's *Prayers and Meditations*.'

'But my new book's about the influence of Modalism on fourth-century Christology – it's got nothing to do with St Anselm at all!'

Lang was unperturbed. 'Then you'd better be writing an article for a learned journal – a reappraisal of St Anselm's ontological argument, perhaps –'

'And I suppose that during a discussion of the ontological argument I casually ask Jardine if I can sift his journal for pearls of wisdom, heavily

14

disguised as impure thoughts on the subject of his wife's companion!'

Lang gave me one of his thinnest smiles. Knowing that my levity had encountered disapproval I said at once, 'I'm sorry, Your Grace, but I honestly don't see how I'm to proceed. If you could issue me with some elementary marching orders –'

This appeal to his authority smoothed the ruffled feathers. 'Ask Jardine about his journal. It's no secret that he keeps one, and as it's unusual to find a clergyman continuing that sort of spiritual exercise into middle age I think you'd be justified in exhibiting curiosity on the subject. I want to know if he uses it as a confessional. Then I also suggest you talk to Miss Christie in an attempt to find out if Jardine writes to her when he's away from home. To be frank, Charles, I'm even more worried about the possibility of indiscreet letters than I am about a journal which is probably kept under lock and key. Men of Jardine's age are capable of almost limitless folly where young women are concerned, and even though I do doubt the existence of any blatant indiscretion there's always the chance that I could be wrong.'

'Surely Miss Christie would burn an indiscreet letter?'

'Not necessarily. Not if she were in love with him – and that's why I want you to take a hard look at this *ménage* to gauge its potential inflammability.' Lang, who had written romantic novels in his youth, began to exercise a baroque imagination. 'For example,' he said, 'it's not impossible that Jardine's wholly innocent but the woman's in the grip of a grand passion. Jardine may long to dismiss her yet be terrified of doing so in case she causes trouble.'

The plot was dramatic but not, unfortunately, implausible. The attentions of passionate spinsters were an occupational hazard for all members of the clergy, and after allowing a pause to signify that I was giving his theory serious consideration I said abruptly, 'Supposing I succeed in finding something compromising. What do I do?'

'Report to me. Then I'll see Jardine and order him to take action himself. He'd make a much more thorough job of censoring his papers than you ever could.'

I was relieved to hear that my activities were not to include sabotage, but nevertheless I still felt a certain amount of shady behaviour was being sanctioned and I decided that the shadiness should be more precisely defined. I said lightly, 'If the journal's under lock and key, Your Grace, I trust you don't require me to pick the lock? Or am I expected to behave like a Jesuit: all things to be permitted for the good of the Church!'

'This is the Church of England, Charles, not the Church of Rome. Good heavens, of course I'm not suggesting you behave in any manner unbecoming to a gentleman!' exclaimed Lang with an indignation which only narrowly failed to ring true, and I knew then he had been hoping I would not press him to define the boundaries of the commission too closely. Naturally he was obliged to repudiate any suggestion that he might be sanctioning shady behaviour. 'All I'm suggesting,' he said with a very passable attempt at innocence, 'is that you "test the water", as it were, before I dive in. My problem at the moment is that my suspicions are so entirely unsubstantiated that I'm quite unable to confront Jardine with them, but if you too find yourself suspicious after sampling the atmosphere at the palace, I shall feel I can approach Jardine without the fear that I'm making some colossal mistake.'

This statement was credible enough, but I decided the time had come to probe how far he was confiding in me. The more he insisted that he believed Jardine to be innocent of any blatant indiscretion the more tempted I was to suspect the Bishop was giving him the worst kind of clerical nightmares. 'Your Grace, is there any possibility at all that Jardine could be in very deep water?'

Lang achieved a patient expression as if I were a wayward child who had asked a foolish question. 'My dear Charles, we're all sinners and the possibility of error must always exist, even for a bishop, but in this case the likelihood of deep water's exceedingly remote. Despite all our differences I'm convinced Jardine's devout; if he'd committed a fundamental error he'd resign.'

This statement too was credible. There might have been loose-living bishops in the past but nowadays no bishop was ever accused of anything worse than senility. However Jardine had not always been a bishop. 'Has there been any scandal in his past, a scandal which was successfully hushed up?'

'No. He would hardly have received regular preferment if that had been the case, Charles.'

'Yet you mentioned his "healthy interest" in the opposite sex –'

'Occasionally at a dinner party he makes it a little too obvious that he finds a woman attractive, but in truth I find that reassuring. If anything were seriously amiss I'm sure he'd be at pains to conceal it.'

This struck me as a shrewd judgement, and in the knowledge that I was once more dealing with the canny Scot who inhabited the bottom layer of his personality I decided to risk prolonging my cross-examination. 'What about the feather-brained wife?' I said. 'Do we know for a fact that he's discontented with her?'

'No. There's a persistent rumour that the marriage has its difficulties but he always speaks of her loyally enough, and the gossip may merely have arisen because they seem an ill-assorted couple. Don't jump to conclusions about that marriage, Charles. Very clever men often marry very stupid women, and just because the Jardines seem intellectually unsuited you shouldn't automatically assume they're unhappy.'

After this wise warning that I should avoid approaching my commission with preconceived ideas I felt there was only one question left to ask. 'When do I leave for Starbridge?'

'As soon as Jardine's prepared to receive you as his guest,' said Lang, well satisfied with my commitment to his cause, and finally allowing the warmth to permeate his thin dry politician's smile.

V

I thought he would leave then but he stayed. For a time we talked of College matters; he wanted to know whether the undergraduates were still susceptible to the evangelical Christianity of Frank Buchman's 'groupists' but I said I thought that influence was on the wane.

'The tragedy of such movements,' said the Archbishop who had sanctioned the Buchmanites in 1933 and had probably lived to regret it, 'is that their good intentions are so vulnerable to abuse. Troubled young men should seek to purge their souls in private confession before a priest, not in the so-called "sharing" of painful experiences with a group who may be spiritually no wiser than they are.' So subtle was his manipulation of the conversation that it was not until he asked his next question that I perceived the drift of his thoughts. 'Do you hear many confessions, Charles?'

'I never seek them. I always stress that the Church of England says only that one may make confession, never that one must. But of course if an undergraduate comes to me, I hear him.'

'And you yourself? I was wondering,' said Lang, finally revealing the core of his curiosity, 'if you might wish to take advantage of this rare private meeting by raising any problem which you feel would be eased by a confidential discussion.'

I allowed only the briefest silence to elapse before I replied, but I knew my silence had been not only noted but reserved as a subject for future speculation. 'How very thoughtful of you, Your Grace,' I said, 'but I'm happy to say that the only serious problem I have at present is to decide what to put in my new book.'

'A problem which I'm sure your intellect will be more than capable of resolving in due course! But may I ask who your spiritual director is nowadays?'

'I still go to the Abbot of the Fordite monks at Grantchester.'

'Ah yes, Father Reid. I wish I had the time to call on him while I'm in Cambridge, but alas! One is always so monstrously busy.' Lang made a theatrical gesture of despair, glanced at his watch and rose to his feet. My audience was drawing to an end.

I asked for his blessing, and when he gave it to me I was aware of his gifts as a churchman; I remembered how his care and concern had sustained me during the difficult years both before and after my ordination; I recalled how his generosity of spirit, glamorously displayed, had sparked my understanding that Christianity could be not a pallid priggish way of life but a glittering realization of one's finest possibilities. People can be led to Christianity by infinitely diverse routes, and there was no denying that I had been led by Lang's worldly success to the creed which rated worldly success unimportant. Beyond the glittering image lay the stark absolute truth. It was a juxtaposition which had fascinated me ever since I had decided to be a clergyman, but as I now looked without effort past Lang's worldly glamour to all the flaws of his powerful personality, I was conscious of amazement that he should have had such an influence on my life. How had this vain, pompous, arid old bachelor ever inspired me to a discipleship which emphasized the humility and simplicity of Christ? The inspiration struck me as little short of miraculous, but then guilt assailed me because although I owed Lang so much I could no longer view him through those rose-tinted spectacles which I had worn with such unquestioning ease in the past.

He departed. The ensuing solitude came as a relief, and retiring at once to my bedroom I stripped off both gown and cassock before pausing to light a cigarette. At once I felt more relaxed, and as soon as I was dressed with the minimum of formality, I returned to my sitting-room, mixed myself a substantial whisky and soda and began to contemplate my mission to Starbridge.

VI

The more I considered the situation the less enamoured of it I became. It would involve me in deception; although it could be argued by any student of moral philosophy that the welfare of the Church justified a little espionage by the Archbishop's henchman, I was averse to involving myself in one of those situations where the end was held to justify the means. When I had cited Jesuitical casuistry earlier, Lang had all but quoted Shakespeare's line: 'This is the English, not the Turkish court,' but nevertheless I did wonder, as I recalled our conversation, what game Lang was really playing.

Jardine had humiliated him during that debate in the House of Lords ten days ago. 'What are the ordinary people of England to think,' the Bishop had demanded in fury, 'when on one of the great moral issues of the day the Archbishop of Canterbury says with a conspicuous lack of courage that he can vote neither for this bill nor against it? Is this leadership? Is this the great ecclesiastical pearl of wisdom which so many people have been eagerly awaiting? Is this the ultimate fate of the Church of England – to be led into the wilderness of moral confusion by a septuagenarian Scot who has apparently lost touch with those whom he purports to serve?'

I thought Lang would want to get rid of Jardine after that performance, and the only way Lang could rid himself of a turbulent bishop without a scandal was to find evidence of a disabling impropriety so that a resignation could be extorted in private. In other words, I suspected that I was being used not merely to safeguard the Church but to promote a secret war between two of the country's leading churchmen.

This was a most unedifying thought. As I followed my Sunday evening custom of making myself a cheese sandwich in the little pantry attached to my rooms, I wondered if I could extricate myself from Lang's scheme but I could see no way out. I had committed myself. I could hardly admit now that I was suffering debilitating doubts. Lang would be most displeased, and incurring my Archbishop's displeasure was a prospect on which I had no wish to dwell. I decided my best hope of resolving the dilemma lay in proving Jardine's private life was as pure as driven snow with the result that the Archbishop's Machiavellian plans would collapse in an unconsummated heap, but the next moment I was asking myself how likely it was that Jardine was an episcopal saint. Even if one ruled out the possibility of a fatal error there was still room for a variety of smuts on the driven snow; the thought of flirtatious behaviour at dinner parties was not encouraging.

I finished my second whisky, ate my sandwich and brewed myself some coffee. Then I decided to embark on some preliminary research by talking to two people who almost certainly knew more about Jardine than I did.

My first telephone call was to a London friend who worked for *The Church Gazette*. We had been up at Cambridge together as undergraduates, and later when I had been Lang's chaplain and Jack had begun his career as an ecclesiastical journalist it had suited us both to maintain our friendship.

'I confess I'm ringing you out of sheer vulgar curiosity,' I said after the conventional enquiries had been exchanged. 'I'm about to stay at the episcopal palace at Starbridge – what can you tell me about its current tenant?'

'Ah, the vampire who feeds on the blood of pompous archbishops! Brush up your theories on the Virgin Birth, Charles, take a gun and shoot straight from the hip – after dinner at Starbridge when the lovely ladies have withdrawn the conversation will be guaranteed to put you through your theological paces.'

'Are you deliberately trying to frighten me?'

'Oh, don't despair of survival! He likes theologians – they give him a good run for his money. But why are you offering yourself to Jardine for shooting practice?'

'I'm beginning to wonder. Tell me more about these lovely ladies I shall meet at the dinner table.'

'The gossips say no man receives an invitation to dine unless he has an attractive wife, but I dare say that's an exaggeration.'

'What's Jardine's own wife like?'

'She's a wonderful, fluffy thing with a heart of gold and a stunning selection of tea gowns. Everyone adores her. Her favourite topic of conversation's the weather.'

'That must make a welcome change from the Virgin Birth. And isn't there a good-looking companion in the household? What do I talk about with her?'

'Don't get excited, Charles – curb your natural inclination to indulge in impure thoughts! Miss Christie's the original ice-maiden. Starbridge is littered with the bones of those who have died of unrequited love for that particular lady.'

'Well, I wasn't seriously expecting to find a nymphomaniac lodged at the episcopal palace – '

'No, Jardine knows when to play safe. Lovely ladies, preferably titled and always chaperoned by their boring old husbands, are more in his line than nymphomaniacs and ice-maidens. No scandal, of course. He just likes to look and chat.'

'No doubt he enjoys the chance to talk of subjects other than the weather.'

'Ah, so you've heard the rumour that the Jardines' marriage has died of boredom, but don't you believe it, old chap! Mrs Jardine's still pretty as a picture and I shouldn't think Jardine gives a damn about her intellect once the lights are out in the episcopal bedchamber.'

'Jack, are you still working for *The Church Gazette*? You're sounding exactly like a hack from *The News of the World*!'

'Nonsense! There's nothing scandalous about a bishop who sleeps with his wife. *The News of the World* would only bat an eyelid if he started sleeping with someone else, but as far as I know – '

'Yes, how much of this prurient rigmarole of yours ifs hearsay and how much is first-hand information?'

'Well, naturally I'm in league with the chaplain but since he always presents his hero as a cross between St Paul and Sir Galahad he's hardly a source of spicy gossip. However I do have first-hand experience of the Jardines. Last March I was invited down to Starbridge to report on a Church committee meeting which was discussing special Coronation services in the southern province – Jardine, as chairman, was playing host. Of course he's rumoured to eat journalists on toast for breakfast but in fact he was very civil to me, and Mrs Jardine was a poppet. She gave me some ginger biscuits and said I reminded her of her nephew.'

'And the luscious Miss Christie?'

'She gave me a cool look and told me where to find the lavatory. But I think you'll like both the Jardines, Charles, and I see no reason why you shouldn't survive your visit with ease. Just gird your loins when the sinful vintage port starts circulating, and take a deep breath if the Bishop begins to hold forth on the Virgin Birth . . .'

VII

I next telephoned a man whom I had met at theological college and who was now the incumbent of a rural parish in the Starbridge diocese. Although our paths had diverged since our ordination we had maintained our friendship by letter and I felt I could express without insincerity the hope that we might meet during my visit. However a meeting was to be impossible; he and his family were about to take their first holiday in five years. Keeping quiet about my spring visit to France I said I was sure Bournemouth would be delightful, but I was still repressing a shudder at the thought of the cheap boarding house which awaited him when he asked why I was visiting Starbridge.

To reveal that the Bishop had invited me to stay at the instigation of Dr Lang would have seemed, in the circumstances, an unforgivable piece of bragging so I merely mentioned my desire to visit the Cathedral library and said I would be calling at the palace as a courtesy. 'What's your opinion of Jardine, Philip?' I added. 'Do you find him a good bishop?'

'I find him an embarrassment, quite frankly. That speech in the Lords! I felt sorry for Lang. A bishop's got no business to attack his archbishop in public.'

'But what's he like when he's doing his job instead of chasing every headline in Fleet Street?'

'Why ask me? I usually only see him once a year for confirmations.'

'But don't confirmations give a good indication of a bishop's conscientiousness? There's a world of difference between a bishop who can barely disguise the fact that he's treading a very well-worn path and a bishop who makes the candidates feel the occasion's as special for him as it is for them.'

'True,' said Philip reluctantly. 'Well, I have to admit Jardine can't be faulted there – although when he first became bishop five years ago he did seem *distrait*. However, I put that down to lack of experience. The next year he was quite different, very much in command before the candidates, very relaxed behind the scenes, but all the same . . . I've heard he can be an absolute terror.'

'In what way?'

'Well, he's supposed to be at his worst when a clergyman wants to get married. He's got a bee in his bonnet about clergymen being ruined by unsuitable wives, and if he doesn't think a clerical fiancée's going to make the grade as a vicar's wife he has no hesitation in saying so. It makes one wonder about his own marriage – rumour has it that Mrs Jardine's delightful but incompetent and that the real power at the palace is her companion.'

'Yes, I've heard about Miss Christie. Jack Ryder paints her as a *femme fatale*.'

'What rubbish! She wouldn't have lasted ten years in a bishop's household unless she was propriety personified!'

'But she's attractive, isn't she? Wouldn't it have been safer to engage a companion who looked like the back end of a tram?'

'Jardine's the kind of man who would baulk at confronting the back end of a tram every morning at the breakfast table.'

'Philip,' I said amused, 'I'm receiving the clear impression that you don't like him, but is this solely because he attacks his archbishop in public and demolishes clerical fiancées? Neither of these unfortunate habits can have affected you personally.'

'No, thank God. Mary and I tied the knot while Jardine was still Dean of Radbury! I don't dislike him, Charles – he's always been charming both to Mary and to me – but I do disapprove of him. I think he's far too worldly, and he's got a very flashy *nouveau riche* streak which should have been ironed out before he was let loose on an income of several thousand a year. I'll never forget the garden party he gave for the diocesan clergy two years ago – talk about extravagance! I was shocked. I kept thinking what all the catering must have cost and calculating how many poor people in my parish could have benefited from the money.'

'My dear Philip! Aren't you being a little churlish about your generous bishop?'

'Perhaps. And perhaps you live in an ivory tower, Charles, and don't know what's really going on in the world. How long has it been since you visited a house where the husband's been unemployed since the Slump, the wife's half-dead with TB and the children have rickets as well as lice?'

There was a silence.

At last Philip said rapidly: 'I'm sorry – '

I interrupted him. 'I'm very conscious, believe me,' I said, 'that I lack experience at the parish level.'

'Nevertheless I shouldn't have implied – '

'It doesn't matter.' There was another pause before I added: 'Well, I'm sorry I shan't be seeing you, Philip. Perhaps next time – '

'Oh yes,' he said. 'Next time.'

But we both knew 'next time' was a long way away.

VIII

On the following morning the Archbishop telephoned to inform me that I should present myself at the palace early on Wednesday evening; Jardine had professed delight at the prospect of offering me hospitality, a profession which Lang cynically suspected derived from a guilty wish to make amends for the bellicose speech in the House of Lords. '. . . and I'm sure he'll give you a warm welcome, Charles,' was the Archbishop's dry conclusion.

'Did he remember meeting me last year?'

'Of course! When I mentioned your name he said: "Ah yes, the young canon from Cambridge who thinks the world began not with Adam and Eve but with the Council of Nicaea!'

So Jardine had at least glanced at the book which had made my name in theological circles. He himself had published no work of historical scholarship, but that never deterred him from writing trenchant reviews of other peoples efforts and I had been surprised as well as relieved when my own book had escaped his characteristic literary butchery. How the escape had been achieved I was uncertain, but possibly he found any discussion of Arianism boring and had decided to rest his pen.

These thoughts about scholarship reminded me that I had not yet decided why I should need to consult the library of Starbridge Cathedral, and aware how important it was that my need should be convincing I spent some time pondering on the problem before I devised a stratagem which would enable me to tell the truth. I had long been contemplating the revision of my lecture notes on medieval thought. I now decided that my undergraduates were going to learn more about St Anselm, and as a conscientious lecturer I naturally felt obliged to cast a glance over Starbridge's early manuscript of *The Prayers and Meditations*.

I suffered a further moment of uneasiness as I contemplated the duplicity inherent in this decision, but then I pulled myself together with the thought that no harm could come to me even if Jardine were steeped in apostasy. On the contrary, Lang was bound to be grateful for my help with the result that I would inevitably emerge from the affair with my future prospects in the Church enhanced.

Casting my last doubt aside I began to prepare for my journey.

So I came at last to Starbridge, radiant ravishing Starbridge, immortalized by famous artists, photographed by unnumerable visitors and lauded by guidebooks as the most beautiful city west of the Avon. I could remember clearly from my previous visit as an undergraduate the medieval streets, the flower-filled parks and the languid river which curved in an arc around the mound on which the Cathedral stood. The Cathedral itself dominated not only the city but the valley. Wider than Winchester, longer than Canterbury, set in a walled precinct which was even larger than the close at Salisbury, Starbridge Cathedral was renowned for embodying in pale stone and vivid glass the most glittering of medieval visions.

The city itself was small, and being encircled on three sides by the river it still gave an impression of compactness despite the recent housing development to the east. It lay snugly in the middle of its green valley like a jewel displayed on velvet, and the smooth slopes of the surrounding hills added to the impression that the landscape had been designed in order to show the city to its best advantage.

The diocese was primarily rural but it included the port of Starmouth with its sprawling slums so there was a dark underside to the tranquillity which formed the stranger's immediate impression of the area. Nonetheless I thought Jardine was probably well pleased with his latest preferment. The diocese was rich; his income was well to the fore among episcopal salaries. London was easily accessible by train, a fact which meant he could keep in close touch with the centres of power, both secular and ecclesiastical, and the bishopric conferred an immediate right to a seat in the House of Lords, a privilege not accompanying the majority of bishoprics where the incumbents had to wait their turn for an ecclesiastical seat to fall vacant. Starbridge was not Canterbury and it was not York but it was plush, privileged and pleasing to the eye, and no doubt there were many among Jardine's episcopal brethren who envied him.

I had decided to travel to Starbridge in my car, not the sports car which I inevitably found myself driving whenever I dreamt of motors, but the respectable little Baby Austin which was cheap to run and easy to manipulate out of tight corners in the busy streets of Cambridge. Whenever I hankered for an MG I reminded myself how fortunate I was to have even an Austin. Most clergymen could not afford a car, and in fact motors were still regarded by the older bishops as an evil which lured parsons on jaunts away from their parishes.

The road began to curve among hills as I approached Starbridge, and soon I glimpsed the Cathedral in the distance. The road curved again, the spire vanished, but at the next twist it was once more visible, slim and ethereal, a symbol of man's inchoate yearning to reach upwards to the infinite. As the road continued to wind I felt as if it were mirroring life itself, granting glimpses of transcendence only to rush on before the transcendence could be fully experienced, but finally the last fold in the road lay behind me and I could see the entire city shimmering in the valley below.

This view over a settlement was very old. The Romans had built their city Starovinium on the ruined encampment of the British tribe the Straobrigantes, and the ancient name still survived in city landmarks and on official documents. The Bishop, who was theoretically married to his diocese, was entitled to use the surname Staro in his correspondence, and I had proof of this tradition in my pocket. Jardine himself had sent a letter to welcome me to Starbridge.

'My dear Dr Ashworth,' he had written in a bold striking hand, 'the Archbishop of Canterbury has informed me that you wish to pursue your studies in the Cathedral library, and may I now confirm that you would be most welcome to stay at the palace from the evening of July the seventh until the morning of the tenth. His Grace thought you would probably arrive by motor, but should you prefer to travel by train, please send a wire to my chaplain, Gerald Harvey, who will arrange for my chauffeur to meet you at the station. His Grace also thought that you would not wish to stay more than three nights, but if you should decide to prolong your visit I hope you will assist me at the early service of Holy Communion in the Cathedral on Sunday. In looking forward to the renewal of our acquaintance, Dr Ashworth, I send my best wishes for a safe journey, and assure you that I remain yours very sincerely, ADAM ALEXANDER STARO.'

The auguries for my visit could hardly have been more favourable. Descending from the hills I drove across the floor of the valley and finally entered the city.

X

The crooked medieval streets were confusing but the way to the Cathedral was signposted and I soon found myself at the gateway of the Close. Slowing the car to a crawl I asked the constable on duty to direct me to the palace; my memory of the Close was hazy.

I drove on, and the next moment the Cathedral was towering above me in an overpowering display of architectural virtuosity. There had been no later additions, no ill-judged alterations. Built during the short span of forty years the Cathedral was uniform, untouched, unspoilt, a monument to faith, genius and the glory of English Perpendicular.

I drove down the North Walk with the vast sward of the churchyard on my right. On my left the ancient houses, dissimilar in style yet harmonious in their individual beauty, provided the perfect foil to the Cathedral's splendour, and as I turned south into the East Walk I experienced that sense of time continuing, an awareness which is never more insistent than in a place where a long span of the past is visually present.

At the end of the East Walk the palace gates stood open and within seconds I was confronting the palace itself, a Victorian 'improvement' on the original Tudor building which had been destroyed by fire in the last century. Dr Jardine's home was a mock-Gothic travesty built in the same pale stone as the Cathedral, but it was not unpleasing. Smooth lawns and ancient beech trees framed the house, and above the porch the arms of Starbridge were carved in the stone in a brave attempt to unite medieval custom with a wayward Victorian illusion.

Parking my car in a secluded corner of the forecourt I extracted my bag and paused to listen. The birds were singing; the leaves of the beech trees were a brilliant green against the cloudless sky; the town beyond the walls of the Close might have been a hundred miles away. Again I sensed time continuing. I was standing in twentieth-century England yet at the same time I felt a mere pace away from a past which contained the seeds of an alluring future, and suddenly I forgot the harsh realities of the present, the horror of Hitler, the agony of the Spanish Civil War, the despair of those whose lives had been ruined by the Slump. I was conscious only of my privileged good fortune as I allowed myself to be seduced by the subtle glamour of Starbridge, and running up the steps to the front door I rang the bell with all the eagerness of an actor who could barely wait for his cue to walk onstage.

The door was opened by a butler who looked like a character from a Trollope novel – a worldly version of Mr Harding, perhaps – and I stepped into a vast dark hall. Beyond some mock-Gothic furniture of varying degrees of ugliness a handsome staircase rose to the gallery. The walls were adorned with dim portraits of nineteenth-century gentlemen in clerical dress.

'If you'd care to come this way, sir . . .' The butler had already taken the bag from my hand when a woman emerged from the far end of the hall. As the butler paused at once I paused beside him, and the woman moved swiftly, smoothly, silently towards us through the shadows.

'Dr Ashworth?' She held out a slim hand. 'Welcome to Starbridge. I'm Miss Christie, Mrs Jardine's companion.'

I took her hand in mine and knew without a second's hesitation that I wanted her.

TWO

'I pleasantly assured him that in my belief, based on the experience of a long ministry, it would be roughly true to say of the married clergy of the Church of England that probably fifty per cent were ruined by their wives and fifty per cent were saved.'

Letters of Herbert Hensley Henson
Bishop of Durham 1920–1939
ed. E. F. BRALEY

I

No one had described Miss Christie to me, and Jack's reference to an ice-maiden had evoked an image of a tall blonde. However Miss Christie was small, no more than five foot two, with slender ankles, a slim waist, reddish hair and black-lashed dark eyes. She also possessed high cheek-bones, a delicately moulded but very firm chin and a subtle mouth which somehow reinforced this hint of a determined character while conveying an impression of sensuality. Her make-up was discreet; her grey skirt and white blouse were restrained in taste, as befitted a lady's companion in a clerical household; I thought her alluring beyond description, and my first coherent thought was: how could he resist her? Yet I knew that this was a wild question which failed to reflect the reality of the situation. Unless he was an apostate Jardine had no choice but to resist, yet such was Miss Christie's allure that for the first time I seriously considered the possibility of apostasy.

She showed me to my room. I managed to maintain a polite conversation as we ascended the stairs, but all the time I was thinking about Jardine in the light of what I now knew of Miss Christie. As I calmed down I dismissed the melodramatic notion of apostasy but I now began to wonder if Jardine's inclination to form harmless friendships with good-looking women was his way of deflecting an inclination which was not harmless at all.

I roused myself from these speculations as Miss Christie led the way into a large bright room sombrely adorned with more massive Victorian furniture. Beyond the window the garden stretched downhill to the river, and on the far side of the sparkling water cows were grazing among the buttercups in the meadows. Starbridge lay east of this outmost curve of the river, and to the west the farmlands stretched across the valley to the hills.

'What a beautiful view!' I said as the butler deposited my bag and departed. Miss Christie had moved to the vase on top of the chest of drawers and was restoring the symmetry of the flower arrangement by adjusting an errant rose.

'The bathroom is at the end of the corridor,' she said, evidently finding my comment on the view too mundane to merit even a murmur of agreement. 'Dinner is at eight but we assemble for cocktails in the drawing-room at any time after quarter-past seven. The water's hot every evening from six o'clock onwards. I trust you have everything you require, Dr Ashworth, but if by any chance something's been forgotten do please ring the bell by your bedside.'

I thanked her. She gave a brief formal smile and the next moment I was alone.

There was a bible placed on the bedside table to remind visitors that despite the grandeur of their surroundings they were in a clerical household, and in an effort to distract my mind from the temptation to meander down carnal byways I opened the pages in search of an edifying quotation. However this random dip produced only Ezekiel's diatribe against the harlot. Still thinking of Miss Christie I ploughed forward into the New Testament and eventually found myself lingering on the text: 'For there is nothing covered, that shall not be revealed; and hid, that shall not be known.'

That seemed like a good omen for an espionage agent. I closed the bible. Then after visiting the regal lavatory, which remained as a sumptuous memorial to Victorian plumbing, I unpacked my bag and sat down with my prayer book to read the evening office.

II

When I closed my prayer book the time was half-past six. I stripped, washed at the basin to erase all trace of my journey, and decided to shave. I did not usually shave twice a day but I wanted to appear thoroughly well groomed, not only to impress Miss Christie but to impress the Bishop. I sensed Jardine might have strong views on the obligation of a clergyman to present a neat appearance to the world; he himself had been very smart, very dapper, when I had encountered him in Cambridge eight months ago.

The evening was warm and the prospect of encasing myself in my formal clerical clothes was not appealing but naturally I had no choice other than to martyr myself in the name of convention. I spent some time in front of the glass as I coaxed my hair to lie flat. I have curly hair which I keep short, but it has wayward tendencies which water can rarely subdue for long. However I never use hair oil. It makes me look like a bounder, and I was always unaccountably nervous in case my appearance reflected the wrong image in the mirror.

Yet that evening I found my reflection reassuring. Here was no bounder, no shady character from a modern 'shocker', but a clergyman who was thirty-seven and looked younger. Playing squash and tennis had curbed an inclination to put on weight as I left my twenties behind, and although I was a little too fond of good food and more than a little too fond of good wine, my appearance proved I had these weaknesses well in control. I saw no heaviness around the jaw, no pouches beneath the eyes, no giveaway lines around the mouth. I looked like the man I wanted to be and the image in the long glass seemed impregnable as I surveyed it in the golden evening light.

Glancing at my watch I saw the time had come for me to make my appearance downstairs. The curtain was about to rise on the stage at Starbridge, and leaving my room I headed for the wings to await my cue.

III

I had no trouble finding the drawing-room. As I descended the stairs I could hear the murmur of voices drifting towards me through the open door on the far side of the hall. A woman gave an attractive laugh, a man protested: 'No, I'm serious! I've always thought *Peter Pan* was a most sinister story!' and I deduced that the conversation had arisen in connection with the recent death of Sir James Barrie.

'But Henry, you can't possibly describe an innocent fantasy as sinister!'

'Why not? Captain Hook reminds me of Mussolini.'

'Everyone reminds you of Mussolini. Oh darling, I do wish you'd forget Abyssinia and look on the bright side for a change – after all, think how well we're doing! We've survived the War, the Slump and the Abdication – and now that dear Mr Chamberlain's poised to turn the country into a vast version of Birmingham with that divinely businesslike efficiency of his, I'm sure we're all set for a rosy future!'

'This sounds like another of Barrie's fantasies. No wonder you enjoy *Peter Pan*, my dear.'

I walked into the room. The first person I saw was Miss Christie. She was standing by the French windows and looking formidably aloof. In contrast the other three occupants of the room were exuding that easy camaraderie which arises when people have enjoyed an unaffected friendship for a long time. By the fireplace stood an elderly man with a frank mild face and that air of self-confidence which can only be acquired from a lifetime spent in privileged surroundings. He was drinking a cocktail which appeared to be a dry martini. Perched on the arm of a sofa a handsome woman was also toying with a martini glass, and beyond her a plump, pretty, grey-haired little woman in a lavish lavender evening gown was selecting a water biscuit from a silver dish nearby.

Everyone turned to look at me. Miss Christie at once moved forward to make the introductions, but she was a long way away and the plump, pretty little woman forestalled her.

'Dr Ashworth!' she exclaimed, beaming at me. 'How nice to see you! I hope your motor journey wasn't too difficult but it must have helped that the weather was fine. Isn't the weather beautiful? All the sunshine's so good for the garden.'

I did not need to be told that I was being addressed by my hostess. 'How do you do, Mrs Jardine,' I said, smiling as I took her hand in mine. 'It's very kind of you to have me to stay.'

'Not at all, it's splendid for Alex to have someone clever to talk to! Now let me introduce you to everyone. Miss Christie you've met, of course, and here – ' she turned to the couple who had been debating *Peter Pan* ' – are Lord and Lady Starmouth who have always been so kind to us ever since Alex was Vicar of St Mary's, Mayfair. They have such a delightful house in Curzon Street and Alex stays there when he has to be up in town for the debates in the House of Lords – oh, heavens, perhaps I shouldn't mention the Lords' debates, especially as you're a friend of the Archbishop's – Lyle, am I dropping some frightful brick?'

'Dr Ashworth,' said Miss Christie, 'is probably only thinking how pleasant it must be for the Bishop to stay with friends whenever he's up in town.'

But in fact I was thinking that the good-looking Countess of Starmouth might well be one of Jardine's 'lovely ladies', faithfully chaperoned by one of the gentlemen whom Jack had described as 'boring old husbands'. However this unflattering description hardly did justice to the Earl of Starmouth who looked alert enough to be entertaining even though he might have been on the wrong side of seventy. Perhaps Lady Starmouth kept him young; I estimated that she was at least twenty years his junior.

'My wife collects clerics,' said Lord Starmouth to me as we shook hands. 'She'll collect you too if you're not careful.'

'I adore clergymen,' agreed his wife with that aristocratic frankness which never fails to make the more reticent members of the middle classes

30

cringe with embarrassment. 'It's the collar, of course. It makes a man seem so deliciously forbidden.'

'What can I offer you to drink, Dr Ashworth?' said Miss Christie, middle-class propriety well to the fore.

'A dry sherry, please.' No ambitious clergyman drank cocktails at episcopal dinner parties.

A young man in clerical garb bustled into the room, muttered, 'Bother! No Bishop,' and bustled out again.

'Poor Gerald!' said Mrs Jardine. 'I really wonder sometimes whether we made the right decision when we installed a telephone. It's so terribly hard for the chaplain when people ring up at awkward moments . . . Oh, here's Willy! Come and meet my brother, Dr Ashworth.'

I was introduced to a Colonel Cobden-Smith, a hale gentleman in his sixties with a pink face, white hair and a cherubic expression. He was accompanied by his wife, a thin energetic woman who reminded me of a greyhound, and by a very large St Bernard dog who padded majestically through the room to the terrace on his way to water the flowerbeds.

'I know nothing about theology,' said Mrs Cobden-Smith to me as soon as we had been introduced. 'I always say to Alex that I know nothing about theology and I don't want to know anything either. As far as I'm concerned God's God, the Church is the Church, the Bible's the Bible and I can't understand what all the arguments are about.'

'Funny business, religion,' mused her husband, uttering this dubious remark with such an ingenuous admiration that no clergyman could have found him offensive, and began to talk about a Buddhist monk he had met in India.

The young chaplain bustled back into the room. 'So sorry, Mrs Jardine, but you know what the Archdeacon's like when he rings up in a panic . . .'

I was introduced to Gerald Harvey. He was a short bespectacled man in his early twenties who seemed to be perpetually out of breath, and I wondered whether the Bishop of Starbridge regularly reduced his chaplain to this state of wild-eyed anxiety.

'. . . and I've heard about your book, of course,' he was saying, 'but I confess I haven't read it because all those ancient arguments about the Trinity simply make me want to tear off my dog-collar and enlist in the Foreign Legion – oh my goodness, there's the doorbell and the Bishop's still not down! I'd better go and see if anything's wrong.'

He dashed away again. I was surprised that Jardine had selected such a plain, unsophisticated and clearly unintellectual chaplain, but before I could speculate on the existence of sterling virtues which would have qualified Harvey for his post, the butler announced the arrival of Mr and Mrs Frank Jennings. Jennings, I soon discovered, had just been appointed to teach dogmatics at the Theological College in the Close. He himself was unremarkable in his appearance but his wife was a pretty young blonde, and remembering Jack's gossip I wondered how far her looks had qualified the couple for an invitation to the episcopal dinner table.

'I found your book most stimulating,' Jennings said to me agreeably, but before he could continue his wife exclaimed: 'Good gracious, Frank, look at that gigantic dog!'

'Alex had a dog once,' said little Mrs Jardine as the St Bernard made a stately return to the room. 'He called it Rhetoric. But we were living in London at the time and poor little Rhet was run over by such a vulgar Rolls-Royce – really, I've never felt the same about motor cars since . . . Do you have a dog, Dr Ashworth?'

'No, Mrs Jardine.'

'Do you have a wife, Dr Ashworth?' called Lady Starmouth, giving me a friendly look with her fine dark eyes.

I was acutely aware of Miss Christie's hand pausing in the act of pouring out glasses of sherry for the newcomers.

'I'm a widower, Lady Starmouth,' I said.

'All clergymen ought to be married,' said the authoritative Mrs Cobden-Smith, offering a handful of water biscuits to the St Bernard. 'They say the Roman Catholics have frightful trouble with their celibate priests.'

'They say the Church of England has frightful trouble with its married clergy,' said a strong harsh well-remembered voice from the doorway, and as we all turned to face him the Bishop of Starbridge made a grand entrance into his drawing-room.

IV

Dr Jardine was a man of medium height, slim and well proportioned, with dark greying hair and brown eyes so light that they were almost amber. The eyes were set deep and wide apart; by far his most arresting feature, they were capable of assuming a hypnotic lambent glaze in the pulpit, a physiological trick which Jardine used sparingly but effectively to under-line his considerable gifts as a preacher. His quick abrupt walk revealed his energy and hinted at his powerful restless intellect. Unlike most bishops he wore his gaiters with *élan*, as if conscious that he had the figure to triumph over the absurdity of the archaic episcopal costume, and when he entered the room he was radiating the electric self-confidence which his enemies decried as bumptious and his admirers defended as debonair.

'Don't be alarmed, everyone!' he said, smiling after the opening remark which had won our attention. 'I'm not about to secede to Rome, but I can never resist the urge to counter my sister-in-law's scandalously dogmatic assertions . . . Good evening, Dr Ashworth, I'm delighted to see you. Good evening, Jennings – Mrs Jennings – now, Mrs Jennings, there's no need to be shy. I may be a fire-breathing bishop but I'm extremely tame in the company of pretty ladies – isn't that so, Lady Starmouth?'

'Tame as a tiger!' said the Countess amused.

'We used to have some good tiger-shoots in India,' reflected Colonel Cobden-Smith. 'I remember – '

'I saw such an adorable tiger at the zoo once,' said Mrs Jardine, 'but I'm sure it would have been so much happier back in the wild.'

'Nonsense!' said the Bishop robustly, accepting a glass of sherry from Miss Christie. 'If the unfortunate animal had been in its natural habitat your brother would have come along and murdered it. Did you arrive in time for Evensong, Dr Ashworth?'

'I'm afraid I was late getting here. The traffic around London – '

'Don't worry, I don't award black marks for missing services. Now, Mrs Jennings, sit down and tell me all about yourself – have you managed to find a house yet?'

As his wife was purloined by the Bishop, Jennings began to tell me about his arduous quest for a property in the suburbs. Occasionally I offered a word of sympathy but for the most part I sipped my sherry in silence, eavesdropped on the other conversations and kept a surreptitious watch on Miss Christie.

Lady Starmouth suddenly glided into my field of vision. 'I think you must be the youngest canon I've ever met, Dr Ashworth! Does this mean the Church is at last beginning to believe it's not a crime to be under forty?'

'The canonry came with the job, Lady Starmouth. When Archbishop Laud founded Laud's College and Cambridge Cathedral in the seventeenth century he stipulated that the College should appoint a doctor of divinity to teach theology and act as one of the Cathedral's residentiary canons.' I suddenly realized that Miss Christie was looking straight at me, but when our glances met she turned away. I continued to watch as she picked up the sherry decanter again but Colonel Cobden-Smith cornered her before she could embark on the task of refilling glasses.

'. . . and I hear you were Dr Lang's chaplain once,' Lady Starmouth was saying. 'How did you meet him?'

Reluctantly I averted my gaze from Miss Christie. 'He gave away the prizes during my last year at school.'

'You were head boy of your school, of course,' said Jardine from the depths of the sofa nearby.

'Well, as a matter of fact,' I said surprised, 'yes, I was.'

'How clever of you, Alex!' exclaimed Mrs Jardine. 'How did you guess Dr Ashworth had been head boy?'

'No boy attracts His Grace's attention unless he shows signs of becoming a walking advertisement for Muscular Christianity.'

'I adore Muscular Christianity,' said Lady Starmouth.

'If Christianity were a little more muscular the world wouldn't be in such a mess,' said the forthright Mrs Cobden-Smith.

'If Christianity were a little more muscular it wouldn't be Christianity,' said the Bishop, again displaying his compulsion to argue with his sister-in-law. 'The Sermon on the Mount wasn't a lecture on weight-lifting.'

'What exactly *is* Muscular Christianity?' inquired Mrs Jardine. 'I've never been quite sure. Is it just groups of nice-looking young clergymen like Dr Ashworth?'

' "Angels and ministers of grace defend us!" ' said the Bishop, raising his eyes to heaven as he quoted *Hamlet*.

'More sherry, anyone?' said Miss Christie, finally escaping from Colonel Cobden-Smith.

'Dinner is served, my Lord,' said the butler in a sepulchral voice from the doorway.

V

The dining-room was as vast as the drawing-room and it too faced down the garden to the river. I had wondered if the gentlemen were required to 'take a lady in' to dinner, but Mrs Jardine gave no instructions and as we all wandered informally into the dining-room I was hoping I might claim the chair next to Miss Christie. However there were place-cards, and a quick glance told me I was to be disappointed. Although I shared with the Bishop the pleasure of being seated next to Lady Starmouth my other neighbour proved to be the formidable Mrs Cobden-Smith and meanwhile, far away on the opposite side of the table, Miss Christie was once more finding herself trapped with the Colonel; to my irritation I saw he was clearly delighted by his undeserved good fortune.

After the Bishop had said grace we all embarked on a watery celery soup, a disaster which was subsequently redeemed first by poached trout and then by roast lamb. The main course was accompanied by a superb claret. I almost asked the Bishop to identify it, but decided he might subscribe to the view that in Church circles a keen interest in wine was permissible only for bishops or for archdeacons and canons over sixty. With a superhuman exercise of will-power I restricted myself to two glasses and was aware of Jardine noticing as I declined a third.

'Leaving room for the post-prandial port, Canon?'

'Oh, is there port, Bishop? What a treat!' I assumed an expression of innocent surprise.

The dinner surged on, everyone talking with increasing animation as the claret exerted its influence. Mrs Cobden-Smith asked me about my background, and having established the exact shade of my class she was sufficiently reassured to give me the benefit of her opinions which ranged from the futility of giving the working classes houses with bathrooms to the folly of listening to the Indian natives who wanted independence. When I could escape from Mrs Cobden-Smith's attentions Lady Starmouth pounced and I found myself being subjected to a far more subtle inquisition. Lady Starmouth wanted to know about my wife, but when I volunteered little information in response to her oblique enquiries she decided to probe my views on a topical subject affecting matrimony; I was asked what I thought of A. P. Herbert's celebrated Marriage Bill which had triggered Jardine's attack on Lang in the Lords.

The knowledge of how much I owed the Archbishop was never far from the surface of my mind. I said politely, 'I'm afraid I disapprove of divorce being made easier, Lady Starmouth.'

'My dear Dr Ashworth, you surprise me! I thought you'd have very liberal modern views!'

'Not if he's the Archbishop's man,' said our host, breaking off his conversation with Mrs Jennings.

'I'm no one's man but my own, Dr Jardine!' I said at once. I felt unnerved as well as annoyed that he had seen straight through my dutifully conservative stance.

'Well spoken!' said Lady Starmouth.

'Do you approve of divorce at all, Canon?' said Lord Starmouth with interest.

This placed me in a fresh dilemma. If I wanted to be entirely loyal to Lang, who followed the teaching on divorce in St Mark's Gospel, I would have to say that I believed marriage to be indissoluble, but I was now anxious to show Jardine that I was no mere sycophantic echo of the Archbishop. On the other hand some loyalty to Lang was essential; I could hardly espouse Jardine's extreme and controversial views. I decided to seek the diplomatic middle course by jettisoning St Mark in favour of St Matthew.

'I believe,' I said, 'that adultery should be a ground for divorce – for both sexes, just as Our Lord said.'

'So you disapprove of the rest of A. P. Herbert's Bill?' said Jennings, coming late to the conversation and manifesting the teacher's desire to clarify a clouded issue. 'You don't believe that the grounds for divorce should be extended to include cruelty, insanity and desertion?'

'Precisely.'

'So!' said Jardine, unable to remain silent a moment longer, his amber eyes lambent at the prospect of debate. 'You would approve a divorce, would you, Dr Ashworth, if a man spends ten minutes in a hotel bedroom with a woman he's never met before – yet you would deny a divorce to a woman whose husband has subjected her for years to the most disgusting cruelties?'

'I'm not denying the remedy of a legal separation in such a case.'

'In other words you'd condemn her to a miserable limbo, unable to remarry! And all because you and the other clerics who tow the High Church line insist on clinging to an utterly fallacious interpretation of Our Lord's teaching in the Synoptic Gospels!'

'I – '

'You don't seriously think Our Lord was talking about divorce as a lawyer, do you?'

'I think Our Lord was talking about what he believed to be right!' I was aware that all other conversation in the room had ceased; even the servants by the sideboard were transfixed.

Jardine said truculently, 'But he wasn't talking legalistically – he wasn't, in advance of Christian history, claiming to be another Moses, the supreme law-giver. He was a life-giving spirit, not a legal code personified!'

'He was indeed a life-giving spirit,' I said, 'and he illustrated the true life of Man – he made clear the principles of right human action, and I think we ignore his teaching at our peril, Bishop!'

'But what exactly was his teaching on divorce?' demanded Jardine, ripping open the hole in my argument. 'The Gospels don't agree! I think the clause permitting divorce for adultery was inserted into St Matthew's Gospel in an attempt to correct the legalistic way in which the early Church had thoroughly misunderstood the teaching of Jesus – '

'That's Brunner's theory, of course, but Brunner's notorious for remodelling Christianity to suit the twentieth century – '

'Brunner's *reinterpreting* Christianity *in the light of* the twentieth century, and what's wrong with that? Every generation has to interpret Christianity afresh – '

'Bishop, are you saying that A. P. Herbert has a license to rewrite St Matthew?'

' – and one of the outstanding aspects of Christianity is that Christ preached compassion and forgiveness, not an inflexible hardness of heart. How long were you married, Dr Ashworth?'

'Three years. But – '

'And during those three years,' pursued Jardine, 'did you have no glimpse of what the state of matrimony could be like for others less fortunate than yourself?'

'That's absolutely irrelevant to the theological point under discussion!'

'You *were* happily married, I assume?'

'Yes, I was – and that's exactly why I'm opposed to debasing the institution of marriage by a set of fashionable divorce laws which go far beyond the teaching of Christ!'

'It's people who debase marriage, not laws – people who would keep a couple yoked together in circumstances which would have made Christ weep! Tell me, how long have you been a widower? It must be hard for you to remain single when you regard marriage as such a blissfully ideal state!'

I hesitated. I was by this time very profoundly disturbed. I sensed I was losing control not only of the debate but of my inner equilibrium, the equilibrium which I had to maintain in order to be the man I wanted to be, and although I knew I had to terminate the conversation I could not see how to do it without a disastrous loss of face.

'Well?' demanded Jardine. 'Why the long silence? Let me ask you again: how long have you been a widower?'

I saw the trap he was setting to expose my hypocrisy but I saw too that there was no escaping it. Pride and prudence combined to make an outright lie impossible. In defiance I said finally, 'Seven years.'

'Seven years!' The amber eyes widened as I gave him the answer he wanted. I felt as if my soul had been X-rayed. Nausea churned in the pit of my stomach. 'You surprise me, Dr Ashworth! You talk so sanctimoniously about the institution of marriage yet apparently you have little desire to marry again! Is this because of a belated call to celibacy? Or are you perhaps not quite such a stranger to marital unhappiness as you would have us all believe?'

He had tied me up in such a knot that I had no choice but to grab the sharpest knife to slash myself free. 'I'm certainly no stranger to marital tragedy,' I said. 'My wife was killed in a car crash when she was expecting our first child, and I often think I'll never recover from the loss.'

There was a silence. The light went out of Jardine's lambent eyes, and for a second I saw the grief mark his face as a memory seared his mind. Around the table no one moved. The room seemed suffocating.

At last Jardine said, 'I'm most extremely sorry, Dr Ashworth. I've no personal experience of losing a wife but I do know what it's like to lose a child. Forgive me for trespassing so intolerably on what must be a very deep and private grief.'

I was so conscious of shame that I was unable to speak. Jardine might not have exposed me as a fraud to his guests but he had exposed me as a fraud to myself, and I knew that to preserve my fraudulent mask I had taken the cheapest way out when I had had my back to the wall.

I was still groping for composure seconds later when the ladies withdrew and Colonel Cobden-Smith immediately announced his intention of retiring to the smoking-room. Lord Starmouth offered to accompany him, and after helping themselves to a glass of port apiece they departed in search of tranquillity after the débâcle at the dinner table.

'I've such a strong aversion to smoking,' Jardine explained to Jennings as the door closed behind the last servant, 'that I insist on confining it to one room of the house.' He turned to me with careful courtesy. 'But perhaps you'd care to join the Colonel and Lord Starmouth, Canon – are you a smoker?'

'Yes, but not when I'm wearing my clerical collar.' My voice sounded astonishingly casual.

'How admirable. And you, Jennings?'

'I'm a non-smoker, my Lord.'

'Even more admirable. Jennings, you may address me as "Bishop" or as "Dr Jardine" but leave "My Lord" to the servants, if you please. I think bishops suffer quite enough from delusions of grandeur without being addressed as if they'd been born to the purple . . . Well, gentlemen, you've just seen me at my worst and now I must make every attempt to display myself at my best. Dr Ashworth – ' he passed me the decanter ' – I beg you to help yourself to the largest possible glass of port and to tell me about your new book. His Grace muttered something about fourth-century Christology and St Anselm, but as there appears to be no connection between the two subjects I confess I'm mystified – or are you perhaps hoping to prove that the seeds of the ontological argument were sown at the Council of Nicaea?' And he gave me his most charming smile.

I smiled back to signal that I had every intention of supporting his attempt to restore a convivial atmosphere, and began to explain my plan to revise my lectures, but it was Jennings, not Jardine, who talked to me about St Anselm. The chaplain interposed a remark about the Cathedral library but sank into silence as the discussion of St Anselm's theology degenerated into the dreariest type of academic debate.

Suddenly I said to Jardine, 'I'm sorry, we must be boring you.'

'Not in the least.' He sipped his port. 'I was merely wondering why you turn your back on the present to bury yourself in the remote past. But perhaps modern Church history would involve you in modern Church politics which is a subject best avoided if your views are unlikely to please the people in power.'

I recognized that this subtly dangerous statement was not an attack but an inquiry; he was giving me the opportunity to state that my career had not been distorted by the most unwholesome form of ambition, and I said at once, 'I happen to find Arianism and Modalism more stimulating than the Oxford Movement.'

Jardine picked up the reference to Anglo-Catholicism. 'Does that indicate a certain ambivalence about the High Church party?'

He was inviting me to disassociate myself from Lang, and suddenly I knew he would once again see straight through any profession of loyalty which was not entirely sincere. 'I was sympathetic to Anglo-Catholicism when I was ordained,' I said in a clumsy attempt at evasion.

'So was I – that'll surprise you, won't it! But I can see now that I was merely trying to reject my Nonconformist background.' He turned suddenly to his chaplain. 'Gerald, I've promised to lend Mr Jennings that book by Brunner, *The Mediator*. Take him to the library, would you, and look it out for him.'

That disposed of Jennings and Harvey. I was alone with the Bishop at last and almost before the door had closed I found myself saying: 'I'm beginning to think you see straight through everything.'

'I have a first-class try. I sometimes think I know what life must be like for a musician who possesses perfect pitch. I have a well-nigh infallible ear for detecting false notes in a conversation.'

'During our debate – '

'During our debate you tried to conceal that your private views on divorce are rather different from your public views. Yes. I know. And that's why I couldn't resist the temptation to tear you to shreds, but I am indeed most sincerely sorry that the debate went so wrong.'

'It's all right. My hypocrisy got what it deserved. Sorry I took such a cheap way out.' The conversation was now so far removed from any dialogue I could have foreseen that I was unable to sustain it. Moving to the hearth, the glass of port in my hand, I pretended to examine the carvings on the chimneypiece.

'Now that,' said Jardine, 'is a very remarkable apology. You're beginning to interest me exceedingly, Dr Ashworth.' Although I had my back to him, I heard the splash as he refilled his glass. 'First of all I was tempted to write you off as just another of Lang's bright young men,' he was saying, 'but the truth's more complicated than that, isn't it? You no longer find the required mask of sycophancy easy to wear.'

I finished my port before saying, 'I'm very much in Dr Lang's debt.'

'Of course you are. Men of power have a knack of building up extensive credit, but if one is in a position of power,' said Jardine, moving over to me with the decanter in his hand, 'one must always be scrupulously careful not to bankrupt one's debtors by demanding inappropriate methods of repayment. More port?'

'Thank you.' I held out my glass with a steady hand.

'May I give you a word of advice? Your first duty, debts or no debts, is not to the Archbishop of Canterbury. Your first duty is to God who created you as a unique individual in his own image, not as a miraculous facsimile of Dr Lang. Be yourself, Dr Ashworth. Be the man God intended you to be, not the sycophant His Grace's vanity would prefer. And now,' said Jardine, having refilled my glass, 'I shall stop preaching and we shall divert ourselves very briefly, before we join the ladies, by ruminating on an issue which to me is of far greater interest than dear old St Anselm's meditations. I refer to the search for the historical Jesus – do you think we can ever see beyond the shining image of the Gospels to the man he really was?'

'I think it can be unproductive to probe behind glittering images,' I said, 'and with all due respect I believe your generation has been too preoccupied with Christ's humanity at the expense of his divinity.'

Jardine smiled. 'You think that in pursuing the concept of the immanence of God in mankind we've wound up losing sight of God and following mankind, as represented by Christ, down a historical blind alley?'

'Exactly. Speaking for myself, I'm much more interested in the modern doctrines asserting God's transcendence and the importance of revelation – I think we should focus on the message Christ presented, not on the shadowy figure behind the glittering image,' I said firmly, and escaping with profound relief into the world of scholarship, I began to talk of the writings of Karl Barth and the challenge of Crisis Theology.

VI

On our return to the drawing-room Jardine announced: 'I'm glad to say that Dr Ashworth and I have quite resolved our differences so there's no need for anyone to remain embarrassed by our debate . . . Lady Starmouth, come outside and take a turn with me on the terrace.'

'Coffee, Dr Ashworth?' called Miss Christie.

'Yes – thank you.' I was just moving towards her with alacrity when I was intercepted by a distraught Mrs Jardine.

'Dr Ashworth, I'm so very sorry – my husband was terribly upset afterwards, I know he was – it was when you mentioned the baby – ' As she broke off I saw to my horror that her eyes were full of tears.

'My dear Mrs Jardine – please – don't distress yourself – '

But Miss Christie had come to the rescue. 'It's all right, darling,' she said to Mrs Jardine, and I was struck by her use of an endearment. 'Dr Ashworth understands. Come and sit down – Mrs Jennings and I were just discussing the choirboys' concert.' And passing me my cup of coffee she steered Mrs Jardine to the cluster of chairs where Mrs Jennings was waiting. I found myself abandoned to the company of the Cobden-Smiths, but Lord Starmouth was no more than six paces away by the fireplace and as our glances met he said without emphasis: 'The Bishop's passions get the better of him sometimes, but he's a good man.'

'One doesn't look for passion in a bishop,' said the Colonel with unexpected tartness. 'Bad form.'

'Very bad form,' agreed his wife, 'but then of course if one's not brought up to know the difference between good form and bad form one's bound to cause chaos in later life.'

'Steady on, Amy!'

'But my dear, Alex is the first to admit his upbringing left a lot to be desired! That peculiar old father and that dreadful little villa in Putney – '

'The great thing about the Bishop,' said Lord Starmouth, 'is that he'll own to the little villa in Putney. A lesser man would simply draw a veil over it.'

'He had the veil firmly in place when he met Carrie,' said Mrs Cobden-Smith.

'Steady *on*, Amy!' The Colonel was now clearly nervous. He shot a wary glance in my direction, but I was more interested in Miss Christie; she had left Mrs Jardine, now happily talking about choirboys to Mrs Jennings, and was approaching us with the coffee-pot.

'Is Carrie all right?' murmured the Colonel as his cup was refilled.

'Yes, all's well, Colonel, don't worry.'

'Dr Ashworth still looks a little white around the gills,' said Mrs Cobden-Smith.

'That hardly says much for the power of the Bishop's port,' said Miss Christie drily, sweeping away again with the coffee-pot.

'That's a very strange girl,' mused Mrs Cobden-Smith, 'but so good with Carrie.'

I said casually, 'She must be a great asset in the household.'

'That hardly does her justice. When I think of that time at Radbury before her arrival – '

'My dear,' said the Colonel with surprising firmness, 'I don't think we'll talk about that at present, if you please.'

I was disappointed, and with reluctance I realized that it might pay me later to cultivate Mrs Cobden-Smith.

I had apparently resumed my role of spy. Did this mean I was regaining my equilibrium after the bizarre scene with Jardine? I supposed it did, yet I had no wish to think of spying and no desire whatsoever to dwell on bizarre scenes. Easing myself away from the Cobden-Smiths I succeeded in cornering Miss Christie at the side-table where she was stacking the coffee-cups on to a tray.

'What time is Communion tomorrow?' I said, offering the most inoffensive question I could devise.

'Eight o'clock. Breakfast is at nine.' She looked past me at the drawing-room door. 'Here come Mr Jennings and Gerald – will you excuse me? I must order fresh coffee for them.'

I lost her, and it occurred to me then that a quiet mild approach was going to make no impression whatsoever on Miss Christie. However if she thought she could brush me aside merely by juggling coffee-cups she had made a big mistake.

I resolved to adopt a much tougher line in future.

VII

It was after eleven when I regained the sanctuary of my room, and having stripped off my clothes I smoked a cigarette as I tried to work out what had happened. Some strange bond seemed to have been forged between me and my host but it seemed to be my duty to ignore it. It was not my business either to like or to loathe Jardine; my task was merely to estimate how vulnerable he was to scandal.

However I found I now had a stronger desire than before not to connive with Lang in any secret plan to oust Jardine from the Bench of Bishops. Jardine was clearly innocent. A man of such integrity would be incapable of living a secret life as an apostate steeped in adultery, and I was also sure he was far too shrewd to engage in any middle-aged folly which fell short of an adulterous liaison. It seemed obvious that he exercised his flirtatious streak harmlessly with his lovely ladies and had long treated Miss Christie as part of the palace furniture.

This conclusion was reassuring enough, but I still had to answer the question of what went on in Miss Christie's mind while Jardine behaved like the good man he undoubtedly was. I reminded myself that Jardine could still be vulnerable to scandal if Miss Christie decided to play the neurotic spinster by transforming herself into a furnace of frustrated passion, and although she hardly gave the impression of being a neurotic spinster I felt there was something odd about her extreme self-containment.

I decided I had a moral duty to investigate Miss Christie further and an absolute moral duty to discover how likely she was to transform herself into a furnace of passion.

No Jesuit could have achieved a more satisfying casuistry. With a smile I stubbed out my cigarette, retired to bed and began to plot my espionage for the morrow.

THREE

'I have seen so many clerical careers arrested, and (to all outward seeming) definitely marred, by the clergyman's marriage, that I never hear of a clergyman's becoming "engaged" without a shiver of anxiety.'

Letters of Herbert Hensley Henson
Bishop of Durham 1920–1939
ed. E. F. BRALEY

I

I awoke violently at seven. Naturally I had been dreaming of Miss Christie. I wanted to smoke a cigarette, but I decided that I had no excuse for breaking any of the minor rules by which I achieved self-discipline, and one of those rules was that I never smoked before breakfast. With an effort I read the morning office. Then making another random dip into the Bible I eventually encountered the appropriate words: 'Seek and ye shall find'.

As I dressed it occurred to me that I still had to seek and find a great many facts about Jardine before I could report convincingly to Lang that the Bishop's private life was as pure as driven snow; my impression of innocence would carry little weight unless it were supported by a thorough understanding of Jardine's psychology, and I could hardly establish a psychological portrait without much more information about his past. Apart from gauging Miss Christie's ability to become a furnace of passion my main task was clearly to talk to as many people as possible about the Bishop without making them suspect they were being interrogated, but I doubted that this would prove difficult. People always enjoy a gossip about a famous man, and when a famous man is personally known to them the temptation to reveal how much they know is all the greater.

Leaving my room, I padded downstairs. I met no one, although I could hear the distant rattling and banging of servants pursuing their early morning rituals. Opening the front door I stepped out into the porch, and the brilliant sunlight flooded into my eyes so that for a second I saw only a shimmering green pattern of beech leaves and grass. Beyond the drive the pale stone of the Cathedral soared into a cloudless sky, and after opening the white gate which was set in the wall of the churchyard I headed along the north side of the building to the porch.

A passing verger directed me to St Anselm's Chapel where the weekday Communion services were held. There was no time to gape at the glory of the nave; I wanted to clear my mind in preparation for worship, and as soon as I had chosen my seat in the chapel I knelt to sharpen my concentration. However I had instantly noted Miss Christie's absence.

This failed to surprise me. Weekday Communion is seldom attended by hordes of laymen, and in fact I saw no one I knew from the palace in the small congregation. Then Gerald Harvey hurried into the row behind me, and seconds later at eight o'clock the Dean and the Bishop appeared, preceded by the verger.

As the service progressed I thought how preposterous it was to imagine a bishop administering the sacrament when he was not in a state of grace, and again I remembered the integrity which had emanated from Jardine during our private conversation over the port.

My moment came to receive the sacrament. Erasing all thought of my commission I focused my mind on the spiritual reality confronting me and it was not until I had returned to my seat that I allowed myself to think again of Jardine. I vowed to remember that my first duty was not to the Archbishop of Canterbury. I asked for the strength to overcome my weaknesses. And at the conclusion of the service I let the familiar prayer of Christ echo in my mind: Let thy will, not mine, be done.

Lang's will immediately became as unimportant as my own. I felt comforted, and rising to my feet at last I left the chapel to find Gerald Harvey hovering in the side-aisle.

'Waiting for the Bishop?' I enquired with a smile.

'No, for you.'

I was impressed by this courtesy and at once I felt guilty that I had written him off as ineffectual. 'How nice of you,' I said. 'Sorry I've kept you hanging about.'

'Oh, you mustn't apologize for taking extra time for prayer!' said Harvey shocked. He was so young and ingenuous that he made me feel old and world-weary. 'How did you like the service?'

I paid the Bishop a suitable compliment and was glad I did not have to be insincere for the sake of politeness. We walked through the porch on to the sward. Beyond the wall of the churchyard the houses of the Close basked in the sun and a horse was drawing a milk-cart slowly along the North Walk. I could hear the birds singing in the cedar tree nearby.

'I must confess the Bishop intrigues me,' I said idly at last. 'What would you say was the fundamental nature of his belief? God-centred? Christ-centred? Rooted in the Trinity?'

'Well, it's all those things,' said Harvey, 'but I suppose he's fundamentally Christocentric. He has an overriding belief not just in Christ's compassion and forgiveness but in Christ's honesty and truth, and that's why he can't bear hypocrisy – he sees it as a re-enactment of the Pharisees' behaviour in the Gospels and he feels called to attack it just as Our Lord did.' He shot me a shy glance. 'Please forgive him for last night,' he said rapidly. 'He didn't mean to hurt you. He just misjudged your sincerity – I think he suspected you'd only adopted your point of view out of loyalty to Dr Lang and of course he was wrong, but anyone can make a mistake, can't they, and he really is the most wonderful man, absolutely the best, believe me.'

I realized belatedly that he had sought my company in order to defend his hero, and I knew I should signal that I was willing to be convinced of Jardine's heroic qualities. I said with interest, 'He's been good to you?'

'That's an understatement!' In his enthusiasm Harvey became confidential. 'When I was at the Cathedral School at Radbury my parents died and Dr Jardine – he was Dean of Radbury then – simply took me over, paid my school fees, had me to stay in the holidays – and it wasn't as if I was one of those appealing children who look like angels and win all the prizes. Then later when I wanted to be ordained I wasn't sure whether I'd be able to pass the exams but Dr Jardine just said, "Nonsense, of course you can!" and when he offered to coach me in his spare time I knew he really believed I could do it. I'd never have passed if it hadn't been for him, and afterwards when he asked me to be his chaplain . . . Well, you can imagine how I felt! Of course I was terrified I'd be no good and in fact I'm sure he could get someone better, but I try very hard and I seem to muddle through somehow.'

'I'm sure you do very well.' It was impossible not to be touched by his honesty, and suddenly I knew why he had appealed to Jardine.

Meanwhile our conversation had taken us through the palace gateway and I was rapidly framing some questions which would take advantage of his confidential mood. 'Tell me about life at the palace,' I said. 'Miss Christie evidently has an important role in the household – she seems very close to Mrs Jardine.'

'Oh, Mrs Jardine thinks of her as a daughter, I know she does.'

'How does she get on with the Bishop?'

'People always want to know that,' said Harvey, pausing to extricate his latchkey as we approached the front door, 'and they're always surprised by my reply which is: "Better than they used to" and not the expected "Magnificently well".'

'There's been friction?'

'Well, not exactly *friction* . . . but they've had their cool spells. The first was after she came to Radbury – that was around the time I started staying with them in the holidays – and then there was a second cool period after they arrived in Starbridge five years ago. I remember saying to Lady Starmouth once that I was afraid Lyle might leave if the Bishop became much cooler, but Lady Starmouth told me not to worry. She said it's not always easy for a married couple to live in close proximity to a third party, and of course Lyle's much more involved with both the Jardines than I am. I'm fairly peripheral in their private life, even though I see so much of the Bishop in his professional role.' He finally found his latchkey but when the front door swung open it became wedged against a pile of envelopes. 'Heavens above, look at all this post!'

'Is this abnormally substantial?'

'Yes, we're still dealing with the correspondence on the A. P. Herbert Bill. We even had to engage additional secretarial help last week,' said Harvey, becoming flustered at the memory, and bustled away into the library as if he feared the envelopes might multiply in his hands.

I made a mental note to ask Lady Starmouth about the difficulties of a married couple obliged to live in close proximity to a young and attractive third party. Then I retired to the dining-room in pursuit of breakfast.

II

I was early. I found no one in the dining-room, but the morning papers were laid out on a side-table and I began to browse among the cricket reports in the *Daily Telegraph*. I was still digesting the unfortunate news that Oxford had defeated Cambridge by seven wickets when Jardine walked in.

'I was glad to see you at the service,' he said after we had exchanged greetings. 'I was glad to be there myself. Sometimes one so strongly needs to wipe the slate clean in order to come fresh to a new day.'

There was a pause while we both thought of the dinner party, its unhappy memory now purged from our consciences, and before either of us could speak again the Starmouths entered the room. They were followed by Miss Christie, immaculate in a navy-blue skirt and white blouse, and at once I noticed the discreet, perfectly proportioned curves of her figure above the waist; I even found myself toying with the erotic image of a pair of empty champagne glasses.

'Good morning, Dr Ashworth,' she said formally, while I was grappling with these most unclerical thoughts, but the next moment she was turning to Jardine. 'Carrie's decided to stay in bed for a while, Bishop, and she's asked me to have breakfast with her.'

The Bishop showed no surprise but Lady Starmouth inquired in alarm if Mrs Jardine were unwell. Miss Christie, however, had already retreated to the hall and it was left to Jardine to answer idly as he turned a page of

The Times, 'It's merely the aftermath of insomnia. At two o'clock this morning, acting out of a strong sense of self-preservation, I was obliged to retire to my dressing-room in order to resume the bliss of unconsciousness. The chief disadvantage of Carrie's insomnia is that she's always overcome with the urge to share it with me.'

My immediate reaction was to reflect that Jack had been right in assuming that the Jardines still shared a bedroom. My second reaction was to accuse myself of becoming more prurient than any reporter from *The News of the World*, and in an effort to beat back all thoughts which were unbecoming to a clergyman I began to consider how I should spend my morning. I would have to go to the library; it would look too odd if I postponed my encounter with the St Anselm manuscript, but I thought I could use the fine weather as an excuse not to linger indoors. During breakfast the Earl announced his intention of fishing in the river at the bottom of the garden while the Countess confessed an urge to paint a watercolour of the long herbaceous border, and I thought both of them might be in the mood for a little casual conversation about our host.

'Do you have any special plans for this morning, Mrs Cobden-Smith?' I asked as I finished my eggs and bacon.

'Oh, I shall write some letters, go to the shops, "fill the unforgiving minute", as Kipling would say ...' Mrs Cobden-Smith spoke with such energy that I immediately felt exhausted. 'Willy will take George for a walk – ' The St Bernard looked hopeful as his name was mentioned ' – and then ... What are you going to do after that, Willy?'

'Nothing, I hope,' said Colonel Cobden-Smith.

'Good man!' said Lord Starmouth.

'Well, at least the clergy are preparing for a morning of unremitting toil,' said Lady Starmouth, and gave me yet another of her radiant sophisticated smiles.

III

The most notorious fact about the work which passes under the name of *The Prayers and Meditations of St Anselm* is that it is uncertain how much of the material can be attributed to St Anselm himself. In 1932 Dom Wilmart had ascribed nineteen of the prayers and three of the meditations to the saint, who had been Archbishop of Canterbury at the time of William Rufus, but the matter was still of interest to scholars and much of the interest had always centred on the Starbridge manuscript which showed the work before the insertion of many of the additions.

After the required exchange of courtesies with the librarian I embarked on my reading. The manuscript was written in a clear hand which I mastered without trouble, but there were slips in the Latin which indicated that the scribe might have been a young monk who suffered from wandering attention. To support this thesis I found some entertaining embellishments in the margin, in particular a sketch of a prancing cat with a mouse in his mouth, and I thought how odd it was that this manuscript, perhaps regarded as no more than a tedious copying chore by its scribe, had survived to become a document of profound importance. The young monk had been dead for centuries but his work for God lived on; idly I speculated how I might introduce the subject into a future sermon, and at once I thought of the famous text from Isaiah: 'The grass withereth, the flower fadeth but the Word of Our God shall stand for ever'.

I took notes for over an hour as I compared the text with my copy of Wilmart's book, and then leaving the library I returned to the palace, parked my briefcase in the hall and strolled outside again into the garden.

I saw Lady Starmouth at once. She was sitting on an artist's folding stool, her sketchpad in her lap, and gazing meditatively at the long border which stretched downhill in a blaze of colour towards the river. When she saw me she smiled, beckoning me to join her, and as I crossed the lawn I could see the Earl fishing in the distance by the willows.

'I thought it was going to be a watercolour?' I said as I saw the pencil in her hand.

'I always do a rough sketch first and I've only just begun – I've been chatting to poor Carrie.'

'Is she better?'

'Yes, but still distressed about that ghastly scene last night. I'm afraid that sometimes she's much too sensitive for her own good and never more so than when the conversation turns to lost babies . . . Did you know about the Jardines' child?'

'Dr Lang only mentioned that they had no children living. What happened?'

'Am I being given the chance to gossip about the Bishop? Yes, I am – how delightful! Do sit down, Dr Ashworth, and help me postpone the dreaded moment when I have to open my paintbox and pretend to be an artist!'

To encourage her I said, 'If you're in the mood to gossip, I'm certainly in the mood to listen – after my clash with the Bishop last night I find I'm gripped by a curiosity to know more about him.'

'In the circumstances,' said Lady Starmouth drily, 'I'd say curiosity was an admirably charitable reaction. Now let me see, shall I launch straight away into the saga of the baby or shall I begin with Jardine's arrival in Mayfair? I warn you, I'm rather a menace when I start talking about the Bishop because I find him so intriguing that I tend to prattle away happily for hours.'

'I'm sure you never prattle, Lady Starmouth – I can only imagine you discoursing alluringly!'

She laughed. 'How wonderful to have such a flattering audience! Very well, let me try to discourse with all the allure at my command!'

Lounging on the lawn beneath the hot sun I prepared to give her my fullest attention.

IV

'Jardine's had the most unusual life,' said Lady Starmouth. 'I'm not sure how much you already know about his career, but twenty-one years ago in 1916 he was promoted from an obscure chaplaincy in North London to St Mary's, Mayfair – and of course that's one of the smartest parishes in the West End. Henry and I did our best to welcome the new vicar, and because he was unmarried I made a special effort to introduce him to suitable girls. Did you know Jardine married late? He was thirty-seven when he met Carrie, but before the move to St Mary's he couldn't afford a wife. Unfortunately he had a most peculiar father who had wound up heavily in debt, and Jardine had to support the family on his small stipend.'

'Someone mentioned a peculiar father – '

'The whole family,' said Lady Starmouth confidentially, 'was most odd. In addition to the peculiar father there was a very strange Swedish stepmother and two sisters, one of whom went mad – '

'This sounds like a Jacobean tragedy.'

'No, they didn't all kill each other – unfortunately – but you're right to relate it to literature. It was like a novel by Gissing about the ghastliness of genteel poverty.'

'Were the Jardines so genteel? What did the peculiar father do for a living?'

'Nobody knows. In fact I've never plumbed the depths of Jardine's lurid family background because he prefers not to talk about it, but the sister – the one who didn't go mad – was painfully genteel, poor thing, a very refined accent and a ghastly way with a teacup – and my guess is that they were all upper-working-class but trying to be lower-middle. God, how crucified so many people are,' said the aristocratic Lady Starmouth carelessly but with genuine feeling, 'by the English class system.'

'Did the whole family accompany Jardine to Mayfair?'

'No, the peculiar father and the mad sister were dead by that time, but Jardine moved into the vicarage with his surviving sister and his sinister Swedish stepmother and immediately began to cast around for a wife – '

' – whom you obligingly provided for him!'

'Not quite! But I did go to the dinner party where he and Carrie met

49

for the first time. The meeting was wildly romantic, love at first sight, and four days later he proposed.'

'*Four days?*'

'Four days,' said Lady Starmouth, enjoying my astonishment. 'Carrie's family were in a tremendous tizzy, of course, because of Jardine's odd background, but on the other hand he had this stunning position as Vicar of St Mary's and that made it hard to object to him as a suitor.'

'Did the family make trouble?'

'They somehow managed to restrain themselves. I suspect it was because Carrie wasn't so young any more and the family had begun to worry that she might wind up on the shelf.'

'It's hard to imagine someone as pretty as Mrs Jardine winding up on the shelf.'

'True, but one of the cruellest facts of life, Dr Ashworth, is that men prefer pretty women to be under thirty. After that women need to rely more on other resources.'

I sensed the implication that Mrs Jardine had no other resources on which to rely, but all I said was, 'So nothing impeded Dr Jardine's stampede to the altar?'

'On the contrary, the Swedish stepmother then made a scene and said she wouldn't live in any house where Carrie was mistress. So she retired with the poor plain sister to a flat in Putney – which Jardine had to pay for, of course.'

'But surely wasn't this a good thing? Isn't it better for a woman to start married life without a stepmother-in-law breathing down her neck?'

'Of course. Carrie was thrilled. But Jardine was dreadfully upset. He adored this stepmother, although God knows why – she was twenty years older than he was and she weighed sixteen stone and she had very pale eyes and a very thin mouth and she spoke with a very heavy foreign accent – oh, she was *sinister*, she really was! After the row I thought she'd refuse to come to the wedding but she turned up looking wrathful – what a deathshead at the feast! The poor sister was hardly cheerful either – she wept throughout the service, but at least she was only crying out of sentimentality. I liked the sister. Poor thing, what a wretched life she had! She died of cancer eventually, of course. I say "of course" because she was the sort of person who inevitably dies of something beastly . . . But I must stop digressing. You're being wonderfully patient, Dr Ashworth, but I really am getting to the baby now, I promise – '

'Don't apologize, Lady Starmouth. I'm enrapt by the sinister step-mother.'

'Well, after the wedding she sank into darkest Putney, thank God, and the Jardines floated off on their honeymoon. When they came back Carrie immediately started planning the nursery, so of course we all thought . . . But nothing happened. However finally the baby started. We were all so relieved, and no one was more relieved than Jardine – apart from Carrie herself, of course. He started talking to Henry about which schools the child should go to and Carrie started adding the finishing touches to the heavenly nursery – oh, what a mistake it is to count one's chickens before they're hatched! Eventually the worst happened and the baby – a boy – was born dead.'

Lady Starmouth paused as if to choose her next words with care. 'I wonder how I can convey to you how dreadful this was for the Jardines. Of course a dead baby is always a tragedy, but in this case . . . You see, Carrie was so absolutely sure that her one talent was for motherhood. It's not easy for any woman to be married to a brilliant man and Carrie thought that motherhood would give her the chance to excel in a way which would command Jardine's very special respect. And Jardine himself was longing for a family. He wanted to recreate the family life which he could remember existing before his mother died – a life which he'd almost certainly idealized but which represented to him some intensely desirable goal of domestic bliss. So both he and Carrie were united by these very urgent and powerful dreams – and that was why it was so terrible when the stillborn child tore those dreams apart.'

She paused again and I allowed the silence to lengthen to signal my sympathy before I asked, 'There were no other children?'

'No, and in a way that was the ghastliest part of all because no doctor could tell her why nothing happened. So she went on hoping and so did he – in fact Alex once told me he went on hoping until . . . well, until no hope was possible any more. There! I'm calling him Alex – very improper, isn't it, to call a man by his Christian name when he's not a member of one's family, but I've known him so long now and we're such good friends and Henry doesn't mind if I call Jardine "Alex" occasionally . . . I expect you've wondered about my friendship with the Bishop, haven't you!' she added, giving me an indulgent smile. 'Perhaps you're even a little shocked!'

'Not at all, I'm deeply envious! I've heard about Dr Jardine's so-called Lovely Ladies, and obviously you're the Lovely Ladies' Leader!'

She laughed. 'I simply must add you to my clerical collection!' she said. 'You're such an exceptionally charming listener!'

'I could listen to you indefinitely, Lady Starmouth. Tell me more.'

She sighed. 'It really is too dreadful how little encouragement I need . . . But what shall I tell you next? I've told you about the ghastly background and the romantic marriage and the stillborn child –'

'Strike a lighter note,' I said, 'and tell me about Dr Jardine's Lovely Ladies.'

'Of course Alex has numerous acquaintances among the opposite sex,' said Lady Starmouth, adding another line to the obscure pattern on her sketchpad, 'but there are only three of us who could truly be described as friends. We all met him in 1916 during his first year as Vicar of St Mary's.'

I was immediately intrigued. 'Why was he so prone to friendship in 1916?'

'Moving to Mayfair was a huge change for him, and at first he was very lonely and unsure of himself.'

'Who are the other two ladies?'

'Sybil Welbeck and Enid Markhampton. Alex liked us because we were all absolutely safe – happily married, churchgoing women, firmly anchored to the conventions ... Heavens, how dull that sounds! But we're all tolerably amusing, I promise you – '

'You hardly need to assure me of that, Lady Starmouth, but what amazes me is Dr Jardine's luck in finding three safe Lovely Ladies all at once! Did he never add to his collection?'

'No,' said Lady Starmouth, examining the point of her pencil. 'He didn't.'

'Was that because he felt you were all so incomparable that no other woman was fit to join your ranks?'

We laughed before Lady Starmouth said easily, 'He married soon after he met us, and perhaps he was afraid Carrie wouldn't take too kindly to any new close friends of the opposite sex.'

'Speaking as a clergyman,' I said, 'I find the whole idea of close friendships with married women fraught with the most hair-raising possibilities.'

'Ah, but you're of a different generation, aren't you?' said Lady Starmouth. 'Such friendships may seem strange now but when I was young they weren't so unusual. The War changed so many things, and one of the first casualties of the new freedom afterwards was the concept of the *amitié amoureuse*.'

'Nevertheless I can't help thinking that if I'd been Dr Jardine I might have had a hard time preventing myself from falling in love with one of you.'

Lady Starmouth gave another indulgent smile but answered seriously, 'I can assure you that Alex has never been in love with either Enid or Sybil or me. At the risk of sounding horribly snobbish, I'll say that we're not in the league which he would consider accessible as far as the ultimate intimacies are concerned.'

I was again much intrigued. 'I'm not sure I understand you,' I said, wondering how I could lure her on over such delicate ground, but Lady

Starmouth had no need to be lured. I had forgotten that the aristocracy, unlike the middle classes, fail to find the subject of sex embarrassing.

'When Alex was growing up,' she said, 'the women in his life were – at most – lower-middle-class. Then his years up at Oxford gave him enough confidence to marry an upper-middle-class girl like Carrie Cobden-Smith. But I think if he'd been offered the chance of deep intimacy with someone from the aristocracy, he'd have backed away. He'd have found the prospect too intimidating.'

I knew at once that this was a vital detail in the portrait I was constructing of Jardine. The Bishop was safe with his Lovely Ladies, not necessarily because of any indestructible virtue on his part, but because there was a psychological barrier keeping him in check. Jardine would be aware of this; a clergyman is taught to know himself well so that he may learn the best way to control his weaknesses and Jardine, liking the company of the opposite sex, would only have trusted himself with women whom he felt were ultimately beyond his reach.

'Talking of lovely ladies,' said Lady Starmouth, adding another line to her sketch, 'have you fallen in love with Miss Christie?'

'Miss Christie!' I was so startled that I sat bolt upright.

'I saw the smouldering looks you were giving her in the drawing-room last night. My dear Dr Ashworth, will you allow me to take advantage of my numerous years of seniority by giving you some friendly advice? Don't bother with Miss Christie. She's spent the last decade proving she's quite uninterested in men.'

I said lightly, 'She doesn't nurse a secret passion for the Bishop?'

'I suspect it's much more likely she nurses a secret passion for Carrie.'

I exclaimed appalled, 'But that's impossible!'

'My poor Dr Ashworth, you *are* smitten, aren't you! Of course I'm not implying the passions's reciprocated – Carrie adores Alex. But you tell me this: why is an attractive intelligent girl like Miss Christie content to remain as a companion when she's had numerous proposals, some of them from very eligible men?'

I said suddenly, 'How do the Jardines explain Miss Christie's continuing spinsterhood?'

'Well, the official story is that she suffered a broken engagement before she met them, and that this left her perpetually disenchanted with the opposite sex. But I find that hard to believe – Miss Christie strikes me as the sort of woman who would consider it a matter of pride to recover completely from a broken engagement.'

'Does Dr Jardine ever talk to you about her?'

'Her name comes up occasionally, but not as much as it used to. Of course there have been moments in the past when he's found the situation a bore.'

I sensed we were approaching the difficulties of a married couple who had to live in close proximity to a third party. 'A bore?' I repeated, anxious to lure her on again. 'Why was that?'

'Oh, I'm afraid it's class again! Alex didn't grow up in a house where certain employees lived *en famille* and the presence of a third party tended to grate on his nerves, but fortunately the move to Starbridge seems to have solved that particular problem. There's more space here for third parties than there was in the Deanery at Radbury – and besides, when all's said and done the Jardines' marriage is quite successful enough to withstand the presence of a stranger . . . Dr Ashworth, my husband's waving at you. I expect he's getting bored with the fish and wants to be diverted – but come back and see me again after you've entertained him!'

We exchanged smiles. I said, 'Am I securely in your collection now?' and when she laughed I scrambled to my feet, dusted some flecks of grass from my trousers and strolled off down the garden to interview my next witness.

VI

'I was hoping a little conversation would disturb the fish,' said the Earl as I approached. 'They all seem to be either asleep or dead.'

Beyond the river the herd of cows was grazing again in the meadows. It was a very English scene which the Earl in his country clothes enhanced, and as I leant against the trunk of the nearest willow I was once more aware of the subtle allure of Starbridge as the morning melted into a shimmering afternoon. It was a day conducive to mirages. I was conscious not only that I was a clergyman pretending to be a spy – or was I a spy pretending to be a clergyman? – but that the Earl was a great land-owner pretending to be a humble fisherman. The Earl himself, with his open countenance, looked as if he were a stranger to play-acting, but the atmosphere of that Starbridge noon was reminding me how hard it was to know the truth about even the simplest individuals.

'I daresay my wife's been chatting to you about the Bishop in an effort to ensure you weren't put off by last night's glimpse of the rough diamond,' the Earl was saying. 'He was undoubtedly a rough diamond when we first knew him, but he's got plenty of gentlemanly polish nowadays when he puts his mind to it.'

'He certainly put his mind to it over the port . . . Were you disconcerted, Lord Starmouth, when a rough diamond turned up at St Mary's in 1916?'

The Earl smiled. 'I was more intrigued than disconcerted.'

'You hadn't met him before?'

'No, but I'd heard of him. He was always writing letters to *The Times*.

54

However I had little idea what sort of man he was until I came home from my club one night and my wife told me the new Vicar had called. She said, "He's got beautiful yellow eyes and a harsh ugly voice and he's not sure how to behave and I'm mad about him!" Well, my wife's always had a soft spot for clergymen so I didn't take her too seriously, but then next Sunday when he preached his first sermon I suddenly saw what all the fuss was about. I was used to dozing during the sermons, but this time I stayed awake all the way through – and in fact at the end I was sitting on the edge of my pew. Damn it, I can even remember the text! It was: "I am not come to call the righteous, but sinners to repentance", and when he was hammering home his message his voice seemed to make the church vibrate and his eyes glowed like a cat's. Extraordinary. Of course I saw at once he was going to go a long way.'

'What did you think when you had the chance for a private conversation with him?'

'I was surprised how shy he was – shy and awkward. He spoke all right; Oxford had ironed out any suburban accent, but he had the trick of either talking too much and too aggressively or else not talking at all. However, that was just nervousness. Once my wife took him up and petted him and tried to marry him off he very quickly blossomed. All he needed was a bit of social self-confidence.'

'Perhaps Oxford had given him a chip on his shoulder.'

'More than likely, yes. The Varsity can be hard going for someone who doesn't have the right background – well, I must admit to a bit of prejudice against him myself during the early days of our acquaintance, but then one day he spoke up to me; it was a criticism, a justifiable criticism too, I might add, and suddenly I thought: it took courage to say that. And I respected him for it. He was no sycophant. He was willing to accept a bit of patronage in the form of my wife's kindness but he wasn't going to let that stop him speaking the truth as he saw it. Very exceptional. A man of high moral principle. He's deserved his great success.'

'How very gratifying it must have been for your wife to see her protégé go all the way to the top of the Church of England!'

'Yes, I always say she made a small but significant contribution to his career. He needed someone who would invite him to the right dinner parties and ensure he developed the essential poise his position required. Mrs Welbeck and Lady Markhampton also helped him in that way, but Evelyn was the one who did the most.'

'Your wife's just been telling me about Dr Jardine's devoted band of Lovely Ladies – I must say, I'm deeply envious!'

The Earl laughed. 'I have moments of envy myself! Do you know either Mrs Welbeck or Lady Markhampton?'

'I'm sorry to say I don't.'

'They're both charming. But to tell you the truth the Lovely Lady I really fancied in the old days was Loretta Staviski. No doubt my wife mentioned her. She's arriving from America next weekend to stay with us, and I'm greatly looking forward to seeing her again.'

There was a silence. The river went on flowing and in the meadows the cows continued to graze. I looked at the Earl, who was still peering into the water for a glimpse of a fish; I looked back at the Countess who was still sketching by the herbaceous border, and at last I heard myself enquire in the most casual voice I could muster: 'No, your wife didn't mention her. Who is she?'

FOUR

'Who does not know that no clergyman, however hard-working and devoted, can maintain his spiritual influence if his domestic life be ill-ordered and unhappy?'

HERBERT HENSLEY HENSON
Bishop of Durham 1920–1939
The Bishoprick Papers

I

When I returned to Lady Starmouth I found her looking critically at her sketch. 'I'm afraid this is no good,' she murmured. 'I seem to have lost my touch . . . How were the fish?'

'According to your husband they're all either asleep or dead.' For a moment I remained motionless, watching her. Then I said casually, 'Lady Starmouth, I hope you won't think me impertinent, but may I ask why, when you were telling me about Dr Jardine's Lovely Ladies, you failed to mention Loretta Staviski?'

Lady Starmouth's reaction was swift. 'Loretta?'

'Your husband's just mentioned her. There were four of you, weren't there? Not just three.'

'Only for a short time, during the War.' Lady Starmouth tore the sketch from the pad, crumpled the paper into a ball and put her pencil away in a wooden box. She said nothing else, and her silence was in such stark contrast to her earlier fluency that I felt obliged to say, 'I'm sorry – obviously I've given you offence.'

'My dear Dr Ashworth –' Lady Starmouth spoke in the voice of one who finds herself in the most tiresome of dilemmas ' – of course you haven't given me offence! I'm merely annoyed with myself for not mentioning Loretta because, of course, it's only natural that you should wonder why I left her out when I was prattling so freely about the Bishop's past. However the truth's very simple. I didn't mention her because Alex hasn't seen her since she returned to America in 1918 so she hardly qualifies now as one of his Lovely Ladies.'

'She hasn't visited England since then?'

There was another silence.

'Forgive me, I'm being intolerably inquisitive – '

'Pardonably inquisitive, you mean. Of course you're wondering why I'm tying myself up in such knots.' Suddenly and most unexpectedly she laughed. 'Good heavens, anyone would think I had a guilty secret to hide whereas all I want to cover up is a little private embarrassment!'

'Lady Starmouth, please don't feel obliged to say another word! I'm only sorry that I – '

'My dear young man, now *you're* the one who's behaving as if there's a guilty secret to hide! I can see that the most sensible thing I can do is to enlighten you before you're tempted to exercise a colourful imagination, but you must promise me you'll be discreet. The story's not scandalous, just sad, and I don't want it repeated.'

'I give you my word I shall hold everything you say in the strictest confidence.'

'Very well, then let me say that Loretta has indeed returned to England for visits since the War, but she and Alex no longer have any communication with each other. I'm sorry to say that although Alex always treated her with absolute propriety Loretta fell in love with him and their platonic friendship went very disastrously wrong.'

II

'Forgive me, Lady Starmouth,' I said, 'but in fact I'd been unable to resist wondering if Dr Jardine's platonic friendships were just a little too good to be true. I still say that any clergyman who dabbles in close friendships with the opposite sex is playing with fire.'

'Well, in this case I have to admit he got singed . . . Dr Ashworth, do sit down again – I find you disconcerting when you tower over me like this. It makes me feel I'm being interrogated.'

I sat down at once on the grass but she cut short my apology. 'No, I know you're not really interrogating me – it's all my fault for encouraging your questions earlier, but before I close up like a clam let me just say a little more about Loretta so that you can see why for her sake I prefer to treat the incident as closed. She and I first met in 1917 but I'd heard about her for years because my mother, who was American, had been friends with her mother in childhood and they'd always kept in touch. When Loretta finally came to England she was in a terrible mess. She'd been married young to this man Staviski who was a diplomatist; when America entered the War he was transferred from Washington to London, and almost as soon as he and Loretta arrived in England the marriage went to pieces.'

'He left her?'

'She left him. But she was the innocent party – he'd made life quite impossible for her, so I had no hesitation in coming to her rescue. She stayed with us while she recovered, and of course she soon met Alex. Well, to cut a long story short I'll just say that she was so successful at concealing her true feelings that for a long time neither Alex nor I had any idea she was in love with him, but eventually the truth surfaced and Alex was obliged to end the friendship. Loretta was dreadfully upset. I felt so sorry for her. It was all horribly awkward and pathetic, just as any unreciprocated attachment always is, and later we agreed never to speak of it again.'

'What happened to her afterwards?'

'When she returned to America she embarked on an academic career and now she teaches history at some college on the Eastern Seaboard. She's never remarried but I still wonder if she might one day. She's much younger than me, perhaps only a few years older than you, and although by fashionable standards she's plain she's by no means unattractive . . . However a lot of men don't like a woman to be too clever.'

But I thought of Jardine, enjoying with Loretta Staviski all the intelligent conversation he was unlikely to encounter at home, and I was unable to resist saying: 'Dr Jardine must have been sorry to lose her friendship – was he never tempted to see her again during her later visits to England?'

'How could he? How could he possibly have renewed a friendship which had been so painful to her and so potentially dangerous for him?'

'But was she herself never tempted to –'

'This *is* an interrogation, isn't it! My dear Dr Ashworth, aren't you taking rather too much advantage of your very considerable charm?'

I privately cursed my recklessness and attempted to beat a smooth retreat. 'I'm so sorry, Lady Starmouth, but many a clergyman has to deal occasionally with the sort of difficulty Dr Jardine faced here, and I'm afraid my personal interest in the subject got the better of me. I do apologize.'

She gave me a searching look but decided to be indulgent. 'I've no objection to a sympathetic interest,' she said, 'but perhaps it's lucky for you that I have a soft spot for clergymen . . . Heavens, here's Mrs Cobden-Smith!' Rising to her feet she folded the stool and picked up her artist's satchel. 'For your penance, Dr Ashworth, you can listen with an expression of rapturous attention to the stories of how she and the Colonel civilized India.'

'You two seem to be having a very cosy little tête-à-tête!' called Mrs Cobden-Smith as she approached us. 'I've just been urging Carrie to get dressed. It's no good lying in bed after a touch of insomnia – I told her to get up and have a busy day so that she'd be thoroughly tired by bed-time. I remember when I was in India – '

'I was only saying to Dr Ashworth how interesting you were about India – but do excuse me, I must go and see Carrie myself,' said Lady Starmouth, and escaped adroitly across the lawn.

My next witness had delivered herself to me with an admirable sense of timing. Fighting my reluctance I smiled at Mrs Cobden-Smith and suggested that we might sit on the garden bench to enjoy the sunshine.

III

'It's nice to sit down for a minute,' said Mrs Cobden-Smith. 'I've been rushing around the town trying to buy horsemeat for the dog and the right cough-syrup for Willy. If Willy doesn't have a dose of cough-syrup every night he coughs like a chimney-sweep and if George doesn't have horsemeat three times a week he gets lazy – and talking of laziness, it seems you've been shirking your work, young man! I thought you were supposed to be closeted in the Cathedral library, not dancing attendance on Lady Starmouth! You're as bad as Alex – he likes to dance attendance too, but of course in his case he's just savouring the fact that Adam Jardine from Putney is now the clerical pet of a peeress. Did you know Alex spent the first thirty-seven years of his life being called Adam? It's his first name. But when Carrie fell in love with him we said to her: "My dear," we said, "you simply can't marry a man called Adam Jardine – it sounds like a jobbing gardener!" So she found out his second name was Alexander and we rechristened him Alex. His stepmother was livid, I can't think why.'

I finally had the chance to speak and I thought I had been offered a promising opening. 'What a coincidence!' I said. 'Lady Starmouth was just telling me about Dr Jardine's stepmother.'

'Everyone was always rather appalled by the old girl,' said Mrs Cobden-Smith comfortably, quite uninhibited by any desire to be discreet about a dead relative of her husband's brother-in-law. 'She was a very strange woman – Swedish, and of course we all know the Scandinavians are peculiar. Look at their plays.'

I ignored this dismissal of the giants of the modern theatre. 'But I'm told the Bishop was very fond of his stepmother.'

'Devoted. Very odd. Carrie hated her, but when Alex's sister died something had to be done about the old girl, who was by then confined to a wheelchair with arthritis and so of course Alex announced: "She's coming to live with us!" Ghastly. Poor Carrie. I can't tell you the havoc that decision caused.'

'How did Mrs Jardine cope?'

'You may well ask,' said Mrs Cobden-Smith, using a phrase which I was soon to realize was a favourite of hers. 'It was five years ago, just after the move to Starbridge from Radbury, and Carrie was going through the – well, it was an awkward time for her – and everything was at sixes and sevens. I said to Willy, "Carrie will have a nervous breakdown, I know she will", but of course I'd reckoned without Miss Christie. The old girl took to Miss Christie in the biggest possible way, gave Carrie no trouble and died good as gold six months later. I said to Willy, "That girl Christie's a miracle-worker".'

'Is there any problem Miss Christie can't solve?'

'You may well ask,' said Mrs Cobden-Smith a second time. 'It was strange how she tamed the old girl, I must say. I remember it occurred to me once that there was a curious resemblance between them – not a resemblance in looks, of course – the old girl weighed a ton while Miss Christie's so small and slim – but there was some odd resemblance of the personality. I suspect that the old girl, when she was young, had that same cool competence which Miss Christie now displays so noticeably. Alex's real mother died when he was six, the father was left with eight children under twelve, or something frightful, and the stepmother restored order to the home – rather as Miss Christie pulled the Deanery together when she first came to Radbury.'

I was now offered a choice of two openings; I was tempted to ask about Radbury, but I was also curious to discover more about Jardine's obscure background. Finally I said: 'What happened to all the other little Jardines?'

'One sister went mad and died in an asylum, three brothers went to the Colonies and died of drink or worse, one brother went bankrupt in London and hanged himself and the last brother simply disappeared. That left the younger sister, who eventually looked after the old girl, and Alex.'

'Dr Jardine obviously had a miraculous survival!'

'It was the hand of God,' said Mrs Cobden-Smith with that matchless confidence of the layman who always knows exactly what God has in mind. 'Of course none of us knows for certain what went on in that family, but I've pieced a few lurid details together over the years and there's no doubt the background was a nightmare. I used to talk to Alex's sister Edith – a nice woman she was, terribly common but a nice woman – and she occasionally let slip the odd piece of information which made my hair stand on end.'

'Lady Starmouth liked her too, said she'd had an awful life – '

'Unspeakable. The father was a lunatic – never certified, unfortunately, but quite obviously potty. He suffered from religious mania and saw sin everywhere so he wouldn't let his children go to school for fear they'd be corrupted.'

'But how on earth did Dr Jardine get to Oxford?'

'You may well ask,' said Mrs Cobden-Smith once more, enjoying her attentive audience. 'It was the stepmother. She finally got him to school when he was fourteen and kept his nose to the grindstone until he'd won the scholarship.'

'In that case,' I said, 'since Dr Jardine owed her so much, wasn't it a rare and splendid piece of justice that she should spend her final days with him in his episcopal palace?'

'I dare say it was,' conceded Mrs Cobden-Smith with reluctance, 'although Carrie didn't see it that way at the time. Thank God Miss Christie tamed the old girl before poor Carrie could have another nervous breakdown!'

'Another nervous breakdown? You mean – ?'

'Dash, I shouldn't have said that, should I, Willy would be cross. But on the other hand it's an open secret that Carrie's a prey to her nerves. I've often said to her in the past, "Carrie, you must make more effort – you simply can't go to bed and give up!" But I'm afraid she's not the fighting kind. I'm quite different, I'm glad to say – I'm always fighting away and making efforts! When I was in India . . .'

I let her talk about India while I waited for the opening which would lead us back to the subject of Mrs Jardine's nervous breakdown. The characters in Jardine's past were revolving in my mind: the eccentric father, the doomed siblings, the surviving sister who had had 'a ghastly way with a teacup', the mysterious Swedish stepmother who had exerted such a vital influence – and then after the years of darkness, the years of light and a new world with new people: Carrie and the Cobden-Smiths, the subtle charming Lady Starmouth, the clever American girl struggling from the ruins of a disastrous marriage –

' – disastrous marriage,' said Mrs Cobden-Smith, remarking how fortunate it was that Carrie had avoided marrying an officer in the Indian Army. 'She would never have survived the climate.'

'No, probably not. Mrs Cobden-Smith, talking of survival – '

'Of course, Carrie's had a hard time surviving marriage to a clergyman,' said Mrs Cobden-Smith, playing into my hands before I could risk a direct question about Mrs Jardine's difficulties at Radbury, 'although the ironic part is that in many ways she's cut out to be a clergyman's wife – everyone likes her and she's a very good, devout, friendly little person, but she should have been the wife of an ordinary parson, not the wife of a fire-breathing adventurer who periodically runs amok through the Church of England. It's a terrible tragedy there are no children. Of course children can drive one up the wall, I'm not sentimental about children, but they do give a marriage a focal point, and although Alex and Carrie are devoted to each other any stranger can see they don't have much in common. How ghastly it was when that baby was born dead in 1918! No wonder Carrie went to pieces, poor thing.'

'Was that when she had her nervous – '

'Well, it wasn't really a nervous breakdown,' said Mrs Cobden-Smith fluently. 'I was exaggerating. A nervous breakdown means someone climbing the walls, doesn't it, and having to be whisked away to a private nursing home, but Carrie's collapse was quite different. She just lay weeping on a chaise-longue all day and when she finally had the strength to leave it she started consulting spiritualists to see if she could get in touch with the dead child – terribly embarrassing for Alex, of course, to be a clergyman whose wife consulted spiritualists, so it was arranged that Carrie should have a little holiday with her parents in the country. That did her the world of good, thank God, and afterwards she was fine until they moved to Radbury.'

'Someone did mention that she found the move a little difficult –'

'Poor Carrie! If only Alex had been made vicar of some quiet little parish in the back of beyond! But no, off he went to Radbury to run that hulking great Cathedral, and Carrie found herself put on public display as Mrs Dean – hundreds of new people to meet, all the residents of the Cathedral Close watching critically to see if she made a mistake, new committees to master, endless dinner parties to organize, Mrs Bishop looking down her nose from the palace, all the Canons' wives trying to interfere –'

'When did Mrs Jardine make the decision to engage a companion?'

'Alex made the decision, not Carrie. Carrie was soon in such a state that she couldn't make any decisions at all – although of course,' said Mrs Cobden-Smith, 'she wasn't having a nervous breakdown. Not really. She just went shopping every day to buy things she didn't need – I think it took her mind off her troubles – and when she wasn't shopping she was always so tired that she had to stay in bed. However finally she bought some really frightful wallpaper – the last word in extravagance – and Alex decided she needed someone to keep an eye on her during her little shopping sprees. Miss Christie turned up and was an immediate success. Alex used to refer to her simply as "The Godsend".'

'The Bishop must have been concerned about his wife,' I murmured, selecting an understatement in the hope of luring her into further indiscretions, but Mrs Cobden-Smith merely said: 'Yes, he was,' and shifted restlessly as if aware for the first time that a stranger might read into her frank comments rather more than she had intended to reveal. I suspected that like most people of little imagination she found it difficult to picture what was going on in any mind other than her own.

'Where does Miss Christie come from?' I said, changing the subject to soothe her uneasiness.

'Rural Norfolk – one of those places where there's lots of inbreeding and everyone talks in grunts. She has a clerical family background, of course.'

'How suitable. But Mrs Cobden-Smith, one thing does puzzle me about Miss Christie: why has she never married?'

'Ah!' said Mrs Cobden-Smith. 'That's what we'd all like to know! There's a rumour that she was once badly jilted, but I think she put that story in circulation to cover up a far less respectable reason for staying single.'

'Oh?' I said. 'And what would that be?'

'I strongly suspect,' said Mrs Cobden-Smith, lowering her voice confidentially, 'that Miss Christie has a lust for power.'

IV

The sense of an absurd anti-climax was so strong that I had to fight a desire to laugh but fortunately Mrs Cobden-Smith was more anxious to explain her theory than to see if I kept a straight face.

'Of course the popular rumour,' she was saying, 'is that Miss Christie's secretly in love with Alex, but that's nonsense because I can't see her being such a fool as to waste ten of the best years of her life being hopelessly in love with a married man. No, you mark my words, Dr Ashworth, she's mad about power. Some women are; not all women want to marry, and I think Miss Christie simply loves being in charge here, running the palace, looking after Carrie, helping the Bishop, meeting all the Church dignitaries and all the aristocratic guests like the Starmouths. In my opinion,' said Mrs Cobden-Smith decisively, 'Miss Christie's merely an unusual example of a modern woman who's wedded to her career.'

Having conquered my *fou rire* I could see now that Mrs Cobden-Smith's theory was not so absurd as I had supposed; it was certainly more attractive than Lady Starmouth's wild assertion of lesbianism. However before I could make any comment Mrs Cobden-Smith exclaimed: 'Ah, there's Carrie – downstairs in time for luncheon, thank God! And there's Willy with George. Will you excuse me, Dr Ashworth? I must see George eats his horsemeat.'

She set off briskly across the lawn, and as soon as I was alone I became aware that I was uncomfortably hot. I decided to cool off in my room before lunch while I reviewed the evidence produced in such profusion by my interviews.

By the time I reached the terrace Mrs Cobden-Smith had disappeared with the Colonel and George, but Mrs Jardine was waiting for me with her warmest smile. Now that I knew more about her the smile seemed poignant, and again I was aware of reality submerging itself beneath illusion in the heat of that Starbridge noon.

'How are you, Mrs Jardine?' I said as I mounted the steps to the terrace. 'I was sorry to hear you were feeling so tired.'

'Oh, I'm much better now, thank you! So stupid about my insomnia,

I must have had too much coffee by mistake last night, and then after I'd gone to bed I started thinking about your poor wife and the baby and . . . Well, you know how it is, I dare say, when one's thoughts go round and round, especially in the early hours of the morning, and suddenly I felt so frightened, I don't know why, I do get moments of panic sometimes, especially when the weather's so hot. Do you think there might be a storm coming, Dr Ashworth? The air's very sultry, so close and threatening, and I feel as if something dreadful's going to happen.'

The sky was cloudless and although the air was hot there was little humidity. I said gently, 'I agree it's very warm – shall we go inside?' and I gestured to indicate she should precede me into the house but Mrs Jardine hesitated, looking uncertainly up and down the terrace. 'I was wondering if we should have drinks out here,' she said, 'but I can't make up my mind. Alex never drinks at midday but my brother and sister-in-law do and so do the Starmouths. Do you drink at midday, Dr Ashworth?'

'Not usually, no.' Beyond the open French windows Miss Christie and the butler were entering the drawing-room. I heard Miss Christie say: 'No, it's too hot outside, Shipton,' and the butler set down his tray of glasses on a side-table.

'Lyle says it's too hot out here,' said Mrs Jardine, relieved that the decision had been taken out of her hands. She called to Miss Christie: 'Dr Ashworth doesn't drink cocktails at midday either, dear, so we'll be one extra for lemonade.'

'Yes, I'd anticipated that,' said Miss Christie, coming out on to the terrace to join us. 'Good morning again, Dr Ashworth. I hope you've been enjoying sunbathing in a clerical suit.'

'I have indeed,' I said. 'In fact the morning's been so enjoyable that I'm resolved to have an equally enjoyable afternoon. Will you come for a drive with me after lunch?'

Miss Christie had given an inch and I had taken a yard. At least no one could accuse me of wasting my opportunities, but Miss Christie showed signs of regretting the conceded inch. Without hesitation she said: 'I'm not a free agent, Dr Ashworth. I have my duties here at the palace.'

'Oh, but I shall only be resting this afternoon!' protested Mrs Jardine. 'Do go for a drive with Dr Ashworth, dearest – why not!'

'Why not indeed?' said a familiar harsh voice, and swinging round I found that Dr Jardine was watching me from the threshold of the drawing-room.

V

There was a pause. I glanced back at Miss Christie but she had already reached the practical decision that it was now less awkward to accept the invitation than to refuse it. She said politely: 'Thank you. A drive would be very pleasant,' and then she escaped past the Bishop into the drawing-room where the butler had just deposited a large jug of lemonade.

'It's abominably hot, isn't it?' said Jardine as I watched both the butler and Miss Christie disappear into the hall. 'Carrie, you look on the verge of sunstroke. Come in at once.'

'I feel so odd, Alex – '

'I propose we launch an immediate assault on the iced lemonade.'

The shade of the drawing-room came as an exquisite relief, but as Mrs Jardine sat down on the edge of the sofa I noticed the nervous movements of her hands and sensed her tension more strongly than ever.

'Well, Dr Ashworth!' said Jardine, passing a glass of lemonade to his wife and holding out a second glass to me. 'Do I assume that the glories of the Cathedral library left you cold? As far as I can gather you've spent the morning talking to one attractive woman and you now propose to spend the afternoon talking to another.'

I said with a smile, 'Having spent well over an hour admiring the glories of the Cathedral library, I felt entitled to spend far less than an hour – '

' – admiring the glories of Lady Starmouth. Quite.' The Bishop was taking care to sound amused but I sensed his amusement was wafer-thin and I began to feel uneasy.

'But I thought you were talking to Amy, not Lady Starmouth!' said Mrs Jardine to me. She sounded abnormally confused.

'Oh, Dr Ashworth's been talking to just about everyone!' said the Bishop, and I could now clearly hear the acid note in his voice. 'He seems to be suffering from an ungovernable urge to display the gregarious side of his nature!'

'He hasn't been talking to me,' said Colonel Cobden-Smith entering the room as I began to wonder if Lady Starmouth had lodged a complaint about my interrogation.

'That's because you've been exercising that unfortunate hound in this appalling heat and offering yourself as a candidate for a heart attack – and now I suppose you'll say you want a pink gin!'

'The heat's so bad for everyone,' said Mrs Jardine in an agony of anxiety before the Colonel could reply. 'I'm sure there's going to be a storm, but according to the weather forecast – '

'Oh, for heaven's sake, Carrie!' exclaimed the Bishop in a paroxysm of irritability. 'Stop talking about the weather!'

Mrs Jardine began to cry.

'Ye gods and little fishes,' muttered Jardine as the Colonel and I stood transfixed, and yelled at the top of his voice: 'Lyle!'

In walked Miss Christie. It was almost as if she had been waiting in the wings for her cue.

'Lyle, Carrie can't take this heat. Do something, would you?' said the Bishop, and stooping awkwardly over his wife he kissed her before murmuring, 'I'm sorry.'

'Darling,' said Miss Christie to Mrs Jardine, 'you must drink all your lemonade at once and then you'll feel better. It's very important to take lots of liquid in hot weather.'

Jardine remarked: 'Maybe I should take lemonade regularly to prevent irascibility after an arid morning in my study. I've just been reading the latest crop of letters on the Marriage Bill from people who think I was the clergyman in charge of Edward VIII's wedding, and I'm now wishing more fervently than ever that my deplorable namesake had been called by any name other than Jardine.'

This was a skilful attempt to manipulate the conversation back within the bounds of normality, but before a more relaxed atmosphere could be established Mrs Cobden-Smith swept in. 'Willy, George won't eat that horsemeat. Do you suppose – oh my goodness, what's going on? Carrie dear, you simply must make more effort! I know the heat's trying, but – '

'Amy,' said the Bishop, 'would you kindly stop addressing my wife as if she were an Indian peasant ripe for civilization by the British Raj?'

'Well, *really*, Alex!'

'Mrs Cobden-Smith,' said Miss Christie with unprecedented charm, 'I wonder if you'd be terribly kind and help me take Carrie upstairs to lie down? You must have had such a broad experience of heatstroke in India and I'd so value your advice – should we call the doctor?'

'Quite unnecessary,' said Mrs Cobden-Smith, greatly mollified, 'but perhaps she does need to lie down. Come along, Carrie.'

The chaplain then chose an unfortunate moment to rush into the room with bad news. 'Bishop, the Archdeacon's on the phone again and he's in a frightful panic!'

'Oh, hang the Archdeacon!' exploded the Bishop. 'And hang that abominable instrument the telephone!' But he seized the chance to make a swift exit from the chaos caused by his irritability.

VI

I was surprised how quickly order was restored. Coaxed by Miss Christie, Mrs Jardine drank all her lemonade and said she felt better. The

Starmouths arrived, and while they debated what to drink I could hear the Cobden-Smiths discussing George who presently made a lacklustre entrance. Miss Christie summoned the butler to replenish the lemonade jug, but before I had the chance to speak to her about our outing four guests appeared from various corners of the diocese and all opportunity for private conversation was curtailed.

Lunch passed smoothly if tediously. I busied myself by being sociable with a large matron whose favourite topic of conversation was the Mothers' Union, and although Miss Christie never looked in my direction I occasionally caught Lady Starmouth's sympathetic glance across the table.

However, by half-past two the party had dispersed and I was preparing in my bedroom for a country excursion far removed from a clerical duty. Off came my clergyman's uniform. Having pulled on my coolest informal clothes I unbuttoned my shirt at the neck, adjusted the angle of my hat and once more turned to survey my image in the long glass. Immediately I wondered if I had gone too far with the informality; I fancied I looked like a commercial traveller taking a rest from hawking some dubious product, but when I decided to wear a tie I felt much too hot. Shoving the tie back in the drawer I undid the top button of my shirt again and made up my mind that I looked exactly what I was: an off-duty clergyman about to take a pretty woman for a drive in the country.

But then I looked in the glass and saw the spy beyond the clergyman, the image beyond the image, and beyond the spy was yet another man, the image beyond the image beyond the image. Reality blurred; fantasy and truth became inextricably intertwined. I told myself I had imagined the distant stranger but as I felt my personality begin to divide I covered my face with my hands.

Sinking to my knees by the bed I whispered: 'Lord, forgive me my sins. Deliver me from evil. Help me to serve you as well as I can.' After that I felt calmer, and when I glanced again in the glass I found that the off-duty clergyman was now the only visible image. He was wearing a severe expression as if to stress that I had no business to let the heat addle my brain, and immediately erasing all morbid thoughts from my mind, I set off to meet Miss Christie.

FIVE

'Experience has made it certain that the clergyman's wife must either throw in her lot unreservedly with her husband's difficult and distinctive career, and reap her reward with a range and depth of personal influence which are unequalled in the case of any other married woman, or she must separate herself from his work and life with consequences ruinous both to his success and to her own credit, and, we must add, to the happiness of both.'

HERBERT HENSLEY HENSON
Bishop of Durham 1920–1939
The Bishoprick Papers

I

Miss Christie was wearing a pale-green short-sleeved frock, which exposed her slim arms, and flat white sandals, which emphasized her slender ankles. Other fleshier curves were erotically concealed beneath the prim cut of her frock. She was sheltering beneath a wide-brimmed straw hat.

'Trying not to be recognized?' I said as we met in the hall.

'I might ask you the same question!'

'Well, at least you haven't said – '

' – "Oh, how different you look out of your clericals!" '

We laughed, and as I led the way outside to my car it occurred to me that if Miss Christie could cope with every conceivable crisis in an episcopal household she could cope with a Doctor of Divinity who was mad enough to be afraid of his own reflection. Conscious of relief, happiness, nervous anticipation and sexual desire in pleasantly stimulating proportions I decided the afternoon was going to be a success.

Miss Christie suggested that we might drive to Starbury Ring, a megalithic stone circle high on the Downs, and after she had directed me out of the city we headed up the valley to the north. The surrounding hills curved with a voluptuous smoothness in the limpid afternoon light. Leaving the main road we passed some farms and once were trapped behind a slow-moving cart, but otherwise nothing deflected our attention from the steadily unfolding views.

Suddenly Miss Christie said, 'I ought to take Mrs Jardine for a drive like this. It would do her good. We could even take a picnic and disappear for an entire afternoon.'

'What about the Bishop?'

'Oh, I'd leave him behind. He hates eating alfresco. His idea of relaxation is to write a letter to *The Times*.'

'I hear that was how he made his name before he became Vicar of St Mary's, Mayfair.'

'Yes, he didn't have much else to do when he was a chaplain in North London.'

I saw the chance to pursue my investigation. 'No one's yet explained to me,' I said, 'why he was living in such obscurity before the translation to Mayfair. What happened to him after he was ordained?'

'He was given a parish in this diocese – in the slums of Starmouth. He stayed there for seven years and made a success of it, but it was desperately hard work and in the end his health broke down.'

'That often happens to clergymen in sordid parishes,' I said, and the next moment I was remembering my friend Philip's accusation that I lived in an ivory tower. Some guilty impulse drove me to add: 'However, you mustn't think I speak from experience. I'm afraid my ministry's always been among the affluent.'

'Christ preached to the rich as well as the poor, didn't he?' Miss Christie said composed. 'And Dr Jardine says that spiritually the rich can be just as impoverished as any family on the dole.'

I glanced at her with gratitude but she was looking out of the side-window at the curving hills. After a pause I said, 'Tell me more about Dr Jardine – what happened when his health broke down?'

'On the doctor's advice he resigned his living and borrowed the money to take a long holiday. The rest helped but he still didn't think his health could stand the strain of another parish so he decided to do some writing and research at Oxford. I expect you know he's a Fellow of All Souls. However his financial difficulties in those says were so acute that he had to have some sort of benefice, and finally the Warden of All Souls got him this obscure hospital chaplaincy in North London – the living was in the gift of the College.'

'I gather Dr Jardine had considerable family obligations in Putney.'

'He was supporting his father, his stepmother and his two sisters,' said Miss Christie drily. 'Although he didn't starve he was hardly well nourished. However the chaplaincy suited him – the hospital was very small, no more than a large alms-house, and as there wasn't much work to do he used to spend the days in the middle of the week up at Oxford.

He wrote some articles, preached various guest-sermons – he already had a reputation as a preacher – and sent letters regularly to *The Times*. Eventually, without Dr Jardine's knowledge, the Warden of All Souls approached Mr Asquith, who was then Prime Minister, and asked him if something could be done to improve the situation since it was obvious that Dr Jardine's health was quite restored. Mr Asquith had been enjoying the letters to *The Times* and he immediately remembered that the new vacancy at St Mary's was in the gift of the Crown.'

'That's what we clergymen call an edifying story,' I said. 'After many vicissitudes the good get their reward.'

'I can't see why you should sound so envious,' said Miss Christie as if she felt she had been too friendly and was now obliged to redress the balance. 'You're obviously in line for the choicest of bishoprics.'

'You think so?' I said. 'I'm flattered. But do you honestly believe I'm fit to be a bishop just because I've published a book on the Early Church and can survive at Cambridge Cathedral without quarrelling with the Dean?'

'Oh, I wouldn't presume to judge your fitness, Dr Ashworth. I leave that to God and Dr Lang.'

I knew I had to demonstrate that I was not prepared to tolerate an asperity drummed up by a guilt that we should be getting on so well. Grinding the car to a halt I switched off the engine, swivelled to face her and demanded, 'Why the hostility?'

She went white. At first I thought she was white with anger but then I realized she was white with alarm. When she protested, 'I'm not hostile!' I said at once, 'No – so why pretend?' and leaning forward I kissed her on the mouth.

This was fast behaviour for a gentleman on a sedate afternoon drive with a lady he had known less than twenty-four hours, and for a clergyman the behaviour was so fast that I felt I was travelling at the speed of light. Indeed my speed so stunned Miss Christie that for the first five seconds after our lips touched she behaved as if she were paralysed. Five seconds is a long time when two mouths are joined in a kiss. However on the sixth second the response came, and contrary to my expectations the response was far from hostile. Her mouth opened beneath mine. At once I pulled her closer, but the next moment she was shoving me aside and with reluctance I let her go. Her face was no longer white but a pale pink. I had no idea what colour my face was but I felt as if I had run a hundred yards at high speed, and my mind was swirling not only with thoughts of empty champagne glasses but with images of bright swords, dark tunnels and other ambiguous objects blighted for all time by Freud.

Miss Christie smoothed her skirt – which I had not touched – and as she did so I noticed that she wore a signet-ring on the third finger of her left hand. Finally she said, 'We met yesterday for the first time. We're not even on Christian-name terms. Aren't you behaving a little curiously for a clergyman?'

'At least I now know you well enough to call you Lyle.'

'Dr Ashworth – '

'My name's Charles. Yes, of course I'm behaving curiously for a clergyman, but whenever someone makes a remark which implies a clergyman should be some sort of stainless-steel saint I want to quote Shylock's speech from *The Merchant of Venice* – you know the one, the speech where he says he bleeds and suffers just as other people do – '

'Well, I wasn't implying – '

'Weren't you?'

'Dr Ashworth – '

'Charles.'

' – I'm afraid I'm simply not a candidate for a whirlwind romance – '

'No, don't pretend you're not interested in me! I saw you listening with bated breath last night when Lady Starmouth asked if I had a wife!'

'I – '

'Look.' I adopted my calmest, most rational manner. 'I could proceed in the conventional way. I could pay you nice, safe little compliments and write you harmless little billets-doux and send you flowers and come down to Starbridge every fortnight to take you out to tea – I could do all that; I'm perfectly capable of behaving like a gentleman and playing the game according to the rules, but where would it get me? Absolutely nowhere. I found that out last night when I made that mild approach and you dodged away around the coffee-cups. Well, dodging around the coffee-cups may be great fun for you, but frankly I'm not prepared to be treated as a minor inconvenience. I want to get to know you very much better as soon as possible – which is why I suggested this drive – '

'Then why aren't we driving? I don't want to spend all afternoon in front of this five-barred gate while you regale me with impassioned nonsense!'

I started the engine and we drove on.

II

Within minutes we had emerged on to a broad plateau, and ahead I could see a track leading away from the road towards the ridge which marked the summit of the Downs.

'Stop the car on the verge by that path,' said Lyle. 'This is where we begin the trek to the Ring.'

'There's no need to sound as if you wished you were chaperoned!' I said lightly as I halted the car once more. 'Now that I've defined exactly where I stand I promise I'll behave like a stainless-steel saint for a couple of hours.'

'What happens after a couple of hours?'

'We'll be back at the palace and you can hide behind the Bishop.'

As I opened the passenger door she said, 'You're very interested in the Bishop, aren't you?'

'Is there anyone in the Church of England who isn't?'

We set off up the track. I wanted to hold her hand but I exercised an immaculate self-discipline and kept my fists shoved deep in my pockets. However I was not dissatisfied with my progress. At least she had neither slapped my face nor called me a cad nor demanded to be returned immediately to Starbridge.

'If you want to know me better,' she said at last, 'why don't you set the pace by helping me to know more about you? Most men usually can't wait to recite their life-histories, but you seem peculiarly reticent.'

'I didn't intend this to be a history lesson. I'd rather talk about the present.'

'What's wrong with your past?'

'It's boring. I was born in the right county in the right residential neighbourhood of one of the right towns. My father has the right sort of profession and my mother indulges in the right sort of hobbies. I went to the right schools and the right university, got myself ordained at the right age and began my right career at the right time with the right man. Then I taught at the right places, wrote the right book and eventually became a Canon of the right cathedral. It's all very dull, isn't it? Dr Jardine's past is so much more interesting than mine.'

All Lyle said was, 'You've left out the right marriage to the right wife.'

'So I have. Careless of me. I suppose that was because she did the wrong thing and died.'

We walked on. The sun blazed on the grassy hills dotted with sheep, and as we moved towards the summit of the ridge the view began to expand in every direction. It was uncannily quiet.

At last Lyle said, 'You don't give much away.'

'Does anyone, even the people who rush to recite the carefully selected facts of their life at tedious length?' I was trying to establish a line of conversation which would tempt her to rebut my argument with disclosures about herself, but she merely said with detachment, 'I agree that the exact truth about people is usually impossible to know, but I think most of the time one can make an accurate guess about what goes on.' She paused to look back across the valley behind us. 'Take the Starmouths, for example,' she said. 'The Earl's a good decent Englishman of the old school who takes a conscientious interest in his estates, does his bit for the country by a regular attendance at the House of Lords, and is devoted to his wife and children. Lady Starmouth probably gets a bit bored with him but she's fundamentally good and decent too so she doesn't rattle around like a society hostess but amuses herself instead with the safest class of men – clergymen, who have a strong stake in sticking to the proprieties. Now, I'm not saying this is the exact truth about either of the Starmouths, but I think the odds are I've given you an accurate thumbnail sketch. I mean, I don't seriously believe, do you, that Lady Starmouth is a secret drug-fiend while the Earl keeps a mistress in St John's Wood?'

'Lady Starmouth is certainly not a secret drug-fiend. But – ' I thought of the Earl's candid admiration of Loretta ' – I don't think I'm as sure as you are about that mistress in St John's Wood. Over the years I've come to the conclusion that it's impossible to make reliable guesses about anyone's intimate life.' Without looking at her directly I was nevertheless poised to analyse her reaction.

But she merely said, 'Isn't the Earl a little old for fun and games in St John's Wood?'

'He might consider a mistress rejuvenating. But no,' I said with a smile as we moved on again towards the summit of the ridge, 'I confess I don't really believe the Earl has a secret love-life any more than I believe Lady Starmouth is burning to seduce the Bishop.'

She laughed. 'Lady Starmouth's whole success with the Bishop lies in the fact that she at least would never play the over-passionate female in his company!'

'Are there so many over-passionate females besieging Dr Jardine?'

Lyle suddenly chose to treat the subject seriously. 'Not now,' she said. 'A bishop's more on a pedestal than an ordinary clergyman, but there were one or two very tricky women when he was Dean of Radbury, and apparently when he was Vicar of St Mary's he was forever fending off society women who were far less principled than Lady Starmouth.'

I said equally seriously, to show that I understood the problems which could exist for certain clergymen, 'But surely troublesome women reserve their most ardent attentions for bachelors?'

'Oh, no doubt life became fractionally less hectic once he was married but unfortunately many women even today are tempted to write Mrs Jardine off as insignificant and imagine that the Bishop's languishing in an unhappy marriage. However that's rubbish, of course. The Jardines may seem to a stranger to be ill-assorted but anyone who knows them well will tell you they're devoted to each other. It's an attraction of opposites.'

We had reached the top of the ridge while she was speaking, and as we paused to survey the view we found that the outlines of the landscape soon faded into the heat-haze. Abandoning the obscure prospect across the valley I turned my attention to Starbury Ring which was now visible less than fifty yards away. The Ring consisted of two dozen tall rocks, planted several thousand years ago for purposes which were no longer known but which at once conjured up images in my mind of human sacrifices and other horrors of heathen worship. I thought how comforting it would be to believe that all bloodstained idolatry in Europe now lay sealed in the past, and for a moment I wished I were a Victorian who still had faith in the doctrine of progress. How delightful it must have been to look forward with confidence to the time when mankind would have achieved its inevitable perfection! How soothing to be able to picture an immanent, cosily accessible God who could be known with the aid of reason and a good education! But now the War had destroyed the illusion of progress, bloodstained idolatry was once more invading Europe, and the powerful mind of Karl Barth had perceived that God was remote, utterly transcendent, capable of being known only by revelation.

'I'm sorry,' I said suddenly to Lyle. 'The sight of pagan stones sent me off at a theological tangent. You were saying the Jardines were devoted to each other –'

'Yes, Mrs Jardine adores the Bishop, and the Bishop, like all men, adores being adored. Of course she gets on his nerves occasionally – well, you saw that this morning, didn't you? – but on the whole he considers a little irritation a small price to pay for a wife who's genuinely good, very popular and thoroughly loyal to him in every way.'

'The Bishop seems to have a most remarkable talent for surrounding himself with adoring women!'

'The talent's probably developed in reaction to his bleak childhood. Adoration was in short supply then.'

'I thought he had a devoted stepmother?'

'She wasn't demonstrative. Until he was eighteen he hadn't a clue how she felt.'

'What happened when he was eighteen?'

'He went up to Oxford, and when he said goodbye to her she cried. It was her supreme moment of triumph, you see. She'd singled him out as the best of the bunch and put him on the road to Oxford, but he'd always thought he was just a hobby for her as she had no children of her own.' Lyle paused before adding: 'I think probably in the beginning he really was just a hobby for her, but after a while she found that her ambition for him gave her the determination to endure a difficult marriage. "It was worth it all for Adam," she said to me at the end of her life. She used to call him Adam. She hated the name Alex, thought it was frivolous, a nasty affectation of the Cobden-Smiths. "Adam's not really Alex," she said to me once. "Alex is just a mask, and beyond the mask there's the Adam nobody knows except me." That was a sinister thing to say, wasn't it? I look at the Bishop sometimes and think: there's an Adam in there somewhere! What a mysterious thing personality is, how eerie, how unfathomable . . .'

We were now standing in the middle of the stone circle. The stones themselves, stark and dark beneath their green-brown lichen, heightened the mystery of the Ring as it stood in that empty landscape, and seemed to bring the remote past deep into the present. I felt as if the Druids were brushing shoulders with Karl Barth as one bloodstained century merged into another in defiance of any conventional conception of time.

'This seems an appropriate place to discuss mysteries,' I said, 'and particularly the mystery of personality. Let's sit down for a moment.'

When we were chastely settled two feet apart in the shadow of one of the stones I offered her a cigarette. 'Do you smoke?'

'Only in my bedroom. But if you're going to have a treat I don't see why I shouldn't have one too.'

'You look like the kind of woman who smokes "Craven A".'

'Oh, so you see me as an adventuress!'

'Let's just say I have trouble seeing you as a companion in a clerical household.' As I lit our cigarettes I noticed that her hands were small and that the large signet-ring emphasized the delicate curve of her finger. The skin on the inside of her wrist was very white.

'Are you sure you're not going to pounce on me again?' she said after her first puff. 'You've got a pounce-ish look.'

'That's because you're so pounceworthy. Now stop egging me on by putting impure thoughts in my head and tell me more about this Swedish stepmother. I'm interested in the influence she must have had on Dr Jardine.'

III

'I first met her at Radbury,' said Lyle. 'She visited the Jardines there a couple of times, but then travel became too difficult because of her arthritis. The Bishop used to visit her in Putney whenever he could but I myself never saw her again until she came to live with us in Starbridge at the end of her life.'

'It's nice to think she ended her days with her Adam in his palace.'

'Another edifying tale? Yes, I suppose it was, although the situation wasn't entirely a bed of roses because poor Carrie was terrified of her stepmother-in-law. However,' said Lyle, effortlessly glossing over the crisis which had shaken the palace to its foundations, 'we all got on very well in the end. Old Mrs J. had decided that God was giving her a chance to redeem her previous coldness towards Carrie.'

'She was religious?'

'Yes, she'd been a Lutheran originally, like so many Swedes, but she'd been married to a man who thought institutional religion was rubbish, so she hadn't been a regular churchgoer.'

'But I thought Dr Jardine's father was a religious fanatic!'

'The fanaticism took an anti-clerical form. He thought all clergymen were instruments of the Devil.'

'How extraordinarily difficult for Dr Jardine!'

'Being married to a religious crank was hardly easy for old Mrs J.!'

'Did she confide in you? It sounds as if she did.'

'Yes, she enjoyed telling a sympathetic stranger about all the ghastliness she'd endured in the old days so that "her Adam", as you called him, should survive his appalling home. Her first big battle was to get him to school. Old Mr J. thought schools were sinks of iniquity.'

'He certainly sounds the most tiresome husband. Did she never consider abandoning Putney and bolting for Sweden? Or did her religious beliefs, such as they were, make an escape out of the question?'

'There's no doubt religious belief played a large part in her decision to stay – she became convinced she'd been sent into the family in order to save that child. "I felt it was a call from God," she said. "I felt no other action was possible." '

'But surely once Dr Jardine was grown up – once he'd got to Oxford – '

'Then the really ghastly problems began. The scholarship only covered his fees, and the beastly old father wouldn't give him any money for his keep. Old Mrs J. used to starve herself so that she could send money from her housekeeping allowance – the old man only climbed down when she was half-dead with hunger.'

I said amazed, 'But wasn't the old man pleased that his son was up at Oxford?'

'He thought all universities were dens of vice. However the Bishop survived and was awarded not only a first but a fellowship of All Soul's – '

'Happy ending!'

'Good heavens, no – quite the reverse! Old Mr J. then said, "I've kept you all these years – now it's time for you to keep me!" and it turned out that as he'd been living beyond his means for years while he pursued a life of gentlemanly idleness, his capital was now exhausted.'

'What an old scoundrel! So Dr Jardine had to keep the family on the income from his fellowship?'

'Yes, for a time he didn't think he could afford to go into the Church but eventually he made the decision to be ordained – '

' – and of course the old man disapproved.'

'I gather the two of them nearly killed each other.'

I said appalled, 'But couldn't the old man see his son was opting for a good straight decent life?'

'Oh, he never thought his son would succeed in living decently, no matter what profession he chose. The old man saw him sinking inevitably into corruption.'

'But this must have been terrible for Dr Jardine!' I was now having trouble finding the words to express my horror, and Lyle was looking at me in surprise. 'Terrible – monstrous – intolerable – '

'It got worse. The Bishop became vicar of the slum parish in Starmouth, and as he was unable to afford to marry and as he desperately needed a housekeeper he turned for help to his father, who was sitting in Putney being waited on hand and foot by a wife and two unmarried daughters. However old Mr J. refused to let either of the girls go to look after their brother. He had an obsession with female purity and thought they'd be ravished the moment they left his household.'

'But surely if the Bishop was supporting them all he had the whip-hand?'

'The old man still wouldn't budge. Said he'd rather starve than risk his daughters becoming fallen women.'

'Didn't the girls have any say in the matter?'

'Don't be silly, this was well before the War and he'd ruled them with a rod of iron for years!'

'No wonder one sister went mad!'

'Mrs J. thought she'd go mad herself, but of course she came to the rescue. She said to the old villain, "If you don't let either of those girls go, *I'll* go", and when he still clung to the girls she went.'

I dropped my cigarette and scuffled to retrieve it before it could burn a hole in my trousers. 'But how could Dr Jardine, as a clergyman, justify depriving a husband of his wife?'

'Oh, the old man wasn't too deprived – she used to go home for a visit every fortnight. Besides, neither she nor Dr Jardine believed, when she originally went to Starmouth, that the arrangement would be other than temporary; they thought the old man would eventually release one of the girls, but as he wasn't rational on the subject he didn't.'

'So she stayed on?'

'Yes, she loved it after the gloom and doom of Putney. She involved herself in parish work, met new people – '

'But what happened – '

' – in the end? She went back. The elder sister began to go insane, and Mrs J. felt morally bound to go home since her husband's need for her had become acute. However once she'd gone Dr Jardine couldn't cope; he was already exhausted by the parish and he couldn't withstand the loss of her help.'

'So when he lost her he broke down!'

'What an extremely ambiguous statement! All I meant was – '

'What happened next in Putney?'

'I've no idea. Mrs J. skated over that, but a year later the sister died in an asylum and the old man went senile. Old Mrs J. told me placidly it was the judgement of God.'

'How did the Bishop deal with the new crisis?'

'By that time he was in North London. The house allocated to the hospital chaplain was small but he rescued his father, stepmother and surviving sister and squeezed them in somehow. The father died six months later. Then old Mrs J. and the sister lived with the Bishop till his marriage.'

I decided it would be politic to prove to her that my mind did not always leap to the most dubious conclusions. 'I can't quite see why old Mrs J. made such a fuss about that marriage,' I said innocently. 'Surely she wanted her stepson to make a good marriage as soon as he could afford to do so?'

'She didn't look upon it as a good marriage. Carrie only had a hundred a year. Also Carrie was a bit old – thirty-two. Mrs J. thought that was suspicious, wanted to know why she hadn't got off the shelf earlier . . . But of course the real truth was that although Mrs J. wanted her stepson to marry, no girl was ever going to be good enough in her estimation.'

'Obviously it was for the best that she decided not to live with them after the marriage. But wasn't she tempted to move closer to Dr Jardine once he left Mayfair? Radbury's a long way from Putney.'

'She was afraid of quarrelling with Carrie. That was why she stayed away until she was too infirm to stay away any more.'

'I see now,' I said, unable to resist angling for an indiscretion by using a suggestive remark as bait, 'that the Starbridge finale isn't just an edifying resolution of the problem of old Mrs Jardine – it even qualifies as a romantic ending.'

Lyle immediately looked annoyed. 'It was a happy ending, certainly,' she said in the tone of voice of someone who considers romance a breach of taste. 'But romantic? That makes a complex and remarkable relationship seem banal.'

'Have you got some grudge against romance?'

'Of course – it's the road to illusion, isn't it?' said Lyle carelessly. 'Any realist knows that.' She stubbed out her cigarette. 'I think it's time we went back to the car – you've got that pounce-ish look again.'

'I suppose you do realize, don't you,' I said, extinguishing my own cigarette, 'that you're pushing me back with one hand yet beckoning me on with the other?' And before she had time to protest I had taken her in my arms.

This time I did not have the advantage of surprise and she had her defences firmly in place. As I pulled her towards me she said: 'No!' in a voice which precluded argument and shoved me aside as she scrambled to her feet.

I caught up with her halfway across the Ring but before I could speak she swung to face me and demanded, 'What exactly are you up to? You take me for a drive so that you can get to know me better and yet all you do is ask questions about the Bishop!'

'But I do know you better now! I know you smoke cigarettes in your bedroom, think romance is the invention of the Devil and have a profound admiration for that formidable lady, the late Mrs Jardine!'

'I wish I'd never told you about her!' said Lyle furiously. 'It's obvious you think she had some sort of obscene passion for her stepson – '

'Wouldn't "romantic affection" be a more accurate description?'

'It was not a romance!'

'Not in a tawdry conventional sense, no. But she sacrificed her life for his, didn't she, and isn't that really the unsurpassable romantic gesture? Dickens certainly thought so when he wrote *A Tale of Two Cities* but no one's yet accused Sydney Carton of an obscene passion for Charles Darnay.'

'I thought Carton sacrificed himself for Lucy's sake, not just for Darnay's. Maybe you should start rereading Dickens!'

'Maybe you should start redefining romance. Cigarette?'

'Thanks. I feel I need one after that exchange.'

When our cigarettes were alight we wandered on across the ridge. The Ring disappeared behind us as the track led over the brow of the hill, and in the distance we could see my car, crouched like a black beetle beside the dusty ribbon of the road.

'I did admire old Mrs J.,' said Lyle, 'because I knew what hell she'd been through for the Bishop, but I have to admit she could be an awful old battle-axe. During her two visits to Radbury she reduced Carrie to pulp, and what was worse she used to enjoy it. Poor Carrie!'

'You're very fond of Mrs Jardine, aren't you?'

'She's the sort of mother I always wanted. My own mother was an invalid – she had a weak heart – and it made her very querulous and self-absorbed.'

'And your father?'

'He was a soldier, one of the clever ones, very quick and bright and tough. He was killed in the War, of course, like all the best soldiers, and when my mother died in sympathy I went to Norfolk to live with my great-uncle. He was an ancient vicar who took me in out of Christian charity because no one else wanted me.'

'How old were you?'

'Twelve. It was 1914. You were wondering about my present age, weren't you?'

'Now that I know you're thirty-five allow me to tell you that I'm thirty-seven. How did you find Norfolk?'

'Dreadfully dull. I ended up writing my great-uncle's sermons just to stave off the boredom.'

'You don't write Dr Jardine's sermons, do you, by any chance?'

She laughed. 'Not yet!'

We strolled on down the track. 'Nevertheless,' I said, 'you've been described to me as the real power at the palace. How would the Jardines get on if you left?'

'Oh, but I'm not leaving,' she said. 'Didn't you know?'

'How lucky for the Jardines! But where does that leave you?'

'Exactly where I want to be – looking after my adopted mother and running the palace for the Bishop. I'm not interested in doing anything else.'

'No, obviously there's no time for other interests,' I said. 'Keeping that marriage glued together must be a very all-consuming occupation.'

She stopped dead. I stopped too, and as we faced each other I knew I had caught her off her guard.

'Don't misunderstand,' I said swiftly. 'I'm not calling you a liar. Earlier you made it plain that the marriage, despite its surface irritations, was a happy one involving that well-known phenomenon the attraction of opposites, and I see no reason to disbelieve that. Lady Starmouth also told me she thought the marriage was a success. But its success depends on you, doesn't it? If you weren't there to do all the things Mrs Jardine can't do, the marriage would go to pieces along with Mrs Jardine – just as it did at Radbury before you arrived with your jar of glue to stick the pieces together again. Well, it's always gratifying to one's self-esteem to feel that one's indispensable, but do you really think that once the Jardines are dead and you're on your own at last you won't look back and regret a lifetime of missed opportunities? Or are you simply going to say, as old Mrs Jardine said at the end of her life, "It was worth it all for Adam"?'

She was so pale that for the first time I noticed the faint freckles across her cheekbones. It was impossible not to conclude that I had shot an arrow into the dark and scored a bull's eye, but all she said in the end was a stony, 'I don't call him Adam.'

'Well, I should hope you don't call him Alex either,' I said, 'or my imagination would really run riot. I've noticed he calls you Lyle whenever he isn't referring to you as Miss Christie and I suppose it's natural enough after ten years that he should follow his wife's example in treating you as a highly favoured employee, but I'd certainly raise an eyebrow if you started calling him by his Christian name.'

'Oh, shut up! You've made quite enough snide remarks for one afternoon!'

'I thought I was making some intelligent observations in an attempt to solve the mystery!'

'What mystery?'

'The mystery you present to any man who admires you, the mystery of why you're content to go through life as a mere companion – '

'I'm beginning to think *you're* the real mystery here, Charles Ashworth, with your interest in the Bishop and your Don Juan manners and the wife you won't talk about and the past you gloss over so smoothly! Why are you going through this elaborate charade of making torrid passes at me?'

'It's no charade. I knew as soon as we met yesterday that I was deeply attracted to you – '

'That's the most unreal opening a sentence could have! You knew nothing about me! You're obviously deep in a romantic fantasy!'

'Why don't you tell me about this broken engagement of yours which has given you such a horror of romance?'

'I'm telling you nothing more!' She was taut with anger. 'Take me home at once, please – I find this entire conversation deeply offensive!'

We walked on in silence, she hurrying as fast as she could without breaking into a run, I lengthening my stride to keep pace with her. At the car I said, 'I'm extremely sorry if I've given you offence but please believe me when I say my admiration for you is genuine.'

'I don't want your admiration.' Wrenching open the door she collapsed in a heap on the passenger seat; evidently I had shocked her to the core.

V

We did not speak throughout the journey back to Starbridge but as I halted my car in the palace drive I said, 'Please give my apologies to Mrs Jardine and say I won't be making an appearance at tea. I must do some work in my room on my St Anselm notes.'

'Very well.' She had regained her composure and although she was still pale her voice was calm.

I wondered how long it would take her to decide – greatly against her better judgement, of course – that she wanted me to make another pounce.

VI

Upstairs in the cavernous Victorian bathroom I filled the bath to the halfway mark with cold water and sat in it for a while as I sluiced away both the sweat of my afternoon's exertions and my very carnal thoughts on the subject of Miss Lyle Christie. Then I returned to my room, pulled on some underclothes and cast an eye over my St Anselm notes, but the glance was a mere formality. I wanted only to give a veneer of truth to my statement that I was missing tea in order to work, and eventually, my conscience assuaged, I began to imagine what I would have said to the Archbishop if he had appeared beside me and demanded a progress report.

I now knew very much more about Jardine than I had known before my arrival and I was certainly well on my way to building up a psychological portrait which would enable Lang to decide whether his enemy was the kind of man who could be disastrously exploited by Fleet Street, but I had still elicited no information about Lang's chief worries, the journal and the possible existence of indiscreet correspondence. I myself was now convinced that Jardine was far too shrewd to commit epistolary indiscretions, but the journal remained an unknown quantity. No one had mentioned it to me yet, but this silence was hardly surprising if the journal were a long-standing hobby which everyone took for granted.

I meditated on the subject for a while but came to the conclusion that Jardine would have been unlikely to use the journal as a confessional during the lifetime of his stepmother. Why confide in an impersonal notebook when one had a confidante who provided limitless sympathy and understanding? I could imagine him tossing off some lines in a frenzy if his stepmother had been inaccessible, but I was sure that a ruthless censorship would have taken place once the sympathetic understanding had been obtained.

I then asked myself if he might have used the journal as a confessional since his stepmother's death, but all my witnesses had testified that after the upheaval surrounding old Mrs Jardine's arrival in Starbridge Jardine's life had been unpunctuated by crises; possibly no confessional had been required. The chaplain had said Jardine had been getting on better with Lyle; Lady Starmouth had remarked that a spacious palace made it easier for a married couple to live in close proximity to a third party; Mrs Cobden-Smith had implied that by this time Lyle had been at her zenith as a miracle-worker. I suddenly remembered my friend Philip saying that Jardine had seemed *distrait* during the first year of his episcopate, and this observation from a stranger harmonized with the facts I now knew: the rocky start to the Starbridge career followed by years when Jardine was able to pursue his calling against a background of tranquillity. I decided that the journal was probably as dull as sackcloth and quite unworthy of a reduction to ashes.

At this point I paused in my meditations to light a cigarette but as I shook out the match my thoughts once more turned to the Lovely Ladies. I had already decided that because of the Bishop's psychological constraint on the subject of class I could tell Lang with confidence that there was no risk of any scandal with an aristocratic Englishwoman, and although the incident with the foreigner Loretta Staviski could certainly be regarded with suspicion, I had believed Lady Starmouth when she had vouched for Jardine's good behaviour. Jardine was popular with the ladies; that sort of clergyman always risked fatally attracting a parishioner, but in the vast majority of cases the clergyman was innocent of misconduct and I was sure that Jardine, newly married and no doubt burning to make a success of his splendid preferment, had had powerful reasons for treating Loretta with propriety.

I had almost argued myself to the conclusion that Jardine was as pure as driven snow, but I had left the most ominous possibility to the last.

I began to think about Lyle.

I had noticed that although she had admitted she regarded Mrs Jardine as a mother she had not said she regarded the Bishop as a father. Yet she had described her own father as 'clever', 'bright', 'quick' and 'tough', all adjectives which could be applied to Jardine. Obviously she was fond of the Bishop; obviously she respected and admired him, but there was no hint in her manner of a schoolgirl's crush or a spinster's frustrated passion, and I was driven to suspect that her feelings here too were filial. In fact I now found I shared Mrs Cobden-Smith's conviction that Lyle stayed with the Jardines not because of a passion for the Bishop but because of a passion for power – and not merely the power of running the palace but the power of keeping that marriage glued together, the power springing from the fact that she made it possible for the Bishop to continue his ministry. What happened to a bishop whose marriage went to the wall? It was a spine-chilling thought, and I thought it was a chill to which Jardine's spine had become well accustomed.

I did speculate about the possible ill effects on Lyle of a broken engagement, but on this point I could form no more than the tentative conclusion that some adverse romantic experience seemed likely. Her response to my kiss indicated she was sexually normal; her repudiation of it indicated an abnormal fear of romantic involvement. Ignorance prevented me from expanding my theory further, but nevertheless I felt I could say to Lang that Lyle's aversion to marriage was more likely to spring from a broken engagement than from any inappropriate feelings towards the Bishop.

Having summed up Lyle's probable attitude to Jardine I turned the relationship around and began to consider Jardine's probably attitude to Lyle. This was easier because as a clergyman I could mentally put myself in Jardine's shoes without any undue strain on my imagination: I had married in haste but had almost certainly repented at leisure, and as the result of my rashness I now had a wife who was capable of being a crippling liability. I was an eminent cleric beyond hope of divorce so the most nerve-racking question in such nerve-racking circumstances inevitably became: how did I survive my marriage? Lyle was the heaven-sent answer, and because Lyle was so vital not only for the welfare of my marriage but for the welfare of my increasingly illustrious career, I would take no risks whatsoever and exercise an iron control over any insane but pardonable desire to flirt. I would, of course, find Lyle immensely attractive, and that would make it difficult to adjust to her presence in the household – I would even tell Lady Starmouth I found the presence of a third party an intrusion on my marriage – but with prayer and willpower and plenty of deliciously *risqué* chats with my safe Lovely Ladies I would control myself, diverting the emotion into harmless channels whenever possible and suppressing the emotion which could not be diverted. I was Adam Alexander Jardine, a mature survivor trained in the hardest of schools, and I was neither weak nor a fool.

That left only one more vital question to be answered before I stepped out of Jardine's shoes. I was a man of volatile temperament with plenty of physical energy and a strong liking for women; did I or did I not live like a monk? I did not. I slept with my wife, who was still pretty, still adoring, still mildly lovable in her own maddening way and – most important of all – still available. Certainly no one else was and married clergymen, like beggars, can't be choosers.

I decided this was not merely a plausible interpretation of the Jardine *ménage* but the only interpretation which made sense. I felt I could now say confidently to Lang: 'The girl, who probably has strong psychological reasons for not marrying, regards the woman as her mother and regards the man as satisfying her hankering for power. The woman regards the girl as her daughter and regards her husband with adoration. The husband regards his wife as a liability but as a source of sexual satisfaction, and regards the girl as a godsend but as sexually taboo. The marriage is entirely safe so long as this triangle is maintained and I see no sign of any approaching catastrophe.'

But of course this last statement would be untrue. I knew now that *I* was the approaching catastrophe bent on breaking up the triangle, and once the triangle disintegrated the marital disaster would be poised to unfold.

I was still contemplating this prospect with appalled fascination seconds later when someone rapped loudly on my door.

I jumped, sprang to my feet and pulled on my dressing-gown. 'Come in!' I called, assuming I was addressing a servant sent to deliver either a telephone message or perhaps a letter which had arrived by the afternoon post, and turned aside to extinguish my cigarette in the ashtray.

The door banged open and the Bishop blazed across the threshold.

'Now, Dr Ashworth,' he said abruptly as I spun round in shock, 'I think it's time you told me the truth – and when I say the truth I mean the truth, the whole truth and nothing but the truth. Exactly why did you come to Starbridge and what the deuce do you think you're playing at?'

SIX

'The sexual appetite (which is the most insistent and the most important of our bodily desires) presses for satisfaction . . . So we start with the certainty that sexual indulgence will be popular and that Christianity will be most difficult precisely at that point.'

More Letters of Herbert Hensley Henson
Bishop of Durham 1920-1939
ed. E. F. BRALEY

I

In the second which followed I saw the Bishop with photographic clarity and noticed that his brown eyes were no longer brilliant but opaque. His mouth was set in a tight line, his hands were clasped behind his back as if to conceal clenched fists and his whole stance radiated pugnacity. 'Well, Dr Ashworth?' he demanded, and his pugnacity was formidable indeed. 'Speak up! What do you have to say for yourself?'

I knew at once that I had to stop him thinking I could be intimidated but unfortunately I was far from being completely unperturbed. Some form of defensive action was clearly called for. 'I'm sorry, Dr Jardine,' I said, 'but I refuse to conduct an interview with a bishop while I'm wearing only my underclothes and a dressing-gown. You must allow me a moment to dress.'

There was a short tense silence. Then Jardine laughed, exclaimed, 'I admire your nerve!' and sat himself down at the table by the window.

Scrambling into my clerical uniform I found I could all too easily deduce what had happened. Lady Starmouth had complained about my interrogation, the chaplain had revealed my interest in the palace *ménage*, Mrs Cobden-Smith had disclosed what an excellent listener I was and Lyle had reported my episcopal obsession. I was about to be exposed as a deplorably unsuccessful espionage agent, but on the other hand my findings were all in Jardine's favour. If I allowed his rage to run its course I might have a chance of pacifying him when he subsided into mere indignation. It seemed the best I could hope for. However meanwhile I had to cope with his rage.

'Thank you,' I said when fully dressed at last I sat down opposite him at the table. 'Now I feel more civilized. First of all, Bishop, let me apologize from the bottom of my heart – '

'Spare me the apologies. Give me the truth. Why are you here?'

'Dr Lang sent me.'

Jardine showed no surprise. 'The Archbishop should take care,' was his acid comment. 'He's showing a talent for ecclesiastical skulduggery unmatched since the days of the Borgia popes. And what was his objective – or rather, what did he tell you was his objective?'

'He's acting to protect you, Bishop. He's afraid his enemies in Fleet Street might use you in an attempt to smear the Church, and he sent me here to estimate how vulnerable you are to scandal.'

'That may indeed be what he told you – but of course the real truth is that he's sent you here to spy on my private life in the hope that you'll find evidence which he can use to compel my resignation!'

'Bishop – '

'Monstrous! Archbishops have been executed for less!'

I felt I had no choice but to attempt my patron's defence. 'Bishop, His Grace doesn't suspect you of any gross failure or even of any serious indiscretion, and I must absolutely insist that he's not trying to get rid of you – '

'No? It sounds to me as if he's recently travelled incognito to the Old Vic to see a performance of *Murder in the Cathedral* – with the result that he's now declaiming, in the manner of Henry II: "Who will rid me of this turbulent priest"!'

'Dr Lang,' I said firmly, ignoring this shaft, 'is worried primarily about the existence of a minor indiscretion which an unscrupulous journalist could distort. He's also worried in case your unusual domestic situation should be misunderstood. Bearing in mind the enormous amount of attention you've been receiving from the press lately, do you really think it's so reprehensible that Dr Lang should send someone he trusts to survey the landscape to make sure you're not vulnerable to the worst form of exploitation by Fleet Street?'

Jardine controlled himself sufficiently to say in an even voice, 'You're making heroic efforts to defend the Archbishop for his inexcusable trespass on my privacy, and I respect your loyalty to him, but didn't it occur to His Grace that I'm perfectly capable of constructing my own defences against any assault from the press?'

'The Archbishop merely wanted to make sure you hadn't accidentally left a chink in your armour.'

'And dare I ask what kind of chink His Grace had in mind?'

'He was concerned in particular about the existence of unwise entries in your journal and the existence of indiscreet correspondence.'

Jardine burst out laughing. Then he exclaimed with the most withering scorn, 'What kind of a fool does he think I am?'

'I know it sounds preposterous, but Dr Jardine, it's a fact that men of your age – even brilliant men of your age – do sometimes go off the rails, and His Grace felt he had to make absolutely sure – not only for the sake of the Church but for your own sake – '

'Quite. Very well, I take your point. I suppose if one's Archbishop of Canterbury one should always allow for the possibility of a bishop going stark staring mad, and His Grace no doubt interpreted my attack on him in the Lords as the onset of lunacy. However let me try and allay His Grace's melodramatic fears as swiftly as possible.' Jardine leant forward, placing his forearms on the table, and clasped his hands purposefully. 'First: my journal. It's not an adolescent's diary reeking of carnal allusions. I comment on the books I've read, record my travels, note the themes of my sermons, remark on whom I've met and generally try to reflect what it means to serve God as a churchman. I won't say I've never used the journal to record personal difficulties because I have, but as I've always excised the pages later and burnt them, you can tell the Archbishop that my journal in its present state would send any reporter from *The News of the World* straight to sleep . . . Or do you find that impossible to believe?'

I said truthfully, 'No, I'd already reached the conclusion that you'd edit your work. I was only wondering – ' I broke off.

'Well?'

'No, my next question would have been impertinent.'

'You may as well ask it. Since I'm apparently surviving the Archbishop's monstrous assault on my privacy without suffering a stroke, one little piece of impertinence from you is hardly likely to dent my miraculous sang-froid. What's the question?'

'I was wondering when you last felt impelled to excise entries from your journal.'

Jardine raised an eyebrow, gave me a searching glance but concluded I was anxious only about the possibility of recent difficulties in his private life. 'You needn't worry,' he said drily. 'My life's been singularly uneventful for some time now. It's been five years since any pages from my journal were consigned to the library fire.'

'Was that when you were still at Radbury?' I said, certain that the answer was no but hoping to egg him on to a further revelation.

'No, I'd just moved to Starbridge – and I trust, Dr Ashworth, you won't graduate from a minor to a major impertinence by asking me what was going on in my life at the time.'

'No, of course not, Bishop.' I thought of Mrs Jardine drifting again towards a nervous breakdown as she grappled not only with the arrival of her stepmother-in-law but also with what Mrs Cobden-Smith had described as 'an awkward time', a euphemism I had translated as the menopause. I could well imagine the Bishop relieving his feelings in his journal as he waited for the arrival of his confidante.

'I had a difficult decision to make,' said the Bishop unexpectedly, 'and I needed to set down the situation on paper in order to clarify my mind.'

That did surprise me. I could not immediately see what decision had had to be made. Possibly he had been debating with himself whether in view of his wife's mental health, he had had a duty to install his stepmother not at the palace but in the best Starbridge nursing home.

'Very well, so much for the journal,' Jardine was saying briskly. 'Let's turn now to my correspondence. There are four women to whom I write regularly. First and foremost: my wife. Whenever we're apart I try to write her a line every day. I'd say that was fairly normal behaviour for a man of my generation who detests the telephone, although a young man like you might think it rather an extravagant use of writing paper. After my wife the next woman on my list would be the incomparable Lady Starmouth to whom I pen a line about twice a week. Our chief topic is clerical gossip, but we also discuss literature and politics – topics which interest Mrs Welbeck and Lady Markhampton to whom I write regularly but less frequently than I write to Lady Starmouth. Am I making myself clear? My correspondence with all three of these delightful ladies, stimulating as it is, can't possibly be described as the kind which would encourage a husband to challenge me to pistols at dawn. You may assure His Grace he has no cause for alarm.'

'May I risk another minor impertinence?'

'You're a brave man, Dr Ashworth. But continue.'

'Do you ever write to Miss Christie?'

'Only when I have essential information to impart. For example, the last time I wrote to her was in May when my wife and I were in London for the Coronation. I sent Miss Christie a line to say that Carrie and I would be staying up in town an extra day in order to dine with some old friends from Radbury.'

'Why didn't Miss Christie go to London with you?'

'That's not an impertinent question, Dr Ashworth, but as far as I can see it's an irrelevant one. I had a part to play in the Coronation ceremony and my wife had a seat in the Abbey. Rather than risk being crushed to death by the multitudes lining the processional route, Miss Christie sensibly decided to stay at home and "listen in" to the proceedings on the wireless. Do you have any other irrelevant questions, or am I now allowed to inquire what kind of report you intend to present to Dr Lang?'

I smiled at him before I said, 'I shall tell His Grace that in my opinion every chink in your armour's sealed.'

'Splendid! And are you also going to inform His Grace that in addition to entering my household under false pretences you've been further abusing my hospitality by playing fast and loose with my wife's companion?'

I felt as if I had been felled on the rugger field by an unexpected tackle. It took a considerable effort to look him straight in the eyes and say strongly, 'I may be playing fast but I'm not playing loose.'

'No? Miss Christie thinks your behaviour lacked stability, and I must say I agree with her. Don't you think you were a little rash to subject a respectable woman to passionate advances less than twenty-four hours after your first meeting with her?'

'No more rash than you were at my age,' I said, 'when you proposed to your future wife on the strength of a four-day acquaintance.'

There was a silence. We stared at each other. Jardine's amber eyes were dangerously bright.

'That was a major impertinence, Dr Ashworth.'

'And so, with all due respect, was your last remark, Dr Jardine. No man, not even a bishop, tells me how to run my private life.'

'What an extraordinarily arrogant statement! Are you saying you're never in need of spiritual direction?'

'I –'

'Who's your spiritual director? Or are you so adrift as to believe you don't need one?'

Beneath the table my fists were clenched. Somehow keeping my voice level I said, 'My spiritual director is Father James Reid of the Fordite monks at Grantchester.'

'Oh, I know the Grantchester Fordites from my days at Radbury – and of course I remember Father Reid, the best kind of cosy old monk, very gentle and saintly and kind. But don't you need someone rather tougher than a cosy old monk to advise you on your spiritual life, Dr Ashworth?'

I said nothing, and when Jardine realized I had no intention of replying he said in a voice which was unexpectedly compassionate, 'Don't think I can't remember what it's like to be thirty-seven and unmarried. But impulsive romantic action isn't the answer, Dr Ashworth, and you're quite intelligent enough to know that for those of us not called to celibacy the pressures of a celibate life can lead to emotional instability unless there's regular and effective counselling by someone who knows exactly what problems are involved.'

Again he paused and again I remained silent. Finally he said, 'Have a word with your bishop. See if he can recommend someone more suitable than dear old Father Reid who's been celibate so long that he's probably forgotten the male organ has a purpose other than urination. Cambridge is a good man, even if he does spend too much time writing theses about whether Ezra came before or after Nehemiah, and I'm sure he'd do his best to help you.'

Once more the silence lengthened but eventually I was able to say, 'Thank you, Dr Jardine. And now, of course, since I've so thoroughly abused your hospitality, you'll want me to leave your house at the earliest opportunity.'

Jardine leant back in his chair and regarded me as if I presented some difficult but fascinating problem. 'My dear Dr Ashworth,' he said as he rose to his feet, 'if you cut short your visit and leave the palace under a cloud, you're going to trigger exactly the kind of gossip Dr Lang is so anxious to avoid. Can't you imagine the report in the gutter-press? "We have it on good authority – " (that would be the eavesdropping second housemaid) " – that a storm erupted in the Cathedral Close at Starbridge when Canon Charles Ashworth was expelled from the palace after an assault on the virtue of the Bishop's attractive young companion, Miss Lyle Christie." (Naturally they would omit all mention of my wife.) "We are reliably informed that the ravishing Miss Christie returned from a motor drive *à deux* with the handsome Canon only to rush sobbing to the Bishop, 'He unleashed his passion at Starbury Ring!' whereupon the Bishop stormed to the Canon shouting: 'Never darken my door again!' . . ." And so on and so on. Oh no, Dr Ashworth! I'm not falling into the trap of asking you to leave! We do, after all, have a duty to the Archbishop to keep up appearances, even if he does insult us both by treating you as a spy and me as a fool.'

During this speech the Bishop had crossed the room. He now opened the door and looked back. 'You will complete your visit, you will behave like a gentleman and you will consider my advice on the subject of spiritual direction,' he said, 'and meanwhile I look forward to resuming our theological discussions over the port tonight. I should very much like to hear your views on the Virgin Birth.' And he walked out, banging the door abruptly behind him.

II

I had been warned off.

I began to wonder how far the Bishop had interfered with Lyle's other romances. Most clerical suitors would have backed away in fright if the Bishop had bared his teeth, but I was far from being a vulnerable young cleric and I was not prepared to be intimidated. Anyone who had Lang's patronage was not obliged to worry about the approval of the Bishop of Starbridge, and I saw no chance of Jardine ever moving into a position which could affect my career; he had too many enemies among the politicians to receive either of the two most exalted preferments, the archbishoprics of Canterbury and York.

Having removed my collar I lit a cigarette to steady my nerves. I was wondering if I could place a sinister interpretation on the fact that Lyle had run straight to the Bishop, but I could only conclude that I should have predicted such a response. Obviously a close partnership between Lyle and the Bishop had developed over the years, and once I had accused her of providing the glue which prevented the Bishop's marriage disintegrating, her natural reaction would have been to warn him that I was bent on rattling the skeleton in his cupboard. In these circumstances it was small wonder that Jardine had decided to rattle his sabre in return, particularly if Lyle had also considered it her duty as a loyal employee to warn the Bishop that I showed signs of wanting to demolish his *ménage à trois*. If the welfare of his marriage and career depended on Lyle he not only had to rattle his sabre; he had to lunge straight for my jugular vein.

However although I was willing to concede that the Bishop's belligerence was understandable I thought his attitude from a spiritual point of view was unhealthy. I had a very Christian desire to remarry. He seemed bent on foiling my current attempt to attain that goal. Moreover both Lyle's welfare and mine could be adversely affected, and after prolonged reflection I found myself unable to resist the conclusion that he was in the wrong.

I suddenly realized I had missed Choral Evensong again, and with an exclamation of annoyance I stubbed out my cigarette, replaced my collar and sat down to read the evening office.

Halfway through the *Nunc Dimittis* it occurred to me that Jardine must often have faced the possibility that Lyle would leave one day; he had not employed a woman who was so unattractive that her future was entirely predictable. I decided that if I were Jardine I would long since have formed a contingency plan which I could put into operation if Lyle handed in her notice, and the contingency plan would revolve around the fact that I would always have a suitable replacement in mind. Large numbers of companions were drawn from clerical homes where there was little money to support girls trained only to be ladies, and as a bishop I would be in a good position to survey the available candidates. Of course it would be difficult to find someone who equalled Lyle's ability to be a godsend, but since an acceptably pleasant, competent woman could probably be tracked down without too much trouble, it could be argued that Jardine was now only fighting to save himself some inconvenience. Lyle's departure would certainly represent an earthquake in the episcopal household, but people do recover from earthquakes; life does eventually return to normal.

Yet anyone would imagine, from Jardine's pugilistic behaviour towards me, that if the earthquake happened at Starbridge all life at the palace would cease.

I told myself I was still smarting from the assault on my jugular vein, and returning to my prayer-book I made a new effort to concentrate on the office, but long before I reached the end the inevitable possibility was seeping into my mind. I told myself to suppose, for the sake of argument, that my plausible explanation of the *ménage à trois* was in fact entirely wrong; I told myself to suppose, again for the sake of argument, that I suspended belief and started to think the unthinkable. If Lyle were Jardine's mistress it would explain both her reluctance to marry and Jardine's pugilism towards a dangerous suitor.

The only trouble with this theory, which seemed at first glance preposterous and at second glance so unpleasantly plausible, was that it fell apart as soon as it was submitted to a close examination. For a start I could not imagine that Mrs Jardine would continue to treat as a daughter the woman who was sleeping with her adored husband. Mrs Jardine was not the cleverest of women, but I thought she would be sufficiently intuitive to know if the two most important people in her life were having an affair. However the real difficulty with the theory remained that I could not see a man of Jardine's integrity leading a spiritual double-life. I was still willing to bet heavily that he was not an apostate, and unless he were an apostate adultery was inconceivable.

Somehow I reached the end of the office and began to prepare myself for dinner. All things were possible, even the unlikeliest of apostasies, but it was a waste of time for me to think the unthinkable unless I found some indication, however small, that Jardine was capable of unthinkable behaviour.

I stopped flattening my hair and stared into the glass.

Other clergymen fell into error. Why not Jardine? Suddenly, for clouded reasons beyond my comprehension, I felt an urge to prove that Jardine had at least once since his ordination been guilty of a serious moral failure – and that was the moment when I first started speculating seriously on the subject of Loretta Staviski.

III

Jardine's threat to discuss the Virgin Birth with me over the port was never realized. One of the lay dinner-guests, Starbridge's most distinguished architect, proved to be a non-smoker who could not be dispatched to the smoking-room, and out of courtesy Jardine at first avoided splitting theological hairs. However after a discussion of the arrests which had recently taken place in the German Evangelical Church the architect said deferentially, 'Talking of clerical matters, Bishop, I hope you won't mind me mentioning the A. P. Herbert Bill. I'm interested in your opinion of it, particularly as I too think that the grounds for divorce should be extended, but I'm still not sure how you justify your views theologically. What makes you so sure that Christ wasn't laying down the law on this particular subject but only stating an ethical guideline?'

This was clearly an intelligent sympathetic layman who deserved to be encouraged. Jardine said kindly, 'Well, the first thing you must remember is that Our Lord wasn't a twentieth-century Englishman brought up in a culture which glorifies the modest understatement. He came from the Middle East and in the culture of his day people communicated important truths by the use of striking word-pictures, statements which we would call exaggerations. A well-known example of this is when Christ says: "It is easier for a camel to go through the eye of a needle, than for a rich man to enter into the kingdom of God". A modern Englishman would merely say: "He can't do it".'

'So in other words what you're saying is – ' But the architect could not quite relate this warning about the un-Englishness of Christ to the teaching on divorce.

'The next thing you should remember,' said Jardine, paying no attention to the interruption as he busily laid the foundations of his argument, 'is that one should always try to see Christ against the background in which he lived. At the time of his ministry there were in fact two opposing attitudes to divorce within Judaism. One group, the Hillel Jews, thought that divorce could be granted even for the most trivial reasons – if the wife burnt the dinner, for instance. The other group held that divorce should be granted only for adultery and only to men – in fact divorce was actually required when a man had an adulterous wife; he had no choice.'

'Good heavens!' said the layman, fascinated by the thought of compulsory divorce. I sensed he had almost said 'Good God!' but had remembered just in time that he was at the Bishop's table.

'Now,' said Jardine, reassured that the layman was still conscious, 'we come to Our Lord. What he was really doing was criticizing the lax attitude of the Hillel Jews by a heavy underlining of the teaching of the stricter school of thought. And the way he phrased this criticism was in the Middle-Eastern way: "fortissimo" by Semitic overstatement, not "pianissimo" by British understatement. He said: "What therefore God hath joined together, let no man put asunder". Of course he was aware that both schools of thought permitted divorce, but he wasn't talking as a lawyer and he wasn't talking about the law. He was attacking the morality of divorce sought for trivial reasons, and he did this by emphasizing the sanctity of marriage.'

'Ah!' said the architect, recognizing a familiar phrase. 'Sanctity of marriage – yes – '

'Let me give you a twentieth-century parallel,' said Jardine, helping him along. 'If I were to tell you that recently in Reno, Nevada, a woman divorced her husband because he squeezed the marital toothpaste tube from the top instead of the bottom, you might well react by saying: "Disgraceful! Marriage should be for life! Shocking debasement of the institution!" But you don't really think that marriage should always be for life; if it breaks down in such a way that its spiritual core is destroyed – if the marriage ceases to be a marriage in any meaningful sense of the word – then you and I and many thousands of others believe that the marriage is spiritually null and should be legally terminated. And *that* in my opinion is the compassionate teaching which must inevitably lie beyond Our Lord's statements stressing the sanctity of marriage.'

'So what you're saying is,' said the layman, who was now, like a promising infant, 'coming along nicely', 'Christ would have disapproved of the divorce law of Nevada but approved of the new divorce law proposed by Mr A. P. Herbert.'

'Precisely!' said Jardine. 'Herbert's Bill has two main purposes: one is to relieve suffering – and do you suppose that Christ, with all his compassion, would have objected to that? – and the second is to reinforce the sanctity of marriage by permitting the dissolution of the marital travesties, the cases where the spiritual core of the marriage has been destroyed not just by adultery but by cruelty, desertion or insanity as well – and do you suppose that Our Lord, who recoiled from the debasement of marriage, would have objected to the elimination of the marriages which had become a mockery? I think not.'

'How clear it all seems!' said the architect, delighted that his personal views, reached by moral inclination, could be justified theologically. 'And how jolly to think of Christ approving of the A. P. Herbert Bill – although I suppose one might deduce that from the fact that the Bill's now certain to become law. Bishop, do we dare say that the success of the Bill's second reading in the House of Lords last month was God's will?'

'Well, it certainly wasn't the Archbishop of Canterbury's will,' said Jardine, 'but then as far as I know His Grace hasn't yet claimed to be God. Dr Ashworth, I'm beginning to think your prolonged silence has a sinister quality. I hope you're not thinking I should be burnt at the stake.'

'No, we'll acquit you of heresy today, Bishop!' I said smiling at him, and at once saw the amusement flare in his eyes.

When one considered all the adverse circumstances, it was most bizarre how much we both liked each other.

Was he an apostate? I still could not believe it, and although his views might be startling to a layman I knew he was only treading a well-worn theological path; an examination of Christ's words in the light of conditions prevailing in first-century Palestine was nowadays considered a thoroughly respectable endeavour in the attempt to look beyond the glittering image of Christ in the Gospels to the historical figure about whom so little was known. Jardine's views on divorce were certainly open to criticism, particularly by the conservative wing of the Church, but he was a long way from a suspect Christianity, and the ardour of his conviction that compassion should be shown to the victims of hopeless marriages indicated a man who believed whole-heartedly in the reality of Christ, not an apostate who was covering up his lost belief with a few clever phrases.

Moreover on this issue Jardine was in distinguished company. Martin Luther had gone even further than A. P. Herbert in urging new grounds for divorce where the spiritual core of the marriage had been destroyed, but the trouble with such liberal views, I always thought, was that once one had embraced them it was hard to know where to stop. Unless one was careful one could so easily reason oneself into claiming that the compassion of Christ justified even divorce on the grounds of a careless squeeze of a toothpaste tube.

'You're looking very pensive, Dr Ashworth!' called Lady Starmouth after my return to the drawing-room.

'I'm still recovering from Dr Jardine's post-prandial wisdom . . .'

My own views on divorce were complex. Despite my public support of Lang, who regarded Herbert's Bill with antipathy, I privately approved the Bill on humanitarian grounds – which meant, in other words, that I was citing the compassion of Christ in order to approve extending the grounds for dissolving shattered marriages. However I did think that theologically it was difficult to argue that Christ would ever have approved of extending the grounds for divorce beyond adultery. Jardine had had a good shot at the argument, but the architect's enthusiastic acceptance of it indicated not the strength of the thesis but the strength of Jardine's gift for manipulating a receptive audience. In my opinion Christ had been a good Jew, not 'liberal' in the modern sense of extending a credo to its outer limits in the name of freedom, but 'radical' in the original sense of cutting back the credo to its roots to rediscover its true spirit. This radicalism was illustrated by his opposition to the Pharisees and his determination to respond not merely to the letter but to the spirit of Judaism, a spirit which encompassed a far stricter view of divorce than that envisaged by Mr A. P. Herbert.

I suddenly realized that Lady Starmouth was saying to me, '. . . and I do hope you'll call on us when you're next up in town!'

'How kind of you, Lady Starmouth! Thank you,' I said, and at once remembered the Earl's information that Loretta was due to arrive in London that weekend.

Across the room Lyle was watching us. She had been avoiding me all evening but now she stepped forward impulsively, and as Lady Starmouth turned away from me to respond to a question from the architect, I eased myself around the back of the sofa to a spot out of sight of the terrace where the Bishop was enjoying a stroll with the architect's good-looking wife.

Lyle reached me a second later. 'I'm sorry this afternoon ended in a mess,' she said rapidly. 'I enjoyed myself up at the Ring. Thanks for the outing.'

So she had decided she was ready for another pounce.

'Have lunch with me tomorrow.'

'Oh, that's quite impossible – the Starmouths are leaving, more guests are arriving and Mrs Jardine will need me all day,' she said without hesitation, but as she nerved herself to look at me directly I thought her eyes were communicating a very different message. At last she added in a low voice: 'I'm sorry. It would have been nice. But I can't.'

'Don't worry, I'll ask you again,' I said. 'Bishop or no Bishop.'

For a moment she was motionless. Then she said in her politest voice, 'Will you please excuse me?' and slipped away before the Bishop could return to the room to make sure nothing subversive was occurring in his absence.

V

I was quite unable to sleep that night. I tossed and turned, I read the most boring genealogies of the Old Testament, I dowsed myself with cold water, I prayed, counted sheep and went to the lavatory. Finally at two o'clock I padded downstairs to the Bishop's library in pursuit of some light reading. Jardine's taste in literature was a varied one and we had already discovered a shared weakness for detective stories.

Reaching the library I switched on the light and began to prowl around the shelves. I was just thinking that the Bishop's book collection was less eclectic than I had anticipated when I discovered a shelf devoted to nineteenth-century novels, including a battered group by Sir Walter Scott. I was delighted. The novels of Scott never failed to lull me into a state of somnolence, and pulling out *Ivanhoe* I idly opened the cover.

To my surprise I found myself confronting a much-inscribed fly-leaf.

At the top of the page someone had written INGRID ASHLEY, 1885, and below this signature another hand, bold and upright, had added: 'My Stepmother gave me this book to keep me quiet, but I solemnly swear I shall never read it because I know that novels are the invention of the Devil. ADAM ALEXANDER JARDINE, 1888 (aged 9).' But this was not the last entry on the fly-leaf. Further down the page the bold upright hand, now imbued with an elegant maturity had written: 'My dearest, just look at this inscription which I wrote to protect myself in case Father found a novel in my room! What a pathetic little horror I was and what a wonderful thing you did, introducing me to *Ivanhoe*, to English literature and to civilization. Let me now return this book to its original owner and say: Welcome to Starbridge! All my love always, ADAM (ADAM ALEXANDER STARO, 1932 – aged 53!)'

A football sounded behind me, and as I spun round *Ivanhoe* slipped through my hands to thud upon the floor.

'Can I help you, Dr Ashworth?' inquired Jardine in his most sardonic voice. 'Is there perhaps some information you still require?'

VI

I somehow managed to say, 'I assure you my espionage has its limits, Bishop. I wasn't making a secret assault on your journal.' To hide my confusion I stooped to pick up *Ivanhoe* as I added, 'I was looking for some light reading to ease the boredom of insomnia.'

'In that case we're driven here by a common goal but personally I'm about to fight my own insomnia with a detective story.' He bent to extract a volume from the bottom shelf. 'Have you read *The Murder of Roger Ackroyd* by the other, more famous Miss Christie?'

'Yes. That's the one where one has to watch the narrator.'

'Precisely. I always find the more I read that story the more intrigued I become by the narrator's omissions and evasions.' He glanced at the book in my hands as he added, 'However perhaps you're better off with Sir Walter Scott. That volume in particular has sentimental memories for me.'

'I was just reading the inscription. Your stepmother must have been a remarkable woman, Dr Jardine.'

'She needed to be remarkable. It's a catastrophe for any family when the mother dies young, and by the time Ingrid entered our lives we were all deeply disordered . . . I suppose your own mother didn't die young, by any chance?'

I was surprised by the question but I answered easily, 'No, she and my father are both still flourishing in Surrey.' Setting aside the copy of *Ivanhoe* I selected Dorothy Sayers' *The Nine Tailors* from the bottom shelf.

'What sort of man is your father?'

This time I was no longer merely surprised but astonished. I said abruptly, 'Why do you ask?' but Jardine only laughed.

'Since you've been making various deductions about me,' he said, 'I've decided to make a deduction or two about you. Lady Starmouth remarked on your evasiveness about your family. Miss Christie commented how profoundly you seemed to sympathize with me when she touched on my difficulties with my father. Naturally I've been wondering if you too have a parent who's a heavy cross to bear.'

'My father did disapprove of my ordination,' I said, 'but we get on very well now.'

'I used to say that when people asked me about my father,' said Jardine. 'It was less painful. However perhaps your father's a great deal less incomprehensible than mine was.'

'Incomprehensible?'

'Isn't lack of understanding responsible for much of the misery in family relationships? I spent years trying to understand my father, but it was only at the end of his life that I finally realized what had been going on.'

I said before I could stop myself, 'Did that make a difference?'

'Of course. With understanding, forgiveness becomes possible . . . You do have trouble with your father, don't you?' said Jardine, but I only answered, 'No, we got over all the trouble a long time ago.'

We were silent, locked in an enigmatic curiosity which lay beyond my powers of analysis, but at last Jardine said unexpectedly, 'Sit down for a moment, Dr Ashworth. I'm going to do something I never normally do. I'm going to talk about my father, because despite all you've said I think you may find my story relevant to that private life which you seem so determined to conceal.'

VII

'My father was the son of an impecunious Cheshire farmer,' said Jardine. 'He ran away to London when he was sixteen with the idea of training to become a clergyman, but he soon discovered that neither the Church of England nor the respectable Nonconformist churches wanted to know a penniless working-class boy with ideas above his station. Finally my father said to himself in a disillusioned rage: to hell with all ecclesiastical organizations and to hell with the priesthood.

'To assuage his sense of rejection he joined an obscure sect where there was no formal priesthood and everyone took it in turns to preach hellfire and damnation. That was when he discovered he had a God-given talent for preaching. Before long he was preaching in the open air on summer evenings, and eventually a rich widow offered to build him a chapel. Later he managed to marry her for her money. My poor father! Since his arrival in London he had been earning his living as a porter in a Putney warehouse but he knew he had no prospect of promotion; in those circumstances was it any wonder that he came to see his gift for preaching as the passport to the gentleman's life which he felt so strongly that a man of his intelligence deserved?

'I wonder if you've ever read *Elmer Gantry*. It's a novel about an American itinerant preacher who . . . well, it's a study of the seamy side of evangelism, the side we orthodox churchmen are ashamed of. It's the story of a preacher who uses his power over women to raise money not for God but for himself . . .

'No doubt you can imagine what happened. My father was without spiritual counselling and of course he fell into the grossest errors. He had this gift from God, the ability to preach, but you know as well as I do, Dr Ashworth, what a dangerous charism that can be. That's why I myself never, never preach extempore. The moment one departs from the written word one's tempted to sway one's audience by playing on the most dubious emotions.

'My father never wrote down a word and he knew just how to keep the richest women fainting with excitement in their pews – and he also, I regret to say, knew exactly how to revive them afterwards in the vestry. Sir Thomas More has a word for it in *Utopia*: waywardness. My father was intolerably wayward with women. His first wife was an infirm old woman who could satisfy only his financial needs, and I'm afraid he convinced himself that all things would be forgiven him so long as he preached the word of God as fervently as possible.

'However when his wife died he did turn away in shame from his old life; he felt he could well afford to retire on the money she'd left, and he decided to devote himself to the study of theology. By that time too he had an additional motive for turning over a new leaf because he'd just met my mother, who was a young girl from a very respectable family, and he knew he'd never be allowed to marry her unless he could offer her a life of absolute propriety.

'I'm sure the marriage was a success, not only because I can remember the happy home my mother created but because I can so clearly remember how he went straight to pieces after she died. He'd seen my mother as a reward from God for good behaviour, poor man, and that was why he felt her death was a judgement; he was at once convinced that he hadn't been forgiven for his past sins after all.

'His guilt now began to crucify him. Is there any guilt worse than that of a man who has used a gift from God in the Devil's service? For a long while he shut himself up in his house and wouldn't go out. He wouldn't speak. He spent the whole time praying. He became wholly obsessed with his past sins, and from there it was but a short step to becoming obsessed with the sins of the world – the world which by rejecting him had set him on the road to corruption.

'You can imagine the effect on eight children of such behaviour. Eventually things came to such a pass that even my father, mentally ill as he undoubtedly was, realized that something would have to be done. By that time he had begun to preach again – though not for money; he thought the least he could do to appease God was to serve him as honestly as he could in the pulpit, so he returned to the chapel of the obscure sect where he had first made his name, and one Sunday he noticed a newcomer, someone who had attended the service out of curiosity, someone who was apparently quite unmoved by his sermon, someone utterly different from all the women who fawned on him afterwards in admiration.

'It was my stepmother. She was employed as a companion to an old lady. She'd taken the position after her husband, a commercial traveller named Ashley, had been so inconsiderate as to die leaving her penniless. She hadn't the money to go home to Sweden but she was saving up for the fare.

'My father persuaded her to remain in England, but heaven only knows how she found the strength to stay once the initial attraction to him had worn off. My father was very, very difficult, far too difficult for any of my brothers to endure. They all left home as soon as they could to earn their living across the river in London, and I was all set to go too – when I was thirteen my favourite brother found me a position as an office-boy in the firm where he was a clerk, but the position fell through and as soon as the news reached us my stepmother turned to my father – I can see her now – and said, "You always said you needed a sign from God before you could allow that boy to go to school. Well, there's your sign, and either that boy goes to school or I walk out of this house and never come back!'

'I went to school. I hated it. I wanted to leave but she wouldn't let me. She was very tough, very ruthless. She said, "Do you want to end up like your father or don't you?" and of course there was only one answer to that. She said: "You're going to lead the life your father never had. You're going to open all the doors which were slammed in his face and you're going to be what he was never allowed to be. And then all the suffering will be redeemed," she said – she was a deeply religious woman – "and all the pain will be smoothed away and everything will make sense and he'll look at you and be so proud and happy at last."

'It was a magnificent dream, wasn't it? But I couldn't see how it was ever going to come true. My father soon became extremely jealous of me – he couldn't bear to think I was leading the life he hadn't been allowed to lead. He was hostile and belligerent. What rows we used to have! How unhappy we made each other! Yet every time I wanted to give up and emigrate to Australia my stepmother would say fiercely, "*You've got to go on!*" and I knew I could never walk away. Besides, by that time I'd seen the truth – I'd seen I was locked up in a dark room and my stepmother was trying to drag me out into the light. So I endured all the appalling scenes, all the endless unpleasantness, and I clawed my way to freedom, but I certainly didn't do it so that his suffering could be redeemed. Oh no! I did it for myself, I did it for her, but as for my father he could have rotted in hell for all I cared. Towards him I was rude, unkind, contemptuous, impatient, angry, bitter, resentful, unloving and once or twice downright cruel. Could any son with a mentally ill father have been more unChristian? I think not. And even after I was ordained I merely covered up my unacceptable emotions with a pious expression and observed my filial duties with gritted teeth.

'So when at the end of his life my father went senile my first reaction was to hope he died quickly. In fact I couldn't understand why God was letting him live. It seemed quite pointless.

'But then he became a little better. He became lucid, lucid enough to know he was near the end, and then he began to talk to me. At first he would only talk about theology, but at last he began to review his life and suddenly I sensed his great urge to tell me every detail of his past – all the pathos, all the futility, all the waste – so that my present would take on a new meaning. And at last as my father talked to me with such painful honesty the miracle of communication occurred and I was able to understand the full dimensions of his tragedy. Then forgiveness was easy, and once I'd forgiven him I no longer saw him as a monster but as the father who had given me a Christian upbringing, no matter how bizarre, and who now wanted to heal our long and terrible estrangement before it was too late.

'He had a favourite text. It was "I am not come to call the righteous, but sinners to repentance". He kept urging me to preach on that text but I didn't care for it; I thought it was so typical of my father with his immense preoccupation with sin, but he was so insistent that at last, to keep him happy, I assured him I'd do as he wished. But I didn't. The next Sunday I preached on another text, and then when I came home I knew he was dead because I saw the blind had been drawn across the window of his room.

'Immediately I felt guilty. I thought: if only I'd preached on that text! And then before I knew where I was, I was feeling guilty about all my cruel words in the past, all my unfilial behaviour, all my appalling lack of understanding and love – indeed I felt so absolutely pulverized with guilt then that I hardly knew how to bear the burden, but what I did know beyond any shadow of doubt was that I had to preach on that text which now seemed to speak directly to me. I felt that *I* was the sinner called to repent, and that a true repentance, a true turning away from my past errors, lay in struggling to become a far better clergyman than my ingrained rage against my father had ever allowed me to be before.

'So that became my own special text, and over the years I preached on it again and again – until when I finally stood as a bishop in Starbridge Cathedral and said, "I am not come to call the righteous, but sinners to repentance!" I knew the past had been redeemed, and that although my father had died when I was an obscure chaplain he lived again whenever I said those words as the vicar, the Dean and the Bishop he had never managed to become. The most moving aspect of that entire ceremony at Starbridge was that my stepmother was still alive to see me sit on my episcopal throne. But there were no hugs and kisses afterwards, no gush of sentiment, no emotional tears. She wasn't that kind of woman. She just said casually to me, "I knew it would be worth it all in the end" and I said equally casually, "Thank God you could never afford the fare home to Sweden".

'Now, Charles Ashworth, this isn't a sermon, and half-past two in the morning is hardly the hour to embark on heavy moralizing so I shall say only one sentence more: put your relationship with your father right because the longer you let it remain wrong the more guilty you're going to feel when he dies . . .'

VIII

Jardine stopped speaking. We were sitting facing each other across his desk, and behind him the books rose in well-ordered tiers from floor to ceiling. The surface of his desk was crowded but not muddled; on either side of the blotter piles of papers lay neatly pinned beneath glass weights, while beside the silver inkstand pens and pencils were arranged with precision in a tray.

'Thank you, Bishop,' I said. 'It was extremely good of you to take me into your confidence like that and I regard it as the highest possible compliment.' I suddenly realized that in my inspection of his desk I had been looking for an item I had failed to find, and the next moment I was unable to resist inquiring, 'Do you have a photograph of your father and stepmother?'

'Of course. Every respectable couple in Putney had their picture taken to mark their engagement.' Opening the bottom drawer of his desk he extracted a photograph and handed it to me. It was a studio portrait of a middle-aged man, bearded but still recognizable as a Victorian version of the Bishop, and a young woman of about thirty, good-looking and sultry with blonde hair, pale eyes and a resolute mouth.

'How attractive she was!' I said startled. 'Somehow I'd expected someone plainer.'

'Oh, she didn't keep her looks. Shortly before I moved to Mayfair she put on weight – thyroid trouble – and became rather withdrawn but I never cared what she looked like. I said to her once, "Whether you're six stone or sixteen stone you'll still be Ingrid", and she said, "Whether you're nine or ninety you'll still be Adam". Nobody calls me Adam any more,' said the Bishop, replacing the photograph in its envelope, 'but that doesn't mean Adam no longer exists. I sometimes think that having two names is like having a split personality. Alex is the Bishop, the famous man in public life – '

'The glittering image,' I said.

' – but beyond Alex there's Adam, still staggering around beneath the burden of that difficult past, still haunted by so many fearful memories, still battling with that filial guilt which can never be completely assuaged – '

'Sometimes I too feel as if I've got a split personality,' I said, 'but my other self doesn't have a separate name.'

Understanding flared in Jardine's eyes. He said abruptly, 'Cut yourself loose from Lang and give your other self room to breathe. Being His Grace's lackey is doing you absolutely no good at all.' He did not wait for a reply but moved to the door with his detective story in his hand. 'I suggest we now make renewed assaults on our insomnia,' he added over his shoulder. 'I apologize for detaining you so long with my unsolicited bedtime story.'

'I've no complaints, Bishop. Quite the reverse. Thank you again.'

We retired in silence to our bedrooms.

IX

I thought of that bearded Victorian version of Jardine with the sultry young woman who had restored order to a chaotic household. Then I thought of that woman, middle-aged but possibly still sultry, leaving her husband to keep house for the stepson twenty years her junior, the stepson who could not afford to marry.

'She said, "It was worth it all for Adam",' I could hear Lyle murmuring in my memory.

'He really is the most wonderful man, believe me,' said the young chaplain, Gerald Harvey, as I slipped over the edge of consciousness and my mind was released from all constraint.

'You don't give much away, do you?' said Lyle to me in a vast church as we waited in vain for the Bishop to marry us. 'You're the real mystery here.'

'Karl Barth has solved the mystery of the historical Jesus,' said Jardine to me as we stood in the centre of Starbury Ring. 'He says you have to watch the narrator in *The Murder of Roger Ackroyd*.'

'I'm so glad I found you, Dr Ashworth,' said Mrs Jardine, the present Mrs Jardine, smiling up at me as we stood by the river at the bottom of the garden, 'because I wanted to tell you that I've found out who killed Roger Ackroyd. It was Mr A. P. Herbert. Isn't it wonderful that Our Lord's approved of the A. P. Herbert Bill? Divorce is always so interesting, isn't it, especially in hot weather.'

'Loretta was divorced,' said the Earl to me over his shoulder as he landed a huge fish. 'Of course she'd been Jardine's mistress for years.'

'No, no, no, Henry!' exclaimed Lady Starmouth who was swimming naked in the river. 'She was never Alex's mistress! He always behaved with propriety!'

'That's what *you* say, Lady Starmouth!' said Mrs Cobden-Smith, appearing with the St Bernard. 'But why should we believe you?'

'I'll tell you what I believe,' said Lady Starmouth, climbing out of the river and revealing a pair of intriguingly spherical breasts. 'I believe Dr Ashworth wants to go to bed with me.'

'I'm so sorry, Lady Starmouth,' I said, 'but I'm afraid I can't. I'm waiting to go to bed with Loretta.'

'I'm your passport to Loretta,' said Lady Starmouth, dressed in a white ballgown as she led me out of the mortuary where my wife lay dead. 'But I shan't introduce you unless you go to bed with me first.'

Lyle said behind me, 'I really do want to go to bed with you. But I'm afraid of the Bishop.'

'Did you go to bed with the Bishop?' I said to the sultry Swedish girl who was waiting for me at the end of a dark corridor, but she said, 'I have to take you to church because I'm such a deeply religious woman.'

'Charles is so religious,' said my mother, who was playing bridge in the nave as Ingrid and I walked into Starbridge Cathedral, 'but despite that he's tremendously successful. His father's so proud of him.'

'I never usually talk about my father,' said Jardine as he mounted the steps to the pulpit. 'My family was deeply disordered.'

'We're such a wonderfully happy family!' said my mother, laughing as she dealt the cards. 'We never exchange a single cross word!'

'You bloody young fool!' cried my father as he broke down the door and burst into the nave.

'I am not come to call the righteous,' said Jardine from the pulpit, 'but sinners to repentance.'

'You narrow-minded bastard!' I shouted at my father.

'I am not come to call the *righteous*,' proclaimed Jardine in a louder voice, 'but *sinners* to *repentance*.'

'No, Charles, no!' screamed my mother.

'*I am not come to call the righteous, but sinners to repentance!*' bawled the Bishop.

'You'll never make a clergyman!' yelled my father at me. 'Who the devil do you think you're fooling?'

'I AM NOT COME TO CALL THE RIGHTEOUS, BUT SINNERS – SINNERS – SINNERS – '

'Father!' I shouted, sitting bolt upright in bed with the sweat streaming down my face. '*Father!* FATHER – '

Silence fell.

The bedroom was very dark. With a shaking hand I switched on the light. Then I slid out of bed on to my knees and began to pray.

X

The Starmouths departed after breakfast the next morning and after we had waved goodbye I asked the Bishop if he could spare the time later for a word in private.

'Of course,' he said, 'but it had better be now before I start work on my sermon.'

'You're preaching on Sunday?'

'At Martins, yes. I'm standing in for the Dean who's been called away to the north to conduct a cousin's funeral. Are you going to extend your visit to assist me at early Communion?'

I was considerably surprised. 'I'm sure,' I said, 'that you'd prefer to withdraw that invitation you made in your letter, Bishop.'

'I can't think why. I'm a Christian, Dr Ashworth, not a heathen politician anxious to blackball you from some exclusive club! Reconsider the invitation and let me know your decision later,' he said, and as we entered his library he changed the subject by adding with a smile: 'I trust I vanquished your insomnia last night!'

'I'm glad to say I was asleep within ten minutes.' I paused before saying with care, 'You were very frank with me then and now I'm going to be very frank with you. I suspect the Archbishop may well be pursuing a personal vendetta, but he never actually commissioned me to find the evidence which would cut your throat and even if I did find it I'd never give it to him. I don't believe cutting throats should be part of my clerical duties. Nor do I believe that a bishop of your calibre deserves to be smeared by the press just because Lang made an exceptionally pompous exhibition of himself over the Abdication. Can you believe me when I say I'm entirely on your side? And if you believe me will you allow me to ask a very impertinent question in order to confirm that you're absolutely impregnable from scandal?'

'Well, you're obviously working yourself up to some truly monstrous piece of impudence, Dr Ashworth, but luckily for you I'm beginning to find your impudence entertaining. What's the question?'

'Is there any communication at present between you and Professor Loretta Staviski?'

SEVEN

'Your treatment of women is a matter of the utmost concern.'
More Letters of Herbert Hensley Henson
Bishop of Durham 1920–1939
ed. E. F. BRALEY

I

Thanks to my elaborate warning Jardine took this new assault on his privacy remarkably well; perhaps, since Lady Starmouth had obviously reported to him every detail of my interrogation, he had even been expecting a question about Loretta. Showing neither surprise nor anger he merely heaved a sigh of resignation.

'My dear Canon, I'm touched by your zeal on my behalf,' he said drily, 'and I hardly like to sound ungrateful since you've been so generous as to assure me of your unqualified support, but isn't your zeal becoming a trifle excessive?'

'Not when one considers that the professor is arriving in England soon and that any Sunday rag in search of scandal is quite cabable of having you watched. If you were to meet Professor Staviski in London – '

'I shan't. I haven't communicated with her for nineteen years, and anyway even back in 1918 there was no scandal. All that happened was that one of my parishioners fell in love with me and I was fool enough not to realize it for some time.'

'Bishop, may I just ask how many people knew about this incident?'

'Only Lady Starmouth.'

'But are you saying,' I was astonished, 'that no one else knew – no one else at all? What about your wife?'

'She was away from home when my friendship with Mrs Staviski reached its unfortunate end. Our child had been born dead, the doctor had recommended country air for Carrie and she was spending a month with her parents.'

'But did no one suspect what had happened? After all, you could hardly have been living in a vacuum in Mayfair!'

'Obviously the essence of the incident's eluded you. Mrs Staviski was flawlessly concealing her true feelings and I merely regarded her as another good friend like Lady Starmouth. Neither of us was generating gossip.'

'But wasn't your wife surprised when Mrs Staviski suddenly vanished from Mayfair?'

'Yes, but it was wartime and a lot of people were coming and going. Also my wife was far from well and too preoccupied with her own troubles to pay much attention to the troubles of others. That was why I never confided in her, of course. It would have been selfish to add to her burdens at that time.'

'How did Lady Starmouth find out?'

Jardine paused, considering the question. Then he said abruptly, 'I'll tell you exactly what happened. Bearing in mind all the circumstances I see no point in keeping you in the dark, and as a clergyman you might even find it instructive to see where I went wrong. This is not a story of moral failure, Dr Ashworth, but of extreme pastoral inadequacy – in other words, this is where we look beyond Alex and Bishop's "glittering image", as you put it last night, and see poor old Adam, struggling to be a good vicar and really making a very great hash of it indeed . . .'

II

'It was surprising how many people called her by her Christian name,' said Jardine. 'I could never make up my mind whether it was because she was a foreigner and thus outside the English social structure with all its petty conventions, or whether it was because the xenophobic British merely balked at the alien surname. However as a clergyman bound hand and foot by the proprieties, I always called her Mrs Staviski until the day our friendship ended. If I call her Loretta now it's not because I was accustomed to do so at the time but because "Professor Staviski" (as she now is) makes her sound like some mad disciple of the Russian Revolution.

'I met her in 1917 when she left her husband and Lady Starmouth enlisted my help. I quickly realized that the marriage had broken down beyond hope of repair – the husband was homosexual – so I decided my duty as a pastor lay not in trying to preserve the marriage but in trying to salvage Loretta, who had been treated so abominably that her self-confidence had been wrecked. Her husband had made her feel she was an object of revulsion to the opposite sex, and I concluded that if she were ever to be restored to a normal life some other man had to repair the damage which had been done. This, I think, was a perfectly rational conclusion but the trouble was that I then elected myself to do the repairs.

'Yes, you may well look at me with amazement, but I wasn't quite so stupid as this statement may lead you to believe. I only met her at Lady

Starmouth's house – or at my own in the presence of my wife – and even when Loretta acquired a flat I never went there without a curate in attendance. I had three curates, and I'd learnt always to take one with me when I paid pastoral calls on lonely ladies in Mayfair.

'But of course I was making a big mistake. I should have realized Loretta wasn't stable enough to cope with platonic friendship. Men and women aren't, after all, intended by God for asexual intimacies and in fact there's a sexual element in all my three long-standing platonic friendships, but the point about Lady Starmouth, Lady Markhampton and Mrs Welbeck is that they're all married, well balanced and happy; their friendship with me is essentially just a decoration on an already satisfying cake. But with Loretta I wasn't merely a decoration. I was the icing, the marzipan, the currants, the raisins – everything. She was a foreigner in London, her separation from her husband cut her off from many people who might have befriended her and she was very much alone. Did I allow for her extreme vulnerability? No, I did not. I called on her more often than I should have done; in an effort to divert her from her troubles I lent her numerous books – but all novels, nothing of spiritual value – and in an effort to restore her self-esteem I paid her numerous compliments. Naturally such folly could have only one conclusion.

'It all ended on a Saturday in September 1918. After breakfast I was just starting work on Sunday's sermon when a wire arrived to say that Lady Starmouth's favourite brother had been killed in action and could I go down to Leatherhead immediately. As you must have discovered by now, that's where the Starmouths have their country home; they have no connection with the city of Starmouth in this diocese beyond the fact that the first Earl's mother was born there and when he was offered his earldom he decided it would be less embarrassing to be called Lord Starmouth than Lord Leatherhead. Loretta used to like that story – Americans are always so ingenuously intrigued by titles ... She was there, of course, with her friend when I arrived at Starmouth Court later that morning. She'd caught an earlier train from London.

'I talked to Lady Starmouth on her own for a while and then we all lunched together. The Earl wasn't there; he was on his way back from Scotland and wasn't expected until much later. After luncheon Lady Starmouth decided to rest and I was about to consider my return to London when Loretta said she had something to tell me and I fell in with her suggestion that we should go for a walk down into the valley. The Starmouths' house is built on a hillside overlooking the River Mole – but perhaps you know that? I've just remembered that you come from that part of Surrey, don't you, and so you've probably often passed the house – it's visible from the main road between Leatherhead and Dorking.'

Jardine paused, his eyes dark with memory, his hands clasped tightly as he leaned forward on his desk. 'We walked to the river,' he said. 'We walked back. It was the first time we'd ever been alone together, far from other people. There was traffic on the road – pony-traps, cyclists, even a motor, but we were alone. Then she told me everything and the friendship ended.' He paused again before adding abruptly, 'She cried a lot. When we got back Lady Starmouth was downstairs. She took one look at Loretta and guessed everything – which in a way was a good thing because she was able to help us both. She helped Loretta get a passage to America, an almost impossible feat in wartime, and she helped me by never once offering a word of reproach. But of course by that time I could see how deeply I'd failed Loretta as a pastor, and so I knew far better than Lady Starmouth how very, very much I was to blame . . .'

III

I allowed a moment of sympathetic silence to elapse before venturing the comment: 'I can certainly understand why you made no further experiments in platonic friendship.'

'I realize that you find the whole concept of platonic friendship fantastic, but then you're a member of the sex-obsessed post-War generation. In my young day a wider range of male–female relationships was possible . . . But I don't mean to make excuses for myself. I did make terrible mistakes with Loretta.'

'But not scandalous ones. There were no letters, I suppose, Bishop?'

'Not after she'd declared her feelings, no. We'd had some harmless correspondence earlier but I burnt it.'

'No entries in the journal?'

'Fortunately I had no pressing need to pour out my remorse on paper because I was able to pour it out to Lady Starmouth instead.'

A thought struck me. 'Did you confide in your stepmother?'

'Ah!' Jardine gave a wry smile. 'I did tell her much later at the end of her life, but in 1918 I said nothing. My stepmother had made such a fuss when I married that I avoided talking to her about my women-friends . . . Dear me, how possessive that makes her sound! Let me at once correct that unfortunate impression by saying that she always wanted me to marry but unfortunately her idea of a suitable wife for me was quite different from my own. That's not an uncommon dilemma for mothers and sons to find themselves in, I believe.' He leant back in his chair with another smile. 'Well, Dr Ashworth? Is the last chink in my armour finally sealed?'

'I think that as far as the press are concerned you really must be impregnable.'

'And apart from the press?'

'Oh, you have your Achilles heel, of course,' I said, rising to my feet, 'but fortunately the way to protect yourself there is very simple. May I suggest you start looking around without delay for a new companion to replace Miss Christie?' And as the smile vanished from his face I made a swift exit into the hall.

IV

So now I knew the story of Loretta. Or, to be accurate, I now knew Jardine's version of the story of Loretta, an account which harmonized dutifully with the account of Lady Starmouth. Of course he had not told me everything; I was prepared to bet there had been a kiss or two by the river in the intervals between the passing pony-traps which he had mentioned so carefully, but nevertheless I suspected he had been reasonably honest with me. A kiss between a married clergyman and a passionate young woman certainly represented the sort of indiscretion Lang had feared, but so far as I could see there could be no conceivable danger to Jardine now, nineteen years later, particularly since no one but Lady Starmouth and old Mrs Jardine had ever known the friendship had gone so wrong.

I was genuinely pleased that Jardine was impregnable from scandal yet at the same time I was unforgivably disappointed that I still had no excuse to think the unthinkable; a minor indiscretion, even though reprehensible, was a long way from a major moral error. My disappointment baffled me. I felt it was irrational that I should want to unmask as an apostate a man I so much admired, and I began to wonder if my two personalities were subtly at war with each other. However that was a mad thought which could not be entertained for more than the briefest of moments, and thrusting it aside I retired to my room to plot my next move.

It was now Friday. I had assumed I would have to leave on the following morning, but since Jardine had been gentleman enough to stand by the invitation in his letter I thought it would be churlish of me not to stay on. Besides I was never a man who wasted his opportunities, and the extension of my visit would give me the chance to see more of Lyle.

Taking a sheet of the palace notepaper from the drawer of the table I sat down and wrote, 'My dear Bishop, Of course I'd consider it a great honour to assist you at Holy Communion and a great pleasure to remain at the palace. Thank you for your continuing hospitality which in the circumstances I find impressively generous. Yours most sincerely, Charles Ashworth.'

But I wondered if he were already regretting his invitation.

The day proved frustrating because I had no chance to see Lyle on her own. After leaving the Bishop's letter on the hall table I made another nominal attempt to work in the Cathedral library but when I returned to the palace I was informed that Lyle had accompanied Mrs Jardine to the station to meet the new guests who were arriving to replace the Starmouths.

There were hordes of people at lunch. I counted eighteen places laid at the extended dining-room table and soon discovered, to my disgust, that Lyle and I had been placed six seats apart. Moreover as soon as the last visitor departed she and Mrs Jardine drove off to open a church bazaar and I was left still debating whether I had been the victim of a conspiracy. Wandering moodily around the town to pass the time, I browsed in the antiquarian bookshops and finally succeeded in attending Choral Evensong.

The guests at dinner were confined to those who were staying at the palace. The new arrivals, four cousins of Mrs Jardine, seemed incapable of talking about anything except fox-hunting, and I could see Jardine was missing Lady Starmouth's sophisticated glamour. However after the cloth was drawn the lay guests were successfully dispatched to the smoking-room and he was able to cheer himself up by discussing the Virgin Birth with me. As I had suspected, he believed in the creed *ex animo* and in his own Modernist way was thoroughly orthodox.

We returned to the drawing-room. Lyle was on duty by the coffee-pot but the Bishop came with me to collect his cup and obstinately refused to take a turn on the terrace with any of the ladies. Possibly he felt all the female guests were too plain to be worthy of such attention, but possibly too he was determined to keep me from enjoying a private word with Lyle.

'Come and sit down, Dr Ashworth!' called Mrs Jardine, patting the vacant space on the sofa beside her as she presided among her elderly female cousins. 'We all want to hear more about Dr Lang!'

I suddenly decided I was the victim of a conspiracy. 'I'm just coming!' I called back, and said swiftly to Lyle as the Bishop looked on, 'What are you doing tomorrow?'

'I'm going out for the day with Mrs Jardine. She wants to take her cousins to the sea.'

'Dine with me when you get back.'

She hesitated but the Bishop said briskly, 'Give yourself an evening off, Lyle, and accept the invitation – unless, of course, you feel Dr Ashworth so blotted his copybook at Starbury Ring that you don't wish to go out with him again. If that's the case then you'd do much better to be frank and tell him so.'

'Thank you, Bishop,' I said. I turned to Lyle. 'Think about it,' I said, 'and let me know.' And leaving her sheltering behind the coffee-pot I joined Mrs Jardine to recall my most flattering memories of Dr Lang.

VI

The next morning I awoke after another turbulent night to find that a note had been slipped under my door.

'I shall be free from seven-thirty onwards this evening,' Lyle had written in a small precise hand. 'If you're uncertain where to dine, may I recommend the Staro Arms in Eternity Street? L. C.'

I decided I had imagined the conspiracy.

Or had I?

I wondered what the Bishop was thinking.

VII

I spent the day forcing myself to work on my St Anselm notes until I reached the point where I could conclude my researches in the University Library at Cambridge. Afterwards, relieved to the point of frivolity, I scribbled experimentally on my notepad and having produced three absurd verses I returned from the Cathedral to the palace where I copied my lines on to a sheet of notepaper.

> 'There was a young lady named Lyle (I wrote)
> Who wanted to run half a mile
> Whenever Charles A
> Said: 'Is there a way
> You can care for me more, dearest Lyle?'

> 'There was a smart bishop named Jardine
> Whose name only rhymes with a sardine.
> He said: 'Go far away,
> You bad Dr A,
> And leave Lyle to serve Mrs Jardine!'

> 'There was a canon called Ashworth from Laud's
> Who aspired to the best life affords.
> He knew to win Lyle
> He must exercise guile,
> So he tried hard to lure her to Laud's.'

Underneath this last line I wrote: 'Sorry this isn't a sonnet, but unfortunately not all clergymen can rival John Donne. Why don't you take a few days' holiday and visit Cambridge soon? Have you ever been punting on the Cam? Have you ever seen King's College Chapel? Have you ever watched the sun set over the Backs? There's a world beyond Starbridge, and I think it's time someone reminded you of it.' Signing my Christian name I added my telephone number before concluding: 'P. S. Bring Mrs Jardine too, if you feel you can't leave her. Why not? The change would do her good.'

Having demolished her most obvious excuse for refusing my invitation I raided the garden for a rose and retired once more to the house. It was mid-afternoon. Jardine was out and Mrs Jardine's party had not yet returned from the excursion to the sea. The butler was probably much surprised when someone rang the bell in the drawing-room, but when he appeared he had his sepulchral expression firmly in place and never even faltered at the sight of the rose in my hand.

'I want to leave this in Miss Christie's room, Shipton,' I said, watching for any sign that might indicate the servants regarded Lyle as hopelessly out of bounds to all admirers. 'How do I get there?'

However Shipton seemed delighted by the prospect of a romance and possibly even more delighted by the prospect of a romance which was inevitably doomed. His sepulchral expression softened; his voice became confidential. 'Miss Christie's room is a little difficult to find, sir. Allow me to show you the way.'

We made a dignified journey upstairs, I bearing the rose, Shipton bearing his modified expression, and I was led through a labyrinth of gothic corridors to a remote room high in the south turret.

'New servants must need a map to get here!' I remarked as he opened the door.

'Miss Christie likes to give the Bishop and Mrs Bishop every privacy, sir, as befits a lady in her position who lives as one of the family. Will that be all, sir, or shall I wait to show you the way back?'

'No, I'll find my own way back, thank you, Shipton, but if I don't return within twelve hours you can organize a search-party.'

'Very good, sir.' He padded away with his gravity intact, and I walked into the room.

It was a high bright octagon, adorned sparingly with an unremarkable collection of furniture. Among the collection was a single bed, covered with a blue counterpane, and on the bedside table was the Penguin edition of Hemingway's *A Farewell to Arms* together with a faded photograph of a bright-eyed soldier in uniform. There was something unbearably poignant about his air of hope and vigour. On the dressing-table stood some silver brushes, a modest tray of make-up and a jam-jar of honeysuckle

116

from the garden. Three pictures hung on the walls, a watercolour of a lake which could have been one of the Norfolk Broads, a framed sketch of a large Georgian townhouse which I suspected was the Deanery at Radbury, and a first-class engraving of the matchless Starbridge Cathedral. I stood there absorbing the scene so that I would be able to picture her in her seclusion when I was far away in Cambridge, and then I laid the rose on her pillow, took the verses from my pocket and left the folded paper beneath the rose's long stem.

On my way out I paused to look at her bookshelves and discovered in addition to the intelligent modern novels the controversial *The Quest of the Historical Jesus*, Albert Schweitzer's attempt to reconstruct the career of Christ within an eschatological framework. It was the only theological volume in the collection apart from her inevitable set of Jardine's books, but it made me wonder if she borrowed other works of theology from the library downstairs. I cast my eye over the Jardine volumes, the anthologies of sermons, his polemic on the doomed Prayer Book reform of the Twenties and his notorious attack on the Malines Conversations, but I found no book which I had not already read. I was interested to see that beyond the Jardine collection there was a copy of A. P. Herbert's *Holy Deadlock* in which the author of the famous Bill had satirized the law on divorce.

I found the tone of her books vaguely worrying. Apart from her novels her collection suggested a mild preoccupation with religion but not, so far as I could see, with personal piety. There was no copy of the Bible visible in the room.

I began to wonder if Lyle were the apostate.

However I knew I could discover at dinner the exact nature of her religious belief. Taking one last look at that deeply private room I opened the door again and began the convoluted journey back to the main part of the house.

VIII

Her first words to me as we met in the hall that evening were: 'How did you find my room?'

'I took a map, a compass, a week's supply of rations and Shipton.'

'I don't like to think of anyone prowling around my room,' she said. 'In fact I hate to think of it.'

'Oh? That must make life awkward for the servants!' I said, smiling at her, and the next moment she was answering rapidly, 'I'm making a fool of myself, aren't I, and being abominably rude as well. Thank you for the rose. It was beautiful. And thanks for the limericks. I'm glad you didn't write a sonnet because I happen to find sonnets a bore.'

We set off for the short walk to Eternity Street where the Staro Arms, a former coaching-inn dating from the fourteenth century, was built around a cobbled courtyard. In the garden beyond, wrought-iron tables shaded by scarlet sun-umbrellas dotted the lawn which sloped to the river, and along the low wall which divided the bank from the garden a row of geraniums stirred in the faint evening breeze. We chose a table which enabled us to see the reflection in the water of the medieval houses on the opposite bank, and soon the waiter arrived with our drinks; Lyle had ordered a Schweppes sparkling lime, garnished with gin and ice, while I had requested a half-pint of Whitbread's pale ale.

'Don't you drink spirits?' Lyle asked.

I did not answer directly but said: 'I think clergymen do better to avoid drinking spirits, just as they should always avoid smoking when they're wearing their clerical collar. Such habits project the wrong image on the ecclesiastical screen.'

'Well, I'm glad you're keen to project the right one tonight. I was afraid you might be feeling pounce-ish again.'

'What a stimulating thought!' I said promptly, but when she gave an exasperated laugh I added to soothe her, 'We're going to have a civilized dinner. We're not even going to mention the Jardines, not unless you want to. We're going to talk about novels and theology and whatever else we find we have in common, and then I can tell you more – if you're interested – about my life in Cambridge, and you can tell me more – if you wish – about life in rural Norfolk, where, so Mrs Cobden-Smith tells me, everyone talks in grunts. In other words we're going to enjoy each other's company and relax with no thought for the morrow.'

'That all sounds much too good to be true,' said Lyle drily, but she was already relaxing, and as we exchanged smiles again I decided I was finally on the brink of making substantial progress.

IX

I myself did not relax until halfway through the meal when I discovered she was not an apostate. She had an unmistakably genuine faith and an intelligent layman's interest in expanding its intellectual perimeter; as I had suspected, she often borrowed books from the Bishop's library. I did say with reluctance, 'I noticed there was no Bible in your room,' but she replied tartly, 'Well, at least I now know you didn't open the drawer of my bedside table!'

I was deeply relieved. No matter how strongly I felt that Lyle was right for me I would have had no choice but to accept that she was wrong if I had uncovered evidence that she was not devout. How could one live with a woman in the closest intimacy unless she were able to understand the fundamental force in one's life? An attraction of spiritual opposites was a disaster for any clergyman.

This hint of my more private spiritual concerns evidently aroused Lyle's curiosity, and at the end of the meal she gave in to the temptation to enquire how I had reached my decision to be ordained. 'And don't just say you were called,' she said. 'Obviously God called you but how did He do it?'

I said easily, 'I'd been a regular churchgoer since my last year at school when Dr Lang had given the prizes and made a speech which had caught my imagination, but although I did toy then with the idea of being a clergyman I knew my father wanted me to follow in his footsteps by becoming a solicitor in the family firm. However after a year up at Cambridge I found the law had no message for me and soon I was feeling so miserable and confused that I wrote to Dr Lang for advice. I decided that if he replied encouragingly it would mean I should consider going into the Church but if he merely replied politely through a chaplain it would mean I'd have to think again.'

'And he replied encouragingly?'

'He wrote a letter in his own hand and asked to see me. He wasn't Archbishop of Canterbury then; he was Archbishop of York, and he invited me to Bishopthorpe for the weekend. Naturally I was overwhelmed. He was so very kind and understanding.' I paused. The contrast between my past and present feelings for Lang was unexpectedly painful.

'So of course you felt you were being called.'

'I knew it. My father was livid but he mellowed later and now he's very proud of my success.' I signalled for the bill and said lightly, 'So much for my calling. I'm afraid it's not very dramatic, is it? No blinding white light on the road to Damascus, no voice speaking from the clouds!'

'I should think it was very dramatic,' said Lyle, 'but on a human, not a divine level. However I suppose it was only natural that your father should have been disappointed when you chose not to follow in his footsteps.'

'Oh, it was no great tragedy,' I said as the waiter brought the bill. 'He got what he wanted in the end. My brother Peter took my place in the family firm and everyone lived happily ever after.'

'Honestly? Or is that another of your extravagant romantic statements?'

'What extravagant romantic statements?'

'Never mind. That was a lovely dinner, Charles, and I enjoyed every mouthful. Many thanks.'

Five minutes later we were walking back along Eternity Street in the moonlight. I had offered to take her to the Staro Arms in my car but she had evidently decided that a drive *à deux* was best avoided – or perhaps the Jardines had only let her out of their sight on condition that she abstained from travelling in my chariot of sin. I had learnt no more about her relationship with them, but I had not forgotten my impression that they were conspiring to chaperone her, and no matter how often I told myself the idea was absurd I was unable to convince myself I was being irrational.

At the antiquarian bookshop which marked the end of Eternity Street we turned right and saw ahead the Cathedral Close's gateway illuminated by the pale light of the street-lamps. The Cathedral itself, massive against the moonlit sky, loomed in the distance and assumed an errie shadowed beauty as we began to cross the sward of the churchyard.

We were silent. It was almost eleven o'clock and the lights in the windows of the houses around us were beginning to be extinguished. At the east end of the Cathedral we reached the white gate in the churchyard wall, and before I raised the latch I hesitated. Simultaneously we moved towards each other and simultaneously we held out our arms for an embrace. The resulting kiss was full, mutual, perfect, and I felt that old, delectable satisfaction that the feminine flesh could be so entirely other yet so entirely complementary to the flesh in which I myself lived and moved and had my being. I was once more aware how small she was, how delicately made, and beyond this awareness I was conscious how densely my desire was spreading through my body as it drove away all doubt, all difficulty and all despair. I wanted to go on kissing her. I wanted to go on generating the heat which fired that exquisite force beyond description, but she broke away, dragging open the gate in the wall and running off along the East Walk.

I caught up with her halfway down the palace drive.

'My God, what a fool I am!' she gasped, pausing to scrabble frantically in her bag for her latchkey. 'What a fool!'

'You're only a fool to say you're a fool! When are you coming to Cambridge to visit me?'

'Never.' She finally found the key. 'I'm sorry, I shouldn't have kissed you like that, I despise myself, I absolutely vowed I wouldn't lead you on – '

'What on earth's going on in this house?'

'Nothing!' As she succeeded in opening the door I saw her eyes were bright with tears.

I grabbed her for another kiss and although she tried to push me away I held her tightly. 'Are you in love with him?'

'Oh, for God's sake! No, of course not!'

'Are you in love with her?'

'*What?*' She was so appalled that she even forgot to struggle.

'Then there's absolutely no reason why you can't be in love with me. Look, darling – '

Voices echoed in the distance, and as the grip of my arms automatically slackened she broke away, rushing over the threshold to safety. I paused to wipe her lipstick from my mouth, and by the time I entered the hall she was already vanishing upstairs.

I closed the door just as the Bishop's departing dinner-guests began to stream out of the drawing-room, and when Mrs Jardine made a confused attempt to introduce me I was obliged to linger in the hall. Eventually the last guest departed but Mrs Jardine, smiling brightly, forestalled my attempt to slip away up the staircase.

'Did you have a nice evening, Dr Ashworth? It's such a good thing for Lyle to get out and about with someone her own age, and I'm sure the outing cheered her up tremendously! She was so depressed about the Coronation.'

The Bishop's harsh voice immediately exclaimed, 'Carrie!'

Mrs Jardine jumped. 'Oh Alex, I'm sorry, I – '

'Lyle's quite recovered from all that now.'

'Yes, of course she has – dearest Lyle, she's always so contented – well, we all are, aren't we? And Dr Ashworth, what a mercy the weather stayed fine for you this evening! It must have been so delightful in the river-garden of the Staro Arms!'

I told myself I was going to solve the mystery of Lyle Christie even if it proved to be my last accomplishment on earth.

X

As I walked to the Cathedral the next morning with the Bishop to assist him at the early service I was not expecting to be engaged in conversation. Silence is preferable before a profound act of worship, but on leaving the house Jardine said casually, 'I'm glad you enjoyed your dinner at the Staro Arms. Rather an attractive example of a medieval inn, I've always thought.'

'Yes, very.'

'And as my wife said last night, it's good for Lyle to get out and about with someone her own age.' As we passed through the palace gateway he fidgeted for a moment with his pectoral cross before adding, 'Why my wife chose to bring up the subject of the Coronation I can't think. It's true Lyle was depressed at the time because she couldn't participate in the event as Carrie and I did, but she stayed at home by her own choice. I offered to get her a ticket for one of the stands in Parliament Square, but she was absolutely resolute in declining . . . Were you yourself in London for the Coronation?'

'I had a seat in the Haymarket.'

'It was a magnificent ceremony,' said the Bishop, 'but I was infernally hot in my cope and the hours of standing about were hard on the older bishops.' He paused but as we reached the Dean's door, the private entrance for the clergy, he said very courteously, 'Well, Canon, I'm delighted to have you with me this morning – welcome once more to the Cathedral!'

I murmured my thanks, but on my way to the vestry I found myself wondering what – if anything – these casual comments on the Coronation had been designed to hide.

XI

Lyle was absent from Communion, and as I helped the Bishop administer the sacrament I felt more bewildered than ever. A kiss with an unmarried man hardly constituted a sin serious enough to remove her from a state of grace. I decided she must have overslept but I remained worried, particularly since I knew she was a regular Sunday communicant, and later I realized that Jardine was worried too. I heard him say to his wife who was waiting for us after the service, 'What's happened to Lyle?'

'She said she was feeling a little frail, poor dear. I told her to go back to bed.'

'But Lyle never feels frail!' In his concern the Bishop sounded outraged.

'Well, no, dearest, not usually, but any woman can have a frail day once in a while.'

'Oh, I see,' said the Bishop blankly.

I stepped closer to them. 'Should we take her the sacrament, Bishop?'

'No, a state of frailty is hardly the equivalent of a state of prostration,' said the Bishop severely, and at once I sensed he disapproved of the reserved sacrament in all but the most extreme cases. As we moved outside I murmured, 'I suppose you're a long way from favouring perpetual reservation, Bishop.'

'Perpetual reservation? Certainly not! I'll have no Popish practices here!' declared the Bishop, and as I realized he was probably behaving exactly like his Nonconformist father I thought what a mysterious force heredity was, spreading like a stain across the texture of the personality.

We returned in silence to the palace.

XII

Lyle missed breakfast but appeared later as we all gathered in the hall to go to Matins.

'I'm all right now,' she said in response to the Bishop's abrupt inquiry. 'It was just a passing malaise.' And when she smiled at me I knew she was anxious to conceal the new tension in our relationship. 'Thanks again for last night, Charles.'

I said, 'I was worried in case the dinner had disagreed with you.'

'I admit those heavenly mushrooms gave me some interesting dreams!'

'I had some interesting dreams too,' I said, keeping an eye on the Bishop who seemed to be abnormally restless. 'Remind me to tell you about them sometime.'

'Are we all ready?' said the Bishop irritably, 'or am I to deliver my sermon by a series of stentorian shouts from the palace doorstep?'

We set off once more to the Cathedral.

XIII

I had been hoping for a first-class sermon and Jardine did not disappoint me. His text was 'For what shall it profit a man, if he shall gain the whole world, and lose his own soul?' and as I watched, knowing he had written out every word though he often gave the impression of speaking off the cuff, I admired him for keeping his God-given talent on such a tightly disciplined rein.

The sermon, perfectly constructed, immaculately delivered, unfolded itself like a complex flower opening its petals before the sun. I always found it arresting to see an expert in any field doing his work well, and Jardine was an expert in homiletics, selecting his intellectual strands sparingly but weaving them with stark skill into a rapier-sharp exposition of Christian teaching. Finally, reaching his peroration, he knotted the intellectual strands into a single dazzling sentence, heightened the power of his delivery and drove home his message with the full force of his oratorical sledgehammer.

I thought, I'll give up my ivory tower. I'll go to Africa as a missionary. Or I'll become a slum-priest.

Then I knew I had been hypnotized by those lambent amber eyes.

On my knees during the blessing I found my thoughts were becoming more rational but remaining revolutionary. I was telling myself that instead of passing the remainder of the Long Vacation at Laud's while I worked on my new book I should instead offer to do a locum so that some overworked country parson could have a holiday. But then the sinner's thought entered my head; the parish experience would look well on my curriculum vitae, and I despised myself.

During the silence following the blessing I prayed urgently: deliver me from temptation; show me the way; let thy will, not mine, be done.

Then the organist launched into a final toccata, and rising to my feet I began to wonder anew about Lyle.

XIV

Later as we all assembled in the palace drawing-room prior to the midday Sunday dinner, I congratulated the Bishop on his sermon and added on an impulse, 'I was hoping to visit a clergyman in your diocese before I left Starbridge, but it turns out he's away on holiday. His name's Philip Wetherall and he's an old friend of mine.'

'Wetherall,' said the Bishop. 'Ah yes. The parish of Starrington Magna. An excellent wife, two well-behaved small children and a very vocal infant.'

'I haven't met the offspring but the wife's splendid, I agree, and Philip himself is so hard-working and conscientious that I was most relieved to hear he was finally having a holiday.' I had no intention of saying more but the other half of my personality evidently felt there was more to be said. Rapidly I murmured, 'I feel guilty about my privileged ministry sometimes.'

Jardine regarded me without expression. When he made no immediate reply I thought he might be considering my intercession an impertinence and my guilt an affectation but suddenly he said: 'I assure you Wetherall hasn't escaped either the eagle eye of my Archdeacon or my own keen interest. But I'm glad you spoke up for your friend, Dr Ashworth; I'm glad to know you're not solely preoccupied with the seamy side of Church politics.'

I managed to say: 'It was a great sermon. It made me think. I want to change course, but . . . not so easy . . . sort of trapped . . . not sure I fully understand – '

'Go to your bishop,' said Jardine. 'Ask him to help you find a new spiritual director in the Cambridge area. And do it soon.'

The butler announced that dinner was served. Across the room the Colonel was finishing his pink gin and Mrs Cobden-Smith was declaring that refrigerators ran more efficiently on electricity than on gas and Mrs Jardine was telling her cousins what wonderful servants she had at the palace and Lyle was glancing at her watch and everyone was rising to their feet.

'But I don't want to go to my bishop,' my voice said to Jardine. 'I don't want him thinking I'm in any sort of muddle – and anyway I'm fine, everything's fine, there's absolutely no need to bother my bishop, no need at all.'

'Come along, Alex!' called Mrs Cobden-Smith. 'The meal will get cold if we have to wait for you to say grace!'

Jardine ignored her. He said in a voice which would have been inaudible to the other people in the room, 'The Fordite monks have a house in my diocese, as I'm sure you know. I'll have a word with the Abbot and ask him to recommend their best counsellor at Grantchester.'

'That's very good of you, Bishop, but – '

'No buts. You absolutely must have proper counselling. Now let's make a speedy move to the table before Amy starts complaining about cold soup.'

I followed him in silence to the dining-room.

XV

I left the palace an hour later. After the round of farewells had been smoothly accomplished and the words of gratitude warmly expressed to my hosts all I said to Lyle in the porch was, 'I'll be back.'

Glancing into the driving-mirror for a final view of the palace I saw she was still standing where I had left her, a small tense figure, enigmatic to the last, disturbingly alone.

XVI

When I reached London some time later, I steered my way through the stifling streets to my club in St James's where I reserved a room for the night. Then leaving my car parked nearby I walked the short distance to the Starmouths' house in Curzon Street.

I was now more determined than ever to see Loretta Staviski in my quest for the evidence which would allow me to think the unthinkable. Rationally I still could not believe that Jardine had fallen into a gross moral error either with her or with anyone else, but I was beyond mere reason. I had sensed the bizarre in Lyle's distress the previous night, the inexplicable in her absence from Communion, the weird in the Bishop's attempt to gloss over her depression at the time of the Coronation and the sinister in his irritability as she and I had exchanged light-hearted remarks before Matins. I was now convinced that some very odd situation indeed existed at the palace at Starbridge, and although the mystery appeared increasingly intractable this only made me more determined to solve it. Taking a deep breath I sallied up the steps to the black front door of the Starmouths' tall cream-coloured house and rang the bell.

However I was destined to be disappointed; Lord and Lady Starmouth, I was told, had departed with their guest for their country home and were not expected back in London until the following Thursday. Retiring to my club I plotted an assault on Leatherhead, read the evening office and supped well off cold mutton and claret.

XVII

Starmouth Court, slumbering in seclusion on its wooded hillside, overlooked a stretch of the Mole Valley which was attractively pastoral. Fields framed the watermeadows by the river, and beyond the fields the hills climbed steeply to give the landscape its balance and grace. It was hard to believe, as I approached the house on the morning after my arrival in London, that I was less than twenty miles from my club in the heart of the West End.

I showed my card to the keeper at the lodge, and when he opened the gates I drove up the steep winding drive. I was intrigued to see the house at close quarters after so many years of distant glimpses; the Queen Anne mansion was handsome, serene and well-preserved, like a wealthy dowager who had lived an uneventful life. Having parked the car I looked back towards the valley but the trees hid the view at ground level and the atmosphere of seclusion was heightened.

A modest young footman opened the door, and after introducing myself I asked for Lady Starmouth.

'I'm sorry, sir,' came the response, 'but Lady Starmouth went into Leatherhead this morning and she isn't expected back until lunchtime.'

I suddenly knew fortune was going to favour me.

'Then perhaps,' I said, 'I could see Professor Staviski if she's at home.'

'I'll inquire, sir. Please come in.'

He took my card and showed me into a small morning-room which faced the drive. I waited. For a long time nothing happened, and I was just wondering if the Professor had gone into hiding in order to preserve her guilty secret when high heels tapped across the hall, the door opened abruptly and at last I saw the woman who had proved such a pastoral disaster for Jardine.

EIGHT

'I was much interested and not a little surprised at her confidence, lack of reticence, and complete detachment from conventional sex-morality . . .'

More Letters of Herbert Hensley Henson
Bishop of Durham 1920–1939
ed. E. F. BRALEY

I

I had forgotten Lady Starmouth's estimate that Loretta was not much older than I was. I had been expecting a woman in her early fifties, a contemporary of Lady Starmouth and Mrs Jardine, so it came as a considerable surprise when I found myself confronted by a woman barely past forty who looked younger; evidently the disastrous husband had been acquired in her teens. I had also been expecting someone plain, partly because of Lady Starmouth's remark that Loretta failed to conform to fashionable standards of beauty and partly because Jardine had portrayed her as a woman lacking in self-esteem, but this woman was smart, well groomed, striking. She had dark hair, swept smoothly into a knot on top of her head, a suntanned complexion and an hourglass figure which I immediately noted and fancied. Behind her stylish glasses her eyes were a vivid blue.

She looked me up and down with that unabashed curiosity which I had found before in American women oblivious of English constraint, and I sensed that she too was noting what she saw and fancying it. I smiled. She smiled back, and at once I knew we had travelled a long way before a word had been spoken.

'Dr Ashworth?' she said in a slightly husky voice as she held out her hand. 'What a coincidence! Evelyn's been telling me all about you.'

This hardly surprised me; Lady Starmouth would have been quick to inform her that someone was taking much too keen an interest in that old friendship with Jardine, but as far as I could tell Loretta seemed quite unconcerned by my questionable invasion of her privacy.

'How do you do, Professor,' I began formally, but she immediately set all formality aside.

'Call me Loretta,' she said. 'Everyone else over here does. Can I call you Charles or will you think I'm a scarlet woman out to vamp you?'

After the straitlaced atmosphere of Starbridge this was heady stuff indeed. 'Please do call me Charles,' I said, 'and if you want to vamp me I'm sure I can give you the appropriate pastoral attention.'

She laughed. 'That's pretty good,' she said, 'for an Englishman. Well, Charles – is it too early for a drink? Yes, I guess it is. But how about some coffee?'

We decided there was nothing wrong with drinking coffee at eleven o'clock in the morning. The servant was summoned, the order given and in response to my polite inquiry about her journey Loretta began to talk about her voyage across the Atlantic. I was soon so intrigued by her story about a Roman Catholic priest whom she had taught to dance the Black Bottom that I almost forgot to inquire after Lady Starmouth.

'She's calling on the local vicar,' said Loretta, lighting a cigarette, 'but I didn't feel in the mood for inspecting some dusty exhibit in Evelyn's clerical collection – with the result that here I am, entertaining the Archbishop of Canterbury's private eye!'

'And of course you're thinking my visit's the most monstrous piece of impertinence – '

'Not in the least! I'm enthralled . . . Sorry, I should have offered you a cigarette – do you smoke?'

'Not in my clerical collar.'

'Maybe I should start wearing a clerical collar – I smoke far too much . . . Ah, here's the coffee.' Our conversation was briefly suspended, but as soon as the servant had gone she added amused, 'Does old Lang rock the Church of England?'

'I promise you that if Dr Lang ever learns of your existence it certainly won't be from me. He merely dispatched me to Starbridge to make certain Dr Jardine's impregnable from scandal, but I've come to the conclusion that although Dr Jardine's made the occasional pastoral mistake there's no question of any serious moral error.'

'Then why are you here? I mean, don't get me wrong – I'm delighted to meet you, but I can't quite see – '

'This is where I make my confession,' I said, smiling at her. 'I've come here out of sheer curiosity because I've become an admirer of the Bishop and I'd like to hear more about those days in Mayfair when he was the same age as I am now. Are you by any chance free for lunch? There's an attractive hotel at Box Hill with a reputation for good food.'

She was intrigued. 'Will you produce a curate to preserve the pro-prieties?'

I laughed. 'I don't have a curate!'

'In that case, yes, lunch would be wonderful – many thanks!' She laughed too. 'Alex used to bring a curate whenever he called at my apartment,' she said, shedding ash from her cigarette with a casual flick of her wrist. ' "Mr Jardine", I used to call him in those days – how we didn't all die of respectability I'll never know but I didn't call him Alex until right at the end when I put my cards on the table and found I'd overplayed my hand.'

I said uneasily, 'Perhaps you'd rather not talk about him.'

'Charles, it's twenty years since I met Alex Jardine and nineteen years since I last saw him. A lot of water's flowed under the bridge since then.'

'Nevertheless – '

'I'm the reassuring proof that contrary to all the sentimental nineteenth-century novels, frustrated romantic love needn't prove fatal. In fact if you want to talk about him I'd enjoy a reminiscence. What a man he was! Of course I can see why I fell for him and it wasn't just because I was lonely after a broken marriage. It was because he didn't regard it as an inexcusable breach of good taste for a woman to be born with brains. Oh, he was such fun! We used to laugh and laugh, even with the curate in attendance . . . But we can talk more about Alex at lunch. Tell me about you. Evelyn said you'd written a book which had mesmerized all the theologians . . .'

Time slipped lissomly away as the conversation glided from my book to a survey of academic life on both sides of the Atlantic. I forgot Jardine. I even forgot lunch until somewhere a clock struck twelve and Loretta said: 'I'd better throw on some rags suitable for a country outing.' And as she rose to her feet she added, 'Maybe I'll follow in Evelyn's footsteps after all and start collecting clergymen! They're obviously much more fun than stamps or antiques.'

I laughed, just as she had intended that I should, but all the time was wondering if in her lavish use of that casual American charm, she was making a determined effort to annihilate those suspicions of mine which so obstinately refused to die.

II

Three-quarters of an hour later I broke my rule of abstinence from midday drinking and took a sip of a very dry Chablis. We were sitting in the dining-room of the hotel two miles away, and beyond the window of our alcove the garden stretched to the river which wound beneath the densely wooded slopes of Box Hill. I had been tempted to order champagne, but no clergyman had any business to be offering champagne to a lady he had known less than two hours. Merely by taking her out to lunch I was once more travelling at the speed of light, and I was well aware that I now had to be careful. I had not misinterpreted Loretta's unEnglish informality. I knew she could never have maintained her friendship with Lady Starmouth if her reputation had been other than exemplary, but her personality was so conducive to unguarded friendship that it would have been easy to make the mistake of assuming she was an adventuress. I suddenly remembered Lyle talking of the mystery of personality during our visit to Starbury Ring, and I thought that although Loretta was emanating an aura of gregariousness the reality beyond this mask was almost certainly more complex than I could at present perceive.

'Is this the moment when I embark on my journey into nostalgia?' she inquired when Jardine's name inevitably recurred in our conversation. 'What a wonderful opportunity to be self-indulgent!'

'Well, if you're absolutely sure you don't mind – '

'A couple more glasses of this beautiful wine and you'll be wondering how to stop the tidal flow of my reminiscences! But let me just ask you this: how much do you already know?'

That was an awkward question. Since I wanted to see how closely her account tallied with the official version, the less I revealed the better. With care I said, 'Dr Jardine mentioned your sad circumstances in 1917 and how he'd tried to help you.'

'I hope he stressed how ruthlessly he observed the proprieties. I don't want you to think he played Edward VIII to my Mrs Simpson.'

'But I've already told you I don't suspect him of any serious error!'

'True. But I still have this nasty feeling,' she said lightly, looking me straight in the eyes, 'that you think we had a swing together from those Mayfair chandeliers.'

'Dr Jardine was newly married and had just received a dazzling preferment,' I said, looking straight back. 'I don't find it so difficult to believe he ruthlessly observed the proprieties.'

The waiter arrived with our soup but as soon as he had departed she said, 'Alex's hands weren't just tied by the marriage and preferment. He had to be particularly careful where I was concerned because in those days a woman who left her husband was socially as dead as a dodo. It's true that the War was hammering away at the conventions, but of course as a clergyman Alex had to keep up the good old pre-War standards and so I wasn't surprised when his wife at first refused to receive me . . . However eventually he persuaded her to invite me to tea in the name of Christian charity.'

'What was your verdict?'

'On Carrie? I thought she was pathetic. There she was with this husband who was just plain dynamite, and all she could do was simper around in a tea gown and talk about the weather! My first reaction was: how does he stand it? I was bored to tears inside of five minutes. However I should have realized that no stranger really knows what goes on in any marriage – God knows, no one had a clue what was going on in mine – and the truth was that Carrie suited Alex down to the ground. He didn't want to be married to a brain-box. He wanted to be married to an ornament who always went to bed looking sizzling in her latest Parisian nightgown. However it didn't occur to me then that Carrie could have her sexy side. I was very young, only twenty-one in 1917, and although I'd learnt a thing or two from my awful husband – whom you British would call a sod – I was still hopelessly ingenuous when it came to interpreting human relationships. I just jumped to the conclusion that the marriage was a failure and that Alex was longing for some extra-marital entertainment.'

'But no devout clergyman could even consider adultery, let alone commit it!'

'Sure, but I was very ignorant and I just thought clergymen were laymen in fancy dress. I didn't realize that a clergyman really does see life a little differently from the average boring old layman who's only interested in chasing sex and money.'

'You weren't religious?'

'Not in the least, and certainly not after a hellish marriage. The War was another reason too why I misread the situation. I'd become quite used to the idea of everybody surreptitiously sleeping with everyone else whenever they could snatch a few days' leave from the horror of the Front – not that I was ever promiscuous; my husband had made me feel no man could possibly do other than throw up in my presence, but when Alex showed no signs of throwing up I naturally started to hope.'

'But you concealed your feelings.'

'Of course. Evelyn would have been shocked if she'd known how I felt, and Evelyn was my life-line – I'd have gone to pieces without her. But in fact concealment wasn't so difficult – one can conceal almost anything if one lives in the hope that eventually one's dreams are going to come true, and my dream was that Alex would have an affair even if there was no possibility of divorce and remarriage. My God, how naïve I was! It truly is the most crippling handicap not to have a religious upbringing. I thought I was so smart but suddenly I found out that a complete dimension of my mind lay undeveloped and that spiritually I was on a par with an imbecile.'

'And now?'

'Now I'm old enough to be less arrogant and more humble . . . Maybe religion comes with age. I don't believe in the Incarnation – sorry, Charles! – so I guess I'm not a real Christian, am I, but I do believe in God now and I certainly admire Christ as a great man so I shan't feel too much of a hypocrite when I got to church with Evelyn next Sunday.'

'Did Jardine try to talk about Christianity to you?'

'Oh sure, and when *he* talked about it I believed the whole story – Incarnation, Virgin Birth, the lot. But then Alex could make you believe anything – and not just because he could mesmerize you with those amazing golden eyes. He had tremendous powers of logic and reason. In fact I always thought he'd have made a good lawyer – the kind who can argue that black really is white and that if you keep seeing black you have some grave defect in your vision.'

I laughed before saying, 'But if you were learning about Christianity from the most persuasive of instructors, why didn't you see that you were wasting your time being in love with a clergyman?'

'How could I see? Love's blind, and my love was blind until one day in 1918 when . . . Has Alex told you about this?'

'About Lady Starmouth's brother being killed in action? Yes. Dr Jardine said he came down to Starmouth Court to call on her, and after lunch when she was resting you suggested a walk so that you could reveal your feelings.'

'That's right,' she said. 'That's the way it was.' She took another sip of her wine. 'We walked down to the bridge over the river . . . How lovely it was! Such pretty country! There's a railroad track running parallel to the river in this valley but it's cleverly constructed on an embankment so it somehow avoids being a blot on the landscape. I remember I was just admiring the view when this little train appeared like a clockwork toy below us and huffed and puffed its way into the woods. We both laughed and said how cute it was – and that was the moment when he realized exactly how I felt about him . . . Why, Charles, how bemused you look! What's the problem?'

'I was trying to work out how you looked down on the railway line from that bridge over the river.'

'Well, we – ' She stopped. 'You know the location?'

'Yes, I do. I was brought up near here at Epsom.'

'Ah.' She sipped her wine composedly. 'Well, then it'll be easier for you to understand what I'm talking about. When we left Starmouth Court we walked along the road to the bridge and then turned off along a path which followed the river-bank. But after a few minutes we turned off that path too and followed a track which led under a second bridge – the railroad bridge – and into a steep field which had a clump of trees in the middle of it. You'll recall the field I mean – it's clearly visible from the main highway.'

'I remember it well, yes,' I said, but I was thinking of Jardine's statement with its massive omission: 'We walked to the river. We walked back.' I heard myself add, 'I remember picnicking in that field when I was a boy and waving at the passing trains.'

'Alex and I waved at our train too. How we laughed! But then the next moment the train was gone and I finally began to understand what being a clergyman was all about.' She paused before saying abruptly, 'Alex said he couldn't abandon the vows he'd made at his ordination. He quoted the Bible, something about how once you'd put your hand to the plough you couldn't turn back, and finally he just said: "I'm not going to end up like my father".'

'Ah!'

'Freudian, wasn't it? But in fact God left Freud far behind in the end. Alex said: "Try to understand. God's not a fairytale. He's real, He's there and I have to serve Him as a clergyman, but I won't be able to serve Him if I break His rules." Then he put it another way. He said, "If I broke the rules I'd be damaging myself, sliding into a divided life which induces a cancer of the soul; it would be the end of my life as I know it and the beginning of a new life where I'd wind up in a hell of guilt, mentally ill and cut off from God." He made it all seem so blindingly obvious – and of course I just couldn't take it. A man who not only had principles but lived up to them! I felt as if my cynicism had been blasted to bits; I felt not only rejected but defenceless, annihilated . . . Poor Alex! I sobbed and sobbed and the scene was – oh, indescribably harrowing! But Alex, from a clerical point of view, was perfect. No wonder he's a bishop now. He deserves to be.'

We had both finished our soup and again conversation ceased as the waiter removed our plates. Then I said, 'I think Dr Jardine deserves to be a bishop too. But then I never seriously thought that anything you said would make me think otherwise.'

I sensed rather than saw her relief.

We settled down to enjoy the remainder of our meal.

III

All I could think was how much she must have loved him not only to defend him to the hilt nineteen years after the disaster but to defend him at such cost to her self-esteem. In fact the most suspicious aspect of the present situation was Loretta's frankness. Even after allowing for her American informality I thought it highly unlikely that she would welcome the opportunity to talk to a stranger about a painful episode which showed her in such a pitiable light.

My imagination accelerated. I pictured Lady Starmouth saying to her: 'My dear, the most frightful thing's happened – a young clergyman's found out about you and Alex, and to make matters worse he's not just any young clergyman – he's the Archbishop of Canterbury's spy!' And I felt I could understand all too clearly why there had been such a long delay before

Loretta had come to the morning-room to meet me. As soon as she had seen the name on my card she had feared the worst and paused to work out the best way to defuse the danger. I could almost hear her saying to herself: 'Charm him and disarm him. Make him think I have nothing to hide.'

Putting a brake on my imagination I reminded myself that still nothing had been proved. Jardine had certainly made a large omission from his narrative, but in the circumstances that was natural; he would never have wanted me to know that he and Loretta had walked deep into the countryside far from all those passing pony-traps. He could still be guilty of nothing worse than a minor indiscretion, but nevertheless my suspicions were now thoroughly roused. I reminded myself that he had been under acute domestic strain in 1918 following the stillborn birth of his child and his wife's nervous breakdown. I reminded myself that Loretta was an attractive woman who had been deeply in love with him. Was it really possible that Jardine, despite his faith in the concept of platonic friendship, had had no perception of the strong undercurrent of sexuality which must have inevitably permeated their encounters?

I thought not. I was now sure he had known of her feelings long before that September day in 1918 and I was sure too that he must have been strongly tempted to reciprocate them. Yet I was unable to see how I could prove these convictions were true. Loretta had clearly reached the limit of all she was prepared to tell me about the incident, and she was quite shrewd enough to sidestep any attempt I might make at cross-examination.

I thought of Jardine, and suddenly I remembered him stooping to pluck *The Murder of Roger Ackroyd* from the bookshelf in his library. Inspiration dawned. I remembered the mystery novel I had read. When a detective wanted to test a theory he was unable to prove, he returned to the scene of the crime and staged a reconstruction.

IV

'. . . so the Bishop of London shouted out: "I say to you that the streets of hell are paved with champagne, fast cars and loose women!" whereupon an innocent voice from the audience called back: "O Death, where is thy sting?" '

Loretta shook with laughter. 'Is that a true story?'

'If it's not it ought to be. Look, I've just had an idea – that was a large lunch and I fancy some exercise. Would you like to come for a walk with me down by the river?'

'That sounds an attractive proposition, but unless you want me to get bogged down in the meadows I'll have to go back to Starmouth Court to change out of these high heels.'

I had anticipated this. 'We'll call at the house, then drive to the river and leave the car at the bridge.'

'The bridge where – '

'I'm sorry, am I being insensitive? If you'd rather not go near that spot again – '

'Oh, for heaven's sake!' she exclaimed. 'Why make a big deal over a love affair that never happened? Let's go and wave at another cute little train!'

I was now sure she was bending over backwards to allay my suspicions. We went outside to my car.

V

I was not looking forward to meeting Lady Starmouth but to my relief the footman told us she was having a siesta. I thought she would decide I was behaving in a very questionable manner for a clergyman, and I was sure she would be deeply suspicious, even deeply annoyed, by my interest in her guest.

Loretta kept me waiting ten minutes in the morning-room. I was just wondering why it was taking her so long to slip out of her high heels when she reappeared not only in different shoes but in an informal sunfrock with a large matching hat. She looked foreign, exotic. The sunfrock had a neckline which was well within the bounds of decency but which nobody could have described as high.

'This is the coolest dress I have,' she said as we stepped outside, and casting me a sympathetic glance she added, 'It's a pity you can't strip off that hot uniform of yours.'

'What a delectably improper suggestion!'

She laughed. 'Relax!' she said. 'I haven't forgotten you're a clergyman!'

'I'm glad at least one of us remembers.' We were both laughing by that time but I knew I had to apply an emotional brake. 'I'm sorry,' I said abruptly as I held open the door of the car for her. 'My tongue's running away with me.'

'Is that a sin?'

'No, just a mistake. Like smoking in a clerical collar.'

'A breach of self-discipline?'

'Yes.' I was surprised by her understanding. 'Exactly.' I said no more and seconds later we were on our way down the drive. On the main road Loretta said unexpectedly, 'God's at the centre of your life too, isn't He? He doesn't just fade away when things are going well, as He does with most people. He's there all the time – and like Alex you *know* He's there.'

I said obliquely, 'The sun's not a mere disc in the sky which you can see whenever you bother you look up. The warmth of the sun permeates the world even on a clouded day, and that's not mere wishful thinking or sensual illusion. You can see the plants reacting to the warmth. It's real.'

'I wouldn't quarrel with that. But I still think the ability to be religious – to keep God constantly in view – is a gift. It's like playing the piano well. A lot of people long to be accomplished pianists but if they've insufficient talent they fail, no matter how hard they practise and how many lessons they take.'

'I agree we're not all born with supreme mystical powers, but on the other hand a certain level of spirituality is within everyone's reach. It's a question of . . . But no,' I said smiling at her, 'I really mustn't lecture you as if you were one of my undergraduates.'

She smiled back. 'Aren't you going to try to convert me to Christianity?'

'The best way to convert someone like you is probably not to adopt an intellectual approach; you'd find the doctrinal arguments mentally stimulating but your soul would remain untouched.'

'Then how would you go about converting me?'

'I'd say you'd be more impressed by action than by words. For instance, back in 1918 what was it that impressed you most about Christianity? Was it Dr Jardine talking hypnotically about the Incarnation – or was it Dr Jardine rejecting you in the face of a very great temptation?'

The car was approaching the river. I could see the bridge ahead of us, but as I glanced sideways at Loretta I sensed her thoughts were far away.

'Christianity did make an impact on me when he ended our friendship,' she said at last. 'I thought that all men – real men – ever thought about was chasing money and women. To find a man – a real man – who thought there was more to life than that . . . Yes, it made me feel I had to try to understand.'

'But understanding proved elusive?'

'Not entirely. I see Christianity as a beautiful dream. But that's what being human's all about, isn't it? That's what sets us apart from the apes. We have beautiful dreams and the finest lives are spent trying to make those dreams come true.'

'To think of Christianity as a dream is to ignore its reality, although perhaps what you're really saying is that the finest lives express man's yearning for transcendent values. That's real enough – but just listen to me! Trust a theologian to make the nobler aspirations of humanity sound dry as dust!'

We laughed, and driving across the bridge I halted the car on the verge. But then some unexpected impulse made me add: 'I agree that a lot of men appear to be interested only in money and sex but I think too that a lot of men would secretly like to believe there's more to life than the materialist's treadmill. However, society forces them to chase worldly success in order to be esteemed, and then they chase women either to forget how unhappy they are chasing success or because they see women as boosting their value in the eyes of the world.'

'So all men's troubles arise from the pursuit of worldly success? That's an interesting theory, Charles! I wonder if I'm beginning to learn a little about you at last!'

I said lightly: 'Am I such a mystery?'

'We're all mysteries,' said Loretta. 'That's what makes life so fascinating.'

I could not deny it.

We left the car and set out on our walk.

VI

The ground sloped from the road to the river which meandered lazily beneath the bridge, and when we reached the path by the bank I paused to shade my eyes with my hand. On either side of the valley the wooded hills shimmered in a heat-haze and on my left the water sparkled hotly in the brilliant light.

Loretta paused too, and as I saw the stillness of her face I said suddenly, 'Are you sure you want to go through with this?'

'That sounds as if we're on our way to get married. Yes, sure I'm sure! Let's exorcize all the past horrors . . . Do they still perform exorcisms in the Church of England?'

'Nowadays it's generally regarded as a somewhat unsavoury superstition.'

'How odd! Is it wise for the Church to abandon exorcism to laymen?'

'What laymen?'

'They're called psychoanalysts,' she said drily. 'Maybe you've heard of them. They have this cute little god called Freud and a very well-paid priesthood and the faithful go weekly to worship on couches – '

'Ever tried it?'

'Sure. My analyst told me that the reason why I kept trying to marry impossible men was because deep down I didn't want to get married at all – and after two years of lying on his couch and reviewing my past I came to the reluctant conclusion that he was right.'

'What extraordinary things go on in America!'

'Maybe. But the fact remains that the analyst exorcized my demon of despair when I was spiritually sick.'

137

'Well, of course the Church provides counselling for the spiritually sick, but *exorcism*! That's a different matter altogether!'

'But is it? Isn't it all one? If no one finds you when you're spiritually sick, don't the demons eventually possess you to such an extent that you end up climbing the walls and screaming for help?'

'But is it really appropriate, in this scientific twentieth century, to call a nervous breakdown demonic possession?'

'I don't see why not. Personally I find it a lot easier to believe in demons and the Devil – especially in this scientific twentieth century – than in God and the angels. If the world's fundamentally evil I'd say the difference between a nervous breakdown and demonic possession is purely a matter of semantics.'

'I'd deny the world's fundamentally evil, no matter how prevalent evil may be. I see you have dangerous tendencies,' I said smiling at her, 'towards the Gnostic heresy!'

'The most dangerous tendency I have is to talk too much. Why on earth did I tell you about my analyst? Now you'll be thinking I'm crazy.'

'My dear Loretta – '

'Maybe it's time I kept quiet for a while.'

The path forked ahead of us, and leaving the river we turned uphill towards the bridge which carried the railway line over a gap in the embankment. I did make attempts to renew the conversation but her replies were monosyllabic, and by the time we reached the bridge we had once more relapsed into silence. Beyond the bridge rose the steep field she had described, the field in which I had picnicked as a boy with my parents and my brother Peter.

'It's odd how close the past seems sometimes,' I said as we paused for breath. Out of respect for the severity of the gradient we had avoided struggling directly uphill and were cutting a diagonal path across the field, but the way was still steep. Ahead of us the spinney, a dark cluster of trees clinging to the hillside, once more stirred my memories; I had retired there to sulk after squabbling with Peter and arousing my father's irritation. 'I feel I've only to look back now over my shoulder,' I said, 'and I'll see myself as a child long ago on that family picnic.'

She made no reply. She was standing motionless, listening, and as I listened too I heard the distant murmur which had caught her attention.

It was the train.

'We were further up the hillside last time – nearer the trees – oh, I must get there, I must, I want it to be just the same . . .' She dashed forward, I hurried after her and all the time the noise was increasing as the train thundered down the valley towards us.

Below the spinney she halted. We could see the train now. It was approaching from the left, and beyond the railway line, beyond the river, beyond the watermeadows I could see the main road and the miniature cars and the Starmouths' house on the hill. The train, looking curiously like an over-sized toy against a painted backdrop, roared closer.

'We must wave!' cried Loretta. 'Wave, Charles, wave!'

We waved. The engine-driver saluted gamely, and as the train swept past, assorted children waved back at us from their window-seats. Then in a flash the episode ended. The train disappeared from sight beyond the far corner of the field, the noise died away and all was quiet again. I turned to Loretta, but my amused comment was never spoken for I saw her cheeks were wet with tears. The next moment she was stumbling across the few yards which separated us from the spinney, and as I stared after her she disappeared among the trees.

I allowed her time to compose herself, but when she showed no sign of reappearing I followed her. The trees were guarded by dense undergrowth; it took me longer than I had anticipated to find a gap in that barrier of bramble bushes, but once I had stepped into the shadows I saw her at once. She had retreated to a secluded spot on the far side of the spinney and was sitting amidst a patch of bracken. I glimpsed the strained lines of her red sunfrock as she clasped her knees in a foetal position, and as I drew nearer I could see her shoulders shaking as she wept. She had taken off her glasses but when she heard me coming she scrabbled to retrieve them.

I knelt down, covering her hands with mine, and the glasses remained unworn. 'Forgive me,' I said, 'I should never have brought you here.'

'I thought I could take it, but . . .' She began to cry again.

I put my arm around her. It was an instinctive gesture born of guilt and I withdrew almost immediately as prudence triumphed over sympathy, but the message had been communicated; she looked up.

'My God, this is strange!' she said in a shaking voice. 'It's just as if you're him and it's happening all over again.'

We stared at each other. Then as I slowly put my arm around her once more I knew beyond doubt that it was not she who had suggested that walk to the river nineteen years ago and not she who had made the first move beyond the bounds of convention.

VII

I said, 'I think I'm going to do something very stupid,' and I kissed her on the mouth. Then I said, 'Of course I'm crazy but I'll think about that later,' and I kissed her again.

All she said when I eventually eased aside the straps of her sunfrock was, 'I don't want you to suffer the torment Alex suffered. Oh God, Charles, if only you knew what we went through – '

'It's different this time. I'm not married.'

'Yes, but –'

I interrupted her with a kiss. More time passed and when at last I paused to slip off my jacket she said no more about suffering but merely reached out to touch my collar.

She whispered: 'I remember the way it fastens at the back.'

And then I knew I could begin to think the unthinkable.

NINE

'I am grieved that you also have to sustain the shock and shame of clerical scandals ... how much clerical failure and scandal I have witnessed. I am sure our way is far more difficult than most men realise: and that of all men we have most need to remember: "Let he that thinketh he standeth take heed lest he fall." '

More Letters of Herbert Hensley Henson
Bishop of Durham 1920-1939
ed. E. F. BRALEY

I

The bracken was cool against my hot skin. I was aware of that coolness as I fought and won the initial battle for control over my excitement which was very deep and very powerful. There was only one awkward moment. It came when I sensed she was ready and moved myself into position between her thighs. She said suddenly, 'You're going in.'

I halted. 'It's too soon?'

'No, no – ' She pulled me close and kissed me with such fervour that disaster nearly intervened. I had to twist my mouth away to regain my control.

When I could speak again I said, 'It's safe? Will I have to withdraw?' but again she said, 'No, no – ' and again she pulled me close until at last I began to penetrate her.

The first ninety seconds were marred by my dread of an early finish, but once I was inside she seemed more aware of that danger and I was conscious of her sensitivity as she matched her response to mine. Gradually the disadvantages stemming from abstinence faded and the rewards became predominant; once the battle for control had been won I knew I could sustain myself for a long time.

'Are you all right?'

'Dumb question!'

'The bracken's hardly a well-sprung mattress.'

'I wouldn't even care if it was concrete.' She raised her mouth to mine and later I heard her murmur, 'It's been such a long time.'

'How long?'

'Three years. I was so tired of the pain of nothing working out . . . And you?'

But I merely drew her into a different position and thrust myself deeper into her hot curving flesh.

II

When we had finished we were too exhausted to do more than lie in silence and watch the blue sky beyond the overhanging branches of the tree above us. My mind was empty. I knew the pain would begin later but meanwhile I was anaesthetized, every fibre of my body satiated and every ache of tension smoothed away. I longed again, as I had longed so often before, for the intimacy of married life, but that reminded me of Lyle and immediately my mind began to divide. I squeezed my eyes shut as if I could erase the present by refusing to look at it, but still my two personalities struggled to separate in a battle which lay beyond my understanding.

'Cigarette?' said Loretta, retrieving a packet from her handbag.

'Thanks.' I was diverted. My mind emptied itself again and the battle was suspended.

After we had smoked in idleness for a time she said, 'How the hell do you manage, not being married?'

'Contrary to popular belief no one ever dies of chastity.' I began to trace the outline of her breasts with one finger.

'True, but let's be honest – chastity can be pretty damned uncomfortable. Why haven't you remarried?'

'Why haven't you?'

'Oh, I'm an easy case to explain.' She too started tracing. I felt her finger slowly circle my chest. 'My analyst and I figured out that (a) most men can't cope with my brains, (b) most men can't cope with my success, (c) I don't like playing second fiddle, (d) I'm not domestic, (e) my husband was enough to put anyone off marriage for life, and (f) I've never really got over Alex; I kept waiting to meet someone who could match him and by the time I realized that wasn't going to happen I was past the age when I felt inclined to compromise.'

'You must have loved him very much.'

'Well, of course we'd have married if it hadn't been for that dumb wife. My husband wouldn't have been a problem because by the end of 1918 he'd drunk himself to death, but you know, Charles, I often wonder how Alex and I would have got along. I'm not fundamentally a religious person and I've got an independent streak which might have made marital life difficult. In fact I think I'd have been a very unsatisfactory wife for a bishop.'

'But if you'd married Jardine at that stage of your life when your mature personality still wasn't completely formed – '

'Yes, I might have adapted, but we'll never know, will we? It's the world of might-have-been . . . like that second marriage you've never made. Why don't you want to remarry?'

'I do.' I stubbed out our cigarettes and began to caress her again.

'Then why haven't you done so years ago? Maybe you're like me. Maybe deep down you don't want to get married at all.'

'But I do! I must! I – oh, don't let's talk about it any more, I hate even thinking of my baffling and intractable problems – '

'But maybe you should. Some problems don't just go away by themselves. They're like demons and they have to be exorcized.'

'Well, I don't know any exorcists and I've got my demons under control,' I said, but as soon as the words left my mouth I panicked. 'Oh my God, what am I doing, what's happening to me – '

'Charles – darling – '

'I'm all right,' I said, ramming myself so deep inside her that she gasped. 'I'm all right, I'm all right, I'm all right – '

I had anaesthetized myself again.

The panic faded.

I settled down to saturate myself in sex.

III

This time the experience began differently. It was darker, more disjointed, but I knew it reflected my inner disorder and she knew it too for she sought in various subtle ways to soothe me. I responded. Slowly I relaxed until at last I was the one on my back in the bracken and her soft flesh above me was a delicious contrast to the hard ground beneath my spine. The only unsuccessful moment came when I guided us into different positions in an attempt to share her finish; we slipped apart and the climax came when I was outside her.

'Damn.'

'It's okay.' She held me tightly in her arms while we recovered and only released me when I reached again for the cigarettes. Eventually I said after meditating on her present pleasure and her past abstinence: 'I suppose it's easier for a woman to cope with chastity.'

'Thanks. I'll think of that next time I'm dying of frustration. I'm sure it'll be a great comfort.'

'I'm sorry, that was appallingly insensitive of me – '

'Funnily enough Alex made a remark like that too. He spoke as if no woman could possibly imagine what hell the celibate life could be.'

'How did *he* manage before he married at thirty-seven?'

'I don't know and later I always wished I'd asked. In the old days Evelyn and I often used to speculate about his early life, but we never reached any firm conclusions.'

'Tell me, how much does Lady Starmouth actually know about you and Jardine?'

'Well, she knew at the end that Alex was just as much in love with me as I was with him – I mean, she saw us, we couldn't have kept it from her, we were in pieces. However there was no question of her not standing by us and doing all she could to cover up the mess. She'd made up her mind that Alex was going to go right to the top of the Church of England.'

'Wasn't she angry with you for jeopardizing him?'

'Livid. But she forgave me. You might not think it, but Evelyn's another of those rare people who really do make an effort to live up to their religious beliefs.'

'How appalled she must have been when I found out about you!'

'She said she nearly died. She apologized to me because she had explained the incident away by depicting me as a tiresome neurotic female and Alex as purity personified, but what choice did she have? I took the same line just now at lunch, but of course . . . the truth was very different.'

'The love was always reciprocated?'

'Always. We fell in love right away when we met in 1917, but my God, how he fought against it! That awful curate whom he used to bring along as a chaperone! And those awful minutes alone at the Starmouths' house whenever Evelyn was called away to the phone – but he never kissed me, not even then. It would have been too dangerous; anyone could have walked in . . . But the worst part was visiting him at home with his wife. I didn't want to go but he felt the fact that his wife had received me would kill any gossip which might be simmering.'

'What were his feelings about his wife by that time?'

'When we were here he said he'd realized on his honeymoon that he'd made a frightful mistake but he was sure the situation would be redeemed when they had a family. Well, the kids didn't happen, did they, though back in 1918 she'd just had a baby and no one knew she'd never conceive again. Alex said it had been a terrible year, the child arriving stillborn, Carrie having a nervous breakdown, he getting no sex for months on end . . . He didn't exactly mention sex in the same breath as Carrie and the baby, but I had no trouble getting the message that sex was important to him. In fact in the end he said, "The marriage could be worse. When

Carrie's well she's very dutiful." Dutiful! Ugh! What a repulsive Victorian euphemism! That was one of the moments when I remembered he was seventeen years older than I was. Anyway I was vilely jealous to think of her having him several times a week and I became more jealous than ever when he told me he'd be happy to make love every night. However he said he thought that would be selfish – probably he was frightened in case she developed a dislike for it. It meant so much to him that he was prepared to exercise a moderate amount of restraint.'

'I simply can't understand how he could have stayed chaste from his ordination till the age of thirty-seven. Surely he must have had lapses!'

'Maybe – but maybe not. Remember Freud. Sex can so often be affected by what's going on in the mind.'

'You think there could be psychological as well as religious reasons for Jardine's chastity during those years?'

'Where sex is concerned,' said Loretta, 'anything's possible. For instance, his father was one of the hellfire-and-damnation school and that kind of guy can make his children feel guilty about sex, particularly if he feels guilty about it himself. Alex might have taken some time to get over that. Then when he was ordained he was so violently Anglo-Catholic (reacting against Dad the Fundamentalist) that he even vowed himself to celibacy, so obviously it took him some time to get over *that*. Then he was given some terrible parish where he slaved himself into a physical if not a nervous breakdown and *that* must have sublimated his sexual energy nicely. But the most important factor of all was that he was never deprived of female companionship for long, and personally I believe that loneliness, rather than lack of sex, is often the reason why celibacy becomes intolerable. He had this stepmother – '

'Here we go again. I keep hearing about this stepmother. I've even wondered if they were having an affair.'

'I'd doubt that.'

'Why?'

'Because I don't think Alex would ever enter into a continuing illicit relationship,' said Loretta, voicing my own insuperable objection to this theory. 'He proved that when he rejected me. It would have been easy for us to have had an affair – after all, I was living apart from my husband in my own apartment – but he wouldn't do it even though he was crazy about me.'

'That's certainly very significant.'

'Any clergyman can have an isolated lapse which he can atone for afterwards,' said Loretta. 'Clergymen are human beings, not angels. But how can a devout clergyman pursue his calling if he continuously lives in sin?'

'He either ends the sin or becomes an apostate.'

'Well, Alex certainly wasn't an apostate when I knew him. He was a believer through and through.'

The *ménage à trois* at the palace was beginning to look innocent again, but the thought of Lyle was still too difficult to endure. Stubbing out my cigarette I turned once more to Loretta, and in the manner of a patient begging his nurse for a pain-killing injection I whispered, 'Love me.'

IV

The strength came as soon as I touched her but she made me wait as she kissed my body and drew her hands over my thighs. At last when I was too strong to bear further delay she yielded; our positions changed; I linked us again and felt her flesh enclose mine as she expelled her breath in pleasure. I clung to her. She stroked my hair and for some seconds I did not move but remained in that position of extreme intimacy. At last I said, 'I want to confide in you.' I had realized I could fuse my two personalities by drawing the past into the present and bringing together within the same boundary of time and space the Charles of Starbridge and the Charles who was lying naked on that Surrey hillside.

'Then go ahead,' she said, still stroking my hair. 'I promise you can trust me.'

The sexual strength slackened as if the power had been switched to other channels. Slipping out I buried my face for a second in her breasts before embarking on the full story of my visit to Starbridge.

The tale took some time to tell but finally I heard myself say, 'You must be appalled by the idea of me making love to you while I'm in love with someone else. I'm appalled myself. I don't understand what's going on, but I'm beginning to think there are two mysteries here, the mystery of what's going on at the palace and the mystery of what's going on in my head – and the most peculiar thing of all is that these two mysteries seem somehow to be connected ... Or does that make me sound completely crazy in addition to being thoroughly immoral?'

Loretta did not respond with a quick reassurance as a lesser woman might have done. Nor did she make any tart comment about Lyle. Instead after careful thought she said, 'No, I don't think you're crazy. And I don't think you're fundamentally immoral either. But I do think you could be fundamentally confused.'

'That's a very generous judgement –'

'I'm not interested in being generous, just in being accurate. Charles, are you sure you're in love with this girl? If one's confused it becomes harder to distinguish between truth and illusion, and in my opinion your instantaneous attraction to Lyle does suggest there might be some degree of illusion going on.'

'I'm quite certain my feelings are genuine.'

'Yes, but . . . Okay, let's leave Lyle and turn to Alex because this is where you seem to be very confused indeed. Your interest in his past borders on the obsessive – it's as if you're seeing him as some kind of symbol impregnated with hidden meanings – '

'What on earth do you mean?'

'I only wish I knew. I feel I'm groping around in the dark but Charles, I'm sure you ought to discuss this with someone who's a great deal more competent than I am to sort out what's going on. Do you have an adviser you can consult? Clergymen usually have someone, don't they – what do you call them – confessors, counsellors, directors – '

'I go to the Fordite Abbot of Grantchester, near Cambridge. The Fordites are Anglican-Benedictines, not Roman Catholic monks, but monks within the Church of England.'

'Fine. See your Abbot and tell him everything.'

'Maybe I should make a short retreat.' I thought about it but the prospect of any spiritual exercise which included confession was so appalling that I could only shudder and press my face against her breasts again. However, when I realized I could only divert myself from the horror of confession by dwelling on the Starbridge mystery I withdrew from her and propped myself up on one elbow. 'In your opinion,' I said, 'what's going on in that *ménage à trois*?'

'My guess would be absolutely nothing – I think you got it right the first time. Lyle keeps the marriage glued together and her presence satisfies the different needs of all three of them: her need for power, Carrie's need for a daughter and Alex's need for an orderly home.'

'I agree that's the only answer which makes sense, but the fact is that the atmosphere just doesn't tally with that explanation. I'm sure there's something going on between Lyle and Jardine, although now you've confirmed my opinion that he'd never enter into a continuing illicit liaison I don't see how they can be having an affair.'

'Okay,' said Loretta briskly, sitting up. 'Let's try and cut through some of this confusion of yours by running through the various possibilities. Possibility number one: Lyle's in love with Carrie.'

'Out of the question.'

'Is it? Very feminine helpless women like Carrie often do wind up in lesbian situations, and you should remember there's always the chance that your feelings for Lyle could be an illusion.'

'Yes, but – '

'The biggest argument against the existence of lesbianism,' interrupted Loretta, taking my side before I could dispute the idea further, 'is that I can't see Alex ever tolerating it. I think we can assume that whatever's going on must somehow succeed in satisfying all three of them. Okay, let's move on to possibility number two: Lyle's crazy about Alex but Alex isn't crazy about her; he's kept the situation in control and nothing's ever happened between them.'

'I can't see any clergyman in his right mind tolerating an infatuated woman in his household,' I said. 'The situation would be much too inflammable. He'd have got rid of her straight away.'

'But supposing he wasn't in his right mind? This is possibility number three. Supposing he's crazy about her but his religious beliefs are keeping him in check?'

'From a clerical point of view that would be even worse than the previous situation – it'd be disastrous for his spiritual health to have such a temptation constantly on his doorstep.'

'So that leaves the final possibility: Alex has lost his mind, thrown all scruples to the winds and is deeply involved in a fully consummated love affair.'

'And that,' I said, 'is impossible for two reasons. The first is that I'm sure Mrs Jardine wouldn't tolerate it, and the second is that he couldn't remain a bishop in those circumstances unless he's an apostate – which we're both sure he's not.'

'I agree that last difficulty seems to be the eternal stumbling block,' said Loretta, 'but I think I can visualize a situation where Carrie would be complaisant. According to Evelyn, Alex and Carrie never gave up hope of having a family – a hope which would give each of them a powerful motive for continuing to have sex. But supposing, once Carrie reached the menopause, she turned against sex on the grounds that it had become pointless. It's not an uncommon thing to happen, and when it does the marriage usually reaches a crisis. That's the point where the husband, if he's a layman, takes a mistress and the wife looks the other way.'

I stared at her. 'I think you've hit the nail on the head,' I said. 'I think that's what happened. From something Mrs Cobden-Smith said I deduced the menopause was going on five years ago, and that was exactly the time when Mrs Jardine was once more on the brink of breakdown.'

'But that was because the old stepmother turned up.'

'Yes, but supposing there was more to the crisis than that. Jardine told me that this was the last occasion on which he recorded personal difficulties in his journal – and he admitted that he'd had an important decision to make. Supposing he was trying to decide whether or not to –'

'I agree it's suggestive. If anything happened I'll bet it happened then, but the big question is: did anything happen? And if it did, how did Alex square his conscience?'

'I'm going to find out. I've got to, *got to* –'

'I know. It's worrying me. Charles, you're much too obsessed about this – '

'How can I not be obsessed with it if I want to marry Lyle?'

'Yes, but . . . Okay, let's have another shot at putting the situation in some sort of rational perspective. The plain truth is that you don't know whether you're in love with Lyle or not. However you think you are and this makes you ultra-sensitive to this mysterious *ménage à trois*. The most likely explanation of the *ménage* is that there really is nothing going on, but because you're not perceiving reality properly you're sliding deeper and deeper into illusion by devising this theory which will explain Lyle's coolness without damaging your own ego. In other words you're saying subconsciously to yourself: she and Jardine are having an affair and that's why she's not responding to me properly. But I think you ought to face the possibility that by reading too much into people's innocent reactions you're winding up imagining this sinister atmosphere at the palace. In fact in my opinion the really relevant question here is not what's going on in the *ménage* but what's going on in your subconscious; for example, why are you so sure Lyle's right for you?'

'She can cope with anything.'

'But that makes you sound like a lunatic in need of a keeper!'

'Does it?' I pulled her into my arms again. 'One more time,' I said. 'Just once more.'

She parted her legs and put her hand gently on my body to guide me in.

V

The knowledge that this was to be my last chance for some unknown time of satisfying myself sexually made me urgent as I gave physical expression to my despair. My misery was compounded by exhaustion and soon I felt the power fading. Loretta moved to restore it but my flesh was already contracting and seconds later I was closing my eyes against the light as I slumped back upon the bracken.

I slept. Then waking suddenly, just as one so often does after a short deep sleep, I sat up and said, 'Jane.' Loretta kissed me on the cheek. In confusion I saw she was dressed.

'I've been asleep,' I said dazed.

'Only for ten minutes. I thought you needed it . . . Who's Jane?'

'My wife.' Absurdly my eyes filled with tears, and terrified by this fresh evidence that I was on the point of disintegration I grabbed the lighted cigarette Loretta was offering me and turned my back on her. As I dressed I was able to say, 'I've proved Jardine was capable of a single lapse. Now

I've got to prove he was capable of a continuing illicit liaison. If I knew he'd been sleeping with that stepmother before his marriage –'

'I'm sure he wasn't. Look, Charles, you've just got to get this obsession in perspective –'

'I suppose he might have fought shy of taking his father's wife. After all, even though there was no blood relationship between them the legal relationship would have brought them within the prohibited degrees –'

'Well, that wouldn't apply in this case, would it?' said Loretta, taking her glasses from her handbag.

I stared at her. 'What do you mean?'

She stared back. 'My God!' she exclaimed. 'Don't tell me you didn't find out!'

'Find out what?'

'Alex's father never married her, Charles. She lived for twenty-five years as his mistress. There was neither a blood-tie nor a legal relationship between Alex and Ingrid Jardine.'

VI

'Alex told me and Evelyn about it once,' said Loretta. 'He was trying to establish a better relationship between Carrie and his stepmother but he wasn't making much progress and he confided in us out of sheer exasperation. Apparently Carrie was taking the line that she wasn't obliged to receive anyone who had lived in sin for twenty-five years.'

'But the father was a religious fanatic! Why on earth didn't he marry her?'

'He hated all formal religion and he hated all clergymen so he kidded himself into believing he didn't need a clergyman reciting the wedding service over him in order to be married before God. He had to marry Alex's mother in church – she was a girl from a very respectable family – but Ingrid was on her own and apparently quite prepared to humour his crankiness; probably there was a very strong sexual attraction going on. Anyway old Jardine summoned her to his bedroom one night, and after they'd said some prayers together and exchanged a few vows he put his signet-ring on her finger, took her to bed and consummated what he was pleased to call his new marriage.'

'Wait,' I said. 'Wait.' My heart was thudding hard. 'Just a moment.'

'God, what is it, Charles? You're as white as a ghost!'

'Did you say a signet-ring?'

'Yes, maybe he thought a real wedding-ring was as unnecessary as a clergyman reciting the wedding service – or maybe the marriage was unplanned and he used the only ring available at that moment . . . Charles, what the hell is it? What's the matter?'

I said, 'Lyle wears a large signet-ring on the third finger of her left hand.'

VII

Eventually Loretta said, 'No. I know what you're thinking but it's impossible.'

'It's the only explanation that fits. Jardine married Lyle informally before God and they now think of each other as husband and wife. They believe they're not living in sin, and that means they can go on receiving the sacrament regularly.'

'No.' Loretta shook her head. 'That definitely has to be a fantasy. Old Jardine had no education and didn't know any better, but Alex would know that kind of marriage had no validity. And anyway, damn it, he wasn't free to marry!'

'Obviously before he talked himself into an informal marriage he talked himself into an informal divorce. Have you heard of the A. P. Herbert Bill? Parliament's about to extend the grounds for divorce but I think Jardine's views go far further than the new law. He believes that a prima facie case for divorce exists whenever the spiritual core of the marriage is destroyed – in fact I'd say he was well in step with Martin Luther who believed that refusal of marital rights should be a ground for divorce. If Mrs Jardine was refusing to have sex – '

'Charles, you're in the stratosphere – for God's sake come down to earth!'

'But I know I'm right!'

'And I know you're wrong! Alex couldn't possibly get himself in such a mess – '

'Didn't you say that where sex is concerned anything's possible?'

'You're out of your mind!' shouted Loretta, but added at once in a calmer voice, 'Okay, I can see the theory's plausible, but try to keep one truth nailed up in front of you: it hasn't been proved.'

'It soon will be – all I've got to do now is go back to Starbridge and talk to Lyle!'

'But even if your theory's true she'll never admit it!'

'Oh yes, she will! I'm going to rescue her.'

'Charles, you're just not in touch with reality! If your theory's true – and I don't think for one moment that it is – then that girl's besotted with Alex. I say that because no woman who wasn't besotted would ever acquiesce in the humiliation of a secret marriage.'

'I think the marriage is breaking up.'

'Oh, my God . . . Look, Charles, before you rush off to Starbridge to make some horrific exhibition of yourself, please, *please* go and see that Abbot of yours – '

'Oh, I have to see him first, I agree. I can't go on serving God as I should until I've made my confession. I'll go back to Cambridge tonight and call on the Fordites tomorrow morning.'

'Promise?'

I promised. She sagged in relief, and taking her in my arms I held her for a long moment.

At last she said, 'Charles, I know we can't meet again; I know you'll have to put things right with God by promising there'll be no repeat performance of this afternoon's drama, but could you write to me? Just once? Otherwise I'll go out of my mind wondering what on earth happened in the end.'

'I'll write.'

We left the spinney. It seemed a long way back to the bridge over the river. We walked in silence as I planned my next assault on Starbridge and she no doubt wondered how to convince me of its futility, but when we were within sight of the car she said, 'Alex began to hurt here – it was terrible. He kept saying he wanted to leave his wife but he knew he'd never survive the guilt which would cut him off from God – and that was the moment when he said: "I don't want to end up like my father". Charles, I'm just so sure he'd never follow in the old man's footsteps – '

'I agree he'd never want to end up mentally unstable and spiritually wrecked, but how far can one exercise control over one's heredity? Of course with God's help anything's possible, but if one turns away from God – '

'I don't think Alex could turn away from Freud. He had a psychological as well as a spiritual horror of immorality.'

'But that's exactly why he'd feel compelled to convert adultery into marriage!'

'I give up. Let's agree to differ,' said Loretta, kissing me as we reached the car, but when we eventually opened the doors we found the interior was so hot that there was no temptation to linger for further embraces, and with reluctance we embarked on our return journey to Starmouth Court.

VIII

Outside the house our hands clasped and on an impulse she said, 'Never think I don't understand how difficult your calling is. Never think I believe you're a bad clergyman just because for once you couldn't live up to your ideals.'

But I only said, 'I've failed you.'

'No,' she persisted, 'you dream the dream. That's all that matters. It's just that in an imperfect world no dream can come true all the time.'

'How comforting life must be for you soft-hearted liberal Deists! But Christianity is much tougher and more virile than that. I ignored the care of your soul in order to exploit you for my own selfish purposes. That's acting without love and compassion. That's sin. That's failure.'

But still she struggled to comfort me. 'You're the one who's hurt here. I exploited you every bit as much as you exploited me.'

'That wasn't exploitation. Your action was a cry for help as you sought an end to loneliness – a loneliness which I've completely failed to alleviate.' I saw her expression change as she realized I had seen much further than she had ever intended, but I was unable to stop myself saying, 'The psychoanalyst helped you. The Christian priest rejected you. What a travesty, what an unforgivable debasement, of the way things ought to be!'

For a moment I thought she would be unable to reply but at last she said unsteadily, 'It's such a beautiful dream!' Then she struggled out of the car and ran into the house without looking back.

I drove down the dark winding drive into the valley.

IX

It was late at night when I reached my rooms in Cambridge, and I was very tired. After a bath I drank some whisky and slid into bed.

I had not read the evening office. I had made no attempt to pray. For a long time I lay still, as if I could retain my equilibrium in the spiritual void by aping unconsciousness, but when I felt the void deepening I left the bed to pour myself another drink. In panic I focused my mind on the Starbridge mystery, that proven distraction from my problems, and later – it was around one in the morning – it began to dawn on me that I had to solve the Starbridge mystery before I could make my confession to Father Reid.

Yet I had promised Loretta I would go to the Fordites before I returned to Starbridge, and I had to keep my promise to Loretta.

I drank some more whisky.

Eventually I decided that I would call on Father Reid but only to arrange a retreat at the end of the week. Then I could go back to Starbridge, and once the mystery had been solved I could concentrate on putting my soul in order in time for the Cathedral services on Sunday.

Happy ending.

I drank another whisky as if I needed help in believing that such happiness was within my reach, and gradually as I thought of Starbridge, radiant ravishing Starbridge, that shining city which contained the key to all my secrets, I knew how deeply I was compelled to prise apart that glittering image in order to confront the stark dark truths beyond. Then in my mind's eye I saw Jardine, not the Adam who hid behind Alex, but the bishop empowered with the *charismata*, the coruscating churchman, just the kind of churchman I wanted to be, but of course I *was* Jardine, I knew that now, and that was why I had to see him again as soon as possible.

'I've got to talk to Jardine,' I said aloud to the whisky bottle as I turned it upside down to shake the last drops into my glass. 'He understands me. No one else does.' And as soon as those words were uttered I knew I could never confide in Father Reid. Seeing Father Reid would be a waste of time but I had made my promise to Loretta and like all good clergymen I never broke a promise. I would see Father Reid for a brief social visit before I departed for Starbridge because I was such a good clergyman, such a brilliant success, and my father was so proud of me and yes, I'd definitely go to see Father Reid and that was final.

In the name of the Father, the Son and the Holy Ghost. Amen.

X

The next morning I took some alka-seltzer, brewed some strong coffee and made myself read the office. I had made up my mind not to go to pieces. The bout of panic had been aggravated by my foolish lapse with the whisky, but now I had regained my equilibrium all would be well.

I drove to Grantchester, the village near Cambridge where the Fordites had their house. I had decided to pass the time with Father Reid by telling him about the St Anselm manuscript; I still intended to arrange a retreat, but now that I was sober I remained more convinced than ever that my confession could be made only to Jardine.

So difficult was it for me to face the painful reality of my situation that I was halfway to Grantchester before I perceived the obvious objection to my plan. Jardine would inevitably decide that our lives had become so entangled that he was disqualified from acting as my confessor. Indeed if he considered himself married to Lyle he was quite unfit to offer me spiritual counselling.

At this point I felt so confused that I stopped the car. I felt unable to speak of Loretta to anyone but Jardine because it seemed to me that only someone who had made an identical error would be able to summon the compassionate understanding necessary for granting absolution. At the thought of Loretta my body stirred restlessly, and that small movement which my mind failed to control at once emphasized the overwhelming nature of my problems. Devoid of effective counselling, confronted by the utter breakdown of my celibate life, knowing myself temporarily cut off from God, I had my back to the spiritual wall.

Panic flooded through me again but I conquered it by bombarding my mind with images of Starbridge. Lyle, Jardine, Carrie – Jardine, Carrie, Lyle – Carrie, Lyle, Jardine –

Driving the last mile to Grantchester I reached the monks' house and turned through the gateway.

XI

The Fordite Order of St Benedict and St Bernard had been founded in the last century when an old rogue named Ford, who had made a fortune in the slave trade, came under the influence of John Henry Newman and suffered a startling conversion to Anglo-Catholicism. Shortly before Newman seceded to Rome, Ford died, leaving all his wealth to the Church of England for the purpose of founding a monastic order. His incensed widow eventually acquired a fraction of her husband's estate, but the Fordite monks had begun as a rich community and the careful management of their resources had ensured that the community became richer still. In this prosperity they formed a striking contrast to attempts by others to lead a cenobitic life within the Church of England, attempts which usually ran into financial difficulty.

There were four houses, all granted the status of Abbey by various benign Archbishops of Canterbury, but with one exception – the boys' school where the title had been retained to impress the parents – the word 'Abbey' was not used by the Order. This was because the Fordites liked to stress their separation from the Roman Catholic orders and considered that the word conjured up unfortunate images of the religious climate in England before the Reformation. Indeed although the Fordites lived a Benedictine way of life their English idiosyncrasies set them apart from traditional Benedictine communities. The title 'Dom' was never used either; people outside the Order were encouraged to address those monks who were ordained as if they were still Anglo-Catholic priests in the world, and apart from the London headquarters, where the Abbot-General lived in disconcerting luxury, there was a notable lack of pomp and pretentiousness in the communities.

The headquarters had once been old Ford's townhouse, the school Starwater Abbey had been his country seat and the Ruydale estate in Yorkshire had formed part of his extensive property investments, but the house at Grantchester had been acquired long after his death for the purpose of specializing in retreats for theological students, and I had stayed there on a number of occasions both before and after my ordination. The house lay on the outskirts of the village made famous by Rupert Brooke's poem, and was set in secluded grounds of five acres where the monks grew vegetables and kept bees. The Fordites' Grantchester honey, recalling the poem by Brooke, was much in demand by visitors to Cambridge.

When I rang the bell that morning the front door opened so swiftly that I jumped. I had an immediate impression of improved efficiency, and the impression was strengthened by the young doorkeeper himself who was exceptionally clean and neat in his appearance. The Fordite habit, with its vague resemblance to the habit of the Trappists, underlines the idiosyncratic nature of the Order; the over-tunic is black and sleeveless but the under-tunic is white with long sleeves which tend inevitably to grubbiness. However this monk's sleeves were sparkling white, as if he were advertising some new soap-powder, and his little brass crucifix gleamed as it hung from his leather belt.

'Good morning!' he said cheerfully, an impressive illustration of the contented celibate life. 'Can I help you?'

Despite all my troubles it was impossible not to smile at him. 'I'm Dr Ashworth from Laud's,' I said. 'I was hoping Father Reid might be free to see me for a moment.'

The monk immediately became grave. 'I'm afraid I must give you some sad news, Doctor – Father Abbot died last week and was buried on Friday.'

I was nonplussed, not merely because my plans were flung into disarray but because I had been fond enough of Father Reid to feel a keen regret that he had been separated from me. 'I'm very sorry,' I managed to say. 'I shall miss him. He was my spiritual director.' I tried to collect my thoughts. Obviously as a canon of the Cathedral I had a duty to see the new authority, express my condolences and offer him my good wishes for the future. 'Perhaps I could see Father Andrews?' I said tentatively, naming the officer who I assumed had taken Father Reid's place.

'I'm sorry, sir, but Father Prior's been transferred to London.'

The young monk's face was now expressionless and suddenly I sensed that a massive upheaval had taken place within those closed community walls. As I recalled my earlier impression of an improved efficiency it occurred to me that a new broom had begun to sweep the house very clean.

'Well, if Father Reid's dead,' I said, 'and Father Andrews has been transferred, who's now in charge?'

'Father Abbot-General has appointed someone from outside our community, sir – Father Jonathan Darrow from our house in Yorkshire.' He opened the door wide. 'Please do come in, Dr Ashworth – our new Abbot wishes to meet everyone who came under Father Reid's direction, and I'm sure he'll see you straight away.'

That settled that.

I crossed the threshold, and although I did not know it I was crossing my private Rubicon.

I was about to meet my exorcist.

TEN

'There is no part of my duty as bishop that perplexes and distresses me so much as the treatment of clergymen who have fallen into some gross impunity.'

Letters of Herbert Hensley Henson
Bishop of Durham 1920–1939
ed. E. F. BRALEY

I

I sat down in the visitors' parlour which was a large plain room containing a table and several chairs. Above the fireplace a crucifix hung on the wall but there were no pictures. A glass panel had been inserted in the door so that no monk could have an unobserved conversation with a female visitor.

It was past the hour of Mass which concluded the early services, and I knew the monks would be engaged in their private tasks before they reassembled for the next service at noon. The house was quiet. The Fordites are not bound to observe a strict rule of silence but conversation is discouraged except during the weekly recreation hour on Saturdays.

Three minutes passed. I was continually rephrasing my words of condolence, and I was still searching for the most appropriate formula when swift footsteps echoed in the hall and the new abbot strode into the room.

He was very tall, even taller than I was, and had a lean but powerful frame. His iron-grey hair was cut very short, his iron-grey eyes saw, I knew, everything there was to see, and the strong striking bone structure of his face was impressive but intimidating in its austerity. It was an irony that the lavish pectoral cross and heavy ring which symbolized his office succeeded in underlining this austerity rather than negating it. An abbot was usually considered the equal in rank of a bishop within the Church of England, and although a bishop had a pastoral duty towards any monks in his diocese, a duty acquired when he was appointed 'visitor' to their cloister, a Fordite abbot was answerable only to his Abbot-General in London and to the Archbishop of the province.

158

'Dr Ashworth?' said the stranger as he paused on the threshold of the room, and added much as the chairman of the board might have addressed a young director who interested him: 'Good morning – I'm Jon Darrow, the new Abbot here.'

He somehow managed to be formal and informal at the same time. The use of the abbreviated first name was striking and led me to assume he had kept his original name on entering the Order. Monks were supposed to choose a new name to symbolize their new life in God's service, but the Fordites regarded this cenobitic tradition as optional.

He closed the door and we shook hands. His clasp was firm, brief, confident. Mine was cautious, uncertain, perhaps even unnerved.

'I'm extremely sorry that you weren't informed of Father Reid's death,' he said, 'but unfortunately he kept no list of those he counselled so it was impossible for me to write to you.' He made the omission of a list sound like evidence of an unpardonably inefficient administration, and I began to wonder if he had ever served in the army. The authority he exuded had a certain 'spit-and-polish' quality; as I tentatively embarked on my set speech I found myself remembering the young doorkeeper's dazzling crucifix.

'I was very surprised – and greatly saddened – to hear the news – it must have been a shock to you all – '

'It was, yes,' said Father Darrow, crisply terminating my unimpressive attempt to express my condolences. 'Father Reid was held in considerable affection by the community and will be much missed.'

That disposed of Father Reid. Still trying to find my bearings I said uncertainly, 'I understand you've been brought in from outside – isn't that rather unusual? I thought that normally the community elected an abbot from among their own number.'

'It's very unusual, yes, and a stimulating challenge both for me and for my Grantchester brethren.' That disposed equally crisply of the unusual appointment. 'Please sit down, Dr Ashworth. I presume you came to see Father Reid about a spiritual matter?'

Uncertainty continued to grip me. I hesitated.

'Let me tell you a little about myself,' said Darrow, sitting down opposite me at the table. 'I think it's often difficult to confide in someone new and untried; spiritual directors are not, after all, something one acquires without thought at the local shop, like a sack of potatoes. I'm fifty-seven years old and I entered the Order when I was forty-three. Before that I was a chaplain in the prison service, and before that I was a chaplain in the Navy – in which, incidentally, I served during the War. I obtained my theology degree at Laud's. For nine years of my life I was a married man and I have a son and daughter, now grown up.' He paused. 'That, I fear, is very much of a thumbnail sketch, but I hope perhaps you may find it illuminating.'

I did. A former Naval chaplain who knew what sex was all about and had even got as far as fathering two children might well be an acceptable alternative to Jardine, and spurred on by the knowledge that I had my back to the spiritual wall I said cautiously, 'Thank you, Father. Yes, that's very helpful. I'm sorry I was so hesitant.' I tried to dispense with hesitancy. 'I came here this morning in the hope of arranging a retreat,' I said, attempting a passable imitation of my usual self-confidence. 'I thought I might return here on Friday, have a talk with you – at your convenience, naturally – and make my confession. Then I'd like to spend some time in prayer and meditation under your direction before leaving early on Sunday morning in order to attend the services in the Cathedral.'

Father Darrow was looking straight at me with his very clear grey eyes. My nerve failed. 'Well, I mustn't take up any more of your time,' I said rapidly, rising to my feet. 'If you have no objection to my plans, I'll – '

'Sit down, Dr Ashworth.'

I sunk back in my chair.

'When did you last make your confession?'

In the circumstances it was a conventional question but that did not make it easier to answer. However I thought that with luck he would accept my information without questioning it. 'Last April,' I said.

'And you made your confession to Father Reid?'

Damn. 'No,' I said casually, trying to pretend there was nothing unusual about such an evasion of one's spiritual director.

'To whom did you make your confession?'

Double-damn. This was very awkward. I cleared my throat and rubbed my nose to give myself time to think. 'I was in France,' I said at last, 'on holiday. I made my confession to a priest in a Paris church.'

'A Roman Catholic?'

'Yes.'

There was a pause. 'You discussed the matter with Father Reid, of course,' said Darrow, 'on your return.'

'Well, as a matter of fact,' I said, 'no, I didn't.'

'When did you last make your confession to Father Reid?'

'Last March, before Easter.'

'How often do you make confession?'

In my confusion I was so preoccupied that my normal practice of confession might be judged inadequate that I failed to realize he was bent on exposing the abnormality of two confessions made in rapid succession. 'Well, I'm not really an Anglo-Catholic, Father, not nowadays, and since confession isn't compulsory in the Church of England – '

'Once a year? Twice? Three times?'

160

'Once a year. During Lent.'

'I see.' There followed a pause as I belatedly realized I had revealed a situation I would have preferred to conceal. Darrow waited, but when I remained silent he said with perfect courtesy, 'Today is Tuesday. May I ask why you wish to postpone your confession till the weekend?'

Triple-damn. I had no wish to start discussing my need to return to Starbridge. 'There's a very important matter,' I said firmly, 'which I have to attend to.'

'A worldly matter?'

I was caught. If I said yes he would accuse me of putting worldly interests before my spiritual welfare. If I said no he would want to know why I was clearly reluctant to discuss a matter which was part of my spiritual life. I stared at him, and as he stared back, grave and uncompromising, I realized with the most profound uneasiness that he was formidable.

'When did you last receive the sacrament?' he said while I was floundering over his last question.

This was easier. With relief I said, 'Sunday.' And driven by the compulsion to polish away the tarnish which he had perceived on my glittering image I added, 'I was staying at Starbridge – at the palace – and the Bishop asked me to assist him at Communion.' This sounded reassuringly impressive, and I was just relaxing in my chair when he said: 'And if your own bishop were to telephone you today with the same request how would you answer him?'

In the silence that followed I felt my face grow hot as I shifted in my chair and stared down at my clasped hands. No reply was possible. I felt humiliated, angry and gripped by a violent desire to walk out. Yet I stayed – and not only because I knew I had my back to the spiritual wall. I stayed because he was mentally pinning me there and I was quite unable to wriggle away.

'What is your Christian name?' said Darrow.

'Charles.'

'Then since you've put yourself under my direction I shall call you by your Christian name – you have put yourself under my direction, haven't you,' said Darrow in a voice which made it clear he expected no argument, and I nodded. At that point I was incapable of shaking my head.

'Very well. Now, Charles, let me summarize the situation for you as you seem to be too confused to see it clearly. You come here and tell me that you wish to make confession. Because you normally make confession only once a year during Lent it would appear that some abnormal difficulty has overtaken you since you attended Holy Communion last Sunday. Moreover since your confession during Lent another abnormal difficulty apparently overtook you last April which necessitated a confession to a

Roman Catholic priest, a most unusual step for an Anglican clergyman to take and a step which you apparently felt unable to discuss with your confessor Father Reid. These abnormal difficulties suggest you need help and obviously you're not unaware of this, but you come here this morning and suggest that you put your spiritual life in abeyance for a few days while you attend to some matter which you insist is of great importance. I put it to you that nothing is more important than that you should make your confession and return to a state of grace at the very earliest opportunity, and I do beg you most earnestly to rearrange your plans so that you can return here either today or – at the very latest – tomorrow morning.'

He stopped speaking. I stared at my clasped hands and as I watched, my fingers began to twist together, interlocking until the knuckles shone white.

At last I said, 'I do realize how odd my behaviour must seem, but there's a mystery I have to solve and until it's solved I can't understand the mystery beyond the mystery, which is the mystery in my mind, and until I solve the mystery beyond the mystery, how can I hope to achieve any real understanding of what's going on?'

I was mouthing gibberish. I broke off in despair but Darrow said, 'What you're saying is that you can't make your confession because your errors are shrouded in mystery; you're saying that until you unravel this mystery you're unable to achieve the understanding which must necessarily precede any truly meaningful repentance.'

'Exactly.' I was impressed as well as deeply relieved by his grasp of the situation. 'Once I solve the mystery in the foreground,' I said with more confidence, 'then the mystery in the background – that is, the mystery in my mind which is driving me into error – will become clear and I'll be able to make an effective confession.'

'But what makes you so sure that this first mystery, the mystery in the foreground, is solvable?'

'Well, it must be.' I stared at him. 'Of course it must be.'

'Must it? In my experience the puzzles of life can seldom be unravelled easily into clear-cut solutions. Suppose you fail to solve the mystery. What then?'

'But there's no possibility I'll fail! All I have to do is to go back to Starbridge and talk to a certain person.'

'But what makes you so sure that the mystery in the background will then be triumphantly illuminated? Supposing, on the contrary, the solution of the first mystery results not in light but in darkness?'

I continued to stare at him. 'How could that happen?'

'What you're really saying is this: you're saying you need a light to illuminate the dark corners of your soul. But one has to be very careful with dark corners of the soul. Too much light too suddenly can be dangerous. The dark corners can hit back and put the light out.'

There was a long silence. Then Darrow rose to his feet. 'I'll take you to the guest-wing,' he said, 'and assign you a room. You shouldn't leave here now. It's too dangerous.'

'Dangerous!'

'You're like a yachtsman with a high fever who insists on steering straight for the rocks. Drop anchor, lie down and get well enough to plot a better course.'

'I can't. I want to but I can't.' I leant forward in a last desperate effort to explain. 'I've got to go back to Starbridge – I can think of nothing but Starbridge – it's as if Starbridge is a huge magnet pulling me so hard that I can't escape, and although I don't want to put my spiritual life in abeyance I must, I can't help myself, I can't do anything until I've solved the Starbridge mystery – but once the mystery's solved and I return to Cambridge – '

'Come straight here, no matter what time of the day or night it is.'

I could not reply, but as I looked again into those grave grey eyes I had the uncanny dread that he was clairvoyant.

I said sharply: 'I'll be all right.' I tried not to make it sound like a question.

I shall always remember what he said next. He spoke his biblical paraphrase as if it were a famous quotation. 'High and wide is the gate which leads to self-deception and illusion,' he said, 'but for those seeking truth strait is the gate and narrow the way and brave is the man who can journey there. How profound is your courage, Charles? And how deep are your reserves of spiritual strength?'

I could not answer. I knew what a weak spiritual state I was in, and unable to meet his eyes I retreated, more confused than ever, to the hall.

All he said as he opened the front door was, 'I'll pray for you.'

I wanted to linger. I could feel the power of his mind pulling me back, but by that time I was being driven by a compulsion which was quite beyond my control and hurrying to my car I set out on the road to disaster.

II

When I returned to my rooms to pack a bag for the journey I found a letter from Jardine had arrived by the second post. Recognizing his handwriting at once I ripped open the envelope.

'My dear Dr Ashworth,' I read, 'I have spoken on the telephone today to the Abbot of Starwater, and he told me that the man you should see at the Fordites' Grantchester house is without question Father Jonathan

163

Darrow. Father Reid, I'm sad to say, is no longer with us and the Grantchester community has only just acquired this new Abbot who has a first-class reputation as a director of souls. He comes from the Fordites' Yorkshire house where he was Master of Novices, but apparently his work has extended far beyond the training of monks. I have also spoken on the telephone today to one of the bishops of the Northern Province who told me he has sent troubled clergymen to Darrow on several occasions and always with the very best results. I do urge you not to delay your next visit to Grantchester, and in trusting that this letter will be of help to you in your difficulty, I remain yours sincerely, ADAM ALEXANDER STARO.'

I remembered Jardine saying how much he hated the telephone. I was impressed by his evident concern for my welfare but I was intrigued too.

I wondered how far he identified with me.

III

So I came once more to Starbridge, radiant glittering Starbridge, and as I approached the city through the pass in the hills I saw again the spire of the Cathedral appearing and disappearing as the road twisted and turned, the vision of truth fleetingly glimpsed but continually erased in the mirrors of fantasy and illusion.

I was again too late for Evensong, but after I had taken a room overlooking the river-garden at the Staro Arms I made myself read the office. Then I extracted the bottle of whisky from my bag, poured myself a stiff drink and lit a cigarette. I was wearing grey trousers with a sports jacket and an open-necked shirt, and as I glanced in the glass I thought I no longer looked like a salesman hawking a dubious product but like an actor who was having trouble remembering his lines.

I had a second stiff whisky. Then I went downstairs to the telephone kiosk in the hall.

At the palace the chaplain picked up the receiver and after the necessary exchange of pleasantries I asked for Lyle. A long delay followed, and I was just wondering if she was trying to invent an excuse for avoiding a conversation with me when her voice said sharply, 'Charles?'

'Darling – ' In my relief that she had made no attempt to evade the call I allowed myself the luxury of an endearment ' – I'm back in Starbridge and I must see you. Can you dine this evening?'

'You're in *Starbridge*?' She sounded dazed.

'I could collect you in half an hour – '

'Just a moment.' As she put the receiver aside I heard her say to Gerald Harvey, 'Where's the Bishop?'

'Lyle!' I shouted but she was gone. I nearly hung up in rage but sheer obstinacy made me stand my ground and seconds later Jardine was exclaiming, 'My dear Canon, why didn't you let us know you were returning? You could have stayed at the palace!'

This confused me. I had been expecting hostility, not hospitality.

'I felt I couldn't possibly impose – after the awkward aspects of my last visit – '

'Nonsense! Come and dine!'

'Tonight?'

'Why not? We'll expect you at seven-thirty. I shall be so interested to hear about your long luncheon with Loretta,' said Jardine, and rang off without waiting for a reply.

IV

Having consumed a third whisky I changed into my clerical clothes and set off on foot up Eternity Street towards the Close. After my long drive it was a relief to forsake the car, but as I reached the palace gates the rain began to fall and I was obliged to sprint the last yards to the front door.

The butler seemed pleased to see me. The unexpected revival of last week's doomed romance would no doubt provoke further enjoyable speculation over the teacups in the servants' hall.

'Are there many guests expected tonight, Shipton?'

'None at all, sir. The Bishop and Mrs Bishop were due to go to London with Miss Christie today but unfortunately their host was unwell and the visit had to be cancelled.'

'So there'll be no one here tonight except – '

' – except the three of them and yourself, sir. Mr Harvey's dining out.' And opening the door of the drawing-room he announced in his most melancholy voice, 'Dr Ashworth, my Lord.'

Jardine was alone by the window, his hands in his pockets, his slim frame emanating his characteristic restless energy, his eyes watching the rain as it streamed against the glass. As I walked in he turned to face me but I saw no hint of distaste or disapproval in his expression.

'Ah, there you are!' he said, moving towards me with his hand outstretched. 'Welcome back to Starbridge. Did you get my letter?'

'Yes – thank you, Bishop. It was extremely good of you to go to so much trouble.' We shook hands. 'I did in fact meet Father Darrow this morning and I've arranged to begin a retreat under his direction this weekend.'

'I'm very glad to hear it, although surprised you saw fit to delay the retreat in order to return here.'

I made no reply but picked up a copy of *Country Life* which was lying on a nearby chair and embarked on a detailed examination of the cover.

'I was of course much disturbed when Lady Starmouth telephoned yesterday to say that you'd abducted Loretta for an excessively long luncheon,' said Jardine, 'but I think it would be best if we avoided discussing your continuing obsession with my past until we're alone together with the port.'

'What a pity,' I said, flicking through the pages of *Country Life*. 'I was hoping for another theological discussion once the ladies had retired. I thought we might debate Luther's view that the refusal of marital rights should constitute a ground for divorce.' And I tossed aside the magazine.

The door opened and in fluttered Mrs Jardine. 'Dr Ashworth!' she exclaimed as Jardine and I continued to stare at each other. 'How nice to see you again – although you seem to have brought some very tiresome rain with you from Cambridge!'

'Yes, I'm afraid that storm you feared has finally arrived, Mrs Jardine,' I said, taking her hand in mind, and as I glanced beyond her I saw Lyle watching tensely from the doorway.

V

Of the three of them Mrs Jardine alone behaved as if my swift return to Starbridge were unremarkable, and during dinner she maintained the burden of the conversation by chatting about subjects of an almost intolerable banality. Lyle was polite but withdrawn; we exchanged only a few stilted sentences, and once the dinner table lay between us I had no opportunity to take a close look at her ring which she was as usual wearing on the wedding finger of her left hand. Meanwhile with a sublime disregard for the tension in the room Mrs Jardine was telling me some long story about how she had forgotten to go to a charity committee meeting because the third child of the Canon in Residence had contracted mumps. She then asked me what kind of charity work my mother did – an awkward question since my mother led an idle life drinking too many cocktails and getting on my father's nerves. However I had only to mention my mother's fondness for fashion magazines and Mrs Jardine was telling me about the fashion show she had organized to raise money for the children of the unemployed dockers in Starmouth.

'Lyle organized it,' said the Bishop, who appeared sunk in boredom at the far end of the table, and suddenly as I remembered Loretta saying that I might be reading too much into people's innocent reactions, I wondered if the tension existed only in my mind; I wondered if this unusually private glimpse of the *ménage* was revealing not the sinister undercurrents I had anticipated but merely the blameless tedium of a well-worn regime.

'No, Carrie did the organizing!' Lyle was insisting to the Bishop. 'I merely hired the hall, instructed the caterers and sent out the invitations.'

I was just wondering what had been left for Mrs Jardine to do when Mrs Jardine herself exclaimed warmly, 'You were wonderful, Lyle!' She turned to me with enthusiasm. 'Does your mother have a companion to help her, Dr Ashworth?'

'Only my father.'

'Maybe we can discuss your father over the port,' said the Bishop, finally unable to resist livening up the dinner by shooting a provocative verbal arrow into the conversation. 'That could prove an interesting debate.'

'More interesting than Luther on divorce?'

Lyle glanced up from her food. I was looking straight at her. Immediately she glanced away and began to dissect her potato.

'Talking of fathers, did I ever tell you about my own father, Dr Ashworth?' enquired Mrs Jardine, swiftly terminating the silence, and no further pause was allowed to develop in the conversation until the end of the meal when she felt obliged to refresh her voice with a sip of water.

At once I said to Lyle, 'When am I going to see you tomorrow?'

Lyle's eyes seemed to darken. I glanced instinctively at the Bishop but to my surprise it was Mrs Jardine who spoke first.

'I'm terribly sorry, Dr Ashworth,' she said, 'but I'm afraid I'll be needing Lyle all day tomorrow, and then on Thursday we go off to Bath and Wells – well, it's Wells actually, but we're staying with the *Bishop* of Bath and Wells because Alex has been invited to preach a special commemorative sermon – what exactly are they commemorating, Alex?'

'I've forgotten,' said Jardine, and instantly laughed at the absurdity. Lyle and Mrs Jardine laughed too, and suddenly I longed to smash the innocuous façade of the conversation. I said abruptly to Lyle, 'In that case I'd like to see you alone this evening before I leave. I want to talk to you about your signet-ring.'

I thought I saw Lyle turn a shade paler but it was impossible to be sure.

'Oh, isn't it a lovely ring!' exclaimed Mrs Jardine, innocence personified, but as she succeeded once more in cloaking the tension with banality I wondered if she were deliberately checking every abnormal turn in the conversation. 'People often remark on it! I remember I had a ring once – '

'Will you tell me later how you acquired that ring?' I said to Lyle.

'Of course she'll tell you!' exclaimed the Bishop with impatience. 'But why wait till later? The subject hardly merits a private interview! Tell him now, Lyle.'

Lyle said composed, 'The Bishop's stepmother gave it to me. It had great sentimental memories for her but she could no longer wear it because the joints of her fingers were swollen with arthritis. I was touched because

I admired her very much, and I wear the ring in memory of her.'

'Ah, how interesting!' I said, pouring myself a fourth glass of claret from the decanter. 'That must be the ring the Bishop's father gave her during their highly unusual wedding ceremony.'

Jardine said at once, 'That'll be all, Shipton,' and both butler and footman withdrew.

As soon as the door closed I said to Lyle, 'I was wondering if the ring meant that you too had been through a highly unusual wedding ceremony.'

'If that's a joke,' said Lyle in a low voice, 'I don't think it's funny.'

'It's no joke and I didn't come here to be amusing.' Draining my glass I reached for the decanter again.

'Dr Ashworth,' said Mrs Jardine with surprising strength, 'I'm very distressed to see you not behaving as a gentleman should. I think you forget yourself.'

'Mrs Jardine,' I said equally firmly as I poured myself a fifth glass of claret, 'I came down to Starbridge to see Lyle but you and your husband are clearly conspiring to prevent me from having any conversation with her alone. In the circumstances can you wonder that my annoyance is verging on anger and that my good manners are becoming frayed at the edges?'

'I don't want to have any conversation with you alone,' said Lyle, immediately responding to the challenge.

'Why not? Because you're afraid you'll give me another adulterous kiss – like last Saturday's kiss which kept you from Communion the next morning because you felt you'd betrayed your husband?'

Lyle was speechless but the Bishop at once leant forward to address his wife. 'It's all right, Carrie,' he said. 'Don't be alarmed. I'm afraid Dr Ashworth is mentally very disturbed indeed.'

'You're damn right I'm disturbed!' I said, tossing the 'damn' into the conversation to smash its normality beyond repair. 'What's happening here would disturb anyone!'

'You're drunk!' said Lyle in contempt, and before I could reply Jardine said curtly, 'Of course he's drunk. He reeked of whisky when he arrived and he's been drinking claret as if it were lemonade. Carrie – '

'Yes, of course, dearest.' She rose with perfect dignity to her feet. 'Lyle – shall we?'

We all stood up, I resting my hands lightly on the table to steady myself, Jardine opening the door for the ladies. As Lyle walked away I shouted after her, 'He's in error! The divorce is a fantasy, the marriage a lie!'

Lyle swept out followed by Mrs Jardine. Neither of them looked back. The door closed.

'Sit down, Dr Ashworth,' said Jardine abruptly. 'It's time you and I had a very serious talk together.'

I never hesitated. I said in fury, 'You "married" Lyle five years ago just as your father "married" your stepmother. Well, that sort of behaviour might have been excusable in your father who was an eccentric uneducated widower who no doubt sincerely believed he was marrying before God, but *you*! You're well-educated, subtle, sophisticated – all the things your father never was – and *you were already married*! How can you sit on your episcopal throne and believe that what you've done could ever have God's blessing? You've cut off a young woman from a normal married life, you've perverted the vows you made at your ordination – no, don't try to tell *me* she's your wife! She's your mistress – and don't try to tell me you're divorced either! You're not divorced, not by the law and not in the eyes of God! You've just wrecked Lyle's life in order to satisfy your own selfish needs!'

I stopped speaking. I was trembling. Grabbing my glass of claret I drained it and reached for the decanter.

'Sit down, Charles,' said Jardine in his calmest voice, and as he used my Christian name I knew that like Father Darrow he was using it because he was a senior churchman trying to help one of his younger brethren in distress.

I sat down abruptly. The claret was smooth in my throat. Overcome with emotion I knocked over my glass accidentally as I replaced it on the table, and as the dregs spread in a red stain across the undrawn cloth, I had the bizarre impression that although I was the one who had launched the attack I was the one who was now bleeding.

Jardine said, deeply concerned, 'Did Father Darrow make no attempt to detain you this morning?'

'Yes, but I knew I had to come back here to solve the mystery – and I've solved it, haven't I? I've finally worked out the truth!'

'My dear Charles, I'm afraid your truth is a fantasy and you've solved absolutely nothing.'

'That's a lie!' I shouted.

'Try to keep calm. I can't help you if you persist in being truculent – and believe me, I'm most anxious to help you extricate yourself from this distressing muddle. I presume it was Loretta who told you about my father's marriage?'

'How can you call it a marriage! Your stepmother just cohabited with him and then left him to cohabit with you!'

'I'm sorry, but I can't permit such a gross distortion of the facts. My stepmother,' said Jardine, 'was in a very real sense my father's wife; certainly they both believed themselves married in the sight of God. It's true that when I finally found out there had been no legal marriage I took a priggish line – I was at the height of my narrow-minded Anglo-Catholic phase – and I did encourage her to leave him; I thought I was saving her from a life of sin by sanctioning her decision to come to Starmouth to keep house for me. But years later when she decided she had to go back I realized she'd always been as good a wife – as dutiful a wife – to my father as any woman who had been married in church. However since most people find it impossible to regard an informal marriage with charity I strongly object to the facts being circulated. I'm most distressed that Loretta was so indiscreet – and naturally it makes me wonder what on earth went on between the two of you yesterday – '

'I followed in your footsteps.' I was having trouble emptying the claret decanter into my glass. 'We went to the steep field to watch the train go by.'

'Oh, so you found out about that! Yes, I did go a little farther with her than I admitted to you – '

'In every sense of the phrase!'

Jardine looked at me carefully. Then he fetched the port decanter from the sideboard and said, 'I'm not going to offer you this because you've had quite enough to drink already, but I don't see why I shouldn't take a glass to fortify myself against your fantasies. Now about this sad little incident in the field – '

' "Sad little incident"? My God, what a way to describe adultery!'

'*Adultery?*'

'Don't you try and deny it!' I shouted. 'I had her myself in the same corner of that spinney where she had you!'

Jardine stared at me. Then he walked to the door, glanced out into the hall to make sure no one was listening and closed the door again. 'Charles,' he said in his gentlest voice as he returned to the table, 'I want you to recall Loretta's words with great care because although people can change very much during the course of two decades I can't believe she would have changed enough to lie to you on this point. Did she actually say that I'd committed adultery?'

I tried to think. My mind was in chaos, but I had a sickening memory of Loretta saying, 'You're going in', and suddenly I knew she had been neither apprehensive nor dubious but surprised.

'Of course,' said Jardine in the voice of one who states the obvious, 'I never penetrated her. The adultery exists only in your mind, Charles.'

VII

'I admit some embraces took place,' said Jardine. 'I admit my behaviour was thoroughly reprehensible for a clergyman. But there was no consummation. How could there have been? How could I have gone on as a clergyman if adultery had taken place?'

All I managed to say was, 'I don't believe you.' But I did.

'I wonder how I can make you see that it's the truth. Perhaps I can make my abstinence more credible if I admit it was due not so much to virtue as to fear, the fear which reflected my horror of waywardness, my horror of ending up like my father. Can't you see? I was incapable of consummating an adulterous union, Charles, psychologically incapable of it.'

I covered my face with my hands.

At last Jardine said, again using his gentlest voice: 'And now let me talk about Lyle. I admit that when she entered my house at Radbury ten years ago I was attracted to her – in that tiresome inconvenient manner which is so common among middle-aged men whose marriages have entered an awkward phase. Naturally I told my wife that Lyle would have to go, but Carrie's nerves were so bad at that time that when she objected I gave way – and not only because I shrank from any course which might have tilted her into a full-scale nervous breakdown; I gave way because I felt Carrie's objection reinforced my own opinion that Lyle was the heaven-sent solution to our troubles. The situation was desperate. I was spending so much time trying to cope with my wife that I could barely cope with my duties as Dean, but when Lyle came I was set free to serve God properly at last.'

He paused. I had uncovered my eyes but could only stare at the red stain on the table-cloth.

'I'm sure you see how inevitable my next decision was,' said Jardine. 'I realized that if Lyle were to remain in my house I could on no account permit even the faintest trace of impropriety in my manner to her. Impropriety wouldn't merely have been stupid; it would have been ungrateful to God, who had sent Lyle to us to ease so much of our sadness and difficulty. You may be thinking that this attitude of extreme propriety towards Lyle was hard for me to adopt, and you'd be right; it was. But curiously enough once the attitude had been adopted it was easy to maintain because my marriage became so much more tolerable. Carrie greatly improved, thanks to Lyle's care, and the result was that we were able to resume our marital relationship after a long interval. That disposed of my last doubts. I knew then it was right that Lyle should stay.'

Again he paused, and as I raised my eyes from the table-cloth to the empty claret decanter I was aware of him sipping his port. 'However,' he said, 'you mustn't think I haven't spent a lot of time worrying about Lyle's welfare. Our triangle would hardly be morally acceptable, would it, if Lyle were unhappy and unfulfilled. But Charles, the point here is that if Lyle really were unhappy and unfulfilled she wouldn't stay. It's impossible for me to explain her aversion to matrimony without breaching her confidence so all I can say is that a psychological aversion, rooted in her past, does exist, but nevertheless Carrie and I have both made great efforts to help her overcome this difficulty – for instance, we've always encouraged her to go out with young men, and I'm sure you'll remember that it was I who urged her to dine with you at the Staro Arms. Of course Lyle's sometimes tempted to indulge in a romantic flutter or two, but the rock-bottom truth is that she likes her life exactly as it is, and if she wishes to remain single she has a perfect right to do so. I quite see that this must be highly frustrating for you, but – '

'I'm going to marry her!' I was struggling to overcome the terrifying conviction that every word he said was true. 'You're telling me all these lies because you're jealous, possessive and deeply in love with her yourself!'

'My dear Charles – '

'If your wife died you'd marry Lyle tomorrow!'

'Let's try and keep this conversation rational, shall we? I admit,' said Jardine, 'that when I first met Lyle I told myself I'd marry her if ever I became a widower, but I soon realized one can hardly spend one's life waiting for one's wife to die! That way insanity lies. The truth was – and still is – that I'm a married man, I'm a clergyman and I'm stuck with the status quo, but at least it's a status quo that enables me to serve God to the best of my ability with the support of a loving dutiful wife of whom I'm extremely fond. As I remind myself daily I'm very lucky to have any workable status quo at all, and need I stress that it would be quite unworkable if I hadn't so far recovered from my initial attraction that I can now regard Lyle with a healthy affection and respect? I think not. The facts speak for themselves. Be reasonable, Charles! I know you're far from being in a rational frame of mind, but isn't is patently obvious that there's nothing improper going on here?'

It was. Yet I found myself quite unable to admit it. I began stubbornly. 'I think – ' but he interrupted me.

'Yes,' he said, 'this is where we get to you and what you think – and this is where we meet two intractable problems. The first is that you're at present too drunk even to face your difficulties, let alone grapple with them, and the second is that although you urgently need counselling I'm quite the wrong person to give it to you. I'm part of the crisis, aren't I?'

I was so incensed that he should call me drunk merely because I had had a little extra claret that I shouted, 'I don't want your damned counselling!' I tried to grab the port decanter but he whipped it away.

'No,' he said severely. 'No more.'

I waited till he had replaced it on the table and then I lunged forward, swiped the decanter from under his nose and began to pour the port into my empty glass.

'You're being very foolish,' said Jardine, 'but you want attention, don't you? You're like a little child who misbehaves in order to get noticed. You say you don't want my counselling but in fact I suspect that's exactly what you're angling for. You're deep in some private fantasy, and – '

'*You're* the one who's deep in some private fantasy if you think you're deceiving me!' I was now so enraged that I hardly knew what I said. 'Do you think I can't see exactly what's going on? You're just fighting tooth and nail to stop your glittering image coming apart at the seams!'

'No,' said Jardine, 'you're the one who's fighting that particular battle, and the glittering image is falling apart before my eyes.' He rose to his feet. 'Let me call my chauffeur and ask him to drive us over to the monks at Starwater.'

'I'm not leaving this bloody room,' I said, 'until you bloody well admit you've been sleeping with Lyle!'

'Charles, you need help. I can't give it to you and you absolutely must let me take you to someone who – '

'You're not washing your hands of me!' I shouted. 'I'm not going to be brushed off, I'm not going to be kicked out, I'm not going to be treated as if – '

'All right! All right, all right, all right . . .' Jardine cast a quick glance at the door to reassure himself it was still closed. 'You want me to be the one who helps you. Very well. I'll do what you want, but I do it greatly against my better judgement and only because you're giving me no choice. Now – ' He drew up his chair in order to sit down at my side ' – let me try to bring you closer to what I fear will be a very unpalatable reality . . .'

VIII

'For some reason,' said Jardine, 'you've picked me to be the central figure in your life at present. We won't call this a fantasy because you evidently find that word hurtful, so we'll just say that you were experiencing certain difficulties in your private life and when you met me I seemed in some mysterious way to provide you with a solution. Obviously you liked the idea – which that old fool Lang had put into your head – that I was an eminent churchman who led a double life. No, that's an understatement. You didn't just like the idea – you were enrapt by it.

'So you arrive in Starbridge and soon you've far exceeded your brief from Lang – after all, it must have quickly become very clear to you that I'm not the sort of man who compromises himself by dabbling in foolish love-letters or keeping an uncensored journal. However you're not interested in Lang's brief, not any more. What you're now interested in is the possibility that behind the glittering image of my ecclesiastical success lies a life steeped in the kind of error which would make even Lang's senile speculations look pale. You embrace this theory with such zest that it becomes necessary for you to prove it, but the interesting part is that the more obsessed you become with proving my guilt the more fervently you swear you're on my side. By this time, of course, you've parted company with reality altogether. By this time you're acting out the most elaborate and fantastic of delusions – '

I had levered myself to my feet. My voice said trembling, 'I refuse to listen to this.'

'But you will. You will, Charles, you will.' The lambent eyes were suddenly so bright that I could not look away. 'Sit down, Charles,' said Jardine and at once I sank back in my chair. 'Charles, listen to me – listen to me, Charles, because I say you can't afford to go on with this fantasy any longer, you must try to face reality, and the reality is that you're ill, mentally ill – '

'No – *no* – '

'Yes, Charles, yes – how could any normal man have misinterpreted my situation in such an extraordinary and bizarre manner? The truth is that the man I am has nothing to do with the man you think I am. You've invented me. I exist only in your imagination. You think you know me so well that you can see numerous resemblances between us, but every one of them's an illusion, an illusion which is necessary to support your longing to believe we're identical. And why do you want to believe that we're identical? Because you think you can justify your own unfortunate behaviour by saying you're only following my example – you feel you can escape from your problems by projecting them on to me. So you place me in front of you as if I were a blank screen and your mind the magic-lantern projector, but in fact it's *your* image, not mine, which you're seeing reflected. The real mystery here, Charles, is not what's going on at Starbridge – that's just a drama you've invented to divert yourself from your problems. The real mystery is what's going on in your soul. Why does an extremely able and successful young clergyman with a brilliant future and an unclouded past suddenly, for no apparent reason, start mentally falling apart?'

I jumped up, knocking over my chair, and as he too sprang to his feet I said, 'You can't talk to me like that, you can't.' I was so dizzy that I had to grab the edge of the table.

'I'm sorry – I've taken a risk in speaking so plainly but I could see no other way of convincing you that you simply must have help. I myself can now do no more but I'm sure the monks at Starwater – '

'You're rejecting me!' I shouted. 'You keep rejecting me! You've rejected me over and over again!'

'My God,' said Jardine, suddenly ashen, 'this is what happened with your father, isn't it? You poor boy, I didn't realize – oh, what a hash I've made of this, I'm so damnably sorry – '

I shoved him aside and rushed from the room.

IX

I have no clear recollection of my journey back to the Staro Arms. All I remember is the hotel receptionist's disapproving stare as she gave me the change for the telephone call. Then I shut myself in the hall kiosk again and asked the operator to connect the line to Starmouth Court.

By the time Loretta came to the telephone I was almost beyond speech but I managed to say, 'Why didn't you tell me the whole truth?'

'What do you mean?'

'He didn't do it, did he? He didn't go in.'

'Wait,' she said. 'Wait. I understand what you're saying and I'm willing to talk, but not on the phone. Where are you?'

'Starbridge.'

'Okay, obviously I can't see you tonight, but tomorrow – '

'I'm coming tonight.'

'But Charles – '

'I've got to see you. If he lied about you I'll know he lied about everything,' I said, and rang off before she could reply.

X

In my room I changed back into my grey trousers, sports jacket and open-necked shirt. I also drank two glasses of water in pursuit of sobriety. Then I packed my bag, paid my bill and left the hotel.

The drive took less time than I had anticipated for there was little traffic at that time of night. Beyond the Surrey border on the ridge called the Hog's Back I felt tired but I cured that by stopping the car and drinking from my bottle of whisky. Staring at the lights which stretched north to London in the valley below me, I thought of Starbridge, its radiance masking unutterable horrors, but that memory was too painful to bear and taking another shot from the bottle I drove on into the dark.

It was after midnight when I reached Starmouth Court but a light was shining in the little morning-room where Loretta and I had first met. I glimpsed her figure silhouetted against the window, and a moment later I was stumbling into her arms.

'Everyone's gone to bed,' she said. 'Come and have a drink. You look shot to pieces.'

In the morning-room she passed me a glass of brandy and I drank half of it straight off. Then I said, 'Just what the devil did go on in that bloody spinney nineteen years ago?'

'We made love.'

'Completely?'

'No.'

'But why the *hell* didn't you make that clear?'

'Oh, for God's sake, Charles, give me credit for at least the minimum of good manners! You were panting to make love to me. How could I say, "Wait a minute!" and regale you with a blow by blow description of what had happened with Alex?'

'But I only went ahead because I thought he'd gone ahead too!'

'My God, that's a bizarre remark!'

'But if I'd known there'd been no penetration – '

'The way he made love that hardly mattered. Alex did tell me that without penetration there was no adultery according to the law of England – remember me saying he'd have made a good lawyer? – but when one's busy having an orgasm the legal niceties don't seem very important. As far as I was concerned I'd made love to him and he'd made love to me and – '

'But he told me the truth.' I could think of nothing else. ' "I never penetrated her," he said. So if he told me the truth about you then he must have told me the truth about Lyle – '

'What did he say?'

I started drinking my brandy rapidly again. 'He called my theory a fantasy.'

'I'm not surprised.'

'Shut up!' I shouted.

She jumped. 'Charles – darling – take it easy – '

I tried to apologize by kissing her but she was unresponsive and the next moment she was removing the brandy bottle to the far side of the room.

'Maybe this is where I start to dream the dream,' she said drily. 'You're obviously incapable of dreaming anything at the moment so I'll have to do the dreaming for you to help you along.' She glanced at her watch. 'How long would it take to get to Cambridge at this time of night?'

'Less than three hours. Perhaps less than two and a half. Petrol will be a problem but there's an all-night garage on the Great North Road.' I swallowed the rest of my brandy. 'Well, if you're washing your hands of me I may as well go.'

'Don't be dumb, I'm coming with you.'

'What!'

'Well, someone's got to look after you, haven't they, and there doesn't seem to be anyone else volunteering for the job!'

'But I wouldn't dream of dragging you all the way to Cambridge!'

'And I wouldn't dream of letting you go alone when you've obviously been hitting the bottle. I'm going to drive you home.'

'But you're an American! You'll drive on the wrong side of the road!'

'Don't be ridiculous! I may have my faults but I'm not incompetent. Excuse me while I just scribble a line to Evelyn – and I'd better call a hotel to let them know I'll be arriving in the middle of the night. Which hotel should I stay at?'

'The Blue Boar. But Loretta – '

'I'll use the phone in the hall. Just a minute, Charles.'

I sank back on the couch, but as soon as I was alone the pain began to pound me and seconds later I was retrieving the brandy bottle.

XI

Somewhere north of Hatfield she said, 'Where does that Abbot live – the one you told me about?'

'Heaven. He died and changed his address. Found that out this morning.'

'Is there a new Abbot yet?'

'You bet there's a new Abbot – as you Yankees would say. He's an ex-Naval chaplain called Darrow who knows all about sex. Married nine years. Became a monk. Amazing.' I took another sip of whisky. I had stopped having drinks now, of course. I just had little sips occasionally.

'He sounds like the kind of guy who could cope with anything. How do I get to the Abbey to deliver you?'

'Keep going to Cambridge. Turn off just before you get there. Little village. Grantchester. Like the poem by Rupert Brooke. My wife used to like his poetry . . . Did I ever tell you about my wife?'

'You said her name once. Jane.'

'Jane, yes. I loved her very much. She was so pretty, so sweet, so good, and I was so unfit, so unworthy, so . . . But Father Darrow will be able to cope. Did I tell you he'd even fathered two children? Extraordinary. How could such a man become a monk, you ask. How could any man become a monk, you ask. Well, I'll tell you. It's a special gift – a "charism", as we say in the Church. In fact Father Darrow is what we in the Church would call "charismatic". He's six foot three and looks as if he practises telepathy in his spare time.'

'Well, start exercising your telepathy, Father Darrow,' said Loretta, 'and lay out the welcome-mat for Charles.'

I took another sip of whisky to help me face the thought of Darrow waiting beyond the welcome-mat, and the car sped steadily on through the night towards Grantchester.

XII

The porch light was shining at the Fordite mansion but the rest of the house was in darkness. Halting the car Loretta switched off the engine and turned to face me.

'I'll leave the car-keys with the bell-hop at the Blue Boar,' she said. 'Have you got that, Charles?'

'Car-keys. Blue Boar. Porter. What funny words you Americans use!'

'Do you have a suitcase in the trunk?'

'No, I have a bag in the boot.' Opening the door I levered myself from the passenger seat and leant against the car as I gazed up at the stars. 'Beautiful,' I said. 'Reminds me of God. Utterly transcendent. Says Karl Barth.'

Loretta was moving swiftly up the steps to ring the bell. Leaving my bag by the front door she ran back to the car.

'Come along, darling. This way.'

'I love you, Loretta. Marry me.'

'No, you're going to marry Lyle. Remember?' She was steadying me as I cautiously navigated the steps.

'But you could cope. You're coping. I love you. That wonderful sex – if I could have you every night – '

' – you'd get tired of me. Look, someone's opening the door. Come on, darling, just another couple of steps. Nearly there.'

A little white-haired monk appeared on the threshold. I had never seen him before but he said: 'It's Dr Ashworth, isn't it? Father Abbot's been expecting you.'

Then I knew Darrow was already exercising his charism.

XIII

Loretta kissed me and said, 'Good luck.'

'I'll never forget you, never,' I said, but she was already on her way back to the car. The engine started, she waved goodbye and seconds later I could see only a pair of red lights vanishing beyond the gateway.

'This way, Doctor,' said the little monk, steering me firmly over the threshold with one hand while he carried my bag with the other. He closed the door by a gentle push of his foot. 'This way.'

I was guided through a door which led into the guest-wing, and manoeuvred with skill to the corridor of bedrooms on the floor above. We finally stopped outside a door where the numeral four was painted on the panel, and the little monk, never relaxing his grip on me for a moment, set down my bag to turn the handle.

'Four's my lucky number,' I said. 'I'm so lucky, so privileged, so successful, it's really amazing how lucky I've always been. Did you know I was one of the Archbishop of Canterbury's chaplains when he was Archbishop of York? My parents were so proud. I come from a wonderful home – I've got wonderful parents, a wonderful brother, everything's always been so wonderful – I've had every possible advantage and yet I don't deserve it, don't deserve it at all because I'm so unworthy, so unfit.' I sat down very suddenly on the bed. The room was small and neat, the bed placed in the corner, the table and chair by the window, the wardrobe against the inner wall, the basin in another corner by the unlit gas fire. There were no curtains, only a black blind, and no pictures. On the bedside table stood a lamp and a bible.

'Now take a little rest on your bed,' said the monk, speaking to me as if I were an exhausted child who had been thoroughly overstimulated by too much excitement, 'and I'll tell Father Abbot you're here.'

'He already knows,' I said, kicking off my shoes and slumping back against the pillows.

The little monk smiled and disappeared.

The room began to revolve.

Closing my eyes I at last escaped into oblivion.

XIV

Someone came into the room not long afterwards but I never saw him. Someone unpacked my bag and put it away on top of the wardrobe, someone put my prayer-book by the Bible, someone put two aspirins and a glass of water on the bedside table. Someone, without doubt, paused to say a prayer for us both.

Then the light was turned out, the door was closed and I was left to sleep dreamlessly in the dark.

XV

I awoke in excruciating pain. My head was hurting, my stomach was hurting, my intestines were hurting, and beyond them my mind was hurting, every grain of it, and my soul was screaming steadily but soundlessly for relief.

But relief was absent and meanwhile I had to grapple with physical humiliation. I got my eyes open. They were aching. I struggled upright but had to bend over low to keep conscious. I crawled to the basin. I vomited. And all the time my soul was screaming steadily but soundlessly for relief.

I crawled back to the bed, saw the aspirins and somehow managed to swallow them, but I was too ill to be helped by pills and the next moment I was vomiting again. I only just managed to reach the basin in time. I levered myself upright, shuddering, shivering, stupefied with the pain, and when I looked in the mirror above the basin I saw myself as if in a distorted glass and recognized the stranger I was too afraid to know.

I backed away, nearly fainted, crashed into the table, slid down by the bed. 'Oh God . . .' The pain was overwhelming me. I wanted to die. I knew it was a sin to pray for death but the pain was beyond all endurance and the never-ending scream of my soul, as it surveyed the enormity of my shattering failures, was finally finding expression in the agonized words which streamed from my mouth like a haemorrhage. 'My God, my God – forgive me, don't leave me, help me, *help me*, HELP ME – '

The door of the room opened and in walked Father Darrow.

PART TWO

THE MYSTERY BEYOND THE MYSTERY

'I am only facing the two quite general, but quite sufficiently rousing facts: that we all of us have "selves" (the enemies of our good true selves) to fight, and that only so fighting are we adult, fruitful and happy.'

Spiritual Counsels and Letters of
Baron Friedrich von Hügel
ed. DOUGLAS V. STEERE

ELEVEN

'You will realise that the care of your health is a religious duty.'
More Letters of Herbert Hensley Henson
Bishop of Durham 1920–1939
ed. E. F. BRALEY

I

I gasped: 'I'm cut off from God.' I was in terror. I was shuddering from head to foot. Tears were streaming down my face. 'He's gone. He's rejected me. He's not here – '

'He's here but you can't see him. You've been blinded.'

'Blinded – '

'It's only temporary but meanwhile you must do exactly as I say. Let's try and get you up from the floor – and on to the bed – that's it – '

'I'm being invaded.' I was shuddering again, gasping for breath. 'Without God – all the demons – taking over – telling me I'm not fit to – '

'Take this.' He shoved his pectoral cross hard into my hand. 'The cross bars their path. No demon can withstand the power of Christ.'

'*But He's not here – *'

'He's here. He's here whenever his followers are gathered together in His name. He's here.'

I looked past the cross and saw the Spirit. It was there in his eyes, absolutely real, immediately recognizable. The demons retreated. I said not to Darrow but to the Spirit, 'Don't leave me.'

'There's no question of abandonment. When you're calmer you'll realize that, so your first duty to yourself – and to God – is to be calm. Keep holding the cross in your right hand and give me your left. That's it . . . And try to breathe better, take deep breaths . . . Good. Now I'm going to say a prayer for you, a silent prayer, and I want you to listen with your mind and try to hear what I'm saying.'

Silence fell. I obediently listened but I heard nothing. However after a while I became aware in my darkness of a strange heat. The cross slipped as my right hand began to sweat, and my left hand, enclosed between Darrow's palms, began to tingle. Thinking it was afflicted with cramp I

183

tried to shift its position but he at once tightened his grip and the tingling continued. I was so fascinated that I made no further movement but sat docilely on the bed with my eyes closed. He had pulled up the chair from the table and was sitting within inches of me but on a higher level.

Slowly my hand was released. I opened my eyes to find he was watching me, and as our glances met he said: 'Did you hear the prayer?'

'No. But I remembered Our Lord saying: "Lo, I am with you always, even unto the end of the world".'

'And now you're calm.' He smiled, quite unsurprised by my reply, and as I belatedly realized that the words of comfort without doubt reflected the essence of his prayer, I saw he was not only satisfied with my progress but pleased with his own uncanny skill. Slowly I said, 'You're a healer. You helped me not only by prayer but by channelling power through your hands. That was the charism of healing.'

'You're very flattering,' he said, 'but one could also say you healed yourself by breathing deeply, concentrating your mind on a fixed task and cutting off the supply of adrenalin which was drowning you.'

I thought about that. He let me think about it. There was no attempt to hurry me. We continued to sit calmly together, I dirty and dishevelled in my grey trousers and crumpled shirt, he crisp and clean in his black habit with the white sleeves. As I continued to clutch his cross I became aware that life was, for the moment, bearable. My soul had stopped screaming. I was experiencing a remission of pain.

At last I said: 'I suppose I'm having a nervous breakdown.'

'Oh, I've always thought that a very unhelpful term – why don't we leave it to the medical gentlemen?' said Darrow carelessly with that touch of confidence excusable in a healer who knows he may succeed where doctors fail, and suddenly he seemed so approachable, so compellingly easy to trust. Before I could stop myself I said, 'I don't want to go to a lunatic asylum.'

'There's no question of you going to a lunatic asylum.'

'You don't think I'm – '

'Obviously you're going through some profound spiritual ordeal but defining it in questionable medical terms is simply a waste of breath; it does nothing to solve the problem.'

I managed to say, 'How does the problem get solved?'

'If I may use the terms you employed so intriguingly yesterday, I'd say we have to examine the mystery and then look at the mystery beyond the mystery in order to locate the source of your pain and heal it. But first we must attend to practical matters. You're going to be here for some time. Are there any engagements you should cancel, any matters which have to be attended to?'

I remembered my car at the Blue Boar and gave him the telephone number of a friend who would remove it to Laud's. As he jotted down the information in a notebook I added that Lang would be expecting to hear from me, but before I could say more I found to my horror that my eyes were filling with tears. 'I can't talk to him.' I whispered. 'I can't talk about – ' But I was unable to finish the sentence.

'Leave him to me,' said Darrow as if the Archbishop were a troublesome schoolboy. 'Is he expecting to hear from you this morning?'

'No, there's no great urgency, but – '

'We'll draft a message for him later. Now, Charles, your next duty to yourself – and to God – is to regain your physical fitness because as far as I know no one's yet tackled a spiritual ordeal successfully when they're worn out and hung over. How much did you drink yesterday?'

I tried to tot up the large drinks and the little sips but lost count.

'Was yesterday just a binge or have you been drinking heavily for some time?'

'A binge. But – ' I hesitated before forcing myself to add, 'I've been drinking more than I used to.'

'How do you behave when you're drunk? Do you become the life and soul of the party? Or do you merely fall asleep? Or do you perhaps become someone you most definitely don't want to know when you're sober?'

'The latter. I become angry and aggressive.'

'The angry stranger . . . Yes, well, we'll take a look at him later but meanwhile you must rest. I absolve you from reading the morning office because you're too sick to do it properly, but I'll bring you a book to look at if sleep proves difficult. Could you keep the aspirin down? No? Very well, I'll bring you some alka-seltzer.'

'If I could have some black coffee – '

'No, I want you relaxed, not stimulated, and besides any liquid serves to flush out a hangover.' Removing my glass he refilled it from the basin. 'Now I'm going to leave you for five minutes,' he said, replacing the glass on the bedside table, 'and while I'm gone you're to put on your pyjamas and get between the sheets.'

I clutched the cross and fought my panic but panic won. 'Don't go.' Shame overwhelmed me. 'I'm sorry – I'm being so stupid, so weak – '

'Michael, whom you met last night, will come at once if you call him. But I'll be holding you in my mind,' said Darrow in the enigmatic language used by those who regard abnormal powers as merely a commonplace aspect of reality, 'and I won't relax my grip. You won't need to call Michael.'

I believed him. Mind triumphed over matter. Darrow was again exercising his charism.

II

On his return he gave me another cross which I could wear instead of his own, and once the alka-seltzer had been consumed he produced the book he had brought from the library. It was *Mystics of the Church* by Evelyn Underhill.

'This is very light reading for a man of your background,' he said, 'and as it was published after you concluded your life as an undergraduate I doubt if you've ever troubled to read it. However a glance at mysticism can often prove to be the shot of oxygen which revives a debilitated theological mountaineer, so if you can't sleep skim through a chapter or two and when I return after the office at noon you can tell me whether or not you find the book mildly diverting . . .'

III

I was asleep when he returned. I had not even opened the book because sleep had overpowered me when I was still waiting for my headache to ease. I was woken at half-past one by the little white-haired monk who brought me a mug of soup, two hunks of bread, a plate of vegetables in a cheese sauce and a dish of plums. A glass of milk also stood on the tray.

'Father Abbot says you're to eat it all,' said the little monk. 'Remember your duty to God to be fit, he says. He says when you've finished you're to have a shower and get dressed and he'll come back and see you at three. The water won't be hot, Doctor, not in the middle of the day, I'm sorry, but Father Abbot says you're not going to be killed by a cold shower.'

I was beginning to feel like an athlete in the hands of a ruthless trainer. Assuring Michael that I could well survive a cold shower I sat up, savouring the absence of nausea, and resumed the struggle to return to normality.

IV

When Darrow returned at three o'clock I was dressed in my clerical suit and seated at the table as I read Miss Underhill's book. I had discovered that I could function normally so long as I did what I was told; no doubt this was why Darrow had given me such precise orders.

'That's better,' he said as he saw me. He was carrying a chair which he placed opposite me at the table. 'Did you forget to shave?' he asked as he sat down. 'Or was there some difficulty – other than the lack of hot water – which made you feel shaving was best avoided?'

'You didn't tell me to shave.'

186

'That's true, but nevertheless you must have considered the idea, if only out of habit . . . Was the difficulty centred on the razor? No, I knew there'd be no risk there. Then it was the mirror, wasn't it? You were frightened, perhaps, in case you saw the angry stranger, the one who takes you over when you're drunk.'

I nodded but had to shade my eyes with my hand to conceal my distress.

'When you understand him better,' said Darrow, 'he won't seem so alarming, but before we concentrate on these problems of yours, let's dispose of the Archbishop of Canterbury. Since you became distressed when his name arose earlier, am I right in assuming he had some connection with the mystery which you went to Starbridge to solve?'

'Yes, he gave me this – this commission – '

'All I need at present is some short message such as: "Commission completed, full details later." Then I can telephone His Grace, give him the message and say that as you've been working very hard lately I've insisted that you make a lengthy retreat – in fact I can even say with perfect truth that I wanted you to begin the retreat earlier but you postponed it because you were so anxious to complete his commission.'

I made a great effort. 'You could say to him: "All's well. Journal safe. No letters".'

Darrow wrote down the message, snapped shut his notebook and said briskly, 'Good. So much for the Archbishop. Now the next thing we have to decide is whether you're fit to begin discussing your problems today.'

'I'm fine now.'

'Fit enough to begin the task of confiding in me informally so that I can help you approach your formal confession before God?' said Darrow, clarifying the issue in case I was under the illusion that a talk between us would mean a mere sociable conversation. 'Fit enough to talk about this commission in Starbridge?'

'Yes.'

'Very well, go ahead and tell me about it.'

There was a long silence. Eventually when the tears blurred my eyes again I said in despair, 'I must be mad because I can't stop crying and men never cry unless they're off their heads.'

'That's a very powerful myth in our culture and a myth which can produce extremely unhealthy results. Which is better: to express grief and pain by using tear-ducts specially created for the purpose or to express grief and pain by enduring a silent secret haemorrhage of the soul?'

I said as the tears began to fall, 'I feel so overwhelmed by the memory of all my unfitness.'

'Very well, perhaps so far you haven't served God as well as you might have done. Perhaps you've even longed to put matters right – '

'I have, yes – oh, indeed I have, I've prayed and prayed for help but – '

'Then your prayers are being answered, aren't they?'

I stared at him. 'Answered?' I looked around the room. I was barely able to speak. 'I've broken down so utterly that I'm unable to continue as a clergyman, and you say *this* is God answering my prayers?'

'Of course. Do you think God's been unaware of your difficulties and the suffering you must inevitably have endured? And do you think He's incapable of reaching out at last to bring you face to face with your troubles so that you can surmount them and go on to serve Him far better than you ever served him in the past?'

I understood but was unable to tell him so, and as I covered my face with my hands I heard him say, 'God hasn't sent this ordeal to destroy you, Charles. He's come to your rescue at last, and here in this village, here in this house, here in this room where you've hit rock-bottom, here's where your new life finally begins.'

V

He cut short the interview at that point, but he rejoined me at five o'clock that afternoon as I was sitting on the wooden seat facing the herb-garden. The air was warm and scented, the sun was shining fitfully and a breeze was stirring the last pages of Miss Underhill's book in my hands.

'I telephoned the Archbishop,' said Darrow, sitting at my side. 'He thanked you for your message which he said was quite sufficient for the time being, and said he was delighted to hear you were making a retreat. He told me he always worried about young clergymen who were unusually successful by worldly standards, and he was sure a retreat could only prove beneficial. Finally he sent his good wishes along with his approval, and said he would be keeping a special place for you in his daily prayers.'

Such affectionate sympathy triggered a guilt that I had rejected him. With great difficulty I said, 'Dr Lang's been very good to me in the past.'

'And in the present?'

'He hasn't changed. But I have. I've drifted away from him. He's not a man I feel in tune with any more.'

'Whom do you feel in tune with now?'

It was no use trying to hide my distress. I merely sat motionless, radiating misery, but when Darrow made no attempt to press me for a reply I became increasingly aware of my need to lance the misery by communicating with him. I said, 'At Starbridge – ' but no more words came, and I was just contemplating in despair the utter failure of my attempt at communication when he said idly, 'I've never met the Bishop of Starbridge, but I heard him preach once when he was Vicar of St Mary's, Mayfair.'

By a miracle of intuition he was transforming my failure into a triumph, and suddenly I sensed the line of communication, fragile but indeniably real, floating between us on the fragrant breeze from the herb-garden.

'That type of preaching is a special gift,' reflected Darrow, 'and like all charisms it can be dangerous if abused. I remember my spiritual director saying to me when I was a young man, "Beware of those glamorous Powers, Jon, the Powers which come from God but which can so easily be purloined by the Devil!" Dr Jardine's a fine preacher and certainly when I heard him he had his gift immaculately disciplined, but I thought he was potentially a dangerous man.'

I shuddered but the line of communication was no longer a fragile thread; it was a thick rope which was steadily hauling me out of the abyss of silence.

'A volatile temperament,' mused Darrow, 'a hypnotic edge to an attractive appearance, a brilliant mind, a God-given genius for homiletics – it's an explosive mixture, isn't it? In fact I've often wondered in recent weeks how I would feel if I were Archbishop of Canterbury and had to deal with a bishop whose latest hobby was creating havoc in the House of Lords.'

My fingers closed on the cross below my neck and it was as if I grasped Darrow's hand at last after my long haul upwards on the end of the rope. I whispered, 'I feel as if he annihilated me,' and slowly, very slowly, I began to talk about my commission in Starbridge.

VI

The talk covered many sessions and was punctuated by periods of rest; I realized later that Darrow could judge with uncanny precision how much conversation I could tolerate without breaking down and how long I needed afterwards for recuperation. However as the days passed I became stronger, and by the time I had completed a detailed account of my first visit to Starbridge I felt anxious to continue the story without further interruptions. It was an irony that I then encountered the formidable obstacle of my afternoon with Loretta. My narrative became disjointed; I lapsed into silence. It was late at night, and the only light in the room came from the bedside lamp which left Darrow's face in shadow as we sat facing each other at the table.

'Just say: "There was an interval",' he said at last but when I remained unable to continue he commented not unsympathetically, ' "Strait is the gate and narrow is the way" – but perhaps a little too strait and narrow for you at present. Very well, we'll leave the story there for a while.'

I realized then that I was being a coward, pointlessly holding my tongue when the nature of my error must by that time have been so obvious, and making a new effort I said: 'You're using that quotation in the context of truth, just as you did when we first met. "High and wide is the gate", you said, "which leads to self-deception and illusion, but for those seeking truth strait is the gate and narrow the way – "'

' " – and brave is the man who can journey there".'

Crawling out from the shadow of my cowardice I told him what had happened in the spinney.

VII

'. . . and it was as if I was giving myself shot after shot of morphia. Every time the morphia wore off I had to give myself another shot because I was too frightened to face up to what was happening.'

'And how would you define what was happening?' Darrow, who had registered no emotion during my confession, now permitted a note of interest to enter his voice as if I had made a statement which was worthy of a detached discussion, and I was so relieved by the absence of censure that I had no trouble replying, 'My celibate life as a widower had utterly broken down and I couldn't see how I was going to go on.'

'How old were you when you married?'

'Twenty-seven. Having no gift for celibacy I was tempted to marry immediately after my ordination, but since marriage then would have put me in a financial strait-jacket and limited my opportunities – ' I broke off in shame. 'How calculating and ambitious that makes me sound!'

'It's not a sin to be prudent. It needn't necessarily be a sin either to be ambitious in God's service.' He smiled at me. 'But if you didn't rush to the altar in the early twenties, how did you solve the problem of chastity at that time?'

'More by luck than virtue. Not long after my ordination I became one of Dr Lang's chaplains, and soon there I was, living at Bishopthorpe with the Archbishop watching over me like a lynx-eyed chaperon – '

'But surely if you had no call to celibacy this role of secretarial monk must have become increasingly irksome?'

'Yes, I left the Archbishop eventually, returned to Laud's where I was a Fellow and began to teach. That was when I began to make a name for myself with my lectures on the Early Church.'

'You were looking for a wife, of course.'

'Yes, but I couldn't find anyone who was entirely right. However then I had the most astonishing piece of luck: Dr Lang recommended me for the headmastership of St Aidan's at Eastbourne, and soon there I was, twenty-seven years old, headmaster of a Church of England public school with a splendid salary – and a wife. She was the daughter of the retiring headmaster and I met her when I went down to St Aidan's for the interview.'

There was a pause but Darrow said nothing and at last, driven by the need to terminate the silence I said rapidly: 'We were married three years and then she was killed in a car accident. She was pregnant. It would have been our first child. The shock was terrible, I . . . well, it took me a long time to get back to normal. I left the school and returned to Laud's to sink myself in research. I wrote a book – '

'I've read it. Very lucid. Arianism disembowelled with a chilling surgical skill.'

'I wanted to disembowel something – it stopped me thinking about what had happened, so I worked and worked until my whole life revolved around that book to such an extent that I began to worry about what on earth I'd do when it was finished. However in the end I didn't have to worry; there was no time. The book was a big success in academic circles and I was awarded my doctorate and suddenly I found myself being lionized – '

' – by the ladies, no doubt, as well as by the enthusiastic scholars.'

'Yes, the celibacy got harder and harder, but somehow . . .' My voice trailed away. Again Darrow waited and at last I was able to say, '. . . somehow I've never quite managed to remarry. Yet I do want to remarry – in fact I'm desperate to remarry, but . . . I don't.'

'It sounds as if you're caught in some mysterious way between the Devil and the Deep Blue Sea. I can quite understand why you might regard the celibate life as the Devil if you've no call to celibacy, but why should you regard marriage as the Deep Blue Sea?'

'But I don't! I was very happy with my wife – my marriage was the most splendid success!'

'Then if the problem doesn't lie in marriage *per se* where do you think it does lie?'

There was a long silence.

'Well, never mind,' said Darrow at last. 'That's not important for the moment. Now I suggest we call an end to the discussion at this point and – '

'The problem lies in me,' my voice said. '*I'm* the problem. I'm so unfit and so unworthy that I feel no woman would ever be able to cope with me.'

'And do the women you meet appear to share this view of you?'

'Oh no! But then they never meet the man I keep hidden. They just meet the man on public display.' I hesitated but added, 'I call him the glittering image because he looks so well in the mirror. But beyond him – '

'Beyond him,' said Darrow, never batting an eyelid, 'stands the angry stranger who appears in the mirror whenever the glittering image goes absent without leave.'

'Yes. He's a destroyer. No woman could cope. Except Lyle. I think – yes, I really do think that Lyle could cope – '

'We'll stop there,' said Darrow.

'She copes with everything, you see – everything – '

'We'll talk about her later but not now – you're exhausted. And anyway before we start discussing the dramatis personae you must reach the end of your story. At present we're still with you and Loretta at Leatherhead.'

I rubbed my eyes futilely at the thought of Loretta but when I whispered in despair, 'Stupid tears. Such a coward,' Darrow said, 'Nonsense! You've begun to squeeze through the narrow gate. You're being just as brave as you could be,' and once again he gave me the strength to go on.

VIII

'. . . and then Jardine said, "Let me try to bring you closer to what I'm afraid will prove a very unpalatable reality," and he began to make this speech . . . I can't describe it – it was a nightmare – he tore up my glittering image and rejected my other self beyond – I'm sorry, that doesn't explain anything – '

'Oh yes it does,' said Darrow.

' – but I can't find the words to convey the horror, the absolute *horror* – '

'You don't have to tell me any more than that for the moment. Just say, "After Jardine had made his speech . . ." '

It was afternoon, that period of the day following the monks' dinner when there were no offices to be sung and they were free to attend to other work. Darrow and I were again sitting at the table in my room. We had hoped to hold the conversation in the herb-garden but the arrival of wet weather had made this impossible, and I was sorry to be confined to the house. At Darrow's suggestion I had been doing a little gardening in the afternoons; monks are always aware how much energy is required to sustain an adequate spiritual life and how much needs to be expended in physical labour.

There were other guests staying in my wing of the building but Darrow thought it would be too arduous for me to be sociable so to my relief I was told to avoid the common-room downstairs and see the other guests only at mealtimes when the rule of silence ensured I could eat in peace. As a special privilege, providing me with an alternative to the seclusion of my room, I was allowed into the enclosed section of the house in order to read in the library, but I read only as Darrow directed; by that time my new examination of mysticism had advanced from Evelyn Underhill,

Dean Inge and Baron Friedrich Von Hügel, and as my reading progressed I was both amazed and ashamed by the shallowness of my knowledge. Having long since decided that I preferred to work in the less spiritually demanding sphere of historical facts I had tended to view mysticism merely as a recurring phenomenon which broke out, like a religious version of measles, whenever orthodox ecclesiastical life became sunk in abuse and inertia. Perhaps also I had felt that the morbid, aberrant aspects of mysticism made it suitable for study only by women, emotional adolescents and eccentrics, and this prejudice had blinded me to the value of a true mysticism stripped of oriental nihilism and Roman superstition.

However I was at present too enfeebled to have much insight into this blindness which had undoubtedly sprung from spiritual arrogance as well as intellectual pride, and it was as much as I could do to read obediently, garden conscientiously and attend the services regularly in the chapel. I was forbidden to attend the night office of Matins because Darrow thought it was more important for my health that I should have an unbroken night's sleep, but I attended Prime at six in the morning, the combined service of Terce and Sext at noon, the combined service of None and Vespers at six in the evening, and Compline at eight. Mass was celebrated after Prime, and each morning I stayed to watch. I wanted above all to receive the sacrament, but I had accepted that I must abstain until my errors were fully understood and true repentance became possible. Darrow and I had discussed the situation once I had told him about Loretta.

'Of course you want to rush into a formal confession and wipe the slate clean without delay,' he had said to me. 'That's only natural. But I warn you, I'd ask some very searching questions before I gave you absolution and quite frankly I doubt if at present you could begin to answer them. For instance I'd want to know exactly why you made love to Loretta. Were you driven solely by what the melodramas call "unbridled lust" or was there in fact very much more going on than the mere gratification of a passing whim? And whether or not the incident was merely the result of lust I'd want to know what guarantee you could give me that such an incident wouldn't happen again – and that, of course, would bring us to the vexed question of your celibacy. How far do you really understand your problem about remarriage? It seems to me we have a lot of detective work to do here before you can view your situation with the degree of clarity necessary for any effective confession.'

He paused as if he thought I might want to argue but when I remained silent he said, 'The point I'm making is that your behaviour with Loretta can't be confessed in isolation because such a confession would inevitably be inadequate. And can you in all conscience receive the sacrament after an inadequate confession of at least one very disabling sin?'

That question could only be answered in the negative, and I saw then how wrong I had been to hope that his absence of censure on the subject of Loretta meant that he intended to be lenient with me. I was used to benign elderly spiritual advisers who bathed me with sympathetic soft-heartedness; to encounter a director who was sympathetic but tough was unnerving. Yet it was also a relief. I knew a firm discipline was necessary as I struggled to regain my health, and because I could acknowledge this truth I felt no desire to rebel against him; on the contrary I found myself increasingly anxious to win his approval and had soon redoubled my efforts to complete the Starbridge narrative as truthfully as possible.

'. . . so Loretta said she'd drive me to Cambridge,' I found myself saying at last. 'I don't remember much about the journey but I do remember arriving here and seeing the stars and talking about the transcendence of God. I think I even mentioned Karl Barth.'

'What an indestructible passion for theology!' said Darrow amused, but as I smiled, relieved beyond measure that my narrative was finally completed, I was unable to resist saying, 'You must be thinking I've behaved like a lunatic.'

'That's an emotional word and singularly unhelpful in this context. I think it would be more accurate to say that you're a normal man and like many normal men you have a set of personal problems which you're obliged to cart around with you wherever you go. However you're also a strong man, strong enough to keep the hatches battened down on these problems, and you go on leading a normal life until one day you arrive in Starbridge. Then everything changes – and it changes because the Star-bridge mystery somehow blasts aside those battened-down hatches and . . . Well, if I were still in the Navy I'd say the Starbridge mystery had kicked you right in the balls.'

I was so relieved by his stress on my normality that I was able to say at once, 'The worst part of all is that I feel as if I'm still being kicked. I didn't solve the puzzle. I still don't know for certain what's going on. I do believe Jardine – I know that rationally I ought to believe him – I know that if I don't believe him I must be – ' I broke off. 'Yet I don't believe him,' I said. 'I can't believe him, I *won't* believe him – '

'Exactly. You're going round and round the mulberry bush in an emotional frenzy which is thoroughly exhausting for you and can serve no useful purpose.' Darrow leant forward, resting his forearms on the table. 'Charles, the first important truth to grasp is that neither you nor I, on the evidence so far available, can solve this mystery conclusively.'

'But I've got to know – I've got to find out – '

'There you go again, burning to rush around the Starbridge mulberry bush in a dance which can only prove unproductive! You've got to break out of that circle, Charles, so let's approach the problem from another angle: why is it so important for you to solve this mystery?'

'It's because of Lyle, of course. I want to marry her so I've got to know what's going on.'

'Very well, let's take a closer look at your feelings for this woman who's at the heart of the mystery. I think this is the moment, Charles, when we finally begin to talk about Lyle.'

TWELVE

'I cannot honestly say that I think the adoption of celibacy would meet our present difficulties.'

More Letters of Herbert Hensley Henson
Bishop of Durham 1920–1939
ed. E. F. BRALEY

I

'It's easy to be sceptical about the idea that a lasting love can spring into being at first sight,' said Darrow, 'but one must always bear in mind that improbable things do happen and your feeling for Lyle might just be one of those improbabilities. In other words, Charles, I've resolved to keep an open mind on the subject. But can you make a similar resolution? Ideally I'd like you to prise your mind open an inch for the length of this discussion.'

I regarded him warily. 'You're asking me to admit I could be wrong about her.'

'Don't feel threatened. I'm not out to undermine your feelings, only to clarify them, because I believe important consequences could flow from the clarification.'

With reluctance I said, 'Very well, I've got my mind prised open an inch. Go on.'

'Let's suppose for a moment,' said Darrow, 'that your feelings are, in fact, an illusion. I think you'd agree that once you'd found out you were deluded there'd be no question of marriage and therefore the mystery of whether or not she's Jardine's mistress would become irrelevant.'

With even deeper reluctance I said, 'That's true. But nonetheless I'm sure – '

'Very well, let's now assume you're not deluded and that Lyle's the long-awaited Miss Right. Then obviously you must know the truth, but how likely is it that you've been able to see Lyle with such clarity so early in your acquaintance with her? Or to put it another way, we know that love at first sight's possible, but exactly how probable is it in this particular situation?'

'I just feel so certain that I can't be wholly mistaken – '

'Then let's consider a third theory. Supposing your feelings for Lyle are based neither wholly in illusion nor wholly in reality but in a mixture of the two. In other words, there may well be some illusion going on but nevertheless you've recognized some quality in Lyle which you correctly believe will make her a good wife for you.'

'But this is exactly what I feel!' I exclaimed. 'I looked at her and knew she could cope with my problems!'

'The most important comment I can make about that statement,' said Darrow, 'is that probably no woman could cope satisfactorily with your problems before you've learnt how to cope with them yourself. The next most important comment I can make is that you've no way of knowing how true that statement is until you can perceive where the borderline between truth and illusion lies. Contrary to what you suppose, the real difficulty here is not what's going on between Lyle and Jardine but what's going on between you and Lyle. You've actually been going round and round in circles chasing the wrong problem.'

'But surely it's vital to discover – '

'It's only vital to discover whether she's his mistress if you first discover that your feelings for her are solidly rooted in reality.'

'But I can't be completely deluded! After all I'm a mature widower of thirty-seven – '

'I agree that's a powerful argument in your favour, but Charles, no matter how undeniable your maturity and experience you should allow for the fact that these troubles of yours might be warping your judgement.'

'You're leading me gently up the garden path,' I said, 'but I still can't see the front door. Are you saying – '

'I'm saying that this problem is all one and that we can't consider your feelings for Lyle in isolation from the remainder of your troubles any more than we could consider the incident with Loretta in that way. I'm saying that the best approach to the entire crisis is not to waste time speculating about what might or might not be going on at Starbridge, but to solve your private troubles, because then and only then will you be able to look at the Starbridge mystery with eyes clear enough to separate truth from fantasy and reality from illusion.'

II

We met again that evening. He took me for the first time to the Parlour, not the Visitors' Parlour with its plain table and chairs but the Abbot's Parlour across the hall, and presently a monk brought us some tea and a plate of oatmeal biscuits.

'Is this a reward for good behaviour?' I enquired amused, after the monk had departed.

'My intention was to give you a holiday before we embark on our voyage among your private problems.'

The room was large and furnished with surprising lavishness in the style of the 1890s. I presumed this decor had been inherited from the original owners of the house and preserved to impress any important visitors who might call on the Abbot. We were sitting on well-sprung armchairs which were upholstered in red velvet and placed on either side of a marble fireplace. Above the chimneypiece hung a passable painting, probably a Fordite investment, of Christ in the Garden of Gethsemane. A magnificent clock, its dial held aloft by two scantily-clad nymphs, ticked discreetly on the mantelshelf. The frieze below the shelf showed pagan hunting scenes containing more dubiously-clad females. I was surprised it had survived the Fordite invasion.

'It's an interesting room,' I murmured politely as he passed me my cup of tea.

'That depends entirely on one's interests.'

We laughed, and suddenly I wondered if he had ordained the holiday for himself as well as for me. I sensed he was glad of my company to relieve the strain of being a stranger in unfamiliar surroundings, and I was just about to ask him to tell me more about himself when he said, 'How are you feeling now about the Starbridge mystery? Is it still revolving unceasingly in your mind or have you finally managed to encase it in a straitjacket?'

'I've got hold of the straitjacket; I do see that it's useless at present to expend further energy on speculation. But I can't quite get the straitjacket on the mystery. What I'd really like to know, Father, is what on earth you make of my story.'

'My opinion isn't important,' said Darrow at once. 'My business is to illuminate the problem so that you can form a rational opinion of your own.'

'I understand that. But – '

'It's also arguable that any opinion I had would be worthless. I wasn't a witness at Starbridge. All I have is your evidence, and your evidence must necessarily be influenced by many factors, some of which may distort the truth no matter how hard you've tried to be honest.'

'Yes, I understand that too. But nevertheless – '

'I can certainly shine a spotlight into the dark corners. But will that help you get the mystery into the straitjacket or will it merely encourage you to go round and round the mulberry bush?'

I tried to put into words my need to have a yardstick against which I could measure my sanity. 'I feel I need a reaction from you,' I said.

'Otherwise I'm going to spend my time wondering if you secretly think – '
I could say no more but I had apparently said enough; at once Darrow
made his decision.

'Very well,' he said, 'I'll turn on the spotlight. There are in fact a
number of points about your story which I feel have a certain significance . . .'

III

'Let's turn the spotlight first on Lyle,' said Darrow. 'Unless she's either
a lesbian or else deeply involved with another man it's hard to see why
she should make such Herculean efforts to keep you at arm's length. After
all, let's be frank; you're extremely eligible. I haven't forgotten that she
may have profound psychological reasons for being set against marriage,
but it seems to me that if she were completely frigid – to use the word in
its psychoanalytical sense – you'd have deduced this during your more
intimate moments with her.'

'Yes, if you feel she's sexually normal your natural reaction would be
to look around to identify the man who has the benefit of her normality,
but Charles, even if this man is Jardine, that still doesn't prove she's
sleeping with him. She could well be in the grip of an unconsummated
passion, and if we're wrong and she does indeed have some shadow on
her psycho – a fear of sexual intercourse, perhaps, which could coexist
with an apparently normal enjoyment of romantic attentions – then she
might feel that an unconsummated passion suited her better than a passion
which was consummated.'

This unpleasantly plausible theory was not new to me but that did not
make it less unpalatable. 'In essence that was Jardine's explanation of Lyle's
spinsterhood,' I said with reluctance.

'Yes, but that proves nothing,' said Darrow at once. 'It could be true –
but if he were obliged to invent a story to explain her abstention from
marriage he'd naturally pick the most plausible story available.' And before
I could comment he added: 'Let's shine the spotlight now on Jardine
himself because the next significant point on my list is Jardine's attitude
to you. I don't think you've quite realized how odd this is. Here you have
a man who has a reputation for being fairly rude fairly often in his relentless
crusade against hypocrisy. However when your Machiavellian purposes
are finally unmasked, does Jardine lose his temper with you? No, he
doesn't. After a formal expression of outrage in which his anger is directed
not against you but against Dr Lang, he apparently makes strenuous efforts
to be civil – indeed he seems to pursue a policy of converting you into a
episcopal pet. Now this is all very admirable but is it typical of Jardine?

Not from what I've heard of him. Why didn't he kick you out of the palace? It's nonsense to say that your abrupt departure would have created unfortunate publicity. Jardine's always having rows with people. He'd just had a row with his Archbishop in the House of Lords. What newspaper would pay the slightest attention if he now had a row with a mere canon? His whole behaviour is most intriguing.'

This was certainly an angle I had failed to perceive in the dimensions of the Starbridge mystery. 'What's the explanation?'

'Let's hear your opinion, not mine.'

'Jardine could have decided to tame me in order to allay my suspicions – and because he didn't want to worsen his relationship with Lang by throwing me out.'

'True. Perhaps too he feared that if he threw you out Lang would suspect the worst. Go on.'

'I've run out of explanations.'

'There's one other possibility,' said Darrow, pouring me some more tea. 'He might have given in to the urge to treat a promising young man as a son. It's a common syndrome among childless middle-aged men and would certainly explain his unusual benevolence towards you.'

I suddenly found I could not drink my tea. I had to replace the cup in its saucer.

'All we can say with confidence here,' said Darrow, watching me, 'is that Jardine acted out of character, a fact which could be significant. And my next significant fact – '

'Yes,' I said, 'where does the spotlight go next?'

'Let's turn it on the signet-ring. Everyone so far, even Loretta, seems to have treated your theory of the informal marriage as if it were the last word in outrageous fantasy, byt the fact remains that it's the one theory which explains how Jardine could enter into a liaison with Lyle and still believe he was avoiding apostasy; the fact that he would be grossly deluding himself is beside the point.'

My relief was so great that I was unable to speak.

'The question I'd like to ask Lyle,' said Darrow when he saw I was beyond speech, 'is that: why did old Mrs Jardine – the stepmother – give her that particular ring? Most women of that generation would own several rings, not necessarily expensive ones but ornamental dress-rings incorporating semi-precious stones. If Mrs Jardine's hands were so afflicted by arthritis she wouldn't have been able to wear any of her rings. Why not pick a pretty feminine ring for Lyle? Why choose this masculine signet-ring unless it had some special significance?'

'That's true.' Excitement restored my power of speech.

'Don't get excited, Charles. The choice of ring proves nothing – old ladies can have strange whims. But nevertheless it's significant,' he said, 'that when at the dinner table you finally began to make statements implying the existence of an informal marriage, no one made any remark such as: "Good Heavens, what's he talking about?" or: "I'm so sorry, Dr Ashworth, but could you repeat that because I think I must have misheard you". Your bizarre statements are received with a notable lack of astonishment – but this may merely have been because everyone was frozen with embarrassment by your lack of sobriety.'

'So still nothing is proved!'

'No, but the next significant fact – Jardine's final explanation of his *ménage* – certainly makes one wonder what can be going on.'

'Does it?' I said confused. 'But he was so convincing! He destroyed my certainty that I knew the truth!'

'That says much for Dr Jardine's powers of persuasion and he may indeed be innocent of wrongdoing, but there's an inconsistency in his story which appears to have eluded you. First of all he says he was attracted to Lyle but he appeased his wife by keeping Lyle in the household. It seems unlikely that any clergyman would decide to steer such a risky course unless he was deeply in love and not responsible for his actions, but let's concede he was at his wits' end about his wife's health; let's assume he spoke the truth when he implied his feelings for Lyle were a mere sexual inconvenience and that he had an overwhelmingly urgent reason for continuing to employ her. He then states that he mastered his feelings so that the *ménage* was able to function successfully. This too seems unlikely, but let's remember that middle-aged men do recover from tiresome minor infatuations, particularly if, like Jardine, they have powerful motives for recovering; in other words, let's once more give him the benefit of the doubt and assume this statement too is true. But then he brings out a really amazing piece of information: he admits that when he and Lyle first met he wanted to marry her. Now, Charles, in my opinion that statement is incompatible with his earlier assertion that she was a mere sexual inconvenience. When a man wants to marry, deep passions are involved which can't conceivably be dismissed as an inconvenient middle-aged itch.'

'So he was probably lying when he said he's mastered his feelings!'

'No, don't jump to conclusions. This inconsistency certainly makes his story less plausible but implausible things do happen and we still have no evidence that he didn't succeed in controlling his feelings at Radbury. In fact his statement that Mrs Jardine improved so much under Lyle's care that she was able to resume the marital relationship has the ring of truth and supports the idea that far from foundering further the marriage took on a new lease of life.'

'But what happened when they came to Starbridge and Mrs Jardine's health deteriorated again? Couldn't Jardine's strong feelings towards Lyle have resurfaced?'

'It's impossible to know. And may I remind you, Charles, that we have no evidence whatsoever that Jardine and his wife aren't still enjoying marital intimacy.'

'But according to Loretta – '

'Loretta submitted a plausible theory about what might have happened to the Jardines' marriage five years ago, but it remains a theory.' Darrow paused to allow me to digest this before adding: 'Charles, the significance of Jardine's disclosure that he once wanted to marry Lyle is *not* that it constitutes proof of gross misconduct. It doesn't. The significance lies in the fact that it reveals a situation which could hardly have been worse for Jardine's spiritual health. Even if there was no adultery in any physical sense, the scope for continuing adulterous thoughts is enough to make any confessor blanch.'

This fact at once seemed so obvious that I exclaimed: 'Why on earth didn't I see that at the time?'

'You were drunk and intolerably confused, but the truth is, of course, that any spiritual counsellor would have told Jardine to get rid of the girl even if the dismissal resulted in another breakdown for Mrs Jardine. One's driven to conclude that Jardine sought no advice and merely went his own way – a very dangerous course for a clergyman to steer in such a very dangerous situation.'

'So the stage would have been set for the kind of gross error represented by the unofficial marriage.'

'Possibly, although there's still no proof that the gross error ever happened. Nevertheless the situation's significant – as significant as that final scene between you and Jardine, the scene which could justifiably be described as a nightmare in counselling.'

I stared at him. Then I gave a convulsive shudder and looked away.

'We needn't talk about it now,' said Darrow at once. 'All I'm implying is that Jardine's gross mishandling of the scene suggests that he might have been shattered by the accuracy of your disclosures, but this again, like all other theories, is non-proven. The innocent explanation is that he was shattered to see a young man whom he regarded as a son in such extreme distress, and his emotional involvement with you destroyed his ability to give effective counselling.'

Still not looking at him I said carefully, 'I want you to explain, please, why you're so sure he grossly mishandled the scene. After all, I haven't told you the details. How could you possibly know whether the disaster was his fault for being inept or my fault for being – ' I gave another shudder.

Darrow said without hesitation, 'Obviously you were in an extremely bad way and obviously something had to be done, but the solution was not to make a long speech which wound you up so tightly that in the end you snapped and rushed off on a journey you were quite unfit to undertake. What he should have done was calmed you down by letting you talk; he had absolutely no business to be making speeches when he should have been listening. Then the next mistake he made was to say what he did say, because whatever was said clearly proved unendurable to you. In that single comment you made earlier on Jardine's speech you said: "He tore up my glittering image and rejected my other self beyond". Now we won't attempt an analysis on that sentence yet, but it seems clear to me that Jardine did something which is psychologically taboo: he dismantled defences which should have been left intact until you were strong enough to dismantle them yourself.'

'Defences . . .'

'Don't worry about that now. Obviously we'll have to discuss the significance of your glittering image, just as we'll have to discuss your whole relationship with Jardine, but we won't discuss them until you're ready to do so, and when we do embark on a discussion I can promise you that the conclusions you draw will be your own, not conclusions which I've imposed on you during a long speech.'

After a pause I said slowly, 'He clearly thought – he made me believe – '

'We'll stop there,' said Darrow, rising to his feet.

' – but in contrast you're treating me as if – '

'Come on, I'll take you back to your room.'

'But tomorrow,' I said, 'I'll talk about him. I know I can talk about him now. You've got faith in me. You take my theories seriously. You don't think I'm – '

'Let's deal with tomorrow when we come to it – you're too tired to talk more at present,' said Darrow, and sinking obediently into an exhausted silence I let him lead me back to my room.

IV

'I want to talk about Jardine,' I said the next day to let him know my courage had not faded overnight.

'We can certainly talk about him if you wish, but I rather thought we might begin this examination of your private troubles by having another look at the vexed question of your celibacy. I'll tell you why: it's because it seems to me to be your most urgent problem. After all, you can probably live without Jardine, but can you live without a wife? The answer would appear to be no.'

I relaxed as the ordeal of discussing Jardine was postponed. We were sitting at the table in my room again, and outside in the garden it was still raining.

'The situation is certainly confusing,' Darrow was adding. 'On the one hand you appear to have no doubt that you're not called to celibacy. But if we take celibacy in its strict sense – abstention from marriage – there's no denying that the celibate life is exactly what you've managed to achieve.'

'But that's not in response to a call from God.'

'You may well be right, but it's a very important point and we've got to be sure. I think you'd agree that so far as marriage is concerned there are two types of churchmen. One set feels that marriage distracts them from serving God as well as they can, and the other set feels that as single men they can't serve God properly because they're continually distracted by loneliness and by wondering (as the naval ratings would say) where the next fuck was coming from.'

'That's me,' I said.

'Possibly, but don't rush to judgement. Now I think you'd also agree that sexual frustration can afflict even those called to celibacy because in both types of churchman the determining factor in their choice between a married and a celibate life isn't always the strength of the sexual drive.'

'Think of St Augustine,' I murmured.

'Think indeed of St Augustine, a celibate who admitted to a strong sexuality. The point I'm making, Charles, is that the urgency of your present sexual inclinations isn't necessarily an indication that you're not fundamentally called to celibacy, and the question I'd now like to ask you is why, at this particular stage of your life, are you having sex? Is it just to scratch the familiar itch or are there more complex reasons?'

'You're remembering that I likened the sex with Loretta to shots of morphia. You're thinking that I might be using sex merely to escape from my problems.'

Darrow said, 'If you are indeed using sex in that way, the danger is that marriage may not solve your problems but compound them. That's why we must be so cautious when considering your mysterious ambivalence about remarriage. Are you in truth suited for the domestic life? Might you be able to serve God better as an unmarried man? These are questions which should be carefully considered if we're to reach an accurate assessment of your difficulty here.'

'I see the point you're making, Father, but the fact remains that I've been a married man and I know beyond doubt that marriage can help me to pray better, work harder and maintain a much steadier spiritual life. At present I'm hopelessly erratic and subject to distraction.'

'All right, so be it; I accept that you're not abstaining from marriage because of a call to celibacy which your private problems are preventing you from recognizing. Now, having established that you do need a wife in order to serve God best, let's probe a little deeper into the mystery of why you can't reach the altar.' He paused and then looking straight at me with his very clear grey eyes he said, 'Tell me, Charles, who's the one who wants to get married?'

The question was so bizarre that I could only stare at him in silence.

'After all,' said Darrow, 'we mustn't forget, must we, that there are two of you.'

I grappled with the implications of this statement for some time but again he made no attempt to hurry me and at last I was able to say, 'It's the glittering image who wants to get married.'

'He's keen to marry the perfect wife and live happily ever after, just as a model clergyman should?'

'*I'm* keen to marry the perfect wife and live happily ever after, just as a model clergyman should.'

'You're the glittering image?'

'Yes.'

'Very well, but what about your other self? Let's hear again what he thinks about remarriage.'

'Yes, I mentioned his attitude the other day, didn't I? He doubts that it's possible for him to marry and live happily ever after because he's so unfit and unworthy that no woman could cope with him. Except Lyle.'

'Yet Lyle, in some mysterious way, is unavailable for marriage. Is it just a coincidence, do you think, that of the two women in your life at present, one is an independent woman uninterested in matrimony and the other seems determined not to become deeply involved with you?'

Again I had to take time to think but eventually I said: 'It's no coincidence. It's part of a recurring pattern. For some years now I've only been attracted to women who aren't available for marriage to a clergyman.' I was unable to stop myself adding, 'Does that sound quite insane?'

'Not in the least,' said Darrow serenely. 'It's most sensible of your other self to take stringent precautions against remarriage if he feels such a step would be a disaster.' He paused before adding: 'It sounds as if he's very much afraid of this potential disaster.'

After a long silence I managed to nod.

'This must be a great burden for your other self. Has he been carrying it long?'

'Seven years.'

'He must be exhausted. Has he never been tempted to set down the burden by telling someone about it?'

'I can't,' I said.

'Who's "I"?' said Darrow.

'The glittering image.'

'Ah yes,' said Darrow, 'and of course that's the only Charles Ashworth that the world's allowed to see, but you're out of the world now, aren't you, and I'm different from everyone else because I know there are two of you. I'm becoming interested in this other self of yours, the self nobody meets. I'd like to help him come out from behind that glittering image and set down this appalling burden which has been tormenting him for so long.'

'He can't come out.'

'Why not?'

'You wouldn't like him or approve of him.'

'Charles, when a traveller's staggering along with a back-breaking amount of luggage he doesn't need someone to pat him on the head and tell him how wonderful he is. He needs someone who'll offer to share the load.'

I considered this metaphor with care.

'Think of me as the porter,' said Darrow, 'and consider the possibility that life might be less exhausting if you unloaded some of your bags on to my empty trolley.'

I considered this extension of the metaphor with even greater care. Finally I said, 'Where do I start?'

'We need to go back seven years, I think, to that time when the burden claimed you. Can you say what happened seven years ago or is it too difficult? If it's too difficult at present we can leave it and talk of something else.'

After a long moment I managed to say, 'My wife died. Seven years ago. She died.'

'Ah yes,' murmured Darrow and waited, but my glittering image only said with composure, 'I'm afraid there's nothing I can tell you that you don't already know.'

'Nothing at all?'

'No, I've already told you, haven't I, how terrible it was when she died, and obviously I'm still affected by my grief. It's as if I don't want to risk involving myself with anyone else who might die and cause me so much pain.'

'I can quite understand that,' said Darrow, 'but isn't the grief in any way alleviated by the memory of the years you had together before she died?'

'Yes, of course,' I said at once. 'We loved each other very much and had three years of perfect happiness.'

'No clouds in the sky?'

'None at all.'

Darrow merely said, 'You mentioned your wife was pregnant when she died. Had she been pregnant long?'

'No, she'd only just found out.'

'I see. And you'd been married three years. That must surely have been a considerable strain for you both.'

'Strain?'

'Wondering month after month why no child came.'

I got up and walked out of the room.

THIRTEEN

'Childless husbands and wives fall easily apart.'
Letters of Herbert Hensley Henson
Bishop of Durham 1920–1939
ed. E. F. BRALEY

I

I went to the bathroom and sat for a minute on the edge of the bath. When I had myself completely in control I returned to my room and found Darrow was still sitting at the table but I gave him no chance to speak. Immediately I said, 'My marriage is of no significance in this context and I don't want to waste your time talking of matters which are of no significance. I know it's ridiculous that I haven't remarried, but all I have to do is to pull myself together and behave sensibly.' As I spoke I was moving around the room, pausing by the bedside table, picking up the Bible, flicking through the pages. The various books streamed past my fingers: Genesis, Exodus, Leviticus, Numbers, Deuteronomy, Joshua –

'Obviously you'd prefer to resume this conversation later,' said Darrow, rising to his feet. 'I'll leave you to unwind.'

'You completely misunderstand!' I said annoyed. 'You're thinking I can't go on but I can – of course I can! And I don't need to unwind – I'm not wound up!'

'Then why are you pacing around like a lion at the zoo?'

I bit back the exasperated blasphemy, smothered the impatient obscenity and flung myself down in my chair again. Darrow too resumed his place but although I waited for his next question he merely embarked on a minute examination of his Abbot's ring until at last I was driven to demand, 'Why don't you say something?'

'I was waiting for you to talk to me.'

'But I've nothing to say!'

'Very well, we'll sit in silence.'

I leant forward and tugged at his sleeve to stop him examining the ring. Then I said, 'I want to go on but I can't unless you ask questions.'

Darrow immediately reverted to his usual close attentiveness. 'Let's leave your wife for the moment,' he said, 'and talk about these ineligible women who have been attracting you since her death. In what way were they unsuitable for a clergyman?'

'They were divorced or separated or agnostic – or if they weren't agnostic they were vague Deists like Loretta.'

Darrow said casually, 'Did you sleep with any of them?'

I was appalled. 'Good heavens, no, of course not! Word would have got around – it would have ruined my career, my whole future – I couldn't possibly have had sex with any of them!'

Darrow said, 'Who's "I"?'

I was silenced.

'We know for a fact,' said Darrow, 'that someone called Charles Ashworth has indeed had sex recently with one of these ineligible women, a vague Deist called Loretta Staviski.'

'That wasn't me.'

'So it was your other self who made love to Loretta. But how does he normally manage if he finds chastity difficult?'

After a pause I said: 'He goes abroad. Holidays. Always abroad. Loretta was an exception because when I'm at home I usually succeed in keeping him locked up.'

'And at the end of these holidays abroad there's always confession to a foreign priest?'

'Of course! Confession, repentance, absolution . . . well, I couldn't have gone on otherwise, could I? And I must go on because nothing must stand between me and my calling. Unless I serve God in the Church my life would be entirely meaningless so it would be quite wrong, wouldn't it, if any longing to serve Him was frustrated just because someone unfit and unworthy who isn't me at all commits an error every now and then.'

'Tell me,' said Darrow, 'were you never able to discuss with Father Reid these difficulties caused by your other self?'

'Oh, but I couldn't! Dear Old Father Reid, he liked me and approved of me so much and I couldn't bear the thought of disillusioning him.' I hesitated but added firmly: 'It would have been cruel.'

Darrow said, 'And what about Dr Lang, who clearly also likes you and approves of you? Did you ever confide in him or did you decide that too would have been cruel?'

I looked at him closely but saw no trace of an irony which would hint at either incredulity or condemnation. With care I said: 'I was chaste when I worked for Lang.'

'I realize that, but what about the time before your ordination when you were already very much Lang's protégé? Were there no wild oats sown during your Varsity years?' .

'But I couldn't possibly have told Lang about that! It would have meant the end of his patronage – he wouldn't have liked and approved of me any more!'

'Charles, would I be reading too much into your remarks if I deduced that liking and approving are very important to you?'

That was an easy question to answer. 'Well, of course they're important!' I exclaimed. 'Aren't they important to everyone? Isn't that what life's all about? Success is people liking and approving of you. Failure is being rejected. Everyone knows that.'

'We'll stop there,' said Darrow.

'Success means happiness,' I said, 'and that's why I'm in fact such a happy person despite these little troubles which are bothering me at the moment. I've always been so successful – a wonderful career, a wonderful marriage – '

'We'll talk again this afternoon,' said Darrow. 'The weather looks as if it might clear up. We might talk in the herb-garden.'

II

'I must apologize for making such a stupid exhibition of myself this morning,' I said as the scent of the herbs floated towards us on the mild air. 'Of course I realized as soon as you left that I'd behaved like a lunatic.'

'You were a little irritable, certainly, but I saw no signs of lunacy.'

'What about all that mad switching about between the two personalities?'

'You were speaking of very difficult matters and I was encouraging you.' Darrow was quite unruffled. 'It was I, not you, remember, who brought the concept of the two personalities into the conversation in the hope that it would bring us closer to the truth.'

I relaxed. 'Nevertheless,' I said, 'I was a fool to pretend my marriage was all sunlit perfection because I'm sure that aroused your scepticism. After all, you've been married yourself; you must know very well that even in the happiest of marriages there can occasionally be a dark corner or two.'

There was a pause while I gripped the arm of the garden seat with my left hand and groped for my cross with my right. Then Darrow said idly: 'When did the first dark corner appear in your marriage?'

'Straight away because there was a problem about money. I regret to say I'd been extravagant, keeping up with the people who mattered, and by the time I met Jane I was in debt. There was no real difficulty because I had the prospect of an excellent salary as headmaster, but starting out in married life is expensive and I didn't want Jane's father to think I couldn't afford to give his daughter the best.'

'Her father approved of you?'

'Very much, yes, so of course I didn't want to upset him by confessing I was in financial difficulty. Well, after the wedding I said to Jane we'd have to be careful for a while – no radical reduction in our standard of living but merely an avoidance of any major expenditure.'

'Sounds reasonable.'

'Yes, but . . . no doubt you cam imagine the dilemma that put us in, Father.'

'I can still remember,' said Darrow, 'the heart attack I almost had when my wife bought the baby's perambulator and told me how much it had cost.'

'Yes, I knew you'd understand, and you can see too, of course, what an awkward position I was in as a clergyman. When I married in 1927 the Church of England's official attitude to contraception was still negative.'

'Very awkward.'

'Jane was devout and when I suggested contraception she was shocked. She'd have accepted it later, after we'd had four or five children and another pregnancy might have been detrimental to her health, but she didn't believe contraception was right for newly-weds. Well, neither did I, but . . . It was difficult, Father. It really was.'

'Did this lead to quarrels?'

'Jane wasn't the sort of person who quarrelled. She just cried and then tried to be brave, but I was terrified she might confide in her father. The old boy was a clergyman of the Victorian school and he thought all contraception was the invention of the Devil.'

'What effect did this difficulty have on your intimate life?'

'Well, Jane wanted to be a good wife so everything seemed on the surface to be all right, even when I began using French-letters, but . . . I knew she was unhappy about the situation and that made me feel guilty – and feeling guilty made me feel angry because I resented being made to feel guilty. Sex got a bit tense. Everything got a bit tense – '

'You were using French-letters all the time?'

'Yes, except occasionally when I ran out of my supply. I couldn't buy them locally because of the risk of being recognized, and I didn't always have the time to make the necessary expedition further afield so sometimes I had to practise withdrawal – but oh, how I hated that! I was always so afraid of an accident – '

'Profoundly afraid? Why? Were you still in financial trouble?'

'No, my financial affairs were much improved. By the time we celebrated our first wedding anniversary I even had a balance in the bank.'

'In that case I presume the subject of a baby again came up for discussion.'

'Yes, Jane wanted to abandon the contraception and I agreed. But then an awful thing happened, Father, every man's nightmare. I began to suffer from premature ejaculation. I'd ejaculate even before I'd penetrated her.'

'How very distressing. What did your doctor say?'

'Oh, I couldn't go to my doctor! I knew him socially – he was a friend of my father-in-law's, and I didn't want anyone I knew thinking I was a sexual failure. Anyway I was all right so long as I was using the French-letters.'

'You're saying you went back to the contraception?'

'Well, I had to, didn't I? Our sex-life had turned into a disaster without it. So I said to Jane, "I'll have to keep on with the French-letters until I can get over this difficulty," and she said: "Just as you think best" – but then I heard her crying in our bedroom – '

'When did you confide in your spiritual director?'

'I didn't. This wasn't a spiritual problem.'

'Are you telling me that this severe marital worry didn't impinge on your life of prayer and your service to God?'

'But I couldn't tell dear old Father Reid! He was so holy – so celibate – how on earth could I have talked to him about French-letters and premature ejaculation? It's just not the sort of thing one talks about to one's spiritual director, is it, and besides ... I didn't want another churchman to know about the contraception.'

'Thinking of your duties as a churchman, may I ask how you were faring as headmaster of St Aidan's while this trouble was going on?'

'Oh Father, in a way that was the worst problem of all – I hated it! I was so bored with all those adolescent boys – I'd forgotten how tedious boarding-school life could be – '

'When did you realize you'd made a mistake?'

'Almost straight away but I felt I couldn't say anything because everyone – especially Lang – was expecting me to make a huge success of it and I couldn't bear the thought of disillusioning them. So I knew I'd have to endure the situation for a minimum of three years – if I'd left earlier people might have judged me a failure.'

'What did Jane think of your unhappiness with your work? She must have been very upset.'

'Oh, I never told her,' I said. 'No, of course I never told her. Like everyone else she was expecting me to be a great success, and anyway she was so upset already that I felt I couldn't bear to upset her further – '

'Where had your intimate life got to by this time?'

'It was all very awkward. Occasionally I dispensed with the French-letter but it never worked. However we both tried very hard to pretend nothing was wrong, so – '

'But surely such a situation couldn't have gone on without some sort of crisis occurring?'

'Jane did become a little depressed. It wasn't a nervous breakdown, you understand – no one ever called it that – but she cried all the time and said she wanted to go and stay for a while with her father . . . I nearly had a fit when she said that, but then she screamed at me that I cared more about what her father thought than about what *she* thought, and I said no, I care terribly what you think, I love you, and she broke down and said how could I be content to go on without a baby, and I said I'm not, I'm not, I want a child as much as you do . . . And then, Father, finally, the terrible truth dawned on me and I realized that was a lie. I didn't want a child. I didn't know why. I still don't know why. I just thought: I can't be a father, I can't cope. But I knew I couldn't tell Jane and I knew I couldn't tell anyone else. A Christian marriage is for the procreation of children, and I wasn't just a Christian, I was a clergyman. But this stranger, the one who lives behind the glittering image, he didn't want a child and he took over my marriage; I – I tried hard to keep him out, I tried so hard, Father, so hard – ' I was breaking down but I dragged myself together. ' "Strait is the gate",' I whispered, ' "and narrow is the way".' I scrubbed my eyes with my cuff and somehow found the strength to go on.

'The odd thing was,' I said, 'that as soon as I'd admitted to myself that I didn't want a child I had no more trouble with premature ejaculation. It was as if that just protected me from fatherhood while I couldn't face up to the truth, but once I'd faced the truth I found I had almost limitless powers of control. I used to pretend with Jane. I'd pretend to reach a climax and somehow managed to hold back till I could get to the lavatory afterwards – '

'But Jane must surely have realized there was no seminal fluid.'

'I don't know. I don't know what she thought, Father. We never talked about it.'

'You were, in fact, by this time deeply estranged.'

'Oh no, Father, everyone always remarked how happy Jane and I were, the ideal young couple – '

'How did the tragedy end?'

I opened my mouth to say, 'It wasn't a tragedy!' but the words were never spoken. I was too overwhelmed with relief that at long last the pain had been correctly identified. I felt as if I had finally exchanged a pair of brutal clogs for a pair of handmade leather shoes. 'Tragedy,' I said. 'Tragedy.' I had to say the word aloud to make sure it was real. I said to Darrow: 'It's the word "success" which is unreal here, isn't it? But I always have to talk in terms of success because tragedy and failure are . . .' I groped for the right word but could only produce '. . . unacceptable.'

Darrow said nothing.

'Tragedies and failures don't happen to me,' I said. 'They're not allowed to happen.'

'Who's "me"?' said Darrow.

'The glittering image.'

'Then whom did this tragedy happen to?'

'My other self.'

'He agrees now, does he, that it was a tragedy?'

'I think he always knew. The suffering seemed so undeserved.'

'Made him feel angry, did it?'

I managed to nod.

'Good!' said Darrow astonishingly. 'It's right that he should be angry if he's been locked up and forbidden to acknowledge his suffering! What could be more unhumane to a suffering man than to imprison him?'

I said confused, 'But I've got to keep him locked up!'

'Yes, but I think,' said Darrow to the glittering image, 'that you need a rest. Being such a ruthless jailer must be the most exhausting occupation. I think the prisoner might be allowed out on parole here in this room – just for a minute or two – so that he can complete the story of the tragedy which he feels belongs to him and him alone. Or does he perhaps feel too angry to talk about it?'

'No, he wants to talk,' I said, 'because he knows you'll understand.' Then I stepped out from behind the glittering image. I felt stark naked, terrifyingly vulnerable but not alone. I came out because Darrow was there to meet me and I trusted him not to recoil in horror.

'The tragedy ended when Jane got pregnant,' I said, and *I* said it, my other self said it, and not just my other self but *my true self*, the real Charles Ashworth said, 'I don't know how it happened but I suppose that for once the coitus interruptus wasn't so interrupted as I thought it was. Then one night I came back to the headmaster's house after an absolutely damnable staff-meeting – oh, how I hated that school! – and Jane was waiting for me with shining eyes to tell me the good news. And then I – my other self – MY TRUE SELF – *I* took over from the glittering image. I said, "My God, that's the last thing I need to hear after another bloody awful day at this bloody awful school," and I poured myself a double whisky. Jane said, "You're not the man I thought I was marrying." Tears were streaming down her face, and immediately I was crucified with guilt. I went over to her, begged her to forgive me but she shouted, "Never!" and hit me and rushed out. I was so stupefied that I didn't at first rush after her – and when I did it was too late. She'd gone to the garage and taken out the car. I couldn't catch her before she drove off and less than five minutes later she'd crashed into a tree – killed instantly – no other car was involved, and the coroner at the inquest said what a tragic accident it was, but of course I always wondered – I always wondered – '

' – if it was suicide,' said Darrow.

I leant over the table, buried my face in my forearms and cried as I had not cried since I had learnt of Jane's death seven years before.

III

'If she was devout,' said Darrow, 'suicide is unlikely.' He had moved his chair around the table so that he could sit at my side.

'But I can never be certain of that and meanwhile I feel her death was entirely my fault – '

'I quite understand why you should feel that, Charles, but it's not a judgement you're qualified to make. We never know all the circumstances of a tragedy, and even if we did we might not have the wisdom to interpret them correctly.'

'But the indisputable fact remains – '

'The only fact which is beyond dispute here is that your wife is dead. God saw fit, for reasons which are hidden from us, to claim her after only a short life in the world, and you must accept this. Your guilt is making you say that this shouldn't have happened, that God made a mistake, but this is arrogance. Say to yourself instead: "Jane is now beyond all pain and this is God's will; I did make errors during my marriage but the best thing I can do now is not to wallow in guilt but to find out why I made these errors so that I can ensure they never happen again." Then Jane's death will have meaning.'

'I did love her,' I whispered. 'I really did.'

'Of course. That's why you're not sitting back and saying, "My marriage was a disaster but thank heaven I escaped!" And that's why you must, in memory of her, reconstruct your life so that you can make the right marriage to the right woman. Your first task, I think, is to understand exactly why your marriage ran into such painful difficulties.'

'But I do understand! It was because my real self was so unfit, so unworthy – '

'Stop!' said Darrow so incisively that I jumped. 'That statement contradicts every word you've just uttered!'

I stared at him. 'I don't understand.'

'In your narrative you made it quite clear that your true self didn't get a chance to speak his mind until that final scene. Who was really running that marriage of yours?'

I could not answer.

'Your marital difficulties didn't begin in that final scene, did they? They began before you were married when you ran into financial trouble – and who got you into financial trouble by luring you into keeping up expensive appearances? Who kept you from seeking help by demanding that no one should know your marriage was in difficulty? Who seduced you into that disastrous headmastership and then insisted that you stayed there? Who came between you and your wife and prevented you from being honest with her? Who initiated this tragedy and then left your real self bearing the burden of all the guilt and the shame?'

But still I could not speak. My emotion was beyond expression.

'You're not the villain of this story, Charles,' said Darrow. 'You're the victim. It's the glittering image who should be locked up in jail.'

IV

There was a long silence while I struggled to adjust to this new perspective on my identity but eventually Darrow added: 'I'm beginning to feel very, very sorry for this true self of yours. Terrible things happen to him but no one knows because he's not allowed to talk about them. He's cut off, isolated by that ruthless jailer. He only ever escapes when the jailer has too much to drink and then he's always so aggressive that he seems thoroughly beyond the pale, but no wonder he's so angry! He's been imprisoned on a false charge by a jailer who should himself be behind bars. Tell me, can you really feel no sympathy for him in his predicament?'

'Yes, but . . . what good would my sympathy do?'

'All the good in the world because if you regard him with sympathy instead of horror then a different image will begin to appear in the mirror. Love and compassion breed understanding and forgiveness, and once a man's understood himself sufficiently to forgive himself for his mistakes, the unfitness is made whole, the unworthiness is redeemed – and that's what we want, isn't it, Charles? We want to restore your belief in your own worth so that you can find the courage to set aside the glittering image and triumph over this tyrant who's tormented you for so long.'

Once more the unwanted tears began to fall. I heard myself whisper, 'Why do I feel so worthless? Why has all this happened?' and Darrow said: 'That's the mystery beyond the mystery – and that's the mystery we've now got to solve.'

V

We met again that evening. The bedside lamp glowed behind Darrow as usual and gave his unremarkable grey hair a distinguished silver sheen. His ineradicable air of authority was heavily muted; I was conscious primarily of his serenity.

'Can you come out on parole again?' he said. 'I'm anxious to hear what you think about that glittering image now that you've had the time to reflect on our last conversation.'

'He's got to be locked up. I can see that. But I can't see how I'm ever going to do it.'

'It's possible,' said Darrow, 'that if we can solve the mystery beyond the mystery he may simply wither away.'

I was intrigued but sceptical. 'I can't imagine him not being there.'

'Been around long, has he?' said Darrow casually.

'Always.'

'He's always been there defining success in terms of winning everyone's liking and approval?'

'Yes.'

'But what about you, Charles? How would your true self define success?'

'Well, of course I do realize,' I said, 'that there's more to life than winning everyone's liking and approval. Success is pursuing one's calling to the best of one's ability. In other words, one dedicates oneself to serving God, and – '

'Which self?'

'One's true self,' I said automatically, and heard my sharp intake of breath. Still grappling with the insight which had been thrust upon me I concluded: 'One dedicates one's true self to serving God and one strives hard to do His will.'

'Or to put it in non-theological terms,' said Darrow, allowing me time to complete the struggle, 'success involves realizing the fullest potential for good of one's true self so that one's life is a harmonious expression of one's innate gifts. Now, Charles, how would you, your true self, define failure?'

'Locking up one's true self in order to live a lie,' said my voice. 'Living out of harmony with one's true self in order to pursue the wrong goals for the wrong reasons. Caring more about other people's opinions than about serving God and doing His will.' I added in shame, 'I can see I've been very much in error.'

'Yes, but the point to note is that your errors haven't arisen because of any profoundly incapacitating unfitness on the part of your true self. He knows – *you* know – exactly what you should be doing with your life, but that glittering image has such a stranglehold over you that you have to devote an enormous amount of time and energy to keeping him happy.'

I explored that summary and finally pronounced, 'I'm like someone who's being blackmailed.'

'Exactly. The glittering image insists that the right people won't like and approve of you unless you give him a luxurious home right in the forefront of your personality, and for some reason you're so addicted to liking and approval that you're willing to give in to this demand in order to satisfy your addiction.'

I thought that over. 'When I know people like and approve of me,' I said tentatively, 'I don't feel so unfit and unworthy any more.'

Darrow looked pleased as if some inarticulate pupil had made an eloquent speech. 'Excellent,' he said. 'And now perhaps you can see why, if we solve the mystery beyond the mystery, the glittering image may simply fade away.'

'It must be a question of breaking the addiction. If I don't feel unfit and unworthy, then I won't be so dependent on people liking and approving of me and I won't need the glittering image to secure their liking and approval.'

Darrow looked pleased again as if the inarticulate pupil had finally reached the top of the class, but before he could comment I said in despair, 'I can see all this intellectually, but – '

' – but emotionally you still can't imagine how you could ever live without your glittering image systematically captivating the people who matter. But I think if we trace him back to his roots and find out how he came into existence we'll begin to see why you feel too unfit and unworthy to go through life without him.'

'But the glittering image doesn't have any roots,' I said baffled. 'I told you – he's always been there.'

'How very remarkable,' said Darrow blandly. 'I've never before heard of a baby who arrived in the world complete with a glittering image.'

I smiled uncertainly at him before saying, 'Supposing we can't find the roots?'

'I don't see why we shouldn't. It's just a question of knowing where to dig. Then once we reach the roots we'll prise them out so that the entire noxious weed can be left to wither away in the sun while the half-strangled starving plant in the flower-bed will be able to flourish at last.'

I considered this prospect in silence and the silence lasted a long time.

'However,' said Darrow watching me, 'digging's hard work and you may not be strong enough yet.'

I said suddenly, 'Is this where the gate gets even straiter and the way even narrower?'

'Yes, but we don't have to approach this new gate yet, Charles. We can just sit and look at it for a while.'

But all I said was, 'I want to go on.'

FOURTEEN

'It is not quite easy to fix an autobiographical paragraph into such a composition as that which I am now addressing to you, but I think it will have to be attempted, for undoubtedly my personal religion has been strongly affected by the eccentric course of my early years.'

HERBERT HENSLEY HENSON
Bishop of Durham 1920–1939
Retrospect of an Unimportant Life

I

It was morning and the light of a clouded day illuminated my room as we sat down again at the table. I had repeated my desire to begin the excavation which would lead to the root of my glittering image, but Darrow had made no immediate reply; I suspected he was calculating how far I spoke out of bravado.

'Well, we won't drill straight away to bedrock,' he said at last. 'Let's first scrape off a little topsoil by talking of Jardine.'

My hand groped for my cross.

'We won't discuss him in detail,' said Darrow quickly. 'I'd just like you to clarify my mind on a single point: did Jardine like you straight away? He obviously liked you very much later or he wouldn't have told you about his father.'

I could think of the early part of my visit to Starbridge without difficulty. 'I don't think he did like me particularly at first,' I said. 'He thought I was just one of Lang's bright young men.'

'Did you want him to like you?'

'Yes, of course.'

'Why "of course"? It could have been a matter of supreme indifference to you.'

'Yes, but during our row at the dinner-table he gave the impression he strongly disapproved of everything I said – '

' – and you didn't like him disapproving of you?'

I hesitated before saying abruptly, 'I hated it.'

'Yet it would be true to say, wouldn't it, that by the end of your visit you'd managed to win his approval despite all the friction caused by Lang's commission and your attraction to Lyle?'

I nodded.

'Very well,' said Darrow, 'we've established that here was an important man many years your senior who liked and approved of you. Now let's leave Jardine and go further back into the past – let's talk about your relationship with Dr Lang. There seems to be a similar pattern here . . . but perhaps I'm mistaken.'

'No,' I said reluctantly. 'Lang and Jardine are two very different men but I was equally successful in winning Lang's liking and approval.'

'Can you describe the relationship with Lang in more specific terms?'

'I was his protégé.'

'Yes, but is there one adjective, do you think, that we can use to describe the attitude of this distinguished man many years your senior who likes and approves of you?'

'Benign.'

'There isn't another adjective you'd choose?'

'No,' I said at once.

'Very well, let's go back a little further to Jane's father, another distinguished man many years your senior who regarded you benignly. When you were telling me about Jane you made it clear how important his liking and approval were to you, and obviously you succeeded in getting on well with him. Did Jane have any brothers?'

'No. The old boy minded that very much, I think.'

'In that case he must have been very pleased to have acquired such a first-class son-in-law.'

I traced a mark on the table with my forefinger and said nothing.

'This is really quite a coincidence, isn't it?' said Darrow. 'Three distinguished older men, all regarding you with exceptional approval! Would you say they had any striking feature in common?'

'The Church.'

'Was that the only common denominator?'

'Yes,' I said at once.

'And when you were up at Cambridge as an undergraduate – I expect there was someone special there too, wasn't there, who took a benign interest in you?'

'Well, as a matter of fact,' I said, 'yes. I became the protégé of the Master of Laud's.'

'Did he have a family?'

'Both his sons were killed in the War.'

'And before you went up to Cambridge I'm sure the headmaster of your school took a special interest, didn't he?'

'Yes, I was head-boy.'

'And at prep school?'

'Yes, I was head-boy there too.'

'And what happened before you went to prep school?' said Darrow. 'Who was the important older man in your life then?'

I looked out of the window, I looked all the way down the garden, I looked far back into the past, and the silence closed around us as the memories stirred in my mind.

'Charles,' said Darrow, 'for some days now I've been watching all the characters in the drama of your life parade across the stage, but there's a very important person who hasn't yet appeared. Is this perhaps the moment when he makes his long-awaited entrance or are you going to save him up for a later scene?'

I laughed. 'By all means let him make his entrance!' I said. 'But in fact my father's not important in this context.'

'If you'd prefer to say no more – '

'Oh, there's no question of that! What do you want to know?'

'Well, perhaps you could just mention in passing how you get on with him – '

'Exceptionally well,' I said. 'He's the most splendid chap and I have nothing but respect and admiration for him.'

'You've always got on well with him, have you?'

'Always. Well . . . I admit there was a little difficulty when I went into the Church – no, let's call a spade a spade and say there was a big row – but we got over all that years ago and now he's proud of my success. I'm very fond of both my parents and I'm very good friends with my brother – in fact I'd say we were an unusually close, happy family.'

All Darrow said was, 'When did you last go home?'

II

I said, 'I don't think I'll talk any more this morning. I'm all right, there's nothing wrong, but I think I'd like time to reflect on the extraordinary coincidence that I keep meeting these benign older churchmen!' I smiled to show him how amused I was, how detached, how absolutely in command of myself, and my self was the glittering image, threatened, fearful, prepared to fight hard to survive.

Darrow said to him politely, 'Just as you like. Shall we hope for sunshine this afternoon in the herb-garden?'

'I suppose you now want me to admit,' I said later as Darrow sat down beside me on the bench in the herb-garden, 'that there are a bunch of terrible skeletons in the family cupboard.'

'Charles, I'm just the porter with the trolley. I'm not here to criticize the quality of your luggage or to order which bag you should put down. My function is simply to offer you the chance to get rid of any bag which you don't want to carry any more, but the decision to keep or discard each bag must be yours and yours alone.'

Having considered this I felt sufficiently reassured to say, 'I'm not a fool. You wanted me to describe all this benign interest from the older men as paternal. You wanted me to admit that the one thing they all had in common was that they had no sons of their own. You wanted me to acknowledge that it's no amazing coincidence that I always seem to have this kind of older man in my life. You want me now to concede there's something wrong with my relationship with my father. But there isn't. There really isn't. We're very fond of each other.'

'Very well,' said Darrow serenely. 'We won't bother to talk about your father. Let's talk instead about all these father-figures you've accumulated over the years.'

'What a bloody awful word "father-figure" is! I exclaimed, and with the word 'bloody' I felt the glittering image slip. A clergyman had a duty to avoid bad language. I suddenly realized my true self had a duty to avoid bad language. I suddenly realized my true self was trying to escape and I needed time to lock him up. I said to Darrow to divert him, 'Are you a follower of Freud?'

'Let's just say I'm an interested observer.'

'I think Freud's rubbish. I refuse to believe all men are in love with their mothers and searching continually for father-figures.'

'Is that what Freud actually says? However let's forget Freud – and let's forget that description "father-figure" which I agree is absurdly lugubrious. How would you yourself describe all these benign older men in your life?'

'Well, obviously they're a substitute for my father, I can see that, but that can't be the whole explanation because my father's attitude towards me is benign too.'

'Do you think it's possible,' said Darrow, 'that you simply enjoy being a son? If your relationship with your father is so good you may be unable to resist the urge to repeat it at every opportunity.'

This suggestion struck me as bizarre. Regarding him with suspicion I said austerely, 'I hardly collect fathers for pleasure.'

'Well, as a matter of fact it did occur to me that being the ideal son must be a somewhat time-consuming and tiring occupation.'

I laughed. 'You'll be telling me next I was so exhausted being a son that I didn't have enough energy to face being a father!'

Darrow laughed too. 'Sounds absurd, doesn't it?'

'Ridiculous!' I traced a pattern on the wooden arm of the bench.

'Perhaps it would be closer to the truth to say that your father didn't make fatherhood seem an attractive occupation.'

'That's a ridiculous suggestion too. He's always been wonderful.'

'The ideal father?'

'Well . . . He has his faults, of course, just as we all do, but by and large – '

'He's wonderful. I see. Now, Charles, there's a question I'd like to ask but you may not wish to answer it. If you don't – '

'I wish you'd stop treating me as a hopeless neurotic!' I said irritably. 'Of course I'll answer any question you care to ask – what do you think I've been doing since this interview began?'

'It's been a glittering performance,' said Darrow.

I at once picked up the Bible, which I had been reading before he had joined me, and began to flick through the pages. Again the books streamed past my fingers: Genesis, Exodus, Leviticus, Numbers, Deuteronomy, Joshua –

'What's this next question of yours!' I said casually.

'Are any of these benign older men like your father or is he in a class of his own?'

'He's nothing like them at all.' I had reached the New Testament, and suddenly one verse rose straight from the page to meet me. 'Strait is the gate,' I read, 'and narrow is the way, which leadeth unto life, and few there be that find it.'

I closed the Bible carefully, very carefully, as if I feared it might shatter to pieces in my hands, and gently very gently, I set the book down on the bench. Then I said to Darrow, 'I'm not telling the truth. I'm sorry. Yes, there's a likeness, a common denominator.'

'The Church?'

'No, my father's an atheist. He sent me to Church of England schools but that was only because he's so obsessed with what he calls "a good straight decent life", and he wanted schools which laid stress on morality. The common denominator between my father and the father-figures,' I said, 'is that they're all moral upright men.'

'Your father's beginning to intrigue me very much,' said Darrow. 'Do you think you could attempt a thumbnail sketch of his personality?'

This seemed a reasonable request and I thought I could grant it without difficulty. 'Why not?' I said, looking him straight in the eyes to show I was undaunted, but I was setting out at last, although I did not realize it, on my harrowing journey to the heart of my glittering image.

IV

'My father's very truthful, very frank,' I said. 'He resembles Jardine in detesting hypocrisy but he doesn't have Jardine's intellect or sophistication. My father despises glamour; he thinks it's bad form, pretentious. He'd distrust that *nouveau-riche* aura of the fast social traveller which makes Jardine so interesting in his palace. My father hasn't the slightest desire to travel socially because he likes life exactly where he is; he thinks that to be a member of the English middle classes is to belong to the best caste in the world.

'At the same time within that caste he's very ambitious. He founded his firm on his own and wound up thirty years later with sixteen partners and a first-class reputation. He's only just retired. Of course Peter and I went to the best schools and of course we all lived in the best part of Epsom. My parents still live there. My mother has higher social aspirations than my father, but although he's always scathing about anyone with a title he wouldn't want the aristocracy abolished because he thinks England should remain quite unchanged. He despises the working classes *en masse* but he's kind to them as individuals – he's good to his servants, good to his employees at the office, because he thinks that's his duty.

'My father's very keen on duty. He thinks that's what being a middle-class English gentleman's all about; one has a duty to work hard, live a decent life, deal honestly in business, set an example to the community and stand by one's family. He despises inefficiency, sloth, slovenliness, disloyalty, crime, immorality and cruelty to animals. He keeps a black Labrador called Nelson and drives a black Rover. He could afford a Daimler but he'd think that was pretentious. My mother gets livid with him on that subject and compensates herself by making regular shopping expeditions to Harrods. "What a nasty pretentious-looking piece of nonsense!" he said when she bought her new fur coat, but in fact he secretly likes her to look smart and expensive because that symbolizes his success – which of course he'd never dream of bragging about; that wouldn't be the done thing at all.

'When I was appointed Lang's chaplain my mother bragged about it to her friends and couldn't even complete a sentence without mentioning the word "archbishop", but my father just said, "My son's got an interesting post. He's a sort of private secretary. Useful start to his career." But he was very pleased. He said to me, "Better than wasting your time in a bloody vicarage somewhere in the back of beyond," and then he said: "For

God's sake don't get drunk or fool around with some girl and get sacked."
When I got the headmastership of St Aidan's he said, "A bit young, aren't
you?" but he was thrilled. He said, "Important step up the ladder. But
don't let it go to your head – no airs and graces, no drinks you don't need,
no stupid flirtations. Never forget that pride comes before a fall."

'Later when I published my book my mother was soon boasting away
as usual and even told my aunt how much money I had been paid on the
advance, but my father overheard her and was furious. He thinks any
public talk about money is vulgar, but in private he likes to know every
financial detail. He said to me, "I suppose the book will only sell a few
copies,' but when I told him it could make money as a text-book he lapped
up all the figures. However he wouldn't let my mother keep my book
permanently displayed on the drawing-room table. "Not the done thing,"
he said. "Flashy. I won't have it." And he put the book away in the
bookcase. My mother was so livid that they had a row – the first row they'd
had over me for years – but she had to give in eventually.

'They used to have rows over me when I was small. He said she
pampered me too much and she said he didn't pamper me enough. I don't
mean they had rows in front of me when I was a child – that would have
been bad form – but once or twice I listened at the keyhole.

'When they had the row over my book they had the row in front of me
– rows are apparently permissible in the presence of adult offspring – and
finally my mother called him a brute and burst into tears. My father said,
"Stupid woman. Storm in a teacup," and stumped off to his study to read
the *Daily Telegraph*. My father doesn't read *The Times*. He thinks it's
pretentious. He likes the *Daily Telegraph* for the sport and the business
news. He doesn't read much, only the occasional biography. "I shan't read
that," he said when I gave him a copy of my book. "Not my cup of tea."
But late that night I went to his study and found him reading it. "Can't
think how anyone takes Christianity seriously," he said. "Amazing how
those Early Church people survived. Personally I'd have thrown the whole
damn lot to the lions." He read the whole book and said, "Quite interesting
but a pity they couldn't have printed it on better paper." That was high
praise, coming from him.

'When I was awarded my doctorate he said, "Well, don't expect me to
call you doctor. As far as I'm concerned doctors are rogues who charge
too much for trying to put their patients in coffins, and thank God you
never wanted to dabble in medicine." My mother loved me being a doctor
and she begged me not to mind about my father's attitude – she said his
aversion to doctors had developed even before I was born and there was
no hope of changing him. It was easier when I became a canon. "Damn
silly title!" said my father. "How long do I have to wait before I can call
you Bishop?" That was when I knew how pleased he was. Then he said,

"You're doing rather well, aren't you? Amazing! Well, if you've got to be a damn clergyman at least I have the satisfaction of knowing you're a successful one. *Well done, Charles!*' he said, and smiled at me.

'I'll never forget that. I was so overcome I couldn't speak. But the next moment he was saying: "Now don't make a mess of it. Keep your nose to the grindstone. Stick to the straight and narrow, watch your alcohol consumption and don't make a fool of yourself over some bloody woman. All your faults and weaknesses won't go away just because you've got some fancy clerical title and can put the letters DD after your name." My mother overheard that last sentence and she was livid. She shouted, "How dare you talk about faults and weaknesses when he's standing there good as gold in his clerical collar?" and my father lost his temper. He said, "Stupid woman, treating him like a saint! Can't you see all that religious rubbish is just an act? He's only in it for the glamour and the play-acting!"

'Well, I wasn't going to let him get away with that but I was in such a state that all I could do was shout, "You bastard! You *bastard*!" and then my mother started to scream and I tried to hit him but she got herself between us and sobbed, "No – please – I can't bear any more suffering – " and my father yelled, "*Shut up, you stupid woman!*" and slapped her and I tried to hit him again but she flung her arms around me and I had to hold her because she was sobbing so violently, but I said to my father, "That was the damndest thing you could possibly say to me and the damndest attitude you could possibly adopt to her and I'd like to take her right out of this house this instant!" And he said, "Take her away and good riddance – at least I'll still have Peter." And somehow that was the last straw. I shouted, "I'm so bloody sick of bloody Peter always being your bloody favourite – *damn* bloody Peter!" and my mother started screaming again but my father just said, "Disgraceful language to use in front of a woman. You're not much of a clergyman, are you, whenever you forget to put on that glamorous act! Well, you never take *me* in, not for a moment," and he slammed the door of his study in my face.

'I banged on the panels but he'd turned the key in the lock and although I begged him to let me in he wouldn't. He wouldn't even reply and I felt absolutely rejected, utterly cut off – and I hadn't done anything except protest against his insults! I couldn't bear it, but I couldn't go on banging at the door because my mother was so upset, weeping and weeping, and so I tried to comfort her by saying I really would take her away but that horrified her. She said, "But I couldn't possibly leave! What would everyone think?" and she said, "We've got to keep up appearances. Nobody must ever know." Then she cried again but finally she said, "We're really very happy – he's just a little difficult now and then, that's all, but you mustn't think he doesn't love us both and you must never think he's not terribly proud of your success." I said, "He's got a very funny way of showing it, and if he thinks I'm coming back here to be insulted in future he's made a big mistake."

'That was last year, last September. I haven't been back. I asked my mother to visit Cambridge but she refused because she was afraid people might think it odd if she came without him, and she has this obsession with keeping up appearances. That's why there's been no divorce, of course. My mother would be too frightened of scandal ever to risk an affair, and my father . . . well, he's not the sort of man who plays around with women. He'd think that vulgar and cheap. Adultery's for cads and bounders, not for strict, strong-principled men like him. I can imagine him thinking to himself: I vowed to be faithful to that woman and I'll be faithful to her even if it kills me – and even if it kills her.

'He did write to me after the row. I can remember the letter word for word. He said, "Of course the stupid woman got the wrong end of the stick. She didn't realize I'd praised you before I warned you about your faults and weaknesses. But praise should be sparing and I'm not here to flatter and pamper you to death. That's not what fathers are for. My duty as your father was to bring you up to be a good straight decent man and once I'd done that – and I did – my next duty was to make damned sure you stayed that way. That's why I regularly remind you of your faults and weaknesses. I'm not in this parenthood business to be loved and doted on. I'm in it to do my duty and be respected. You wouldn't respect me if I allowed you to go to the dogs and I wouldn't respect myself either." Then he signed himself: "Your affectionate Father," and added: "PS Visit us again soon if only to keep your mother happy."

'There wasn't a word of apology. I wrote back and said I wasn't going to return unless he apologized for scoffing at my vocation and calling me a fraud. He wrote back and said he was waiting for me to apologize for using filthy language in front of my mother and trying to hit him. I didn't write back. So that was that. However, finally Lent arrived, and when I saw Father Reid – dear old Father Reid! – he said, "I think you're a little bit in error here, Charles. I don't think calling Mr Ashworth a bastard is compatible with the commandment "Honour thy Father", and besides, if we're mocked for our vocation we must always turn the other cheek and accept the suffering."

'Well, by that time I was feeling thoroughly miserable about my father so I hardly needed any extra pressure to coax me into writing to him again. I sent a friendly letter apologizing, inviting him to bring my mother to Cambridge for a visit and offering to put them both up at the Blue Boar. He wrote back saying he'd come so long as I wasn't expecting him to attend any mumbo-jumbo in the Cathedral. That finished it. He was so damn rude. I didn't write back. I just tried to put him out of my mind, but that wasn't so difficult because I was very busy with my undergraduates, and even after they'd gone home for the Long Vacation I had yet another distraction because Lang arrived with his commission. And when I came at last to Starbridge ... well, as soon as I met Jardine my father ceased to be important any more.

'Jardine killed the pain. They all did, all those older men with no sons of their own who thought I was worthy of special attention. They killed the pain of knowing my father dislikes me. I'm just a duty as far as he's concerned. I thought that if I was a success I'd finally make him like me – I've worked and worked and worked at being a success because I know success is the only language he really understands – but even though I try to talk to him in his own language he doesn't hear me; in fact it's almost as if he refuses to hear me – oh, how unjust it is! How unfair! It makes me feel so angry, Father, so angry, so hurt, so resentful, and all that anger goes round and round in my mind until I feel I can't bear the pain of it any longer – and when the pain becomes unbearable I hate him, yes, I do – *I hate him* – oh God forgive me, I know it's wicked but I've so often been so unhappy – so often when I was growing up I found myself hating him, so often when I was growing up I found myself being vilely jealous of my brother for being the favourite, and all that hatred and jealousy made me feel so guilty – oh, how I despised myself, because of course I do love my father, I do – I love him all the time I'm hating him but the whole relationship's such a back-breaking burden and now I can't carry it a second longer, I've got to put it down. I *want* to put it down but I don't know how to do it, and that's why you've got to help me, Father, you've got to help me, *you've got to help me* –'

228

FIFTEEN

'I think there is probably in most lives a point at which private confession is both natural and salutary, very largely because it is felt to be the fitting and almost inevitable beginning of a new spiritual chapter in personal life.'

HERBERT HENSLEY HENSON
Bishop of Durham 1920–1939
Retrospect of an Unimportant Life

I

I was tugging at my cross and suddenly as the clasp snapped the chain slid through my fingers. I gasped but Darrow scooped it up and thrust it back between my shaking hands. I could barely see. My throat seemed to be swelling so fast that my supply of air was impeded. I felt as if I were standing naked before an icy wind.

'I can't breathe – '

'Oh yes you can,' said Darrow, and shoved me back hard against the bench to straighten my spine. Automatically I cried out, my windpipe relaxed its spasm and the air flowed again into my lungs. 'And again,' said Darrow. He gave me another shake to help the next breath along; I felt as if I were being resuscitated from drowning.

'Why am I so cold?' I had begun to shudder from head to toe.

'Shock. You opened the cupboard door and looked directly on the skeleton inside. Now, Charles – ' He sat down again beside me ' – keep holding the cross and give me your free hand. I'm going to say a silent prayer, just as I did on the morning after your arrival, and this time I want you not only to continue taking those deep breaths but to think of the heat of those Palestinian summers when Our Lord exercised the famous charisms – preaching, teaching, healing . . . and all in the heat, all in the warmth, all in the sun.'

The silence fell, and gradually I found I could feel the sunlight on my face as I sat motionless on the bench. Behind my closed eyelids I saw the sun-baked Palestinian landscape, but then the scent of the herb-garden brought me back to England and for a brief moment I saw Jane smiling at me. I remembered I was working to give her death meaning by my own rebirth, and as I realized that all I now needed was courage I felt the warmth begin. It seeped through my hands to my arms, through my arms to my heart, through my heart to my mind and through my mind to my soul.

I opened my eyes at exactly the same moment as Darrow opened his.

'You heard, didn't you?' he said.

'Yes. Courage. A new life. And Jane was there.'

Darrow smiled but was silent and suddenly I was saying: 'You saw her. You must have done. I know you did. Why don't you admit – '

'You mustn't tempt me, Charles. Do you remember me telling you of the spiritual director who said, "Beware of those glamorous Powers"? It's so easy to make a gift from God look like a charlatan's parlour-trick . . . But now forget the parlour-tricks and look around you. Do you know where you are?' And as I looked blankly at the herb-garden he added, 'No, look in your mind. The strait gate is behind you; you're in the middle of the narrow way at last.'

I sat there, outwardly calm but inwardly still shattered by the aftermath of shock, and it was a full minute before I was able to say, 'Will he start fading away now?'

'Not yet. We're looking on the roots but they're deeply embedded and we have to dig a little deeper before we can remove them successfully.'

'But I'm going to be all right – you're going to sort everything out – '

'No, Charles, *you're* the one who's going to sort everything out. But only when you're rested and fit.' He took off his Abbot's cross and gave it to me. 'Put that on and let me take the one with the broken chain. I'll get that repaired and you can have it back tonight.' He paused as I thanked him but then he said casually, as if he could no longer resist the temptation to help the healing process by a flash of unorthodoxy: 'That was a pretty locket Jane was wearing.' And rising to his feet with all the showmanship of a conjuror who had just produced a rabbit from a hat, he sauntered forward to inspect the nearest bed of the herb-garden.

II

The effect – as no doubt he had anticipated – was to divert me entirely from my shock and to restore me at a stroke to normality. I jumped to my feet and evidently the rapid movement served to remind him that I might be liable to panic. At once he said, 'I'll get someone to sit with you,' and I realized that despite his flamboyant parlour-trick he remained the careful priest, pleased with his healing skills but humble enough to

230

realize that they should be supplemented by a more conventional care. 'You shouldn't be alone at the moment.'

'I'm all right.' I was still so enrapt by the display of his 'glamorous Powers' that I barely heard him. 'Father, she's happy, isn't she?' I said, but immediately I was overwhelmed with embarrassment. 'I'm sorry, I know what happened. I wasn't seeing her as she is – I was remembering her as she was, and you looked across and saw my memory.' In shame I added, 'Forgive me for sinking into the error of superstition, but I suddenly had a great urge to communicate with her.'

'That's a healthy sign.' He showed no anger. 'I suspect you've been suppressing all thought of her for years, so if you now seek to commune with her memory it suggests that the burden of guilt is beginning to lift.'

'It's because I'm at last doing something to put matters right – wiping out the man who made her unhappy – '

'Yes, the glittering image has certainly taken a pounding today, but now you need time to recuperate. If you're strong enough – and only if you're strong enough – we'll resume the attack this evening.'

III

That evening we exchanged crosses following the repair of the broken chain, and as he replaced the Abbot's cross on his chest I thought how ill its lavish splendour accorded with his austere, occluded, tightly disciplined personality.

'Well?' he said as we sat down at the table. 'How are you feeling after this morning's haemorrhage?'

'Haemorrhage!'

'Is that an exaggeration? You lost a lot of emotional blood, and sometimes,' said Darrow, embarking on another meticulous examination of his ring, 'after an ordeal like that one can suffer a reaction. One can feel guilt and anger, guilt that one's betrayed one's most private secrets, anger that one's been lured into speaking the unspeakable.'

We considered this possibility in silence but at last I said: 'I do feel guilty – but not because I've told you my most private secrets. And I do feel angry – but not with you for luring me into self-revelation. I feel angry with myself because I wanted to give you a fair picture of my father yet I ended up by delivering that vile tirade. And I feel guilty because I failed to convey to you what a wonderful man he is and how much I admire and respect him.'

'There was no failure,' said Darrow. 'You did convey those feelings clearly.'

'I did? But at the end when I said I hated him – '

'If all you felt was hatred you wouldn't be here. You'd have walked away from him years ago and heaved a sigh of relief that you'd finally escaped from his clutches. But you can't walk away, can you? During the past year you've tried but you've merely made yourself thoroughly miserable.'

'It's as if . . .' I strained to identify the elusive words and at last ventured: 'It's as if he's got some colossal hold over me.'

'Of course. We're very much at the mercy of those we love, and never more so than when those we love don't love us quite as we would wish in return.'

'But he doesn't love me at all.'

'Who's "me"?' said Darrow.

'My true self. He doesn't love and approve of me as I am, and that's why – '

Darrow waited.

' – that's why I have to become someone else. But he doesn't even like the glittering image!'

'He respects him, though, doesn't he? And so long as you're slaving away fulfilling his definition of a successful man you stand a hope of hearing him say once in a while, "Well done, Charles!" '

'Yes, but he thinks it's all an act.'

'This is where your father resembles Jardine. He has a knack of spotting a performance that doesn't quite ring true, and so there are inevitably times when he sees straight past your glittering image and starts disapproving of you all over again – as he did during that last terrible quarrel.'

Shading my eyes with my hand I traced a line on the table and said, 'He tore up my glittering image and rejected my other self beyond.' Suddenly I could no longer see. I had to use both my hands to shade my eyes.

Darrow said: 'That was a cruel thing to do, wasn't it?'

I nodded. 'But it wasn't his fault.'

'No?'

'No, it was my fault. If I hadn't been so unfit and unworthy he wouldn't have needed to disapprove of me so strongly. You see, he's so straight, so upright, so decent – if only I could convey to you what a hero he is – '

'Charles,' said Darrow, 'your father may indeed be a remarkable man in many ways, but if he's at the root of your glittering image – if he consistently rejected your true self so that you were obliged to become someone else – if he was in any degree responsible for launching you on that road which finally resulted in your arriving here one night dead drunk and spiritually shattered – his status as a hero is very much open to debate.'

It had never occurred to me before that my father's heroism could be debatable. I wrestled with this revolutionary idea for some time before saying firmly, 'He can't be entirely to blame.'

'That seems fair. I must say, I entirely disapprove of the Freudian tendency to blame all a child's troubles on his hapless parents ... Very well, let's assume you should share at least some of the responsibility for arriving here wrecked in the middle of the night. But how much of the responsibility should you shoulder?'

I could only say in despair, 'All of it – I can't blame my father for anything. If I wasn't so unfit and unworthy – '

'Who says you're unfit and unworthy?'

'I do. How else can one explain my father's attitude towards me?'

'That,' said Darrow, 'is the big question, Charles.'

I stared at him. 'But of course I'm unfit and unworthy!' I said. 'And of course my father's right to despise me for it. When I think of my recent errors – that drinking bout – Loretta – '

'Never mind your recent errors for the moment. Let's concentrate on your more normal behaviour. You work hard, don't you – try to do what's right – aim to lead what your father would call a good straight decent life?'

'Yes, but – '

'Then is it realistic to treat you as a drunken wastrel who's perpetually poised to go straight to the dogs? And is it fair? You're not really such a bad chap as all that, are you?'

I tried to speak but nothing happened.

'Well, I mustn't put thoughts in your head,' said Darrow. 'If you want to believe you're a bad chap you have a perfect right to do so, but I'd like you to consider very carefully how far this belief chimes with the actual evidence provided by your life. I'd also like you to consider the indisputable fact that your father is not the Pope speaking *ex cathedra*; he's not infallible. No matter how heroic he is he's still capable of making mistakes, just like any other human being.'

I managed to say, 'I'd like to believe I'm not such a bad chap. Sometimes I do believe it.'

'How do you feel about your father's judgement then?'

'Angry. But that's wrong, isn't it? I must turn the other cheek and forgive him.'

'Yes, you must – eventually. But how can you possibly forgive him at present when his attitude towards you is so inexplicable?'

'It's not inexplicable. My father adopts this attitude towards me because I'm so unfit and unworthy,' I persisted but even as I spoke the words began to assume a curiously hollow ring.

'This is indeed how you've always explained your father's attitude,' said Darrow, 'but supposing, just for the sake of argument, this explanation's dead wrong?'

The psychological chain binding me to my self-hatred was suddenly wafer-thin. I said, 'My father certainly *thinks* I'm unfit and unworthy. That's undeniable. But – '

'But?' said Darrow, coming to meet me as I struggled out of the dark into the light.

'It's just possible . . . it's not wholly out of the question . . . in fact it's within the bounds of probability – ' I drew a deep breath and said, 'He's made a mistake.' The chain snapped apart as the truth overpowered me like an avalanche, but after the avalanche came the silence and into the silence came the first faint whisper of the massive questions which I had never before been able to hear. Eventually I found I could say the questions aloud. 'Why does he have this low opinion of me?' I said baffled. 'What have I done to deserve it?' and as I spoke I felt as if I were turning some great psychological corner to confront a strange new landscape in my mind.

'And that,' said Darrow, 'is the mystery beyond the mystery beyond the mystery. Congratulations, Charles. Now we're indeed beginning to make progress.'

IV

'Your father certainly seems from your narrative to be strong and high-principled,' said Darrow when we met later, 'but he also seems to be dangerously proud. Pride is always dangerous. Pride coupled with a strong inflexible character can be lethal.

'Part of your father's pride, I think, would be manifested in the way he brought you up. Once he'd made a commitment he'd stick to it through thick and thin and he seems to have been saying to himself (if I may borrow the phraseology you yourself used), "I'll bring Charles up to be a good straight decent man even if it kills me – and even if it kills him." That sort of inflexible determination, though it can be admirable if riveted to a moral principle, is potentially destructive because it's incapable of adjusting to changing circumstances. Perhaps your father was justified in being strict with you when you were small – bright children often need a firm hand – but it seems he was incapable of modifying his attitude when you grew up.

'Now we come to the heart of the matter. There you are, clever, nice-looking, successful beyond any father's wildest dreams. Most fathers would be grovelling at your feet in sentimental adulation, so why should your father be sunk in this incorrigible pessimism? Of course one must make allowances for his character – his hatred of boasting, his natural English reserve, his admirable horror of spoiling you. One might suppose he's incapable of being demonstrative towards a son, but since you tell me your father displays an all-too-human paternal partiality towards your brother one feels driven to wonder why he's so inhibited in showing paternal partiality towards you.

'Now let's see where we've got to. We've speculated that your father adopted this attitude towards you when you were very young; this is supported by your impression that the glittering image has always been there. We've deduced that because of his inflexibility he was later unable to change his attitude, even when you turned out well, but we still don't know why he was compelled to adopt it in the first place. We know he was a conscientious father who was consumed with the desire to bring you up to be a good man, but we don't know why he's apparently unable to believe his success here is permanent. We can assume, I think, that he would act with the best of motives, but we don't know why he's wound up treating you so unfairly. Perhaps the whole mystery can be summed up by asking: how has this particular road to hell been paved with your father's good intentions?'

Darrow stopped speaking. We were sitting again in the herb-garden but I was by this time oblivious of my surroundings. I was too busy channelling my mental energy into the mystery as if it were a piece of research which demanded absolute concentration.

'How much clearer everything seems,' I said, 'but that means, para-doxically, how much more mysterious. I feel as if I'm seeing the outline of the mystery for the first time.'

'Then let's now step past the outline to examine the mystery at close quarters. Tell me about your brother. Is he older than you?'

'No, he's two years my junior and I suppose one could describe him as a sunny-natured version of my father. He's married with three children and lives near my parents in Epsom.'

'Is he clever? It's hard not to imagine you outshining him on every front.'

'He's certainly no fool; he's a partner in my father's firm, but he's limited in his interests and we don't have much in common.'

'How did his early career compare with yours?'

'I did outshine him. I often suspected my father felt driven to favour Peter in order to compensate him – in the same way as my mother felt driven to favour me in order to compensate me for my father's harshness.' I hesitated before adding, 'However explaining the family relationships in terms of favouritism fails to convey their complexity. For instance, although I'm my mother's favourite neither of us are comfortable with each other. She's much more relaxed with Peter.'

'You're not close to her?'

'I hate to say it but I find her a strain. It's because she's very effusive – but not in a natural way. In fact she always makes me want to cringe and protest: "For Heaven's sake treat me normally instead of putting on this act!" Yet it's not an act. The emotion's genuine enough but she can't express it in a relaxed manner.'

'Yet you said she was relaxed with Peter.'

'He doesn't seem to affect her in the same way. In fact the atmosphere Peter generates with our parents is entirely different, but I suppose this must happen frequently in families where the two children are unalike.'

'I agree this is a fairly common phenomenon, but has it ever struck you in your own case as seeming distinctly abnormal?'

'Well, I remember one instance in particular: I was visiting them soon after I was ordained – it was before Peter was married and he was still living at home. I was watching the three of them when they were in the garden and I was indoors. My father was laughing, Peter was sprawled happily in a deck chair – even my mother was looking relaxed. Then I walked out of the house to join them and it was as if a curtain had come down over the scene. Peter didn't change. He went on sprawling in his deck chair, but my father said "Here comes the clergyman" in a typical sardonic voice and my mother said with that awful false brightness of hers, "Let's all have cocktails!" and I felt – '

'Yes?' said Darrow. 'How did you feel?'

'Like an unwanted guest.' It was too difficult to go on.

'Odd man out? I'd been thinking,' said Darrow, coming to my rescue, 'how different you must be from the other members of your family and how awkward this must have been for you when you were growing up.'

The knowledge that he understood enabled me to say, 'When I was fifteen I even wondered . . . Well, Father, don't laugh, I know this sounds melodramatic and ridiculous, but I even wondered if I were adopted.'

'That sounds rather a sensible explanation to me. Who said it was melodramatic and ridiculous?'

'My father.'

'Ah!' said Darrow. 'I see. Your father made you feel melodramatic and ridiculous, just as he made you feel unfit and unworthy.'

There was a silence while I grappled with the huge implications of this statement but at last I said resigned, 'No, this time there's no question of my father making a mistake. I really was being stupid. You see, what happened was this . . .'

V

'I'd been wondering for some time if I were adopted,' I said, 'and finally I decided to inspect my birth certificate to see if there were any clues there. My father kept all the family documents in a file in his study so it was a simple matter to make a raid one night when everyone was asleep. I found no hint of any irregularity on my birth certificate, of course, but in the file I came across the certificate of my parents' marriage and then I did make a discovery which astonished me: my parents had married a year later than I'd thought. I knew the month and day of their wedding because they always celebrated their anniversary, but I thought they'd married in 1898. I'd never realized they were married in 1899 and that I'd arrived – in 1900 – only seven months after the wedding.'

'Premature?'

'That was my first reaction but no one had ever mentioned me fighting for life in my cradle. Then I wondered if I'd been conceived out of wedlock with the result that my father had been forced to marry my mother, but somehow I couldn't see him seducing a girl from a respectable family. And at that point I remembered my father's sister mentioning cattily once that my mother had been considered fast when she was young, and immediately it occurred to me that I might have been fathered by someone else.'

'Did you go back to your aunt for further information?'

'No, I didn't like my aunt. I might have gone to my mother, but I was in the throes of a sex-obsessed puberty and I balked at the prospect of asking her intimate questions. So in the end after much soul-searching I went to my father. I'd convinced myself he'd be relieved to tell me the whole truth at last.'

'How did he respond?'

'He was livid. Mortally insulted. "Never heard such melodramatic ridiculous nonsense in my life!" he said. 'How dare you doubt my paternity after I've been slaving away all these years to give you a decent upbringing!" Well, as you can imagine, Father, I was completely cowed.'

'Of course you were, but did he deign to explain – '

'Yes, he had a thoroughly convincing explanation for my early arrival. He said that in 1899 everything was going wrong for him; it was before he founded his own firm, he was unhappy in his work and although he wanted to marry my mother he'd given up hope of her accepting him. So on an impulse he volunteered for the Army – the Boer War was brewing all that summer – and when my mother realized he could be sent overseas to fight she became aware how much he meant to her and she finally agreed to marry him. Well, in the end the Army rejected him because of his eyesight, but for a time both he and my mother believed they were to be separated so they rushed to the altar as soon as possible – and in all the drama the conventions slipped; he did have her for the first time before they were married. "Very reprehensible," he said, "but I was so carried away that she'd agreed to marry me and so worried in case I had to leave before the wedding that I lost control and blotted my escutcheon." '

'So what conclusions did you draw from this conversation?'

'I believed him. He was so dogmatic, so positive, so convincing – '

'Was he hurt?'

'Hurt!'

'Well, if my son had questioned his paternity in that way,' said Darrow, 'I certainly wouldn't have been dogmatic or positive. Neither would I have been livid or mortally insulted. I'd have been deeply upset and extremely worried about why he found our relationship so unsatisfactory that he was driven to search for painful explanations. Tell me, did you ever discuss this with your mother?'

'He absolutely forbade it. He said, "Your mother's a very emotional woman, she feels guilty that you were conceived before the wedding, she suffered agonies of embarrassment when you arrived early, and you're never on any account to mention the subject to her." '

'So his testimony is unsupported.'

'Yes, but I'm sure he was telling the truth.'

'What makes you so certain?'

I finally voiced the conclusion I had drawn years earlier after great pain and difficulty. 'I'm certain,' I said, 'because I believe that if he wasn't my real father the truth would have surfaced when I decided to go into the Church. I can't begin to describe the awfulness of the rows we had, but the one thing he never did was disown me.'

Darrow was silent.

'I realize that illegitimacy is the obvious explanation of the mystery,' I said, 'but it can't be the right one.'

Darrow remained silent for a moment before saying: 'Very well, where have we got to? We've already established that your father's attitude to you doesn't arise from the fact that you're profoundly unfit and unworthy. We've now established that it doesn't arise from the fact that he's not your natural father. What, then, is your final explanation of the mystery?'

'Well, I suppose all one can say is that sometimes, even in the best of families, a parent has an antipathy towards one of his children and this creates tensions within the family.'

'I agree such cases do happen,' said Darrow, 'but unless the parent is either mentally ill or sunk deep in poverty, there's always a reason for the antipathy. For example sometimes the child reminds the parent of someone unpleasant – Great-Uncle Cuthbert who beat him when he was little, perhaps, or Great-Aunt Matilda who deprived him of chocolate in childhood. Do you perhaps remind your father of any such disagreeable antecedents in the family tree?'

'I don't see how I can. I'm not like anyone in our family. That's the point, isn't it? I'm such a stranger.'

238

'How curious,' said Darrow, 'because your father seems to look at you, Charles, and see someone he knows.'

I was astonished. 'Does he?'

'It's all there in your narrative. Take a moment to think about it.'

I reviewed my story with meticulous care. Then I said cautiously: 'It's as if he's not seeing me – my true self – but a glittering image. Yet it's not *my* glittering image. It's a far more sinister glittering image than mine.'

'Exactly. Your father's big aim in life – as he's always telling you – is to bring you up to a good straight decent man, but his very insistence on this seems to suggest he's terrified he'll fail. He looks at you and can hardly believe you've turned out so well – in fact he daren't believe it, he behaves as if he's scared to death something could still go wrong. He thunders to you on the subject of drink. He exhorts you not to get in a mess with women. There you stand before him, a good straight decent man in a clerical collar – in fact you've been called to a profession which ensures that you're just about as good and straight and decent as you can get – but your father doesn't see the clerical collar, Charles, and he doesn't see you either. He looks beyond you in his memory and he sees a wastrel, someone who drinks too much, someone who gets in a mess with women, someone who ruins himself, someone whom perhaps your father once resented and feared ... And who do you think that is, Charles? If the description doesn't tally with any member of your family, whom do you think it fits?'

'My real father,' I said, and saw a new world shudder loose from the chrysalis of the old.

SIXTEEN

'He impressed me as wise, patient, discerning, experienced and unquestionably sincere, a genuine pastor. His counsels were worth having and I have never forgotten them. I could not doubt that, if all clergymen were as well qualified as he, there would be few who would not benefit by "opening their grief in private confession".'

HERBERT HENSLEY HENSON
Bishop of Durham 1920–1939
Retrospect of an Unimportant Life

I

'We could be entirely wrong,' said Darrow. 'The deduction seems obvious enough from the evidence but any evidence can be subject to mis-interpretation.'

My mind was so absorbed by the thought of the stranger who had been conjured up out of the most opaque corners of my narrative that I could only say, 'I know we're right.'

Darrow at once anchored me to reality. 'You know no such thing. What you do know, on the other hand, is that you can go to your parents to demand the truth and the odds are that one of them's bound to reveal it. At this stage of your life they can't claim they're justified in lying to protect you.'

'Do you suppose that was why my father lied to me when I was fifteen? But why should he have wanted to protect me? It would have been more in character if he'd leapt at the chance to tell me the truth once I'd voiced my suspicions!'

Darrow said nothing.

'And why did he marry my mother in such terrible circumstances?' I demanded, my incredulity mounting. 'What a fantastic thing to do! And then to bring up the child as his own – and never to betray the secret despite considerable provocation ... Why, I can't imagine how or why any man could do such a thing!'

'That's exactly the sort of remark people often make to a man who becomes a monk,' said Darrow. 'They entirely overlook the fact that where a call from God exists any other course of action becomes unthinkable. Your father may have felt called to perform this unusual and difficult action – he may have believed, for reasons which seemed to him to be incontrovertible, that he had no choice but to marry your mother and assume responsibility for you.'

'But my father's an atheist! He wouldn't even hear a call from God, let alone believe in one!'

'What a heretical statement! Are you saying an atheist can limit God's power to call men to do his will?'

'No, of course not, but – '

'What sort of an atheist is your father anyway? It sounds to me as if he's a man who's too proud to admit there could be more to the world than he can discern with the aid of his senses yet too honest to be entirely comfortable with his arrogance; his attacks on Christianity and the Church suggest he's trying to convince himself as well as others that religion has nothing to offer.'

'I'd agree with that, but despite his secret ambivalence I still can't imagine him responding to a call from God. After all, a call can't take root and endure unless there are fertile conditions prevailing in the psyche, and I find myself quite unable to conceive what his motive was here.'

'The answer's patiently obvious. If you can somehow manage to discard your preconceived notions you'll find the facts permit only one conclusion.'

I stared at him. 'I can see he might have made the original decision because he loved my mother – although what an amazing gesture of love that would have been! – but why didn't he tell me the truth when I was fifteen? I can't see why on earth he should want me to go on believing he was my father if he didn't care about me.'

'Precisely,' said Darrow, rising to his feet. 'Good. Well, we'll call a halt to the conversation there, and this evening we'll – '

I grabbed his sleeve. He sat down again. 'But my father doesn't care about me,' I said. 'That's the point. He doesn't care.'

'What evidence can you provide to support that statement?'

'Well, I told you . . . I explained . . .'

'You told me things which made me suspect he could be obstinate, pig-headed, misguided and rude, but I can't think of a single thing you said which made me think he was indifferent to you. Uncaring fathers don't lash themselves into a frenzy of anxiety every time they imagine their sons are going to the dogs.' He stood up once more. 'Think about it,' he said over his shoulder, 'and we'll talk again this evening.'

'Of course,' I said when we met later in my room, 'no matter what the solution of the mystery is, he *is* my father. Fatherhood is much more than initiating a process of reproduction.'

'That sounds like a promising approach to a very difficult dilemma. But let's assume our theory's right and that somewhere in the world there's a man who could claim to have begotten you. How would you feel about him?'

'Hostile. He nearly ruined my mother and must have caused her enormous pain.'

'True. Go on.'

'He walked out on me when I was an embryo and has never made any attempt – so far as I know – to show the slightest interest in me.'

'True again.'

'However . . .' I hesitated before concluding carefully, 'If he's alive I'd like to meet him, just once, for a quick look. Then I can put him aside and get on with my life, but if there's no meeting I suspect I'll always wonder what he was like and I might wind up being obsessed by him.'

Darrow said neutrally, 'Adopted children usually do have a psychological need to meet their natural parents. Very well, what do you think your next step should be?'

'I want to leave here as soon as possible in order to visit my parents and find out if our theory's true. But when do you think I'll be ready to make my formal confession and receive the sacrament again?'

'I'm already impressed by the realistic approach you're displaying to this new dilemma. Has the moment finally come, I wonder, when you can give me a realistic assessment of your reltaionships with Lyle, Loretta and Jardine? If you can accomplish that to my satisfaction, then I promise I'll hear your formal confession without delay . . .'

III

'Let's start with Lyle,' said Darrow after I had assured him I now understood my errors well enough to profess a valid repentance. 'Tell me what you think was actually going on beneath the storybook romance.'

Without hesitation I said, 'When I arrived in Starbridge I was in despair about my inability to lead a successful celibate life, and I was intent on discovering not just a woman I could marry but a woman who could cope with the worthless person I believed myself to be. I thought myself to be worthless in this context not merely because my father had a low opinion of me but because I'd made Jane unhappy; however I couldn't think of

Jane because that was too painful, so I told myself that everything would come right so long as I found a problem-solving miracle woman. Naturally I was indulging in fantasy – how obvious that seems now! – but I was so desperate to marry and put an end to my bouts of fornication that I had to believe I could make my fantasy come true.'

'That's an excellent beginning,' said Darrow. 'Go on.'

Much encouraged I said, 'The odds were heavily against the possibility that Lyle was Jardine's mistress but nevertheless I suspect that in my subconscious mind I'd pictured them in bed together and thought: a girl who could maintain a clandestine love-affair with an eminent church-man is just about the only kind of woman who would have a hope of coping with me. Probably I thought this before I ever met Lyle, but when I saw her this wild deduction about her suitability was re-inforced because I did find her exceedingly attractive. And to cap it all – to make the psychological situation perfect – she was in a mysterious way unavailable and for years I'd only been attracted to unavailable women.'

'You can see clearly now, no doubt, why you chased the unavailable women despite your genuine desire to remarry?'

'I had an equally genuine desire not to remarry because I was terrified I might drive another woman to suicide. I hadn't come to terms with Jane's death at all, and the tragedy acted as a block in my mind.'

'Good. Very well, so you fell for Lyle – '

'I fell for her hook, line and sinker, and whether or not this was all a huge illusion I still don't know. I'd like to believe my feelings are in some way rooted in reality, but I do concede now that I'll have to see her again when I'm in a much more stable frame of mind before I can finally decide whether she's right for me.'

'That's most impressive, Charles – what an improvement on your earlier extravagant declarations! Now can you approach Loretta with a similar realism?'

I knew this would be harder. After a pause I said: 'What a good friend she was to me at the end! I shall always remember that rescue of hers with gratitude, but apart from that . . .' My voice trailed away but Darrow made no attempt to intervene and after another pause I was able to confess: 'My afternoon with Loretta was a disaster – although I must be honest, mustn't I, and admit the sex was magnificent. However that's just judging the incident from a physical point of view. Emotionally it was a disaster for me because it ploughed up my feelings for Lyle and put me in the biggest possible muddle. Mentally it was a disaster for me because the new muddle pushed me nearer the brink of breakdown and made me sink myself more obsessively than ever in the Starbridge mystery in order to divert myself from my problems. Spiritually it was a disaster for me because it cut me off from God and magnified my guilt as a clergyman to such an extent that I was unable to respond to your initial attempt to help me. And pastorally it was a disaster for me because I exploited a woman who was lonely and ignored a soul's unmistakable need for care. How can I do other than regret an incident which was an emotional, mental, spiritual and pastoral disaster? All physical gratification becomes sour and futile when isolated in such a wasteland.'

Darrow said, 'Can you put into words, do you think, why you were tempted to make love to her? Or are you implying this was solely an act of physical gratification?'

'That was the most obvious motive, but I can see now that I was driven by other forces too. For instance I was in a state of extreme spiritual weakness brought on by my private troubles; I'd been working harder to preserve my glittering image than to serve God. Then I was also in a state of profound emotional turmoil and I used Loretta to anaesthetize myself from my problems. And finally . . . well, this is the crux of the matter, isn't it, Father? I thought she'd had full sexual intercourse with Jardine, and my identification with him at that point was so strong that I just thought: if he had her I'll have her; if he can do it, then why on earth shouldn't I?'

Darrow leant back in his chair. 'Very well, now can you tie up the last loose end and tell me how you view your relationship with Jardine as you look back through the strait gate from the narrow way?'

'Yes, of course,' I said and once more paused to collect my thoughts, but this time they proved uncollectable.

'Never mind,' said Darrow. 'I wasn't really expecting you to expound on Jardine tonight.'

'I know what I want to say but I can't quite – '

'You've done extremely well, but now you need to rest. Get a good night's sleep, Charles, and tomorrow I think we'll finally succeed in putting the Bishop in his place.'

IV

'So far as I can make out,' I said after a sleepless night, 'there are two aspects of my relationship with Jardine. First of all I seem to see him as an exceptionally compelling father-figure.'

Darrow nodded. 'Can you see why he should have this exceptional appeal?'

'I need older men to give me the approval my father withholds and Jardine entered my life at a time when I was completely estranged from my father.'

'Yes, but what made Jardine more compelling than, for example, Dr Lang?'

'Well, I can see now that as far as I'm concerned Lang and Jardine aren't so unalike as they seem to be,' I said with reluctance. 'They're both eminent churchmen and they both have glamour.'

'Ah, now we're progressing.'

'Lang seems . . . well, it sounds unkind but he seems like a worn-out gramophone record now, a pompous stagey old bachelor who has no message for me any more. But certainly when we first met I thought he had great glamour. Jardine, on the other hand, not only has glamour but he's far from being a pompous old bachelor; he's a racy married man who has problems with women. I not only liked him but I came to identify with him – and that brings me to the second aspect of our relationship: I came to regard him as a double.'

'Before we deal with that, tell me why you've chosen father-figures who are glamorous and clerical.'

'I suppose I'm rebelling against my father who hates clerics and despises glamour. He thinks Lang's hopelessly theatrical and if he were ever to meet Jardine he'd say, "Fellow's not quite a gentleman. Bit too flashy with the vintage port. Bit of a bounder with the ladies." '

'All right, so far so good. Now let's take a look at this curious *doppelgänger* situation. Can you explain how you came to regard Jardine as a double?'

'This is where I get into difficulties. As far as I can make out – ' I stopped. Darrow waited. In front of me on the table my hands began to twist in their clasp. 'As far as I can make out,' I forced myself to say, 'this is the part where I went stark staring mad.'

'Oh yes?' said Darrow casually. 'Were you violent – physically violent, not merely verbally abusive?'

'No.'

'Were you performing bizarre acts, like taking off your clothes in public?'

'Good heavens, no!'

'Did you hear voices, see visions and think that little green men were out to kill you?'

'No, of course not!'

'Well, you could have been mad, I suppose,' said Darrow, 'but you certainly weren't stark staring mad, and personally I doubt whether we can convict you of anything worse than emotional stress. What I suggest is that we now put aside for a moment this thesis that you were stark staring mad and take a look at what was actually going on. Exactly when did you start doubting your sanity?'

'It was during that last scene with Jardine, the scene where he made his speech – '

'Ah yes, the speech he made when he should have been listening!

However, I'm sure it was an oratorical masterpiece. After all,' said Darrow expressionlessly, 'if there's one thing we all know about the Bishop of Starbridge it's that he has a very powerful and persuasive tongue.'

It was as if a spell had been broken. 'He could make you believe black was white,' I said, and suddenly I found I had the courage to look at the memory without flinching. As my hands stopped writhing in front of me I leant forward on the table and began to describe how Jardine had laid waste my equilibrium.

V

'. . . and I know I'm not describing this well, Father – it's so hard to find the words – but Jardine made me feel my whole identification with him was a grand illusion.'

'Obviously he was very convincing. But how did he raise the possibility that you were deluded?'

'He said I was using him as a mirror – only he didn't use the metaphor of the mirror. He talked of a blank screen and a magic-lantern. He said I was imposing on him – projecting on to the blank screen – feelings and situations which existed only in my mind.'

'The Bishop seems to have been reading Feuerbach. But go on.'

'He said that in my mind I'd picked him to be my hero and was justifying my own bizarre behaviour by saying I was only following his example.' I shuddered at the thought of Loretta. 'There was some sort of horrible truth in that – '

'Projection theories always seem difficult to rebut until one realizes that the whole truth has failed to be projected. We know now that your behaviour, bizarre or otherwise, didn't arise solely from a desire to mirror Jardine; we know that you were driven by a variety of other factors including your estrangement from your father and your wife's death. However let's go on with this thesis of Jardine's that you were the magic-lantern projector and he was the blank screen. Did he actually say that the resemblances between you were non-existent?'

'He said that I'd imagined him and that the man he was had nothing to do with the man I thought he was – and that's madness, isn't it, when one can no longer distinguish between reality and illusion? He made me feel as if I'd imagined the entire Starbridge mystery, he made me feel – '

'Yes, try and say it out loud – '

' – rejected. It was as if a door had slammed in my face. I felt as I'd felt during that last row with my father when he'd slammed the door of his study and locked it, but this was infinitely worse because in addition to feeling rejected I also felt stark-staring – '

'Were you aware of his eyes while this was going on?'

I was abruptly diverted from the nightmare of insanity. '*His eyes?*'

'Think carefully. Were you looking directly at him?'

'Yes.' I shuddered at the memory but managed to add, 'His eyes are light brown but he can make them glow until they seem amber. They were amber then.'

'And was there a point in the conversation when he repeated a phrase several times, a phrase such as "listen to me"? Or was there a point when he repeated your name perhaps three times in one sentence to secure your attention?'

I said slowly, 'Yes, there was. At one stage I said, "I refuse to listen to this," but he said, "You will – you will, Charles, you will. Sit down, Charles – sit down and listen to me – listen to me. Charles – "'

'Ah yes,' said Darrow nonchalantly as if we were discussing behaviour which was commonplace. 'I thought so. He was using a hypnotic technique to heighten the power of his charism – a technique which can occasionally be useful but which is always fraught with danger. I believe I now understand what happened. A charism which manifests itself in oratory can operate like a wireless, and Jardine had not only switched on this wireless but turned up the volume knob as high as it would go. The effect would be unusually devastating because you were drunk and in a severely weakened state, but Charles, now that you're stone-cold sober and in a far stronger frame of mind you should have no trouble turning down the volume knob and finally switching the wireless off.'

I was greatly intrigued but all I could say was, 'I can't quite find the volume knob.'

'It's his assertion that you imagined the resemblances. All you have to do is explode it.'

'But how?'

'Make a list of the apparent resemblances and we'll see whether or not they're valid.'

I said cautiously but without difficulty, 'The wife who got so depressed that she had to go back to her parents for a while – that was what Jane threatened to do and what Carrie Jardine actually did. The wife who was dutiful about sex – although this didn't stop the marriage from running into problems. The Jardines' period of childlessness followed by the birth of their dead baby, a period which corresponds to my years of contraception followed by the loss of the unborn child. Jardine's aversion to the celibate life, an aversion he confessed to Loretta, which corresponds to my own feelings about celibacy.'

'Admirably put. There you have several genuine resemblances between you and Jardine. Can you see any more?'

I said with growing confidence, 'Jardine comes from a lower social class than I do, but his long climb to the top of the social tree has resulted in him winding up with two personalities – a fact which suggests that like me he has trouble preserving a unified identity. He himself admitted to me that Alex is the glittering image and Adam is the man beyond, the man he likes to keep secret because Adam's made so many mistakes. Like me he normally doesn't talk about his past – and in particular he doesn't talk about – '

'Yes? Go on, Charles – '

'His father,' I said. 'His father.'

'And there you have the most dramatic resemblance of all.'

My confidence was now complete. 'His father problem was on the surface very different from mine,' I said, 'but in essence it was the same. Jardine had felt unloved and rejected by his father until the old man was near death.' I paused as I remembered my nocturnal talk with Jardine in his library. 'It was strange how Jardine sensed I had problems with my father,' I said. 'I merely pursued my usual policy of reticence but unlike everyone else Jardine had the personal experience to know what that reticence meant.'

'In other words he saw himself in you – the identification process was working in reverse.'

'Yes, I'm sure now that this was why he didn't throw me out of the palace when he discovered I was Lang's spy – I intrigued him so much that he couldn't resist the urge to let me stay on so that he could get to know me better and later, after he had confided in me about his father, I became convinced that he was the only man I knew who had the experience to look beyond my glittering image and sympathize with the man I really was. That was why his rejection at the end was so terrible to me.'

'In other words,' said Darrow, 'the psychological recognition was mutual and real. The resemblances between you were not only numerous but striking. So much for Jardine's accusation that you were projecting a fantasy.'

The relief was so overwhelming that it was some time before I could say, 'How could I have believed him?'

'You were hypnotized into believing you were mad and then you were too terrified to confront the memory to realize his thesis was false.' There was a toughness in Darrow's voice but he eradicated it. Without expression he added, 'Clearly the charism was abused.'

Having finally faced my memory of the scene I was able to voice the most sinister possibility of all. 'Could he have deliberately sent me over the edge in order to protect himself?'

'He could,' said Darrow, 'but on the other hand if he saw himself in you it seems unlikely that he would have been deliberately destructive.

248

The most likely explanation is that in the distress caused by his involvement with you he lost control over the charism.'

'But surely his use of hypnosis can only be sinister?'

'Not necessarily. He may well have resorted to hypnosis with the best of intentions – to calm you down. However where he made his big mistake was to assume that if he confronted you with certain realities you'd be able to pull yourself together. From a counselling point of view, as I told you earlier, this was quite the wrong approach, and the error was compounded by his lurid presentation of what he believed those realities to be, but Charles, let me stress that despite the abysmal mess he made of the scene there's still no proof that he was engaged in covering up an affair with Lyle. All the disaster proves is that even an experienced bishop should never attempt to counsel someone when all his better instincts caution him against it.'

There was a silence while I digested this truth but finally I said, 'At least I can now see the scene in its true colours. I can't tell you how much better I feel.'

'I'm very glad, but don't start relaxing too soon because we're not quite home yet. We've established that you should on no account think you were mad just because you identified yourself with Jardine. But what happened when you pursued this identification to its limits? Can you take another look at that incident with Loretta?'

'I suppose this is where I convict myself of being emotionally disturbed even if I wasn't certifiably insane. I wanted him to be guilty of adultery. When I found he hadn't penetrated her I felt cheated. And in the end I wanted him to be sleeping with Lyle – I wanted it even though the thought was unendurable.'

'And why did you wish these sins upon him?'

'I felt that if he could be guilty and still be a brilliantly successful churchman, then I could too. I thought . . . I was so afraid . . .'

'Yes? You're almost there, Charles. One last hurdle – '

'I was so afraid my vocation was breaking down and I couldn't bear to think of it. All I want is to serve God in the Church but everything seemed to be falling apart – my celibacy, my career, my whole life – and in those circumstances Jardine became – Jardine symbolized – '

'Symbolized – '

' – he was a symbol of hope – and in the end he was hope personified, my only hope, my last hope . . . I thought: if only he could be guilty, I'll be all right – if he can go on, I can go on . . . And that was why – that was why – '

'When he rejected your identification with him, he wasn't just rejecting you as a father, was he?'

'No, he was destroying my last hope of serving God in the Church, damning me to the hell of broken vows – and oh God, I couldn't bear it, Father, I couldn't bear it, I couldn't bear it, I couldn't bear it . . .'

VI

'It was very terrible for you,' said Darrow, pulling his chair around the table so that he could sit beside me. 'But you can see now, can't you, how you used this valid identification with Jardine to drum up defences which would keep your fears about your vocation at bay. You were afraid not of losing your faith in God, which I suppose is the commonest fear of clergymen with such beleaguered psyches, but of losing your ability to serve him in the Church.'

I was able to say, 'I believe now that eventually I'll be able to go on in obedience to those vows I made at my ordination, but the past months have been such a nightmare of fear and doubt – '

'Of course they have. And of course you can now understand how that nightmare burgeoned in your mind until it reached intolerable proportions. It began not merely because your father had convinced you that you were unfit and unworthy, a man who was only acting the part of a clergyman, but because you felt your father's scepticism was to a frightening degree becoming justified. You *were* worried about your increasing need for alcohol, and you *were* finding yourself in increasing difficulties with women – but why was this happening? Not, contrary to what your father might think, because of some genetic curse. It was happening because you were under increasing psychological strain. The glittering image was becoming more and more of a burden – no wonder you wanted to drink to escape from him! – and you had this crucial problem, which you couldn't master, about your inability to face remarriage. The tension caused by this problem remorselessly drove you into errors – errors which only made you feel more unfit, more unworthy – and the inevitable result was that you became imprisoned in a downward spiral of despair. In the circumstances the wonder is not that you became emotionally disturbed but that you didn't do so much earlier, and in my opinion you must be absolutely dedicated to serving God; a lesser call would have disintegrated long ago.'

When I was calmer I said, 'It was almost as if I knew I couldn't break down until I'd found someone who could be guaranteed to glue me together again.'

'One of the saddest aspects of your story is undoubtedly that you felt unable to confide in anyone before you met me, but before either of us makes the mistake of becoming too self-satisfied with the results of our meeting let's remember that although your troubles have been clarified they haven't yet been resolved. You have some hard work to do now on

250

the home front, but we can discuss that later. At present there are more immediate matters to consider.'

'My formal confession?'

'Yes, it can be brief, since we've already discussed your errors in such depth, but you must still approach the task with care; I'm going to make some suggestions about prayer and meditation. Then once your confession's been made we can discuss what you're going to do on your return to the world. I think it's extremely important for you, both emotionally and spiritually, that we draw up a very meticulous battle-plan.'

VII

I made my formal confession before God that evening, and Father Darrow, granting me absolution, assigned me a short penance which I performed in the chapel before I went to bed. I had expected a severe penance, possibly even a protracted one, but Darrow said that the severe, protracted ordeal of my informal confession to him had formed a penance which now only required completion with prayer.

The next morning, for the first time since my arrival, I was able to participate in the mass.

All the Fordite services were conducted in the vernacular, and although the form of worship represented the apex of the High Church wing of the Church of England, the language stressed that sharp division from Rome which formed the hallmark of the Fordite monks. The chapel was ornate, but the lack of emphasis on the Virgin set it apart from any church under the Pope's jurisdiction. I could not see the entire chapel because visitors were allowed only in a section of the transept, but the stained glass which was visible to me stressed the life of Christ and the single work of sculpture consisted of a crucifix.

I received the sacrament. I had been so buoyed up by my anticipation that it was a shock when after the first seconds of overwhelming comfort I experienced the panic of despair. I started fearing I might fall into error the moment I left my secure retreat; I began to worry that I would still be unable to face remarriage and fatherhood; I tormented myself with the dread that my feelings for Lyle were entirely illusory, that the liberating theory of my paternity was mistaken and that I was indeed utterly unfit to serve God as a clergyman.

My new hope shattered. My frail self-confidence crumbled. After the service I stumbled back to my room, pulled the blind and lay face downwards on the bed with the cross pressed against my chest as I struggled to repel the demon despair. The demon and I wrestled for some time. He never entirely vanquished me but he made exhausting attacks. I was immobilized. I needed all my strength to bar his path to my soul.

Darrow found me after his chapter meeting. He walked in, took one look at my prostrate form, pulled up the blind and said: 'On your feet, Charles. Kick the demon in the arse and let's get down to work.'

The mood represented by the symbol of the demon immediately dissolved into the framework of my mind. I slunk to the table.

'I thought I'd be all right now,' I said with shame. 'I thought I'd be strong as an ox and brave as a lion and ready to stride out of your front door singing "Onward Christian Soldiers".'

Darrow laughed. 'Some frightened citizen of Grantchester would undoubtedly have summoned an ambulance! No, Charles, I'd be most perturbed if at the present stage of your profound ordeal you were to stride out of here singing a militant hymn.' And he added as we both sat down at the table: 'In a way I'm glad you've had this setback because now you'll have no trouble believing me when I say I think you should stay here a few days longer. Spiritually you're still extremely weak, and since taking the sacrament isn't by itself going to restore you miraculously to full strength, I'm going to set you some spiritual exercises.'

I tried not to look alarmed. Even in the most ardent days of my training for the priesthood I had never been keen on work which offered me no chance to excel with my academic gifts.

'You probably won't need to remain here longer than a week,' said Darrow, 'but for the next twenty-eight days I want you to rise at six in the morning and spend one hour in reading, prayer and meditation as I shall direct. You may have a cup of tea or coffee to wake you up but no food during this hour, please, and no cigarettes.'

My heart sank. I was never at my best early in the morning and before approaching an hour of spiritual exercises I felt I needed a three-course dinner, several cigarettes and a stiff whisky. Laymen think clergymen have an inexhaustible ability to pray and meditate, but in fact unless one is a monk trained to spend a large portion of each day in worship few clergymen have either the time or the energy for a full hour of solitary spiritual hard labour. Every morning I said my prayers and read the office, but these activities resembled a short spiritual sprint; what I was now being required to do was to run a spiritual mile, and I knew very well that I was out of training.

However my resolve to rebuild my life to give meaning to Jane's death compelled me to say to Darrow, 'I want more than anything to get fit. I'll do whatever you say.'

'Let me explain what I'm aiming for: I want to help you restore the balance to spiritual life which your private problems have inevitably distorted. In your pursuit of a success which would impress your father you've probably tended to channel too much energy into your work as a scholar; I'm not saying you haven't been conscientious in your public worship and private prayer, but have you been more than merely conscientious? I feel you should now devote more time to cultivating your inner life so that you can achieve more than a mere outward semblance of your vocation.'

'I'm beginning to see why you've been leading me through a course of reading on mysticism.'

'There were two reasons for that. The first was that you seemed to be too much preoccupied with the transcendence of God – a common failing among admirers of Karl Barth, I fear – and I thought you needed to be reminded of the mystics' doctrine of synteresis, the idea that a divine spark exists in every human being – '

' – and that God's immanent as well as transcendent.'

'Exactly. Mysticism provides a middle way between a Liberal protestantism stressing the immanence of God and Barth's crisis theology stressing the transcendence.'

'And your second reason for directing me to the mystics?'

'I wanted to see how you reacted to a stress on the relationship between man and God which can exist beyond the rituals of formal worship, and during our subsequent discussions I began to suspect you weren't using your spiritual gifts, such as they are, to their full capacity – with the result that your misguided belief in your unworthiness had been reinforced. And that's another reason why you now need to spend time each day in training and rehabilitation; you need the boost to your self-esteem that the achievement of a balanced spiritual life will provide.'

I was unable to stop myself saying: 'I feel so depressed that I'm in such a weakened state.'

'Then it's all the more important that we should build up your spiritual strength. Now, Charles, you clearly need some hard physical work if you're to avoid spending the morning moping on your bed – come into the garden with me and let's see if we can discover some small useful tree which is crying out to be cut down . . . '

VIII

There was no tree crying out to be cut down but there was a large patch of ground which was asking to be dug up. I dug and I dug and I dug. After a while I felt better, and later as I took a shower I remembered Lady Starmouth saying with a smile, 'I adore Muscular Christianity!' Her remark seemed a terrible irony now that I could acknowledge what a debilitated Christian I had become but when I looked in the glass and saw not my glittering image but my true self I thought that one day, a long way off in a future almost impossible to imagine, an approving reference to Muscular Christianity might not seem so misplaced.

It was an encouraging thought, and I knew then that I was starting to hope again, starting to rebuild my shattered confidence.

IX

Darrow spent our afternoon session assigning me my books for the exercises and discussing the most effective techniques for meditative reading. 'We'll start the meditations with the Synoptic Gospels,' he said, 'because I want you to focus your attention on Christ and then we'll move on to St John's Gospel so that you can focus on the Spirit. You're too theocentric, possibly because your psychological problems have made you preoccupied with God as Father. I've noticed a marked imbalance in your whole perception of the Trinity.'

I began to feel alarmed again. I might be a Doctor of Divinity but now I felt like a student about to fail an examination, and suddenly I found myself desperate to pass. Supposing I were unmasked as a complete spiritual failure? The thought of abject failure was appalling enough, but the thought of disappointing Darrow was intolerable. In panic I cast around for a solution which would protect me in my vulnerability, and when Darrow returned to my room that evening, the glittering image said to him: 'I do wish you'd tell me more about yourself, Father! There's so much I'd like to know.'

As soon as the words were spoken I felt myself relaxing. This was an infallible technique for acquiring the goodwill of older men; I would ask them about their past, I would listen with the ardent interest of the model disciple and I would be rewarded by a gratifying display of paternal benevolence which would be blind to all the faults and failings I was so desperately anxious to conceal. 'Tell me about your days in the Navy!' I urged Darrow with all the warmth and charm I could muster, but although I waited with confidence for the response which would anaesthetize my fear of unfitness, Darrow was silent. At first I thought he was merely pausing to set aside his counsellor's mask and when he smiled at me I was sure he was about to become confidential, but then he said gravely, 'No, Charles. If I'm to help you best I must continue to be to a large extent impersonal. I can only be your spiritual director. Nothing less. And nothing more.'

Another silence fell as I painfully perceived the machinations of my glittering image, but at last Darrow said with a firmness which enabled him to be gentle without sounding condescending, 'This isn't a rejection, Charles. Quite the contrary. I'd be rejecting you if I allowed you to put our relationship on a footing which would merely reinforce these psychological difficulties which have plagued you for so long. One of my most vital tasks at present is not to prove to you that you need a father-figure; it's to prove to you that you can do without one.'

I nodded. After a while my true self was able to say, 'Don't think I'm unaware how absurd it is for a man of my age to need a father-figure constantly in the background.'

'I'm sure that once you're at peace with your father a great many difficulties are going to be resolved. But I'm equally sure, I'm afraid, that this peace isn't going to be easily attained.'

In an effort to overcome my embarrassment by changing the subject I said rapidly, 'Is this where we start drawing up the battle-plan for my return to the world?'

'Perhaps it is,' said Darrow, who had of course gauged the exact depth of my distress and wanted to support my effort to counter it. 'Very well, let's visualize your approaching visit to your parents in Epsom . . .'

X

'Your task here,' said Darrow, 'is to put your relationship with both your parents on a new basis. Establishing the facts about your paternity isn't just going to satisfy your very pardonable curiosity; it's going to provide an atmosphere of truth in which a new relationship with your parents can be created.'

'Yes, Father.'

'No, Charles, don't just sit back and say: "Yes, Father" like an obedient novice! Work hard, think hard, be constructive – '

'How do I approach this task of creating a new relationship?'

'That's better. Your task is to approach them as a good Christian, and that reminds me of something you said during your narration of the Starbridge story. Didn't you confess that you felt guilty about your lack of parish experience? Well, here's your chance to take over from the local vicar and minister to your parents' spiritual health.'

'But my dear Father – '

He gave me a steely look. 'You think your parents aren't worth ministering to? You think that just because they don't go to church they're unworthy of your rarefied spiritual attention?'

'No, of course not, but – '

'Is being a priest just a matter of letting off the occasional homiletic firework and writing books on the Early Church?'

'No, Father. One preaches the Gospel by living one's calling.'

'Precisely. Go down to Epsom and live your Christian message. You need never mention God. You needn't even wear your clerical collar. Just turn up on your parents' doorstep and show them by your actions what you believe in.'

'Yes, but Father, whenever I visit them I do always try so hard – '

'To do what? To be the perfect son, doing his duty to those two cardboard figures labelled "Father" and "Mother"? Put aside that glittering image, Charles – and put aside their glittering images too! Look beyond the cardboard façade and discover those two strangers who have kept themselves hidden from you even as you've kept yourself hidden from them. What's really going on in your parents' lives? How's your father coping with retirement – always a great hurdle for any successful man? How is he, the atheist, facing the prospect of imminent extinction? And your mother – how's she facing old age and the prospect of a declining appearance? How's *she* coping with your father's retirement – always a disturbing change for any wife? How lonely is she? How much does she miss you and how much does she long to confide in you? Charles, you have this challenging pastoral situation on your hands; are you going to spend your summer at Laud's, comfortably insulating yourself from your twentieth-century problems by seeking exile once more in the remote academic past, or are you going to come down from your ivory tower at last and serve God in a place where you may well be needed more than you've ever been needed in your life?'

I felt as if God had called me not with a whisper but by a blast on the trumpet, and I hung my head in shame to think that I could have been so deaf for so long.

SEVENTEEN

'The marks of Jesus are silently impressed on His true disciples in the normal procedure of the life in society as well as in the crises of suffering and martyrdom.'

HERBERT HENSLEY HENSON
Bishop of Durham 1920–1939
Retrospect of an Unimportant Life

I

'It won't be easy,' said Darrow. 'Your father will no doubt be objectionable as usual and your mother will probably make you cringe, just as she always does, but keep calling on them, Charles. Devote your summer to it. Then in the end caring may generate understanding; understanding may generate forgiveness and once you've forgiven them you'll be at peace with them both at last.'

I said abruptly, 'That reminds me of Jardine. When he was talking about his father he said, "With understanding forgiveness becomes possible".'

Darrow relaxed his professional neutrality far enough to say: 'My rock-bottom opinion of the Bishop's spiritual perception goes up a notch,' but at once he looked as though he regretted his frankness and before I could comment he was adding swiftly, 'And now, no doubt, you're anxious to extend the battle-plan from Epsom to Starbridge.'

I tried to choose the words which would show him I understood my position. 'I do realize,' I said, 'that my parents must come first; I must sort out Epsom in order to gain the equilibrium which will enable me to sort out Starbridge. However – ' I hesitated but could only confess, 'I hate the thought of putting Lyle in abeyance.'

'I agree this is a most difficult point,' said Darrow at once, and encouraged by his sympathy I made a new effort to express my feelings.

'I think I'd find it easier to put Lyle in abeyance if there was a limit set to the time I had to wait,' I said. 'Assuming I do well with my parents – '

'They'll probably still need the lion's share of the remainder of the Long Vacation. Why don't you pick a date at the end of September for your reinspection of Lyle?'

257

Six weeks seemed a long time to wait but I said without hesitation, 'Very well, but meanwhile could I write to her to re-establish contact?'

'That's a fair question but I don't see why you should assume I can answer it better than you can. Let me ask you some further questions to help you make up your mind. For instance, what would a letter achieve beyond re-establishing contact? How would you feel if she failed to respond? Would you feel more frustrated than ever? Might this anxiety deflect you from your parents who should now be your first consideration? Might you be tempted to rush off to Starbridge for another bruising encounter with the Bishop?'

I was obliged to admit these were all disturbing questions. 'Perhaps I should do nothing for the moment,' I said with reluctance.

'We'll keep the matter open and discuss it regularly. Then I'm sure a satisfactory solution will evolve ... And talking of evolution, Charles, I think you're fit enough now to hear some information I've been keeping from you about the evolving situation at Starbridge. On the morning after your arrival here Jardine telephoned me.'

I was shocked by the nervousness of my reaction. 'Did he tell you I was mad?'

'He was much more anxious that I should tell him you were safe. Of course he was frightened in case you'd smashed yourself up in your motor; if you had, part of the responsibility would undoubtedly have been his.'

'Did he phone again?'

'Three days later, yes. He wanted to know how you were getting on. I said, "How kind of you to enquire, Bishop – Charles is in better health and benefiting from a quiet time with us." I was curious to see if he'd press me for further information.'

'And did he?'

'He certainly went fishing. He said, "Charles was in a very distressed state when he left us. I was most concerned because he seemed to be dabbling in some incredible fantasies." I then made some mild noise such as "Hm" and inflected it so that it could mean almost anything – whereupon he lost his nerve, changed course and asked me how I was settling down in Cambridgeshire.'

'So he did try to convince you I was mad!'

'I don't think so,' said Darrow with that serenity which never failed to reassure me. 'If that had been his aim I think he'd have tried a direct approach by insisting you'd been raving, but he was clearly more concerned to get information than to make slanderous accusations.'

'But of course he's sacred you'll believe me!'

'Of course, but that would apply whether he was guilty or innocent, wouldn't it? Even the holiest of bishops would blanch at the thought of a canon spreading a story of episcopal adultery through the hallowed cloisters of the Fordite monks!'

Gradually I felt myself relax. 'I'm sorry,' I said. 'I'm behaving stupidly.'

'Not at all. It's just as natural for you to worry about Jardine convincing me that you're mad as it's natural for Jardine to worry about whether you're convincing me he's an adulterer. But Charles, my purpose in relaying this news of Jardine was not to make you anxious; I was trying to make the important point that time hasn't stood still at Starbridge since you rushed away from the Bishop's dinner table. I think you're tending to see Lyle and Jardine and their relationship – whatever that may be – as frozen in time, but the situation at the palace will be constantly evolving, just as your situation here has been evolving, and that's another reason why I think you should wait a little longer before you make your final circuit of the Starbridge mulberry bush. You flung a big stone into that particular pond, Charles; stand back now until the ripples reach the edge of the pond and you can see what's been washed up at your feet. I think you may well find that the wait will pay significant dividends later . . .'

II

My first attempt at the spiritual exercises went entirely wrong. The opening half-hour had been allocated to reading at a normal pace passages from St Augustine's *Confessions* and *The Imitation of Christ* by Thomas à Kempis, two famous works which naturally I had studied earlier in my career but which had for some time remained unopened in my library. This task seemed simple enough but when I finished in fifteen minutes I realized belatedly that I had been reading at the abnormal speed developed by my academic work, and to make matters worse I found on rereading the pages that some of the paragraphs were unfamiliar. I felt disconcerted by this proof of poor concentration, but it was not until I moved on to my assignment of meditative reading that my problems began in earnest. I had been given a short passage from St Mark's Gospel to consider, not an interesting section like the Little Apocalypse which would have involved me in some challenging scholarly thoughts on Jewish eschatology, but the few verses which described the healing of Jairus's daughter. The story was excruciatingly familiar, and after five minutes I found all my attempts at meditation had run aground on the rocks of boredom.

To pass the allotted time I translated the verses first into New Testament Greek and then into medieval Latin, but I was acutely aware that I was not supposed to be exercising my scholarship, and it was with mortification that I approached the last quarter of an hour which had been allocated to prayer. This section was easier, as I was in the habit of praying, but I was so upset by my failure to meditate competently that I found my concentration was wandering again and my prayers lacked depth.

I saw then how adrift I was unless the scholarly side of my intellect was engaged, and although I was no stranger to a broader religious awareness I realized that over the years my experience had narrowed instead of expanded. I liked my religion to take a cool, hard, analytical form and then I was capable of feeling very devout indeed, but without the prop of my intellectual power I was lost. I told myself I was not temperamentally suited to meditation; my gift was for studying and teaching, not for sitting around brooding over the spiritual resonances of one tiny section of St Mark's Gospel.

However I knew I could never utter such unacceptable thoughts to my mentor, and after prolonged anxiety I decided that the only course I could take was to concede my failure but to stress that a vast improvement was both imminent and inevitable.

We met after his chapter meeting.

'Someone suffering from malnutrition often has trouble taking normal food at first,' he said mildly after I had admitted my difficulties, 'but the important thing is that you had the desire and the will to stay at the dinner table and confront your plate for the duration of the meal. Let's take a detailed look at what happened so that I can adjust the diet for you.'

After a post-mortem of the entire ill-fated hour he extended the time allocated to simple reading, kept the time of prayer unchanged but reduced the meditative reading to eight minutes. However the length of the material remained the same. 'If you were in training,' he said, 'you could take twenty-five minutes over that passage – which is about as long as most people can profitably spend on this sort of reading – but don't get discouraged; I don't expect too much from you yet.'

However I found I could not bear this oblique confirmation of my failure. At once the glittering image said before I could stop him, 'Don't worry, Father – I'm sure I'll soon master these little difficulties!' and at once I knew I was making the same mistake as I had made when I had tried to reduce my relationship with Darrow to a purely personal level. I tried to find the words to retract the remark in all its false absurdity, but in the end of was Darrow who spoke first.

'Charles,' he said, 'you don't have to be a huge success in order to win my liking and approval. So long as you do your best – no matter how mediocre your best is – my liking and approval are guaranteed.'

There was a silence as the glittering image, battered but not yet dead, subsided once more into my subconscious but still I was too shaken to reply.

'Let's face the truth here,' said Darrow, and again his firmness allowed him to be gentle without sounding condescending. 'You are in many ways a very ordinary young clergyman. You have a certain modest spiritual gift which you've neglected, and you now have to pay it attention by developing it as far as you can, but I'm not looking for any glamorous success here, Charles – I don't expect you to transform yourself into St Ignatius Loyola in order that I may pat you on the head and say, "Well done!" What I'm hoping is that you, the real Charles Ashworth, will struggle doggedly on at this task which is so very far from easy for you, and eventually achieve a possibly small but nevertheless solid improvement in your spiritual life. *Then* I shall say: "Well done, Charles!" but I won't be setting the seal of approval on any glamorous playacting; I'll be demonstrating my faith in your true self. Keep smashing that glittering image, Charles. It's the enemy within. Keep smashing it until you can finally excavate the roots by remaking your relationship with your father.'

Deeply ashamed of my dishonesty I promised him I wanted only to live in the truth.

III

I spent another five days with the Fordites before I felt confident enough of my strength to risk returning to the world. My second attempt at the exercises proved equally humiliating but now that I was relieved of the burden of trying to become a latter-day St Ignatius Loyola I found I could concentrate better; I was no longer distracted by the worry of what Darrow would think of my failure.

Day by day Darrow made further adjustments to my spiritual diet, and gradually I stopped being nervous of the post-morten and welcomed it instead. His questions clarified my thoughts, pinpointed my weaknesses and gave me an additional incentive to concentrate when the exercises were in progress. It soon became evident that he always knew when I was trying as hard as I could and when I was unwittingly drifting into inertia, and once I trusted him never to underestimate my efforts or to overestimate my ability I was able to surrender myself willingly to his discipline and bend my whole will towards achieving the balanced spiritual life which my problems had so effectively prohibited.

We only discussed the Starbridge situation once more before I left Grantchester. On the evening before my departure I said to him, 'I've been thinking again about whether I should write to Lyle, and I've come to the conclusion that if I want to do the normal thing here I should write not to Lyle but to Mrs Jardine. After all, she was my hostess at that terrible dinner and the least I can do now I'm better is to apologize for my drunken behaviour.'

Darrow merely said, 'What would you expect such a letter to achieve beyond reassuring them of your good manners?'

'It would reassure them of my stability. It seems to me that if I shoot off a passionate polemic to Lyle now she'd simply dismiss it as further evidence that I'm round the bend.'

'Very well, by all means write to Mrs Jardine, but tell me, Charles, are you still disturbed by the need to put Lyle in abeyance?'

'Disturbed but resigned. I do accept that my parents must come first.'

'I'm sure they'll prove a substantial diversion . . . And how do you feel now as you prepare to face the world again?'

'Nervous. But hopeful because I know I'm taking positive action, working for my own rebirth. I won't let you down, Father, I promise.'

'It's not I whom you mustn't let down.'

'I realize that. But aren't I allowed to see you as a symbol?'

Darrow said lightly: 'It's dangerous to see people as symbols! I think you'll be on much safer ground if you simply regard me as a priest doing the work God's assigned to him.' He stood up, added, 'Come to the Abbot's Parlour after breakfast so that I can give you my blessing,' and then before I could reply he was moving swiftly from the room.

IV

The next day we parted in plain style in that lavish parlour. I knelt to receive his blessing, and as I stood to shake his hand he said, 'This is where a new phase of your ordeal begins, Charles. I'll be praying hard for you until we meet again.'

It was difficult to thank him adequately but I tried to imbue the conventional phrases with the gratitude no words could ever had expressed. I also tried to give him back the borrowed cross but he waved it aside. 'No,' he said, escorting me to the front door, 'you'll need that a little longer, I think.'

I thanked him again, slipped the cross around my neck and walked away from him into the world.

V

After taking a bus into the city I entered my rooms at Laud's as the Cathedral clock was striking eleven. For one long moment I stared at those familiar but curiously alien surroundings where my glittering image had toiled so arduously to promote the myth of his perfection, but at last I closed the door, set down my bag and walked to the desk to telephone my parents.

Before I lifted the receiver I removed my clerical collar and opened my newly-purchased packet of cigarettes. The first taste of the cigarette evoked an image of the proverbial nectar of the gods, and leaning forward in my chair with my elbows on my desk I inhaled in a trance of satisfaction as I flicked through the pile of correspondence which had accumulated. As usual there were too many bills but several undergraduates had sent me diverting postcards from places scattered throughout Europe and an unknown American professor had written a friendly letter about my book. Ignoring the pile of theological journals and Church newspapers I embarked on my call to Epsom before glancing at the copy of *The Times* which I had just bought. China was still fighting Japan. The Spanish were still fighting each other. The Devil was still stalking Germany. So much for the world. I was just thinking that life in the cloister, despite the lack of women, did have a great deal to offer, when the telephone bell stopped ringing in Epsom as my parents' long-suffering adenoidal parlourmaid finally picked up the receiver.

'Hullo, Ada,' I said after she had announced herself as the Ashworth residence. 'You sound in good form.'

'Mr Charles – well, what a lovely surprise! Just a minute, your mother's out having her hair done but your father's at home – I'll get him out of the greenhouse.'

I inhaled deeply from my cigarette. Minutes passed, and I was about to transfer the receiver to my other hand to relieve the muscles which had begun to ache with tension when a series of noises at the other end of the line culminated in my father saying abruptly, 'Charles?'

'Good morning, Father. I – '

'What's all this? Are you in some sort of trouble?'

My heart began to thud at a brisk pace. 'I can't imagine why you should say that,' I said, and somehow succeeded in burning a hole with my cigarette in the front page of *The Times*.

'And I can't imagine why else you'd telephone when we're apparently quite beneath your notice these days! Well, I don't suppose you want to speak to me. Your mother said she'd be back by twelve. That means one. I'll tell her you telephoned.'

'Wait!' I was dimly aware that for some reason I was grinding out my half-smoked cigarette. 'Father, I want to come down to Epsom for lunch tomorrow – I was planning to arrive around noon with a bottle of champagne – '

'*Champagne?*'

'Yes, I want to bury the hatchet – ' I was now shredding the cigarette to pieces in the ashtray ' – and I thought the burial would be worth celebrating.'

'Nasty, pretentious drink, champagne – except at weddings. No need to waste your money. Just turn up tomorrow at noon with a civil tongue in your head and you can be sure the hatchet will be buried six feet deep. Then we can drink a glass of my best sherry and that'll be that.'

'Yes, Father.'

'You should guard against extravagance, Charles. No need to behave as if you're a member of the fastest set in town.'

'No, Father.'

'Tomorrow at noon, then. Your mother will be very pleased. But make sure you drive carefully and don't wreck your car pretending you're a motor-racing hero,' said my father severely, and hung up the receiver before I could grope for a reply.

VI

I thought of Darrow and took several deep breaths as I held my cross. Then shrinking from all thought of my parents I embarked on the task of attending to the many mundane matters which had accumulated in my absence. Later, on my way to the bank, I paid my respects to my car which was standing safely in the Laud's forecourt. I felt as if I had come back from the dead; the sense of beginning a new life was becoming stronger.

That evening I wrote Lang a long friendly letter apologizing for my delay in reporting to him, and padded the pages with some carefully selected details of my retreat. That gave me the opportunity to praise Darrow and compose a scholarly paragraph on mysticism. Sandwiched between the irrelevant paragraphs I wrote: 'In respect of your commission I found no evidence that all was not currently as it should be, and Your Grace will be reassured to know that the complete absence of any proof must render our man safe from hostile forces east of Temple Bar.' I also added on a less dramatic note: 'Of course if you wish to see me to discuss this matter further I'll come to Lambeth immediately, but I fear there's little I can add beyond the fact that I encountered a most generous hospitality during my visit which passed, in many respects, far more pleasantly than I had anticipated.'

I had now finally escaped from my role of archiepiscopal spy. Sealing the envelope I left my rooms, posted the letter in the pillar-box by the Cathedral and still savouring my liberation from the burden which had triggered the onset of my great ordeal, I returned thankfully to College to dine.

VII

At the end of the evening I poured myself a small whisky to help me sleep but it tasted so vile that I threw it away. The result was that for hours sleep proved elusive, and when my alarm clock rang at six I could hardly open my eyes. However before I could sink back into unconsciousness I remembered Darrow, and seconds later I was struggling out of bed to make coffee.

The exercises seemed bafflingly difficult again, the texts remote, my meditations arid, and as I struggled to concentrate I could think only how odd it was that I should be groping my way so clumsily towards my new life in that room where the glittering image had so adroitly displayed his techniques for acquiring his shallow success. And suddenly in my despair that I should now be so slow and awkward I longed more fiercely than ever for my new life. The longing had no words but I knew I was praying for a strength which had to be granted from without, not dredged up from within where my resources were so enfeebled. It was as if I were saying, 'Let me live!' and the next moment Jane was returning to me in my memory. I could see her running across the beach on our honeymoon towards the sea, I could hear her urging joyously: 'Come on, Charles, *come on*!' and as the early morning sunlight pierced the window at Laud's the dead text was pulsating with life before my eyes. 'Look, Charles – the tide has turned!' I heard her call, and as the book slipped from my hands I was aware of her love bearing me forward on the tide of my deliverance to the brilliant darkness which lay eternally beyond.

VIII

I reached Epsom punctually at noon on that Saturday morning and headed for the outskirts of the town where my parents lived near the race-course. Their house, built at the end of the last century, had six bedrooms, three reception rooms and an acre of garden but my father had resolutely refused to move after his children had left home. This was his house, earned by his own hard work, and he was sticking to it until he was carried out feet first – or so he told my mother whenever she pined for a smart modern bungalow to cocoon them snugly in their old age. Attached to the house was an Edwardian conservatory, called 'the greenhouse' by Ada, which had long been the centre of my father's aspirations as a horticulturist and was now the ruling passion of his life. As I turned the car into the drive that morning and saw the sun shining on the glass roof I wondered if he had yet succeeded in his ambition to grow oranges larger than plums.

I emerged from the car and pulled on my jacket. I had decided not to wear my clerical clothes, since my father so often made snide remarks about them, and was instead dressed in a pale grey suit and a plain shirt accompanied by my old school tie. I hoped I looked formal without being pretentious, smart without being flashy, well-bred without aspiring to be more than middle-class. In other words I was trying hard to convince my father that no matter what the truth was about my paternity he had not laboured at fatherhood for over thirty-seven years in vain.

Ada opened the front door, and as she stood flat-footed and shining-eyed on the threshold my father's dog Nelson pranced barking across the floor.

'That dog!' said Ada crossly as Nelson waved his front paws at me in excitement, and in response to my enquiry about her health she produced the reply that her bunions were killing her. However this was a traditional response; Ada's bunions had been killing her for at least twenty years, and after expressing the equally traditional words of commiseration I was finally able to ask, 'How are my parents?'

'Ever so pleased you're visiting, Mr Charles. Madam went out early this morning and bought a new dress. Make sure you notice it but don't say I – whoops! Here she is! God bless you, Mr Charles, lovely to see you . . .' She thudded away towards the kitchens as my mother made a theatrical descent of the stairs.

'Charles – darling!'

My mother was a woman in her late fifties, still slender, with dark hair, dark eyes and a smart haggard look which was not unattractive. Her chief hobby was her appearance which she maintained with an unflagging dedication. I was sure she dyed her hair and equally sure the idea that she might descend to such vulgarity had never occurred to my father who adopted a naïve attitude to the more esoteric mysteries of the female sex. Her taste in clothes was expensive yet restrained; she was wearing a navy-blue dress accompanied by an unobtrusive strand of pearls.

'I'm glad to see you still haven't lost the secret of eternal youth,' I said, smiling at her. 'I like your dress.'

'Darling, what wonderful flattery – I adore it!' As we kissed I noticed she was wearing a delicate scent, and suddenly I pictured her devoting her entire morning to burnishing her glittering image for my benefit. 'And Charles, how divine you look without that clerical collar! Or will it make you cross if I say that? I mustn't make you cross . . . But come outside – I thought we'd have drinks on the terrace and I'm going to mix some champagne cocktails as a special treat. I know that silly old man told you not to bring champagne – how typical! – but why shouldn't we have some champagne, I'd like to know? I was so thrilled you'd decided to visit us – and so was *he* although he'd never admit it. Honestly, Charles, since he retired he's been exactly like a bear with a sore head – '

'I suppose he must miss the office a lot.'

'Well, why should he? He's got his horrid conservatory! I keep asking him to grow orchids but he won't; it's sheer bloodymindedness. He could perfectly well grow orchids if he wanted to.'

'How's Peter?'

'No help at all, I'm fed up with Peter at the moment. The least he could do is drop in every week to have a drink with your father and talk about the office but he's always working late or going to the Test Match or playing golf or whizzing off to a smart dinner party with Annabel. Of course I blame Annabel for being too possessive; I always did think she was a thoroughly selfish girl – oh, there's the telephone. Maybe it's Peter ringing up in remorse after neglecting us for so long. Darling, go and dig your father out of that ghastly conservatory and tell him we're about to have drinks.'

Nelson accompanied me through the door on to the terrace and padded at my heels as I walked around the side of the house. However outside the conservatory, which he knew from experience was too warm for his comfort, he sat down in the shade to wait. Meanwhile my heart had begun to thud at a brisk pace again. I felt as if every step I had ever taken in my life had led to this moment when I would open the conservatory door and face once more but with new eyes that fierce mysterious man who had brought me up.

I reached the door. I opened it. I crossed the threshold into the sultry heat. I was reminded of a jungle being colonized by a single ruthless British soldier intent on building his own private empire on which the sun would never set.

'Ah, there you are,' said my father from the far end of the conservatory. 'Glad to see you've arrived in one piece. That stupid woman says she's going to make champagne cocktails – why you're not utterly ruined by her petting and pampering I can't imagine, but there we are, she means well and it's not every day she has the excuse to waste my money on champagne. Where's your dog-collar? Nice to see you looking like a normal chap for a change. Suppose it's too much to hope that you've given up that damnfool superstitious pantomime that calls itself the Church of England.'

I touched the cross hidden beneath my shirt and walked on down the conservatory to meet him.

EIGHTEEN

'Then as to success of life, I think that all turns on the meaning attached to success. From one point of view, I do not doubt that my professional career may fairly be described as successful, but that is not the point of view which at any time has secured my acceptance.'

HERBERT HENSLEY HENSON
Bishop of Durham 1920–1939
Retrospect of an Unimportant Life

I

My father was seventy years old but could have passed for a man in his early sixties. He had a trim neat upright figure, not tall, and he moved with none of the hesitation of old age. His hair, which had once been a mundane brown, was now an equally mundane pepperish-white; short, straight and ruthlessly parted it receded sharply on either side of his high forehead. The eyes behind his glasses were blue. He had a long straight nose and a sharp pugnacious chin. His mouth drooped at the corners when he sulked and tightened into a thin-lipped line when he was angry but he had a swift rare pleasant smile which revealed that he had kept his teeth; my father hated dentists almost as much as he hated doctors and was convinced they were charlatans intent on making money by the most dubious means.

As I approached him I saw he was wearing his scruffiest gardening clothes. 'Thought I'd change while your mother's pampering you over the first round of those damned cocktails,' he said as we shook hands. 'Did she send you to fetch me?'

I told him about the telephone call which might have come from Peter, and my father, giving an eloquent sniff, began to scoop a small pile of earth from the work-bench into an empty flowerpot.

'Mother said you hadn't seen much of Peter lately,' I added, removing my jacket in acknowledgement of the heat.

'He's been too damn busy. I'm just fit for the scrap-heap, of course, now I'm retired. And that stupid wife of his has been giving him

268

extravagant ideas by bullying him into taking a holiday on the Riviera. "What's wrong with England?" I asked him but he just laughed as if I were senile. He never bothers to keep me up to date with what's happening at the office. Wish to God I hadn't retired but I always said no one should stay at the helm after the age of seventy so I had to stick to my guns and practise what I preached. And now what have I got? One son who doesn't answer my letters, another son who prances off abroad and a wife who nags me to grow orchids! It's enough to make one puke. I'm fed up with the whole bloody business of being alive. Roll on extinction, I say, and thank God there's no after-life. That really would be the last straw.'

'I'm sorry I didn't answer that last letter of yours, Father,' I said. 'That was wrong of me. But can I now renew my invitation to Cambridge? I'd be very pleased if you and Mother – '

'Can't leave my plants. Various things at a critical stage. Need daily attention.' My father scooped up the last fragments of earth and pressed them ferociously into the flowerpot before demanding, 'Why all the sweetness and light? What's going on? Why are you here? Are you in debt?'

'My dear Father – '

'You don't have to soften me up before you ask for a loan. Come on, Charles – out with it! I knew as soon as you telephoned yesterday that you were in some sort of trouble – '

'I have indeed been in very great trouble,' I said, 'but it has nothing to do with money and I'm getting better now.'

He pushed the spectacles high up on the bridge of his nose so that he could stare at me through the lenses. 'You've been ill?'

'I've been through a time of severe strain but I'm now, with the help of my new spiritual director, beginning to – '

'Your new *what*?'

'Spiritual director. A specialist in spiritual health. Like a doctor of the soul.'

'Very nasty. Sounds like quackery. You ought to be careful, Charles. Some of these quacks can do a lot of damage.'

'I assure you he could hardly be more respectable – he's a clergyman as well as a monk, and – '

'A monk! I don't like the sound of this at all, Charles. No man in his right mind would be a monk. But what's the matter with you? Lost your faith?'

'No, I'd lost my spiritual way but I'm finding it again, and Father Darrow – the monk – thinks you can be of enormous importance in helping me along the road to recovery. That's actually why I've come here today.'

We stood facing each other, my father still holding his trowel, I still holding my jacket while my shirt stuck to my back. My heart was now thudding more briskly than ever.

'Well, of course I'll help you in any way I can, Charles. That's what fathers are for. But this all sounds damned odd to me and I'm not sure I understand what's going on. Stop talking about spiritual this and spiritual that and put it in plain no-nonsense English. Have you had a nervous breakdown?'

'Father Darrow refused to call it that. Perhaps one could say that my entire way of life broke down so that I found myself unable to go on without pausing to solve a number of severe problems.'

'Severe – oh, rubbish, Charles! That nasty monk's been putting a lot of nonsense into your head! You don't have any problems – you're making the biggest possible success of that peculiar profession of yours!'

'That was the problem.'

'My God, don't tell me you're going to chuck everything up and rush off to be a missionary in Africa!'

'No, before I can even begin to reassess my calling I have to get my soul in order, and that's why –'

'There you go again, talking in ghastly clerical whimsy-language! Why the devil you can't just say you're in a bloody muddle, I don't know. God, how you worry me, Charles! For years and years I've slaved to bring you up to be –'

'You did a wonderful job, Father. Before I say what I'm going to say next I want to tell you how very much I admire you and how very grateful I am to you for all you've –'

'What the *hell's* all this? Nasty sentimental maundering – talking like a damned foreigner – pull yourself together, Charles, and for God's sake stop embarrassing me!'

There was a pause. I looked at him and knew the hour had come – and suddenly as he looked at me I saw he knew it too; he knew that no fierce rebuke could stop me now from saying what had to be said. We stood there in the stifling conservatory, in that little jungle which he was doggedly colonizing with his incorruptible British spirit, and it was as if we both saw the sun setting on the empire which he had been so valiantly sustaining for so long.

I said, 'I've got to know. I can't live with the uncertainty any longer. Help me – you said you'd help me – that's what fathers are for, you said –'

'I'll help you best by telling you to wash your hands of that bloody monk and stop acting like a bloody actor in a bloody melodrama!'

'Are you my natural father?'

The sun finally set on the empire and the night began to fall.

II

My father turned away to face the work-bench again so that I could see his face only in profile, and then slowly, very slowly, he took off his spectacles. I felt as if I were seeing an actor remove his mask at the end of some long Greek tragedy. Then slowly, very slowly, like the old man he was, he sat down on a wooden stool and stared with unseeing eyes at the spectacles in his hands.

At last he said in a tired voice, 'So it was all for nothing.'

'How can you conceivably say that?' I was shattered. Automatically, hardly knowing what I did, I upturned a giant flowerpot so that I could sit down at his side.

'Didn't want you ever to know. Thought if you guessed it would mean I'd failed and if I'd failed it would mean everything was a mockery – the marriage, all my ideals, everything. But you guessed. So I've failed. And it's all been for nothing.'

'I don't think you've failed,' I said. 'I'll never think you've failed. And if I don't think you've failed then it can't all have been for nothing.'

He moved abruptly away. I knew why. He was terrified that he might prove unable to keep the depth of his distress to himself. The silence lengthened as he turned his back on me and pretended to examine one of the vines, but at last he said, 'I suppose you want to know everything.'

'I must. I'm sorry.'

'Well, don't blame me if you don't like it!' said my father, making a frail attempt to recapture his characteristic truculence. 'If you think he was a bloody hero you're making a very big mistake.' And then before I could reply he said in a rush, 'His name was Alan Romaine . . .'

III

'Alan Romaine,' said my father. 'Alan Romaine. Typical. Just the sort of name he *would* have. Maybe he picked it out of a French novel. Wouldn't surprise me. Nothing about him ever did surprise me. Alan Romaine . . .

'He was a doctor. But not your ordinary decent quack who runs gamely around the local houses with a stethoscope and is always a bit pressed for time. This quack was special. He had grand ideas. He was going to play the hero in a big London hospital and later he was going to have rooms in Harley Street where all the titled women could consult him about their aches and pains. He knew people. He name-dropped. He was about to begin a specialist's training in gynaecology at Bart's but that summer he had a little time to fill in so he came down to Epsom as a locum. Romaine liked Epsom. Near London . . . scene of the Derby . . . racing . . . smart people . . . glamour . . . just his sort of place. Once he'd arrived he settled down in double-quick time and prepared to conquer everyone in sight.

'He was only twenty-seven. Obviously he'd done well. Plenty of brains. First-class at cricket and tennis. Modest, though – knew how to behave. All the women from nineteen to ninety treated him as a Greek god but because he was such a sportsman he was popular with the men too – all the men except me. I just took one look at him and thought: bounder. Cad. Too flashy by half. And I wondered about him. He never spoke of a family. Nobody really knew anything about him. He was a gentleman, of course, but . . . not to be trusted.

'He drank quite a bit. No one seemed to notice but I did. Once at a dinner when the ladies had withdrawn he had a third glass of port after a heavy raid on the claret decanter and I said to him, "You're drinking rather a lot for a doctor, aren't you?" That made him angry. "Poor old Ashworth!" he said. "So old, so staid, so dull!" But I said, "You'd better watch your step. Hard-drinking bounders don't wind up in Harley Street. They wind up in the gutter." For a moment I thought he was going to throw his glass at me but instead he laughed and said, "You're just jealous – and don't think we can't all guess why!"

'As you know, I'd wanted to marry your mother for some time,' said my father, turning away at last from the vine and moving back to the work-bench, 'but I was much older than she was and I wasn't glamorous. I was just a plain man who wore glasses and worked hard. Of course I had my ambitions but unlike Romaine I didn't go around advertising them, and meanwhile I wasn't happy in my job and I was tempted to make a complete change. I was also tempted to turn my back on Epsom for a while – I couldn't bear the thought of being an onlooker when Helen married a man whom I felt sure was no damned good – and when it seemed to me that the marriage was inevitable I decided to volunteer for the Army.

'As you no doubt remember I gave you a censored version of that decision when you were fifteen. However what I didn't tell you was that the Army decided straight away that they didn't want me. There was no interval while they made up their minds; they just weren't interested in a thirty-two-year-old civilian with poor eyesight. Well, I was glad in the end that I didn't have to leave the law but sorry to be stuck in Epsom while Helen was still steering this disastrous course – and don't think I hadn't tried to alter that course, because I had. But she'd just told me to leave her alone. Finally I said, "Always remember, whatever happens, that I love you and I want to marry you." Perhaps I had a premonition that he'd jilt her. But on the other hand I'm not the sort of fellow who gets premonitions.

'And then . . . she came to me. I'd already heard from the Army but I hadn't actually told anyone that I wouldn't be leaving Epsom after all. She came to my house and broke down, broke down utterly, it was very terrible. I wanted to go after him and . . . But I knew I had to put first things first. He could wait. She couldn't. She'd come to ask me what to do. I don't believe she really thought I'd stick to my guns and marry her. She just wanted to know what on earth she was going to do. Romaine – ' My father stopped.

I waited. By this time I was standing, leaning back against the work-bench and gripping the edge with both hands.

My father turned to face me. 'He was already married,' he said. 'He called it a "Jane Eyre" situation. Typical. He was equating his own sordid behaviour with a romantic novel – ugh! It revolted me. Anyway there he was with a wife hopelessly insane in an asylum, and there was Helen, completely ruined – oh, it was all so wrong, *so wrong*, I couldn't stand to think of it, and I knew at once I had to put things right. Well, what other choice did I have? I couldn't have let evil win. That would have been quite contrary to all my principles. I thought: I'm going to prove good always does win through in the end . . . Silly really, I can see that now, but at the time I felt no other course of action was possible, and my decision was strengthened when she said – ' My father stopped again. Then he replaced his spectacles, looked me straight in the eyes and said, 'She told me Romaine had offered her an abortion.

'I said, "*You will not have an abortion under any circumstances whatsoever.*" Of course I'd realized that she wanted someone to tell her not to do it because she must have known in her heart that it would have been a disaster for her. I told her she'd never get over having murdered her own child – and that was true, I knew it was, I knew Helen, I knew how sensitive she was underneath all that brittle gaiety. I said, "You'll marry me and no one's ever going to know." Oh, how relieved she was, poor girl! She cried and cried and said she'd be the best possible wife to me . . .

'I had one interview with Romaine. I made sure I was absolutely sober and utterly in control of myself. Then I went to him and said, "You're leaving Epsom and leaving England. Forget Harley Street. Forget all those glamorous dreams. You're going abroad within a month or, by God, I'll see you struck off the medical register – and if you ever dare come near Helen again," I said, "you can be bloody well sure you'll regret it." I'll always remember that moment. He was dead white. He'd been drinking, of course. I could smell the brandy. But he was quiet. And suddenly I felt as if I were looking at someone whom no one in Epsom, least of all poor Helen, had ever really known.

'Well, the next day after he'd pulled himself together sufficiently to strike a glamorous pose, he announced that he felt called to work in Africa and so off he went, the noble young doctor, romantic to the last . . . and I was left to pick up the pieces.

'I pretended that I was on the brink of leaving for my military training so we had a good excuse for marrying straight away, but she insisted on having a white wedding and that meant a few days' delay while the gown was made. I tried to persuade her that we couldn't afford to wait but she said it would look too odd if she wasn't married in white and whatever happened we had to keep up appearances. However finally we got to the altar, and that night after I'd consummated the marriage I said: "That's that. You're both mine now – which means that you're never, never under any circumstances going to mention that man's name again and you're never, never under any circumstances going to tell anyone that child's not just as much mine as any future children you may have. That child," I said, "is going to be my child from this moment onwards and I'm going to bring him up to be a good straight decent man even if it's the very last thing I ever do."'

My father paused. Taking off his spectacles again he began to polish them with a grubby handkerchief. 'So much for the preliminaries,' he said tersely, 'but then the trouble really began . . .'

IV

'Well, of course,' said my father, 'it was all rather different in the end from what I'd expected, but then I'm not sure now what I did expect. I don't think I'd looked much beyond the honeymoon, but Helen found pregnancy a great trial. Couldn't face marital intimacy most of the time. I told myself it was just her condition but . . . I suspected she was pining for Romaine.

'Then you arrived and she worried herself to death about what people would think – she'd convinced herself you'd be conveniently late but no, there you were on time. She wouldn't go out for a while, wouldn't see anyone, cried in her room – and it wasn't just because she was afraid people were talking about her. It was because she had finally woken up to the realization that she'd jumped out of the frying-pan into the fire – she'd avoided ruin but now here she was tied to a husband whom she . . . well, she wouldn't have married me if she'd had a choice. She never loved me as much as I loved her, and all the time . . . well, I felt increasingly sure she was pining for Romaine.

'She decided to have another child as soon as possible, and I knew why. It was because she couldn't stand the guilt, the guilt that she couldn't love me as she should, and she wanted to make amends but although she became obsessed with the thought of another baby she didn't conceive straight away. More tears, more unhappiness, more awful guilt – however finally, thank God – she had Peter and that put everything right for a while, but the marriage never really ran smoothly. She tried hard, but . . . I knew she didn't love me and I started to get resentful. And of course all the time there you were, growing up, the constant reminder, the cuckoo in the nest . . . poor little chap, not your fault. You were a nice little fellow too. I said to myself: I'm not going to take it out on him . . . But I'd look at you and I'd remember Romaine.

'Then suddenly one day I realized that my own boy was getting overlooked because you were such an exceptional little chap. You really did have great charm. Everyone used to pat you on the head and dote on you, and no one doted more than your mother. But finally I woke up and saw you were getting very spoilt and pampered with ideas quite above your station so I knew there had to be no pampering from *me*, not if I wanted to be a good father, but of course your mother didn't understand, silly woman, thought I was taking it out on you. I wasn't. I just didn't want you growing up like him and I thought I saw all the ingredients there . . . So I got very strict and your mother called me a brute and we started having bloody awful rows, always over you, but I won, I shut her up, I even hit her sometimes, terrible, very wrong, shouldn't ever strike a woman, but I wasn't going to stand any nonsense from anyone in my household, not after all I'd been through, and anyway the net result of all this was that I wound up keeping you down with one hand while I paid special attention to Peter on the other. Not a good situation, but I didn't want my boy growing up thinking himself inferior because he had this exceptional older brother. Of course you hated me paying attention to Peter, you hated anyone paying attention to Peter, you liked the whole world revolving around you so that you could preen yourself in the limelight. Silly little fellow, but not your fault. You couldn't help everyone cooing over you, but I knew I had an absolute moral duty to keep the balance, and besides . . . I was so afraid you'd turn out like Romaine.

'However as time went on I got both you and your mother under control and you really did begin to show exceptional promise. Very gratifying. But naturally I never believed it would last. I found myself becoming haunted by the worry not only that your heredity would triumph despite all my efforts to muzzle it but that you'd somehow succeed in discovering the truth about your paternity and go straight off the rails. You gave me a nasty moment when you realized you'd arrived so soon after the wedding, but I'd been prepared for that crisis so I was able to knock it on the head straight away. There's nothing more unstable than a moody adolescent, and I was sure you'd have gone to the dogs in no time if you'd found out then that I wasn't your natural father after all.

'You looked like Romaine by then. I used to see your mother gazing at you and I knew she was remembering, just as I was. I'd feel so angry then, so bitter, but I'd cheer myself up by thinking: if that boy turns out well at least there'll be something redeemed from the mess. So I kept on at you, urging you to keep to the straight and narrow, until finally there you were, safely up at Cambridge reading law, and I thought: I've done it. That boy's turned out properly and he's all set to lead a thoroughly decent life, no glamour, no playacting, no fantasy. But then – my God! You sidled home and told me *you wanted to go into the Church*! No wonder I nearly had a fit. I didn't think you were in touch with reality. You'd always been a bit of a romantic idealist – thank God the War ended before you could throw away your life dying gallantly in action! I thought this Church nonsense was just a pose, like Romaine telling everyone he'd felt called to be a doctor in Africa, and my God, that was the closest I ever came to letting the cat out of the bag about your paternity.

'But of course I didn't do it. Well, I couldn't have done it, could I? It would have been like hitting a man when he was down. There you were, wallowing in emotion, talking drivel about God – how could I have done anything but kept my mouth shut? You needed to be protected, not disowned, and besides . . . if I'd said to you then: "You're not my son," it would have been a lie because by that time you *were* my son. *I'd* brought you up, *I'd* knocked my values into you, *I'd* made you what you were . . . But now you were telling me that what I'd made you was a bloody clergyman! God, what an irony! I hardly knew whether to laugh or cry.

'Well, I battered away at you to try and save you from yourself, but you dug in your toes and wouldn't budge. I had to admire you for sticking to your ideals, and finally I thought: well, at least it's a good straight decent life. But then I thought: how's he ever going to stand it, living as a curate, unable to afford to marry, he'll go to the dogs, start drinking too much, get in a mess with some woman, and then all my hard work will have been for nothing and my marriage will be more of an unredeemed disaster than ever. But I'd underestimated you, hadn't I? You weren't the average ineffectual young padre who gets stuck in some remote rural hamlet preaching sentimental mumbo-jumbo. You were special. You had grand ideas. You name-dropped. And of course you wound up as the Archbishop's favourite poodle. Typical. Couldn't help admiring you. But oh my God, how you reminded me of Romaine . . .

'I couldn't believe it would work out. I kept waiting for you to get in a mess, but you didn't – you landed that amazing post at St Aidan's and you married that thoroughly nice girl. Wonderful. But then I started worrying in case the marriage went wrong, thought she might perhaps have been a little *too* nice for you, thought you might later fancy someone tougher and more alluring . . . No peace, you see, not even then. When I married your mother and took you on I thought fatherhood would end promptly on your twenty-first birthday, but it didn't. Parenthood only ends with the grave. I went on worrying myself silly about you, but there you were, still doing well, and I could always cheer myself up by thinking: never mind, I did at least make a success of that boy. You were like a symbol in the end, a symbol that my ideals had triumphed over all the tragedy . . .'

'But then last year . . . that awful row . . . I felt so depressed. I thought: maybe I've failed after all. I did cheer up a bit when you sent us that invitation to visit Cambridge for Easter, but the whole letter was much too smooth and I knew some old clergyman had been getting at you during Lent. I can always spot insincerity a mile off. So I wrote back that stiff reply in the hope that I'd needle you into writing something genuine, but no, you got up on your high horse and stayed there.

'Then I suddenly felt very old. I'd just retired. I had no work to go to any more, nothing to distract me from my unhappiness. You were estranged from me, Peter was too busy enjoying the life I'd once led to pay me much attention . . . I felt rather jealous of Peter, being young, leading the life I still wanted to lead . . . I was a bit sharp with him once or twice. Mistake. He took offence. Silly boy, henpecked by that awful Annabel of his . . . I suppose he's happy. Maybe he's miserable. Who knows? All I know is that *I'm* bloody miserable stuck in Epsom day after day with your mother, but poor Helen, I do feel sorry for her in so many ways. She's had a disappointing sort of life, not the life she had in mind. She would have liked a more glamorous husband, someone romantic, someone . . . well, someone like Alan Romaine.

'We never mentioned him, never, not even during all our rows over you, but he's always been with us. He's still with us. He's here now, invading my conservatory, smashing everything up . . . And after this, I suppose,' said my father turning on me fiercely, 'you'll want to trace him! I can just see you going all sloppy and sentimental, thanking God you've found your real father at last – so much for God! I slaved for years and years to be a decent father to you and now bloody Romaine will saunter along and reap the benefit! Disgusting! But that's typical of life, isn't it? The real bounders always bounce along into a happy ending while the decent fellows get trodden in the dust. Good doesn't triumph over evil, not in real life, good gets ground down and spat upon. Law of the jungle. No God. Nothing. Beats me how anyone can believe otherwise.'

He sank abruptly on to the stool again and groped to remove his spectacles for another polishing. I waited to allow him time to steady himself; I bent my head so that he would think himself unobserved as he furtively wiped his eyes on the grubby handkerchief; but then I sat down at his side once more, and leaning forward I gently covered his trembling hands with my own.

V

High heels clacked in the distance like gunfire to warn us of my mother's approach. We both started, both glanced at the door. I was quite beyond speech by this time, but fear galvanized my father into action, and shoving away my hands he struggled to his feet.

'Not a word, Charles. *Not a bloody word.*' He spoke in a fierce whisper, his face set in its hardest lines, every muscle of his frame rigid with determination. 'Your mother's not to know you know. Absolutely not. *Never.* And if you so much as breathe one syllable of this conversation to her, I'll – '

My mother tip-tapped through the conservatory doorway before he could complete the sentence. 'Well, really, you two!' she exclaimed in exasperation. 'What are you up to? I'm waiting to drink champagne cocktails! Eric, go and change out of those filthy clothes and let Charles escape from this ghastly hell-hole of yours!'

I somehow achieved a smooth intervention. 'Was that Peter on the phone?'

'Yes, he sent his regards to you and said he was so sorry he wouldn't be able to see you before you rushed back to Cambridge but he and Annabel were just off to a garden party at Richmond.'

'Typical!' said my father. 'No time for his family!'

'When's he going to come and see Father?' I said before my mother could put all the blame on Annabel.

'Tomorrow evening at six. You see, Eric? I knew it was nonsense when you said yesterday he'd forgotten you!'

'He's just coming to keep me quiet. "Better keep the old buffer sweet," he's saying to that awful Annabel, "or he might do something nasty with his will." Well, I don't care if he comes or not. It's all the same to me.'

'Silly old man!' said my mother, grimacing at me to convey he was irritating her beyond endurance. 'What nonsense you talk!'

But my father elbowed her rudely aside and stumbled off at a rapid pace into the garden.

VI

'Well, of course he's become absolutely impossible,' said my mother. 'I'm at my wits' end – have been for some time actually – and really, darling, when I heard you were coming today I almost started believing in divine providence because I feel that if I don't talk to someone soon about how awful life is at the moment I'll start climbing the walls. Quick, come to the terrace and let's have a drink while he's changing.'

'He seemed fairly pleased to see me – '

'So he damn well should! I said to him this morning: "You'd better cheer up before Charles comes or he won't come down here again in a hurry," but he only said: "He won't come down here again in a hurry anyway, so why should I bother?" Ghastly old man, moping around like death personified, and it's so frightful for *me* being tied to someone who spends his whole time looking as if he's trying to find a coffin to lie in. Heavens, I'm not even sixty yet, and he makes life so dreadfully depressing . . . I wish to God he hadn't retired. He doesn't know what to do with himself, apart from pottering around in that frightful conservatory – and I'm sure the heat there's bad for him. He could have a heart attack. Maybe that's what he wants. I don't know, God knows what he wants, but I know what *I* want, and that's a decent holiday. Peter and Annabel are taking the children to the south of France, such a lovely idea, but Eric poured cold water on it and as good as told Peter he was an unpatriotic nitwit for wanting to take a holiday outside England – well, no wonder Peter took offence, I don't blame him, although I do think Annabel stirs him up. There's something very *common* about Annabel, but then we all know, don't we, that her father made his money out of trade.'

We had by this time reached the wrought-iron table shaded by a white umbrella, and I was pouring the cocktails from the jug. 'I'm sorry things are so difficult,' I said as I sat down beside her and lit her cigarette.

'Never mind, darling, let's drink to a happy visit – mmm, what lovely champagne! Now don't let me rattle on about all my ghastly problems – tell me about yourself. I must say, you're looking a little thin and peaky! I do hope you haven't been working too hard.'

'I've just concluded a long retreat with the Fordite monks at Grant-chester.'

'Poor darling, no wonder you're looking peaky! It's a miracle you're not worn to a frazzle – like me. Honestly, Charles, I can't get over how amazing it is that you should turn up. I kept hoping and hoping you would and I was going to write but I didn't want to pester you and I was so afraid of being one of those ghastly mother who *cling* – and everyone knows nowadays that clinging mothers can do so much damage. Of course Eric's always accused me of spoiling you but I've tried so hard to be sensible, I really have, and the last thing I want is to be a nuisance or a burden or – oh hell, I'm embarrassing you, I can see I am, I'm saying all the wrong things but I'm so nervous, in such a state, please, plase don't be cross . . .' And she began to cry.

'My dearest Mother . . .' I dragged my chair around the table so that I could put my arm around her shoulders. 'I'm so very sorry – how dreadful to think you were afraid to write to me and how appalling to think I've left you alone for so long – '

'Oh, I'm all right,' she said, drinking half her cocktail. 'Heavens, I don't want to make you regret you've come! Everything's absolutely fine really – except that sometimes I think I can't go on any more – ' She broke down again.

'How difficult is he? Is he just surly or – '

'No, he doesn't hit me, not nowadays. My God, he used to get so angry – but I did try so hard to be a good wife to him, I really did . . . It was just that whatever I did never seemed to be enough. Sometimes I used to despair so much that I'd tell myself I'd leave when you and Peter were grown up, but when it came to the point I was too frightened. He'd have been beastly about the divorce and I couldn't face being socially ostracized . . . Perhaps if I'd met some decent man . . . But I never did. All the decent ones were happily married.'

'All of them? What about earlier in your life?'

'When you and Peter were little? Yes, there were one or two men who were very keen – although I was never unfaithful because I was so afraid Eric would find out and he'd already threatened me about that. "If you're once unfaithful to me," he said, "that's it. Finish. And don't think you'd ever see either of your sons again." Well, that settled it, didn't it? Actually I think Peter might have managed without me, but you . . . oh, I couldn't have left you. No, no, that was quite impossible. I stayed with him because of you in the end – it was like some ghastly punishment but it didn't matter, I accepted it, I'd have done anything for you and you needed me, I knew you did, especially as Eric could be so . . . oh, how I hated him sometimes! But there was no question of leaving, and besides, I never in fact met anyone whom I could love as I wanted to love . . . as I knew I could love – ' She stopped.

'You mean,' I said after a pause, 'there was a memory which acted as a yardstick?'

'Yes, I met a man once . . . before I was married . . . first love . . . and no one I met later ever measured up to him. It was as if I could see them only in black and white whereas this memory was in glowing colours.' She drank deeply again from her glass.

'What happened to him?'

'I don't know. He had to go away, but it was so strange, Charles, because I always thought . . . I always thought – '

' – he'd come back.'

She nodded, struggling with her tears again. Her mascara had smudged. The powder was streaked. I could see the deep lines on her face. 'But he didn't,' she said levelly. 'Stupid of me to indulge in romantic dreams, wasn't it? But Eric always says I'm a stupid woman.'

'Father makes a lot of wild statements that are unjust. Perhaps he feels that life's been unjust to him and he wants to hit back.'

'Life unjust to him? But he's had a wonderful life, so successful! He's had everything he's ever wanted!'

'Yes, but . . . well, never mind Father for the moment, I'd much rather talk about you. Tell me more about this first love of yours.'

'Oh, darling, I can't. Eric would be so angry if he knew I'd even mentioned it to you, and besides . . . some things really are better not discussed.'

'Are you sure? I've just spent days discussing my life with the clerical equivalent of a psychiatrist and I feel much better.'

'Charles! Darling, what's wrong? Oh, if only you knew how much I worry about you – is the trouble to do with Jane? I know how terribly her death upset you, I've sensed you bottling up your grief all these years, never speaking of her – oh Charles, I did so long to help, but somehow I never knew what to say . . . I loved Jane. I cried and cried when she died – '

'My dearest Mother – '

'I did, Charles, I did! Such a good nice girl she was, always so kind to me, not like bloody Annabel who treats me like a drunken hag. Well, I know I do drink too much sometimes – and particularly when I have to face Annabel, but I'm all right, Charles, I'm all right – '

'I'm going to come back here next week and stay for a couple of days. I think it's very important that you should talk to me in detail about all your unhappiness – '

'Oh, if only you knew how much I long to confide in you!' she said. 'But I mustn't. Eric would make life hell if he thought I'd been confiding in you behind his back.'

'Eric's already making life hell. Let's see if we can change the gramophone record. Come on, Mother, we probably have at least another ten minutes together before he reappears – have a second cocktail and tell me all about this first love of yours who affected you so deeply for so long.'

VII

'I mustn't say his name,' said my mother, 'because Eric said it was never to be mentioned again, but when I was a young girl still in my teens I thought it was the sort of name every romantic hero ought to have . . . Now I know what you're thinking, darling. You're thinking: what fools young girls are about men! But it wasn't as simple as that. I was going through a ghastly time and it was as if this man's wonderful glamour and his whole great spirit of high romance were in some magical way a negation of all the dreadful things that were happening to me.

'You'll remember me telling you that when I was eighteen I went to Germany for six months to be "finished". Well, I always pretended it was great fun but the truth was I hated it. I hadn't wanted to go but Great-Aunt Sophie said it would be better if I went away from home for a while because my mother was so ill by that time with her TB and my father was keeping this mistress ... My dear, nobody would think anything of it now, but this was 1898 and Aunt Sophie was deeply Victorian. Nobody explained about the mistress, of course, and I didn't understand why I was being sent away – oh, I was so unhappy! But in the spring of 1899 I was allowed to come home again because the mistress had left Epsom and now not only my mother was at death's door but my father was dying of cancer. I expect you remember hearing most of this before, darling, but I wonder if you've ever stopped to think how absolutely frightful it was for me.

'Well, Papa eventually died – I think old Dr Barnes killed him with morphia in the end – and there I was, nineteen years old, in this house which was exactly like a morgue. My mother went on dying by inches and Aunt Sophie creaked around in her corsets and everything was prayer-books and hushed whispers and I used to feel as if I were suffocating.

'And then ... that summer ... old Dr Barnes broke a lot of bones in an accident and this young doctor came to Epsom for three months to take his place.

'I soon met him. He came to attend my mother in her illness. I remember I was embroidering yet another useless sampler when I heard the noise of wheels in the drive and on going to the window I saw this young man jump down from the pony-trap with his Gladstone bag. Then he caught sight of me – but he didn't just touch his hat and move on. He swept off his hat and he raised his hand and he smiled and ... It was the breath of life, Charles. I ran all the way to the front door to let him in.

'He was a tremendous success in our set. Everyone liked him except Eric but everyone knew Eric was jealous. I'd known Eric for years ... and respected him ... but he seemed so terribly old, over thirty – imagine! – and although I wanted to marry, to escape from home I honestly couldn't see myself marrying an old man. I didn't truly know Eric then, of course. Later I discovered all his wonderful qualities and ... well, I married him, didn't I? But earlier ... after I'd met this other man ... I couldn't think of Eric at all.

'Eric said I was just infatuated with the man's looks but he was wrong.

Of course this man was divinely attractive. But I fell in love with him mainly because he was the only person who seemed to understand what hell I was going through. He said he'd been going through hell himself because someone he loved very much had recently been certified insane. He said, "Life's so frightful in so many ways, so many terrible things can happen even to the best people, and that's why it's so important to live to the hilt while one can and snatch all the happiness that's available."

'I said, "That's how I feel too."

'It was rather a solemn moment, but then he kissed me – for the first time – and he laughed and he said, "I have this *irresistible* urge for champagne – let's raid the cellars and filch a bottle!" Oh, he was such fun! It was only three in the afternoon – a preposterous time to drink champagne, but Aunt Sophie always took her afternoon rest till four so no one was breathing down my neck. We crept down to the cellar and found a bottle of champagne and sneaked off to drink it in the summer-house – oh, how we laughed and oh, what fun it was! But terribly naughty, of course – Aunt Sophie would have died. I said: "I feel terribly naughty!" and he said, "So do I! Isn't it amusing?" and he laughed again and began to recite some lines from Browning – that poem about how one mustn't miss one's opportunities – "The Statue and the Bust". I can remember him lounging on the summer-house love-seat with the glass of champagne in his hand as he quoted: "The sin we impute to each frustrate ghost is the unlit lamp and the ungirt loin . . ." Then suddenly he set down his glass and said, "I feel a delicious urge to start lighting lamps and girding loins!" Oh God, how romantic it was, how exciting, I adored it, I was absolutely swooning . . .

'Well, as I've said, it was all terribly naughty and of course it couldn't last, and after a few meetings . . . well, to cut a long story short,' said my mother, finishing her second cocktail rapidly, 'it turned out that he was already married – the one in the asylum was his wife – so nothing came of my big romance and eventually he went off to Africa while I married Eric and settled down. But Eric always hated that episode in my past, and that's why you must never, never let him know that I've – oh God, here he is. Not a word, darling, promise me – *not a word* –'

'I suppose you're still drinking those disgusting cocktails,' said my father, emerging on to the terrace with a glass of sherry in his hand. 'Another bottle of good champagne murdered . . . Helen, why are you looking so odd?'

'She's wondering why she feels no remorse for committing the murder!' I said lightly but neither of them smiled, and in the silence that followed this trivial but flawlessly smooth response I sensed they both looked at me and saw Dr Romaine.

Despite the depth of my emotional turmoil I worked as hard as I could to make the lunch a success. I kept the peace whenever they began to bicker, I asked after their friends, I listened to interminable stories about Peter's omissions and the iniquities of Annabel. Finally we discussed the Coronation, and once the discussion had led inevitably to Dr Lang, who had played such a leading role in the ceremony, we were soon talking about the Church of England's performance during the House of Lords' debate on the A. P. Herbert Bill.

'I adore that Bishop of Starbridge!' said my mother. 'He's the only one who seems to know what marriage is all about, and there was a madly attractive photograph of him in last week's *Illustrated London News*.'

'Bishops have got no business being attractive to women,' said my father. 'That man's paid to be a eunuch in gaiters, not Rudolph Valentino in a mitre. And anyway, what does he think he's doing, attacking his boss in public? Shady sort of behaviour, if you ask me, but then they say Starbridge isn't a gentleman. Never went to the right school.'

'Do you know him, Charles?' said my mother.

I embarked on a heavily censored version of my recent activities in Starbridge, and the rest of the lunch passed in an atmosphere of hushed delight as my mother savoured the thought of me staying at an episcopal palace and my father mentally marked another lofty cross on the graph of my ascending career. However after my mother had reluctantly observed the convention of the ladies' withdrawal at the end of the meal, my father said as he lit his pipe, 'I shouldn't get too involved with Starbridge, if I were you. It might get you into hot water with Canterbury. Or as you clerics would say: stick to Cantuar and leave Staro well alone. You seem to be mixing with some very dubious people at the moment, Charles, and I'm especially worried about this peculiar monk.'

'But I promise you he's a first-class chap, Father – there's no need whatsoever for you to worry!'

'Well, of course I'm bloody well going to worry! I spend my life worrying about you, Charles, and now I'm going to worry more than ever – my God, how I got through that meal just now I'll never know, but I've got to keep up appearances because whatever happens your mother must never, never know we've discussed Romaine.'

'Why not?'

'*Why not?*'

'Yes, why not? Isn't it high time the three of us sat down and discussed him so that he can be exorcised once and for all?'

'I've never heard such a mad suggestion in all my life! Of all the idiotic, ridiculous – '

'Father, I do wish you could talk to this monk of mine – I really think he might help us both here. Why don't you come up to Cambridge and – '

'I can't leave my plants, and anyway I absolutely refuse to talk to some mad meddlesome old monk who should have been put in his coffin and buried years ago!'

'He's fifty-seven.'

'That's worse. An old monk's bad enough but a middle-aged monk's a disgrace. Why isn't he living with a wife and several children in a nice house with a tennis-court?'

'Well, now that his wife's dead and his children are grown up he's decided he can serve God best by – '

'The man's obviously unbalanced. I refuse to see him – and I refuse to go to Cambridge.'

'Never mind, I've already told Mother that I'd like to come back here next week and stay for a couple of days. I think it's extremely important that we – '

'Don't make me laugh! You won't come back – we won't see you for dust now! You'll be too busy chasing bloody Romaine!'

I said, 'If he's alive I'd like to meet him – just once, to satisfy my curiosity. But you don't seriously think, do you, that I'd ever want to be friends with someone who was willing to murder me when I was an inch long?'

'My God, you astonish me sometimes, Charles! How could a man with your brains make such a bloody naïve remark? For God's sake stop and think before you open this frightful Pandora's Box! The rotter'll charm you and ruin you – I can see it coming – '

'My dear Father, I'm not a nineteen-year-old virgin female!'

'Wish you were. Then I could lock you up to keep you safe. My God, if you go down the drain now after I've spent nearly thirty-eight years slaving to keep you on the straight and narrow – '

'I can't go down the drain – Darrow's put in the plug, and if only you'd talk to Darrow you might start believing I'm not such a potential rake as you think!'

'Well, of course I don't think you're a – '

'Yes, you do, it's monstrously unfair! I know you don't mean to be unfair – I can see now that you don't mean it – but you just can't help yourself and it's all because Romaine's haunting this family like an unexorcized ghost – '

'Well, you won't exorcize him by digging him up and taking a look at him – you'll simply get in an even worse muddle than you're in already! For God's sake, Charles, go and talk to your mad monk before you do anything catastrophic – perhaps you'll listen to him even if you won't listen to me!'

'I certainly intend to talk everything over with Darrow when I see him again tomorrow, but he's not mad, he's one of the sanest men I've ever met. Now please, Father – no more quarrels! Put out that awful pipe and let's join Mother in the drawing-room . . .'

IX

At three o'clock when I left, my mother hugged me and said with tears in her eyes, 'You really will come back next week, won't you, Charles?'

'Yes, I promise.' I kissed her and felt the tears spill on to her cheeks as she held me close.

'For God's sake!' exclaimed my father in a paroxysm of embarrassment. 'Stop weeping over the boy! Disgusting!'

'Oh, shut up, you brute!' my mother shouted at him, and ran sobbing into the house.

'Stupid woman,' said my father. 'I can't stand that sort of nonsense. It's very bad for you and not at all how a mother should behave. Parents shouldn't let their children know when they're feeling upset and emotional. Irresponsible. Not the done thing at all.'

We shook hands without speaking. Then I said, 'Goodbye, Father. God bless you,' and his mouth, already well turned down at the corners, began to tremble.

I got into my car and drove away.

X

I drove straight to the Epsom public library. The medical directory was waiting for me in the reference section and my hand was steady as I drew the book from the shelf.

Through my mind flickered the multitude of fates which might have overtaken Romaine. He had died of drink in Africa, died a hero's death in the War, died of old age in England after a long debilitating exile. Alternatively he was alive but no longer a doctor. He had been struck off the register years ago for hard drinking and seducing patients; he was keeping a tobacconist's shop in Eastbourne or a bookshop in the Charing Cross Road or a public house in Cornwall; he was in a lunatic asylum, an old peoples' home, a bed-sitting-room; he lived in a mansion with his fifth wife and ten children. Any fate was possible, but if he were alive and still practising in England as a doctor he would be listed in the book which was now in my hands.

The directory opened at the letter M. M for Mother, poor Mother, how she had suffered. N. N for Nativity, my birth on time too soon after that pathetic white wedding. O for the Orgasm which had created me, P for the Penis which had begotten me, Q for the Questions where is he, what became of him –

I reached the letter R. Of course he was probably dead. Or if he were alive he might well be abroad, settled happily in the Colonies.

ROM – ROMA – ROMAI – ROMAINE –

He was still alive.

ROMAINE, ALAN CHARLES –

Charles! My father could never have known the second name; he would have killed her if he had known.

– OAKTREE COTTAGE, STARVALE ST JAMES –

I had heard of Starvale St James. It was not far from my friend Philip Wetherall, the vicar of Starrington Magna. It was a village less than twenty miles from Starbridge.

I had to sit down. I sat there for a long time while people padded to and fro among the bookshelves in the quiet room, but at last I replaced the directory, left the library and embarked on the long drive home to Cambridge.

NINETEEN

'The difficulty of arriving at the truth when one had nothing but human testimony to depend on, is both apparent, and, from a religious point of view, terribly disconcerting.'

HERBERT HENSLEY HENSON
Bishop of Durham 1920–1939
Retrospect of an Unimportant Life

I

The telephone was ringing as I entered my rooms that evening, and when I picked up the receiver my brother Peter said, 'Charley, it's me. How did you survive your visit to the Governor?'

'Just let me feel my pulse and make sure I'm still alive.'

He laughed but said urgently, 'Charley, what do you think's going on? Mother seems to be hitting the gin bottle for six every day, the Governor's deep in his beastly jungle of a conservatory and nothing I do is ever right. The Governor seems to hold it against me that I don't discuss the office with him in detail, but Charley, he *can't* expect to keep up with everything now he's retired! He's got to learn to let go, but somehow I haven't the heart to say that – poor old boy, I feel so sorry for him, even though he's being distinctly beastly to me at the moment. Annabel says I should take a firm line but somehow . . . I can't bear the thought of hurting the old boy. Annabel doesn't quite understand, and honestly, Charley, what with Annabel nagging me on the one hand and the Governor being beastly to me on the other I feel in the mood to emigrate to Australia.'

'I'll deal with the demented parents if you can deal with the militant wife. I'm returning next week for a couple of days to sort them out.'

'Thank God. I knew you'd come to the rescue in the end, Charley – don't think I didn't have faith in you, but the truth is I've been in such despair – '

'Hold fast, Peter, and cancel all your plans to emigrate. The Church of England's finally on its way.'

II

I fell into bed, slept till six, silenced my jangling alarm clock, spent the required hour on my exercises, dressed in my cassock, attended Communion in the Cathedral, breakfasted, returned to the Cathedral for Matins and the Sung Eucharist, saw my bishop afterwards for ten minutes' conversation, accepted his invitation to midday Sunday dinner, escaped at three, discovered one of my undergraduates had turned up with his parents at Laud's, gave them tea in my rooms, returned to the Cathedral for Evensong at six, rushed back to College, threw a few essential items in a bag, staggered to my car, drove to Grantchester and arrived exhausted but still conscious at the Fordite mansion at half-past seven that evening. I had already arranged to stay the night, and the little white-haired monk, welcoming me like an old friend, said he had kept the same room for me. It seemed like the nearest earthly approximation to heaven I had encountered for some time, and on attaining my sanctuary I kicked off my shoes, collapsed on my bed and lay inert as a beached whale for some minutes.

When Darrow arrived all he said was: 'Obviously you've been working hard.'

We smiled at each other. I had sprung to my feet as he entered the room, and now we shook hands. His first question was, 'You've kept up with your exercises?'

I was aware of his priorities; his concern for my spiritual health preceded his curiosity about my parents.

'Yesterday I felt I might be getting somewhere,' I said, 'but this morning I was back in the desert after my view of the oasis.'

'No doubt you were distracted by yesterday's events. And your paternity?'

'We were right. My father is Eric Ashworth but I was begotten by a disastrous doctor called Alan Romaine.'

III

We did not talk further then; he had merely come to the visitors' wing to welcome me, but later he returned and we had a long session together. His final verdict was, 'You've done well with your parents and made more progress than I thought you would in such a short time. But where do you feel the battlefield now lies?'

'Starvale St James.'

Darrow was silent.

'Is that wrong?' I said, my confidence immediately dented.

'It's neither right nor wrong; it's merely inevitable. If I hesitate it's not because I disapprove but because I'm trying to decide the best way to approach this subject which is a very dangerous one and potentially a breeding ground of painful illusions.'

I was even more disturbed. I felt obliged to confess: 'My father was thoroughly alarmed by the whole prospect and called it a Pandora's Box, but I thought he spoke out of prejudice and jealousy. Of course he thinks that Romaine's bound to send me straight to the dogs.'

'Of course. I'm afraid we must expect your father to revert to his favourite nightmare when he's under strain, but what assurance did you give him that you would approach your Pandora's Box sensibly?'

'I told him what I told you the other day: I just want to see the man once. Then I can sit back and say: "There! I've done it!" And that'll be that.'

'You make Dr Romaine sound like a sightseer's landmark, Charles, but is he really on a par with Buckingham Palace and the Tower of London?' And before I could answer he added, 'Why are you so determined not to see Romaine more than once?'

'It would be disloyal to my father, who I've now discovered didn't reject me at all but tried hard year after year in his own muddled, well-meaning, pigheaded way to be the best of fathers to me. I don't need another father in my life now, and I certainly don't need a broken-down old quack who tried to murder me when I was an embryo.'

'Then why go and see him at all?'

I was taken aback. 'But I must!' I exclaimed. 'He's the source of my life – I must just see – '

'Yes, there's a psychological need. So you're in this awkward position, aren't you? You want to be involved yet you don't want to be involved.'

'I don't in the least want to be involved!'

'If that were true you wouldn't want to see him.'

'All right,' I said, becoming heated. '*All right*. I'm getting involved, but my involvement's going to be minimal. After all, he rejected me – tried to kill me – '

'That, I agree, is rejection. But do we actually know whether he would ever have performed the abortion? How much in earnest was he? It's a question your father can't answer because he wasn't there.'

'I concede that I've only heard my father's side of the story – '

'No, you've heard your mother's side as well, and the two views of Romaine are very different, aren't they?'

'But that's why I want to see him! I want to hear his own version of what happened!'

'Exactly.' Darrow sat back satisfied in his chair. 'You're searching for the truth; that's why you want to interview Dr Romaine and that's why, despite all your father says, the interview should take place. You need to establish a view of reality which will enable you to live comfortably with these difficult facts which you've uncovered this weekend.'

'But all I need is one interview,' I persisted. 'Then I can turn my back on him and walk away.'

'And may I ask,' said Darrow, 'exactly what you hope to achieve as a priest by rejecting him as you believe he once rejected you?'

There was a silence. The knot of tension expanded as my anger became infused with guilt. 'Are you suggesting,' I demanded at last, 'that I turn him into a grotesque father-figure whom I keep locked up in a cupboard and inspect at regular intervals?'

'I'm suggesting you try to keep an open mind in a very difficult situation. Although Romaine's a stranger he did nonetheless strike the spark which put you in the world and this means that in a very real sense he's with you as long as you live. So obviously you've got to learn to live with him now that he's been identified, but how can one live successfully with a person if one remains in a state of anger at the thought of all his wrongdoing?'

After another painful pause I said: 'What do I do?'

'What do you think?'

I had to drag the words out of my conscience. 'I must forgive him.'

'Yes,' said Darrow, 'you must forgive him in order to be at peace with him – and that may well be very hard indeed. So don't think of this visit to Starvale St James as a little holiday to see a bizarre landmark, Charles. Think of it as a large rack in your continuing ordeal – and then, I suspect, you'll approach the meeting in something which resembles a realistic frame of mind.'

Silence fell as I considered my quest in this new light. Finally I said, 'Supposing I can't cope with him and wind up ruined, just as my father prophesies?'

'Ah, now we're getting somewhere. Here comes that demon, your fear that you're unfit and unworthy.'

'Supposing I like him but he doesn't like me?'

'Here comes that demon, your fear of rejection.'

'Supposing he doesn't even remember I exist?'

'Unless he's suffering from amnesia I doubt if he'll have forgotten the catastrophe at Epsom which destroyed his hopes of a Harley Street practice,' said Darrow drily, but I was barely listening. I was finally peering into my mind with a clear eye and being horrified by what I saw. I heard myself say, 'I want him to like me so that I can hurt him by rejecting him, and I want to hurt him not just to pay him back for my mother's suffering but to prove to my father – and to myself – that I'm a loyal son . . . But just listen to me! What a muddle I'm in, I'm raving – '

'Better to be honest. Then you'll know exactly how hard you'll have to work to achieve a genuine forgiveness.'

'What an appalling situation!' Feeling close to despair I asked him if I could stay at his house longer than we had planned so that I could spend the following day thinking and praying under his direction. 'Then I'll leave very early on Tuesday morning,' I added, 'and drive down to Starvale St James.'

'So be it. Very well, Charles, get some sleep and tomorrow we'll start arming you against the demons.'

IV

Without making a huge detour I was unable to avoid Starbridge on my journey to Starvale St James, but as I descended from the hills shortly before noon on that Tuesday morning I saw that the Cathedral was no longer glittering like an opulent decoration on a wedding-cake but shrouded in a mist which was seeping through the watermeadows; here was no mystical sun-drenched city but merely a bedraggled county town in the rain. Winding my way into the market-place I took the short cut through Butchers' Alley to avoid the shopping lanes around St Martin's-in-Cripplegate. The main gates of the Cathedral Close flashed past me as I drove over the crossroads into Eternity Street, and then I was heading past the Staro Arms, across the West Bridge and into the open country beyond the river. In my driving mirror I watched the spire of the Cathedral recede and tried to imagine what everyone would be doing at the palace. I thought of Darrow saying, 'You threw a big stone into that particular pond', and at once in my imagination I saw the ripples still travelling inexorably to the edge.

These thoughts diverted me for ten miles, but when I saw the name of my destination on a signpost I spent the remainder of the journey trying to steady my nerves. I reached the village at twenty-one minutes past noon. The rain had stopped, the mist had dispersed and the sun was trying to shine. Halting the car I asked for directions and was told that Oaktree Cottage lay beyond the church at the far end of the street.

My destination proved to be a rambling house with a thatched roof; I guessed that the building had once been two cottages which some enterprising builder had knocked into one. A drive led from the lane through a well-kept garden where an ancient gnarled gardener was scratching peacefully at a border, and ignoring the sign which directed patients to the surgery at the side of the house I approached the front door. My fingers slipped on the bell. Automatically I wiped my hands on my jacket as I waited for a response, and after the inevitable eternity had appeared to pass the door was opened by an elderly parlourmaid. 'Good morning.' I said, handing her my card. 'Is Dr Romaine at home?' But before the parlourmaid could reply a woman's voice called from the shadowed hall beyond, 'Who is it, Withers?'

'Dr – Mr – Dr Ashworth, M'm,' said the parlourmaid who clearly believed any clergyman who wanted to be addressed as 'doctor' was behaving perversely, and handed my card to a plump golden-haired woman who now stepped forward into the light.

'Dr Ashworth – I'm so sorry, have we met? Your face looks familiar, but I can't quite – '

'No,' I said. 'We haven't met. Mrs Romaine?'

'Yes ... Thank you, Withers,' she said abruptly, dismissing the parlourmaid. She spoke in a no-nonsense contralto with a faint North-Country accent. The golden hair was cunningly dyed. 'Do come in, Dr Ashworth.'

'I was hoping for a brief word with your husband,' I said as the door closed behind me. Naturally I had prepared a speech to meet all possible permutations of the situation which would confront me on Dr Romaine's doorstep but for a moment I feared I was going to forget my lines. By this time Mrs Romaine was giving me a very hard look indeed. 'He knew my parents in the old days before the War,' I heard myself say after an awkward hesitation, 'and when I discovered he lived here I thought I'd look him up. The vicar of Starrington Magna is a friend of mine and I'm not unfamiliar with this part of the country.'

Mrs Romaine decided to replace the hard look with a hospitable smile. 'How nice of you to call! My husband's still out on his rounds, I'm afraid, but he should be back soon. If you have the time to wait – '

'Thank you.'

'You'll have to excuse me,' she said, leading the way into the drawing-room, 'but I'm just about to go out to lunch. I'll leave your card in the hall for my husband and make sure Withers tells him you're here – would you like a glass of sherry while you wait?'

I declined the glass of sherry. She told me not unsociably to make myself at home, gave me one last hard look and departed.

I glanced around the room. It was expensively furnished to accord with the oak-beamed ceiling and the inglenook fireplace, but all the furniture appeared to be modern reproductions of traditional styles. Various knick-knacks in questionable taste were scattered along the mantelshelf but there were no photographs. On the wall hung several bad prints set in heavy gold frames, of the famous Constable paintings of Starbridge Cathedral, and on the floor the carpet felt plush to the point of sponginess as I walked to the window. I was unable to resist the conclusion that my mother would have judged the room vulgar in its moneyed attempt to ape a lady's drawing-room, and I knew she would have dismissed my hostess by that most damning of all middle-class epithets, 'common'.

Turning my back on the window with its view of the picturesque cottage garden I paced up and down until at last, like a drowning man, I saw my life flicker past as if that part of my self which Darrow had called my beleaguered psyche were engaged in some complex attempt to trace how I had arrived in Starvale St James at this precise moment of my life. My memory was just recalling my installation service in Cambridge Cathedral with photographic clarity when far away across the hall the front door casually clicked open and equally casually banged shut.

I froze. There was a pause. I heard the parlourmaid's voice followed by a man's murmur, but after that there was a long, long silence. I knew at once – I needed neither to see nor to be told – that he was staring with incredulity at my card, but at last his footsteps crossed the hall, the drawing-room slowly swung wide and in walked Dr Alan Romaine.

V

I at once experienced that sinister shock which follows a glimpse of oneself in a distorted mirror, and I knew then why Mrs Romaine had given me such a hard look once she had had the chance to register the details of my appearance. The man before me was a long way from being my double but nevertheless I felt I was being offered an uncanny glimpse of myself as I might appear in the unimaginable 1960s.

He was my height, six foot one, and far from being a 'broken-down old quack' he was in a moderately good state of preservation. I recognized my curly hair, transformed from brown to grey but still displaying unruly tendencies; since baldness runs in families I was relieved to see that although his hair was sparser than mine it was still plentiful. I recognized the dark eyes with the creases at the corners, the mouth with the humour lurking subtly at the edges, the deep cleft in the chin which in childhood would have been described as dimpled. He was far heavier than I was; with his athlete's figure run to seed he must have weighed fifteen stone to my twelve and a half, but he carried himself well and in his unhurried graceful movements I glimpsed the charm which had enchanted Epsom in 1899.

I stood stock still in the middle of the room with my fists clenched at my sides and no doubt I looked the picture of extreme tension, deep distrust and appalled fascination. He paused by the door and looked the picture of relaxed amusement, his mouth curling humorously at the corners and his eyes bright with interest. I thought of my father saying as he fought his tears, 'The bounders always seem to bounce their way to a happy ending'. I thought of my mother saying, 'It was like some ghastly punishment'. I looked at this debonair stranger who was apparently unmarked by tragedy, and I loathed him.

He glanced down at my card, then looked up again with a quizzical smile and said, 'Dr Ashworth!'

'Yes. Good morning, Dr Romaine.'

Our voices were identical in timbre but different in inflection. Inflections are acquired by a child from those people who bring him up, and in my mind my voice was saying with Eric Ashworth's fierce stresses: still caddish, still flashy, still gliding along the glamorous road – *disgusting*.

Meanwhile his voice was saying with an admiration which repelled me, 'A Doctor of Divinity at Cambridge! How proud your mother must be . . . And how is your mother, may I ask? I hope she's well.'

'She's very well,' I said. 'So's my father. Both my parents are well.'

I did remember Darrow talking of forgiveness. I did remember my hours of prayer and discussion at Grantchester. I did remember my resolve to open my Pandora's Box with a steady Christian hand, but at that moment I was beside myself with rage. I wanted only to brandish my loyalty to my father in every sentence.

'Still flourishing in Epsom? Splendid!' said Romaine warmly, but he had turned away from me and although the lines of humour still shaded his mouth a stillness touched his face for a moment. Then he dropped my card on to a side-table and gestured gracefully to the cluster of decanters nearby. 'Let's have a drink!' he said with a smile. 'Or do you believe alcohol's the invention of the Devil? Our local vicar's very fierce on the subject – in fact he berates us so unmercifully so often on the subject from the pulpit that I always find myself longing to take a swig from the largest bottle I can find.'

'You're a churchgoer?'

'Yes, I'm a churchwarden.'

In the silence that followed I felt as if God had rapped me across the knuckles. Rage, remorse, guilt and misery began to shudder sickeningly through my beleaguered psyche in a series of emotional tidal waves.

'Whisky, sherry or gin?' Romaine was saying agreeably.

'Sherry. Thanks.' It hardly seemed possible that I could speak but I not only spoke; I even sounded casual.

'Well, this is the most astonishing surprise!' said Romaine equally casually as he handed me my glass. 'How did you find out where I was?'

'I looked you up in the medical directory.'

'Of course! What an idiotic question – maybe I'm finally going senile. I see now that the question I should have asked was: when did your mother tell you about me?'

'Oh, it wasn't my mother who told me,' I said. 'It was my father.'

'Dear me,' said Romaine, shooting the barest fleck of soda-water into his double-whisky, 'how extremely difficult . . . My dear chap, do sit down – the chairs aren't nearly as frightful as they look. Have a cigarette – I hope you smoke as well as drink?'

'Not in my clerical collar.'

'What magnificent self-control! I smoke like a chimney, terribly bad for me – ' He was lighting a cigarette as he spoke ' – what a bore one's bad habits are, but on the other hand how dull life would be without them . . . Now where were we? Ah yes, your father – such an extraordinary man! I underestimated him, of course, thought he was a dry-as-dust old fogey who enjoyed being a crosspatch, but the main problem in those days was not that I underestimated Ashworth but that I overestimated myself. I thought I could walk on water.'

'Walk on – '

'Water, old chap. Terrible delusion. Only the very best fellows like your father can walk on water. The rest of us just sink like stones. Did he tell you about our final meeting?'

'Yes, he – '

'I thought he would, and I'm sure he didn't do himself justice. He was superb. I can see him now as if it were yesterday, very dapper in his wing-collar, not a hair out of place. What an executioner! And after he'd hung, drawn and quartered me he simply pulled on his gloves, donned his top hat and strolled away while I was left wondering whether to shoot myself. However I didn't have a gun, I passed out with drink before I could borrow one, and when I recovered I found myself gripped by the most ungentlemanly desire to survive . . . But that's typical of life, isn't it? It's only in novels that the villain meets that scintillating bloodstained end which conveniently puts him out of his agony. In real life God much prefers him to toil away trying to live with what he's done – and talking of God, I must say I'm absolutely *delighted* that you should be a clergyman! Much more fun than being a doctor – all those interesting sermons to write and a beautiful church to work in and a nice wife whom everyone likes . . . You're married, of course?'

'My wife died in a car accident.'

'How very terrible . . . Children?'

'No.'

'Ah. I've been married three times,' said Romaine after drinking deeply from his glass. 'I – but no, I'm talking too much and I mustn't be a thundering bore. One of the worst things about getting old is that one's so often afflicted with the urge to talk garrulously about the past.'

I said, 'I've come here to indulge that urge, Dr Romaine. I see no point in not being frank; I want to hear exactly what happened.'

'Exactly? No comfortable euphemisms? Just the plain unvarnished truth?' He hesitated as if weighing the challenge but he remained unflustered. Then he said: 'Very well, but hold on to your clerical collar, my dear chap, because this is where your Christian charity really gets exercised to its limits.' And sinking into the nearest armchair he crossed one leg over the other and embarked with the most appallingly charming insouciance on the narrative I so urgently needed to hear.

VI

'I was mad, of course,' said Romaine. 'Nowadays some kindly GP would have referred me to an alienist and I'd have spent numerous happy hours lying on a couch while I talked interminably about my childhood, but in those days one was judged sane unless one was raving so I got away with pretending to be normal. I was always pretending to be something or other. When I was a young man I pretended to be a romantic hero, and I suppose, looking back on my life, that was the most disastrous role I ever played.

'It all began when I was a child and started playing the poor little orphan. However I'm not going to tell you some long story about how when I was seven my mother died in childbirth and my father expired in bankruptcy and even my toys were seized by the wicked bailiffs – it's all true but I wouldn't like you to think I had a Dickensian childhood because when I was orphaned I went to live in Starbridge with a doting maiden aunt who provided me with a delightful home, a nursery full of new toys and a nanny who thought I was the cat's whiskers. Did I go down on my knees every night and thank God for my astonishing good fortune? I did not. Like the horrid spoilt child I soon became I took it all for granted and thought my aunt's sedate little house in the shadow of the Cathedral was the last word in dreariness. As far as I was concerned wealth and success, not painstaking respectability, was the key to security; I never forgot the painstakingly respectable little room where my father had blown his brains out.

'However I didn't want to think of my father blowing his brains out so I pretended it hadn't happened, and at school, when I invented some interesting clerical connections for myself based on my aunt's staid circle in Starbridge, I discovered I had a flair for telling stories which everyone believed. So then I realized that I didn't have to be stuck with my unromantic past because all I had to do to be accepted by the right people was to pick the right role to play.

'Up at Oxford I played the dashing young aristocrat, but I didn't have the money to sustain that for long and besides I did genuinely want to pursue that middle-class profession, medicine. However I didn't want to be just any old doctor. I wanted to go down in history as the doctor who had done the most to save women in childbirth. I was always so angry that my mother had died in her misguided attempt to give me a sibling, and perhaps the only way I could master the anger of bereavement when I was young was to put the blame on medical science and then vow to put right what had gone wrong.

'Eventually I wound up at Bart's to complete my training. How my aunt paid for it all I'll never know but she paid until I qualified – at which point she died happy with no money in the bank. I was so disgracefully spoilt by that time that when I heard she was dead my first reaction was: damn it, whom can I touch now for a loan? It took money to be a fashionable medical genius, and besides I liked to cut a dash up in town when I mixed with the right people.

'Detestable, wasn't I? But take heart – Nemesis was waiting in the wings. I met this girl. She was a patient. I was still doing general work before embarking on specialization and at that time I'd been assigned temporarily to what would nowadays be called the psychiatric ward. The girl was brought in suffering from delusions. She was very pretty – and very rich. The brain specialist thought the girl's prognosis was poor, but I didn't believe that. I just thought: silly old fool, I can do better than he can. I thought I could cure anyone, especially a pretty girl with a rich father; I saw the shining water in front of me and I said to myself: lovely! I'll walk on it! It never even occurred to me that such a thing couldn't be done.

'I told your mother I was the victim of the "Jane Eyre" syndrome – a latter-day Mr Rochester who married his wife for the best of motives in complete ignorance of her insanity. What a lie! And how deluded I was to think I could cure the incurable – although unfortunately I did manage to achieve a temporary cure. I made love to the girl in the old-fashioned sense of holding her hand and gazing soulfully into her eyes, and I got her out of hospital. She really did seem miraculously better. In fact she seemed just as sane as I did at the wedding, but of course the truth was we were both lunatics living in a fantasy. She attacked me with a knife on our honeymoon; a week after she was locked up she had a further relapse and never spoke rationally again. All the income from the marriage settlement was diverted to pay for the best asylum and the best doctors, so within a month of the wedding I was penniless again – and shackled, at the age of twenty-seven, to a woman who could live another fifty years.

'That was reality – and of course I couldn't begin to face it. I was a man who liked women, and the private life of a doctor is almost as restricted as the private life of a clergyman. How was I going to manage? I had no idea. I couldn't even begin to imagine. So I just thought: it didn't happen; it'll go away if I don't think about it. And like all people who need to keep reality at bay I started to drink too much.

'I got out of London. I was due for a break anyway before I began my specialist's training and I'd already decided to do a locum because I needed the money, but what a huge relief it was to escape to Epsom to help out poor old Dr Barnes! No one knew at Epsom, not even Barnes himself. He'd merely applied to Bart's for help, and when they referred me to him they didn't mention my marriage.

'So I went to Epsom and began a new life. I thought: it's just as if I'm a bachelor. I wasn't clinically mad but I was certainly deeply disturbed – although please don't think I'm making excuses for what happened next. Nothing could excuse what I did, but I just want to explain in accurate terms what was going on. Well, I met your mother and . . . Poor girl, what a rotten time she was having! I felt so sorry for her because no one seemed to understand what hell she was going through, her mother dying by inches and that old great-aunt clanking around like a walking coffin. I admired your mother so much for not developing some hysterical illness as so many young girls did in those days when everyone was too well-bred to scream with frustration. That's a brave girl, I thought, a girl of character, intelligent, sensitive – and very lovely . . . I started having fantasies that my wife would die – and after a while it was reality which seemed the illusion and only the fantasies which seemed real.

'Helen had a hard time facing reality too, and in my fantasies she saw an escape from the painful dreariness of her daily life. Later – much later – I realized what a good thing it was that I hadn't been free to marry her. I nearly destroyed her with my fantasies; I *would* have destroyed her if we'd ever married. She needed someone who could offer her the sort of reality she deserved, a decent home, a normal family life, stability – and all I could offer her was a string of day-dreams which hadn't a hope of coming true.

'Well . . . where do I go from here? You know what happened next – here you are to prove it. But perhaps you're wondering how on earth I let it happen. Had I never heard of that wicked word "anticonception"? Yes, of course I'd heard of it, but I believed that sheaths – which in those days were pretty damned awful – were for use only with loose women as a prophylactic against VD. Sheaths weren't *romantic*, you see, and I was moving in this fantasy of high romance. I was also still trying to tell myself I could walk on water – which meant, in this context, that I thought I could achieve perfect control in a situation where control is famous for its absence . . . What a dangerous belief for a man who's fallen into the habit of drinking too much! Certainly that was the last time I ever fooled myself I could walk on water.

'After your father had hung, drawn and quartered me I went abroad, not to be a noble soul in darkest Africa – that was just the story I spun to make my Epsom friends tell me how wonderful I was – but to South

Africa, to the Boer War. I stayed out there till the war's end but I didn't win any romantic medals because I was working in a safe dull military hospital. At the end of the war I decided to stay on but as I couldn't afford to set myself up in private practice I volunteered to work in a Roman Catholic missionary hospital in Rhodesia. Well, all went smoothly at first but then I got in an awful mess with a nun – there's something about those white wimples which absolutely brings out the worst in me – so I ended up as a ship's doctor on a liner bound for India. I won't bother you with my Indian adventures but I got in a mess there too and eventually I wound up in Hong Kong – drinking far too much, I regret to say, and unable to hold down a job in one of the good hospitals. I ended up working for a protestant mission in the slums where I had to deal with a lot of diseases which I prefer not to think about, and the result was I drank harder than ever because I hated my work yet couldn't scrape up the money to move on.

'But then the miracle happened.

'This nurse came to the clinic. She was Chinese and a Christian. She took one look at me and decided I needed rescuing and I took one look at her and decided I wanted to be rescued. I spun my usual line – "Sleep with me and all my problems will be solved" – but that cut no ice whatsoever. I was very impressed. Then I said, trying to convince her that I wasn't such a bad chap after all, "I only drink because I'm lonely," and she said, "Oh no, you don't! You drink because you feel guilty and you can't forgive yourself for what you've done."

'There's something very wonderful about the Chinese; they'd got the world sorted out when we were just dancing around Starbury Ring in blue woad. And there's something very wonderful about a Christian, a real Christian, the kind that practises what it preaches. I said, "I *can't* forgive myself," but she said, "Christ can," and quoted Confucius. My God, I was mad about her! Eventually I said, "Can't we just pretend my wife's already dead?" But she told me we couldn't pretend to God and if he wanted me to marry her he'd arrange it. And damn it all – well, you can guess what happened, can't you? Two weeks later a cable arrived from England to say my wife was dead.

'So I married my Chinese lady. She was a lot older than I was so there couldn't be any children, but nevertheless for ten years we did live happily ever after. I stopped drinking altogether and finally got a job in a good hospital again. I used to work on maternity cases, and I was happy for the first time in years . . . But then my Chinese lady died and everything fell apart. I felt I couldn't bear to remain in Hong Kong without her, and I knew it was time to come home.

'I won't bore you with all the dubious adventures I had as I earned my passage back to England on a series of hair-raising old tubs, but eventually

I did wangle my way within sight of the White Cliffs of Dover. I was forty-five and the War was on.

'As soon as I was settled, working in an East End hospital which was dealing mainly with casualties from the trenches, I hired a private detective and sent him down to Epsom to find out what was going on. Back came the report that Mr and Mrs Eric Ashworth were living with their two sons, Charles and Peter, in a very nice house on Epsom Downs. Then I had to make a decision. Did I wreck everyone's lives all over again or didn't I? Well, I knew what my Chinese lady would have said. She would have told me that if I really wanted to redeem the past I'd put aside my selfish curiosity and leave the Ashworth family to continue their lives in peace. Of course if your mother had been a widow I'd have raced to Epsom to look her up, but as it was . . . No, I felt I had no right to interfere.

'After the War I got a better job in a hospital in Manchester – I was always a little uneasy in London in case I bumped into Ashworth – and there I met my present wife, another nurse. I can honestly swear with my hand on the Bible that I didn't know, when I proposed to her, that her father was making a small fortune out of manufacturing corsets.

'Eventually the old man died and Bea found herself with "a few thou of the ready", as the swells say, so we hit on the idea of leaving Manchester and pursuing the ideal country life in a thatched cottage. I had this hankering to return to the Starbridge area; it's funny how at the end of one's life one yearns to return to the beginning . . . But it's a nice spot, isn't it? And whenever I get the urge to yawn I remind myself I could still be working in a slum clinic and getting through a bottle of whisky a day. But don't think I'm complaining! Far from it! I'm always telling myself how wonderfully lucky I am and what a lot I've got to be thankful for.'

I knew that way of approaching reality. I had adopted it often enough myself when I had wanted to pretend that all was well in my life, and as I watched him pour himself a second double whisky I said suddenly, 'Do you and your wife have children?'

He added another fleck of sodawater to his glass before he turned to face me. 'No,' he said. 'I've never had children by any of my three wives. But I regard that,' he added, raising his glass to his lips, 'as all part of the judgement.'

And then I looked past his glittering image to the sadness which lay opaquely beyond.

'Have another drink,' said Romaine. 'I'm afraid I'm rather hitting the bottle, aren't I, but I'm beginning to feel as if I've been walloped by a sandbag. Do have some more of that appalling sherry! I was in such a state earlier that I forgot to warn you that it was sweet and not dry.'

'No, I won't have any more, thank you. I think I should leave so that we can each recover from our separate sandbags.'

'Oh, but you can't possibly leave yet – I want to hear all about you! I say, I've just had the most delectable idea: let me pour away this ridiculous whisky and bring up from the cellar the most magnificent bottle of Vueve Clicquot which I've been saving for a rainy day!'

'Thank you,' I said, 'but I must refuse. I've got a long drive ahead of me.'

'Well, you shouldn't drive on an empty stomach. Stay to lunch!'

I said with difficulty, 'You must excuse me, Dr Romaine. But I must go.'

'Ah well,' he said, drinking half his double whisky, 'just as you wish. But before you run off do please tell me when I can hear you preach. I'd so much like to come to Cambridge and "sit under" you, as they used to say when I was young.'

'I'm not the Canon in Residence at the moment. I shan't be preaching until the first Sunday of next month.'

'Splendid, I'll come up for the weekend. Where does one stay in Cambridge?'

'The Blue Boar is the most convenient hotel, but – '

'I'll telephone for a reservation. Now, you needn't think you have to entertain me – in fact you needn't even see me if you don't want to, that's all right, I understand. Just because I lost my head a moment ago and started talking about champagne you mustn't think I'm dead set on being a drunken old bore, making your life a misery. I'll just slip up to Cambridge, slip into the Cathedral to hear you preach and then slip away again – no fuss, no bother, no mess – '

I heard myself inviting him to dine with me in hall after the morning services.

When he escorted me to my car he said: 'How wonderful it must be for Ashworth that you've done so well! And your brother – has he done well too?'

'He's a partner in my father's firm.'

'Lucky Ashworth! But then my Chinese lady would just say that the good get their reward. What an amazing man he was! When I was working in the slums of Hong Kong and getting through a bottle of whisky a day, I used to think of him surging triumphantly through life in his wing-collar. He haunted me, you know, and so did your mother – they've both haunted me all these years . . . I suppose your mother's still very lovely to look at?'

'She's kept her looks remarkably well, yes.'

'I'm very glad, but I wouldn't want to see her again because I'd rather remember her exactly as she was. Sometimes,' said Romaine casually, 'it really is far wiser not to risk resurrecting the past.'

I merely looked at him. I thought of my mother, longing year after year for him to come back, and no reply was possible.

At once Romaine realized he had made a mistake. 'However of course I'm so very glad you came here today!' he said, obviously fearing I had interpreted his remark as a personal rebuff. He had taken his right hand out of his pocket but when he realized I had no intention of shaking hands with him he pretended to flick a speck of dust from his cuff. 'It was such a wonderful surprise!' he added desperately. 'I feel so excited that I've met you!'

'In that case it was lucky that Ashworth stopped you aborting me, wasn't it?' I said, slamming the car door, and drove off with a roaring engine to blot out all possibility of a reply.

IX

I was in such turmoil that two miles outside the village I halted the car on the verge and switched off the engine. Gripping my cross I tried to pray but I was too upset. I wanted only to wipe Romaine from my mind, but there he was, imprinted for ever, a smooth, tough, wily old survivor who apparently knew exactly how to tug at my heartstrings. I thought of his valiant effort to gloss over his touching offer of champagne; I thought of his brave attempt to hide his distress when he realized I was determined not to shake his hand; I thought of his pathetic panic when he realized he had aroused my animosity, and I felt that my equilibrium, so painfully acquired at Grantchester, had been demolished. I could cope with his charming mask merely by disliking it, but the pathos beyond defeated me. I felt threatened by it. I was quite prepared to work out an intellectual formula for forgiveness which would put my beleaguered psyche at rest while enabling me to be a good Christian, but I did not want my emotions involved. My instinct was to lash out, push him away.

I decided that the sooner I returned to Darrow the better but meanwhile

I was a long way from Grantchester, I had had no lunch and I knew Darrow would have advised me to eat before wrestling further with my problems. Starting my car again I drove back to Starbridge.

By the time I arrived all the restaurants serving lunch had closed but I prevailed on the lounge-waiter at the Staro Arms to bring me sandwiches and coffee. After the meal I felt better. Reflecting that Darrow might well have recommended exercise at this point, I decided to take a walk along the river, but when I reached the West Bridge and saw the spire of the Cathedral I knew I had to make another attempt at prayer. I felt I urgently needed to pray not only for the strength to master my troubles but for forgiveness. I had hurt that pathetic old villain in Starvale St James, and I wanted to lighten the burden of my guilt before I resumed my journey.

Remembering that my earlier attempt to pray in the car had been a failure I wondered if I was being superstitious in assuming that a spiritual competence would miraculously return to me once I stepped on to consecrated ground, but superstitious or not I felt the pull of the Cathedral, and the next moment I was turning back along Eternity Street.

I had given Darrow my word that I would keep well away from the palace, but as it was now nearly half-past three I calculated that the possibility of meeting either Lyle or the Jardines was acceptably remote. Jardine usually spent his afternoons fulfilling official engagements, Mrs Jardine, if she were at home, would be having a rest before tea, and Lyle would probably be relaxing in the garden after her usual busy morning. Thinking hard of Lyle I reached the crossroads at the end of Eternity Street, and I was still thinking of her as I passed beneath the arch into the Close.

Minutes later, as I entered the Cathedral, the cool dim light was immediately soothing, and savouring the pervasive air of peace I moved slowly down the nave towards the chancel.

At the far end of the south transept lay the chapel set aside for private prayer, its carved screen supplemented by curtains which covered the spaces in the wooden tracery and ensured the privacy of those praying within. Opening the door I stepped softly inside. I had expected to find myself alone but a woman was kneeling in prayer and as I came in she glanced up.

We both gasped. For one long moment we remained motionless, staring at each other, but when Lyle began to grope her way to her feet I said rapidly, 'I'm sorry – I'm disturbing you,' and retreated in shock to the transept.

TWENTY

'Now one word in your ear. Perhaps I am mistaken: but I have sometimes thought that there was a suggestion in what you say and write, of some private and special worry of your own. If that be so, don't suspect me for one moment of the impertinence of pushing into your affairs: but I have a genuine affection for you, and should be glad to help you in any way that was in my power.'

More Letters of Herbert Hensley Henson
Bishop of Durham 1920–1939
ed. E. F. BRALEY

I

'Charles – ' She stumbled after me but I had stopped before she called my name. Far away in the nave I could hear the faint drone of a guide as he showed a party of visitors around the Cathedral.

'Tell me I'm not hallucinating,' said Lyle, still stupefied. 'What are you doing in this part of the world?'

'I had to see someone in Starvale St James.' Pulling myself together I added, 'Look, we can't talk here – let's go into the cloisters.'

The massive door opened reluctantly as I heaved the handle, and we passed from the transept into the sunlit quadrangle beyond. In one corner of the grassy square a garden-seat had been placed in memory of some Edwardian benefactor, and at my suggestion we sat down facing the cedar tree which shaded the lawn.

'This is the most extraordinary thing to happen,' said Lyle, still dazed. 'It's like a sign.'

'It's certainly an opportunity to say how very much I've been thinking of you. Did Mrs Jardine get my letter?'

'Yes, that was like a sign too – the letter made you seem real again. I was beginning to think I'd imagined you.'

'My dearest Lyle . . .' I was quite unable to stop myself taking her hand in mine and she was apparently quite unable to stop herself tightening her clasp on my fingers. 'Forgive my long silence.' I said, 'but I was in a colossal muddle when we last met and Father Darrow's been busy unravelling me.'

'We were all so relieved when we heard you were safe with the Fordites . . . Is Father Darrow really as clever as everyone says he is?'

'It would be impossible for me to praise him too highly.'

She said unexpectedly, 'I wish I had someone like that to talk to,' and at once I was concerned for her. The cry for help was muted but unmistakable. Realizing that she would be reluctant to tell any of her numerous clerical acquaintances about a problem which concerned a bishop I said tentatively, 'Perhaps an Anglican-Benedictine nun might help. I'm sure the Abbot of Starwater could recommend – '

'I hate nuns. I'm not wild about monks either, but if Father Darrow lives up to his reputation, perhaps . . . But he wouldn't want to see a woman, would he?'

'I'm sure he'd see anyone in an emergency.'

'Oh, this isn't an emergency!' she said at once. 'I'm fine.'

'That's what I used to tell myself before I ended up drunk on Father Darrow's doorstep.' I was now deeply concerned. 'Lyle, if things get impossible phone me at any time of the day or night and I'll do my best to help – and don't think this offer means I'm playing Casanova all over again because I'm not; I'm just trying to be something that resembles a clergyman, and if you ever do need my help I promise I shan't demand any romantic payment in return.'

She gave me a searching glance before saying cautiously, 'You're different.'

'You never really met me before. I was hiding behind a mask – the mask I call my glittering image – but Father Darrow's helping me to put that mask aside so that I can be the man I really am.'

I saw the comprehension flare in her eyes. 'Oh, if only you knew,' she whispered, 'how much I long to put aside *my* glittering image and be the woman *I* really am!' But before I could reply she was saying abruptly, 'What on earth does Father Darrow make of all this?'

'It's not his primary business to have opinions. His task is to see I form rational opinions of my own.'

We were silent at last, and into our silence seeped the Starbridge mystery, billowing between us like a dark cloud to sever our communication. Glancing at her watch she stood up. 'I must get back. Carrie will be needing me.'

'Lyle – '

Her eyes were suddenly dark with emotion. 'Don't ask any questions.'

'Let me at least give you some additional numbers in case I'm not at Laud's when you phone.' I found the receipt from my lunch at the Staro Arms and wrote on the back my parents' number in Epsom and the

Fordites' number in Grantchester. Then I added, 'If I don't hear from you I'll get in touch in mid-September in the hope of arranging a meeting at the end of the month. What's the best way of communicating with you. Shall I write?'

'No, don't do that,' she said quickly. 'Gerald gets to the post before I do and he tells the Bishop everything. A letter with a Cambridge postmark would be quite impossible to explain.'

I somehow refrained from an appalled comment and said in the most neutral voice I could muster, 'What's the best time to phone?'

'The afternoons. If you get Gerald hang up, but if Shipton answers ask for me and if I'm not in I'll ring you back. Say you're Donald Wilson – he's an old flame of mine who rings up occasionally, so I wouldn't have to explain any call from him.'

I was unable to stop myself exclaiming: 'You talk like a prisoner!'

'Of course I'm a prisoner! We're all prisoners of our circumstances, but for God's sake, Charles, *for God's sake*, don't storm the palace in a quixotic attempt to rescue me – '

'Don't worry, Father Darrow's taught me that the most effective help is always offered, never imposed.'

We had left the bench and were moving down the north side of the cloisters, but when we reached the door into the transept she stopped. 'It's best if we say goodbye here.'

'Very well.' I wanted to kiss her but knew she would recoil; she was already glancing nervously over her shoulder to see if we were being observed. Instead I took her hands in mind, and for a second an unmistakable reality blazed between us before dying amidst the miasma of despair which emanated from her.

I said: 'Don't forget. You can phone any time of the day or night.'

She nodded. I released her, and as we both stepped back into the transept I paused to watch her walk away towards the nave. I watched her until she had finally disappeared from sight through the door into the north porch, and then, feeling more deeply disturbed than ever, I returned to the chapel to pray.

II

I felt too exhausted to complete the long journey to Cambridge that day so I spent the night in London at my club. Having anticipated a possible absence from home I had brought with me in my overnight bag the books which I needed for my exercises, but even after a night's rest concentration proved elusive.

Darrow was not immediately available when I arrived without warning on his doorstep later that morning, but after half an hour I was escorted to the Abbot's Parlour where he was waiting for me. Aware that I might be diverting him from more urgent work I apologized for my unexpected appearance and said I would return later to discuss Romaine. 'But something very strange happened yesterday,' I said, 'and I did just want a quick word with you about Lyle.'

'Sit down, take your time and please give me at least a brief summary of your meeting with Romaine before you vanish in a puff of smoke.'

Realizing I was creating a fevered impression I made an effort to be calm. 'I didn't acquit myself well in Starvale St James,' I said. 'Romaine manages to be both a smooth wily old survivor and a vulnerable battered old man. He was pathetically thrilled to see me. I hated that. I hated him. But the worst part of all is that I've invited him to Cambridge next month and I can't wait to see him – and if you can make head or tail of all that, Father, you deserve some sort of cenobitic medal.'

Darrow merely asked, 'What did you do afterwards?'

'I stayed sober,' I said, and recounted my movements up to the moment before my meeting with Lyle.

'At least you dealt with yourself competently when you were in distress,' was Darrow's not unsympathetic comment. 'Very well, we'll return to Romaine later. Now what's all this about Lyle?'

I told him every detail of my meeting with her, and when I had finished he looked so grave that I felt obliged to say, 'Father, I swear I didn't break my promise and go looking for her.'

'No, of course you didn't. Don't misunderstand. I'm not concerned about the meeting, which seems to have been unexpectedly beneficial; I'm concerned about her welfare. However at least you've thrown her a life-line, and that could well prove vital.'

'Would you, in fact, agree to counsel her?'

'I'd counsel anyone in an emergency, as you so rightly told her, but beyond that . . . No, it wouldn't be advisable, Charles, for two reasons. One is that I'm counselling you and therefore I couldn't approach her in a truly detached frame of mind. And the other reason is that a difference in sex can often create difficulties in counselling, even if the two people concerned approach each other with the best will in the world and the purest of motives. She'd be better off with a nun than a monk.'

'She says she hates nuns.'

'When people make extravagant statements like that they may merely be struggling to voice a despair which can't be easily expressed. What Lyle may mean is that at present she feels her problems are beyond discussion with either a nun or indeed with anyone else.'

'Surely the fact that she has such severe problems must mean – '

'We can't know for certain what it means. It certainly seems as if Lyle's involved with both the Jardines in a way that's emotionally and spiritually bad for her, but this still needn't mean she's Jardine's mistress.'

'But even if she's not his mistress he must still be in error to allow such an unhealthy situation to persist,' I said. 'Obviously he's fooled himself into believing that the situation's not unhealthy, but then his error with Loretta proves, doesn't it, that he can be capable of gross self-deception.'

'I was wondering when you were going to notice that.' Darrow sounded so relieved that he no longer had to keep his opinion to himself in order to maintain his neutrality that I was at once able to conclude, 'I suppose I was so disturbed by my own error with Loretta that I didn't pay sufficient attention to Jardine's but it's nonsense, in spiritual terms, to say that he didn't commit adultery with her.'

'Dr Jardine spoke as a good lawyer,' said Darrow drily, 'but not, I'm afraid, as a good clergyman. Your own error with Loretta was severe but Jardine's was infinitely worse: a married clergyman, engaged in gaining a very carnal knowledge of one of his own parishioners – the whole episode's a clerical nightmare, and it makes one realize, I think, Charles, how shrewd His Grace the Archbishop has been over this business. Obviously he senses that Jardine's capable of colossol error and equally obviously, as we can now see, Dr Lang is justified in fearing a scandal, but Charles, none of this need mean Jardine and Lyle are lovers. So keep calm, don't rush to judgement and try hard to accept that for the moment, as far as Lyle's concerned, you've done all that you can do.'

III

That evening I returned to Darrow to discuss my meeting with Romaine and we talked for some time.

'I do understand,' said Darrow at last, 'why you should feel hostile, but if you're not averse to seeing him again perhaps this indicates that you may feel more benign later.'

'I doubt it. He's such an awful old villain.'

'I'm quite prepared to believe you when you say that, Charles, but could you explain to me why you feel he's so awful and so villainous? You've actually made him sound delightful.'

'Have I?'

'Well, haven't you? He tried hard, it would seem, to be truthful with you; certainly he didn't go out of his way to paint himself in a flattering light. He was nice about your parents. He bathed you in approval by saying how glad he was that you were a clergyman, and finally he could barely be restrained from diving into the cellar for the Veuve Clicquot. Is this really such iniquitous behaviour?'

'It was all an act to ingratiate himself with me! But I never forgot for one moment how he made my parents suffer.'

'There's no doubt he did cause your parents considerable suffering,' said Darrow, 'but according to your account he suffered in the long run just as much as they did and possibly more.'

'So he should. He wrecked their marriage.'

'Who says their marriage is wrecked? It seems to me, from what you tell me, to have survived many outstanding difficulties. After all, here they are after nearly forty years, still living beneath the same roof, still on speaking terms and still, so far as we know, being faithful to eath other. I'm not saying their marriage hasn't been difficult, but can one truly describe it as wrecked?'

'It seemed pretty wrecked to me on Saturday!'

'Obviously they're going through a bad time, but like most couples who survive thirty-eight years of matrimony they probably have their good times as well as their bad times. After all, has their marriage really been such unadulterated hell? Your mother's had the kind of affluent sociable life she likes and your father's had an attractive wife who's been a devoted mother to his children. Meanwhile the children themselves are a credit to their parents and are no doubt a source of much happiness as well as the occasional bout of misery. To me this all sounds reassuringly normal – although I'm not denying that there are abnormalities present. But I think you should consider very carefully how far these abnormalities have vitiated the marriage, Charles, before you start blaming Romaine for a marital disaster.'

I was silent. I felt as if the truth had slithered through my hands and was weaving a new pattern which lay beyond my grasp.

'It's undeniable that Romaine's had an adverse effect on your parents,' said Darrow at last, 'but is this entirely his fault? How much of the responsibility should be assigned to your father, who by so ruthlessly suppressing the tragedy gave it this golden opportunity to fester at leisure? And your mother – how much is she to blame for clinging with such tenacity to this very romantic but possibly dangerously deceptive memory of her first love?'

After a moment I said, 'She told me she always thought he'd come back. The thought of her waiting year after year seems so – ' But I left the sentence unfinished.

'That's certainly tragic and you have every right to find it upsetting, but I think we should guard against assuming that everyone would have lived happily ever after if Dr Romaine had tried to revive his disastrous love affair when he returned to England. We should remember that Dr Romaine himself appears convinced that your mother was lucky not to marry him, and we should remember too, I think, that he's far better acquainted with the exact nature of their love affair than either you or I could hope to be. When he made his decision to stay away it seems he was trying to do what he thought was right, not only for himself but for you and your parents as well. It was a sad decision, certainly, but can you honestly say it was a wicked one?'

'No. But I still say he's an awful old villain and I hate him.' I shuddered, crossed myself and whispered, 'God forgive me.'

'Tell me,' said Darrow suddenly, 'did he frighten you? We often hate the things we fear.'

I was silent.

'Did he unnerve you in some way? After all, to confront one's unknown progenitor could well be a deeply unnerving experience. Was there a likeness?'

I winced.

'A strong likeness?' said Darrow, and added with a striking flash of his psychic intuition, 'Was it like looking in a mirror?'

I shuddered from head to toe and covered my eyes with my hands.

IV

'I looked at him and he was just like me and I had to listen to him talking about all the drink and the women and how he'd made such a mess of his life – I saw him through my father's eyes, and – '

'That's all very well, Charles, but you have a perfectly good pair of eyes of your own – use them! Stop looking at Romaine through your father's eyes and make your own judgement!'

I finally let my hands fall from my face. 'But my father must be right!'

'Why? He's wrong about you – we've agreed that you're a much better chap than he's ever been willing to allow. So why shouldn't he be at least partially wrong about Romaine?'

'But Romaine's drinking – the messes with women – '

'Yes, these are telling points against him, but now look beyond the image of the drunken wastrel and see if you can catch a glimpse of the man your father's far too prejudiced to acknowledge.'

I made a great effort and after prolonged thought I was able to venture cautiously, 'He had ideals when he was young. He wanted to redeem his mother's death by saving other women. I saw no evidence that he's not a successful country doctor.'

'So his professional life hasn't all been a failure even though he failed to fulfil his early promise.'

'His personal life hasn't been entirely a failure either. He had his Chinese lady – and it was a Christian marriage – and apparently he's still a Christian – '

'How admirable! Despite all his difficulties he hasn't sunk into cynicism or despair. Would it be fair to say, do you think, that he behaved in a Christian manner towards you?'

After another pause I said, 'I doubt if he was driven by conscious religious considerations. Yet I can't deny he was kind.' To my horror Romaine's villainy began to dissolve. 'He understood everything,' I said in despair. 'He understood how I felt about my father. He understood why I needed to know about the past. And finally I think he even understood that I couldn't cope with him and had to get out.' There was a pause before I could add, 'Despite all my resentment on my parents' behalf I was afraid that once we started drinking champagne I'd find myself liking him, and I can't afford to let that happen – it would be so disloyal to my father and I've got to be entirely loyal to my father or he'll be more convinced than ever that I'm unfit, unworthy, bound to go to the dogs, and so long as my father believes that, I'll feel driven to hide behind my glittering image in order to cope with him – and once I'm back behind my glittering image I really will go straight to the dogs – '

'I agree that at present you need all your emotional resources to deal with your father,' said Darrow. 'Until he can accept the real Charles Ashworth and trust him not to make a mess of his life the glittering image won't wither away. But once you succeed in healing this exhausting relationship with your father, Charles, I have a feeling you won't need to see Romaine as an awful old villain any more.'

V

When I had recovered my equilibrium I exclaimed, 'How ironic that after years of chasing father-figures I should now have two fathers fighting for my attention!' and Darrow laughed before saying, 'Very well, let's leave Romaine there for the moment and turn back to your father. Unfold your next battle-plan.'

'I'm going down to Epsom tomorrow for forty-eight hours. However I fully expect it to be hell because once my father hears that I've met Romaine he's bound to be at his jealous worst.'

'I can quite see,' said Darrow, 'that your father will be tempted to behave badly if he's insecure about your affection for him, but you must be firm, Charles. You have a duty to be good to your father, but you're under no obligation whatsoever to allow him to dictate to you on the subject of your acquaintances.'

A single word in this last speech had so riveted my attention that I could only repeat incredulously, '*Insecure*? But my father's the last man on earth to be insecure! He knows perfectly well that he's got this colossal hold on me!'

'He knows nothing of the kind. All he knows is that you've got a colossal hold over *him*. He sees you as justifying his difficult marriage. He sees you as providing the ultimate proof of whether or not he's been a successful father. Every move you make is of vital significance to him. You've just spent several months holding yourself aloof. Now you seem all set to walk off into the golden sunset with Romaine. Your father's terrified. You've correctly diagnosed that he's jealous, but the source of his jealousy doesn't lie in a mere petty resentment, Charles. It lies in an overpowering fear that you'll reject him in favour of this glamorous stranger, just as your mother once did.'

'But at our last meeting my entire behaviour was directed towards reassuring him that I shall continue to think of myself as his son!'

'He can't believe you mean it. He's irrational with terror. In fact your father now appears to have two distinct difficulties: one is that you'll reject him utterly in favour of Romaine and the other is the nightmare which keeps the glittering image alive – the nightmare that you'll go to the dogs. I think you can probably reassure him in the end about Romaine, but the second difficulty presents more of a problem because no matter how often you promise him you're not going to the dogs he'll never believe you. He needs someone outside the family, I think, to put his mind at rest there.'

'If only I could coax him to see you! But meanwhile what on earth am I going to do with the poor old devil when I arrive in Epsom tomorrow?'

'Let's include your mother in this battle-plan too – she always tends to get overlooked, but she's insecure too, isn't she, Charles? She's frightened of being a burden and a bore to you, frightened you don't love her half as much as she loves you. Here you have two people with an indentical need: reassurance. You've got to let them know that you do love them, but on the other hand you mustn't pamper them, Charles. You must be yourself, not the ideal son spawned by your glittering image. Be genuine, be loving and truthful – and then you'll be a far better son than any glittering image could be.'

All I could say helplessly was, 'Pray for me, Father – '

'Of course.'

VI

The next morning a letter arrived from Starvale St James.

'My dear Dr Ashworth,' Romaine had written in a slanting hand which bordered on illegibility. 'Of course I would never have gone through with it but your mother was talking of killing herself. I couldn't have stood by in silence. It was a desperate moment, so desperate that neither of us was responsible for what was said. I beg you to pity us both in our terror and shame, even if true forgiveness is at present impossible. Of course nothing I have just written detracts from your father's magnificent behaviour in dissuading your mother from tragedy – behaviour for which, during the course of time, he has been so justly rewarded by your very evident loyalty and devotion to him. Please believe me when I write that I do not in any way aspire to take his place in your affections; that would, as I clearly realize, be impossible. All I hope for is the occasional meeting and the chance perhaps to know you a little better than I do now.

'I suspect you thought I had consigned you and your mother rather too ruthlessly to the past, but sometimes one has to be ruthless in order to avert further suffering. Thirty-eight years ago I nearly ruined your mother's life. Certainly I ruined my own for many years afterwards. In those circumstances how could I have embarked later on a course of action where there was even the smallest risk of compounding the suffering I had already caused? Of course when I eventually returned to England I wanted to see you, but I felt I had forfeited all right to do so. I felt I had to content myself with the knowledge that you were safe with your mother, who no doubt loved you, and that you were being brought up in a good home by a man whom I knew to be decent and honourable. That in itself seemed to be a miracle, and the idea that I might lay claim to either you or your mother in those circumstances appeared to me to be not only selfish to the point of wickedness but contemptuous of God's grace to the point of blasphemy. So I stayed away and I'm sure I was right to do so, but you mustn't think the decision was either lightly made or easily forgotten.

'I shall look forward so much to hearing you preach in September, and in sending you my best wishes may I assure you that I shall always be yours very sincerely, ALAN ROMAINE.'

I read the letter twice. Then I took off my collar, lit a cigarette and read it again. Eventually after several false starts I wrote: 'My dear Dr Romaine, Thank you for your kind understanding letter which was far kinder and more understanding than my erratic behaviour on Tuesday deserved. Please forgive me for the pain I must have caused you, and please believe me when I write that I too am looking forward to our September meeting when I hope to show you that I'm neither so boorish nor so rude as you might justifiably imagine me to be. Yours sincerely – '

I paused to consider my signature. Then gritting my teeth I acknowledged our relationship by omitting my surname and merely signing myself CHARLES.

314

VII

'. . . so of course you thought he was wonderful,' said my father, ferociously lashing a tomato plant to a stake.

'You couldn't be more wrong. I found him extremely upsetting and if you don't believe that, come to Cambridge and talk to Father Darrow.'

'I can't leave my plants,' said my father automatically, but added without pausing for breath, 'I can't believe the mad monk approves of this stupid hobnobbing with Romaine!'

'He did remind me of my duty to you – '

'I should bloody well hope he did! For over thirty-seven years I've slaved – '

'But he also said – '

'I don't want to know what he said, I disapprove entirely of that monk, I think he's a bad influence on you. Now come along, Charles, stop slouching among the flowerpots and let's see if your mother's mixed a new batch of disgusting cocktails. I only hope to God she hasn't murdered another bottle of champagne . . .'

VIII

'Funnily enough,' said my mother after my father had retired to change from his gardening clothes, 'your visit last weekend must have done him good because he's been much better – and if he's better I'm better. I just couldn't stand living with someone who behaved as if he was perpetually looking for a coffin to lie in, but now he seems to be thinking that it could be worth his while not to die yet after all . . . Darling – ' She hesitated before adding in a rush, ' – has something happened to you? I think it must have done. You seem different somehow . . . older . . . wiser . . . gentler – oh Charles, have you fallen in love again? Your father would be so angry if he knew I'd been pestering you with nosy questions, but I do so long for you to be happy with another nice girl – '

'I do have someone, yes, but please keep it a secret because it may come to nothing. There are great difficulties.'

'Oh, I shan't tell a soul!' She was touchingly pleased that I had confided in her. 'Darling, I do so hope it works out. I know the difficulty can't be that she's divorced or already married because of course, being a clergyman, you couldn't allow yourself to look twice at anyone who's in that situation, but is she perhaps shackled to a lost love as I always was?'

I smiled. 'Perhaps.'

'It was so strange the way you brought up that subject last Saturday and insisted on talking about it. It was almost as if . . . almost as if . . .

But no,' said my mother, 'my imagination's getting the better of me, but when I looked back on our conversation I really did feel it was as if – '

We looked at each other for a long moment.

' – as if you already knew,' said my mother, and as she read the expression in my eyes I stepped forward to take her in my arms.

IX

'I can't believe it – you mean you *saw* him – you actually *saw* him – but what did he say, what on earth happened, did he ask after me?'

'Yes, he said he was sure you'd kept your looks – '

'Oh, I must see him!' cried my mother. 'I must! To think that he's alive – and in England! Has he only just come back?'

'Well, not exactly – '

'How did you find him? Was he listed in the medical directory? At first I used to search for his name in each new edition but eventually I told myself that was futile – I was so sure he'd contact me if ever he came back, and now that I know he's finally here – and asking after me – '

'Mother darling, I do beg you for your own sake not to take too romantic a view of this! He's married to an efficient-looking blonde with a Lancashire accent, and I'm quite sure she wouldn't welcome – '

'Was he pleased to see you? You're so like him! Oh, he must have been so moved, so overcome – I'm going to cry,' said my mother, and did.

I was still desperately trying to stem this tidal wave of feminine emotion when the drawing-room door opened and in walked my father.

'Good God!' he exclaimed as he saw my mother weeping. 'You'll drown that boy yet! Disgusting! Pull yourself together, you silly woman, and behave yourself! What the devil's going on?'

My mother sobbed more loudly than ever and I felt obliged to kiss her before turning to face my father. 'I'm extremely sorry,' I said, 'but she guessed that I knew about Romaine and I've just told her about my meeting with him.'

'You bloody fool!' said my father, scarlet with rage. 'How dare you disobey me like that!'

'Shut up!' screamed my mother. 'I'm sick of you being cruel to him just because he reminds you of his father!'

'My father,' I said, 'is the one who's standing here behaving like an irrational jealous child. Now listen to me, both of you – '

'Never heard such colossal impudence in all my – '

'Be quiet, Father, and listen to me. Alan Romaine – '

'*I will not have that man's name mentioned in your mother's presence!*'

' – ALAN ROMAINE,' I said, outshouting him, 'has had a life which has

exuding self-confidence but racked by the dread that the approaching scene might be a failure.

'Glad to see you're looking calmer after that shocking exhibition,' said my father as we finally met by the net-post. 'Encourages me to think you haven't gone completely off your head. Now listen to me, Charles. Your mother and I have been talking things over and we take your point so there's no need for you to be upset any more – and no need to keep shouting that you love us. Very embarrassing, that. Bad form.'

'Yes, Father. I only wanted to make myself absolutely clear – '

'Quite. Now this is what your mother and I have decided: we'll all go on exactly as before. We won't talk about it, of course – '

'My dear Father – '

' – but that'll be because there won't be any need to talk about it – everything's been said. So although we'll go on as before, everything will be different.'

'Well, I suppose that does sound more promising, but – '

'I'm sorry, Charles, but your mother and I are quite agreed that although we're very glad you went off your head and spoke your mind we'd really much rather it didn't happen again.'

'But how are you and Mother going to get on when I'm not here? Don't you think it would be better if – '

'Are you going to have the unpardonable impertinence to tell us how to conduct our marriage? May I remind you that we've been at it for thirty-eight years so we must be doing something right! I know your mother very much better than you do, Charles, and I can tell you that the last thing she wants is to hear me dredging up the past in the name of honesty. What your mother wants,' said my father severely, 'is that you should show her a little extra kindness occasionally to make her feel she's not fit for the scrap-heap now she's pushing sixty. However you seem to have grasped that at last, thank God, so there's nothing else I can say on that point. You obviously didn't realize it earlier, but she felt lonely when you shut yourself up in your ivory tower, and of course when you refused to come home *I* got all the blame. Well, naturally I became depressed! Who wouldn't be depressed if they had a wife who was miserable and a son who treated his parents as if they were fit for the dustbin?'

'I really am very sorry about the estrangement, Father – '

'Of course you are. So am I. If we weren't both sorry we wouldn't be here talking to each other. But Charles, if you really want to make amends for worrying me half into the grave, you'll now wash your hands of that rotter Romaine before he ruins your life, wrecks your career and sends you straight to the dogs!'

'Oh, good heavens – '

'Well, what does the mad monk really say about Romaine, I'd like to know? I can't believe he approves of this reckless excavation at Starvale St James, but on the other hand maybe he's mad enough to approve of anything. Did he put you up to that scene just now?'

'He told me to be firm, genuine, loving and truthful. Is that a crime?'

'Nearly killed your mother. Felt a bit queasy myself, to tell you the truth. I think I'd better come to Cambridge after all and get this monk under control. He's beginning to frighten the life out of me.'

'What about your plants?'

My father stooped to pat Nelson. 'Peter might look in on them for a day or two. Of course I'd have to leave him very careful instructions, but the plants can't all die, can they? Some of them would be bound to survive.'

I recognized the unfamiliar note of optimism and knew another tide had turned. I too stooped to pat Nelson, but all I said was, 'I'll make the reservation at the Blue Boar.'

XI

After lunch when my father had retired to his conservatory I said to my mother, 'Forgive me for being so brutal earlier about Romaine, but I was in such a state trying to cope with Father.'

'Yes, I realized that in the end.'

I put my arm around her and we sat in silence for a while. 'Is Alan's wife attractive?' she said at last. 'A blonde with a Lancashire accent sounds perfectly horrid, and I can't imagine him being married to someone common!'

'That's because you can only picture him as he used to be. Mother, I do understand how much you must want to see him, but I honestly think – '

'Oh, I don't want to see him if he doesn't want to see me,' said my mother quickly. 'That would be frightful, so humiliating.'

'I'm sure that in many ways he would like to see you but perhaps he has a better grasp than you have of the pain involved. What would it really be like if you met him again? Would it be romantic? Or would it underline the tragedy and make even your cherished memories unbearable?'

She was silent, struggling to comprehend the situation in its entirety, and as I saw her set her fantasies aside at last I tried to find the words to comfort her.

'At least if you remember him as he was,' I said, 'you still have your cherished memories.'

She nodded. 'I think you saw the truth earlier when you talked of the two Alans. It's as if the Alan I loved died and now today's Alan is someone else altogether.'

320

'Well, that's a sad way of putting it, but – '

'Life often is sad, isn't it? But never mind, I had my great romance, nobody can take that away from me, and I still have you to remind me of it. Darling Charles,' said my mother as I tightened my arm around her, 'how very kind you were to Eric, treating him exactly as if he were your real father. No one realizes better than I do what a difficult man he is, but he'll be quite all right, you know, so long as you show him a little kindness every now and then.'

I kissed her and promised to be kind.

XII

My parents travelled to Cambridge by train on the last weekend in August and stayed at my expense at the Blue Boar. After lunch on Saturday my mother obediently retired to her room to rest while I drove my father to Grantchester; I had explained to her in private how important it was that my father should have a word with Darrow on his own.

'We won't stay long, will we?' said my father restlessly as we left Cambridge. 'I don't want to stay long – in fact I wish now we weren't going at all.' And he added in his most fractious voice, 'Can't think why I let you talk me into this visit, Charles.'

'Father, you volunteered to come of your own free will – '

'Must have been off my head.'

We met Darrow in the Abbot's Parlour, and when he took my father off to show him the garden I went to the chapel for ten minutes to pray. They rejoined me in the Parlour later; my father had an uncharacteristically tranquil look but Darrow was characteristically serene.

'Interesting fellow,' said my father afterwards as we drove back to Cambridge. 'Served in the Navy. Nearly drowned at Jutland. Worked after the War in a prison where they hanged murderers. Doesn't approve of capital punishment. Very interesting. Didn't like being a monk at first. Said he hated being ordered around after all those years of being his own boss. He started out as a monk here in Grantchester but he got kicked out to their farm in Yorkshire because they thought he had too good an opinion of himself and needed to have his nose rubbed in the mud. He said he hated milking cows but liked being trained as a carpenter. I asked him why he stuck it and he said he knew it was the only way he could serve God once he didn't have to provide for his children – he said it was one of those situations where a man feels he has absolutely no choice but to act in a certain way. Reminded me of when I decided to marry your mother. Interesting. Very interesting . . . Of course he's off his head, but he's off it in the most intriguing way. Did you know his son's an actor?'

'My dear Father, do you realize you've learnt more about Darrow in a thirty-minute visit than I've learnt after hours and hours of conversation?'

'We talked about our sons and about how bloody awful it is being a parent. He said he used to worry and worry about Martin – that's his son – in case the boy went to the dogs. Tricky business, being an actor. I asked him if he still worried about Martin and he said, "No, I gave that up five years ago when he came to see me and said he had a small part in a West End play. I thought: here's this boy, doing well, happy, coming to see me regularly, why torture myself imagining a decadent life which may never happen?" Darrow says he still has the occasional twinge of anxiety, like passing toothache, but nothing compared with the agony he used to suffer. Very interesting. Most interesting chap. Made me think a bit, I can tell you.'

My father paused. I waited, my hands gripping the steering-wheel, my gaze riveted on the road ahead. Eventually my father said in a casual voice, 'We mentioned you, of course, in passing, but we didn't say much. Naturally I said how worried I was about you as you were burrowing away digging up a man whom I knew to be an absolute rotter, but Darrow just said, "Worrying takes an enormous amount of time and energy. Are you quite sure the time and energy couldn't be put to better use?" So I said, "How?" and he said, "Trust him and show that you trust him," and I said again, "How?" Then Darrow said, "Let him dug up the rotter. Trust him to rebury the bones as he thinks fit." But I said, "Supposing he makes a mess of it?" And do you know what Darrow said next? He said, "He's your boy. You've brought him up. You've made him what he is. Why should he make a mess of it?" And do you know, when he put it like that I couldn't think of an answer. I did mutter something like, "Well, if he's off his head anything could happen," but Darrow said the main reason why you'd got in such a state recently was that you didn't trust yourself. "But if *you* trust him," said Darrow, "then he'll believe he's trust-worthy and everything will straighten itself out. Children are very much influenced by their parents," said Darrow, "and that's why we fathers have an absolute moral duty to make sure not only that our opinions are correct but that we make those correct opinions crystal clear." Most interesting fellow. Wasted as a monk, of course. Tragic. He might have made a good lawyer. I can just see him having a clever way with the clients and making useful contributions to the partners' meetings.'

It was the highest possible compliment. I was so lost in my admiration of Darrow's skill that I nearly missed the turning to Laud's.

'Well, thank God you're not an actor, Charles,' said my father comfortably as we approached the College. 'Then I really would have something to worry about, wouldn't I? But since you're a clergyman I suppose I can just sit back and let you get on with it. After all, despite everything you've managed to turn into a mature sensible sort of fellow, and with that interesting mad monk keeping you on course I see no reason why everything shouldn't come right in the end.'

That concluded the life of the glittering image. It began to die, and as I remembered Darrow's metaphor I saw the whole noxious weed, complete with its excavated roots, start to wither away in the sun.

I somehow succeeded in parking my car in the College forecourt. 'Thank you, Father,' I said. I wanted to say more but no words came, and all the time the glittering image was withering away, no longer needed, dying on every level of my mind.

'Now don't start behaving like a nasty emotional foreigner again, Charles, because my nerves couldn't stand it. In fact just take me to your rooms as quickly as possible and give me a stiff whisky, there's a good chap, before my nerves give out altogether. God knows it's not every day I meet a mad monk.'

The glittering image finally expired but I wasted no time saying a requiem over the corpse. I smiled at my father, said, 'I think we could both do with a drink,' and we headed in harmony for my rooms.

XIII

'My only regret,' I said later to Darrow, 'is that I couldn't have hidden behind a bush in the garden and witnessed that miracle you wrought with my father.'

'What miracle?' said Darrow amused. 'He was an easy case – a simple decent man, not stupid, who was burning to know how he could put matters right. Of course I'm not claiming I solved all his problems, but at least I offered him a new way of looking at the problem which was foremost in his mind ... And talking of Romaine, are you still feeling nervous about his visit to Cambridge next weekend?'

'Yes – although now that I don't have to spend all my energy trying to convince my father I'm not going to the dogs, maybe I've got a chance of survival.'

Darrow said frankly, 'Romaine could certainly make heavy demands on your new reserves of strength. I think a little nervousness is not unjustified.'

'I wish he wasn't coming.'

'Cheer yourself up with the knowledge that he's bound to try hard to make the occasion a success.'

'That's what I'm afraid of. If it's a success what do I do with him afterwards? I still can't see how to fit him into my life.'

'Worry about that later. The situation may seem much clearer after you've talked to him on Sunday . . .'

TWENTY-ONE

'Friendship, however begun, is a voyage of discovery, full of perils and surprizes.'

More Letters of Herbert Hensley Henson
Bishop of Durham 1920–1939
ed. E. F. BRALEY

I

Romaine sent me a note to say he hoped to reach the Blue Boar on Saturday evening but would not expect to see me until after the morning services the next day. I spent much time wondering whether I should call at the hotel to offer him a drink but decided I was being sufficiently hospitable by inviting him to dine in hall on Sunday. However that conclusion made me feel mean so to assuage my guilt I arranged that a bottle of whisky should be waiting in his room to greet him on arrival. As soon as this arrangement had been made I started worrying in case I was corrupting a heavy drinker.

In the midst of these tortuous psychological gymnastics I embarked on writing a sermon. I toiled away, constructing what I hoped would be a homiletic masterpiece, but was constantly racked by doubt. Were there too many obscure references? Did I sound hopelessly priggish? Was my thesis sufficiently stimulating to stave off the coughing of bored choirboys and the somnolence of elderly worshippers? Laymen have no idea what anxiety clergymen can suffer as they engage in their struggle to communicate the word of God, and even another clergyman might have had difficulty imagining the degree of anxiety I was now enduring as I struggled to communicate the word of God not only to my congregation but to the stranger whose ineffectual contraceptive skill during adultery had somehow resulted years later in the appearance of yet another clergyman in the Sunday pulpit.

The Bishop was absent, having been invited to preach in Durham, and the other two Canons were on holiday, but the Dean was there to share the work of the Sunday services with me. Matins began; I noted Romaine in the congregation and at last after the third hymn I mounted the steps into the pulpit and declared my text from Isaiah: ' "The grass withereth, the flower fadeth, but the Word of Our God shall stand for ever." '

II

'I always think that's the most moving text,' said Romaine later as we walked back to Laud's. 'I feel it puts all the triumphs and tragedies of life into a proper perspective, and of course that was your theme, wasn't it? Or at least one of your themes – it was all so interesting and I liked the story of the monk who drew a cat carrying a mouse in its mouth in the margin of the manuscript. My Chinese lady liked cats; in fact I thought a lot of her as you spoke – and I thought of your mother too and of how I'd quoted Wordsworth to her – I was always quoting Wordsworth to your mother, Wordsworth and Browning – and when you said, "The grass withereth" I thought of that passage about the "splendour in the grass" until past and present seemed to merge and I felt most uncommonly emotional. Well, as a matter of fact, I *am* rather an emotional sort of chap. I tell myself it's the French blood. My grandfather came over here to teach French to a London merchant's family and then he married an English girl and stayed on – oh God, there I go again, droning on about myself! It's time you got a word in edgeways. How did you set about constructing that splendid sermon? How hard you must have worked! I'm sure it took a long time to write.'

We eventually reached my rooms at Laud's.

'What a marvellous place!' said Romaine, gazing around at the very ordinary main chamber which served as a drawing-room, dining-room and library. 'How comfortable you've made it, how conducive to bookish labours! And look at your beautiful prints of Cambridge! If I had a fortune I'd spend it all on pictures – so isn't it lucky that my present fortune, such as it is, belongs entirely to my wife who has very proper ideas about how it should be spent! I'd have squandered the lot in no time.'

I offered him a drink before we went down to hall to dine.

'Well, I don't mind if I do,' said Romaine, 'although I feel a bit of a cad filching whisky from you after you've been so uncommonly handsome as to decorate my hotel room with a bottle of Johnnie Walker Black Label. What a treat! My wife doesn't approve of expensive whiskies and she watches the level in the decanter like a hawk – and quite right too, of course. I need someone to keep me in order.'

'Did you tell her about me?'

'She guessed. When she first met me seventeen years ago I was rather more like you than I am now. Her first question when she returned home after your visit was, "When the hell did *that* happen?" but when I said soothingly, "Oh, that was just a little awkwardness in Epsom in the Naughty Nineties, my dear," she nearly hit the roof. "Don't try to tell me it was a little awkwardness when it was obviously a bloody catastrophe!" she said, putting me in my place, so I found myself confessing everything. "And how many more little awkwardnesses are going to crawl out of the woodwork, I'd like to know?" she demanded in a voice of thunder, so I said meekly that there weren't any more because this little awkwardness had taught me a lesson I'd never forgotten, and she then made that exasperated noise which in books is always written p-s-h-a-w. I have to tread very carefully there, I'm afraid, poor Bea, because it's a great sadness to her that she's been unable to give me children. I knew from the start that it would be much better if I came on my own to Cambridge this weekend because you'd simply remind her that some other woman had succeeded where she'd failed . . . But here I am, prattling on about myself again! Now, my dear Charles, this time you really must get a word in edgeways. Are you working on a new book?'

It was the question which my father had never asked. Halting in the midst of pouring myself a sherry I demanded, 'How did you know I'd already written a book?'

'I thought that as you were a Doctor of Divinity you might have published something stunning, so I telephoned Blackwells at Oxford and ordered your book as soon as they told me about it. I must say I was most entertained by your account of all those frenetic debates which raged about the Trinity! When one thinks of all the awful things that go on today – Hitler, Mussolini, the Spanish Civil War – one can't help but enjoy escaping into a faraway world where the one big topic of conversation was whether the Son was of the same substance as the Father!'

Here was someone who understood. The temptation was irresistible. Handing him his whisky I began to talk about the Council of Nicaea.

III

'That really was the most splendid meal, Charles, and the claret was out of this world – how you resisted the temptation to have more than one glass I just don't know. I say, I did enjoy myself! But should I slink off to the Blue Boar now? I don't want to get in your way if you've got more important things to do.'

'I'm free till Evensong at six.'

'Can I come to that too?'

'My dear Dr Romaine – '

'Charles, I insist that you call me Alan. After all, since you were so generous as to sign yourself by your Christian name in that nice little note which brought tears to my eyes – '

'My dear Alan, if you want to come to Evensong, who am I to stop you? But first I suggest we have coffee – black coffee – '

'It's all right, I'm actually extremely sober – I could operate now and not even make a slip of the knife. Shall I tell you about the time I took out that very curious appendix in Bombay?'

'Well – '

'No, I don't think I will, I mustn't put you off doctors for life . . . Oh, here we are again, back in this nice room – did you have a house when you were married, or a flat? No, don't answer that, I don't want you to think I'm prying into your marriage – and talking of marriage what do you think of the A. P. Herbert Bill – the Matrimonial Causes Act, as it now is? Divorce for insanity at last! Thirty-eight years too late for me, but at least I have the satisfaction of knowing some other young fool won't have his life wrecked just because he thinks he can walk on water. But what an exhibition the Church made of itself in the House of Lords! The only one who talked any sense was the Bishop of Durham – oh, and the Bishop of Starbridge, of course. Now *there's* a man after my own heart! Have you met him?'

I began to talk about Dr Jardine.

IV

'Jolly nice brandy this is, Charles. Black coffee's never quite the same without brandy, I always think, and I'm glad to see you're having a little drop to pep you up for Evensong. Well, this is all absolutely fascinating. Probably it's just a schoolgirl's crush of Miss Lyle's, you know – unconsummated. Shall I tell you why I say that?'

'Tell me.'

'If she'd been sleeping with him it would have burnt itself out by this time. It's only the unconsummated passions of this world which go on and on like a never-ending gramophone record, and personally I always think it's better to leap into bed and have done with it – although of course I shouldn't say that to a clergyman. God, what a dreadful clergyman I'd have been! It was bad enough trying to behave like a doctor . . . Shall I tell you about the woman with the very curious breasts in Rangoon?'

'Tell me anything you like. Have some more brandy.'

'Don't mind if I do, old chap. Marvellous host you are – but aren't you having any more yourself?'

'I don't want the Dean defrocking me after Evensong. Look, Alan, I shouldn't have told you about Lyle – I must be going round the bend – '

'My dear Charles, *don't worry*. I'm the soul of discretion – you talk to Bea. She has no idea who's sleeping with who in Starvale St James, but I know it all right down to the last bedpost – '

'But I should at least have kept my mouth shut about Jardine – '

'Why? I'm thrilled to think he might have had a luscious young girl to cheer him up after a disastrous marriage – although in fact I suspect it's more likely he picked an older woman to soothe him, just as I picked my Chinese lady. I put my money on that mysterious Swedish stepmother, even if she did weigh sixteen stone. I rather like buxom women myself. Shall I tell you about – no, I most definitely shan't. Got to keep myself in control.'

'I seem to have lost control altogether. I can't think why on earth I – '

'I shall take great pride in proving my magnificent discretion, and meanwhile I'm absolutely delighted that you've got an attractive girl lined up – but how are you going to lure her from that palace? Of course if you weren't a clergyman I'd tell you to seduce her as soon as possible; once you'd got her into bed she'd soon forget about Jardine, even if she was his mistress.'

' "Get thee behind me, Satan!" '

'I mean it, old chap! Any young sprig of thirty-seven can knock spots off an old warhorse of – how old's Jardine?'

'Fifty-eight.'

'Well, there you are. Past his prime like me. I can still do it, of course, but I'm really only at my youngest now in the early mornings – and Bea can't stand looking at anything, let alone me with my pyjama flies open, before she's had her first cup of tea and read the headlines of the *Daily Express*. But that's marriage, isn't it? One long compromise . . . What did you say your wife's name was, Charles?'

'No, I'm sorry but I'm not going to tell you about Jane, not yet. I've already told you quite enough for one afternoon – '

'Let me slink off to the Blue Boar and give you a breather.'

'Drink up that brandy and I'll take you for a walk along the Backs.'

V

'The Dean's sermon wasn't nearly as good as yours, Charles, but never mind, it was a very pleasant Evensong. Now I expect you've been thinking: how on earth am I going to get rid of the old bore, but don't worry because the Old Bore is now going to slink off to the Blue Boar and commune in reverent silence with that delectable bottle of Johnnie Walker – '

'Come back to College and we'll have some bread and cheese in my rooms. I don't like to think of you all alone with a delectable bottle of Johnnie Walker. My conscience tells me you need to be saved from that sort of fate very firmly indeed.'

'Oh, I love being saved!' said Romaine. 'Thank you so much – I say, can I have another sip of that nice brandy with my bread and cheese?'

VI

'. . . so I go and see this monk two or three times a week and I talk about things and he sorts me out when I get in a muddle . . . well, all right, just half a glass more – I don't usually drink twice a day – '

'A little extra claret will be very good for you after all your hard work. Now before I slink off to the Blue Boar – '

'I've heard that one before.'

' – you must tell me all about this monk. I'm so glad you've got someone to talk to, Charles, because life's so bloody difficult sometimes, no one knows that better than I do, and I can see so clearly how difficult it must have been for you growing up with . . . well, with problems – '

'Oh, shut up and have some more claret. I wish I'd never told you about my damned problems, I can't think why I'm telling you all these private and personal things, I'll hate myself after you've gone – '

'No, don't do that. Go and see your monk instead and tell him how bloody awful I was, drinking you out of house and home and clinging to you hour after hour like some elderly incubus. Then once you've expended all your anger on me you'll feel better.'

We looked at each other over the claret decanter in the twilit room. After a long moment I said, 'You're very shrewd, aren't you? I've spent all day giving myself away and now you've got me neatly summed up.'

'Nonsense! Human beings are much too complicated to be summed up neatly after a few hours' acquaintance. Let's just say we've spent the day exchanging clues about ourselves – and meanwhile think of all the fun we've had, thanks to your kindness and generosity!'

'I just can't imagine how I'm going to cope with you – the whole problem's got quite out of control – '

'Impossible,' said Romaine firmly, 'because there's no problem in the first place. You don't have to cope with me. I'll just go on pottering around Starvale St James and occasionally popping up to Cambridge to hear you preach and eventually I'll drop dead and that'll be that. Bea will have to cope if ever I become senile or bedridden, and all you'll have to do in those undeniably sordid circumstances will be to give Starvale St James the widest possible berth.'

'Not a chance. I'll be there at the death-bed feeling muddled up.' I drank deeply from my glass.

'Oh, I shouldn't like that at all,' said Romaine. 'I'd be very cross. Promise me no death-bed visits! So Victorian, so dreary, so *dull*!'

'Not necessarily. I'd bring a bottle of champagne.'

'My dear boy, what a lovely thought! It reminds me of Chekhov. Did you know that on his death-bed Chekhov tossed off a glass of champers and died with a beatific smile on his face?'

We started to laugh. At last I said, 'Forgive me. I've been intolerably rude again.'

'You put everything right by offering to bring me champagne on my death-bed! Don't worry, Charles, I understand. I know you don't need me in your life at the moment – I'm just distracting you from the things that are really important, but I'd like to think that one day I might be useful to you in some way. After all, God must have brought us together for a purpose, mustn't he, and if he'd wanted us to remain strangers he wouldn't have made it so easy for us to be friends. In fact in my opinion what's happening is crystal clear: he's redeeming my past by showing that something good came out of all that tragedy and failure, and he's giving you – for reasons we don't yet know – someone else in your life whom you can trust to be loyal to you no matter what the circumstances. Is that really such a sinister prospect? I don't think so, and if you talk it all over with that monk of yours I'll wager you a bottle of Johnnie Walker he agrees with me. And talking of Johnnie Walker I know you're thinking the time really has come when I should slink off to the Blue Boar – '

'Sit down,' I said. 'You need to be saved again. It's time for another round of black coffee.'

VII

At three o'clock the following afternoon I once more turned up on the doorstep of the Fordite monks and sank into the nearest chair in the Visitors' Parlour. I had had a strenuous morning, celebrating Communion in the Cathedral's Lady Chapel, parting from Romaine at the Blue Boar and attending a chapter meeting presided over by an irritable Dean who was in the middle of a quarrel with the Head Verger. Lunch had been spent soothing the Master of Laud's (also embroiled in a quarrel with the Dean) and responding tactfully to the assertions of the Master's wife that all clergymen should be celibate. (The wife of the Dean was universally unpopular.) It was with profound relief that I escaped afterwards to Grantchester.

'I can't imagine why you thought the situation would become clearer once I'd seen Romaine again,' I said irritably to Darrow after I had given him an account of Romaine's visit. 'I feel in a worse muddle than ever. I don't deny I like the old villain, but he still frightens the life out of me.'

'Some degree of distrust may well be healthy at this stage – in fact I'd be far more worried if you'd whole-heartedly embraced him as a father-figure and were displaying unmistakable signs of hero-worship.'

This comment encouraged me. Once I was assured of my stability I found I could try to analyse my feelings with more precision. 'I do feel much better about my parents,' I conceded. 'No doubt they'll continue to drive me to distraction but at least I feel I've created an atmosphere of trust and truth which will enable me to deal with them without hiding behind my glittering image. But Romaine! I've got no confidence there at all.'

'Are you still seeing him as evidence that you're doomed to go to the dogs?'

'No, that view just represents my father at his most irrational, I can see that now.'

'But nevertheless Romaine still frightens you.'

'Perhaps it would be more accurate to say he makes me feel acutely anxious. He really *is* an awful old villain, Father – I'm sure I'm not imagining it – '

'I think it's most unlikely that this judgement is entirely the product of your imagination, but you could be exaggerating out of sheer fright. Can you single out any detail which made you feel uneasy?'

'He didn't attend any of the Communion services.'

'Ah. Yes, I'd wondered about that too.'

Again I was sufficiently encouraged to analyse my feelings further. 'After all,' I said, 'there he was, hanging on my every word at Matins and Evensong. Perhaps he felt the sung Eucharist was too High Church for him, but why didn't he turn up today or yesterday at Early Communion? Wouldn't you think he'd be eager to be first at the rail as I administered the sacrament?'

'Maybe he has a very protestant inclination to attend mass only occasionally. But yes, I do think it's odd he didn't decide that yesterday should be one of those occasions.'

'Well, once I began to wonder if he was in a state of grace,' I said, finally finding that I could approach the root of my distrust, 'I began to wonder if he was entirely happy with his wife who not only holds the purse-strings but guards the whisky decanter. I know he's a churchwarden and ought to be respectability personified, but I've got a nasty suspicion that his Christian beliefs might not necessarily prevent him pursuing a life of adultery, heavy drinking and goodness knows what else. But perhaps I'm being completely unjust to him.'

'Perhaps, but I don't think you're being ridiculous, Charles, or even excessively cynical. Your suspicions strike me as being real possibilities. Supposing in fact that you're right; how far would this shady private life of his impinge on your own life far away in Cambridge?'

'That,' I said, greatly relieved that I could at last not only perceive but voice the truth, 'is what makes me anxious. If his marriage breaks up or if he finally gets struck off the register for sleeping with patients, I'd have to help him – but what a prospect! Tell me how I can stop myself having nightmares about him turning up ruined and penniless on my doorstep one day!'

'You could try telling yourself the nightmares may never happen.'

'I wish I felt as sanguine about that as you apparently do.'

'Well, consider, Charles. Romaine, as you yourself have told me, is a wily old survivor and wily old survivors, like wily old cats, usually have a very keen sense of when to make a mess and when to keep their paws clean. After many vicissitudes Romaine now has a comfortable home, a pleasant practice and a wealthy wife who provides him with a guaranteed source of whisky and sex. This, from Romaine's point of view, is as close to heaven as he's likely to get on this earth and he's going to fight any temptation which will represent a one-way ticket to hell. I think you can allow yourself some cautious optimism here, Charles, I really do.'

For the first time since the start of the interview I was able to relax in my chair. 'Awful old villain!' I said. 'But what fun we had! And at the end ... Well, I couldn't help feeling moved when he said God was redeeming the past by bringing me into his life. Of course I know it sounds appallingly sloppy and sentimental, but at the time – '

' – at the time Dr Romaine was making a masterly attempt to capture your heart, and who can blame him? I must say, he sounds on very familiar terms with God, but then one never quite knows with laymen whether that indicates arrogance, reverence or ignorance.'

'He seemed reverent enough but of course he fell into the layman's trap of assuming he knew exactly what God has in mind. However since Romaine and I have only just met and we've no real perspective on what's going on, any discussion of God's purpose here can at present only be improfitable – or at least,' I added, fearing he might think me too dogmatic, 'so it seems to me.'

But Darrow said without hesitation, 'I agree,' before asking, 'When are you seeing him again?'

'The shrewd old villain took care not to make me feel persecuted – he didn't pin me down to any date. But he'll be back. Of that I'm quite sure.'

'Clever Dr Romaine! And while we're on the subject of his shrewdness I must confess I thought he made some interesting comments on the Starbridge mystery. Ought we to have a quick word about Lyle, do you think, before you leave?'

He had realized that since my parents were under control and Romaine had been safely dispatched to Starvale St James, the Starbridge mystery was now grinding back into the forefront of my mind.

Leaning forward I put my three parents behind me at last and prepared to tackle the next stage of my ordeal.

VIII

'I know I want to marry her,' I said. 'I knew for certain when we met in the Cathedral. There's genuine feeling on both sides, and I'm sure that when we next meet she'll tell me exactly what's going on.'

'Will she? I wonder. The whole problem is riddled with the most serious difficulties, and before you make your final circuit of the Starbridge mulberry bush it's vital that you understand what those difficulties are. Can you come back and see me tomorrow?'

But I could not. My calendar was beginning to fill as the new term approached, and I was also burdened by my duties as Canon in Residence.

After we had agreed to meet on Wednesday evening Darrow said, 'Now be frank with me: are you tempted to rush off to Starbridge – or at the very least to telephone Lyle without delay?'

'I suppose the only honest answer to both those questions is yes. I know I threw her that lifeline and since she hadn't used it I can assume there's no crisis, but nevertheless I'm so very worried about her, and I was wondering – ' I hesitated but was unable to stop myself concluding, 'I was wondering if you could see anything. Can you look across at Starbridge with your mind and – '

Darrow said severely, 'Charles, you'll treat me as a priest, if you please, and not as a charlatan in a fortune-teller's booth on some seaside pier.'

'I'm sorry, but sometimes I feel so tormented – '

'Yes, don't think I don't understand how difficult this waiting is for you.' He took pity on me. 'If I knew what was going on I'd tell you,' he said, 'but my powers are in many respects very limited. I've a certain flair for picking up impressions from someone I can see, but I've never been much good at long-range intuition unless the other person in the psychic conversation is emotionally close to me.'

'Do you ever see the future?'

'Yes, but there are many futures and not all of them come true.' He leant forward on the table as if he wanted to reach out to ease my torment.

'On Wednesday we'll picture the futures,' he said, 'and meanwhile try not to put yourself on the rack by picturing the present. Remember that you could be seeing the wrong picture, and even if it happened to be the right one you'd be unable to erase it. But the future is a different matter. You can draw a picture, erase it and draw another. What I'd like to do is to help you draw several pictures so that you can have a comprehensive insight into what may happen.' He stood up to close the interview. 'You've recently found the strength to endure the present by re-examining the past, Charles, but now that the past has been reviewed and reassembled, it's time to endure the present by viewing and assembling the future. And once that's been done, past, present and future will be set free to converge and the result will be the solution of the Starbridge mystery – although the solution may be a mystery in itself, leading to other mysteries, because as I said to you once the mysteries of life are rarely capable of clear-cut solutions . . . But I must stop talking like a mystic or – God forbid! – like a charlatan on a seaside pier, and urge you, as I must, to have faith in your gathering strength and above all to trust in God who alone can repel the demon of anxiety which is now tormenting you . . . let me say a prayer now to help you in this ordeal, and afterwards I'll give you my blessing.'

My torment was eased. Minutes later I was driving back to Cambridge, but long before I reached my rooms at Laud's I found I was strong enough to face the possible futures which lay waiting for me.

IX

'First of all,' said Darrow when we met two days later, 'I want to remind you of the four major reasons why you shouldn't go cantering off immediately to Starbridge on the nearest white horse to rescue your damsel in distress.'

'Four major . . .'

'Yes, I did wonder if you'd managed to count them all. Now Charles, it's not enough to say grandly that you want to marry this woman. You must give me a competent analysis of the situation to prove you know exactly what you're doing.'

I was immediately determined to demonstrate the rational equilibrium which he himself had helped me acquire. 'I mustn't rush off to Starbridge,' I said, 'first of all because we haven't yet reached that date you set at the end of the month. In other words, I'm still too close to the disaster at the palace and I should wait a little longer to ensure that I can see Lyle without illusion.'

'Good.'

'This applies even though I'm now convinced, since the meeting in the Cathedral, that my feelings are based on reality and that I want to marry her.'

'Even better. Go on. Reason number two?'

'She's a mature adult of thirty-five. I can't charge into her life uninvited – especially as she's asked me not to do so. I must stick to my plan to have a discreet meeting at the end of the month and trust her to phone me if she needs help before that.'

'Well done. Go on to reason number three.'

'I'm stumped. So much for my competent analysis.'

'Let me put the question more specifically: why is it so important that you should allow Lyle every opportunity to end the *ménage* without your active intervention?'

'I might make a bad mess if I intervened.'

'True, but I was thinking of a more distant future. Supposing you and Lyle marry but things go wrong between you. Then she could always turn around and say, "You drove me into leaving when I didn't really want to go." ' Seeing my expression as this glimpse of an unpalatable future was revealed he added swiftly: 'We'll come to the possible marital difficulties later. Now what's the fourth major reason why you mustn't go cantering off to Starbridge on the nearest white horst?'

'I'm sorry, I'm completely failing this test – '

'No, you got the first two reasons right, but they relate only to the present. Think of the future; you may in spite of everything find you don't want to marry her – yes, I know that's unlikely but you must face the fact that it's still a possibility, and if you intervene actively now in the Starbridge *ménage* you're going to find marriage virtually impossible to avoid. Let me just clarify my mind on one point: have you ever mentioned marriage to Lyle?'

'No, but of course she knows that's what I want.'

'Yet you're not hopelessly compromised and if the worst came to the worst you could still back away.'

'Yes, but – '

'I know you think I'm being perverse, Charles, but the truth is you don't know yet which way this mystery's going to break, and if the worst comes to the worst it may well break in a way which would make the idea of marriage to Lyle untenable.'

'You think it would be untenable if I found out she was Jardine's mistress?'

'Let's hear your views, not mine.'

I was silent for a moment before saying, 'I could cope with that if I was convinced the affair was over. I wouldn't hold the immorality against her because I'm sure she wouldn't have slept with him unless she'd honestly believed she was his wife. She'd be like someone who married a bigamist in all good faith.'

'That's a fair judgement. Very well, you're not going to recoil if you find out she's been fooled into adultery. But supposing your plausible theory of the informal marriage is in fact dead wrong. Supposing they're both apostates, both keeping up the pretence of being good Christians while knowingly committing adultery. What then?'

I said slowly, 'I couldn't marry her. Marriage with an apostate would be impossible – there'd be no shared spiritual life – no clergyman could consider it ... Of course if she repented and wanted to return to the Church I'd forgive her and do my best to help, but no matter how far I forgave her it would be very debatable whether I should marry someone capable of living for years in adultery and continually abusing the sacrament. For the sake of the Church and my word a devout wife is essential.'

'In other words, the idea of marrying Lyle would have become untenable. Now I can see you're thinking that this possibility is too remote to worry about, but are all your problems really solved if she's a mere innocent victim who genuinely believes she's Jardine's wife? You may well picture yourself coasting across calm seas into a golden sunset in those circumstances, Charles, but in fact all manner of storms could be waiting for you. Think hard and see if you can identify these storms one by one.'

I was aware that I was being put to the test again. 'Jardine's memory could prove intrusive,' I suggested cautiously.

'Yes, that's a hazard in all cases where the partner's been married before, of course, and it's not insuperable but nevertheless it should be considered. Go on.'

'I think I might be haunted by the secret fear that she was switching horses – backing me because I could ultimately offer her more than Jardine. In other words, I'd be afraid she didn't love me for myself, and then my fear of rejection might crawl out of the woodwork again.'

'Good. You're doing well on this test, Charles. Keep going.'

'It's possible that I might always wonder if I knew the full story of that relationship with Jardine, and if I doubted that I'd scraped the whole truth from the bottom of the barrel, I might start to feel insecure.'

'Excellent.'

'I'm not sure I can go any further except to point out the obvious fact that somewhere along the line I'd have to deal with Jardine and that could prove a great stumbling-block.'

'Jardine, I agree, presents appalling problems. We'll get to him in a moment. Is that really the end of your list of difficulties? So far you haven't mentioned one of the most crucial problems of all.'

'Haven't I?' I tried not to sound despairing.

'You've been considering the situation entirely from your own point of view, but what about Lyle? Let's again assume your theory's true and that she considers Jardine to be her husband. If she leaves him she's inevitably going to suffer some degree of guilt, no matter how justified she is in ending the liaison. Possibly she'll also suffer shock and grief – certainly there'll be a period of considerable emotional difficulty. Now, how is she going to cope with these feelings? How are *you* going to cope with them? How is your marriage going to survive their destructive effects? Charles, I'm not saying this problem's insuperable but is *is* formidable. You've got to be very, very sure you love her and very, very confident of your own emotional and spiritual stamina as you set out to conquer not just this problem but indeed all the problems we've so far enumerated.'

He paused to enable me to digest this warning and eventually I said, 'I'll have to persuade her that she needs expert counselling. Maybe she'd be better off with an alienist than a nun.'

'I wonder. The trouble with psycho-analysts is that they can tiptoe around in a patient's childhood for years without getting anywhere near the spiritual dimension of the problem. I'm still convinced your best hope is to find a nun skilled in counselling who's been married or who's survived a long debilitating love affair – or both.'

'How do I find her?'

Darrow said unexpectedly: 'I'll have a look for you. I'm due to pay the Abbot's annual call soon on the Abbess at Dunton, and when I go I'll seek her help.'

Conscious of Lyle's prejudice against nuns I said, 'It's a difficult problem.'

'It is indeed and I'm sorry to burden you with it, but I'm sure you see how important it is that you should look beyond the golden sunset to glimpse what sort of marriage might be waiting for you in the dark below the horizon – if, that is, Lyle agrees to marry you. Another possible future is that she won't be able to bring herself to do it; she could choose to remain in the *ménage*.'

'I'd make an intervention if that happened.'

'If Lyle's psychologically unable to leave, an intervention would probably be useless. However let's meet that difficulty when we come to it because it may never happen. What *will* happen is a confrontation between you and Jardine at some stage; I regard that as inevitable.'

'If I eloped with her I wouldn't have to see him at all.'

'He'd want to see you after the wedding.'

'What for? Surely not to give me his blessing!'

'Why not? He might see Lyle's desertion as a punishment from God and visualize converting you into a son-in-law as a form of atonement.'

'That's disgusting!'

'But not impossible, and we're surveying possible futures. Consider his psychology: I suspect Jardine collects son-figures just as you used to collect father-figures, and that one of the reasons why the two of you got on so well together was that you were each fulfilling the other's neurotic needs – you were both chasing a father-son relationship. If he now gives his blessing to your marriage he not only atones for any past sin with Lyle and keeps Carrie happy by retaining Lyle in the family; he also permanently acquires a splendid son-figure whom he already likes immensely. And in addition, of course, he acquires the possibility of adopted grandchildren, a possibility which will be equally welcome to Carrie – '

'I'd emigrate to Australia before I let all this happen!'

'I sympathize entirely – if this unhealthy *ménage* is allowed to survive, even in a reconstructed form, it could be emotionally disastrous for Lyle and spiritually very dangerous for you both, but you do see, don't you, Charles, that from the Jardines' point of view a *ménage à quatre* could be an attractive possibility?'

'Well, obviously there's got to be a clean break with them – '

'Yes, but how easy is that going to be to achieve if Jardine is bent on creating a *ménage à quatre* and Lyle is anxious to retain both Jardines in her life? The fact is this situation could quickly jeopardize your marriage, and if you do decide to go ahead it's vital that you and Lyle agree long before you reach the altar exactly what your relationship with the Jardines is going to be.'

After a long pause I heard myself say: 'Well, I've got the whip-hand, haven't I? I could ruin him in one sentence to the Archbishop.'

'I was wondering when you were going to think of that.' Darrow leant forward. 'It wouldn't work, Charles – for two reasons. One is that Lyle would never forgive you and never forgive herself for Jardine's downfall. And the second reason is that if Jardine adopted a tough stance and denied everything Lang couldn't force him to resign without a huge scandal – which is the one thing Lang wants to avoid.'

'So Jardine gets away with adultery – again!'

'Not necessarily. Leave Jardine to God, Charles. God will deal with him far more efficiently than either you or the Archbishop of Canterbury.'

'Well, God certainly seems to have turned a blind eye so far!' I said, but as soon as the words had left my mouth I was horrified. 'I'm sorry, forgive me, but I was just so angry at the thought of Jardine getting away with all this and enjoying a supremely successful career – '

'Yes, the anger's clouding your mind; if you calm down I think you'll see that you're jumping to conclusions that are very much open to debate. After all, what do we really know about Jardine's past? We do know there was a gross error with Loretta, but are you so sure he got away with it? What does "getting away with it" actually mean here? Jardine certainly met with worldly success after he parted from Loretta, but how far did that contribute to either his happiness or his spiritual welfare? The effect was to drive his marriage still deeper into trouble because his wife couldn't cope with her new responsibilities, and Jardine's misery must inevitably have increased. Indeed if you equate worldly success with "getting away with it", Charles, I think you're on shaky ground.'

I gestured to indicate I had no argument to offer.

'It's dangerous to make a judgement when one can't know all the facts,' pursued Darrow, 'and since only God can know all the facts one can only conclude that it's best to leave the judgements to God. For instance, who knows but God when Jardine's present troubles really began? One might speculate that they began with his marriage, but why did he rush into that fatal marriage in the first place? Surely no mature man in his right mind proposes to a woman only four days after their first meeting! Such behaviour hints at instability, at some form of mental distress. Was there indeed an unhealthy situation with the stepmother? If one were speculating about a judgement one might advance the theory that the marriage itself was a retribution stemming from some previous error, but we don't know, do we? And we'll never know. It's impossible to know the whole truth about anyone, Charles, and all we can do is pray for as much enlightenment as God sees fit to grant us. So be cautious with Jardine. Beat back the demon anger. Even if he's entrapped in the grossest of errors you should still approach him with charity and refrain from judgement.'

After a prolonged silence I said with reluctance, 'I suppose I should also still guard against the temptation to assume that adultery's taking place.'

'Yes, because it remains non-proven – and the last possibility here, of course, is that there's no adultery but Lyle's nevertheless locked up in an unhealthy psychological relationship with both Jardines which is preventing her from having a normal life of her own.'

'But even if that were true the situation would still be fraught with difficulty, wouldn't it? I'd still have to deal with the Jardines, still have to deal with Lyle's guilt – the guilt that she was leaving them – '

' – and you'd still have to deal with the dread that you never got to the bottom of the mystery and that maybe she did sleep with him after all. No, I agree this is hardly an improvement on the other possibilities – in fact one could even argue that it would be easier to deal with Lyle's unwitting adultery than with some bizarre neurosis which keeps her in the Jardines' thrall.'

'If the adultery exists it must be bizarre enough in itself. Think of the complications!' I shuddered before adding abruptly, 'Have we now exhausted the possibilities or are there any futures still to be considered?'

'There's always the future we can't predict. For example, Jardine might drop dead. But I think we've covered the futures which are forseeable on the present evidence.'

'It's certainly a daunting prospect.' I looked up into his eyes. 'But if I make the wrong decision after this conversation it certainly won't be your fault.'

'I'll pray there'll be no wrong decisions. And talking of prayer we must discuss your spiritual life before you go. I want you in prime spiritual condition for this finale of your great ordeal, Charles, because I'm quite sure you're going to need all the spiritual strength you can get.'

X

I remember very well when the end began. It was September the fourteenth, the day before I was due to telephone Lyle to arrange a meeting at the end of the month. I had spent the morning attending a conference of the University's theological faculty to discuss a new policy on tutorials; two of the professors had had a row about the Pelagian heresy, and that afternoon as I attended to some correspondence in my rooms I was just wondering idly if I could bring Pelagius into my next sermon when the telephone rang beside me on the desk.

I picked up the receiver. 'Ashworth.'

'Charles – '

It was Lyle. I rose to my feet as if I had been jerked by a rope. She said, 'I need you.'

'Where are you?'

'London. I want to come to Cambridge.'

I glanced at the clock on the chimneypiece. 'There's a train from Liverpool Street at three-twenty. I'll meet you at Cambridge station.'

'Thank you,' she said crying, and hung up.

The last ripples from my big stone had finally reached the edge of the pool and now apparently it was Lyle herself who was about to be washed up at my feet. At once I wondered if Darrow had foreseen this indefinably sinister end to my weeks of waiting, and the next moment I was telephoning the Fordites' mansion at Grantchester.

PART THREE

THE CALL

'. . . the possible final calls of individual souls are completely known to God alone, and to the soul itself, with some real knowledge, only and when it has advanced considerably on the spiritual way.'

Spiritual Counsels and Letters of
Baron Freidrich von Hügel
ed. DOUGLAS V. STEERE

TWENTY-TWO

'A perverted, confused or defective moral sense is yet reverently to be handled, after the manner of the Redeemer, Who would not quench the smoking flax or break the bruised reed.'

More Letters of Herbert Hensley Henson
Bishop of Durham 1920–1939
ed. E. F. BRALEY

I

Darrow was not available. 'Father Abbot's gone visiting,' said the monk who answered the telephone. He made visiting sound as if it were an act of great daring fraught with dangerous possibilities. His voice sank to a whisper. 'He's calling on the Abbess at Dunton.'

I saw us all moving into position like figures on a chessboard, I seeking Darrow, Darrow seeking a counsellor for Lyle, Lyle on her way to Cambridge to seek help. 'When is he expected back?'

'Six o'clock. Doctor.'

'Please tell him I rang.' I replaced the receiver, thought for a moment, then telephoned the Blue Boar to reserve Lyle a room for the night. My next task was to cancel my social engagements, and once that had been accomplished I asked one of my fellow canons to substitute for me at the Cathedral for a couple of days on condition that I returned the favour when he himself was in residence.

Having concluded these essential telephone calls I glanced at my watch. Then clasping my cross for comfort I calmed myself by reading the evening office. I still had over two hours to wait.

II

The train drew into the station shortly before five o'clock and I was on the platform to meet Lyle as she left the last carriage and stumbled awkwardly into my arms. She was carrying only a shoulder-bag.

'Your luggage – ' I was afraid she had left it on the train.

'I don't have any. I came up to London only for the day.' She was very pale but appeared calmer than I had expected. There was no sign of tears. 'Before I caught the train here I sent the Jardines a wire to say I was staying overnight. I didn't say where or why.'

I kissed her briefly, led her outside and told her about the room waiting at the Blue Boar. 'But we'll go to Laud's first,' I said, 'and I'll make you a cup of tea.'

'I'd rather have a whisky,' came the flat reply, and as I swung to face her she said: 'Yes, ladies' companions don't drink whisky, do they? But I want to put aside my mask now, Charles – the glittering image, as you called it – and then when you see me as I am – ' Suddenly she was fighting her tears ' – perhaps you won't want me any more but at least I'll have set you free to find someone else.'

I said as I started the car, 'Whatever happens in the future I promise I'll help you through the present crisis.'

But she was apparently too overwhelmed to reply; she could only avert her face from mine as she struggled for composure, and in silence we drove to Laud's.

III

'Maybe brandy would revive you more effectively than whisky,' I said when we reached my rooms.

'I think it would, yes. Thanks. With soda.' She began to search her bag for a cigarette. After I had given her a light she added, 'I haven't even said thank you for responding like this. I must be wrecking your social calendar and Cathedral duties.'

'You're more important than calendars and cathedrals.' I handed her the glass of brandy, and after siphoning some sodawater into a glass for myself I sat down not on the sofa beside her but in the nearest armchair. I was wearing my collar so I was unable to smoke. Instead I sat well forward in the chair and gripped the glass with both hands. Outside in the quad the sun was shining. My rooms were very quiet, very peaceful.

'Sorry,' said Lyle, 'I seem to be in a sort of coma. I want to talk but I can't quite see where to begin.'

' "Begin at the beginning", as the King said in *Alice in Wonderland*, "and go on till you come to the end". Have another swig of brandy.'

'The trouble is I'm not sure where the beginning begins . . . Charles, could you sit beside me? Or have you planted yourself in that chair not just to reassure me you won't pounce but to help you to behave like a – whoops! I nearly said "eunuch". The glittering image is slipping. Ladies' companions in clerical households aren't supposed to know what such words mean.'

'Surely if they read the Bible and have access to a dictionary they'd find their innocence rather hard to preserve?' I said mildly, and when she laughed I sat down beside her and gripped her trembling hand in mine.

'All that biblical sex!' she exclaimed, and suddenly I sensed she had seen the way forward into her narrative. 'That awful use of the verb "to know"! I remember saying to my great-uncle in Norfolk: "Everyone in the Old Testament seems so well acquainted!" I didn't know anything about sex till fairly late – well, I didn't want to know. My mother said to one of her friends once when I was listening at the door, "Of course no girl would ever face marriage if she *knew all*," and my God, the way she said it! I crept away and vowed I'd never marry, never, never, never. I didn't want children anyway so marriage seemed not only repellent but pointless. I told you my mother was an invalid, didn't I? "I was all right before I was married," she used to say, "but after the child was born I was never the same again." What a nightmare! Marriage, motherhood and *knowing all* – ugh! I grew up wishing I'd been born a man.

'However when I was twenty-four and still living at that ghastly rectory in Norfolk I thought: there's got to be more to life than this, I'll go mad soon, I'll die of boredom unless I can make something happen. And I started thinking rationally about marriage. I was spurred on by the fact that my great-uncle was clearly on his last legs, and once he died I knew I'd be turned out into the street with no money. So I thought: maybe I should give marriage a try. Well, it just so happened that one of my admirers at that time was the son of one of the well-to-do farmers in the neighbourhood, not some blockheaded yokel but a well-spoken boy, reasonably educated, and I thought he could be a solution to my problem. I liked the idea of helping him run the farm one day, and there was a nice house attached to the farm too, Georgian, not some two-up, two-down hovel – it had *possibilities*, and I did so long for a real home of my own at last. I calculated that his parents wouldn't last more than ten years, his sisters would soon be married off and then I'd be free to rule the roost. So the only hurdle was: could I cope with *knowing all*?

'Well, I weighed everything up – I'm horribly calculating, Charles, you'll like me less and less as this narrative progresses, but I've had to be calculating, had to be tough – how else could I have survived after Daddy had gone off to die a hero's death in the War? Bloody wars! Bloody heroes! Why the *hell* couldn't he have come home instead of leaving me alone like that? He left me with nothing, *nothing* except a mother who wilted uselessly on a chaise-longue, and once she was gone I had to endure that ghastly hole in Norfolk with no money, no decent education, no real companionship, just cast-off clothes, boredom and despair – my God! I spent my youth feeling like a kitten flung into a rain-barrel to drown.

'However there I was, paddling away and somehow keeping my head above water, and I thought I could use Thomas to crawl out of the rain-barrel. But as I was so afraid of *knowing all* I said to Thomas: "Before I can possibly decide whether or not to marry you I must know exactly what marriage entails." Actually I thought it was a most sensible suggestion, but of course he was horrified. He was a respectable young man pursuing the respectable girl from the vicarage – only to find she'd turned into a trollop! He broke off the friendship in a fine flurry of self-righteousness, but he came crawling back later. Well, men usually do, don't they? They can seldom bear to resist a good offer when it comes to sex . . .

'Anyway I wound up in Thomas's hay-loft *knowing all*, and naturally it wasn't nearly as bad as the nightmare concocted by my imagination. I think what surprised me most about it was the sheer banality. I wasn't revolted, just amazed that anyone could be bothered to do it more than once. I certainly knew *I* didn't want to bother – no, thanks! – so I had to tell Thomas that marriage simply wasn't on. Poor Thomas! But I don't feel sorry for him, not now, because I know that if we'd married I'd have made him very miserable.

'Well, then the blow fell, my great-uncle died and the Church served me notice to quit the vicarage. But I didn't sink into despair. I was too angry. I thought: that damned bishop in Norwich ought to do something about me! So I went to see him and demanded a job. The Bishop fluttered around in a purple panic, but by coincidence one of his guests at the time was the Bishop of Radbury, and the Bishop of Radbury thought at once of his new Dean.

'I went to Radbury for my interview. Do you know the Deanery there? A beautiful Georgian townhouse with ten bedrooms, much nicer than Thomas's faded rural home – oh, as soon as I arrived I knew the situation had *tremendous* possibilities! I was nervous of meeting Mrs Jardine, but as soon as I saw her I recognized the type and was confident I could cope. Mrs Jardine was a much sweeter, much more lovable version of Mummy – the sort of female designed by God to decorate chaise-longues and drive husbands to drink – or to die a hero's death in some hellish war. However I could see Carrie liked me so I knew the first hurdle had been overcome. But then I had to have my interview with the Dean.

'Carrie took me to his study. I was expecting to meet a white-haired portly old buffer – have you ever noticed how many eminent clerics are white-haired portly old buffers? – so you can imagine how I felt when I first set eyes on Adam Alex Jardine.

'He was forty-eight. I was twenty-five. I took one look and finally realized what *knowing all* was all about. I think I actually went weak at the knees – can you imagine it! One never expects a clergyman to have an effect like a matinée idol, yet it's by no means a rare phenomenon – I remember reading once about a Victorian clergyman who inspired all the women in his congregation to faint in their pews, and I thought at once: that's like Alex Jardine. Clergymen have extra allure too because they're trying to lead a decent life, and every woman secretly dreams of a real stunner who can somehow stop himself rolling around in the mud like all the other swine – although of course she wants him to roll around in the mud with her. I'm sorry, Charles, are you absolutely appalled by my frankness? Maybe you'd better have some brandy too. But this is it, Charles, this is what I'm like behind my mask – cool, calculating and obsessed with sex. All that well-chilled propriety was just an act.

'Well, if this were a D. H. Lawrence novel, Jardine and I would have straightaway leapt into bed together, but life isn't quite so simple as either the modern novelists or the Victorian novelists seem to think it is. In real life people are much more shadowy, and life is much more uncertain, more unpredictable, more mysterious; people can be a lot worse than they are in novels, but they can be a lot better too.' She paused. Then she said: 'Alex – ' and paused again.

The two intimate syllables hung in the air between us. The curtain came down on the first act, the curtain went up on the second, but all I said as I added a dash of brandy to my sodawater was, 'Go on.'

IV

'Alex was – and is – a good man,' said Lyle, holding out her glass for a refill. 'That's the point I want to make crystal clear because unless you understand that you'll understand nothing. He's good – and he's devout. If it had been otherwise he couldn't have survived, Charles; he wouldn't be where he is today.

'But I didn't understand that when we first met. You see, although I'd spent so much time in a clerical household I knew next to nothing about either devout clergymen or a truly religious life. My great-uncle was so old and only interested in butterflies; he just regarded being a clergyman as having a safe roof over his head and a duty to be polite to his neighbours. As for religion I thought it was something people did on Sundays. I had rather a grudge against God, in fact, for allowing Daddy to be killed. Intellectually I knew about Christianity but spiritually I was illiterate so when I realized Alex found me attractive I just sat back and waited for him to make a pass. After all, other men always had. But the next thing I knew was that Alex was trying to get rid of me.

'I couldn't believe it. I was stunned. It made me realize how ignorant

I was and how the world was so much more complicated than I'd imagined. I felt very cheap. It was as if someone fine had shone a spotlight on me and revealed this revolting heap of flesh and bones . . . Do you remember how St Augustine felt about himself when he realized how he looked in the eyes of God before his convertion? Well, I felt like St Augustine. And like him I hated myself and just wanted to be a good Christian. I can't honestly say I was immediately transformed by the call of God because I wasn't. I went on being much the same but I grew up a bit, became a little humbler, a little more aware of my own ignorance, a little more determined to find out what being a Christian was really all about.

'Meanwhile I wasn't sacked after all because Carrie had had hysterics at the thought of losing me, and suddenly I felt so sorry for Alex having not only this ghastly problem of his wife – of course I'd soon summed up the marital situation – but also this ghastly problem of me smouldering away under his nose that I thought: if I really love him I'll help him out. So I told him I hadn't come into his household to wreck his career but to make it possible for him to go all the way to the House of Lords. I was so nervous that I sounded rude and defiant, and at first I thought Alex would explode with rage but he didn't. In the end he laughed. He laughed and said, "What a girl!"

'Then he became businesslike. "You've been frank with me," he said, "and that took courage. Now I'll be frank with you. All I want is to serve God to the best of my ability but my problems keep getting in the way. If we can form a partnership in which you take care of my problems and leave me free to serve God, then I swear you need never be homeless again. But the only way we can form a partnership, Miss Christie, is for us both to forget about turning our life at the Deanery into some wild cross between *Barchester Towers* and *Lady Chatterley's Lover*. Am I making myself absolutely clear?" I assured him that he was. "Very well, I'll give you a new three-months' trial," he said, "and we'll see how we both get on." I said, "Splendid!" and we shook hands.

'That was how it all began. Innocent, wasn't it? And both of us only trying to be good and decent. The streets of hell aren't paved with champagne, loose women and fast cars, as that old fool Bishop Winnington-Ingram said once. They really are paved with the very best intentions.

'Of course Alex should have stuck to his guns and dismissed me. But Carrie . . . poor darling sweetest Carrie . . . If I hadn't been there to run the Deanery and soothe her out of her nervous breakdown she'd have ruined his career. I couldn't help being fond of Carrie – and it wasn't just because she was so hard to dislike; it was because she really did love me as a daughter. Never having wanted children myself I had no idea until then what hell women go through when they want to have children and can't, and Carrie had been through hell. Alex had suffered too but he was in a better position to cope; he had his work to occupy him and he always had plenty of chances to work off his frustrated fatherhood among the choirboys and ordinands who trooped past him continually, but Carrie had no one to mother until I came.

'I asked her why they'd never adopted, but Alex had taken the line that one never quite knew what one was getting with a strange baby and he'd rather take an unofficial interest in people who were older. Well, that was all right for him, but it was tough on her. However she never argued with Alex, not by that time; she'd tried arguing with him in the early days of the marriage about his stepmother, but by the time I arrived at the Deanery Alex was God, in her eyes, and his word was law. Ironically that was part of the marital problem. Alex needs to be screamed at occasionally – he can't stand it when Carrie disintegrates into floods of tears because it makes him feel so guilty that he can't love her as he should. What a pathetic marriage! I felt so sorry for them both, locked together for life with nothing in common but their incompatibility and their double-bed . . .

'I expect you want to know where my obsession with sex had got to by this time, and the answer is: coming along nicely. As usual there was always some man writing me sonnets, but I couldn't look at anyone but Alex and I used to soak myself in fantasy; I'd lie in bed and have what the clerics call "impure thoughts". You're probably wondering how I stood the frustration, but in fact unrequited love can be great fun – ask any schoolgirl with a crush. One burns and one yearns in blissful comfort, and nasty brutal old reality never intrudes at all . . . The truth was I felt wonderful, doing a job I liked, seeing the man I loved every day, enjoying stunning sex every night in my imagination – and when all was said and done that was exactly where I wanted to enjoy it; despite my feelings for Alex I still couldn't rid myself of the nasty suspicion that real sex, even with him, was bound to be a disappointment, so the situation which had evolved at the Deanery actually suited me very well. I must be honest and admit I had my moments of jealousy but they didn't happen very often, and that was Carrie's shining triumph. You see, she's the most Christian of us all – she loves Alex, she loves me, she's always so kind and good . . . In the end it wasn't Alex who brought me to a full Christian belief. It was Carrie, poor stupid helpless Carrie, but she showed me how to live a Christian life, and in the end I found myself loving her far more than I'd ever loved my vain whining self-centred mother.

'And so we came at last to Starbridge . . . But are you understanding what I'm trying to say? I think you have some idea that I'm the innocent heroine enslaved by the wicked Jardines, but you see, Charles, it isn't like that at all. Alex and Carrie are both good and devout. *I'm* the villain of the Starbridge mystery, and here's where my villainy really begins . . .'

V

I said as I lit her second cigarette: 'Is it really a story of heroes and villains? Surely real life is never so simple as that!'

'Yes, I did say earlier, didn't I, that real life is so much less clear-cut than it is in novels . . .' She was calmer now. Her fingers were no longer trembling and the clasp of her hand was firm. 'I feel better,' she said. 'I wonder if that's the brandy or the confessional? I suppose it must be the brandy because I haven't confessed anything yet except what a sex-obsessed adventuress I am.'

I said mildly, 'Do you realize that if you were a man your initiative in getting a good job, your ingenuity in keeping it, your desire to make a success of your work, your preoccupation with sex (a preoccupation which is hardly unusual among those not called to celibacy) – all these things would be considered either admirable or, at the very least, normal?'

Without warning her eyes filled with tears. 'You mustn't make excuses for me. I'm so rotten, so undeserving, so unworthy – '

'Ah yes!' I said. 'I used to play this scene before Father Darrow stepped in and revised my script. Cheer up! You may be unworthy but I doubt if you're more unworthy than I am and anyway maybe we can have an interesting time being unworthy together. But let's get back to your story. You came at last to Starbridge – '

The interval was over and the curtain went up on the third act.

VI

'We came at last to Starbridge,' said Lyle, drawing deeply on her cigarette, 'and almost at once the crisis began. It had actually been brewing for some time. I was thirty, Alex was fifty-three and Carrie was forty-eight – and Carrie had begun the change of life. Physically this was nothing dramatic; she wasn't prostrated by dire symptoms, but mentally she went to pieces because the hope of a baby had kept her going in a difficult marriage. Alex is *not* the easiest of men to live with, and although she adored him he'd often given her a rough time with his quick temper and sharp tongue. However the desire for children had given her the strength to be what Alex calls "dutiful" – what a sickening Victorian word that is! – and although sex had never meant much to her she'd more or less managed to meet her obligations whenever she wasn't having a nervous breakdown. But how was she now going to face a childless future? That was the big question, and the problem was compounded by the fact that she was terrified of leaving Radbury where (thanks to me) she had her life in control, and moving to a whacking great palace with twelve servants at

Starbridge. Of course she still had me to help her out, but I couldn't save her from being put on display as "Mrs Bishop" throughout the diocese.

'All this was desperate enough, but the turn of the screw came when Alex's sister died and his stepmother had to be imported to the palace. Carrie didn't hate old Mrs J. – I honestly don't think Carrie could hate anyone – but Carrie was wholly convinced she couldn't cope with her. Mrs J. gave her what I think is called an inferiority complex, and made Carrie feel stupid and miserable. Old Mrs J. herself, of course, was a very tough lady indeed and she didn't just hate Carrie; she despised her.

'However when old Mrs J. arrived she actually behaved very well – she was so pleased to be back with her Adam – and the real trouble arose not from her hostile behaviour but from the fact that Carrie couldn't believe old Mrs J. was genuinely trying to be benign – you know how persecuted people feel when they're on the verge of collapse. I badgered the doctors for help, and after dishing out the pills one of them even suggested a psychiatrist, but Alex reacted as if the man had recommended witchcraft. Alex thinks psychiatry's rubbish, a sort of heresy on a par with spiritualism.

'Then finally the crisis reached its climax. Carrie, who was by now refusing to leave the palace and face the world, told Alex she had to have a separate bedroom. No more sex. What was the point, she said, when nothing could come of it. Well, Alex could live without the hope of children but he couldn't live without the hope of sex. I knew that. Carrie told me everything by that time – poor darling, she had no one else to confide in, but when Alex found out that she'd talked to me about their intimate life he nearly hit the roof. We had a row and he accused me of cultivating an unhealthy confidential relationship with Carrie. I said that was nonsense and he knew it. "You're lucky she confides in me and not in someone else," I said, "because you know very well I'll keep my mouth shut till the Day of Judgement." He said, "I ought to get rid of you," and I said, "Oh, don't be such a damned fool!" He liked that. Alex likes a woman who can talk back to him. He said, "What on earth am I going to do?" and I said, "Stop being such a pig-headed Victorian and get her to a psychiatrist".

'So he took her up to London – well, we all three went – and the psychiatrist was a nice man but of course he never got anywhere near a cure; he couldn't wave a wand to postpone the menopause. However she liked him so we all began to hope, and when he suggested that a little holiday might be beneficial the three of us trekked off to Bournemouth for a few days.

'Carrie in fact *was* a little better; the psychiatrist wasn't a complete failure, and when I coaxed her out of the palace to buy clothes for the holiday she was almost her old self again. Alex thought she was cured. Talk about wishful thinking . . . I said, "You *are* booking three rooms at the hotel, aren't you, Dr Jardine?" and he said: "That's a very impertinent question, Miss Christie, and not one which I feel obliged to answer." Well, we got to the hotel and of course he'd booked a double room for them. I knew it would be a disaster and it was. On the first night Carrie came to me in tears when he was having a bath and said could she spend the night with me in my room. She was in such a state, practically in hysterics, and when she sobbed that she didn't dare face Alex to tell him I said at once: "Don't worry, darling, *I'll* tell him."

'They had a bathroom adjoining their bedroom – Alex always likes to be extravagant in hotels. I sat down in my dressing-gown on the edge of the bed and listened to him splashing away and eventually he wandered out with only a towel tucked around his waist. He didn't see me at first. He just assumed Carrie was there and he said, "The Bishop of Durham has a good story about how he was once accidentally bathed in Sweden by a youthful masseuse – what a pity this hotel doesn't provide such an interesting facility!" Funny how clearly I remember him saying that; I suppose it's because I also so clearly remember thinking: this is it, I've taken her place, he's talking to his wife and I'm listening to him talk. And *that* was the moment when I knew I wanted real sex at last.

'A second later Alex turned and saw me. He went ashen. Then he very carefully put on his dressing-gown and tightly tied the cord.

'I told him what had happened. He said, "I'd better talk to her," and I said, "I don't think that would be a good idea at all – better to leave her where she is tonight and tackle the whole problem afresh in the morning." He said, "And where are you going to sleep, may I ask?" and I said, "Well, I'm very used to filling in whenever Carrie can't cope and this is all in a day's work for me. Why don't I fill in here too?" And Alex – darling Alex – said, "My dear Miss Christie, we seem to have wound up in the pages of *Lady Chatterley's Lover* – may I suggest we return immediately to the pages of *Barchester Towers*?" And he added, "Please go to your room and tell Carrie she must come back and sleep alone here in this bed while I sleep in the armchair by the fireplace. Tell her I shan't be cross, shan't lose my temper, shan't utter a single word of reproach because I'll be much too busy going down on my knees and asking God to extricate us all from this highly embarrassing, utterly catastrophic and apparently insoluble mess."

'Wasn't he wonderful?

'I went back to my room and swore to Carrie she had nothing to fear. Then I told her exactly what I'd said to Alex. Her first reaction was: "But of course! The perfect solution!" and she kissed me. Her second reaction was: "But it wouldn't be right and Alex would never do it." However, the next moment she was saying, "It's so strange though, because I feel it *ought* to be right – do you feel that, Lyle?" and I told her I did. We all in the end felt it was right. But none of us could see how it could be morally done.

'We cut short the holiday and returned to Starbridge with the excuse that Carrie wasn't feeling well, but in fact Carrie was much better. She's seen the light at the end of the tunnel and so had I, but I was so worried about Alex because I knew he was in despair. However after days of confiding in his journal and getting nowhere Alex finally scrapped his iron rule that he should never discuss his marital life with his stepmother, and of course old Mrs J. sorted us out in no time. She *quite* understood that Alex couldn't live without the hope of sex, and she saw me as playing her own role in a re-enactment of her big romance with Alex's father. But the past never quite repeats itself, does it? Alex's father had been a widower, and Alex was still very much a married man.

'But old Mrs J. had been brought up a Lutheran and she knew that Martin Luther had believed refusal of marital rights should constitute grounds for divorce. She'd also spent twenty-five years living with Alex's father who thought that clergymen were unnecessary, the legal bureaucracy was an impertinence and that any couple could marry themselves before God without conforming to all the man-made rules of Church and State. Old Mrs J. had absolutely no doubts about what Alex should do, Carrie had no doubts, I had no doubts –

'But Alex was absolutely tormented.

'Finally Mrs J. gave me her wedding ring – this ring, my signet-ring. Alex was there. She'd asked to see us both and we were in her room. She said to him, "I want her to have my ring and I want you to put it on her finger."

'She more or less married us. But in the end Alex had to do it more tidily; he's got a very legal streak and he likes ambiguous situations to be properly defined before being neatly filed away. He fetched Carrie. It was late at night by that time and Carrie was getting ready for bed but she came along in one of her stunning negligées – she looked better than she'd looked for months. I was wearing my evening clothes, a rather funereal black dress, but Alex took a rose from Mrs J.'s vase of flowers and fixed it alluringly on my décolletage. He was wearing his episcopal clothes, apron, gaiters, pectoral cross, the lot. Mrs J. was in her usual gunmetal grey. What an odd crowd we must have looked! And what a strange scene it was! Alex made a short speech setting out the position – I think he needed to make a speech to convince himself that what he was doing was right, and of course by the time he'd finished it all seemed so right that one wondered why no one had ever thought of setting us a precedent. He told Carrie he wished to divorce her for refusal to consummate the marriage and said it was his honest belief that this refusal rendered their marriage a purely nominal affair; the spiritual core of the marriage had been destroyed, leaving only the legal formalities, and as far as these were concerned, God certainly didn't need a gaggle of lawyers to sanctify the dissolution of a spiritual nullity; mutual consent alone was sufficient to dissolve any man-made ties.

'Alex promised Carrie that he would always maintain her and that for as long as she lived she would be his wife in the eyes of the world. He then asked her if she had any objection to what he'd said, and she answered no, she loved him very much and she was sure this was the best solution; she promised to do her utmost always to be a good wife to him in public. Alex said, "Then before God I declare my marriage to Caroline dissolved," and after a pause he gave her a kiss and asked her if she wanted to stay on while he married me. She said, "Oh yes, dearest – I put on my best negligée!" and we all laughed but it was a tense moment because we were all so close to tears. Old Mrs J. said suddenly, "Fetch some champagne, Adam, and some glasses for afterwards." She knew he was temporarily too overcome to go on. So off he went to recover and Carrie went to the lavatory and I sat down by Mrs J.'s wheelchair and Mrs J. held my hand.

'When Alex came back with the champagne we got married. Again he did it formally, spelling out all the details, saying it must be a secret marriage while Carrie lived. I agreed to the terms, we exchanged vows and he put the ring on my finger. Carrie cried, of course, in her role of "mother of the bride". It was all very peculiar and emotional. I hugged her and asked her to keep on loving me. She just said, "How could I stop? I'll always love you both and want you to be happy."

'After we'd all had a glass of champagne, ruthless old Mrs J. ordered Carrie off to bed so that she could be alone with us. Then she kissed me and said, "Now I can die knowing Adam will be happy at last"·– and she did die, but not for another few months so she was actually able to see how happy he was with me.

'Meanwhile Alex and I had concluded the wedding-night by going to bed together. It wasn't like my fantasies – he was in such a state he was impotent at first. He said, "I'm afraid this isn't like *Lady Chatterley's Lover* after all," but I said, "Well, it certainly isn't like *Barchester Towers*!" Then we laughed and everything was all right.'

Lyle stubbed out her cigarette. It had been a long time since she had looked me in the eyes and now she still kept her face averted from mine as she said rapidly, 'I'm sorry to take my time over this but I want you to understand exactly how it was.'

'That's what I want too. Shall I make some tea now? If we go on tossing off the brandies like this we'll be insensible before the final curtain.'

She finally dared to look at me. I gave her a reassuring smile. Then releasing her hand I rose to my feet and moved to the pantry to fill the kettle.

Lyle said when I returned, 'Is the story turning out as you anticipated?'

'It is and it isn't. I guessed the bare facts, as you know, but I hadn't visualized the huge emotional strain involved – and I hadn't anticipated how everyone would play their parts. Of course I saw Jardine as the instigator – '

'No, it was me, in the beginning. Then old Mrs J. pushed him over the edge at the end. I wish you could have met her, Charles. She had the most tremendous influence over Alex.'

'What exactly – '

'I don't know,' said Lyle. 'I've played the model wife, waiting for him to confide, but Alex has always remained reticent.'

'Maybe there's nothing to confide.'

'I'm sure there's something. I suspect they had one of those intense relationships where sex is either unnecessary or unimportant – sibling relationships can occasionally fall into that category, can't they, although I'm sure Ingrid and Alex never saw themselves as brother and sister. I know he never saw her as his mother either – he told me he could remember his own mother too clearly, and anyway Ingrid wasn't maternal. While he was growing up he would have seen her as his father's wife, but when he found out about the informal marriage – that was when Ingrid left home to keep house for him – I suspect he just saw her as the unattached woman who loved him. I still doubt if they ever slept together – Alex is so devout – but who knows? If the relationship was entirely innocent, why can't he talk freely about it to me? And why did he rush into that marriage as soon as he could afford to do so – as if he felt it was vital that he should put himself once and for all beyond the reach of temptation?'

'Perhaps something started in Starmouth, finished when she went back to the old man and then started again later in North London after the old man died.'

'I just don't know. You could equally well argue that he rushed into marriage because he feared the platonic relationship was finally becoming sexual. A man can't marry his father's wife, can he, and even though Ingrid's marriage was so peculiar Alex did in the end believe it to be valid in the sight of God. So he couldn't marry her – and as he was a devout clergyman no other relationship was possible, but I'll tell you this, Charles: although we can't know for certain whether she and Alex were ever lovers I'm quite sure that old Mrs J.'s loathing of Carrie was fundamentally rooted in jealousy.'

'Was she never jealous of you?'

'She seemed to decide straight away that it was pointless. In 1932 when

I married Alex she was over seventy, she knew she hadn't long to live and all she wanted was to see her Adam happy. Anyway she liked me. We got on. She adored the wedding – in fact, if I was going to advance a really bizarre theory I'd say she got tremendous vicarious excitement out of pushing me at Alex and imagining us in bed together, but who knows what she really thought? Who even knows where reality lies? Think of all those philosophers – Berkeley and Hume and – '

'I'd much rather think of you. Do you take sugar in your tea?'

'Now *that's* reality! No, thanks. Just milk.'

I poured out the tea. 'So far,' I said, 'I still can't see any heroes or villains in this story, only victims.'

'Victims of God?' she said. 'Or victims of the Devil?' And she added unexpectedly, 'That's a charism, isn't it – the ability to distinguish the manifestation of God from the manifestation of the Devil in ambiguous circumstances. Alex told me it's called the charism of the discernment of spirits.'

We were silent for a moment, but then I said, 'Ring up the curtain on the next act and let me test my powers of discernment.'

TWENTY-THREE

'Personally I incline to think that wherever a situation emerges in which the cohabitation of the husband and wife cannot reasonably or equitably be required, there a prima facie case for divorce must be held to exist.'

'Before one could rightly order these folk to go apart, we must be well assured that they are not in spiritual fact *married*. In the region of essential morals we cannot stake everything on the presence or absence of the legal certificate.'

More Letters of Herbert Hensley Henson
Bishop of Durham 1920–1939
ed. E. F. BRALEY

I

'For a long time,' said Lyle, sipping her tea, 'everything was fine. Or perhaps I should say it was fine despite the peculiar circumstances which in fact made everything very difficult indeed. The first major problem was secrecy; I moved my bedroom to that remote nook in the south turret, but Alex thought it might look odd if he changed his bedroom arrangements at the same time, so he and Carrie continued with their shared room although now he always slept in the dressing-room. Then later they got twin beds so that they could occasionally sleep within the same four walls and present a façade of marital intimacy to the servants.

'The danger to our secrecy in fact came from another quarter altogether. Alex and I had had five years' experience of suppressing our feelings for each other, but it wasn't so easy to maintain a bland façade once we were also indulging in great intimacy – it was the switching backwards and forwards which was so tricky. We developed a strict rule that we should never under any circumstances embrace except in my room – and that was tough because we longed to snatch a kiss sometimes, but it just wasn't worth the risk. We also developed the golden rule that we were never to neglect Carrie – in fact Carrie was quite a problem to us at first because we felt guilty about her; we couldn't help feeling guilty even though we

359

both knew she'd consented to the divorce of her own free will. Carrie was also a problem in another way, poor darling – both Alex and I were terrified she'd be indiscreet. I watched her like a hawk in the early months, but in fact Carrie never once let us down – she was so very conscious how vital it was that she should never make a mistake.

'The other major difficulty at first was the sex. This may surprise you – I expect you imagined us plunging away happily for hours, but we were both paralytic with fear in case I started a baby and for a long while after that first night we didn't go the whole hog at all. The advantage of that was that I was able to get used to intimacy without being overpowered by it, but eventually I went up to town, to the Marie Stopes Clinic, pretended to be a legally married woman and got myself a Dutch cap. After that everything was fine, but the sex always had its slightly sordid side – the hole-in-the-corner side of the clandestine love affair. For instance we both used to worry about the sheets so finally we always lay on a shawl which I could wash myself . . . Oh heavens, Charles, forgive me for dragging in these details but I want to be truthful, I want you to see the absolute grinding *reality* of it all – '

'It's much better that you should be entirely frank. Tell me, did Jardine never get caught going to your room? I'd have worried about that if I'd been him.'

'Well, he seldom came at night. He reckoned that people always suspect the worst if a man goes creeping around the corridors at night in his dressing-gown but no one bats an eyelid if a man wanders casually around fully dressed in broad daylight. Usually Alex would visit me in the early morning, around six. The room next to mine had been converted into a bathroom so I never had to worry about a maid arriving with hot water in the mornings, and in the winter I lit the fire myself to "spare the servants" – that went down well in the servants' hall – so in fact no housemaid ever came near my room until my bed was made between nine and ten. Early mornings were always the best time – or we'd meet sometimes in the early evening when everyone was changing for dinner . . . But when we met it was always as lovers, never as husband and wife. At the beginning that was all very exciting, but later I began to long for a whole night with him, like a real wife. However he always said that was impossible; some wretched vicar might blow his brains out or the Cathedral might burn down – and then there'd be hell to pay if the Bishop wasn't found sleeping in the right bed.

'I expect you can guess where all this is leading, can't you? I became discontented. The discontent came on gradually, so gradually that for a long time I wasn't aware of it – but the more successful I became as Alex's unofficial wife the more ardently I longed to be "Mrs Bishop" in the eyes of the world; it was as if our situation had had the seeds of its own destruction built into it from the beginning.

'The discontent affected my spiritual life – I expect that as a clergyman you were wondering about that. Well, I was fine after the marriage; Alex had told me that there was absolutely no possibility that we were committing adultery and so of course I believed him. Why not? Damn it, he *was* the Bishop! So I had no pangs of conscience on that score and turned up at Communion every week, but when I became unhappy . . . and the good fortune began to go sour . . . it wasn't so easy. I began to wonder dimly if I was being punished . . . But I didn't like to talk about my uncertainty to Alex – not just because I was ashamed of doubting him but because Alex, if the truth be told, isn't a born counsellor. He's sympathetic and he's not incapable of intuitive understanding, but he finds it hard to resist the temptation to make a brilliant speech which solves the problem by temporarily converting one to his point of view. I knew that if I raised any doubts Alex would efficiently talk me out of them, but I didn't want someone to talk; I wanted someone to listen, and there was absolutely no one I could turn to.

'Then a very odd thing happened. As I've already said, I'd never been maternal but one day when I was out in the town I saw this baby in a pram and suddenly I thought: if I was a real wife I'd have one of those. And immediately I pictured this adorable little boy with golden eyes saying, "Mummy! Mummy!" and holding out his arms to be loved. Can you believe it? I couldn't – not at first. I thought: how could I be so hopelessly sentimental? But then I saw that the baby symbolized all the important things of life which I'd longed for yet never managed to get. It wasn't just a case of being overwhelmed by the maternal instinct, although I think the urge to have a baby becomes more powerful as a childless woman grows older and realizes her time is running out – indeed I now suspect my early antipathy to motherhood began to be eroded by the maternal drive as soon as I entered my thirties. But I didn't think of that when I saw the baby in his pram. All I knew at that moment was that I was face to face again with the deprivation I had endured all my life. I'd been deprived of my father, deprived of any sort of normal existence in a family, deprived of a *real* husband – and now when I saw I was once more being cheated of love, a baby's love, a simple *uncomplicated* love devoid of lies and deceit, the kind of love most women take for granted – well, I couldn't bear it. I felt as if I were the kitten drowning in the rain-barrel all over again.

'I turned to Alex for comfort but he was useless – he just got upset. He said, "Do you think I don't want your child more than anything else in the world?" but that sort of emotional statement was no help to me at all; it only made me feel worse than ever, and finally we had a row. That upset Carrie. She always knew if anything was wrong between us. One day I found her crying. She wouldn't tell me at first what the matter was but eventually she said: "I expect you're wishing I was dead so that you could marry him properly." I felt dreadful then, absolutely annihilated. I flung my arms around her and said no, no, never, never . . . But of course I often did wonder how long she was going to go on.

'Can you see how ghastly this situation was becoming? I felt as if someone – God or the Devil – had taken a giant spoon and was slowly stirring us up. I began to feel so muddled, muddled about Carrie, muddled about Alex, muddled about the marriage . . . Finally I went off sex. Alex hated that – and not just for purely selfish reasons but because he thought, poor Alex, that there was so little he could really give me that the least he could do was satisfy me in bed. It took me a while to realize that, but once I understood – oh, I felt so guilty, so unhappy that *he* was unhappy, and of course I let him talk me back into bed in the end. It was then – when he seduced me back – that he . . . No, I can't put it into words. Some things really are too bizarre to be talked about. But he made sure the sex was better than ever.

'Yet can you see how the triangle was coming apart at the seams? We all loved one another, but we were none of us happy any more. By this time – it was last May – what I couldn't bear was seeing Carrie play Mrs Jardine in public – opening fêtes, presiding at charity committee meetings, getting all the attention from the important clerics and their wives at the big services . . . It was intolerable. I could feel myself becoming angrier and angrier, more and more bitter – *I* did all the hard work, *I* kept him happy in bed, *I* was the one he loved – and yet I was no one, just the ageing spinster who was rumoured to cherish a pathetic secret passion for the Bishop – oh, I often wanted to scream with rage and frustration, and all my feelings came to a head at the Coronation when Carrie got the wife's seat in the Abbey. Suddenly something snapped inside me and I poured out all my rage to them both . . . Then I hated myself because they were so dreadfully upset – and I knew at once not only how much I loved them but how absolutely *bound* I was to them both. It was loving the two of them at once – in such very different ways – which was so enslaving, and the weight of their joint love seemed to pin me in position so that there was no possibility of escape.

'Well, we patched up the quarrel, but I wouldn't go with them to London. I sat at home and thought and thought . . . I was in one of those awful states where one's thoughts go round and round in circles. Carrie could die tomorrow or she could live another twenty-five years. How much longer could I go on as I was? Was my marriage valid in God's sight or wasn't it? I could still tell myself it was but I was certainly beginning to wonder if I were entrapped in some frightful fraud. I was thirty-five years old, time was passing by and was I ever going to get my adorable little boy with the golden eyes or was he going to remain an unborn dream? I nearly went mad, torturing myself with those sort of thoughts, and all the time – all the time – I told myself: I can never leave them.

'And then . . . into this terrible situation when God – or the Devil – was really tightening the screws of my emotional rack . . . Well, you know what happened next, don't you – '

'Enter Dr Ashworth,' I said, 'on his shining white horse. Can I pour you some more tea?'

II

'Well, I thought I was on the rack before you arrived,' said Lyle as I refilled our cups, 'but that was nothing – that was just the introduction to the torture-chamber. I took one look at you and thought – much as I'd thought when I'd seen the baby in the pram: I'd like one of those. A handsome, young Canon with a golden future . . . I could see it all, right down to the new curtains I would order when I was Mrs Bishop at last in an episcopal palace which was really my own.

'But then the guilt hit me like a hammer and I despised myself. I thought: if I were a real wife I'd never succumb to such wicked dreams. And I felt so unfit, so . . . oh, so polluted by everything . . . But I made up my mind to fight the temptation very hard and be a good wife to Alex so that he and Carrie would never know how vile and disloyal my thoughts had been.

'But you weren't prepared to make fidelity easy for me, were you? My God, how you frightened me! You frightened us all. One of the worst moments was when I found you'd invaded my bedroom with the rose and the limericks. I kept all my contraceptive paraphernalia locked up in a jewel-box so I knew that was safe, but the tell-tale shawl was just stuffed in a drawer, and if you'd searched my room . . . the stains . . . I was practically gibbering with terror.

'However Alex calmed me down. We had a conference, he, Carrie and I, and he said, "There's only one way to handle this and that's to act as if nothing's wrong. The more hostile we get the more Ashworth is going to think we've something to hide." Then he said to me, "Be as cool to him as you always are with the infatuated chaplains and he'll soon see he's wasting his time.'

'Of course Alex knew you posed a more serious threat than an infatuated chaplain but he did trust me not to be unfaithful, and at that stage you were just a colossal nuisance. However at the same time – and this was *very* bizarre – he seemed to find you fascinating. He talked about you a lot. He was convinced you had serious problems, all to do with women and your father – well, I just thought he was looking at you and seeing his own reflection; I didn't take him seriously, and meanwhile I was busy trying to convince myself that you were merely a dashing Doctor of Divinity who fancies himself with the ladies. However after that lovely evening at the Staro Arms I found it was impossible to remain cool and detached. That kiss outside the Cathedral . . . God knows how I didn't pass out. I wanted to leap into bed with you and make love till dawn.

'But as soon as I got back to my room I was crucified by my guilt again. I felt I'd betrayed Alex, betrayed myself – and the next morning I knew I couldn't face Communion. Of course Alex smelt a rat. We had no opportunity for private conversation before you left, but later he demanded a meeting and it was frightful. He'd guessed what had happened and he was beside himself with jealousy and rage . . . But we ended up making love and afterwards he said: "You're my wife before God. Never forget that." And I didn't see how I ever could . . .

'Well, we were just recovering from your visit when the real ghastliness happened and you reappeared. I don't have to tell you how horrific that dinner was. It was bad enough that you'd guessed the truth, but what was worse was that you were obviously very drunk and very disturbed and might have bellowed your suspicions from the rooftops. I was also horrified to discover that Alex had been right in deducing you had problems, because it was now obvious that you were in a very bad way indeed.

'After you'd left Alex said, "We deny everything. The man's quite clearly unbalanced. It'll be his word against ours and we're the ones who'll be believed." But then the bizarre element surfaced again – what a lot of bizarre elements there are in this story – or is life itself simply more bizarre than anyone's prepared to admit? – and he began to worry himself into a state about you. He was frantic in case you'd killed yourself driving while drunk. He couldn't stop worrying. He kept saying it was all his fault and that his charism had been taken over by the Devil – oh God, it was frightful! I packed Carrie off to bed and sat up with him while be crucified himself with guilt – and *all over you*. He even said you were just the sort of son he'd always wanted – and this was only a couple of days after he'd said he hated you for trying to steal me! Honestly, Charles, there was only one person who was more mixed up about you than I was at that moment, and that was Alex Jardine.

'Well, finally I got fed up with all this self-flagellation – I was worn out by that time – and I suppose I betrayed impatience. Immediately he changed course; he remembered again that you were a rival and he said: "Oh by the way, here's something that'll interest you – Ashworth admitted he slept with Loretta yesterday – are you sure he didn't sleep with you last weekend?" '

'Oh, my dearest Lyle – '

'We had a huge row. I thought he was lying. Then I realized it was true. And I felt so horribly upset and muddled and hurt – '

'Darling, I – '

'It's all right, I don't care now whether you slept with her or not – well, I do care, but I don't think it's important. Obviously you were in some very peculiar emotional state, and if you did sleep with her I'm sure it was a moral lapse you'd never normally have. But when Alex told me I felt absolutely slaughtered – and of course I was livid with him too for accusing me of infidelity when I'd tried so hard to be faithful to him.

'The next thing that happened was that Alex discovered you were with the Fordites and he nearly expired with relief. But he was still terrified you might run to Lang with your suspicions when you'd recovered, and of course he *hated* the thought of Father Darrow knowing everything. Alex worried and worried . . . How he kept going with his work I've no idea. I turned up at the services as usual but that was just to keep up appearances. I was so confused, so unhappy . . . I didn't see how I could go on much longer, and one afternoon I went to the Cathedral to beg God to help me, but I couldn't pray, I was so cut off. I just knelt there in the chapel and said God, God, God, over and over in my mind . . . It was as if I'd dialled a number and was listening to the bell ringing – and I didn't really expect an answer, but then the miracle happened because someone picked up the receiver at the other end of the line.

'You came in. Do you remember me saying it was like a sign? I knew at once I had to leave Alex, but the only trouble was I couldn't see how I was ever going to do it.

'I told Alex I'd seen you. I didn't think we'd been seen by anyone I knew, but the last thing I wanted was for him to hear of the meeting from someone else. I also thought he'd appreciate my honesty, but he didn't and there was an awful scene because he couldn't believe the meeting had been accidental. I tried to tell him the marriage was over, but I couldn't . . . He had such power over me, I can't describe it, maybe no words could ever describe it, all I can say is that I had to give in to him, *had to* . . . And so it went on.

'Well, as the days passed Alex realized you hadn't told Lang and he began to feel better. So did Carrie. But I . . . oh Charles, this is where the going gets very difficult – '

I tried to put my arms around her but she pushed me away. 'No,' she said, 'you don't understand. The going can't be made smooth by a well-meaning kiss.' As she spoke she rose to her feet and turned her back on me; I sensed she was nerving herself to confront some profound ordeal.

'Tell me what I can do,' I said. 'If you want my help in changing your situation at the palace – '

'It's already changed irrevocably.' As she succeeded in summoning the nerve she needed she turned to face me again. 'My life at the palace has ended. There's no choice now. I have to leave.'

I knew what she was going to say a second before she said it. 'You're – '

'I'm pregnant,' she said, and covered her face with her hands.

III

In three seconds I saw it all, the inscrutability of God, the redemption of past tragedy, the backbreaking road into a barely conceivable future. Time completed some eerie circle; I was my father, Lyle was my mother and the embryo was me, waiting for the one man who had the will to give it the future God required. Yet all was subtly changed; I was not my father, Lyle was not my mother and the embryo was not and could never be me. The game was the same but the cards had been reshuffled and it was hard to perceive the dimensions of the hand I had been dealt. All I knew was that I was being called to play that hand. Of that I had no doubt whatsoever.

I touched the cross on my chest and took Lyle in my arms as she started to cry.

'I'll help you,' I said.

She clung to me wordlessly. I stroked her hair, and then the shock began to bludgeon me, hammering my mind until I felt almost too battered to think. But I managed to form a prayer. I asked that I might be granted the grace to perceive the way forward, and the familiar words 'Let thy will, not mine, be done,' were immediately comforting.

'Let's be practical for a moment,' I said at last. 'First of all, are you quite sure about this?'

'Yes, although it hasn't been medically confirmed.' She drew away from me to extract a handkerchief from her bag. 'I'm never more than twenty-four hours late. I knew at once what had happened. I felt different too, couldn't face coffee, it was just as if someone had thrown a spanner in the works and put everything slightly out of alignment.' She blew her nose. 'Today I went to the Marie Stopes Clinic and asked them if they could do a pregnancy examination, but they said it was too soon . . . Yet I know the baby's there.'

I thought of false pregnancies and the power of the mind over the body. 'When do you think it happened?'

'The day I met you in the Cathedral.'

'But what happened to the contraception?'

'I didn't use it – that's why I know exactly when the disaster occurred. It was one of those rare occasions when he came to my room at night.

Usually I always put the cap in before I go to bed so that when he arrives in the early morning I don't have to dash off unromantically to the bathroom, but that night although I was ready for bed I hadn't put the cap in and I was caught by surprise. Then before I could put matters right we were having our row over you, and afterwards . . . when he began to make love to me . . . oh Charles, I felt so helpless, so muddled, so absolutely *despairing*, that I didn't care about the contraception, I was beyond caring – '

'Have you told him about the baby?'

'No.' She found the packet of cigarettes in her bag and clumsily shook one free. 'I haven't told either of them – I felt I couldn't cope with their reactions when I could barely cope with my own. As you've probably realized by now, the great characteristic about my relationship with the Jardines is that I'm always the one who has to cope. Nobody copes with me – and of course that's why I'm here. I felt you could cope, tell me what to do – '

'How do you feel about the child?'

'I'm appalled. Sanity's reasserted itself, I can see my surrender to the maternal drive as irresponsible behaviour and now I'm visualizing myself burdened not with an adorable little boy with golden eyes – that was just a sentimental dream – but a plain little female crosspatch. Unless, of course, I have an abortion – '

'Absolutely not!' I said inevitably, and saw time encircling us both as the past repeated itself in a series of endless permutations. 'It would be utterly wrong!'

'Oh, it's so damn easy for you to stand there and say that – you're a man!' cried Lyle, taking a very different line from my mother. 'I don't think any man has the right to preach sanctimoniously about abortion!'

I had been unprepared for this feminist shaft. It made me realize how imperfectly I still knew her. 'No man has the right to preach sanctimoniously about anything,' I said, 'but I'm not preaching and I'm not being sanctimonious. I'm trying to give you realistic advice. This is the child of a man you loved and it's a child that in the past you've very much wanted. Wouldn't an abortion be a psychological as well as a moral disaster here?'

Her defiance crumbled; she broke down utterly. 'Oh God, I'll never survive this, never – I thought I could but now I don't see how I ever can – I can't cope, Charles, I just can't cope – '

'But I can,' I said. 'I've been preparing for this for a long time, perhaps all my life. I can cope with you and I can cope with that child. You're going to marry me, Lyle.'

IV

I told her briefly about my parentage. She was amazed, stunned and finally appalled as she saw the situation from my own perspective.

'But, Charles . . . Oh God, I don't know what to think! Obviously I've never understood the first thing about you – a man who could make such an offer without being coerced must be so utterly different from the sort of man I imagined you to be – oh no, I can't let you do it, I can't – your offer's the most wonderful piece of idealism, but – '

'What's wrong with idealism?' I said, holding her close as she broke down again. 'If there were no idealism we'd all be grovelling around in the mud with the animals. And anyway the best sort of idealism, the workable kind, is always firmly grounded in reality. I think I'm being exceedingly practical. I know you're the woman I want. You come to me with this huge handicap but as far as I can see I'm in a unique position to cope with it successfully. Of course the marriage will be plagued by the most unusual difficulties, particularly at first, but I think that with strength and will and by the grace of God the difficulties can be overcome. Why not? I'm supposed to be a Christian. Clearly I'm now being called to live out the Christian message of love and forgiveness in a very special way and besides . . . loving you as I do, how could I conceivably walk away?'

She could not answer. She merely clung to me again with a new intensity, and I knew how my father had felt long ago when he had witnessed my mother's overpowering gratitude and relief.

But I steered a different course from my father. I said: 'We need help and we need it now. I want you to come with me to see Father Darrow.'

V

Darrow was still out when I telephoned so I took Lyle first to the Blue Boar where I confirmed her reservation and ordered some sandwiches.

'I couldn't eat,' she said.

'Well, I can and you certainly should. Make an effort,' I said firmly, remembering how ruthless Darrow had been with me on the subject of nourishment, so we sat in the lounge and ate chicken sandwiches. Lyle managed half a round and I consumed the rest; we divided the tea more equally between us.

'I've changed my mind about being keen to meet this man,' said Lyle at last. 'I quite understand why you need to talk to your spiritual director about the future, and obviously I have to be there too because I'm now part of that future but to be frank I don't like the idea of him at all.'

'I assure you there's no need to be nervous.'

'I'm not nervous. I just feel that any woman can't help but regard a monk as a personal insult. What happened to his wife? Alex dug up the fact that he'd once been married.'

'I've no idea what happened to her – Darrow's told me very little about himself, but that's in accordance with all the rules for good counselling. And talking of counselling . . .' I mentioned that Darrow had been looking for a sympathetic nun but Lyle again displayed antipathy.

'I couldn't talk about this to any woman,' she said. 'I don't even like women – apart from darling Carrie, and I don't like her particularly, I just love her.'

This statement was so convoluted, so indicative of mental distress and psychological difficulty, that I thought it wiser to say nothing. I wondered how Darrow would approach the problem.

We drove to Grantchester, and as I turned the car into the Fordites' drive Lyle shuddered.

'Darling . . .' Halting the car I leant over to give her a kiss. 'Try not to regard this particular monk as a personal insult! I'm sure he's not a misogynist.'

'Then what's he doing shut up in this place? How I hate the thought of people being incarcerated in closed orders! It's so damned eerie and unnatural.'

I began to be seriously worried. All counsellors had their failures, and Darrow himself had made it clear that he preferred not to counsel women.

The happy young monk who had welcomed me to the house on he occasion of my first encounter with Darrow greeted us cheerfully and showed us into the Visitors' Parlour. 'Father Abbot's just back,' he said. 'He won't keep you long.'

'Poor old Darrow,' said Lyle when we were alone. 'I hope he won't wilt at the prospect of coping with your next huge problem.'

'Darrow's tough enough to cope with anything.'

'Well, he can cope with you but he'd better not try to cope with me! The last thing I want is to be coped with by someone who's given up sex.'

The hostile note in her voice was now unmistakable, and I was just searching feverishly for the words which would soothe her when footsteps rang out in the hall.

Lyle at once looked as if she were about to face a firing squad. 'It's him, isn't it?'

'Lyle, think of him as a friend – '

'But he's not a friend,' she said, very pale. 'He's the enemy, I know he is, I know it – '

And then in walked my exorcist to confront all the demons I had so persistently failed to recognize.

TWENTY-FOUR

'The power of self-deception is great in the case of all men, but I incline to think that it is greatest in the case of a popular official such as a Bishop, who never hears anything but his own voice, and the sycophantic acclamations which it evokes.'

HERBERT HENSLEY HENSON
Bishop of Durham 1920–1939
Retrospect of an Unimportant Life

I

I had a surprise when I saw Darrow because he had not yet changed back into his habit after his outing in the world, and he was still wearing his clerical suit. The monk's habit had created an illusion that his personality merely formed part of a communal identity, but in clerical clothes the illusion of conformity was lost and his individuality became striking. He looked even more authoritative, even more confident – and he looked restless too, like an adventurer who was accustomed to sailing regularly in uncharted waters. It was as if his cool analytical serenity, which was such a feature of his monk's character, had been given a brasher, more volatile edge, and suddenly for the first time I could see him not only as a chaplain in the Navy but as a novice driving his superiors to such distraction that he had been exiled to Yorkshire to milk cows.

Beside me I heard Lyle's sharp intake of breath, and as I realized that shock had temporarily overcome her hostility I knew she was astonished because Darrow was so different from the 'white-haired portly old buffer' whom she had probably imagined. Darrow himself took one look at her and stopped dead. I stepped forward.

'Father, may I introduce Miss Lyle Christie. Lyle, this is father Jon Darrow.'

Darrow said swiftly, 'How do you do, Miss Christie. Please sit down.' He did not offer her his hand but instead pulled out a chair from the table for her.

'Thank you.' Lyle sounded very cool, very suspicious. I knew the meeting had started badly but I was unable to locate the source of the awkwardness until Darrow said: 'If I'd known Miss Christie was with you, Charles, I'd have paused to change into my habit. A monk should be a monk, not a somewhat eccentric clergyman with an ostentatious cross on his chest – it creates a disconcerting impression. Now, before I leave you in order to change, can I offer you some refreshment? Perhaps Miss Christie would like some tea.'

Lyle firmly declined the offer of tea. I uneasily declined the broader offer of refreshment.

'Then if you'll excuse me for a brief interval – ' He was gone.

As soon as the door had closed Lyle swivelled to face me. 'Why on earth didn't you warn me he was like that?'

'He's a striking sort of chap, isn't he? My father thought he should have been a lawyer.'

'A *lawyer*? Good heavens, no! He should have been an actor – I can see him as a very sinister Prospero in *The Tempest*, or possibly as a very hypnotic Claudius in *Hamlet*, the sort of Claudius who makes it crystal clear why Gertrude could think of nothing but going to bed with him – '

'My dearest Lyle!' I was astonished. It had never occurred to me that a woman might see Darrow as sexually attractive. I had assumed he would seem too chilly, too austere, but I had forgotten that woman are susceptible to an authoritative manner, particularly when that manner is wielded with an air of buccaneering self-confidence.

'I can think of nothing more bizarre,' Lyle was saying fiercely, 'than that a man like that should be a monk. It must be an act – that's *his* glittering image! – and underneath it I'm sure he's not monkish at all. Did you see how he absolutely recoiled when he saw me? Obviously I represent the biggest possible temptation to him – Jezebel reborn!'

I decided the time had come to take a firm line. 'The reason why Darrow stopped dead when he saw you,' I said, '(and I deny that he recoiled) was first because he was genuinely surprised to see you here and second because he knew straight away you'd dream up all kinds of ridiculous fantasies about him unless he was wearing his sexless monk's habit!'

'But how can a man like that live without sex?'

'Darling, I hate to say it but I'm afraid you're prejudiced here by the fact that you've been on intimate terms with a cleric who couldn't cope with chastity – '

'That's right – throw Alex in my face!' cried Lyle, having worked herself up into a nervous rage. 'I wish to hell I hadn't come to this beastly place!' And she burst into tears.

I was still trying to comfort her, still wondering how on earth Darrow was going to deal with us, still reminding myself that I could hardly expect to live happily ever after in a problem-free paradise, when Darrow himself walked back into the room.

Lyle leapt to her feet and marched up to him. 'I think you'd better see Charles alone,' she said. 'I'm not running away – I just don't want a monk probing around in my past, that's all, and to prove I'm not a coward I'll tell you straight away that I'm pregnant and Charles has said he'll marry me and of course he's quite mad and mustn't be allowed to ruin himself like that. I don't care what happens to me, I'm too rotten to bother about, but Charles is good and decent and he doesn't deserve to be dragged down in this vile mess – and if you're as wonderful as everyone's always saying you are, you'll want to step in and save him from me.'

'Lyle – ' I began in despair but I was interrupted.

'Miss Christie,' said Darrow, 'what I want is of absolutely no importance here. The important thing is what God wants. Are you an apostate?'

'No!' shouted Lyle, tears streaming down her face.

'Then you'll accept that your first duty is to God, and that duty at this moment is to be calm so that you can hear Him if he wishes to communicate with you, Charles, give her your cross. Miss Christie, take the cross and hold it tightly . . . That's right . . . and keep holding it . . . Yes, you're being tortured by the demons of shame, guilt, despair, rage and terror, but no demon can withstand the power of Christ – yes, keep holding it . . . and now sit down here . . . Charles, you sit down too and put your arm around her . . . That's it . . . and now I'm going to sit down beside you both and we're all going to pray that in the name of Jesus Christ Our Lord these demons may be cast out and vanquished . . . and not just for your sake, Miss Christie, but for Charles's sake and for the sake of the child . . . Close your eyes and breathe very deeply . . . and evenly . . . and listen to my silent prayer, listen for any word from God, listen and listen very carefully . . . Lord, hear our prayer.'

Lyle had squeezed her eyes shut and was shivering against me as I held her. I longed to tell Darrow to help the healing process with the power which he could channel through his hands, but although I never spoke he still heard me. He said severely, 'Charles, concentrate on our prayer, please,' and I said at once, 'I'm sorry.' At first I thought concentration would be impossible, but Darrow's training had not been wasted, and after praying hard I opened my eyes as he opened his. The words were faith and trust. I had heard them clearly.

Beside me Lyle gave another shudder and opened her eyes.

Darrow leant forward. 'Did you hear?'

'No, I heard nothing.' She rubbed her eyes. 'But I know I have to have faith in God and trust Him to look after me.'

'That's it. What did you hear, Charles?'

'You were praying for faith and trust. I believe that I must trust you to help us and that I must have faith that I'll be able to serve God here to the best of my ability.'

'Exactly. And it's God we all have to serve, isn't it, Miss Christie? I must serve God by helping you both to reach a correct response to this terrible ordeal, Charles must serve God by doing what he believes God's calling him to do and you must serve God by channelling all your energy into perceiving what he requires of you.'

Lyle said shakily, still clutching my cross, 'I want to marry Charles. But I'm afraid that's selfish and wicked and may not be God's will at all.'

'It's not selfish and wicked to want to find the best possible solution to your dilemma. But what you must be certain of is that marriage with Charles is the best solution.'

There was a silence. Then Lyle sobbed, 'Oh, Alex, Alex . . .' and once more broke down in tears.

III

'Hold her close,' said Darrow to me, and I was suddenly aware of his care that there should be no physical contact between himself and Lyle. I drew her to me again and kissed her cheek. She was still clutching the cross, and as I kept my right arm around her shoulders I covered her left hand with my own to confirm her grip.

When she was calmer she said to Darrow, 'Alex is such a good man – you mustn't condemn him.'

'It's certainly not for me to condemn him,' said Darrow, 'or for Charles either. Clearly we're dealing here with a tragedy where people have suffered greatly, but although I talk of suffering and tragedy, Miss Christie, you'll know as a Christian that out of every disaster can come a new beginning, a new hope, a new faith – and not just for you but for the Jardines too.'

'But they can't manage without me!'

'Beware of falling into the trap of thinking that there's only one possible future, a future which is unfavourable to the Jardines. Such an assumption is actually a form of vanity; the truth is that no one's indispensable, so look to the future with humility and then I think you may be able to hope – and not only for yourself but for them as well. Think of our prayer just now. You must have faith in God and trust him to look after all three of you in the difficult days ahead.'

Lyle seemed soothed. After blowing her nose on her handkerchief she said in a low voice, 'My marriage isn't valid, is it?'

'Ah,' said Darrow, 'yes, let's sort out exactly where you stand. If you married Dr Jardine in good faith you'd be adjudged an innocent party now that the marriage has turned out to be invalid. You would only fall into serious error if you went on with the marriage once you knew it to be no marriage at all.'

'So it was all a lie.'

'I suspect we'd come closest to the truth if we called it an enormous piece of self-deception by Dr Jardine. Let me first explain why the marriage can't be valid. The defect is probably not in the marriage ceremony itself; it's arguable that in certain circumstances it might be possible to contract a marriage valid in the sight of God without the assistance of Church and state. For instance, if a man and woman were marooned on a desert island and wished to live in a Christian marriage I don't think they could be called sinners if they exchanged vows reverently before God and set about being a good husband and wife. Dr Jardine's father and stepmother apparently considered themselves on a desert island in Putney and certainly she would have been regarded as the old man's common-law wife, but their spiritual position is debatable and would depend very much on old Mr Jardine's motives. However possibly he acted sincerely and reverently. We'll never know. What we do know is that old Mr Jardine was free to marry but his son, unfortunately, was not.'

'But Alex thought – he was so certain – and Mrs Jardine, his stepmother, she thought – and she was so certain – '

'I'm sure they were sincere in believing they were right. But old Mrs Jardine was evidently capable of considerable spiritual elasticity – to put it kindly – and Dr Jardine had apparently performed his famous trick of converting black into white with an elasticity which wasn't spiritual at all.'

'But Carrie refused him his marital rights – Martin Luther thought – '

'Martin Luther wasn't God. Nor is that view of his on divorce consistent with the law of England.'

'But if the spiritual core of the marriage has been destroyed – '

'I know there's a vocal party within the Church which believes that various circumstances can destroy the core of a marriage and constitute a spiritual dissolution, but refusal of marital rights isn't one of those circumstances, and despite Mr A. P. Herbert's new law it isn't by itself a ground for divorce. Moreover I think it's impossible to argue here that the core of the marriage had been destroyed when Mrs Jardine was still standing by her husband through thick and thin in order to save his career. An aspect of the marriage had certainly broken down, but in every other respect one could hardly find a more loving and loyal wife, and indeed I would judge it indisputable that Dr Jardine had no remedy at law.'

'But before God – the compassion and forgiveness of Christ – '

'I trust we'll all be praying that God looks upon Dr Jardine with compassion and forgiveness, but it's quite unthinkable in spiritual terms, Miss Christie, that a bishop should be able to contract a valid marriage after an informal divorce by mutual consent. In fact many would say he couldn't justifiably remarry even after a formal divorce.'

All Lyle said was, 'He was so sure.'

'Yes,' said Darrow, 'there was indeed great self-deception. He deceived himself into thinking that his marriage was spiritually null. He deceived himself into thinking that any marriage could be possible after an informal divorce. He deceived himself into thinking he was above the law of England and he deceived himself into thinking that a cohabitation bordering on bigamy was acceptable in the eyes of God. He also deceived both you and his wife by allowing you to think he was entitled as a bishop to make up his own spiritual rules as he went along and negotiate with God as he thought fit. This is the sin of pride and shows a degree of spiritual unhealthiness conducive to gross error.'

Lyle was too overwhelmed to do more than whisper, 'What's to become of him?' She started to weep again.

'That's a question which none of us can answer, but like you he has a choice of futures and we must all pray that he's guided to take the right one. However at present you're more important than Dr Jardine. Do you want to continue talking now or would you prefer to rest and return tomorrow?'

'What more is there to say?' Lyle put down the cross in order to wipe away her tears. 'I know now I'm free to marry Charles – I know the truth in its entirety at last – '

'Yes, you do. But does Charles?'

She stared at him. So did I. I demanded at once: 'What do you mean?'

Darrow stood up, moved around the other side of the table and sat down opposite us in the counsellor's conventional position. All he said was, ' "Strait is the gate and narrow is the way".'

The signal passed between us and suddenly I felt the dread sink to the pit of my stomach, but Lyle did not understand. She looked at him fearfully. 'What do you mean?'

'Never forget,' said Darrow to her, 'that I want above all to help you and Charles to reach a correct solution here in accordance with God's will. And remember that this can't be done unless we know the whole truth.'

'But I've told Charles the whole truth! I have, haven't I, Charles?'

'It certainly sounded like the whole truth to me,' said my voice. I sounded emphatic but strained.

'Then in that case, Miss Christie,' said Darrow, 'you'll have no objection to enlightening me on one or two points which I still find obscure.'

Lyle continued to look at him fearfully. Then she said to me: 'I'm not sure what he means, Charles, but he seems to be implying I've deceived you in some way.'

'I don't think he means that,' I said with care. 'After all, he doesn't know what you've told me. Think of him as holding up a torch to illuminate the dark corners – and always with your welfare in mind.'

She considered that. 'All right,' she said finally to Darrow. 'Ask away. What do you want to know?'

'Well, the first and most obvious question,' said Darrow with great gentleness, 'is: when did you decide to have this baby?'

IV

I thought she was going to faint. I felt unsteady myself. Before she could reply I said rapidly to Darrow, 'It was an accident.'

But Darrow's first concern was for Lyle. 'Charles, go into the hall and ask Barnabas to fetch a glass of water.'

'No!' gasped Lyle. She clung to me. 'Don't leave me alone with him!'

Darrow himself promptly called for the glass of water.

'Now, Miss Christie,' he said as he returned, 'have you considered your reply?'

She leant forward, her forearms on the table, her face hard and set. 'I'm not telling you the details of my sex-life. You must get your vicarious thrills in some other way.'

'Lyle!' I exclaimed but Darrow said tersely, 'Be quiet, Charles. Miss Christie – '

'You're prejudiced against women!' cried Lyle. 'You're seeing me as a sex-obsessed bitch who's ruined one good man and is about to ruin another!'

'This is the demon of your guilt,' said Darrow. 'Pick up that cross again from the table.'

'You're trying to prove to Charles that I'm just a calculating adulteress!'

'This is the demon of your shame and self-hatred. Pick up that cross.'

Lyle leapt to her feet and shouted, 'Shut up! You're nothing but a fraud, hiding here in this vile house because you're frightened that if you went out into the real world you'd seduce every woman in sight, so how dare you have the bloody impertinence to interfere in my private life, how dare you! Well, I won't let you vent your frustration on me like that, I won't let you destroy my last hope of happiness, *I won't let any man wreck my life* – '

'This is the demon of your rage,' said Darrow, 'but the rage isn't in fact directed against me. Tell me, how many other men apart from Dr Jardine have so painfully disappointed you?'

Lyle gasped, grabbed the cross and hurled it at him, but as I leapt appalled to my feet Darrow caught the cross and sprang up so violently that his chair fell backwards with a crash.

'How many women did you put through hell before you castrated yourself with that bloody habit?' screamed Lyle, face contorted, her whole frame shuddering. 'I hate you, *I hate you*, I HATE YOU!'

I tried to reach her but I was paralysed with shock. I felt as if some huge force had exploded, leaving a chasm between us, but the next moment Darrow was bridging the abyss. Moving swiftly around the table he said with great strength: 'This torment must end. In the name of God – in the name of Jesus Christ – THIS TORMENT MUST END!' And he slipped the chain of the cross over her head as she flailed her arms to push him away.

'No, no, no – ' She was screaming very loudly, but when he took her in his arms at last, the screams ceased, her whole body shuddered convulsively and she fainted.

V

The young monk arrived a second later with the glass of water.

Darrow said sharply, 'Get the brandy.'

'Yes, Father.' He thrust the glass into my outstretched hand and ran.

Darrow had lifted Lyle on to the long table. He moved swiftly and efficiently, laying her out full length and patting her waist with caution. 'Thank heavens – no sadistic corset,' was his only comment.

I roused myself from my stupefaction, set down the glass and demanded: 'Father, what on earth's going on?'

'It's all right, she'll recover in a minute. Now before she comes round give me some quick answers to some quick questions. The contraception – is she claiming it failed?'

'There was one occasion when she left herself unprotected.'

'Was Jardine aware of the omission?'

'She implied not.'

'Do either of the Jardines know of her condition?'

'No. Incidentally the pregnancy isn't yet confirmed but she seems very certain. Father, I still don't understand what's happening – '

'Don't worry, Charles, I don't really believe this is a conspiracy between all three of them to produce a wanted child, but we've got to be sure . . . Ah, she's coming round. Now keep quiet and leave this to me – yes, come in, Barnabas – Charles, pour out a little brandy, please.'

'Will that be all, Father?' said Barnabas, intrigued by the woman prostrate on the table.

'Yes. Out,' said Darrow, and Barnabas fled.

Lyle moaned.

'You're all right,' said Darrow, stooping over her. 'Have some water first. Then you can have brandy.'

Lyle said: 'Am I having a miscarriage?' She sounded dazed and childlike.

'No,' said Darrow firmly. 'Give her the water, Charles.'

She drank obediently and after she had sipped the brandy Darrow said: 'See if you can sit up without feeling faint.'

She tried. I was still supporting her. When there were no ill effects she looked at Darrow. 'I said terrible things to you,' she whispered. 'I remember.'

Once more Darrow used the ancient symbolic language to express profound psychological truths. He said with complete authority: 'The demons were very strong but they're gone now. You're not well yet but you're going to be well because now the healing can begin.'

'Supposing the demons come back?'

'They can't so long as you're in touch with God. When you lost touch the demons were free to walk into your soul, but you won't lose touch now.' He added to me, 'Give her another sip of brandy.'

Lyle sipped and said, 'I feel better.'

'Good. Charles, help her back into her chair.' He made no move to return to his own chair but leant informally against the edge of the table.

Lyle said suddenly to him. 'I want to talk to you.'

'You want to tell me the truth about the baby?'

'But you already know, don't you?'

'Charles doesn't know and we both have to look after Charles here.'

'I love Charles,' said Lyle, still speaking directly to Darrow. I might have been a hundred miles away. 'I want to be the best possible wife to him.'

'And that's why you must be honest, isn't it? He's given you the gift of his love and you must give him the gift of your honesty to prove you're worthy of him. Very well, let's talk about this baby.'

Looking steadily at Darrow Lyle said, 'I don't know exactly when he was conceived.'

'You gave up the contraception?'

'Yes. I wanted to get pregnant.'

'The only way out, was it?'

She nodded. Her eyes shone with tears.

'Can you tell me how you reached this decision that pregnancy was the only solution to your problems?'

Lyle said, 'I'd gone to the chapel in the Cathedral but I couldn't pray because I was so cut off. Then Charles came. I knew then I had to leave the Jardines, but I couldn't see how I was ever going to be strong enough to end the marriage. Charles doesn't understand this part – the bizarre part – and I can't put into words the quality of the hold Alex had over me, but – '

'When did the love-making change?'

'Earlier this year. I went off sex. I felt in such a muddle about everything. But Alex talked me out of it. *Alex talked* – ' She broke off.

' – and then the sex seemed exciting in a new way.'

She nodded painfully again. 'I can't explain to Charles, I don't want to explain – '

'Yet he must know. Otherwise he'll torture himself by trying to guess what you're concealing.' He turned to me. 'I'm afraid Dr Jardine was again abusing his charism. He used hypnosis to enhance his power and then channelled the power into the sexual act with the result that the act became not so much an expression of love as an erotic subjugation of a prisoner by her captor . . . Do you recognize that description, Lyle?'

She managed to nod.

'Very well, we've explained to Charles that your mind was clouded and your will impaired by this hypnotic and profoundly unhealthy relationship. However when you met Charles in the Cathedral he temporarily acted as a barrier between you and Dr Jardine with the result that you were able to catch a glimpse of your situation in its true perspective – and then you knew the relationship had to end. But once Charles was gone – once the barrier had been removed – you were again vulnerable to Dr Jardine's will.'

'Yes, that night when he came to my room I knew I wasn't going to be able to refuse him, but by chance the contraception wasn't in place, and . . . suddenly I saw that all I had to do was nothing. I was incapable of taking positive action by saying: "I can't go on"; I was only capable of remaining silent, being passive, and while he was making love to me I thought: if I had a baby he couldn't keep me, not all the talk in the world would keep me, if I had a baby I'd have to go. And I made up my mind never to use the contraception again. Poor little baby, I did want him so much but I should never have conceived him under those circumstances – so wrong – I shouldn't have done it – '

'It's easy to be wise in retrospect, not so easy when one's enduring a desperate crisis . . . How did you see the future evolving once you were pregnant?'

'I thought I could get Charles to marry me. I knew I'd have to tell him I was pregnant – I never thought of deceiving him on a really colossal scale – but I decided to tell him the pregnancy was the result of a single ghastly lapse.'

'Tell me how you set about coaxing Charles to propose.'

'I kept saying how calculating and sex-obsessed I was, implying he wouldn't want to know me once he knew what I was really like – I thought that would make him even keener. Attractive men are always fascinated by a woman who can give them a challenge.'

'But even so, surely you were worried that he'd baulk at the last fence when he heard about the baby?'

'Oh yes – I thought I'd have to force his hand at the end, but you see, I was luring him up the garden path until I could deliver the *coup de grace*. And then . . . Oh God, oh God, he forestalled me – '

'How?'

'He told me about his parents,' said Lyle crying. 'He talked about his ideals, he stood by me, he lived his faith – oh, and then I felt so ashamed, so mean, so cheap, so absolutely vile – I could hardly speak I was so crucified with guilt, but I knew then I loved him. I hadn't loved him before. I'd found him physically attractive, but the truth was – '

'Yes – one last hurdle, Lyle – '

'I hated him, I was so angry with him, I wanted to make him pay – '

'And that was because – '

'He slept with Loretta,' said Lyle, tears streaming down her cheeks. 'I thought he'd just been amusing himself with me, I thought I'd been deceived, I thought he'd let me down – men have always let me down, even Daddy let me down, going away and never coming back, and I couldn't bear Charles betraying me when I liked him so much. I thought: I'll have my revenge on him, I'll make him pay, I'll tell him he's got to marry me or else I'll create a scandal by saying the baby's his. I was all set to do it, I'd drummed up the nerve, and there I was, mad with anger and loathing and wickedness, absolutely *infested* by those demons you recognized just now, and then . . . What was it you said at the beginning of our conversation – '

'No demon can withstand the power of Christ.'

'Yes, Charles was so good, so straight, so Christian – the demons all fell away and I was able to love him but then the demons came back, they tried to reclaim me because they knew I was so undeserving of a man like that, they did reclaim me but by a miracle you cast them out – oh Father, help me, please help me, I've been so sick – '

Darrow said at once, 'If you can see that, you're already getting better.'

'I just wish so much that all the terrible things I've done could be wiped out!'

'That may not be so difficult as you fear. Once a true repentance has been achieved the way's open for the start of a new life.'

'But not with Charles. There'll be no new life with Charles now – I'm going to lose him, aren't I, Father? I'm going to lose what I want the most and it'll be a just punishment for all my lies and deception and wickedness.'

Darrow said nothing. He merely turned to face me, and I shall always remember that at the end when the final decision had to be made he was not only silent but inscrutable. The decision had to be mine and mine alone.

'If you can forgive me for Loretta,' I said to Lyle, 'I can forgive you for wanting revenge. And even if you can't forgive me I'd still forgive you anyway now that I know just how deeply you've suffered.'

'Oh Charles – Charles – '

'Let's go back to the hotel and make some wedding plans.'

TWENTY-FIVE

'The retrospect has much in it that is humiliating and that calls for repentance; but Christ, in His limitless mercy, has endured me all these long years, and I cannot doubt that He will be with me to the end.'

Letters of Herbert Hensley Henson
Bishop of Durham 1920–1939
ed. E. F. BRALEY

I

Lyle and I did talk about our wedding but not for long. She was exhausted, and at nine we parted in the foyer of the hotel. The following morning I rescued her from the dining-room where she had been trying to eat breakfast and we returned to Grantchester; she went for a walk around the village while I saw Darrow on my own.

'She's still tired,' I said in response to his opening question, 'but she's much calmer.' I hesitated before adding, 'How soon did you realize what was going on in her mind?'

'I could tell at once she was in difficulty, and when I realized she was using me to express all her anger towards the opposite sex I wondered if you yourself could be immune from that hostility . . . She needs much more help, Charles.'

'Did you find a nun?'

'Yes. Fiftyish, widowed, very intuitive, very humane.'

'I only wish I could believe that Lyle will ever agree to see her.'

'I think that when the present appalling tensions have eased she may well feel a new need to confide.'

'How I wish you could continue to counsel her!'

'It would be too dangerous. You yourself witnessed the sexual edge the scene developed when she was disturbed, and if I attempted to counsel her on my own . . . No, Charles, such a session would only confuse her – and incidentally it would be extremely unwise for me. Monks are very ordinary men in many ways and were quite definitely not designed by God to counsel pretty women on their private lives.' He smiled at me before adding, 'Outline your next battle-plan.'

'We're going down to Starbridge. She needs to collect some essential possessions and I think it's best if she parts from the Jardines as soon as possible. I'll see him on my own first, of course.'

'How do you think he'll behave?'

'That's exactly the question I was going to ask you. What do you think, Father? I'm not asking for a demonstration of clairvoyance now, just a prediction based on the evidence.'

'Most of the time that's all clairvoyance is anyway.' Darrow considered for a moment. 'He'll be stunned – but not, I think, by the news that Lyle's leaving him; he must have been well aware for some time that they were in difficulties. But he'll be stunned by the news of the child, and the first question he's going to ask is how often he can see it. This is where you meet the problem of what part the Jardines are going to play in your marriage, Charles.'

'Lyle accepts that there must be a complete break,' I said, 'and I confess that on this point I'm implacable. They've got to stay well away, and if they think they can come and coo regularly over my child in its pram they'll have to think again.'

Darrow examined his Abbot's ring and was silent.

'Am I being unChristian?' I said uneasily.

'Not necessarily. What do you think?'

'I think God's called me to make this marriage – which will certainly begin by being very difficult – and therefore my first duty is to make sure the marriage works. And I don't believe it'll work if the Jardines are allowed in.'

'I must admit,' said Darrow, 'that I think this is the only conclusion you can reach while you and Lyle are both recovering from your ordeals and learning to love each other, but guard against inflexibility, Charles. Remember what difficulties your father's inflexibility caused when he was unable to jettison his conviction that you were an exact copy of Romaine.'

Now it was my turn to be silent. Finally Darrow asked, 'What are you going to do about the wedding?'

'That's another difficult problem. We're both agreed we want the quickest, quietest wedding possible – I shall get a special licence, of course – but from the point of view of gossip it'll look odd if Lyle's not married from the palace.'

'Will it? Don't lose sight of the fact that she's their employee, not their daughter, and employers and employees frequently fall out. Of course there's bound to be some degree of tittle-tattle if the Jardines aren't present at the wedding, but people have short memories and it'll soon be forgotten. The great thing is to behave confidently, as if you're taking the most natural course in the world – and that leads me to my next suggestion:

why not get Dr Lang to marry you in the chapel at Lambeth? What could be more thoroughly respectable than being married by the Archbishop of Canterbury? And that would also help to explain the Jardines' absence; everyone knows Lang and Jardine are estranged.'

This struck me as a suggestion bordering on brilliance. 'But how much would I be obliged to tell Lang?'

'Nothing.'

'But what if he questions me about Lyle's relationship with Jardine?'

'My dear Charles, you're a clergyman – you're under no obligation whatsoever to repeat a word of Lyle's recent confessions to anyone, even to the Archbishop of Canterbury! All you need say is that both the Jardines were making such heavy demands on Lyle that she was quite unable to have any life of her own. This is so obviously unhealthy and undesirable that no further comment needs to be made.'

My mind cleared. I realized then how exhausted I was by the strain of the past twenty-four hours, and Darrow's clarity of vision was even more comforting than usual.

He said suddenly, 'Are you going to wait till the pregnancy's confirmed before you set the wedding date?'

'No,' I said, knowing he asked the question to see if I were toying with the idea of escape. 'I want to marry her anyway, pregnancy or no pregnancy, and the sooner the better.'

He was satisfied. 'And how do you feel now,' he said, testing me again, 'about being a father yourself?'

I smiled at him. 'Now that I'm not wasting my time trying to be the perfect son to all my father-figures, I'm sure I'll have the energy to tackle parenthood!'

Darrow nodded but when he made no comment I realized he expected me to go on. 'I made myself so unhappy being the perfect son,' I said soberly, 'that I had a horror of creating anyone who might have to go through what I went through. And my father always made fatherhood seem such a colossal trial that I became subconsciously terrified of the burden it would entail.'

Darrow nodded but continued to wait.

'I couldn't cope with my marriage,' I said. 'I couldn't cope with my family, I couldn't cope with myself. Of course I shied away from coping with anyone else, especially a child who would be dependent on me. But now I can cope, father. It won't be easy. It'll often be very hard, but the truth is I don't feel unfit and unworthy here. I believe that this is the family life God has called me to undertake – perhaps to prepare me for a call to serve him in some other field – and that through this great ordeal he's made me fit and worthy for this very special purpose.'

Darrow leant back in his chair as if he had safely steered a ship into harbour after an exceptionally arduous voyage, but all he said in the end was, 'May God be with you – and I'm sure He will. Well done, Charles.'

II

When we returned to Laud's I packed a bag for the visit to Starbridge and then while Lyle and I sat facing each other on either side of my desk I telephoned the palace. Gerald Harvey at once connected me to the extension in the library; as soon as Jardine responded I embarked on my prepared speech.

'I'm telephoning to tell you that Lyle's agreed to marry me,' I said flatly. 'I'm speaking from my rooms at Laud's but we're about to leave for Starbridge so that I can call on you this evening to discuss the situation. I'll come to the palace at six-thirty.'

A deep silence followed this declaration of war but at last Jardine said levelly, 'I'd like to speak to Lyle, if you please.'

'Until six-thirty – thank you, Bishop,' I said, and terminated the call. I had no intention of giving him the opportunity to talk to Lyle unless I was able to monitor both sides of the conversation.

'What did he say?' said Lyle frightened.

I told her.

'Did he sound shattered?'

'Not particularly.' Ignoring her pallor I added to divert her, 'Did you write the letter?'

Opening her bag she produced an unsealed envelope which she handed to me.

'May I?' I said politely before I extracted the letter within. I thought it was important that my behaviour remained civilized as the pressure to become dictatorial increased.

'Of course,' she said.

She had written to confirm that she wished to marry me and to inform him about the child. It was a cold stark little letter; I suspected she had not dared admit any emotion for fear it might have permeated the entire message.

'Is it all right?' she asked nervously.

'Fine.' Sealing the envelope I slipped it into the inside pocket of my jacket and in silence we embarked upon our journey.

III

So we came at last to Starbridge, sunlit sinister Starbridge, the city which had concealed such a tormented reality behind its brilliant glittering image. The sun shone on the Cathedral again as we descended from the hills, and the waters of the river sparkled in the hot September light. Our separate rooms were waiting at the Staro Arms but I did not pause to unpack my bag. I drank some water to refresh myself and then left for the palace. Lyle saw me off. As we parted she was unable to stop herself saying desperately, 'Be kind to him.'

I at once wanted to lay waste the entire palace, but I gave a brief nod, beat back my jealousy with one last kiss and walked out of the hotel into Eternity Street.

IV

By the time I reached the palace I was more tense than ever but I had every emotion tightly in control. I had given Darrow back my borrowed cross at our last meeting, but I had bought a cross of my own which I was wearing beneath my shirt, and during the walk through the Close I touched the outline repeatedly to maintain my equilibrium.

On reaching the palace I was shown at once to the library.

Jardine was standing by the window and it was not until the door closed that he turned to face me. His face was pale and set. He looked tough. I stood my ground.

'Good evening, Dr Ashworth.' Evidently he had decided not to rake up memories of our previous meeting by calling me Charles.

'Good evening, Bishop.'

He gestured that we should sit down and once more we faced each other across the desk. Eventually after an awkward pause he said with care, 'I hope Lyle's well. I've been worried about her for some time.'

'She's better now that she's made up her mind to marry me.' I waited for him to defend himself; I was poised to deliver all the arguments against his informal marital arrangements; I was ready to grapple with the full force of his charism as we wrestled in debate. But he eluded me.

'The most important thing,' he said, 'is that Lyle should be restored to full spiritual health.' And he touched the cross on his chest. At once I knew he was tapping it for the strength to go on, and suddenly I feared he was going to undermine my enmity and plunge me once more into confusion.

'I'd very much like to see Lyle,' he said, 'because I think it's important that I set her free to be happy in her new life. I'd like to tell her that at best we contracted what the lawyers call a voidable marriage, a marriage which the parties can set aside if they choose, and I'd like to make it clear that I do release her from those vows she made five years ago. I'd also say that although of course I shall miss her very much she's on no account to feel guilty about leaving me, and I'd say that because as I survey the events of the last few months it seems very obvious, Dr Ashworth, that you were sent into our lives for a purpose, and that I would indeed be the apostate you doubtless think I am if I failed to understand that it's entirely God's will that Lyle should now become your wife.'

I was beyond speech. I was unable to decide whether he was being immensely clever, scheming to tame me into a pliable son-in-law, or immensely heroic, relinquishing the woman he loved in the best possible way, and I had the terrible suspicion he was being heroic.

'I'm not an apostate,' he said when he realized I was too confused to reply. 'I reached my decision to marry Lyle because I thought I discerned God's approval. The rational arguments for the decision were weak but I'm a clergyman, not a lawyer, and I came to the conclusion that God had provided me with this strange solution to my troubles to enable me to continue to serve him to the best of my ability. Obviously events have proved that I was in error. "Truth is the daughter of time," as the saying goes, but five years ago I did what I honestly believed to be right, right for me, for Carrie and for Lyle.'

He paused but when I still offered no comment he fingered his cross again and said, 'It seems in retrospect that my error was very grave, but our errors are so often rooted in circumstances over which we have no control, and the foundation of my error here goes back a long way, as no doubt you realize. My father and stepmother had such a powerful influence on me, and although I've always congratulated myself on escaping from the world into which I was born I see clearly now that my whole career has inevitably been coloured by my heredity and the very singular environment of my youth. However please don't think I'm trying to make excuses for myself; I'm not. I'm merely trying to put my behaviour in a truthful perspective because I believe it's important that you shouldn't look at me and feel perpetually disillusioned with the Church. I'm not the first churchman to fall into error and I certainly shan't be the last, but you should understand that I'm not an emissary of Satan but merely a devout man who's made an appalling mistake.'

He stopped speaking again, and again I found I was impressed yet sceptical. The situation called for the charism of the discernment of spirits, but at that moment I was quite unable to tell whether his speech came from God or the Devil.

'Lyle will be concerned for Carrie and myself,' said Jardine. 'That's inevitable and that's another reason why I'd like to see her. I want to explain that we'll be all right. I shall, of course, resign my bishopric. I shall make some excuse about ill-health and retire to a distant village – somewhere near Oxford would suit – where Carrie and I can live quietly. I've always wanted to write a serious theological study instead of sermons and polemics, and retirement will give me the necessary time to do so. As for Carrie, no doubt she'll come into her own at last. She never enjoyed being the wife of a successful clergyman, but now I foresee her taking an active part in village life and becoming vastly popular while everyone secretly moans about her tiresome irascible old husband ... And once Carrie's happier than she's been for years our marriage may well take a turn for the better. At least I shall hope so, and perhaps in such changed circumstances I shan't hope entirely in vain.'

I now had the confusion in my mind under control. With the strength developed by Darrow's training I had achieved sufficient concentration to wipe the blackboard of my consciousness clean so that God could write upon it if he wished. Then I prayed again for the gift of discernment.

At last Jardine said, 'When are you getting married?'

'Very soon. I'm getting a special licence.'

Jardine looked puzzled. Cautiously he said: 'Forgive me – I've no wish to interfere, but is it really advisable to rush into this? I speak as a man who himself married in haste, and I do most strongly urge you not to follow my example.'

Without speaking I produced Lyle's letter and gave it to him.

He groped for his reading-glasses. When he opened the envelope the signet-ring fell out and I saw him flinch before he slipped it in his pocket. I went on watching him and eventually I heard the sharp intake of breath as he reached the crucial sentence. The next moment he was levering himself to his feet. On the side-table stood a decanter of brandy, the silent witness of the strain he had endured since receiving my telephone call that morning, and he now poured himself a stiff measure into the tumbler which I knew had already been used. All he said in the end was, 'I've got to be alone.'

I withdrew to the hall. I was still channelling my concentration into keeping the blackboard of my mind clear, but although I continued to pray for enlightenment I remained confused. As Darrow had so truthfully pointed out, I was in many ways a very ordinary clergyman and I now felt quite out of my spiritual depth. Again I prayed for the grace of God which would transform my weakness into strengh, and again the familiar prayer of Christ echoed in my mind: let thy will, not mine, be done.

The door of the library opened. I had probably been in the hall no longer than five minutes but it seemed that a far longer time had passed. From the threshold Jardine said, 'Come back, please,' but he was turning away as he spoke and it was not until I had rejoined him in the room that

I saw his eyes were bloodshot. The gift of discernment at once over-whelmed me; looking past the mask of her heroic resignation which that faultless speech had so effortlessly projected, I saw not the Devil's emissary but only a good man struggling to master the most profound emotions.

'Thank you for letting me have those few moments alone,' he said, and I was just thinking how self-possessed he sounded when I realized he was unable to continue. However when we were both seated again he managed to say, 'I'm sorry, I feel so overwhelmed, I still hardly dare believe it, it's as if the whole tragedy's been redeemed – it even makes Lyle's loss easier to bear because of course this is the most miraculous compensation – '

I suddenly saw what was going to happen, and as I heard Darrow saying, 'Leave Jardine to God, Charles,' the chalk began to write at last on the blackboard of my mind. I could hardly bear to read the message but I knew I was powerless to erase it. I was bound by my call, and only one course of action lay open to me.

'I've always wanted a child,' said Jardine. 'I hink it's the one thing, even now, that I want the most. It was so hard to accept when God withheld the blessing of living children from my marriage, and I've often felt acceptance would have been easier if there had been no children at all. That stillborn baby . . . That agonizing glimpse of a future that never happened . . . It was almost unendurable to know one had created a child only to lose him before he'd even drawn breath in the world.'

I could only watch him in silence, and in my mind the chalk was finally still.

'And how wonderful that you should want to marry her!' said Jardine, too absorbed by his emotions to notice my lack of response. 'In the circumstances that too's miraculous – everything's miraculous – I felt so destroyed by this disaster but now I can start to hope again.' Clumsily he poured himself some more brandy. 'After your telephone call this morning,' he said, 'I didn't know how I was going to bear her loss but gradually after much prayer I realized that my chief task was not to think of myself but to help Lyle by setting her free. So I resolved to put on a brave front – but it was so hard because I knew how much you must despise me – oh, how shaming it was when you walked into the room this evening, how terrible it was to look at you and *know that you knew* . . . Forgive me, I can see I'm embarrassing you by my frankness, but I've suffered so much, never think I haven't suffered, and that's why this news is so wonderful because it transforms all that suffering and makes it bearable at last.' He hesitated before adding diffidently, 'I shall look forward so much to watching him grow up.'

I said nothing.

His expression changed. He had recognized his executioner but could not quite believe the execution was at hand. 'I trust,' he said, 'I'll be allowed to see the child from time to time.'

I felt as if were seeing a man facing a firing squad where all the bullets were being fired in slow motion, but when I spoke it was not because I wanted to but because I had no choice; the message had to be delivered.

'I'm afraid you must take it as settled,' I said, 'that the child will be mine and not yours. I'm sorry, but I've been called to make this difficult marriage and because of the nature of the liaison you had with Lyle I don't see how I can possibly risk allowing you to play any part in my married life. It's out of the question – ' I hesitated but made myself add ' – for the present.'

He grabbed at the lifeline. 'But in the future – '

'We'll see. It depends very much how Lyle and I get on and that in turn depends on how conscientiously you keep out of our lives.'

'I needn't see Lyle. But if I could occasionally see the child – with the help of an intermediary – '

'No. Don't get carried away by the sentimental notion that your biological connection gives you the right to treat my child as yours.' I could hear my father's fierceness in my voice. Touching my hidden cross I made a new effort to be calm. 'Obviously he'll have to know the truth some day,' I said, 'and when he does know he'll want to see you, but until then you must keep your distance unless I feel it's safe to allow you to draw closer.'

He struggled with his emotions and it was some time before he was able to say, 'Could Lyle perhaps send me a photograph occasionally?'

'Lyle will send you absolutely nothing,' I said, 'and I forbid you to communicate with her.' I had to steel myself to add, '*I'll* send the occasional photograph.'

He tried to thank me but I cut him off. Having been compelled to take a tough stance I did not want him making me feel guilty by displaying humility.

Eventually he said, 'Am I not to see Lyle – even to say goodbye?'

'I'll bring her here after dinner tonight, and you can make your set speech to her in my presence. Meanwhile perhaps Mrs Jardine would be good enough to pack some clothes for Lyle to take away – and when we have our new address in Cambridge I'd be obliged if you'd forward the rest of Lyle's possessions at my expense.'

He nodded. I assumed that there was no more which could possibly be said but as I rose to my feet he added unexpectedly, 'Would you like a drink before you go? This interview must have been almost as great an ordeal for you as it's been for me.'

'Thank you, Bishop, but since I was so drunk when you last entertained me here I feel the least I can do now is abstain.'

We both smiled, and suddenly against all the odds the spark of our compatibility flared between us. On an impulse he said: 'I'm sorry I made such a mess of counselling you that night – I did want to help but I was so cut off from God by all my fear and dread that I had no help to give. I'm afraid it was a very great spiritual failure.'

'We all have our spiritual failures.'

'Well, make sure you learn from mine.' He led the way to the door. 'At least you've stopped asking impertinent questions,' he said casually over his shoulder. 'No doubt I should be thankful for small mercies.'

'I could think of quite a few more impertinent questions to ask,' I said, trying to match his lighter tone in order to soften my earlier severity, 'but I see no reason on earth why you should answer them. You're never going to tell anyone the real truth about your stepmother, are you?'

'And what, dare I ask, do you consider "the real truth" to be?'

'I think it was she who was the love of your life. No one else. I think Lyle was really only a substitute, someone your stepmother sanctioned when she knew she hadn't long to live. I think if you'd really loved Lyle you couldn't have lived chastely under the same roof with her at Radbury.'

'What singularly bizarre theories you conjure up out of your singularly fertile imagination, Dr Ashworth!'

'Life sometimes *is* bizarre, Dr Jardine – '

' – and sometimes it's merely innocent. Ingrid was my father's wife. The story begins and ends in that single sentence.'

'But what a complex and ambivalent sentence it is!'

Jardine smiled at me again. It was painful to see the amusement return to those hypnotic amber eyes when they were still bloodshot. It merely underlined the pathos I had no desire to witness. 'So you've resumed your customary impertinence!' he said. 'I'm glad to see that you at least have emerged from our battle unscathed!'

'No one ever emerges from a battle unscathed. I'll return later with Lyle,' I said, and walked out feeling bruised beyond endurance and battered beyond belief.

V

I presided over the final dissolution of Jardine's *ménage à trois* later that evening. It was a sad, difficult meeting. Jardine spoke his piece but at a far more halting pace than he had achieved earlier. Lyle cried. I allowed her to embrace Carrie but afterwards terminated the meeting abruptly. By this time Jardine was ashen, beyond speech, and both women were in tears. Stowing in the car the numerous bags which had been packed for Lyle I drove off at a great pace down the palace drive and pursued an erratic course out of the Close. Lyle wept soundlessly all the way to the Staro Arms.

After the porter had brought the bags to her room I ordered brandies for us both and we sat on the window-seat in the gathering dusk. The golden light of the sunset had almost faded and I remembered Darrow talking of the darkness below the horizon which would represent the reality of marriage after the euphoria of the engagement.

As we sipped our brandy Lyle said rapidly, 'I expect you want to sleep with me. You can if you like. It doesn't really matter if we anticipate the wedding, does it?'

'Yes, it does,' I said. 'It would be like smoking a cigarette when I was wearing a clerical collar. There are some things clergymen just couldn't do if they want to be respected, and if I'm ever to put right that disastrous error with Loretta – '

'Please don't say any more about that.' She groped for my hand. 'You've explained. I understand. We've forgiven each other for all the awfulness there. I only thought that perhaps – '

'Well, of course I want to sleep with you,' I said, 'but let's be realistic for a moment. You're offering out of guilt because you're ashamed you revealed at the palace how deeply you still care for him. If I accepted your offer I'd be accepting because I wanted to drown my insecurity by subjugating you physically, just as he did. But think, Lyle – just think! Do we really want to start our married life on those terms?'

She shook her head and gripped my hand harder than ever.

'You want to wait, don't you?' I said. 'You've had quite enough of quasi-marriages. You've yearned all these years to be a real wife, just as I've yearned all these years to make a second marriage, and why should we now settle for anything less than the genuine article?'

'I thought you might want to try me out.'

'What for? We hardly need premarital sex to tell us that at first the physical side of marriage is going to be difficult! What matters is not that we confirm this obvious fact before marriage but that after the wedding we're prepared to try hard to overcome the problem.' I kissed her before adding, 'Besides, we both need time. You're exhausted. So am I. Let's finish our brandy, crawl into our separate beds and pass out. It may not be the most romantic ending to a gruelling day but I'm quite sure it's the most sensible one.'

'I don't think it's so unromantic,' said Lyle, 'I think if you didn't love me so much the gruelling day would have an even more gruelling ending.'

But in a flash of insight I saw my behaviour in a more complex and murky light; I recognized my desire to do what was right and my anxiety to protect her from further stress, but I recognized too my secret dread of being compared with Jardine and found wanting. However that piece of self-knowledge was at present too difficult to master. Closing my mind against all troubled thoughts I embraced her in the gathering dusk, and later when I glanced out of the window I saw that although the night had fallen at last, the stars were beginning to shine.

VI

Dr Lang married us in the chapel at Lambeth two weeks later in the presence of my parents, my brother, my sister-in-law, my two nieces, my nephew and a friend of Lyle's, an ancient charming clergyman who had been a Canon of Radbury Cathedral during the Jardines' tenure of the Deanery. He gave the bride away while Peter acted as best man. Lang conducted the ceremony with his usual theatrical dignity and as he declaimed a short homily extolling the glories of nuptial bliss for those not called to the celibate life it occurred to me that he might have guessed rather more about my life as a widower than I had cared to imagine. The Archbishop remained the canny Scot beneath his pompous English façade, and I reminded myself that time had proved Dr Lang right in his estimate of the Bishop of Starbridge.

In the circumstances it seemed wiser not to have a prolonged honeymoon, so I decided we should go away for no more than a weekend to a small hotel which I knew in the Cotswolds. We arrived there shortly before dinner, and later when Lyle said how much she had enjoyed the simple but carefully cooked meal I knew she was trying as hard to make me believe she was happy as I was trying to be convinced. I told myself I should feel comforted that she so strongly shared my desire for the weekend to be a success, yet when we finally retired to our room I found I still needed reassurance. I heard myself saying rapidly, 'Look, if you can't face it, for heaven's sake say so. We mustn't start playacting and being dishonest with each other.'

Lyle said, 'I want sex. And I want sex with you. And I want sex with you now. Then maybe we can put a stop to this excruciating tension.'

This was certainly unvarnished honesty and I did my best to achieve an equally candid response. 'I feel exactly the same,' I said, but I was hurt by her lack of warmth. I thought that if I had been Jardine she would have called me darling and held out her arms.

A long unpalatable vista opened before me into my difficult marriage, but I pulled down the blinds in my mind to blot it out. I had hardly spent seven arduous years of flawed celibacy only to be squeamish on my wedding-night, yet the demon of doubt was now crawling through my thoughts. I looked at Lyle, who appeared to be making such a brave attempt to sever herself from the past, and I wondered if she were even now secretly longing for Jardine. And as soon as this terrible thought had entered my head I was tormented by the dread that she would always have secrets which would cut me off from her, secrets which she would never reveal.

I touched my cross and asked myself instead how far it was ever possible to know the whole truth about another human being. I thought of Jardine's final ambivalent silence about his stepmother, a silence which might well indicate not guilt but a desire to keep a cherished part of his life utterly private; no one would ever know now what had happened there, and perhaps it was right that no one ever should. I thought of Darrow saying, 'All we can do is to pray for as much enlightenment as God sees fit to grant us,' and suddenly I realized that Darrow was an even greater mystery than Jardine, a man who concealed all his secrets in order to disconnect himself from his past in the world. What lay behind his call to be a monk? Had he been happily married? Had he been a successful father to his children? Had Lyle been right in her intuitive conviction that the state of celibacy was unnatural to him, and if she was right was his life a continuing struggle to maintain that serenity which always seemed so unforced? The likelihood was that I would never be able to answer any of these questions, and yet my relationship with Darrow was hardly vitiated because he was in so many respects an enigma.

I saw then that Lyle would always have her mysteries, and I saw too that the way to live with them was not to torture myself in pursuit of elucidation but to accept them as a limit set on my knowledge by God for his own purpose. The demon of doubt receded, and releasing the cross I began to prepare for bed.

VII

I was face to face at last with my secret dread that I would be unable to match Jardine's illicit but alluring distortion of his charismatic power. Another searing vista opened into the future, and again the vista had to be blotted from my mind. I was being tormented now by that old demon my fear of inadequacy, and rolling away from Lyle I groped in the dark for the cross which I had left on the bedside table.

As I slipped the cross around my neck I remembered Darrow again. I saw us in the herb-garden, remembered how the word 'courage' had echoed in my mind, and suddenly without words I was able to ask for patience, for strength, for the will to endure all my difficulties and the wisdom to surmount them.

The demons departed as my mind stood open before God, and once more I passed through the strait gate to set out along the narrow way in response to my mysterious call. My new life in God's service stretched before me; I knew there could be no turning back. I could only go on in the absolute faith that one day his purpose would stand fully revealed, and in the light of that faith the darkness of my anxiety was extinguished. The glittering image of the apparent world dissolved into the great truths which lay beyond and the truths were not a beautiful dream, as Loretta had thought, but the ultimate reality. Love and forgiveness, truth and beauty, courage and compassion blazed with a radiance which far outshone the cheap glitter of illusion, and I knew then with an even deeper conviction that in serving God man only fulfilled his need to strive to live in that eternally powerful light. St Augustine's famous words echoed in my mind: 'O God, thou hast made us for thyself, and our hearts are restless until they rest in thee.'

At once I was at peace; my self-confidence returned, and as I claimed my wife and child at last I thought as my father had thought before me: they're both mine now.

Afterwards I said carefully to Lyle, 'I think you really might come to love me one day,' and at once she said, 'Darling!' and held out her arms.

Without doubt some difficult hurdle had been overcome. I wondered what the next one would be.

I fell asleep and dreamed of a little boy tormenting me with his lambent amber eyes.

AUTHOR'S NOTE

The character of Charles Ashworth is fictitious.

The character of Alex Jardine is based in part on the life and career of Herbert Hensley Henson (1863–1947), one of the leaders of the Church of England in the early twentieth century. Henson was the son of a self-made businessman who retired early and proceeded to live beyond his means while he devoted himself to an eccentric and gloomy evangelical religion. Young Henson's mother died when he was six and three years later his father 'remarried', although no record of the marriage has ever been found. When Henson was fourteen his German stepmother finally persuaded his father to send him to school, a step which set him on the road to Oxford where he was to become a Fellow of All Souls. He was ordained at the age of twenty-three; when he became Vicar of Barking in Essex his stepmother moved to the vicarage to keep house for him. After years of obscurity during which he was obliged to support his family and was consequently too poor to marry, he received his vital preferment: he was appointed Rector of St Margaret's Westminster and became a Canon of Westminster Abbey. Relieved at last from financial anxiety he then married Isabella Dennistoun and a stillborn son was born to them two years later. There were no living children of the marriage. Henson became Dean of Durham in 1912, and in 1916 a young woman, Fearne Booker, arrived at the Deanery to assist Mrs Henson; she remained with the Hensons for over thirty years. In 1918 Henson was appointed Bishop of Durham where he remained until his retirement in 1939. His stepmother spent her final days with him at his episcopal residence, Auckland Castle. It must be stressed that no impropriety existed between either Henson and his stepmother or Henson and Miss Booker.

The personality of Lyle Christie is my own invention and any resemblance to Miss Booker is coincidental.

William Cosmo Gordon Lang was Archbishop of Canterbury from 1928 until 1942. In 1938 during a debate in the House of Lords on Abyssinia, Henson opposed Lang with an unprecedented degree of fierceness, but their tendency to disagree had already been revealed to the public; a year earlier during the Lord's debate on the Marriage Bill Lang had merely adopted a position of neutrality but Henson had spoken in favour of extending the divorce laws with an eloquence which was later recorded with grateful admiration by the Bill's author, A. P. Herbert.

Glittering Images is the first in a series of novels about the Church of England in the twentieth century. The next novel, *Glamorous Powers*, opens in 1940 and focuses on Jon Darrow.

Glamorous Powers

PART ONE

THE VISION

'Ecstasy or vision begins when thought ceases, *to our conscious-ness*, to proceed from ourselves. It differs from dreaming, because the subject is awake. It differs from hallucinations, because there is no organic disturbance: it is, or claims to be, a temporary enhancement, not a partial disintegration, of the mental faculties. Lastly, it differs from poetical inspiration, because the imagination is passive. That perfectly sane people often experience such visions there is no manner of doubt.'

W. R. INGE
Dean of St Paul's 1911–1934
Christian Mysticism

ONE

'The apparent suddenness of the mystical revelation is quite normal; Plato in his undoubtedly genuine Seventh Letter speaks of the "leaping spark" by which divine inspiration flashes on him.'

W. R. INGE
Dean of St Paul's 1911–1934
Mysticism in Religion

I

The vision began at a quarter to six; around me the room was suffused with light, not the pellucid light of a fine midsummer morning but the dim light of a wet dawn in May. I was sitting on the edge of my bed when without warning the gold lettering on the cover of the Bible began to glow.

I stood up as the bedside table deepened in hue, and the next moment the floorboards pulsed with light while in the corner the taps of the basin coruscated like silver in the sun. Backing around the edge of the bed I pressed my back against the wall before any further alteration of consciousness occurred. Firm contact with a solid object lessens the instinctive fear which must always accompany such a radical transcendence of time and space.

However after the initial fear comes the equally instinctive acceptance. I had closed my eyes to lessen the terror of disorientation but now I forced myself to open them. The cell was still glittering, but as I watched the glitter faded to a shimmer until the scene resembled a view seen through the wrong end of a telescope, and I could perceive my body, remote and abandoned, pressed against the wall by the bed as if impaled there by invisible nails. I looked aside – I could see my body turning its head – and immediately the darkness, moving from right to left, began to erase the telescopic view. My eyes closed, again warding off the fear of disorientation, and this time when I reopened them I found I was once more moving in a normal world.

I was myself, inhabiting my body as usual and walking along a path through a wood of beech trees. Insofar as I was conscious of any emotion

I was aware of being at ease with my verdant tranquil surroundings, although I felt irritated by the persistent call of a wood-pigeon. However eventually the pigeon fell silent and as the path began to slope downhill I glanced to my left at the chapel in the dell below.

The chapel was small but exquisite in its classical symmetry; I was reminded of the work of Inigo Jones. In the dull green light of the surrounding woods the yellow stone glowed a dark gold, a voluptuous contrast to the grey medieval ruins which lay behind it. The ruins were in part hidden by ivy, but as I moved closer I could see the slits in the wall of the tower.

Reaching the floor of the dell I faced the chapel, now only fifty yards away across the sward, and it was then that I noticed the suitcase. Standing at the edge of the trees it was sprinkled with labels, the largest being a triangle of red, blue and black design; I was too far away to read the lettering. Afterwards I remembered that I had regarded this suitcase without either curiosity or surprise. Certainly I never slackened my pace as I headed for the chapel, and I believe I knew even then that the suitcase was a mere image on the retina of my mind, a symbol which at that point I had no interest in interpreting.

Hurrying up the steps of the porch I lifted the latch, pushed the righthand half of the double-doors wide open and paused to survey the interior beyond.

There was no transept. A central aisle stretched to the altar at the east end. The altar-table was stark in its austerity, the only adornment consisting of a plain wooden cross, but again I felt neither surprise nor curiosity. Evidently I was as accustomed to this sight as I was accustomed to the fact that the nave was only three-quarters full of pews. Walking across the empty space which separated the doors from the back pew I could smell the lilies which were blooming in a vase beneath the brass memorial plaque on my right. I gave them no more than a brief glance but when I looked back at the altar I saw that the light had changed.

The sun was penetrating the window which was set high in the wall to the left of the altar, and as the ray began to slant densely upon the cross I stopped dead. Unless I stood south of the Equator I was witnessing the impossible, for the sun could never shine from the north. I stared at the light until my eyes began to burn. Then sinking to my knees I covered my face with my hands, and as the vision at last dissolved, the knowledge was branded upon my mind that I had to abandon the work which suited me so well and begin my life anew in the world I had no wish to rejoin.

Opening my eyes I found myself back in my cell. I was no longer pressing against the wall but kneeling by the bed. Sweat prickled my forehead. My hands were trembling. There were also other physical manifestations which I prefer not to describe. Indeed I felt quite unfit to begin my daily work but so profound was my state of shock that I automatically embarked on my morning routine, and minutes later I was leaving my cell.

Perhaps I have erred in starting this narrative with an account of my vision. Perhaps I should instead have offered some essential biographical details, for the repeated mention of the word 'cell' has almost certainly conveyed the impression that I am an inmate of one of His Majesty's prisons. Let me now correct this mistake. For the past seventeen years I have been a member of the Anglican brotherhood of monks known as the Fordite Order of St Benedict and St Bernard. I may still be judged eccentric, anti-social and possibly (after this account of my vision) deranged. But I am not a criminal.

In order that such an abnormal experience can be put in its proper context and judged fairly, I must attempt a thumbnail sketch of my past so let me state at once that in many ways my life has been exceedingly normal. I was brought up in a quiet respectable home, educated at various appropriate establishments and ordained as a clergyman of the Church of England not long after my twenty-third birthday. I then married a young woman who possessed what in my young day was described as 'allure' and which a later generation, debased by the War – the First War, as I suppose we must now call it – described as 'It'. For some years after my marriage I worked as a chaplain to the Naval base at Starmouth, and later I volunteered for duty at sea with the result that much of my ministry was spent away from home. In fact I was absent when my wife died in 1912. For another seven years I continued my career in the Navy, but I judge it unnecessary to recount my war experiences. Suffice it to say that after the Battle of Jutland I never felt quite the same about the sea again.

Accordingly in 1919 I left the Navy and became the chaplain at Starmouth prison. The advantage of this change was that I was able to see more of my children, now adolescent, but the disadvantage was that I became aligned with an authority empowered to administer capital and corporal punishment, two practices which are entirely contrary to my conception of the Christian way to treat human beings. However I endured this harrowing ministry as best as I could until finally in 1923 the hour of my liberation dawned: with both my children launched on their adult lives I was able to retire to the Cambridgeshire village of Grantchester, where the Fordites had a house, and embark on my career as a monk. I had known the Abbot, James Reid, since my undergraduate days at the

University two miles away, and although I had lost touch with him some years earlier it never occurred to me not to seek his help when I was at last free to join the Order.

I shall gloss over the disastrous beginning of my new life and simply state that after three months at Grantchester I was transferred to the Fordites' farm at Ruydale, a remote corner of the North Yorkshire moors where the monks lived more in the austere style of Cistercians than Benedictines. Here I embarked on a successful cenobitic career which reached its apex in 1937 when I was transferred back to Grantchester to succeed James Reid as Abbot.

This brief autobiographical recital – remarkable more for what I have omitted than for what I have deigned to reveal – is all I intend to disclose at present about my past. No further disclosures are needed, I think, to show that my ministry has always demanded a strong constitution, absolute sanity and considerable reserves of spiritual strength. In short, although I write as a monk who has visions I am neither an hysteric nor a schizophrenic. I am a normal man with abnormal aspects – and having abnormal aspects, as Abbot James had assured me when I was a troubled young ordinand, was what being normal was all about.

'But beware of those glamorous powers, Jon!' he had urged after we had discussed my gifts as a psychic. 'Beware of those powers which come from God but which can so easily be purloined by the Devil!' This had proved a prophetic warning. For the next twenty years, while I remained in the world, my life was one long struggle to achieve the correct balance between the psychic and the spiritual so that I could develop properly as a priest, but it was a struggle I failed to win. There was little development. I did become a competent priest in the limited sense that the world judged my ministry to be effective, but my spiritual progress suffered from inadequate guidance and an undisciplined psyche. As Father Darcy told me later, I was like a brilliant child who had learnt the alphabet but had never been trained to read and write. However this situation changed when I became a monk, and it changed because for the first time I found the man who had the spiritual range and the sheer brute force of personality required to train me.

I have reached the subject of Father Darcy. Father Darcy is relevant to my vision because he made me the man I am today. I must describe him, but how does one describe a brilliant Christian monster? Father Darcy was unlike any other monk I have ever met. No doubt he was also unlike any monk St Benedict and St Bernard ever envisioned. Both intensely worldly and intensely spiritual (a rare and often bizarre combination) this modern cenobitic dictator was not only devout, gifted and wise but brutal, ruthless and power-mad.

As soon as he became the Abbot-General in 1910 he embarked on the task of waking up each of the four houses which had been slumbering on their comfortable endowments for decades. Having dusted down each monk he reorganized the finances and courted not only both Archbishops but the entire episcopal bench of the House of Lords in an effort to increase the Order's worldly importance. As a private organization it was not directly connected to the Church of England, even though since its birth in the 1840s it had received the somewhat condescending blessings of successive Archbishops of Canterbury, but Father Darcy's diplomatic ventures ensured that he and his abbots were treated with a new respect by the ecclesiastical hierarchy. Meanwhile the spiritual tone of the Order had been markedly raised, and by the time I became a monk in 1923 the Fordites were well known for the guidance and counselling given to those who sought their help. The restored tradition of Benedictine scholarship was also being noticed with approval.

It will be obvious from this description that Father Darcy had the charism of leadership but in fact he possessed all the major charisms and these gifts from God were buttressed and enhanced by a perfectly trained, immaculately disciplined psychic power which he had dedicated entirely to God's service. He was a formidable priest, a formidable monk, a formidable man. But he was not likeable. However Father Darcy cared nothing for being liked. He would have considered such a desire petty and self-centred, indicative of a disturbed psyche which required a spiritual spring-cleaning. Father Darcy cared only about being respected by those outside the Order and obeyed by those within; such respect and obedience were necessary in order that he might work more efficiently for God, and Father Darcy, like all successful dictators, put a high value on efficiency.

My habit of calling him Father Darcy is new. Only people outside the Order call us monks by our surnames preceded by the title 'Father', if the monk be a priest, or 'Brother', if the monk be a layman. For the last thirty years Father Darcy had been addressed by his monks as 'Father Abbot-General' but after his death a month ago it had become necessary to adopt another designation in order to distinguish him from his successor, and to me, 'Father Cuthbert' had merely conjured up a picture of a cosy old confessor unable to say boo to a goose. In accordance with the constitution of the Order which decreed that all monks were equal in death, he had been referred to throughout the burial service as 'Cuthbert' but whenever this word had been uttered something akin to a shudder of horror had rippled through the congregation as if Father Darcy were still alive to be enraged by the familiarity.

All the abbots attended the funeral. Cyril came from Starwater Abbey, where the Fordites ran a public school; Aidan, my former superior, came from Ruydale, and I came from Grantchester. Francis Ingram, Father Darcy's right-hand man, organized the funeral and offered us all a lavish hospitality at the Order's London headquarters, but he did not conduct the service. That task fell to Aidan as the senior surviving abbot.

'It's hard to believe the old boy's gone,' said Francis Ingram afterwards as he helped himself to a very large glass of port from the decanter which was normally reserved for visiting bishops. 'What a wonderful capacity he had for making us all shit bricks! It's going to be uncommonly dull without him.'

Monks are, of course, supposed to refrain from using coarse language but sometimes the effort of keeping one's speech free of casual blasphemy is so intense that a lapse into vulgarity is seen as the only alternative to committing a sin. It is a notorious fact of monastic life that without the softening influence of women men tend to sink into coarse speech and even coarser humour; when I returned to Grantchester in 1937 as Abbot I found a community so lax that their conversation during the weekly recreation hour recalled not the cloister but the barracks of the Naval ratings at Starmouth.

My promotion in 1937 was unorthodox, not only because monks who follow the Benedictine Rule are supposed to remain in the same community for life but because the monks themselves normally elect an abbot from among their own number. However Father Darcy had decided I could be of more use to the Order at Grantchester than at Ruydale, and Father Darcy had no hesitation in riding rough-shod over tradition when the welfare of the Order was at stake.

'Many congratulations!' said Francis Ingram when I arrived at the London headquarters to be briefed for my new post. 'I couldn't be more pleased!' Of course we both knew he was furious that I was to be an abbot while he remained a mere prior, but we both knew too that we had no choice but to go through the motions of displaying brotherly love. Monks are indeed supposed to regard all men with brotherly love, but since most monks are sinners not saints such exemplary Christian charity tends to resemble Utopia, a dream much admired but perpetually unattainable.

It was not until the April of 1940 when Father Darcy died that Francis and I saw our meticulously manifested brotherly love exposed as the fraud which it was. I have no intention of describing Father Darcy's unedifying last hours in detail; such a description would be better confined to the pages – preferably the uncut pages – of a garish Victorian novel. Suffice it to say that for two days he knew he was dying and resolved to enjoy what little life remained to him by keeping us all on tenterhooks about the succession.

It is laid down in the constitution of the Order that although abbots are in normal circumstances to be elected, the Abbot-General must choose his own successor. The reasoning which lies behind this most undemocratic rule is that only the Abbot-General is in a position to judge which man might follow most ably in his footsteps, and the correct procedure is that his written choice should be committed to a sealed envelope which is only to be opened after his death. This move has the advantage of circumventing any last-minute dubious oral declarations and also, supposedly, removing from a dying Abbot-General any obligation to deal with worldly matters when his thoughts ought to be directed elsewhere. However Father Darcy could not bear to think he would be unable to witness our expressions when the appointment was announced, and eventually he succumbed to the temptation to embark on an illicit dénouement.

There were four of us present at his bedside, the three abbots and Francis Ingram.

'Of course you're all wondering how I've chosen my successor,' said the old tyrant, revelling in his power, 'so I'll tell you: I've done it by process of elimination. You're a good man, Aidan, but after so many years in a Yorkshire backwater you'd never survive in London. And you're a good man too, Cyril – no one could run that school better than you – but the Order's not a school and besides, like Aidan, you're too old, too set in your ways.'

He paused to enjoy the emotions of his audience. Aidan was looking relieved; he would indeed have hated to leave Ruydale. Cyril was inscrutable but I was aware of his aura of desolation and I knew Father Darcy would be aware of it too. Meanwhile Francis was so white with tension that his face had assumed a greenish cast. That pleased Father Darcy. Aidan had been a disappointment, Cyril had been a pleasure and Francis had been a delight. That left me. Father Darcy looked at me and I looked at him and our minds locked. I tried to blot out his psychic invasion by silently reciting the Lord's Prayer but when I broke down halfway through he smiled. He was a terrible old man but he did so enjoy being alive, and in the knowledge that his enjoyment could only be fleeting I resolved to be charitable; I smiled back.

Immediately he was furious. I was supposed to be writhing on the rack with Francis, not radiating charity, and as I sensed his anger I realized that in his extreme physical sickness his psychic control was slipping and his spiritual strength was severely impaired.

He said to me: 'And now, I suppose, you've no doubt whatsoever that you'll step into my shoes! Proud arrogant Jonathan – too proud to admit his burning curiosity about the succession and too arrogant to believe I could ever seriously consider another candidate for the post! But I did consider it. I considered Francis very seriously indeed.' He sighed, his rheumy old eyes glittering with ecstasy as he recalled the next step in his process of elimination, 'How hard it was to choose between the two of you!' he whispered. 'Francis has the first-class brain and the skill of the born administrator, but Jonathan has . . . well, we all know what Jonathan has, don't we? Jonathan has the Powers – those Glamorous Powers, as poor old James used to call them – and they made Jonathan the most exciting novice I ever encountered, so gifted yet so undisciplined, yes, you have all those gifts which Francis lacks, Jonathan, but it's those gifts which make you vulnerable as you continue to wage your lifelong battle against your pride and your arrogance. Francis may be less gifted but that makes him less vulnerable, and besides,' he added to Cyril and Aidan, 'Francis has the breeding. Jonathan's just the product of a schoolmaster's mésalliance with a parlourmaid. He'd serve cheap port and young claret to all the important visitors, and that wouldn't do, wouldn't do at all – we must maintain the right style here, we're a great Order, the greatest Order in the Church of England, and the Abbot-General must live in the manner of the Archbishop of Canterbury at Lambeth. So all things considered,' said the old despot, battling on towards the climax of his dénouement, 'and following the process of elimination to its inevitable conclusion, I really think that the next Abbot-General should be a man who can distinguish vintage claret from a French peasant's "vin ordinaire".'

He had lived long enough to see the expressions on our faces. Sinking blissfully into a coma he drifted on towards death until an hour later, to my rage and horror, the Abbot-General of the Fordite monks became none other than my enemy Francis Ingram.

It would have been hard to imagine a superior less capable of dealing with my vision.

III

My antipathy to Francis was undoubtedly the main reason why I did not confide in him as soon as I had received my vision, but possibly I would have been almost as hesitant to confide in Cyril or Aidan. For twenty-four hours after the vision I was in shock. I believed I had received a call from God to leave the Order, and this belief at first triggered a purely emotional response: I felt an elated gratitude that God should have revealed His will to me in such a miraculous manner, and as I offered up my thanks with as much humility as I could muster I could only pray that I would be granted the grace to respond whole-heartedly to my new call.

However eventually this earthquake of emotion subsided and my intellect awoke. Reason tried to walk hand in hand with revelation and the result was disturbing. My first cold clear thought was that the vision was connected with my failure to become Abbot-General; it could be argued that since the Order, personified by Father Darcy, had rejected me I was now rejecting the Order, a rejection which, because it had been suppressed by my conscious mind, had manifested itself in a psychic disturbance.

This most unsavoury possibility suggested that I might have fallen into a state of spiritual debility, and as soon as I started to worry about my spiritual health I remembered that I was due to make my weekly confession on the morrow.

My confessor was Timothy, the oldest monk in the house, a devout man of eighty-two who possessed an innocent happiness which made him much loved in the community. After my installation as Abbot I had picked him to be my confessor not merely because he was the senior monk but because I knew he would never demand to know more than I was prepared to reveal. This statement may sound distressingly cynical, but I had been brought to Grantchester to bring a lax community to order and since in the circumstances it would have been inadvisable for me to display weakness to anyone, even the holiest of confessors, I had decided that the temptation to set down in the confessional the burden of my isolation should be resisted.

As I now contemplated my duty to set down the burden represented by my vision I knew that the most sensible solution was to circumvent Timothy by journeying to London to lay the problem before my superior. But still I balked at facing Francis. Could I make confession without mentioning the vision? Possibly. It was the easiest solution. But easy solutions so often came from the Devil. I decided to pray for guidance but as soon as I sank to my knees I remembered my mentor and knew what I should do. Father Darcy would have warned me against spiritual arrogance, and with profound reluctance I resigned myself to being at least partially frank with my confessor.

IV

'. . . and this powerful light shone through the north window. As the light increased in brilliance I knelt down, covering my face with my hands, and at that moment I knew – ' I broke off.

Timothy waited, creased old face enrapt, faded eyes moist with excitement.

' – I knew the vision was ending,' I said abruptly. 'Opening my eyes I found myself back in my cell.'

Timothy looked disappointed but he said in a hushed voice, much as a layman might have murmured after some peculiarly rewarding visit to the cinema: 'That was beautiful, Father. Beautiful.'

Mastering my guilt that I had failed to be honest with him I forced myself to say: 'It's hard to venture an opinion, I know, but I was wondering if there could be some connection between the vision and the death of Father Abbot-General last month.'

Since he knew nothing of Father Darcy's deathbed drama I fully expected a nonplussed reaction, but to my surprise Timothy behaved as if I had shown a brilliant intuitive insight. 'That hadn't occurred to me, Father,' he confessed, 'but yes, that makes perfect sense. Father Abbot-General – Father Cuthbert, as I suppose we must now call him – was so good to you always, taking such a special interest in your spiritual welfare, and therefore it's only natural that you should have been severely affected by his death. But now God's sent you this vision to help you overcome your bereavement and continue with renewed faith along your spiritual way.'

'Ah.' I was still wondering how I could best extricate myself from this morass of deception when Timothy again surprised me, this time by embarking on an interpretation which was both intriguing and complex.

'The chapel was a symbol, Father,' he said. 'It represents your life in the Order, while the mysterious bag beneath the trees represents your past life in the world, packed up and left behind. And your journey through the chapel was an allegory. You opened the door; that represents your admittance to the Order as a postulant. You crossed the bleak empty space where there were no pews; that signifies those difficult early months when you began your monastic life here in Grantchester.' Timothy, of course, could remember me clearly as a troubled postulant; one of the most difficult aspects of my return to Grantchester had been that there were other monks less charitable than Timothy who took a dim view of being ruled by a man whom they could remember only as a cenobitic disaster. 'But you crossed the empty space,' Timothy was saying tranquilly, 'and you reached the pews; they represent our house in Yorkshire where you found contentment at last, and the lilies placed beneath the memorial tablet symbolize the flowering of your vocation. Your walk down the central aisle must represent your progress as you rose to become Master of Novices, and the bright light at the end must symbolize the bolt from the blue – your call to be the Abbot here at Grantchester. But of course the light was also the light of God, sanctifying your vision, blessing your present work and reassuring you that even without Father Cuthbert's guidance you'll be granted the grace to serve God devoutly in the future.' And Timothy crossed himself with reverence.

It was a plausible theory. The only trouble was I had no doubt it was quite wrong.

V

Having revealed my most urgent problem in this disgracefully inadequate fashion, I then embarked on the task of confessing my sins. 'Number one:

anger,' I said briskly. My confessions to Timothy often tended to resemble a list dictated by a businessman to his secretary. 'I was too severe with Augustine when he fell asleep in choir again, and I was also too severe with Denys for raiding the larder after the night office. I should have been more patient, more forgiving.'

'It's very difficult for an abbot when he doesn't receive the proper support from all members of his community,' said Timothy. He was such a good, kind old man, not only in sympathizing with me but in refraining to add that our community had more than its fair share of drones like Augustine and Denys. My predecessor Abbot James had suffered from a chronic inability to say no with the result that he had admitted to the Order men who should never have become professed. The majority of these had departed when they discovered that the monastic life was far from being the sinecure of their dreams, but a hard core had lingered on to become increasingly useless, and it was this hard core which was currently, in my disturbed state, driving me to distraction.

Having mentally ticked 'anger' off my list I confessed to the sin of sloth. 'I find my work a great effort at the moment,' I said, 'and I'm often tempted to remain in my cell – not to pray but to be idle.'

'Your life's very difficult at present,' said Timothy, gentleness unremitting. 'You have to deal with the young men who knock on our door in the hope that they can evade military service by becoming monks, and then – worse still – you have to deal with our promising young monks who feel called to return to the world to fight.'

'I admit I was upset to lose Barnabas, but I must accept the loss, mustn't I? If a monk wishes to leave the Order,' I said, 'and if his superior decides the wish is in response to a genuine call, that superior has no right either to stop him or to feel depressed afterwards.'

'True, Father, but what a strain the superior has to endure! It's not surprising that you should be feeling a little dejected and weary at present, particularly in view of Father Cuthbert's recent death, and in consequence you must now be careful not to drive yourself too hard. You have a religious duty to conserve your energy, Father. Otherwise if you continue to exhaust yourself you may make some unwise decisions.'

I recognized the presence of the Spirit. I was being told my vision needed further meditation and that I was on no account to make a hasty move. Feeling greatly relieved I crossed 'sloth' off my list and rattled off a number of minor sins before declaring my confession to be complete, but unfortunately this declaration represented yet another evasion for my two most disturbing errors of the past week had been omitted from my list. The first error consisted of my uncharitable behaviour during a disastrous quarrel with my son Martin, and the second error consisted of my unmentionable response to the unwelcome attentions of a certain Mrs Ashworth.

VI

After making this far from satisfactory confession to Timothy I retired to the chapel to complete my confession before God. Later as I knelt praying I became aware of Martin's unhappiness, a darkness soaked in pain, and as I realized he was thinking of me I withdrew to my cell to write to him.

'My dear Martin,' I began after a prolonged hesitation, 'I trust that by now you've received the letter which I wrote immediately after our quarrel last Thursday. Now that four days have elapsed I can see what a muddled inadequate letter it was, full of what *I* wanted (your forgiveness for my lack of compassion) and not enough about your own needs which are so much more important than mine. Let me repeat how ashamed I am that I responded so poorly to the compliment you paid me when you took me into your confidence, and let me now beg you to reply to this letter even if this means you must tell me how angry and hurt you were by my lack of understanding. I know you wouldn't want me to "talk religion" to you, but of course you're very much in my thoughts at present and I pray daily that we may soon be reconciled. I remain as always your devoted father, J.D.'

Having delivered myself of this attempt to demonstrate my repentance I was for some hours diverted from my private thoughts by community matters, but late that night I again sat down at the table in my cell and embarked on the difficult task of writing to Mrs Ashworth.

'My dear Lyle,' I began after three false starts. I had been accustomed to address her by her first name ever since I had once counselled her in an emergency, but now I found the informality grated on me. 'Thank you so much for bringing the cake last Thursday afternoon. In these days of increasing shortages it was very well received in the refectory.

'Now a word about your worries. Is it possible, do you think, that your present melancholy is associated in some way with Michael's birth? I seem to remember that you suffered a similar lowering of the spirits after Charley was born in 1938, and indeed I believe such post-natal difficulties are not uncommon. Do go to your doctor and ask if there's anything he can do to improve your physical health. The mind and the body are so closely linked that any physical impairment, however small, can have a draining effect on one's psyche.

'I'm afraid it's useless to ask me to heal you, as if I were a magician who could wave a magic wand and achieve a miracle. The charism of healing is one which for various reasons I avoid exercising except

416

occasionally during my work as a spiritual counsellor, and as you know, I never counsel women except in emergencies. This is not because I wish to be uncharitable but because a difference in sex raises certain difficulties, as any modern psychiatrist will tell you, and these difficulties often create more problems than they solve. May I urge you again to consult Dame Veronica at the convent in Dunton? I know your aversion to nuns, but let me repeat that Dame Veronica is the best kind of counsellor, mature, sympathetic, intuitive and wise, and I'm sure she would listen with understanding to your problems.

'Meanwhile please never doubt that I shall be praying regularly for you, for Charles and for the children in the hope that God will bless you and keep you safe in these difficult times which at present engulf us all.'

Having thus extricated myself (or so I hoped) from Mrs Ashworth's far from welcome attentions I then wasted several minutes trying to decide how I should sign the letter. The Fordites, though following a Benedictine way of life, are Anglo-Catholics anxious to draw a firm line between themselves and their Roman brethren so the use of the traditional title 'Dom' is not encouraged. Usually I avoided any pretentious signature involving the word 'Abbot' and a string of initials which represented the name of the Order, but sometimes it was politic to be formal and I had a strong inclination to be formal now. However the danger of a formal signature was that Lyle Ashworth might consider it as evidence that I was rejecting her, and I was most anxious that in her disturbed state I should do nothing which might upset her further. An informal signature, on the other hand, might well be even more dangerous; if I had been writing to her husband I would have signed myself JON DARROW without a second thought, but I could not help feeling that a woman like Lyle might find an abbreviated Christian name delectably intimate.

I continued to hesitate as I reflected on my name. Before entering the Order I had chosen to be Jon but abbreviated names were not permitted to novices so I found I had become Jonathan. Yet so strong was my antipathy to this name that later, as I approached my final vows, I had requested permission to assume the name John – the cenobitic tradition of choosing a new name to mark the beginning of a new life was popular though not compulsory among the Fordites – and I had been greatly disappointed when this request had been refused. I suspected Father Darcy had decided that any pampering, no matter how mild, would have been bad for me. It was not until some years later when I became Ruydale's Master of Novices that I was able to take advantage of the fact that shortened names were not forbidden in private among the officers, and a select group of my friends was then invited to use the abbreviation.

As time went on I also dropped the name Jonathan when introducing myself to those outside the Order who sought my spiritual direction, and now I had reached the point where I considered the name part of a formal 'persona', like the title Abbot, which had been grafted on to my true identity as a priest. I thought of Lyle Ashworth again, and the more I thought of her the more convinced I became that this was a case where Jon the priest should disappear behind Jonathan the Abbot, even though I had no wish to upset her by appearing too formal. I sighed. Then shifting uneasily in my chair I at last terminated this most troublesome epistolary exercise by omitting the trappings of my title but nevertheless signing myself austerely JONATHAN DARROW.

VII

Neither Lyle nor Martin replied to my letters but when Dame Veronica wrote to say that Lyle had visited her I realized with relief that my counsel had not been ineffective. However I continued to hear nothing from Martin and soon my anguish, blunting my psyche, was casting a stifling hand over my life of prayer.

By this time I had exhaustively analysed my vision and reached an impasse. I still believed I had received a communication from God but I knew that any superior would have been justifiably sceptical while Francis Ingram would have been downright contemptuous. It is the policy of the religious orders of both the Roman and the Anglican Churches to treat any so-called vision from God as a delusion until proved otherwise, and although I was a genuine psychic this fact was now a disadvantage. A 'normal' man who had a vision out of the blue would have been more convincing to the authorities than a psychic who might be subconsciously manipulating his gift to reflect the hidden desires of his own ego.

I wrote yet again to Martin and this time, when he failed to reply, I felt so bitter that I knew I had to have help. I could no longer disguise from myself the fact that I was in an emotional and spiritual muddle and suddenly I longed for Aidan, the Abbot of Ruydale, who had looked after me with such wily spiritual dexterity in the past. As soon as I recognized this longing I knew I had to see him face to face; I was beyond mere epistolary counselling, but no Fordite monk, not even an abbot, can leave his cloister without the permission of his superior, and that brought me face to face again with Francis Ingram.

Pulling myself together I fixed my mind on how comforting it would be to confide in Aidan, and embarked on the letter I could no longer avoid.

'My dear Father,' I wrote, and paused. I was thinking how peculiarly repellent it was to be obliged to address an exact contemporary as 'Father' and absolutely repellent it was to be obliged to address Francis as a superior. However such thoughts were unprofitable. Remembering Aidan

418

again I made a new effort to concentrate. 'Forgive me for troubling you,' I continued rapidly, 'but I wonder if you'd be kind enough to grant me leave to make a brief visit to Ruydale. I'm currently worried about my son, and since Aidan's met him I feel his advice would be useful. Of course I wouldn't dream of bothering you with what I'm sure you would rank as a very minor matter, but if you could possibly sanction a couple of days' absence I'd be most grateful.' I concluded with the appropriate formula of blessings and signed myself JONATHAN.

He replied by return of post. My heart sank as I saw his flamboyant handwriting on the envelope, and I knew in a moment of foreknowledge that my request had been refused. Tearing open the letter I read:

'My dear Jonathan, Thank you so much for your courteous and considerate letter. But I wonder if – out of sheer goodness of heart, of course – you're being just a little too courteous and a little too considerate? If you have the kind of problem which would drive you to abandon your brethren and travel nearly two hundred miles to seek help, I suggest you journey not to Ruydale but to London to see me. I shall expect you next week on Monday, the seventeenth of June. Assuring you, my dear Jonathan, of my regular and earnest prayers . . .'

I crumpled the letter into a ball and sat looking at it. Then gradually as my anger triggered the gunfire of memory the present receded and I began to journey through the past to my first meeting with Francis Ingram.

VIII

I first saw Francis when we were freshmen at Cambridge. He was leading a greyhound on a leash and smoking a Turkish cigarette. He was also slightly drunk. During that far-off decade which concluded the nineteenth century Francis looked like a degenerate in a Beardsley drawing and talked like a character in a Wilde play. In response to my fascinated inquiry the college porter told me that this exotic incarnation of the spirit of the age was the younger son of the Marquis of Hindhead. The porter spoke reverently. Even in those early days of our Varsity career Francis was acclaimed as 'a character'.

I wanted to be 'a character' myself, but I was up at Cambridge on a scholarship, my allowance was meagre and I knew none of the right people. Francis, I heard, gave smart little luncheon parties in his rooms and offered his guests caviar and champagne. Barely able to afford even the occasional pint of ale I nursed my jealousy in solitude and spent the whole of my first term wondering how I could 'get on'.

'If you get on as you should,' my mother had said to me long ago, 'then no one will look down on you because I was once in service.'

I was just thinking in despair that I was doomed to remain a social outcast in that bewitching but cruelly privileged environment when Francis noticed me. I heard him say to the porter as I drew back out of sight on the stairs: 'Who's that excessively tall article who looks like a bespectacled lamp-post and wears those perfectly ghastly cheap suits?' And later he said to me with a benign condescension: 'The porter mentioned that you told his fortune better than any old fraud in a fair-ground, and it occurred to me that you might be rather amusing.'

I received an invitation to his next smart little luncheon-party and put myself severely in debt by buying a new suit. The fortune-telling was a success. More invitations followed. Soon I became an object of curiosity, then of respect and finally of fascination; I had discovered that by devoting my psychic gifts to the furtherance of my ambition the closed doors were opening and I had become 'a character' at last.

'Darrow's the most amazing chap,' said Francis to his latest 'chère amie'. 'He reads palms, stops watches without touching them and makes the table waltz around the room during a seance – and now he's taken to healing! He makes his hands tingle, strokes you in the right place and the next moment you're resurrected from the dead! He's got this droll idea that he should be a clergyman but personally I think he was born to be a Harley Street quack – he'd soon have all society beating a path to his door.'

By that time we were in our final year and I was more ambitious than ever. It was true that I was reading theology out of a genuine interest to learn what the best minds of the past had thought about the God I already considered I knew intimately, but I was also possessed by the desire to 'get on' in the Church and I saw an ecclesiastical career as my best chance of self-aggrandisement; I used to dream of an episcopal palace, a seat in the House of Lords and invitations to Windsor Castle. Naturally I had enough sense to keep these worldly thoughts to myself, but an ambitious man exudes an unmistakable aura and no doubt those responsible for my moral welfare were concerned about me. Various members of the divinity faculty endeavoured to give me the necessary spiritual direction, but I was uninterested in being directed because I was fully confident that I could direct myself. I felt I could communicate with God merely by flicking the right switches in my psyche, but it was a regrettable fact that my interest in God faded as my self-esteem, fuelled by my social success, burgeoned to intoxicating new dimensions.

'How divinely wonderful to see you – I'm in desperate need of a magic healer!' said Francis' new 'chère amie' when I arrived to 'dine and sleep' one weekend at her very grand country house. A widowed twenty-year-old, she had already acquired a 'fin de siècle' desire to celebrate her new freedom with as much energy as discretion permitted. 'Dear Mr Darrow,

I have this simply too, too tiresome pain in this simply too, too awkward place . . .'

I was punting idly with the lady on the Cam two days later when Francis approached me in another punt with two henchmen and tried to ram me. I managed to deflect the full force of the assault but when he tried to use the punting pole as a bayonet I lost my temper. Abandoning the lady, who was feigning hysterica and enjoying herself immensely, I leapt aboard Francis' punt and tried to wrest the pole from him with the result that we both plunged into the river.

'You charlatan!' he yelled at me as we emerged dripping on the bank. 'You *common* swinish rotter! You ought to be castrated like Peter Abelard and then burnt at the stake for bloody sorcery!'

I told him it was hardly my fault if he was too effete to satisfy the opposite sex, and after that it took five men to separate us. I remember being startled by his pugnacity. Perhaps it was then that I first realized there was very much more to Francis Ingram than was allowed to meet the eye.

In the end his henchmen dragged him away and I was left to laugh at the incident, but I only laughed because at that moment my psychic faculty was dormant and I never foresaw the future. A month later the lady, who had been telling everyone I had miraculously cured her abdominal pain, became violently ill, and in hospital it was discovered that her appendix had ruptured. She died twenty-four hours later.

I knew that because I had temporarily removed the pain she had refrained from seeking medical advice until it was too late, and as the enormity of the catastrophe overwhelmed me I perceived for the first time the danger in which I stood. Contrary to what I had supposed my psychic powers made me not strong and impregnable but weak and vulnerable, a prey to any passing demonic force. I had used my powers to serve myself and the result had been tragedy. I now realized I had to use my powers to serve God, not merely in order to be a good man but in order to survive as a sane rational being, and as I finally recognized a genuine call to the priesthood I stumbled through the meadows which separated Cambridge from Grantchester and knocked on the door of the Fordite monks.

IX

At that stage of my life I had no thought of being a monk. I was merely desperate to obtain absolution from someone who, unlike the stern authorities at Laud's College, might hear my confession with compassion, and if anyone had told me that one day I would myself enter the Order I would have laughed in scorn.

It would be edifying to record that my spiritual problems were solved once I came under the Abbot of Grantchester's direction, but although James Reid was the holiest of men he was quite the wrong director for me. I liked him because he was fascinated by my psychic gifts and this, I regret to say, enhanced my pride by making me feel special. The result was that I fell into the habit of using my powers to manipulate him until we had both fooled ourselves into believing that we had achieved a successful 'rapport'. In retrospect the truth seems obvious: I was still so spiritually immature that I could only tolerate a director who cocooned me in indulgence, and beyond my genuine desire to devote my life to God's service, my psyche was as disruptive and undisciplined as ever. The years of my troubled priesthood had begun.

I saw no more of Francis after we came down from Cambridge, and for a time I was so absorbed by my preparations for ordination that I never thought of him, but five years later when I was a married Naval chaplain I heard the astonishing news that he had entered the Order. He began his monastic career at the Starwater house, some forty miles from where I worked at the Naval base in Starmouth, but I had lost touch with the Fordites by that time and I saw no reason why I should ever meet Francis again.

However word of his progress continued to reach me as he rose with lightning speed to the office of Bursar, no mean post in a place like Starwater Abbey where there was a large school to run and complex accounts to be kept. He was still at Starwater when I myself entered the Order in 1923, but as my career was unfolding at Ruydale we never met. Nor did we correspond. He represented a past which I could remember only with shame, and I suspected that I represented a similar burden of guilt to him. But then in 1930 he was transferred to the London headquarters in order to assist its ailing Bursar, and in a flash of foreknowledge I knew that our lives were drawing together again after completing some enigmatic circle in time.

Our reunion came sooner than I had anticipated. I underwent a period of crisis which I have no intention of describing so I shall only record that it concerned the house-cat, Whitby, and nearly terminated my career as a monk; Father Darcy had to be summoned to Yorkshire to set me back on the spiritual rails. I recovered from my crisis, but six months later Father Darcy decided to reassure himself that I had fully surmounted the disaster which was now known as 'The Whitby Affair', and I was summoned to London for an inspection.

The summons was most unusual. No one ever visited London from Ruydale except Aidan, who was obliged to travel there once a year for the Abbots' Conference, and although I was apprehensive at the prospect of being inspected by Father Darcy I was also flattered that I was to receive special attention. However when I arrived in London in a state of wary but not unpleasant anticipation it was a rude shock when I found myself welcomed not by the Guest-Master but by the new Bursar, Francis Ingram.

'So you're still as lean as a lamp-post!' he exclaimed. 'But what happened to those owlish spectacles?'

'My sight improved with age. What happened to the greyhound?'

'He died of a surfeit of champagne.'

We laughed, shaking hands as if we were the oldest of friends, but I was unnerved by his aura of hostility. It lay like a ball of ice beneath the warmth of his welcome; to my psychic eye it was unmistakable, and immediately I heard myself say: 'Perhaps we should agree to draw a veil over the past.'

'Should we? Personally I think it's more honest to face one's disasters and chalk the whole lot up to experience. After all,' said Francis, suddenly fusing his middle-aged self with the undergraduate of long ago, 'Wilde did say that experience was the name men give to their mistakes.'

I said with as much good humour as I could muster: 'Still quoting Wilde? I'm surprised our superior permits it!'

'Then perhaps now's the moment to make it clear to you that I'm the favourite with a licence to be entertaining,' said Francis at once, and as he smiled, making a joke of the response, I recognized the demon jealousy and knew our old rivalry was about to be revived in a new form.

I said abruptly: 'You've told him about the past?'

'How could I avoid it? As soon as the rumour reached London that you'd got up to something thoroughly nasty with a cat I said: "That reminds me of my salad-days." And then before I knew where I was –'

'He'd prised the whole story out of you.'

'But didn't he know most of it anyway?'

'I admit I told him about the Cambridge catastrophe, but I never mentioned you by name! And now, of course, he's decided it would be amusing as well as edifying to batter us into brotherly love – he's summoned me here not just to put my soul under the microscope but to purge us of our ancient antipathy!'

This deduction proved to be all too correct. Every evening after supper Father Darcy would summon us to his room and order a debate on a subject of theological interest. The debates lasted an hour and were thoroughly exhausting as Francis and I struggled to keep our tempers and maintain an acceptable level of fraternal harmony. Afterwards Father Darcy would pronounce the winner, dispatch Francis and embark on a fresh examination of my spiritual health. By the end of the week I was so worn out that I could hardly drag myself back to Yorkshire.

Before my departure I said in private to Francis: 'I hope the old man doesn't intend to make a habit of this. All I want is a quiet life at Ruydale.'

'Dear old chap!' said Francis. 'You don't seriously expect me to believe that, do you? After a few years of living on the Yorkshire moors a man of your ambition would feel like Napoleon marooned on St Helena!'

'I don't think that's funny, Francis.'

'I'm hardly delirious with amusement myself.'

'Obviously you see me as a rival, but I assure you – '

'Don't bother. I'm not in the mood for hypocrisy.'

'What's this – a nursery tantrum? I've never seen such an unedifying exhibition of jealousy in all my life!'

'And I've never seen such a plausible performance of a holy man devoid of ambition, but my dear Jonathan, just answer me this: has it never occurred to you that for a holy man devoid of ambition you seem to be carving out a quite remarkably successful career?'

I turned my back on him and walked away.

X

It is a relief to record that this disgraceful scene was not repeated; no doubt Francis was afterwards as ashamed of our hostile exchange as I was, and when we met again he even took the initiative in apologizing for the incident.

I paid six more visits to London before I was transferred to Grantchester, and each time Father Darcy pitted us against each other in debate, dragged our antipathy into the open and, in a metaphorical sense, rubbed our noses in the mess to discourage us from further antagonism. I was reminded of how one house-trains a cat. In the end Francis and I were so chastened by this remorseless spiritual purging that we almost became friends, but I never felt I knew him well. My psychic faculty, blunted by the antipathy which we both learnt to master but not erase, was dead in his presence. I received no insights which would have offered me the key to his character, nor could I perceive the texture of his spiritual life. Our debates had revealed his powerful intellect, but I came to the conclusion that although he was intellectually able he was spiritually limited and that this fact lay at the root of his jealousy. He was quite intelligent enough to know his limitations, more than intelligent enough to conceal them whenever possible and certainly human enough to resent a man who displayed the gifts he secretly coveted but knew he would never attain. He was also, I soon realized, deeply envious of the effortless psychic understanding which existed between Father Darcy and myself, and when I realized how much he depended on our mentor's approbation I found my self driven to question the propriety of their relationship.

Father-son relationships are as forbidden in the cloister as the notorious 'particular friendships' which prurient laymen find so titillating, but I thought that Father Darcy, in characteristic fashion, might be riding roughshod over the rules in order to give Francis some form of psychological security which could prove beneficial to his character. I was not jealous. I had no desire whatsoever that Father Darcy should treat me as a son; I had a tough enough time surviving his attentions as a spiritual director. But I did wonder if Father Darcy were taking an unwise risk, and I wondered too, as time passed, if he were using Francis to gratify some immaculately concealed emotional need.

I knew I was of intense interest to Father Darcy but the interest was essentially detached; I was just the parlourmaid's son who had presented him with the challenge of a monastic lifetime but who could nonetheless be kept at arm's length in Yorkshire. But Francis was the man from his own class with whom he could feel at ease, the man who had to be transferred to London not merely to supervise the Order's financial affairs but to keep the Abbot-General company in his old age. Such a situation was all very comfortable for Father Darcy, but was it good for Francis? I often considered this question but could never answer it with any degree of confidence. Perhaps Francis needed this special attention in order to make the most of those limited spiritual gifts. It was possible. With Father Darcy any bizarre monastic situation was possible – as I realized all too clearly when he lay on his deathbed and declared that his successor must be a man who could tell vintage claret from 'vin ordinaire'.

Francis took care to say to me afterwards: 'I'd like to think that despite the old man's appalling final antics we can somehow contrive to be friends.'

'Of course. Why not?' I said equably before retreating to my cell to seethe with rage.

'I fear I shall still worry in the future about you and Francis,' confessed Aidan to me after the funeral, but I only answered with all my most fatal arrogance: 'I can't imagine any difficulty arising which can't be easily resolved.'

Less than two months later I received my summons to London and I travelled there in the knowledge that I was deep in difficulties which were incapable of an easy resolution. Moreover after years of rivalry Francis now had me where he wanted me: in a position which was utterly subject to his will.

It was a bitter pill to swallow.

XI

Journeying beyond the walls of one's cloister was always a disturbing experience – I shall never forget my first journey from Ruydale to London when I encountered the amazingly exposed legs of two flappers on the train – and now I found myself more disturbed than ever. But this time I barely noticed the female passengers. I was too busy reading *The Times*. It seemed the French had collapsed; Pétain had ordered a cessation of the fighting and was in touch with the Nazi command. For weeks the countries of Europe had been falling to the Nazis and now after the collapse of Denmark, Norway, the Netherlands and Belgium it appeared that France too had been conquered. Without the French we would be quite alone. More than fifteen hundred years of Christian culture hung by a thread and the Devil's breath was hot upon our necks.

I found myself thinking that the chaos in the world mirrored the chaos in my psyche. I saw my career as a monk hanging by a thread, and as I forced myself to acknowledge that my vision could have been a delusion I was aware of the demonic menace which always had the power to annihilate me. A second later I was trying to recover my equilibrium by telling myself I should put my trust in God, but the trouble was, as I well knew, I was quite unable to put my trust in Francis Ingram.

Unless I wanted to be judged an apostate I could not leave the Order without his permission, and that meant my entire future rested on his ability to exercise the charism of the discernment of spirits, the gift from God which enabled a man to perceive whether a situation was divinely or diabolically inspired. Francis, as I had long since decided, was spiritually limited. This did not mean he was incapable of exercising the charism of discernment, for with God's grace even the most unlikely people can display charismatic powers, but it did mean that I had ample opportunity to worry about how far he was capable of placing himself in God's hands so that he might act as a channel for the Holy Spirit. Francis was a clever, cunning, monk. But was he a good one? I found I could derive no reassurance from reflecting that Father Darcy would hardly have willed the Order to a monk who was merely a first-class administrator. Sickness had undermined Father Darcy's powers at the end of his life, and it was more than possible that in a moment of weakness he had given way to the temptation to leave the Order not to the best monk he ever trained but to the best son he never had.

These lowering thoughts occupied me throughout my journey on the underground railway from Liverpool Street Station to Marble Arch. Then I pulled myself together as best I could, gathered up a few scattered shreds of faith and trudged north through the brilliant June sunshine to the townhouse which had once belonged to the Order's founder, Mr Horatio Ford.

'My dear Jonathan, how wan you look!' said Francis in his most theatrical voice as I entered the room where he conducted his daily business. 'But then the news in this morning's *Times* is enough to make anyone blanche. I confess I'm seriously tempted to buy a wireless in order to hear Mr Churchill's broadcast tonight – only the thought of Father Darcy turning in his grave deters me.'

'If Father Darcy were alive he would already have discovered what kind of wireless the Archbishop keeps at Lambeth Palace and he'd be busy ordering a better one from Harrods!'

We laughed. The interview seemed to have begun in a promising spirit of amity, but I was acutely aware that the amity was no more than skin-deep.

When I had first met Francis in his gilded youth I had been reminded of that famous acid description of Julius Caesar: 'He was every man's woman and every woman's man.' But despite this appearance of ambivalence he had paid carnal attention only to the opposite sex and it was not until years later, when I became enamoured with modern psychological theories, that I suspected he was a homosexual who had indulged in heterosexual affairs to conceal his true inclinations not only from the world but from himself. Later still, when I had become far more cautious in applying modern psychology to complex characters, I became less confident of this facile diagnosis and wondered if the effete airs of Francis' youth had merely been part of a mask he had assumed in order to draw attention to himself; I even wondered if the mask had been his way of damping down strong heterosexual inclinations which he believed might disrupt his life disastrously. But whatever the truth was about his sexuality the fact remained that in his maturity no one could have called him effete. He was a tall man, though not as tall as I was, and the passing years, stripping aside the air of decadence, had substituted a flamboyant air of distinction. He had fine dark eyes, expressive dark eyebrows and a remarkable head of silver hair which he wore longer than a monk should, no doubt out of vanity. I was surprised Father Darcy had permitted it. The Fordites may have dispensed with the medieval custom of the tonsure, but they are still expected to keep their hair decently short.

As I entered the room and we embarked on our friendly opening remarks he moved gracefully around the corner of his large handsome desk to meet me. The room too was large and handsome, littered with the antiques old Ford had left behind, and, as Father Darcy had once boasted smugly: 'More than a match for any of the Archbishop's private chambers at Lambeth.' Father Darcy had been dangerously bold in his belief that to attract worldly respect the Order should present a worldly façade, and personally I deplored such a policy. The Abbot-General's office in which I now stood was in the enclosed part of the house which meant that no one outside the Order ever saw it, but nevertheless it was furnished as lavishly as the Abbot-General's parlour where important visitors were received. There was even, I regret to record, a peculiarly gross chandelier hanging from the centre of the ceiling.

After we had laughed with studied heartiness at the thought of Father Darcy ordering the latest wireless from Harrods, we moved swiftly through the formula of cenobitic greeting like actors in a well-rehearsed play. As Francis paused by the desk I knelt, touched his abbot's ring with my lips and then rose to shake his hand. A moment later we were both seated facing each other across his desk.

'I'm sorry to hear you have a difficulty with your son,' said Francis, idly picking up my letter in which I had requested his permission to visit Yorkshire. 'What's the trouble?'

'As it happens I've now decided that Martin isn't my main worry at present.' I had to will myself to add: 'My major difficulty lies elsewhere.'

Francis, who had been rereading the letter, at once glanced up. 'Oh?' he said. 'And what, may I ask, is your major difficulty?'

I said: 'I want to leave the Order,' and at that moment the die was cast.

TWO

'When Tertullian, who was not a mystic, says that most men apprehend God by means of visions, we realize how natural it seemed to the ancients to believe that these experiences were a genuine and by no means unusual revelation.'

W. R. INGE
Dean of St Paul's 1911–1934
Mysticism in Religion

I

I had expected a theatrical reaction but none came. Not a muscle moved in Francis' face; his fine eyes were unreadable. Finally he dropped the letter on his desk, donned a pair of spectacles and produced from a drawer a clean sheet of foolscap. Then after dipping his pen in the ink he wrote at the top of the page: 'JONATHAN DARROW: 17th June, 1940,' and said casually: 'I assume that when you say you want to leave the Order this isn't a mere whim that's tickled your fancy?'

'I'm sorry, I expressed myself badly. What I want is of course quite irrelevant. But I believe this is what God wants.'

Francis underlined his heading and asked: 'When were you first aware of this call?'

'May the seventeenth.'

Francis raised an eyebrow, ostentatiously examined his desk-calendar and allowed a pregnant pause to develop. But eventually all he said was: 'How did you become aware of the call?'

'I had a vision.'

A second pause ensued and was allowed to reach a far more advanced stage of pregnancy. Francis took off his spectacles, dangled them between his thumb and forefinger and glanced at the chandelier as if each crystal had demanded a careful inspection. Then replacing his glasses he pushed them down to the tip of his nose and looked at me over the frames. Francis had a whole series of such mannerisms; I always found them excessively irritating.

'You had a vision.'

'Yes.'

'You had a vision of profound importance on the seventeenth of May and yet it's only now that you deign to confide in your superior?'

'I felt I needed time for reflection.'

'How arrogant! You have what can only be described as a disruptive experience which must inevitably have affected your spiritual life, and yet you coolly decide you're in a position to reflect on the experience at leisure!'

I said at once: 'I was in error. I'm sorry.'

'So you should be.' Pushing back his glasses to the bridge of his nose he wrote: 'Reflects for a month but now admits the arrogance of his failure to confide in me immediately.' On completing this sentence he added in his most acid voice: 'And now I suppose you'll tell me that you've failed to confide in your confessor! Incidentally, who is he?'

'Timothy.' Remembering that Francis had not yet visited the house at Grantchester I offered the most fundamental description I could devise. 'He's our senior monk, a very good, holy old man.'

'Cosy for you,' said Francis. 'I'm only surprised Father Darcy sanctioned someone so pliable, but then I suppose he thought you couldn't go too far astray so long as he was alive to keep an eye on you.'

I said nothing.

'Very well,' said Francis, writing the word 'VISION' on a fresh line, 'you'd better tell me what happened,' and I began my account of the abnormal in the most normal voice I could muster.

II

When I had finished Francis drew a line under his last note and stared in silence at the written page. 'Is that all?' he said abruptly at last. 'There weren't, for example, six naked women dancing merrily in the glade?'

'Absolutely not!'

Unexpectedly Francis smiled. 'I was only thinking that apart from the ending, which I admit is spectacular, it's a dull sort of vision, isn't it? No naked ladies, no heavenly choirs, no disembodied voices exhorting you to great spiritual feats.'

'I'm sorry, I'll try to have a more entertaining vision next time.'

He laughed. I was tempted to relax but sensed that he wanted to lure me off my guard. 'Tell me,' he was saying idly, 'how often do you have these visions?'

'On average about once every four years. A far more common experience is foreknowledge, a flash in the consciousness which lasts no more than a couple of seconds.'

'How accurate are these flashes?'

'There's a high margin of error. But the correct predictions can be striking.'

'But you admit you're often wrong.'

'Certainly. I believe the future is foreknown to God but not foreordained – or in other words, I believe there are many futures but the future which actually happens in finite time is one which can be shaped by the exercise of man's free will. I think my failures occur when man steps in and alters the pattern.'

'Quite. But I really must resist the temptation to be diverted,' said Francis, 'by an enthralling discussion of determinism and free will. Now if we may return to your visions – ' Francis sighed as if he found the word a heavy cross to bear ' – do they always relate to the future?'

'Not necessarily. They may represent the present or past seen from another angle. Or if they do relate to the future, the past may be present as well. It's as if I'm moving in a dimension of reality which exists beyond time as we understand it.'

'How do you classify this present vision as far as time's concerned?'

'I think I've seen the future. There was nothing of the past or present in it at all.'

'And maybe nothing of the future either. But before we get bogged down in scepticism,' said Francis, allowing me no chance to comment, 'give me an example of a vision which was rather less enigmatic than this one. I feel I need some yardstick of comparison.'

After a pause I said: 'In my last vision – not this present one, but a vision I had in 1937 – I found myself back in the prison where I worked before I entered the Order. I was walking down one of the main halls, but then I turned out of the past into an unfamiliar corridor and entered a large room which was certainly like no cell which exists in the prison service. About a dozen prisoners were confined there but they didn't see me so I knew that in this particular dimension of reality I wasn't physically present. At the same time I felt deeply involved; perhaps I was psychically present in my prayers. Then as I drew closer I realized the prisoners were grouped around a man who lay dying and that this dying man was being tended by a priest whom I recognized. It was Charles Ashworth, the Canon of Cambridge Cathedral and the Tutor in Theology at Laud's. I act as his spiritual director. Then I felt the evil emanating from the walls and as I automatically began to recite the Lord's Prayer the vision ended.' I paused before adding: 'Over the years I've become increasingly certain that I saw a scene in a future prisoner-of-war camp.'

'Where's Ashworth at the moment?'

'Still safe in England. But he's become an army chaplain.' Before I could stop myself I was prejudicing my case by voicing the opinion I so much wanted to believe. 'However there's a good chance that the vision won't come true; I think it may have been a psychic aberration brought on by the strain of my translation to Grantchester.'

Francis immediately pounced. 'What makes you so sure that this latest vision isn't a mere psychic aberration?'

I kept calm. 'The light shining through the north window was the light of God. The knowledge imprinted on my consciousness formed a divine revelation. Unlike the Ashworth vision I felt no doubt afterwards, no confusion.'

Francis said sharply: 'What did Timothy think?'

'He saw the vision as an allegory, but he was handicapped by the fact that I concealed the revelation at the end.' I recounted Timothy's interpretation.

'And do you dismiss this allegorical approach entirely?'

'I'm sure I was in a real place – but I concede there may have been symbolism present. I don't believe the suitcase existed on the same level of reality as the chapel. I suspect it represented travel, or possibly change.'

'Tell me why you're so convinced that you were moving in a landscape which actually existed.'

I said without hesitation: 'The quality of the detail. I was unusually distinct. In the chapel I even smelt the scent of the lilies, and such an experience is most unusual in a vision. The sense of smell is nearly always dormant.'

Francis made a long note before extracting a fresh sheet of foolscap from his desk. Then he said: 'After the vision had ended, what sort of state were you in?'

'I was trembling and sweating. The amount of psychic energy required to generate a vision always produces a powerful physical reaction.'

'Were you sexually excited?'

Silence. I was acutely aware that the longer I took to reply the more questionable my hesitation would seem but several seconds elapsed before I could say: 'Yes, but that doesn't mean anything.'

'That's not for you to decide.' Francis wrote on his fresh sheet of foolscap: 'Possible evidence of sexual trouble,' before he glanced up in time to catch me reading his writing. 'Jonathan, would you kindly desist from flaunting the perfect sight you've been fortunate enough to acquire in middle age and abstain from any attempt to decipher my notes? That's an order.'

'I'm sorry.'

'The correct response to an order from your superior,' said Francis, 'is: "Yes, Father." And by the way, are you aware that since this interview commenced you haven't once addressed me in an appropriate manner?'

'I'm sorry, Father. Please forgive me.'

432

There was a pause. Having flexed the muscles of his new power and found them in good order Francis allowed himself a discreet sigh of satisfaction before he picked up his pen again. 'Very well, let's continue with the subject of sexual intimacy – or, to use the coarse abbreviation of the younger generation, "sex". How many women are there in your life at present?'

'There's my daughter – '

'Let's leave Freud out of this, shall we?'

'There's the Abbess at Dunton. She's a splendid old lady of seventy-eight whom I see when I pay the Abbot's traditional call on the nuns once a year.'

'And let's leave out the old age pensioners too. Is there any woman under forty whom you've been seeing regularly?'

'Only Mrs Charles Ashworth, the wife of the theologian I mentioned just now.'

'Is she attractive?'

'Not to me. In fact I rather dislike her. May I stress at this point that my vision has absolutely nothing to do with women and sex?'

'Why are you getting so ruffled on the subject of women and sex?'

'I'm not getting ruffled! I'm simply impatient because – '

'When did you last see Mrs Ashworth?'

Silence.

'Jonathan?'

'I last saw Mrs Ashworth,' I said, 'on the sixteenth of May.'

'The day before your vision.'

'Yes.' Now it was my turn to gaze up at the chandelier as if every crystal had demanded a meticulous inspection.

'And apart from the visit of Mrs Ashworth,' said Francis as the nib of his pen whispered across the page, 'what else happened on the sixteenth of May?'

'Nothing much. There were the usual minor irritations – Augustine, one of my drones, fell asleep in choir and another drone, Denys, had to be reprimanded for raiding the larder.'

'Just another dreary monastic day – but outside in the world it wasn't dreary at all, was it? It was painfully exciting. Chamberlain had just fallen, Churchill had taken over as Prime Minister, the British Army in France was heading for the ordeal of Dunkirk – '

'In such circumstances it was a relief to be diverted by my drones.'

'Your drones and Mrs Ashworth. Was she your only visitor that day?'

'No.' I hesitated before adding neutrally: 'My son came to see me.'

'Ah yes,' said Francis. 'Martin. Obviously now is the moment when you should tell me about your current difficulty with him.'

I glanced down at my hands and to my horror I saw their outline begin to blur. Willing my abbot's ring to remain distinct I managed to say: 'It was nothing. We had a disagreement but that's irrelevant to the subject under discussion.'

'That's not for you to judge.' As my vision cleared I saw him write 'MARTIN' and underline the name twice. 'Has anything else happened to upset you lately – apart, of course, from Father Darcy's death and your failure to become Abbot-General?'

By this time I had myself so tightly in control that I never even flinched. 'No, Father.'

Francis removed his spectacles and to my profound relief I realized the interview was drawing to a close. 'Well, Jonathan,' he said dryly, 'You've certainly given me food for thought. I trust you've made adequate arrangements for your prior to hold the fort in your absence?'

'I did tell him that I'd almost certainly have to stay overnight – '

'Overnight?' Francis regarded me incredulously. 'Did you really think this matter could be settled in a few hours?'

'No, of course not, but I thought that after you'd cross-examined me you'd merely suggest various avenues of prayer and meditation before sending me back to Grantchester to reflect further on the problem.'

'I see. That's what you'd do, would you, if you were the Abbot-General?'

After a pause I said: 'Yes, Father.'

'But you're not the Abbot-General, are you?'

'No, Father.'

Francis pushed his telephone across the desk towards me. 'Ring your prior and tell him you're going to be away for a week.'

III

I had to cancel not only a number of counselling appointments but an important retreat for theological students. I felt sorry for my prior, burdened with the necessity of making numerous awkward telephone calls, but he brushed aside with admirable alacrity the apology I felt he deserved.

While I was speaking to Bernard Francis was engaged in writing a letter. 'Take this to the infirmary,' he said when he had finished. 'The first thing to do with any monk who had visions is to give him a thorough medical examination. I've told Ambrose you're a psychic so he won't immediately jump to the conclusion that you're off your head, but I've forbidden him to ask you about the contents of your vision and I forbid you to reveal them.'

'Yes, Father.'

'When Ambrose has finished his examination you'll probably be in time to make an appearance in choir. I shall expect to see you in the chapel and also afterwards in the refectory. As for the afternoon, you must spend it in prayer. I suggest you meditate on the subject of truth and pray for the courage to be entirely honest with me during the ordeal which lies ahead for us both. Then at four o'clock you'll return to this room and I shall inform you how I intend to proceed.'

'Yes, Father.'

He made a gesture of dismissal and at once I departed for the infirmary.

IV

I had first met Ambrose the Infirmarian in 1923 during the turbulent opening year of my monastic life; when Father Darcy had removed me from Grantchester I had spent the night at the London headquarters before being dispatched to Ruydale. After an indescribable scene in the punishment cell and another equally harrowing ordeal in which I had been obliged to kneel in a humiliated state in front of the Abbot-General's table in the refectory while the brethren ate their supper, I had been dumped in the infirmary to be repaired and Ambrose had given me the welcome reassurance that the Christian spirit was not entirely absent in that rich repulsive house.

Later I had met him on my unorthodox visits to London after the Whitby affair. He had sought my company during the Saturday recreation hour, and I suspected he was interested in me because he had heard I possessed the charism of healing. He was in correspondence with Wilfred, the Infirmarian at Ruydale, a man who unlike Ambrose had had no formal medical training but who nonetheless possessed considerable gifts as a healer, and Wilfred had probably let slip a detail or two which had stimulated Ambrose's curiosity. However since I was forbidden to discuss my ill-fated career as a healer this curiosity had remained unassuaged.

'Good morning, Father!' he said, meticulous in respecting my office even though before my final preferment he had been one of the brethren invited to call me Jon. 'I heard you were visiting us today but I didn't realize I was going to have the pleasure of talking to you.' And when he had read Francis' letter he said with an admirable serenity: 'Do you normally enjoy good health?'

'Very good health,' I said, and at once wondered if I sounded too firm. Psychics are sensitive on the subject and never more so than when their powers are being critically examined.

Ambrose asked a number of mundane questions about my bowels, bladder, heart, eyes and teeth before enquiring if I were prone to suffer from headaches. Immediately I knew he was toying with the idea of a brain tumour.

'I never have headaches,' I said.

'Never?' said Ambrose mildly.

Realizing that I was sounding thoroughly implausible I changed course and admitted to the occasional headache.

'Have you ever suffered from epilepsy?'

'Absolutely not!'

'Quite so, quite so,' said Ambrose, very soothing. 'But I'm sure you understand that the question has to be asked. I must say, it certainly sounds as if you're unusually fit for a man of your age – and what age would that be exactly, Father, if you'll forgive my asking?'

I was caught unprepared. To my surprise I found the question annoyed me, and my surprise was followed by an emotion which I can only describe as a rebellious embarrassment. I said abruptly: 'One's as old as one feels and I feel no more than forty-five.'

When Ambrose looked astonished I saw the stupidity of my evasion and regretted it. Flatly I said: 'I've just had my sixtieth birthday.'

'Congratulations! I trust the milestone didn't go unmarked?'

'No, my daughter wrote and my grandchildren sent cards.'

'What about your son?' said Ambrose, and at once I knew he had been briefed to make an inquiry about Martin.

'He came to see me.'

'How nice!' Ambrose began to take my blood pressure. 'What's he doing nowadays? I suppose he's too old to be called up.' At that time compulsory enlistment only encompassed men up to the age of twenty-seven.

'No doubt he'll eventually be assigned to some non-combatant task. He's a pacifist.'

'I admire these young men for having the courage of their convictions,' said Ambrose generously. I knew his favourite nephew was in the Air Force. 'What terrible times we live in! I feel I know now exactly how St Augustine felt when he witnessed the civilized world collapsing and saw the barbarians at the gates of his city. Indeed sometimes,' said Ambrose, listening to my chest with his stethoscope, 'no matter how deep one's faith it's impossible not to feel depressed.'

We had reached the subject of depression. After Ambrose had completed his tour with the stethoscope, peered down my throat and congratulated me on having kept all my teeth, I said firmly: 'Before you ask the question you've already framed in your mind, may I assure you that I'm not in the least depressed?'

Ambrose gave me a quizzical look. 'I was actually going to ask if you'd been aware of overworking lately.'

I opened my mouth to say no but instead forced myself to admit: 'Perhaps.'

'Overwork can lead to exhaustion and then depression becomes a danger, even with people who aren't normally depressed. Any trouble getting to sleep?'

'Not usually.'

'And getting up? I was wondering if, when this vision began, you were lying in bed and wishing you could stay there all day.'

After a pause I said: 'I wasn't lying in bed when the vision began. I was sitting on the edge.'

'Ah. And what exactly happened? I'm not asking for details of the vision, I hasten to add, but merely for a description of the signs which preceded it.'

'My visual perceptions altered. Colours became very bright.'

'Did you at any time lose consciousness?' said Ambrose, still surreptitiously clinging to the notion of epilepsy.

'No. My visions are always one continuous experience, the abnormal consciousness flowing directly out of the normal consciousness and back again.'

'Is it at any time an out-of-the-body experience?'

'Yes, in the transitional period between the normal and the abnormal I can look down on my body from above.'

'Well, that's all very orthodox for a psychic, I suppose,' said Ambrose, compensating for his obsession with epilepsy by accepting my descriptions calmly. 'When did you start having these experiences?'

'I've always been psychic in the sense of being able to receive flashes of foreknowledge. But the psychic energy required to generate the visions didn't develop until I was fourteen.'

'The age of puberty? By the way, that reminds me – I'd better examine you for possible prostrate trouble.'

We had reached the subject of sex. I kept quiet and waited.

'No sign of disease,' said Ambrose presently. 'Good. But I wonder if you have any more mundane problems in that area? For instance I had a man in here the other day who was plagued by early-morning erections. Of course nothing could be more common than an early-morning erection, but this man suffered such discomfort that he found he could only obtain relief by masturbating, and as he was a priest this put him in a difficult spiritual position.'

'Self-abuse hardly results in an easy spiritual position for a layman either, Ambrose.'

We both laughed.

'Of course a lot of monks would give their back teeth to have such problems,' remarked Ambrose, washing his hands. 'It's curious, isn't it, how a man likes his equipment to be in working order even though he's taken a vow not to use it? I find that psychologically interesting.'

I made no comment.

'I'm told that this vision of yours was accompanied by certain sexual manifestations,' said Ambrose, forced by my silence to abandon his discreet approach. 'I presume this means you had an erection.'

By this time I was getting dressed. Buckling the belt of my habit I said: 'It's unhelpful, Ambrose, to press the connection between the sexual force in the body and the psychic force in the mind. There may indeed be some sort of link, but exactly what that link is can only be a matter of speculation and in my opinion any sexual manifestations which occur are essentially irrelevant.'

'They're not indicative of sexual frustration?'

'One of my most striking visions,' I said, 'occurred during my marriage when I was regularly enjoying my marital rights.'

'Then I'd certainly agree sexual frustration couldn't have been involved on that occasion, but what about this present incident? Has celibacy been uncomfortable for you lately?'

'Certainly not, and personally I'd have taken a very sceptical view of that monk who could only solve his physical problem by masturbating! I hope you had the good sense to tell him to apply cold water more liberally and work harder.'

'So with regard to your present vision – '

'It had nothing to do with sex, Ambrose.'

'But nevertheless it was accompanied by – '

'Why are you laying such stress on this trivial physical phenomenon? Sexuality should be accepted without fuss, not turned into an object of morbid speculation!'

'Yes, Father. Did you ejaculate?'

'Ambrose, I know you're asking these ridiculous questions with the best will in the world, but I really think – '

'I'm sorry, I didn't mean to upset you – '

'I'm not upset!'

' – but I'm merely anxious to get everything quite clear in my mind. Now, if these sexual manifestations are irrelevant, am I right in thinking that the visions have nothing to do with any event, sexual or otherwise, which may be taking place in your life at the time?'

I willed myself to be calm and recalled my duty to be honest. 'No, that's not right,' I said with reluctance. 'There's usually an event which seems to act as a trigger.' I hesitated before adding: 'In 1937 I had a vision about a young priest whom I'd just helped through a grave spiritual crisis. It seemed clear afterwards that this crisis, which had absorbed me deeply, had acted as a stimulant, triggering this psychic glimpse of one of his possible futures.'

'And may I ask if you've identified the trigger of this latest vision?'

I said flatly: 'There was no trigger. The vision came from God.'

We sat in silence for a moment. I sensed that Ambrose was anxious to signal not only his respect for me but his reverence for any gift from God, and because I was aware of his sympathy I managed to control my anger when he eventually asked: 'Have you felt persecuted lately?'

'No. And I haven't been hearing voices either. I'm not a paranoid schizophrenic.'

'The most difficult patients, as any doctor will tell you,' said Ambrose, smiling at me, 'are always the ones who like to run their own interviews and dictate the results to their unfortunate physicians.' He stood up before adding: 'However I have to admit that in my opinion you're physically very fit for a man of sixty, and I'm not surprised you feel no older than forty-five.'

At last I was able to relax. 'Thank you, Ambrose!' I said, smiling back at him, but after I had left the infirmary I realized he had ventured no opinion on my mental health at all.

V

'I've been reading your file,' said Francis when I returned to his room at four o'clock that afternoon. 'Of course I'd read it before – I plucked it from the safe as soon as the old man had breathed his last – but in the light of the present situation I find it doubly fascinating.'

Father Darcy, like all efficient dictators, had kept files on those subject to his authority so that he always knew who was likely to cause trouble. The information had been acquired not only from the regular reports of his abbots but from his annual visitations to their houses.

I said dryly: 'I doubt if a fascinating file should be a source of pride.'

'That shows a promising spirit of humility.' Francis, entrenched behind his theatrical mannerisms, began to flick idly through the assorted papers in the bulging cardboard folder, and suddenly I wondered if he were feeling insecure, playing for time while he steadied his nerves. 'The part I enjoyed most,' he was saying amused, 'was the section about Whitby the cat. Whitby! Was he named after the Synod?'

'Of course.'

'You'll be surprised to hear Father Darcy gives him a favourable mention. "A very superior animal," he writes, "much admired by the community." '

I said nothing, but the mention of Father Darcy seemed to give Francis the confidence he needed and he embarked on the necessary speech. 'This is how I intend to proceed,' he said briskly. 'Every afternoon at this time you'll come here and we'll discuss certain aspects of your situation. Let me hasten to reassure you that at this stage I've no intention of behaving like either a prosecuting counsel or a member of the Spanish Inquisition; I merely want to shine a torch, as it were, into various obscure areas to try to widen your perspective on what I suspect is a very difficult and complex reality. Then I'll send you back to Grantchester for further reflection.'

'Yes, Father.'

'After a month of further reflection,' said Francis, soothed by my immaculate docility and steadily gaining in confidence, 'if you still feel called to leave the Order, you must return here so that I can wheel on the rack, take you apart and poke around among the pieces. It'll be very unpleasant but I've no choice; I'm responsible as your superior for the care of your soul, and I can't possibly release you from your vows until I'm absolutely certain that this call comes from God and not from – but no, we won't talk of the Devil. Father Darcy would, but I'm not Father Darcy, and to be honest I think he was a great deal too obsessed with demonic infiltration and very much too fond of exorcism.'

This confession intrigued me. It was the first time I had ever heard Francis disagree with our mentor or hint at his own private spiritual attitudes. Cautiously I said: 'Father Darcy was a psychic and it's easier for psychics, I think, to talk symbolically of forces which they can perceive so clearly but which normal people find opaque.'

'Oh, don't misunderstand!' said Francis at once. 'I'm not one of those liberal theologians who cheerfully write off the Devil as passé! Obviously demonic infiltration exists – look at Hitler. But you're not Hitler, Jonathan, and I think that any corruption of your call is going to come from the dark side of your personality within you, not from the dark forces of the Devil without.'

'Father Darcy would say – '

'Father Darcy would say the Devil could be at work in your psyche, but that would just be his old-fashioned Victorian shorthand for what you and I know to be the disruptive force of the subconscious mind.' Francis, who had discarded his theatrical mannerisms as his confidence increased, now leant forward across the desk to hammer his point home. 'So let me repeat: it's not the Devil we have to fear here but a dislocation of your personality, possibly brought on by emotional strain or overwork or some cause which is at present hidden from us.'

There was a pause while I debated whether it would be wiser to make no comment but finally I was unable to resist saying: 'A dislocation of the personality is by no means always incompatible with a genuine call. Indeed

440

in some cases a call can't be heard until some dislocation occurs to open the spiritual ears.'

Francis immediately felt intimidated. 'I trust you're not intending to carp and snipe at everything I say.'

'No, Father, I'm sorry.'

'It may indeed be the case that God is calling you by putting you under psychological pressure,' said Francis irritably, 'but how can we tell that until we uncover the exact state of your psyche and see whether the pattern reveals the hand of God or the self-centred desires of your disturbed ego?'

'Quite.' As I assumed my meekest expression, Francis suddenly realized that if he persisted in his ill-temper I could outflank him by taking a saintly stance which would make him look both petulant and foolish. His innate cunning triumphed over his insecurity; at once he altered course.

'Once I believe your vision is a gift from God,' he said with a smile, 'I'll be the first to shake your hand and give you my blessing. But meanwhile . . .' He gave a theatrical sigh '. . . meanwhile I have a duty to be sceptical.' Effortlessly he began to exude an aura of benign concern. 'Now Jonathan, I'm not going to give you orders about how you should spend your time in between our daily interviews, but I do urge you to relax as much as possible. Ambrose thought a little holiday would do you no harm at all – ' This was the first proof I had that Ambrose felt ambivalent about my mental health ' – so please don't exhaust yourself in excessive spiritual exercises. Oh, and I forbid you to fast. I don't want you having visions brought on by lack of food.'

The interview having thus been terminated on a relentlessly friendly note, I retired with relief to my cell.

VI

My cell was in fact not a cell at all but one of the distressingly well-appointed bedrooms set aside for visiting abbots. It lay on the same landing as the Abbot-General's sumptuous bed-chamber, and faced west across the immaculately tended grounds which were bordered by a high brick wall. Our founder Mr Ford, an adventurer who had made his fortune from slave-trading before his miraculous conversion to Anglo-Catholicism in the 1840s, had lived in style on his ill-gotten gains, and his Order, supported from the start by the greater part of his massive wealth, had husbanded their resources with skill.

I have no wish to imply that there is anything wrong with a monastic community which skilfully husbands its resources; on the contrary, every abbot has a duty to make ends meet. But I found it unedifying that a religious order should spend such a large part of those skilfully husbanded resources on maintaining such a luxurious headquarters. I was offended not merely by the antiques in the Abbot-General's office. The atmosphere of debilitating affluence permeated the entire house and even the novices were pampered by having linoleum on the floor of their scriptorium. As I returned to my grossly over-furnished chamber that afternoon I wondered, not for the first time, how I was expected to pray in it, and to counter my disgust I embarked on some alterations.

My first act was to take down the three pictures and put them in the wardrobe. I like paintings but when I am at work I find them distracting. Then I rolled up the carpet, which was woven into a pattern so exquisite that I had already wasted far too much time gazing at it, and tackled the bed, which I knew from past experience during the annual abbots' conferences was soft enough to give me back-ache. Having stacked the mattress against the wall I replaced the coverings on the base, which was reassuringly hard, and sat down at the table.

I closed my eyes but not to pray; I was sharpening my concentration in order to plan how I might best master Francis, but the next moment, realizing that I was behaving like some buccaneering politician engaged in a seamy struggle for power with his party's leader, I checked myself in shame. How unedifying! I resolved to order my thoughts along more salubrious lines, but the more I tried to think like a priest the more I despaired of ever being able to concentrate in that distracting house, and at last, abandoning my room, I sought refuge in the garden.

I felt better outside. At first I merely strolled around the lawn and savoured the sunshine but later my feet carried me through the gates of the cemetery until I found myself standing by the cross which marked Father Darcy's grave.

Desolation overwhelmed me. I felt lost and adrift, unnervingly vulnerable – and the next moment I was experiencing not only a painful grief but a painful rage that I should have been so abruptly abandoned.

The emotion lasted no longer than a second but I was shocked by the glimpse I had received into such a dark desperate corner of my psyche. I even glanced over my shoulder as if I feared Francis might be spying on me in my weakness, but of course there was no one there and finally, pulling myself together, I withdrew to the chapel to pray.

VII

At four o'clock on the following afternoon I presented myself once more at the Abbot-General's office, and the gross china clock which squatted on the marble mantelshelf chimed the hour as I halted before my superior's desk.

'Today we're going to examine your vision in more detail,' said Francis, motioning me to be seated. 'So let me start by asking you this: are you sure the chapel was in England?'

I was sufficiently startled to say: 'It certainly never occurred to me that it wasn't. The light was so English – that dull greenish light which is so typical of a cloudy English day.'

'Presumably the greenish light means the trees were in leaf. But was it spring or summer?'

'Summer. It was too warm to be spring.'

'If you were aware of the warmth,' said Francis, writing busily, 'were you also aware of your clothing? Were you wearing your habit, which we know is hell in hot weather, or were you enjoying the bliss of trousers and a shirt?'

I was intrigued but had to confess: 'I don't know.'

'Then let's approach the memory from another angle. You said yesterday – ' He consulted his notes ' – that there were steps leading to the doors of the chapel. Did you raise the skirt of your habit as you mounted these steps?'

'No,' I said at once, and added without thinking: 'How clever of you, Francis!'

He looked at me over the top of his spectacles. 'Father.'

'Father. I'm sorry.'

There was a pause before he continued: 'So it seems you weren't wearing your habit. But that's not evidence that you weren't still a monk. You may have been on an authorized visit to this place, in which case you'd be wearing a clerical suit, just as we all must whenever we journey outside the cloister. So my next question is inevitably: what was your purpose in going to the chapel?'

'I've no idea.'

'Was it your impression that the chapel was in regular use?'

'Yes. The lilies – '

'Obviously the lilies prove that it had been visited recently but was there any evidence that the building was being used for worship? The lack of orthodox altar furnishings seems odd.'

'I agree but I'm sure it wasn't deconsecrated. Perhaps I was going there for private prayer.'

'The place seemed familiar to you?'

'Yes, I felt no surprise either when I saw the chapel below me in the dell or when I opened the door and saw the interior.'

'Why do you consistently refer to it as a chapel as if it were owned by a family or an institution? Couldn't it have been some isolated country church?'

'In my experience isolated country churches are always medieval. This building was Victorian even though it was built in the style of Inigo Jones.'

'What makes you so sure it was a Victorian imitation and not the work of the master himself? I thought Victorian architects were in love with medievalism, not classicism.'

'Then this must have been the exception that proves the rule. The pews were typically Victorian. Of course they could have been added later, but – '

'If you know so much about the chapel why don't you know what this ruined building was behind it?'

'I'm sure I did know exactly what it was, but my mind's now a blank. Could it have been an ancient castle?'

'In a dell?' Francis was sceptical. 'Castles are usually built on mounds.'

'Perhaps it was a much older church, then – a church which for some reason had been allowed to fall into ruins.'

There was a pause while we both pondered on this mystery but eventually Francis said: 'As we know neither the name nor the vicinity of this place it would be well-nigh impossible to track down, but even if we found the chapel really did exist that still wouldn't prove your vision came from God. All the discovery would prove is that you're capable of a certain type of clairvoyance.' Drawing a line below his last note he dipped his pen in the ink again. 'Let's leave the chapel now and turn to this bag which you believe to be a symbol. Am I right in assuming this wasn't a bag you've ever owned?'

'I'd never have owned such a piece of luggage. It was expensive – and somewhat feminine, pale beige with dark brown corners. In fact it was the sort of suitcase one would associate with a wealthy woman.'

Francis raised an eyebrow. 'Are you sure you've never seen it before?'

'I was sure at the time. But on reflection . . . Yes, it's not impossible that I've seen it before. I suspect that when my vision required the symbol I didn't invent the suitcase but plucked the forgotten memory from my subconscious mind.'

'But why that particular bag?'

'Because it was striking enough to lodge in my memory. After all, one never usually looks at a bag twice.'

Francis laid down his pen, took off his spectacles and idly contemplated the chandelier. 'Supposing,' he said, 'just supposing you've got this entirely wrong and it's the bag, not the chapel, which exists in reality.'

'I'm absolutely sure – '

'Yes,' said Francis, at once leaning forward on his desk and looking me straight in the eyes, 'you're a great deal too sure of yourself here, Jonathan, and I think you should proceed with more mental flexibility and very much more humility. Go away now and ask yourself the following questions: first, what was your connection with the chapel? The assumption that you were going there for prayer is plausible, I agree, but it actually explains nothing. What were you doing in that environment? And what were you thinking about during that walk through the woods? Your mind seems to have been unusually vacant. Does your lack of surprise when you saw the chapel indicate that the scene was familiar to you, or is it in truth an example of the curiously dreamlike quality which permeates this experience of yours? If this were a real glimpse of the future, why weren't you thinking of your current problems, the current people in your life, possibly even of your current approach to God? I put it to you that you were drifting along like a somnambulist, and I think you should consider whether Timothy was really so far off the mark when he interpreted the vision as an allegory. Ask yourself if the ruined building might symbolize what you, in your recent disappointment over your lack of preferment, might consider your spent career as a monk. Ask yourself if this chapel, modern but built along classical lines, might represent your subconscious longing for an entirely new career in the Church. Ask yourself if the evidence that you weren't wearing your habit is in fact a manifestation of your subconscious desire to discard it. And finally ask yourself why you should have seen a bag which apparently symbolizes not travel and change to you (yesterday's explanation) but (so you now confess) wealth and women. Think on all these questions, Jonathan. Think carefully. And return here at four o'clock tomorrow.'

THREE

'The danger (of hallucinations) is recognized by the best mystical writers.'

W. R. INGE
Dean of St Paul's 1911–1934
Mysticism in Religion

I

I had by this time planned a course of reading and meditation to occupy the hours when I was neither crossing swords with my superior nor attending services in the chapel. The Fordites have imprinted their own idiosyncratic stamp on the Divine Office of the Benedictines, merging Terce with Sext and None with Vespers, but several hours of each day are still spent in choir; a monk must never forget that his chief work is to worship God. However beyond the hours of worship lie the hours of service to others, and normally I was heavily occupied not only with looking after my community but with giving counsel to those outside the Order who sought my spiritual direction. It was odd, even disconcerting, to find myself suddenly with no work on my hands beyond the hours spent in choir. I might have been advised to rest but anyone who has ever attempted to lead a celibate life knows how important it is to keep oneself constructively occupied, so after a prolonged perusal of the library shelves I selected some books which I judged would engage my mind without unhealthily overexerting it.

I chose Dame Julian of Norwich's *Revelations of Divine Love*, not merely because it was one of my favourite classics but because I felt I would be cheered by the writings of a sane practical good-humoured person whose visions had been recognized by the Church. As a masculine counterpoise to Dame Julian's robust femininity I also chose *The Cloud of Unknowing*, another of my favourite works. Feeling I should then emerge from the woods of mysticism into the more arid plains of modern theology I avoided the works of Karl Barth, whose preoccupation with God's transcendence is fundamentally hostile to mysticism, and was about to select the latest book by Reinhold Niebuhr, who parted company with Barth in several important ways, when suddenly I spotted Dean Inge's *The Philosophy of Plotinus*.

I was amazed. Plotinus had been a great religous philosopher with a vast influence on Christian Neo-Platonism, but he had been a pagan and Father Darcy had always refused to have Inge's celebrated masterwork in the house. However on opening the cover of the first volume I found the words 'Cuthbert Darcy' inscribed on the fly-leaf. The old fraud! It seemed he had acquired the copy secretly and kept it in his room where it had been discovered after his death. Silently paying tribute to Francis' broadminded good sense in placing the work in the library, I added both volumes to the collection already in my hands and prepared to retire to my cell, but on my way out I caught sight of a new section devoted to modern psychology.

Francis and I, enjoying a rare moment of unity, had succeeded in convincing our mentor that not all psycho-analysts should be burnt at the stake, and rising to unprecedented heights of eloquence we had argued that we had a religious duty to understand as much about the human mind as was possible in the light of the latest scientific theories. When Father Darcy had declared that the Devil was corrupting intellectual progress by the writings of his servant Freud I had even summoned the courage to say to him sternly: 'Remember Galileo.' The Church has been put in some ridiculous positions in the past by turning up its nose at the scientists.

However although Father Darcy had given us permission to read the books we felt were important, he had been adamant that we should keep any work on psycho-analysis under lock and key, and the sight of Francis' collection now standing bravely on the shelves was certainly a surprise. An even greater surprise was that I felt ambivalent. On the one hand I approved of Francis' resolution to bring the Order openly into the twentieth century, but on the other hand I was aware that monks were very ordinary men in many ways and might not automatically benefit from such intellectual modernism; I could well imagine my drones feasting on certain passages with a curiosity which was more salacious than spiritual. To my horror I saw Francis had even displayed the volumes of Havelock-Ellis on human sexuality. This work was not without interest to a serious student of human nature, but there were parts of it which even I, the crusader for modern knowledge, had felt inclined to burn. Certainly I believed such a work could only have an unwholesome effect on the average monk.

I suddenly realized I was perturbed to a degree more complex than might have been anticipated, and retiring to my room I tried to analyse my feelings further. After a while I realized I was worried that Francis might be tempted to compensate himself for his spiritual limitations by relying too heavily on psycho-analytical theory. It was a chilling thought.

Psycho-analysis can be a useful tool and it had certainly given me numerous important insights during my work as a counsellor, but it is not a substitute for religion and it should always be a servant, never a master. If Francis intended to rely on Freud and Jung instead of on God as he exercised the charism of discernment, then both he and I could well be heading straight for the most profound disaster.

II

'No doubt you've composed a host of brilliant answers to the questions I posed yesterday,' said Francis when I returned to his room on the following afternoon, 'but since my aim at present is not to initiate a debate but to illuminate your situation, I propose we move on to the next topic and discuss your failure to become Abbot-General. I trust you're not going to deny you were disappointed?'

'No, Father.'

Francis picked up his pen. 'What steps did you take to adjust to this disappointment?'

'I had a long talk with Aidan before the funeral and made a full confession to him. That helped. Aidan's a wily old fox. He never said anything so obvious as: "You've got to forgive the old boy in order to be at peace with his memory," but he paved the way to forgiveness by persuading me to admit how much I'd have disliked being Abbot-General and how far more suitable you were for the job.'

Francis leant back in his chair. Perhaps he thought his expression was merely quizzical but I found it cynical to the point of being offensive. 'Why would you have disliked being Abbot-General?'

'Too much administration. Too much vapid socializing with the upper echelons of the Church. Not enough time to counsel men outside the Order. Not enough time to meditate in solitude.'

'A small price to pay, surely,' said Francis, 'for such enormous gratification to your self-esteem.'

'My ego isn't so insatiable as you seem to think! After my talk with Aidan I was happy enough to remain Abbot of Grantchester.'

'But were you?' said Francis. 'That's the next big question, isn't it? The world beyond our cloister has been turned upside down, the barbarians are at the gates and it's a very unpleasant fact of life, as Machiavelli knew all too well, that war can be immensely stimulating. It kicks people out of their well-worn ruts, offers adventure and provides all manner of enthralling changes – unless, of course, one happens to be in a monastery. Then life becomes increasingly drab.'

'I hope you're not implying – '

'Do you deny that the War's been a depressing influence on your work? You lost one of your best young men the other day, didn't you?'

'Barnabas, yes. He's gone into the Army.'

'It's always a harrowing experience to lose a good young monk. And meanwhile you still have more than your fair share of boring old drones – Augustine who falls asleep in choir, Denys the glutton – and what was the name of that monk you told me about once, the one who always has to wash his hands when the clock strikes noon?'

'Clement. But a monastery wouldn't be a monastery without its share of harmless eccentrics!'

'Tedious eccentrics. And meanwhile there you are, active as ever but beached like a stranded whale in your Grantchester backwater – '

'I hardly think you can describe a place which is only two miles from one of the great universities of the world as a backwater!'

'Don't try and tell me the War hasn't affected Cambridge! My spies inform me that Air Force officers are now billeted in the Colleges and undergraduates are being sucked into the war machine – with the inevitable result that fewer people must be coming to the house to make a retreat or seek counselling. And meanwhile your tedious administrative tasks are increasing – all the irritating war-time regulations have to be mastered, interminable forms have to be filled in – '

'Bernard likes doing all those sort of things.'

' – and your frustration must be growing daily. What a contrast to the last war when you were on active service as a chaplain! Then you were making a positive contribution to the war-effort, but now all you can do is twiddle your thumbs in your Grantchester backwater amidst all your boring old men – '

'That's a gross misrepresentation!'

' – and it would be only natural, wouldn't it, if you occasionally longed to get out into the world and make some vital contribution to the fight to save England from the Nazis?'

'But even if I went out into the world,' I exclaimed, unable to resist the temptation to outshout him and falling straight into the trap he had constructed for me, 'I couldn't be a chaplain in the Navy again!'

'No.' For the second time Francis leant back in his chair and regarded me cynically. 'You couldn't. You're too old, aren't you? You're sixty. *Sixty*! Jonathan – ' The trap sprang shut ' – why didn't you remind me that the day preceding your vision happened to be your sixtieth birthday?'

I could only say stiffly: 'I didn't think it was important.'

'No? Could you really regard it as just another birthday? When I was sixty last February I was so sunk in gloom that the old man had to shake me, metaphorically speaking, until my teeth rattled and remind me that to mope about one's age is self-centred, futile and a prime example of that morbid introspection which can so seriously impair one's spiritual health. But the old man wasn't there to shake you till your teeth rattled, was he, Jonathan? He was dead – and that, of course, leads me to my last big question of the afternoon: exactly what effect has his death had on you? It seems to me that you've lost the one spiritual director who was capable of keeping you on the rails.'

'That's not true. Aidan's always shown great skill.'

'Aidan's skill lay in translating the old man's orders into action. Father Darcy ruled your career from the moment he removed you from Grantchester seventeen years ago, and perhaps now that you're without him you're beginning to feel lost, confused, adrift – even unbalanced – '.

This was a line of attack which had to be instantly terminated. 'I must insist – '

'No, indeed you must not! You're not here to be dogmatic and opinionated!' Francis, wielding his power with the efficiency of a giant cat bent on disembowelling his prey, was at his most formidable. In self-defence I assumed an expressionless silence, and as the pause lengthened I sensed Francis deciding how he might best complete my demolition. Finally he said in the most mellifluous voice he could muster: 'I can see you're a trifle upset, Jonathan. Would you like me to tell you a little fairy-story to help calm you down?'

The giant cat was closing in for dinner. With a sinking heart I resigned myself to the inevitable.

III

'Once upon a time,' said Francis, 'there was a hero, but he wasn't a prince as most heroes are in fairytales; he was a monk. At his christening long before he became a monk, two fairies were present. The good fairy gave our hero a range of unusual gifts which would one day make him an outstanding monk, but the bad fairy made him proud, arrogant, stubborn, wilful and opinionated. Our hero grew up and had an interesting career in the Church but it was blighted because despite his gifts the bad fairy's curse made him unable to develop them to the full. However when he at last became a monk the miracle happened and he met his fairy godfather, the godfather who knew how to wave the magic wand so that all those nasty qualities bequeathed by the bad fairy could finally be overcome.

'Our hero endured many vicissitudes but thanks to his fairy godfather, who constantly waved the magic wand, our hero flourished, became happy in his new life and eventually allowed himself to hope that he might climb right to the top of the monastic tree. But then one day a terrible thing happened: the fairy godfather retired to live in fairyland, and our hero suddenly found himself not only abandoned, deprived of the magic wand, but also blocked from reaching the top of the monastic tree.

'Because he was a good monk he did his best to go on as usual, but slowly the bad fairy tiptoed back into his life and all those unfortunate flaws in his personality began to emerge again. Our hero became restless and dissatisfied. He fought to overcome these feelings by diverting himself with hard work, but this only made him exhausted and once the exhaustion began he slipped into a depression. Then slowly, very slowly, as life in the monastery became increasingly dreary, he began to think how nice it would be to abandon the soporific routine of his monastic life and ride off bravely, just as all heroes should, to join the great crusade against the Devil which was currently being waged in the world beyond the walls of his cloister.

'But of course he knew he couldn't leave the Order just to satisfy his own desires so he slogged heroically on – until a really terrible thing happened, so terrible that it sent him into a panic. He had a birthday, a particularly nasty birthday for a man, the sort of birthday which made him realize he wasn't just middle-aged any more, he was OLD. And before he could stop himself he was thinking in terror: I'm old, I've got nothing to look forward to except a few more years of living in this dreary backwater and I can't bear it, I've got to get out, I've got to *live* by joining in the Crusade somehow and proving I'm not as old as the calendar says I am! Because he was such a good monk he did attempt to suppress this thought but at that moment the bad fairy pounced, sneaking into his subconscious and showing him the perfect way to escape from his dilemma. And on the morning after that terrible birthday he had a beautiful vision, just as beautiful as any vision from God should be, so beautiful that he had no doubt at all, in his pride and arrogance, that he was being called to leave the Order.'

Francis stopped speaking. With a supreme effort of will I maintained my silence, while far away on the mantelshelf the hideous china clock ticked so abrasively that I longed to smash it to pieces.

'Now, Jonathan,' said Francis, smiling at me with great charm, 'having, I trust, soothed your nerves by spinning you that quaint little tale which of course you'll deny has any relevance to your current situation, I shall conclude this interview by asking you to meditate on the following questions: how vulnerable are you as a monk now that you've been deprived of your mentor? How vulnerable are you as a man who's just turned sixty? Why did you so fiercely deny to Ambrose that you might be seriously depressed? Why did you resent Ambrose asking about your age? Why, when Ambrose began to talk about carnal matters, were you first withdrawn, then evasive and finally downright annoyed? Why have you been so busy insisting both to Ambrose and to me that everything in the garden's lovely when it's quite obvious that some very nasty weeds have begun to flourish in the flower-beds? Forget that pride of yours for a moment, Jonathan! Try and see yourself for once as the vulnerable man you really are instead of as the superhuman mystic whom your vanity requires you to be – and then perhaps we may have some hope of unravelling this most complex of mysteries . . . Now go away, please, and when you return here tomorrow I trust you'll have made up your mind to display very much more honesty and infinitely more humility than you've deigned to display so far.'

IV

Retiring to my room I sat for a long time on the edge of the bed. It was not until after Compline that I was able to read a chapter of Dame Julian's 'Revelations' and feel comforted. 'And at the end of our woe,' Dame Julian had written, 'suddenly our eyes shall be opened and in clearness of light our sight shall be full; which light is God, our Maker and Holy Ghost, in Christ Jesus our Saviour. Then I saw and understood that our faith is our light in our night; which light is God, our endless day.'

I thought of the light of God in the chapel, and at once my faith was renewed. As a good monk I accepted that I had to consider all Francis' repulsive and degrading insinuations, but my will to survive his attacks was now as iron and it was in a new mood of obstinate defiance that I knocked the next day on his door.

V

'I knew this is going to be just as tedious for you as it'll undoubtedly be for me, Jonathan,' said Francis in his most businesslike voice as soon as I was seated, 'but I'm afraid that today we'll really have to discuss sexual matters.'

'I was wondering how long you'd be able to keep off the subject of Havelock-Ellis! Are you sure it's wise to allow all your men access to his work?' I was well aware that this critical response represented a gross impertinence, but I was becoming a little tired of standing by meekly while Francis flexed the muscles of his power.

For a moment I thought he would lose his temper but he controlled himself, and despite all my animosity I was impressed. Dealing with a recalcitrant monk was never easy; dealing with a hostile abbot would without doubt be a nightmare, and the temptation to wield one's power repressively, evenly violently, would be strong.

'No monk in this house is permitted to take a book from the psychology section of the library without my permission,' he said at last, 'but I thought it right that everyone should be able to see what's on offer. I wanted to avoid the hypocritical situation sanctioned by Father Darcy in which a select group of men is granted unlimited freedom in their reading while the superior continues to declare virtuously that only devotional and theological books can stand on the library shelves. Now if you've satisfied your urge to be obnoxious in order to prove to me that you're under strain, may we proceed with this interview?'

Finding myself wholly outmanoeuvred by this honest and dignified reply I could only say: 'I'm extremely sorry, Father. I'm afraid I was in error. Forgive me.'

'Very well, but let me take advantage of your penitent mood by turning immediately to the subject of your celibacy; perhaps your penitence will encourage a frank response. Have you any comment to make about your past difficulties here?'

I said cautiously: 'The difficulties weren't serious. My chief problem as a monk has been in accepting authority, not in doing without women.'

'Nevertheless I see from your file that there's been at least one occasion during your career in the Order when you've longed – and I quote your own words, recorded with startling fidelity by Father Darcy – "to chuck it all up and fuck every woman in sight".'

'I assure you I don't usually use such language, but I was extremely upset when I made that remark and having worked for years among working-class men who used that sort of word with monotonous regularity – '

'My dear Jonathan, just because you've always taken a "holier-than-thou" attitude to my own occasional lapses into vulgarity, there's no need for you to go into such a paroxysm of embarrassment now that I've caught you out in a rare verbal indiscretion! The truth is, as you well know, that so long as you avoid blasphemy and talk like a gentleman in front of your subordinates I don't care a fig about your language. And now if we may return to the subject of your sexual frustration – '

'I see no point in dwelling on it. All normally-sexed monks feel frustrated occasionally.'

'Quite. But would it be fair to say, do you think, that these bouts of difficulty with your celibacy coincided with periods of emotional stress in other areas of your life?'

I said obtusely: 'I'm not sure I understand you.'

'I think you do but you're playing for time while you try to drum up an innocuous response. Very well, let me be more precise: we all have our different ways of coping with emotional disturbances. When I was in the world I used to cope with them by drinking too much, but I seem to remember you were never greatly interested in food and drink. Your solace always lay elsewhere.'

'Only when I was a very young man. But after my call to the priest-hood – '

' – you turned over a new leaf, yes, of course you did, but nevertheless isn't it a fact that when you experienced emotional turbulence as a monk you also experienced a period of difficulty with your celibacy?'

'Well – '

'And isn't it a fact that in the emotional stress which followed Father Darcy's death you might have expected to experience yet another bout of discontent with the celibate life?'

I said abruptly: 'I thought you assured me at the beginning of these conversations that you didn't intend to behave like a prosecuting counsel.'

We stared at each other.

'So!' said Francis. 'You sidestep the question! May I remind you that we'll get absolutely nowhere unless – '

'I was aware of sexual tension but it wasn't an urgent problem. It didn't interfere with my work – indeed I worked harder than ever in order to take my mind off the difficulty.'

'And no doubt this aggravated the exhaustion which led to your depression.'

'I deny – '

'Yes, you would, wouldn't you? But never mind, we've somehow succeeded in establishing that you felt sexually tense. Now let's turn again to that young woman Mrs Charles Ashworth. How often has she been coming to see you and why does she come?'

I had been prepared for this assault. I said: 'I helped her husband through a profound spiritual crisis in 1937 and she was part of that crisis. Without breaking the secrecy of the confessional it's impossible for me to say more than that as the result of the crisis I know facts about them which no one else knows, and in consequence I'm important as a confidant to them both. Indeed Mrs Ashworth has apparently come to see me as a comforting presence in her life. There's no question of counselling – I've referred her to Dame Veronica at Dunton – but occasionally Mrs Ashworth finds it helpful to visit me for a short talk and I always try to be available to see her.'

'But surely,' said Francis, 'if you "rather dislike" the woman – your own words – aren't these visits a bore? Why do you continue to make yourself available?'

I had anticipated this question too. 'I feel it's something I can do for Charles,' I said. 'It's not an easy marriage for either of them and in my unusual position I have the opportunity to exert a stabilizing influence.'

'Is Mrs Ashworth so unstable?'

'I was referring to the marriage.'

'And I'm referring to Mrs Ashworth. Any woman in an unstable marriage is liable to be emotionally volatile. Are you in fact telling me that you've been having regular private interviews with a disturbed woman while you yourself were suffering from sexual tension?'

'That gives an entirely false impression – '

'I think not. Could you explain, please, why you've been pursuing a course of conduct which must inevitably have been bad for your spiritual health?'

I knew I had to proceed with great care. After a pause I said: 'Perhaps I feel guilty that I dislike her and this guilt makes me feel obliged to bend over backwards to be charitable. To tell the truth, I never wanted her to marry Charles. But on the other hand I fully accepted that he felt called to make the marriage, and since this meant I had to master my dislike in order to accept God's will, my continuing antipathy makes me feel guilty; I feel I'm failing to respond to God's will as I should.'

Francis merely said: 'Why do you dislike her?'

'I think she's a tough ambitious little baggage who's fundamentally only interested in herself.'

'Tell me what happened at that last meeting.'

Obediently I embarked on an account of my interview with Lyle. '. . . and then she left,' I concluded in my most colourless voice.

'Did she shake your hand?'

'No.'

'There was no physical contact of any kind between you?'

This was the one question which I had prayed he would never ask. The ensuing silence seemed intolerably loud.

'Dear me,' said Francis, removing his spectacles, 'how very difficult this is. Jonathan, I'm sorry but I'm afraid I shall really have to ask – '

'It was a very trivial incident,' I said rapidly. 'As I opened the door of the visitors' parlour she exclaimed: "Thank you for always being so kind to me!" and then she stood on tiptoe, and kissed me on the cheek and swept out into the hall. Naturally I knew I couldn't possibly see her alone again, so later I wrote to her and – '

'Did you respond to the kiss in any way?'

'No, of course not!'

'I'm not just talking of a voluntary response. Was there any involuntary reaction?'

'Don't be absurd!' I said before I could stop myself but added at once: 'Forgive me, Father, that was the height of disrespect. I'm sorry.'

Francis ignored the apology. 'Why is my question absurd?'

'Well . . .' To my horror I found myself floundering.

'You were in a state of sexual tension, some saucy little baggage comes along and pecks you on the cheek – '

'My sexual tension had been dowsed by my anxiety. I was worried in case anyone had seen us, I was angry that she should have behaved like a trollop and I was repelled by my fundamental dislike of her.'

'Jonathan,' said Francis, 'you may honestly believe in the truth of every word that you're saying; I'm inclined to think that you do. But I want you to go away and reflect carefully about where the truth actually lies here. Are you sure you've really explained why you dislike this woman so much? why does an affectionate peck on the cheek turn a clergyman's respectable wife into a trollop? Why did you become so over-heated just now when I suggested you might have responded involuntarily to this most fleeting and harmless of kisses? And last of all I'm going to ask you this: can you deny that only a few hours before your vision your sexual tension had been exacerbated and your emotional equilibrium undermined by your encounter with this woman?' He paused but when I remained silent he waved his hand in dismissal and I retired, seething with angry humiliation, from the room.

VI

Once again I found myself unable to do anything except sit on the edge of my bed. I had long since drawn up a timetable of work in which simple reading and prayer were interspersed with 'lectio divina' and meditation, but now I found that my will to maintain this admirable discipline had begun to flag. Hoping for comfort I turned to Dame Julian again but this time her joyful optimism had no message for me and halfway through one of my favourite passages I realized I was thinking not of her 'showing' but of Francis' appalling 'fairy-story'. Earlier I had protected myself by refusing to dwell upon it, but now, shaken by Francis' remorseless exposure of the Achilles' heel represented by my sexuality, I found my defences had been impaired. In desperation I thrust aside *The Revelations* of Dame Julian and sought to distract myself with the unknown author of *The Cloud of Unknowing*.

But no distraction was forthcoming. Almost immediately I read: 'Oftimes the devil feigneth quaint sounds in their ears, quaint lights and shining in their eyes, and wonderful smells in their noses; and all is but falsehood.'

Snapping the book shut I gave a convulsive shudder and dragged my way down to the chapel for Vespers.

VII

'I lied to you yesterday,' I said to Francis when we met again. 'I'm sorry. I know very well I've got to be entirely truthful in order to help you reach the right decision.'

Francis never asked what the lie was. That impressed me. Nor did he make any attempt to humiliate me further by embarking on a justifiable reproof. That impressed me even more. Instead he motioned me to sit down and said abruptly: 'It's a question of trust, isn't it, and you don't trust me yet.'

I forced myself to say: 'I do want to trust you.'

'Well, at least that's a step in the right direction.'

'And I do accept that you're a first-class monk – '

'No, you don't. You accept that I'm a first-class administrator and you accept that the old man gave me a first-class training, but I've still to prove I'm a first-class monk, and that's why it's just as vital for me as it is for you that I should deal with your crisis correctly. I know perfectly well that you believe the only reason why I became Abbot-General was because I knew how to exploit the old man's secret longing for a son. Well, now I have the chance to prove the old man wasn't completely off his head and that I really am the right man for the job, so accept that I have a powerful motive to behave properly here, Jonathan, and do please discard your fear that I'll be unable to wield the charism of discernment unless you regularly throw in a lie or two to help me along.'

Yet again I was impressed. I heard myself say: 'It takes courage to be as honest as that. Thank you. I can't promise you I'll succeed in matching your honesty, but I can promise I'll do my best to try.'

'Then put on your boxing-gloves,' said Francis, not ill-pleased by this exchange, 'and let's step back into the ring for the next round.'

VIII

'Today,' said Francis, 'we're going to talk about your son.' Flicking through the pages of my file he added: 'There's not much on record about either of your children. Abbot James noted a few details when you entered the Grantchester house and later when you were at Ruydale Father Darcy made a note – ah yes, here it is – remarking that it was fortunate you were in a remote part of England where your children could only rarely visit you. "Frequent family visits," writes Father Darcy, "would not have been good for Jonathan's emotional equilibrium and would have provided a severe spiritual distraction." Have you any comment to make on that judgement?'

'Father Darcy knew that like any conscientious father I tend to spend an unnecessary amount of time worrying about my children's welfare.'

'But was there so much to worry about once you'd entered the Order? Your daughter's marriage has been a success, you've always said, and your son's certainly not been a failure as an actor.'

I said: 'I'm very proud of both my children.'

'Nevertheless it must have given you a jolt when Martin decided to go on the stage.'

'It was hardly a bolt from the blue. He'd always excelled at acting, and when he decided to make a career of it I felt it would be churlish to stand in his way.'

'What a model father! If he'd been my son I'm quite sure I shouldn't have behaved with such saintly resignation . . . How old was he?'

'Eighteen. It was the year I entered the Order. Martin was determined to support himself by taking part-time jobs while he was earning a pittance in repertory. My daughter was married. I was free to go my own way.'

'Eighteen's very young. Are you absolutely certain there was no row when he declared his thespian intentions?'

'Martin and I don't have rows! Our relationship has always been excellent!'

'Yet last month, on the day before your vision, you and he had what you described as a "disagreement". Will you now tell me, please, exactly what happened?'

I had rehearsed this moment many times. 'He disclosed to me that he wasn't leading a Christian life. Naturally I was upset.'

Francis looked at me over the top of his spectacles. 'He's thirty-five now, isn't he? Isn't that rather old to be sowing wild oats?'

I said nothing.

'What's the problem? Trapped in an eternal triangle?'

I heard myself say in an obstinate voice: 'Martin must choose how to live his life. He's a grown man and I've no right to interfere.'

'But if the life he's chosen to live is unChristian – '

'Well, of course I pray for him to be brought back to Christ. Of course.' Despite my rehearsals I was finding the conversation difficult to sustain.

'Has he been leading this unChristian life for some time?'

'Apparently.'

'Yet you had no idea?'

I shook my head.

'Despite your so-called excellent relationship with him?'

I wanted to shout: 'You bastard!' and hit him. The violence of my reaction shocked me. Bending my head I stared down at the obscene luxury of the Indian carpet.

After a pause Francis said gently: 'I'm sorry. Obviously the revelation was a great shock to you,' and I knew my defences had been destroyed. I could cope with Francis being worldly, cynical, aggressive, snide and downright bloody-minded. But I could not cope with him understanding my misery and being kind.

I stood up. That was wrong. When a monk is seated in the presence of his superior he should never stand until he has been given permission to do so, but now, compelled to turn my back on Francis in order to conceal my emotion, I crossed the room and stood facing the clock on the mantelshelf. My voice said: 'I made a mess of that scene with Martin. I should have communicated by showing compassion, by forgiving. How can anyone be brought to Christ if Christ's representative fails to display a Christian face?'

As I stopped speaking I found I was focusing my entire concentration on the clock in an effort to expel my pain by projecting it in a stream of power from the psyche. The clock's hands quivered; I saw the pendulum falter, and as the present began to grind to a halt the past overwhelmed me, not the recent past but the distant past when I had prostituted my powers in order to 'get on' up in Cambridge. 'I can make your watch stop just by looking at it . . .' The girls had worn watches as brooches in those days, and half the fun of stopping a watch had lain in the erotic adventure of putting a hand on the feminine breast to jolt the mechanism back into action.

In panic I realized I had allowed my psychic discipline to slip. My voice said shattered: 'I've stopped the clock,' but Francis at once retorted: 'Nonsense, it just gave a hiccough. It does that sometimes,' and to my relief I realized that the pendulum was still moving. I said confused: 'I thought – ' but Francis interrupted me.

'Now Jonathan, it's no good trying to play that old parlour-trick because I'm well aware that you never stopped any of those watches in the old days – you merely hypnotized all those gullible girls into thinking that you did. Come back here, sit down and behave yourself – you're acting like a half-baked novice.'

This robust approach, so reminiscent of our mentor, at once steadied me. I returned to my chair.

'Have you heard from Martin since the quarrel?' said Francis after allowing me a moment to regain my composure.

'No, but I've written and I know that eventually he'll write back. Martin's always been so good at keeping in touch and sharing his world with me.' But of course he had not shared it. Grief threatened to overwhelm me again.

'How old was he when his mother died?'

'Seven. Poor Betty . . . After the scene with Martin I thought how upset she would have been about him, and I kept thinking of her, thinking and remembering –' I broke off. Then I added abruptly: 'Forgive me, I'm digressing. My marriage has nothing to do with my present crisis.'

But Francis only said: 'Hasn't it?' Yet you've just confessed that it was most vividly resurrected in your mind shortly before you had your vision,' and as we stared at each other in silence we were interrupted by the rapid clanging of the chapel bell proclaiming an emergency.

IX

'Air raid drill,' said Francis casually. 'We'd better set a good example by retiring speedily to the crypt. I must say, Jonathan, you've picked the most tiresome time in the history of the world to embark on a spiritual crisis.'

After the drill had unfolded in a tolerably well-ordered manner there was no time to resume our interview before Vespers and I found I was greatly relieved by the postponement. I was beginning to be alarmed for the future. If Francis' preliminary talks could so effortlessly destroy my equilibrium, how would I fare when his inquiry became an inquisition? Fear and dread ravaged my psyche, and touring my room I put away all small objects in the chest of drawers. I was afraid that I might be on the brink of generating that activity popularly attributed to poltergeists, an activity caused by bursts of energy from a powerful but poorly disciplined psyche under stress; at such times this energy can move objects, often with considerable force, and if the psyche cannot control itself sufficiently much damage can occur. During my troubled early months in the Order, it had been the poltergeist activity, breaking out in the Grantchester community with alarming violence, which had driven Abbot James to seek help in bringing my disturbed psyche under control.

Memories sprang to life in my mind; I saw myself as a forty-three-year-old postulant summoned to the Abbot's office for an interrogation. I had planned exactly what to say to James to win his soft-hearted sympathy, but when I entered his room I found my plans had gone astray because James was absent and behind his desk sat a stranger, a man in his early sixties, hard-eyed, thin-lipped, ice-cold. The coldness was so extreme that it seemed to burn with heat, and as I at once recognized the powerful psychic aura I experienced a curious mixture of fright and relief. The fear was because I knew this was the one man I could never manipulate and I felt powerless; the relief was because I knew he would heal my disorder. In fact so great was my relief that I forgot to wait for permission to speak but said rapidly: 'I'm causing the trouble but I can't help it because my meditation techniques don't work.'

He sat in his chair and looked me up and down. Then he said: 'Do you know who I am?' and without hesitation I replied: 'You're the Abbot-General.'

'I'm not just the Abbot-General,' he said. 'I'm the one man who can get you out of this spiritual cesspit of yours. Now answer me this: do you want to be a monk or don't you?'

When I immediately answered: 'I don't just want to be a monk – I want to be the best monk in the Order,' he smiled.

'What ambition!' he exclaimed. 'But of course your pride would hardly let you settle for less.' Then the smile vanished, the aura of ice intensified and he said: 'Stand up straight, fold your hands properly, keep your mouth shut until you've been given permission to speak and wipe that arrogant smirk off your face. You've been three months in the Order – are you so unteachable that you haven't yet learnt how to behave? No doubt you think you're such a wise mature priest with your Cambridge degree and your twenty years in Holy Orders, but I'm here to tell you now that psychically you're no better than an ignorant spoilt child and that as a monk you're at present only capable of play-acting.'

He waited in case I dared to argue with him but I was speechless. This interview was far removed indeed from my cosy chats with Abbot James.

'Shall I explain to you,' said the brutal stranger, 'what's really going on here? Like many people whose psychic powers are freakishly well developed you're used to manipulating people whenever you want your own way. What you want here is to be petted and pampered so you've entranced your Abbot, you've tied your poor Novice-Master into a humiliating knot, and now, just like a spoilt child, you're calling attention to yourself by being disruptive in the hope that by causing chaos you'll make everyone realize how special you are!'

'But I swear I'm not doing this deliberately – '

'Of course that's what you swear! You've hypnotized yourself into believing in your own innocence, hypnotized yourself into believing you can't control these ridiculous outbursts of energy! But this is where the hypnosis ends if you want to survive as a monk. We've no room in the Order for confidence tricksters who perform psychic parlour-tricks! What you've got to understand is that there'll be no spiritual progress unless you learn humility and obedience, no hope of acquiring true charismatic power unless you starve that crude psychic force of yours of the pride which makes it so destructive. How can you expect God to use you as a channel for the Holy Spirit when you not only invite but welcome the Devil into the driving-seat of your soul?'

I attempted a defence. I said I was not wicked, merely disappointed and unhappy. I told him the community was lax, that Abbot James was weak and that the Novice-Master was a fool.

Then the stranger rose to his feet. He was not a tall man but at that moment he seemed twice as tall as I was. I flinched. I believe I even took a step backwards. But he never raised his voice. He simply said: 'And who are you to pass judgement on this community? Obviously you're in an even worse state than I'd feared and radical measures will have to be taken. You must be taught a lesson in humility, a lesson you'll never forget, and afterwards you must begin your life as a monk all over again elsewhere.'

Then he had taken me to London and after a night spent in the punishment cell where I had been taught the lesson I would never forget, I had been dispatched to Ruydale to make my fresh start.

The memory terminated. I returned to the June of 1940, but I continued to think of Father Darcy and after a while I closed my eyes so that I might imprint his image more accurately on the retina of my psyche. To attempt to call up his spirit was out of the question; such practices are dangerous as well as arrogant and in my opinion the Church is entirely right to discourage them. It is not for us to interfere in our hamfisted way with the great reality of eternal freedom which lies beyond our brief existence in the prison of time and space, and such discarnate shreds of former personalities which linger within the prison walls are usually either trivial or demonic.

So I made no attempt to summon Father Darcy but when I had constructed his memory as accurately as possible I tried to imagine his response to my current dread that stress would seriously impair my psychic control, and at once the word DISCIPLINE was firmly imprinted on my mind. Finding my timetable I stood looking at it. Then sitting down at the table I opened my bible, made an intense new effort to concentrate and began to read St Paul's mighty epistle to the Romans.

X

'Further to our conversation which was so rudely interrupted,' said Francis the next day, 'I'd just like to clarify a couple of points about this unfortunate interview with your son. Presumably you were very distressed after he left. What did you do?'

'I dashed off a letter of apology to him. Then I forced myself to make my usual appearances in the chapel and in the refectory, but after Compline I retired to my cell again and read *Romans*. That always calms me. I think of St Augustine and Luther reading it and going on to change the course of history; it makes me feel I'm close enough to draw strength from people of great spiritual power. I didn't sleep before the night office but by the time I went downstairs to the chapel I knew I was in control of myself again.'

'And after the office?'

'Then I admit I had difficulties.' I paused to drum up the courage to be honest. 'Once I was faced with the task of sleeping all the symptoms of stress returned. I felt isolated, unhappy . . . If I'd been a married man I'd have turned to my wife for consolation.'

'But as you weren't a married man – '

'I behaved like an ill-disciplined novice and consoled myself, as I implied earlier, with my wife's memory.'

'You mean – '

'I gave way to temptation, obtained the relief I needed and fell asleep around three. How Father Darcy would have despised such a failure of the will! I shall always remember him saying that the body should be an obedient servant, not a tyrant balking at the most rudimentary discipline.'

'Personally I always found Father Darcy's lectures on the power of the will deeply depressing. After his hypnotic persuasiveness had worn off I was left contemplating my weaknesses in despair.'

'I was certainly depressed when I awoke the next morning at five-thirty – and not just because of the failure of my will. I was depressed because I'd allowed myself to get into such a state that a failure of the will was inevitable, and I was still sitting on the edge of my bed, still well-nigh immobilized by my depression, when the vision began.'

Francis said with great delicacy as if he feared one careless word might shatter this miraculous frankness: 'When you said just now that you obtained the relief you needed, am I to understand . . .' His delicacy was so extreme that he left the sentence unfinished.

I thought I could understand his difficulty. 'You doubt that a sixty-year-old man who was emotionally worn out and sexually spent at three o'clock in the morning could manifest the symptoms of sexual excitement during a vision less than three hours later.'

'Not at all,' said Francis with an urbanity I could not help but admire. 'It's a fact that psychics may command unusual reserves of energy, and anyway where sex is concerned anything's possible, even for sixty-year-old men who ought to be decently exhausted. If I hesitated it wasn't because I was boggling at your energy reserves but because I was thinking that if you did achieve a complete release earlier it does support your belief that the vision wasn't triggered by a purely physical frustration . . . You're sure you're not slipping in a little inexactitude to help me along?'

'I hope I'm now beyond the stage of deliberately misleading you.'

'Then I shall merely conclude the interview by asking you to reflect further on the fact that Martin plunged you into a severe emotional disturbance. The question you should ask yourself, I think, is not: "Was this emotional disturbance the direct cause of my vision?" Of course you're determined to believe that question can only be answered in the negative. So perhaps it would be more profitable if you asked yourself instead:

"Exactly why was I so disturbed by Martin's disclosure? What did it mean to me on the profoundest psychological level?" You might also ask yourself if there was any hidden significance in the fact that you later began to dwell with a great intensity on the memories of your marriage. For example, when you were manipulating those memories in a certain way were you merely seeking a release from tension, or were you perhaps expressing a desire to recapture a time when you were leading such an active sexual life that your wife was annually pregnant?'

I stared at him. 'Are you implying that subconsciously I felt so disappointed in Martin that I was smitten with the urge to go out into the world and beget a son to replace him?'

'You find that an unlikely explanation of your vision?'

'I find it ludicrous!'

Francis twirled his glasses. I was reminded of an angry cat swishing his tail.

'I'm sorry,' I said at once. 'That was disrespectful. But I must insist that Martin's still my much-loved son and I've never – *never* – felt so dissatisfied with him that I've longed for a replacement.'

Francis twirled his glasses again and swept open my file. It took him some seconds to reach the passage he had in mind but eventually he found it and paused to look at me. 'I'd like to read you an extract from Father Darcy's report on the Whitby affair,' he said. 'I think you'll find that it's remarkably pertinent to our present conversation.' And clearing his throat he read in a studiedly neutral tone: ' "Jonathan then became very distressed. He said: 'I suddenly saw myself as a layman would see me – a pathetic middle-aged monk, starved of women, deprived of a normal masculine life, who was crying, actually *crying* over a cat.' Then Jonathan said: 'Suddenly I hated my life as a monk, hated it – I wanted to chuck it all up and fuck every woman in sight. I thought: here I am, still only fifty years old and feeling no more than forty; I could be out in the world with a young second wife; I could have another daughter, a daughter who wasn't forever reminding me of Betty – and best of all I could have another son, a son who wasn't an actor, a son I could talk to, a son who wouldn't constantly torment me with anxiety. What am I doing here?' said Jonathan. 'Why am I living this impossibly difficult life?' And I said: 'You're here because you're called to be here. You're here because God requires you to serve him in this hard difficult way. You're here because if you weren't here your personality would disintegrate beneath the burden of your weaknesses. You're here because it's the only way you can survive.' Then he broke down and cried: 'But how do I bear it?' and I answered: 'Think of the novices who have so recently been entrusted to your care. Think of others, not yourself, and you'll find not only liberation from the dark side of your soul but fulfilment of your ability to do great good and live in harmony with your true self.' After that I made him kneel down and I laid my hands on his head and at last the demonic spirit of doubt departed and he was healed." '

Francis closed the file. Then still using his most neutral voice he said: 'And there you have it all: the emotional disturbance, the profound difficulty with your celibacy, the desire to leave the Order and beget a second family – and finally the healing by the one man who was able to keep you on the spiritual rails, the man who's no longer here to give you the help you so obviously need.' He allowed a long silence to develop before adding casually: 'Tomorrow's Sunday and I always try to spend the hour between four and five in meditation. But come here directly after supper, Jonathan, make a new resolution to tell me no more lies and then we'll have our last talk before you depart on Monday morning.'

XI

'I'm worried about your weekly confession,' he said when we met the following evening. 'Of course you could make one of your bowdlerized confessions to Timothy, but I really feel that would be most unsatisfactory and as I'm reluctant that anyone else in the Order should know about your crisis I find I've no alternative but to volunteer my own services as a confessor. I needn't remind you of your right under the Order's constitution to decline to make confession to your superior; if you find my suggestion unacceptable I'll ask Ambrose to hear you, but if you could somehow see your way towards waiving your constitutional right I admit I'd be greatly relieved.'

I could not help but sympathize with him in his predicament. 'You forget that Father Darcy ordered Aidan to be my confessor after the Whitby affair,' I said. 'I'm well used to making my confession to my superior.'

'Quite. But one of the vows I made to myself when I became Abbot-General was that I wouldn't ride rough-shod over the monks' constitutional rights as often as Father Darcy did. However if you're willing to waive this particular right without being coerced . . .'

He allowed me time to prepare, and retiring to the chapel I recalled the episodes of pride, anger and falsehood which had punctuated my life that week. Then I returned to his office and the difficult exercise began. I was surprised when it proved easier than I had feared. He kept unexpectedly quiet, refraining from all the obvious comments, and gradually I began to respect his refusal to gloat over me while I was vulnerable. With a certain amusement I wondered if this compassionate behaviour arose not from his desire to be a good priest but from his instinct to act like a gentleman; I could well imagine him deciding that the waiving of my constitutional

465

right was a sporting gesture which demanded that he should be equally sporting in return.

I was granted absolution and assigned, a very moderate penance. I thought Father Darcy would have judged this much too soft and perhaps Francis too was afterward convinced he had erred on the side of leniency, for as soon as we embarked on our final conversation he became waspish.

'I want to end these talks where we began – with your vision,' he said abruptly. 'There's one glaring omission in your account, and I'm sure I don't have to tell you what that omission is.'

'It wasn't revealed to me what I'm to do when I leave the Order.'

'If you leave the Order.'

'If I leave the Order. I'm sorry.'

'If this vision is from God,' said Francis, examining a well-manicured fingernail in an elaborate charade of nonchalance, 'wouldn't you have expected to receive at least a hint about what you're supposed to do next?'

Cautiously I said: 'I believe further enlightenment will be forthcoming.'

'How wonderfully convenient.' Francis held his left hand at arm's length and gave the chosen fingernail another meticulous inspection. Then suddenly he discarded the mask of nonchalance, leant forward purposefully across the desk and said: 'Now listen to me, Jonathan. You cannot – and I mean *cannot* – ignore your intellectual faculties in favour of a woolly-minded mysticism when your future has to be considered; you should remember that the best mystics have all been distinguished by their sane practical attitudes to life. As soon as you return to Grantchester pull yourself together, confront the reality of this alleged call of yours and try to visualize what kind of life would be waiting for you outside the Order. You're a sixty-year-old priest. You've been out of circulation for seventeen years. At first you're inevitably going to find the world confusing, exhausting, depressing and – for the most part – uncaring. Of course we know you can always find work. We know I can always ring up the Archbishop and say: "Oh, by the way, Your Grace, my best abbot's about to leave the nest – find him a nice little nook in some cosy Cathedral Close, would you?" We know you're not going to be reduced to eating bread-and-dripping in a sordid lodging-house in between bouts of waiting in the dole-queue, but Jonathan, if you're going to survive in the world with your equilibrium intact, you absolutely must feel that you're doing what God's called you to do. Otherwise you'll get depressed and fall victim to Monks' Madness, and we both know what that means, don't we?'

We did. It was a notorious fact that monks who left the Order often found themselves psychologically compelled to recuperate in the most unfortunate of ways from their years of celibate seclusion.

'Oh, and while you're grappling with your possible future in the world,' said Francis as an afterthought, 'do ask yourself what you'd do about women. It's a very important subject and one which must be faced realistically.'

'I'd remain celibate.'

'Perhaps you didn't hear me correctly. I said: "It's a very important subject – " '

'Marriage distracts me from serving God.'

'In that case you'd better stay in the Order. Oh, go away, Jonathan, before I become really irritable with you, and for goodness' sake take your brain out of those second-rate mystic mothballs so that you can do some constructive thinking! Nothing annoys me more than to hear a clever man talk like a fool.'

I rose to my feet. 'Do you wish to see me before I leave tomorrow?'

'Yes, come here after breakfast so that I can give you my blessing.'

He was so fractious that he made the blessing seem a sinister prospect. Leaving the room I began to count the hours which remained until my departure.

XII

France had fallen, and in England the air-raids had started. At Liverpool Street Station I bought a copy of *The Illustrated London News* in order to see a summary of the week's events, and read about the night attacks on the eastern counties. So the long-awaited, inexplicably delayed battle for Britain had begun. Yet I thought the delay might prove significant. God had appeared to withdraw but as always had been eternally present and now the infusion would begin, the outpouring of grace into those facing the blast of the demonic force, the bestowal of courage and endurance which would ultimately triumph over the nightmare of militant idolatry. Our ordeal had begun. The suffering lay before us, but beyond the suffering lay the power of the Spirit, overflowing eternally, in the metaphor of Plotinus, into the muddied waters of mankind, and against that power the ship of idolatry would ultimately shatter. I could see the shattering. It was not a matter of speculation but of 'gnosis', of knowledge; I knew. Yet still I shuddered at the thought of the ordeal ahead of Britain, standing alone at the edge of a demoralized, demon-infested Europe, and the next moment Britain's ordeal was again fusing with my own until it seemed not merely a struggle for survival but a great spiritual quest which could only be described in the ancient language of religious symbolism.

I saw the powers of light withstanding the recurrent invasions of the forces of darkness, the perpetual conflict of finite existence played out amidst the Eternal Now of ultimate reality. Britain wanted peace yet was obliged to go to war to preserve its cherished value; I wanted to serve God in tranquillity yet was obliged to wage a continuous battle against the qualities which marked the opaque side of my nature, and when I saw myself as a microcosm of the conflict which permeated the very air I breathed, I was conscious of the Devil, not the charming little creature rendered so endearingly by medieval artists, but the unseen climate which periodically bruised my psyche as it sensed the vibrations and emanations of the weather-patterns which so many people were apparently unable to perceive. God too can be experienced as a climate, and part of the psychic's 'gnosis' lies in being able to read the barometer which reflects not merely the ebb and flow of demonic forces but the unchanging presence of the kingdom of values, the world of ultimate reality which lies beyond the world of appearances.

It was not until I dismounted from the train at Cambridge that I temporarily abandoned all thought of demonic infiltration. I also abandoned *The Illustrated London News*; I did not want my men to know I had been reading a magazine. It was a rule of the Order that the abbots should read *The Times* each day so that they might inform their men during the weekly recreation hour of events in the world, but this was regarded as a necessary duty whereas browsing through even the worthiest magazine could only rank as a distraction.

Resisting the slothful urge to take a taxi I travelled by motorbus from Cambridge to Grantchester and finally, to my profound relief, walked up the drive of my home. I realized then how much I hated that luxurious house which flourished like an anachronistic weed in the heart of drab, dirty, debilitating London. My Grantchester house was neither old nor beautiful; it had been erected late in the nineteenth century by an East Anglian merchant who had shortly afterwards been obliged by his bankruptcy to sell the place to the Fordites, but in its secluded setting at one end of the village it stood in unobtrusive harmony with its surroundings. Returning to it after my enforced absence I found it refreshingly quiet, modest and serene.

'I've kept all the copies of *The Times* for you, Father,' said my admirable prior, welcoming me warmly in the hall. 'I thought you might have been too busy in London to read the newspaper.'

I refrained from telling him that Francis had not offered his copy for my perusal. Reading a newspaper would have constituted intolerably frivolous behaviour for a monk who was supposed to be concentrating on his spiritual problems.

My relief that I was home expanded into pleasure. My best men were all so glad to see me and even the sulkiest drone achieved a smile of welcome. After dinner I briefly interviewed my officers, attended to the most urgent correspondence, dealt with a couple of domestic matters and toured my five-acre domain of flowers, vegetables, fruit-trees, herbs and bee-hives. In the herb-garden the cat came to meet me and I picked him up. A black cat with a white spot on his chest he had been called Hippo after St Augustine's city, and was a dull affectionate animal like the drone who was responsible for his welfare. After stroking the fur behind the ears I set the creature down again but he was captivated; he padded after me as I completed my tour of the garden and even mewed in protest when I eventually shut the back door in his face.

The bell began to toll in the chapel. I displayed myself in choir, but suddenly as I savoured my happiness that I should once more be worshipping God in my familiar place, I remembered my new call and shuddered. How could I bear to leave? My happiness was at once displaced by misery.

However in my own home I found it easier to regain my equilibrium. Reminding myself that my departure was by no means certain I spent some time reading (the accumulated copies of *The Times* were a great solace) and later made a satisfactory attempt at meditation. When I returned to my cell after matins that night I was tired enough to feel confident that I would fall asleep without difficulty, and indeed as soon as I had closed my eyes I felt my mind drift free of the fetters which I had subconsciously imposed upon it during the difficult week I had spent in London. I began to dream.

XIII

I dreamt of Whitby, proud arrogant Whitby, who had stalked through the backyard at Ruydale with his tail pointed triumphantly at the sky. Prowling prancing Whitby, living in his monastery but padding off to the nearby hamlet whenever the celibate life became too uncomfortable, clever cunning Whitby, a little battered and scarred like all successful tomcats but still as striking as a racy buccaneer, tough tenacious Whitby who worked hard and deserved his pleasures, lean lithe Whitby, wonderful Whitby – what a cat! Whitby was walking through my dream towards me but suddenly he faded into a black cat, not Hippo of Grantchester but Chelsea, my mother's favourite cat, serene elegant Chelsea who washed her paws so fastidiously on the hearth. My mother was there too, serene and elegant just like Chelsea, and she was talking to me without words, saying everything she was too reserved to say aloud and making me feel so sorry for my father who was excluded from these conversations because he was unable to hear us in our silence. 'How lonely you must be with him!' I said to my mother in my dream, but she answered: 'No, I have you and Chelsea.'

'My own children can't hear me when I talk to them,' I said to her, and in my dream time was abruptly displaced because my mother had never lived to see her grandchildren. 'The cat can't hear either.' And as I spoke I saw the stupid ginger cat, my children's cat whom my daughter Ruth had named Goldilocks – which was a ridiculous name for a cat although I had never said so – but whom Martin, enrapt by different fairy-tales, had always called Pussy-Boots. In my dream Betty was slopping some milk into a saucer for the cat and as she stooped I could see past the open neck of her nightgown. 'You look like a cat facing a bowl of cream!' she said laughing, and as I took her in my arms the ginger cat watched us, a stupid cat, not trained to be clever, but unfortunately I was away too much at sea to ensure his education.

'You're going to talk to me about that cat,' said Father Darcy, walking into the scriptorium at Ruydale, and suddenly there was Whitby, proud arrogant Whitby, leaping through the window with an exuberance which made the novices laugh, and Aidan was saying: 'I'm not sure I understand; I'm not even sure I want to understand; but whatever's going on must stop.'

Then in my dream Ruydale dissolved into London and I was searching the Fordite headquarters for Father Darcy. I searched every room, floor after floor, but he had disappeared and finally I had to confess to Aidan: 'I can't go on without him. It's too difficult.' But before Aidan could reply in walked Lyle Ashworth, small and slender in an open-necked nightgown, and as she lay down on the bed I turned to Aidan to say: 'I lied to Francis – I did have an erection after all,' but Aidan had vanished and when I turned back to the bed I found that Lyle had been replaced by Betty. Betty had taken off her nightgown and the next moment I was consummating my marriage, sunk deep in the folds of the most exquisite pleasure, and yet all the time I was so lonely, so isolated, so ravaged by unhappiness and despair –

I woke up sweating.

The room was filled with the dawn light. For some time I prayed for the further revelation which would validate and clarify my vision of the chapel, but no message imprinted itself on my mind and at last, rising reluctantly from my knees, I trudged to the basin to shave.

XIV

I shall not record the mental torment of the next four weeks as I examined each of my interviews with Francis and lurched from confidence to doubt and from despair to hope. Suffice it to say that I meditated on my crisis as conscientiously as I could and somehow, amidst bouts of the most crippling anxiety, contrived to present a semblance of normality to my community as I went about my daily work. Day after day I prayed for a further divine communication, but God, the utterly transcendent God of Karl Barth's repellent anti-mystical theology, appeared to have withdrawn from that scrap of finite time in which my soul was imprisoned and no matter how hard I prayed for a manifestation of his immanence I was disappointed.

In Europe God also appeared to be absent. The Germans slaughtered thirty thousand people in Rotterdam, bombed the Channel Islands and abolished the famous motto of France, 'Liberty, Equality, Fraternity'. In their shock and fear the British seemed to find such events almost impossible to digest; they twittered about tea-rationing (my drones were very cross) and talked righteously about the evils of the 'chatterbugs' who threatened the national security by their gossiping. But we all listened to Churchill with a new intensity. I fell into the habit of reading aloud his speeches, printed in *The Times*, to my men after breakfast; the national peril was so great that I did not think it right that they should be obliged to wait a full week before hearing the news in the Saturday recreation hour. Monks may live apart from the world but they do not reject it, and day after day we prayed for all those whose lives were being ravaged by the war.

However I was eventually diverted from this urgent work by the inevitable summons from Francis. Three weeks after my return to Grantchester I received a communication which read: 'Please confirm that you will return to London on Monday to re-examine the matter which we discussed last month,' and at once I sent an obedient message in reply.

The most arudous part of my ordeal was now confronting me.

I began to steel myself for the inquisition.

XV

'So here we are again,' drawled Francis, 'in spite of Hitler's attempts to interrupt us. I suppose that if the Germans invade they'd shoot all monks on sight? Atheistic Nazism combined with the German folk-memory of Luther's repudiation of religious orders certainly doesn't encourage optimism on the subject.'

'At least you'd be spared the ordeal of interrogating me.'

'So I would. But perhaps I'm to be spared it anyway. Have you finally succeeded in taking your mind out of those mystic mothballs and deciding your vision was a delusion?'

'I'm sorry but –'

'No, don't bother to apologize. I never seriously allowed myself to hope that you'd walk in here, prostrate yourself at my feet and announce: "I was deluded." ' Francis swept back his mane of silver hair and allowed himself a theatrical sigh of resignation. Then he said curtly: 'Very well. Come back at four this afternoon and I'll start the task of taking you apart.'

FOUR

'St John of the Cross even said of a nun who claimed to have had conversations with God: "All this that she says: God spoke to me; I spoke to God, seems nonsense. She has only been speaking to herself."'

W. R. INGE
Dean of St Paul's 1911–1934
Mysticism in Religion

I

'Before I wheel on the rack,' said Francis when we met five hours later, 'I must give you the chance to rebut all the insinuations I made during your last visit, but please, Jonathan, *please* don't offer me any fey mystical claptrap. I want rational propositions from you, not romantic waffle. Now first of all, what makes you think this vision was real and not a fantasy triggered by an emotional disturbance?'

Without hesitation I said: 'Apart from the north light at the end there was no obvious distortion of reality – no six naked women, as you put it, dancing in the glade. If the vision had been triggered by a sexual difficulty I feel some form of sexual symbolism would have shown up.'

'What about the rich woman's bag?'

'I don't believe that was a sexual symbol. If it were then I suspect the lid would have been open to reveal a feminine garment such as a nightgown.'

'Very well, but let's stay with the subject of your sexual difficulties. I concede there was no sexual symbolism in the vision but that might have been because you'd obtained physical relief earlier that night. How can you be sure that the vision wasn't triggered by a far more complex sexual malaise arising from a disintegrating adjustment to the celibate life?'

'Primarily because I've been through much worse times without any vision being triggered. The truth is this difficulty with my celibacy wasn't as bad as you're trying to make out.'

'And Mrs Ashworth?'

'With all due respect I think you should guard against turning that

473

particular molehill into a mountain. Obviously I find the woman more attractive than I want to admit and obviously I've been protecting myself from that weakness by stressing my dislike of her, but I'm not in love with the woman, I'm never likely to be in love with her and such attraction which exists is only of the most trivial kind.'

'So might the ageing Antony have said when he saw the still youthful Cleopatra – but I take your point. And now we've reached the subject of ageing let me ask you this: why are you so sure that your current crisis isn't the result of your panic when you awoke on the morning of your sixtieth birthday and realized old age was staring you in the face?'

'There was no panic. I'm a mature man, not an elderly adolescent clinging to a lost youth! I admit I disliked the idea of being sixty, but what's so abnormal about that? You yourself admitted that you spent three days sunk in gloom after your own birthday this year – how are *you* enjoying being sixty years old?'

'Well, as a matter of fact,' said Francis, 'I'm now enjoying myself immensely. But I dare say that's because I've been fortunate enough to acquire this fascinating new career as the Abbot-General.'

Conversation ceased. As Francis caressed his spectacles languidly I was appalled to realize that my fists were clenched. Surreptitiously I relaxed my fingers one by one.

'Congratulations!' I said at last. 'That was a neat twist of the thumbscrew. Are we reaching the point where you wheel on the rack?'

'Let's first see how well you defend yourself against the charge that you're attempting to storm out of the Order in a fit of pique because you failed to become the Abbot-General.'

'I'm neither a fool nor a bad monk. I've got enough brains to see I'd be very miserable here in London, and I'd never request to be absolved from my vows out of mere injured pride.' I hesitated but when Francis remained silent I added: 'For seventeen years I've had the strongest possible call to the cloister, and on the one occasion ten years ago when I really did long to leave my longing had nothing to do with my lack of preferment. On the contrary, at the time of the Whitby affair I'd just been made Master of Novices and my future in the Order was rosy.'

'But on that occasion you had Father Darcy to steer you through the crisis to safety – and that brings us to the next point: how do you deny the charge that this vision is simply a spiritual aberration brought on by the loss of your mentor?'

I had long since decided that I had no choice but to grasp this particular bull by the horns. 'I could only rebut that charge by proving there's nothing wrong with my spiritual health,' I said, 'and since we both know that my spiritual health has recently been impaired by emotional stress, I can't offer a water-tight defence. All I can say is that it never once occurred to me that I couldn't survive in the Order without my spiritual director. Think of my pride! What would Father Darcy have said if I'd chucked in the sponge in such a pusillanimous fashion? No, of course I had to go on. There was no choice.'

There was a silence while Francis began to polish his spectacles on the skirt of his habit. I could not decide whether he had no idea what to say next or whether he was trying to rattle me by keeping quiet.

'I suppose,' I said to show him I was unrattled, 'you now want me to say something about Martin.'

'You're inviting me to wheel on the rack?'

'No rack's necessary. I'm willing enough to talk – and willing enough to concede that he thoroughly upset me. In fact I'm even willing to concede that he could have triggered the vision. But I don't think he did, and I'll tell you why: if he'd been the trigger I believe the vision would have been different – for instance, I'm sure he would have appeared in it, just as Charles Ashworth appeared in my vision of 1937. And there's another point which is important here: why should Martin's problems make me want to leave the Order? Even if I were in the world I could do no more than pray for him, and I can do that equally well in the cloister.'

'True. But this is where we wonder if you're subconsciously longing to rebel against old age and wipe out your disillusionment with Martin by taking a young second wife and begetting the ideal son.'

'You can't seriously think I'd be quite such a fool!'

'Fortunately for the human race matrimony and procreation aren't confined to fools.'

'Yes, but to embark on both at the age of sixty when I know I can serve God best as a celibate – '

'Why shouldn't God now wish you to serve him as a married man?'

'But I've had no indication of that!'

'You've had no indication of anything! All you've experienced is this mindless urge to leave the Order, and it's quite obvious that this could have been triggered by one or more of a number of circumstances – '

'*There was no trigger.*' I tried not to raise my voice but failed. 'This vision came from God!'

'You still have no doubts about that?'

'Absolutely none!' I said with a dogmatism guaranteed to inflame any superior past endurance.

'How arrogant!' exclaimed Francis. 'How wholly lacking in humility! How utterly devoid of any willingness to admit you could be wrong!' As he stood up I too rose to my feet and we faced each other across his desk. 'Go to your cell,' said my superior, 'and don't come out of it – unless there's an air-raid – until you're due to return here at four tomorrow. I find your attitude profoundly unedifying.'

'Yes, Father.' Walking out I somehow resisted the temptation to slam the door.

II

I wondered if he intended me to fast, but my supper arrived on a tray and later Ambrose appeared, inquiring about my health. Evidently Francis was taking no chances with my mental equilibrium by allowing me to slide into physical debility.

The knowledge that I had deftly repelled Francis' efforts to undermine my confidence was very cheering; settling down to enjoy my solitary confinement I read, meditated, prayed and retired to bed in a mood which could almost be described as complacent.

However my complacency began to fade when I returned to his office on the following afternoon and was obliged to wait outside the door for ten minutes before he gave me permission to enter. Such a petty exhibition of power I found very irritating and my irritation increased when he ordered me into the room only to keep me standing in front of his desk while he finished writing a memorandum. I was beginning to seethe with anger when I realized that any loss of temper would constitute a victory for him, and at once I willed myself to be calm.

Eventually he motioned me to sit down. Then he said abruptly: 'Now listen to me. There are two things I want to make clear. Number one: I'm convinced this vision of yours had a trigger. And number two: the existence of a trigger doesn't necessarily imply the vision didn't come from God.'

I assumed what I hoped was my politest expression and said nothing.

'You believe,' pursued Francis, 'that in order to prove this vision's from God you must maintain that it has no connection with anything which was going on in your life at the time. However I'm now certain that this approach is erroneous.'

Still I said nothing, but I was aware that my polite expression was becoming strained.

'I'm not denying that God's capable of sending people visions out of the blue,' resumed Francis, ploughing on purposefully. 'All I'm saying is that I don't think this is likely in your case, and I say that because, as you reminded me yesterday, your call to the cloister was so strong. I think God would have had to prepare the ground before he gave the blast on the trumpet; otherwise you would have been either deaf to the blast or convinced you were mistaken. So from the point of view of discernment the crucial question becomes: what was the vision's final trigger? I think that once we can answer that question we'll be a lot closer to solving this mystery.'

By this time I had given up trying to look polite and was concentrating on achieving a meek expression.

'Jonathan, I find it unnerving when you give a bravura performance of the model monk. Could you please stop acting and venture a comment which isn't entirely lacking in honesty?'

'I find your opinions very interesting, Father, but I can't help wondering if you might be mistaken. If a final trigger had existed I'm sure I'd be able to identify it.'

'How typical!' said Francis in disgust. 'You think you can do anything, don't you – even read your subconscious mind! It never occurs to you in your arrogance that your subconscious mind may be beyond the reach not only of your intellectual powers but of your tiresome psychic powers as well!'

'Well, of course I'm as capable as anyone else of suppressing a truth I've no wish to face, but all I'm saying is – '

'All you're saying is that you intend to be as arrogant and obstinate as ever! Very well, let me now ask you the question I would have asked yesterday if you hadn't driven me into losing my temper: during your month of reflection at Grantchester did you receive any further enlightenment on the subject of what this call's all about?'

'No. But I'm convinced that if I leave the Order I'll be led to the chapel, and once I get there – '

'Stop!' Francis held up his hand. Then he said incredulously: 'Can I possibly have misheard you? Is it conceivable that you seriously believe you'll be led to this place? You imagine a latter-day Star of Bethlehem will be hanging over the chapel, perhaps, to guide you on your way?'

'No, Father. All I'm saying is – '

'That's enough! Be quiet!'

Silence. I folded my hands together and waited.

'I can see it's a complete waste of time talking to you at the moment,' said Francis. 'I'm beginning to think old age has softened your brain. Go to the workshop and ask them if they can let you have some wood to play with. When people are mentally disturbed they're often encouraged to work with their hands.'

'Yes, Father.' I did succeed in making a dignified retreat but I could not help thinking as I left the room that this time Francis had fared far better in the interview than I had.

III

In the workshop where four monks made church furniture I introduced myself to Edward the master-carpenter, and informed him that I had been ordered to work with wood. He looked incredulous. Manual labour is encouraged at all levels of the Order and I did my share of gardening alongside my brethren at Grantchester, but nonetheless an abbot is hardly expected to seek work as an artisan.

'I was trained by Alfred at Ruydale,' I said.

Edward became deferential. 'What would you like to do, Father?'

I did not answer the question directly but said: 'Is it too much to hope that you've got some seasoned oak to spare?'

He had the oak. It seemed like a sign. With the wood in my arms I moved in exhilaration to the work-bench and embarked on my first carpentry assignment for ten years.

IV

'I hear you're making a cross,' said Francis the next day. 'Amusing for you. How long will it take?'

'Longer than it should. I'm out of practice.'

'What's so difficult about making a cross?' said Francis, deliberately provocative. 'Can't you just bang a couple of bits of wood together?'

'No, Father. I have some very beautiful oak and I want to make the cross out of that one piece, taking every chance to display the grain of the wood to its best advantage.'

'Well, I suppose that's all very soothing for your equilibrium – maybe I should take up carpentry myself. I've got a novice hearing voices, a visiting bishop who's in a muddle about pacifism, four young shirkers who swear they're called to be monks, Harrods trying to sell me something called a radiogram instead of a modest wireless, twenty unanswered letters requesting advice on topics ranging from the sublime to the ridiculous – oh, and I nearly forgot! An abbot whose psychic powers are running riot! When you return to your cell, Jonathan, go down on your knees and thank God you were spared the ordeal of being Abbot-General.'

'Yes, Father.'

'Very well, go away, I'm too busy to bother with you at the moment. I'll send for you in a day or two.'

Exerting an iron will to control my temper I retired once more to the workshop.

V

'I hear you've finished the cross, Jonathan. Of course it's a replica of the cross you saw in your vision, so I suppose all you now have to do is build the chapel, isn't it? Then I can shine a torch through the north window and you can claim a miracle.'

'That's right, Father. But before I build the chapel I was hoping we could resume our talks.'

'Getting impatient? Patience is in many ways the most difficult of all virtues, Jonathan, and one which I feel it would pay you to cultivate.'

'Yes, Father.'

'Perhaps you might have another vision while you wait. It would pass the time.'

'Yes, Father.'

'Jonathan, doesn't it occur to you that this humourless docility is the height of veiled insolence? I detest it – the least you could do to placate me would be to smile at my witty remarks!'

'What witty remarks, Father?'

'Very funny. All right, get out. The Lord Abbot-General is quite definitely not amused.'

VI

'Curiosity stirred in my mind this morning, Jonathan, and it occurred to me to wonder what you've been doing since we last met four days ago. Any more enthralling psychic dramas?'

'No, Father. I've been helping Edward to make an altar-table.'

'Maybe I can solve your entire problem by ordering you to remain here as a carpenter. Obviously the strain of being an abbot sent you off your head.'

'Naturally I shall obey any order you care to give me, Father.'

Francis made a noise which sounded like 'Arrrgh!' and slumped back in his chair. 'Very well, Jonathan, let's have a truce. Sit down.'

Once more we sat facing each other across his desk. I was beginning to feel tense again although the relaxation provided by the carpentry had strengthened me mentally, just as Francis had no doubt intended; a nervous collapse would only have made the task of discernment more protracted. Perhaps he had also intended to strengthen me mentally by severing me from the outside world; I had received no invitation to 'listen in' to the wireless which had finally been acquired to give him immediate news of the continuing crisis, and I had been granted no access to *The Times*. However fortunately for my sanity the monastic grapevine was active. The postman and the milkman were clay in the hands of the doorkeeper, who with impressive journalistic skill jotted down a few pertinent sentences and delivered the scrap to the kitchens. It usually reached the workshop shortly before the office at noon.

'I've reached the conclusion that we must make a completely different approach to this problem of yours,' Francis was saying. 'As things stand we're now firmly entrenched behind fixed positions and no further progress is possible, so we must abandon our survey of the recent past, I think, and turn to the more distant past in our quest for enlightenment.'

Dutifully I said: 'Yes, Father,' and assumed an interested expression.

'What I now want to do,' pursued Francis, changing the nib of his pen, 'is to compare your new alleged call to leave the Order with your old call to enter it and uncover the common denominators.'

I was sufficiently startled to exclaim: 'But there aren't any!' However I added at once: 'I'm sorry. That's not a helpful attitude and I must do my best to be more constructive.'

Francis said after an eloquent pause: 'Thank you, Jonathan.' Throwing the old nib in the wastepaper basket he dipped his pen in the ink and wrote at the top of a new page of foolscap: 'THE CALL TO BE A MONK'. Then he undid the ribbon which bound my file and opened the folder to reveal the earliest entry.

'The first point of interest about your original call,' he said, 'is that it's poorly recorded, but I suspect I know why. You were accepted as a postulant by your predecessor in the Abbot's chair at Grantchester, and we all know now that dear old James Reid, God rest him, was so soft-hearted that he welcomed into the Order almost anyone who knocked on his door. I'd wager your call was never comprehensively investigated. In the end that didn't matter, since your call was genuine, but no doubt when you quickly became so disruptive poor James thought he'd made a disastrous mistake.'

I felt obliged to say: 'He did stand by me – even when I came to blows with the Master of Novices James resisted the demands that I should be thrown out. When he called in Father Darcy it wasn't because he wanted to get rid of me but because he thought the poltergeist activity demanded a first-class exorcist.'

'How Father Darcy must have enjoyed himself! But as soon as he met you, he knew James was right about your potential, didn't he? So he didn't investigate your call in detail either. He was much too busy shaping your future to waste time burrowing into your past.' Francis picked up a page from the file and added: 'Let me read you part of James' opinion recorded after his preliminary interview with you in 1923 when you were still outside the Order. He writes:

' "Jon tells me that he's wanted to be a monk ever since his wife died in 1912. He loved his wife very dearly and they had nine happy years of marriage which were blessed by the gift of two children: Ruth (born 1904) and Martin (born 1905). Jon is clearly devoted to his children and during the eleven years since his wife died he has worked hard to support them even though his call to the cloister was becoming increasingly strong. He tells me that despite his happy marriage he realized that a life of domesticity, charming and rewarding though it might be in many ways, proved difficult to combine with his unusual and distinctive spirituality, and when his wife died he knew he must remain celibate in order to serve God best. He is also convinced that in the world he will always be tormented by the temptation to marry to satisfy his carnal inclinations, and he believes that only in a monastery will he be able to serve God without distraction and develop his spiritual gifts to the full. In my opinion he is patently sincere, mentally well-balanced despite his psychic powers and is obviously a man of high intelligence and considerable pastoral ability. In the past he has been led astray by a desire to exploit the glamour inherent in those psychic powers, but I believe that with sufficient training and dedication a truly charismatic power can be developed for the service of God. I told him I would accept him as a postulant, and I believe that in time he will prove a considerable asset to the Order." '

Francis closed the file. For a long moment we looked at each other in silence. Then he said mildly: 'Jonathan, I don't want to appear cynical but it sounds to me as if you manipulated that unworldly man with all the skill your "glamorous powers" could command. During those nine years of happy marriage, what exactly happened which made you feel the trip to the altar was the one journey you never wanted to repeat?'

VII

'James spells out the truth clearly enough,' I said. 'I came to realize that despite my successful marriage I could serve God best without the distraction of family life.'

'But was your marriage really so happy as James apparently believed it was?'

'No, of course not. My marriage was like the vast majority of marriages; sometimes it was heaven and sometimes it was hell. Betty and I enjoyed the heaven, survived the hell and on the whole rubbed along very tolerably together. I certainly felt I was entitled to present the marriage to James as a success.'

'Tell me about the times when the marriage was hell.'

'You're most unlikely to understand how unimportant our difficulties really were. If you'd ever been married yourself – '

'Oh, good heavens!' Francis was suddenly at his most theatrical. He groaned, shaded his eyes with his hand and twisted his mouth into a mournful grimace. 'I did hope I'd never hear a monk of your calibre try to trot out that hoary jibe of the snide layman. If you're not careful you'll drive me to trot out the equally hoary jibe of the Roman Catholic priests that the onlooker sees most of the game.'

Despite my tension I laughed and apologized.

'I can see I must tiptoe up to this delicate subject by another route,' said Francis. 'How did you meet your wife?'

'After I was ordained in 1903 I went to work at the Mission for Seamen in Starmouth, and a week later I met Betty in the park. She saw me, failed to look where she was going and stumbled over a patch of uneven ground. Naturally I rushed to assist her.'

'Just like a romance from Mudie's Library. What was her background?'

'Her father owned a tobacconist's shop.'

'Dear me, how awkward! What did your schoolmaster father think of your desire to marry below your station?'

'How could he complain? He'd married a parlourmaid – as Father Darcy never ceased to announce to all and sundry whenever he wanted to rub my nose in the mud and induce a spirit of humility.'

'Am I to deduce that you married a working-class woman because you wanted a wife who was just like your mother?'

'No, you can forget your obsession with Freud and deduce that I married a working-class woman because I couldn't afford to marry a lady on my modest salary as a chaplain.'

'If you had no private means I'd have thought that any marriage would have been out of the question for a young man of twenty-three. Surely your father advised you to wait!'

'My father was a quiet scholarly man who didn't find it easy to talk to me – indeed I both mystified and frightened him. His predominant reaction to my desire to marry seemed to be relief that I wanted to settle down.'

'And your confessor – who, of course was none other than dear old James himself at our recently-founded Grantchester house – what did he think of your decision?'

'He was the one who urged me to marry as soon after my ordination as possible.'

Francis said dryly: 'It's amazing how dangerous these unworldly holy men can be. However I mustn't be too harsh on poor old James – after your shady career at the Varsity I suppose it was inevitable that he should doubt your ability to stay chaste for long . . . Did you continue to see him regularly between your ordination in 1903 and your entry into the Order twenty years later?'

'No, there came a point when I realized he was incapable of counselling me, so I decided to dispense with a confessor.'

'You mean you had no direction at all?'

'Oh, I was never completely adrift! I always had some older priest with whom I could discuss spiritual matters but I never made a formal confession and I never talked in detail about my private life.'

'In other words you abandoned Anglo-Catholicism.'

'Not entirely. It was easy enough to drift back into the fold later when I realized I wanted to be a monk. I never lost my admiration for Bishop Gore and the High-Church party.'

'What was the matter on which James failed to give you acceptable counsel?'

'Contraception.' I hesitated but when Francis merely waited I said: 'Betty could barely manage two children under two. The strain was affecting her health as well as our marriage, and when she threatened to seek an abortion if she became pregnent again I saw contraception as the lesser of two evils.'

'Meanwhile James, I suppose, had told you to behave like a eunuch. How far were you able to share the spiritual aspects of this dilemma with your wife? Was she devout?'

'No. She believed in God as children believe in Father Christmas – with a mindless innocence. Religion for her was little more than a charming superstition.'

'How very difficult for you!'

'Not at all,' I said at once. 'She supported me by coming to church on Sundays and she was very good in bed. What did I have to complain about?'

'Well, Jonathan, I'm just an ignorant old bachelor, as you tried to tell me a moment ago, but I seem to remember hearing somewhere that there should be more to marriage than sexual intercourse and I'm quite sure there should be more to being a clergyman's wife than turning up in church on Sundays. Tell me, was your wife intelligent?'

'No, she was really rather stupid. But that didn't matter. I prefer to discuss intellectual matters with men, and anyway when a man gets home after a hard day's work the last thing he wants is to hear his wife expounding on intellectual or spiritual matters. He wants a kiss and a hot meal and the latest report on the domestic front, preferably the more banal the better.'

'The wife you're describing seems to be little more than a housekeeper,' said Francis. 'Or is it a glorified parlourmaid?'

'If you're still clinging to the theory that I wanted to marry a woman just like my mother, I assure you that you couldn't be more mistaken! Betty and my mother were utterly different.'

'Tell me about this mother of yours. Were you the only child?'

'Yes, but she didn't spoil me. She trained me much as she used to train her cats – firmly and without sentimentality.'

'How old were you when she died?'

'Fourteen. Can we stop this digression now, please, and return to more relevant matters?'

'Why are you becoming so flustered about your mother?'

'I'm not flustered! It's just that one doesn't always welcome the opportunity to share cherished memories, particularly if one's in the middle of an inquisition. Why are you so obsessed with the Oedipus Complex?'

'You don't ask the questions, Jonathan; you answer them. Why do you suppose you married a woman who was so utterly different from your mother?'

Losing patience I said with sarcasm: 'No doubt you'd advance the theory that when I failed to find my mother's replica among the women I met through my Cambridge acquaintances, I married my mother's opposite in despair.'

'Never mind the theory I'd advance. Let's hear you advance a theory of your own.'

'I don't have a theory; I have knowledge. I married Betty because I loved her and although the marriage had its difficult aspects I must absolutely insist that it was happy and successful.'

'But my dear Jonathan,' said Francis, 'can't you see that you're trying to harmonize two statements which are fundamentally incompatible? On the one hand you're insisting that you were happily married – yet on the other you're insisting that the marriage made you so maimed spiritually that you were unable to serve God to the best of your ability. I put it to you that either you were happily married and not spiritually maimed; or that you were spiritually maimed and unhappily married. But a priest like you can't possibly be both spiritually maimed *and* happily married. That would be a psychological impossibility.' He terminated the interview by laying down his pen. 'Now go away and consider what I've said, please, and when you return tomorrow I trust you'll be a good deal more explicit about your curious marriage than you've deigned to be today.'

VIII

After supper I retired to my cell to examine the new development in my ordeal. I could now perceive the dimensions of the rack, just as I could sense that Francis was steering me towards it, and I knew I had to take defensive action. I felt no guilt in admitting this because I knew Francis was on the wrong track; my duty at this point was clearly not to wave him on his way but to do my best to steer him back on to the right road.

I sat plotting how I might best deflect him and escape the rack. Of course I could not tell lies. I had to be as truthful as possible but that meant I had to calculate with precision where the boundary between the possible and the impossible lay. It would be unfortunate if I were to discover in mid-sentence that I had allowed myself to be strapped to the rack despite all my efforts to avoid it.

I saw then that the next interview would be fraught with danger, and on the following morning in the workshop I barely glanced at the doorkeeper's daily news. The war beyond the cloister was receding in my consciousness. I was too busy fighting a desperate private war of my own.

IX

'I'm sorry you thought I was being so paradoxical yesterday,' I said to Francis when we next met. 'With your permission I'd now like to explain my marriage in a more comprehensible way.'

Francis kept his expression bland and motioned me to continue.

'What I was really trying to imply,' I said, 'is that I was probably as happy with Betty as I would have been with any other woman. The problem wasn't Betty; it was marriage itself – the whole business of living in close proximity to another person. The truth was I shouldn't have married at all, but as I was neither a eunuch nor a homosexual it never occurred to me at the tender age of twenty-three that I'd be better off as a celibate. So I married and was often very happy. It's true that I did find my spiritual vitality was being sapped, but since I loved my wife and children I was prepared to tolerate that. All marriages involve some degree of compromise and mine was certainly no exception.'

But Francis merely said: 'I do see the distinction you're trying to make when you blame your discomfort on the institution of marriage rather than on your wife, but nevertheless if living in close proximity to another person was so difficult for you one can't help but wonder if that other person might be part of the problem. Forgive me for asking, but did you in fact marry her for any reason other than the sexual and the economic?'

'No, but that doesn't mean the marriage was doomed. Most marriages founder over either money or intimacy. It was our modest bank balance and our intimate relationship which held the marriage together.'

'Well, there wasn't much else to hold it together, was there?' said Francis bluntly. 'She shared none of your intellectual interests; she was spiritually illiterate; she came from a different class, a fact which must have complicated your professional and social life in all kinds of difficult ways – '

'But I've told you – I didn't care about any of those disadvantages! All I wanted was a morally acceptable outlet for my sexual inclinations – '

The trap sprang shut.

'How very humiliating for your wife,' said Francis brutally, and at once I was slammed on the rack.

<h1 style="text-align:center">X</h1>

Francis saw his shot had hit the mark and allowed me no time to regain my equilibrium. 'Tell me more,' he said, 'about how unsuited you were for matrimony. I can quite believe that an immature young man who treats his wife merely as a cheap sexual receptacle would make a far from ideal husband.'

I tried to devise a strong response but I was unable to think clearly. I began to twist my abbot's ring round and round on my finger.

Francis said briskly: 'The truth is, isn't it, that you made each other very miserable. When did you first realize you'd made a mistake?'

'You're completely misrepresenting the situation – '

'How can I be when you admit marriage left you cold?'

'It didn't leave me cold. It left me deprived of psychic space. That's different. It wasn't Betty's fault. As I keep telling you, it was marriage, not Betty, that made me unhappy.' I had stopped twisting my ring but my fingers were tightly interlocked. 'Even before I entered the Order,' I said, 'I needed a great deal of time alone in order to meditate and pray, and frankly I had no idea that the daily routine of marriage would be so hostile to any attempt to sustain a rich inner life. Nothing had prepared me for such chaos. My parents were quiet people; our home was very orderly, very peaceful, very conducive to developing a talent for using solitude constructively. But as soon as I married I found myself in a different atmosphere. Betty was seldom still. She was always rushing hither and thither, continually invading my psychic space, laughing, crying, endlessly chattering ... And then the children came. Of course I was pleased and proud, but the noise, the mess, the constant destruction of any interlude which encompassed peace and order – '

'You were born into the wrong class, Jonathan. My parents cheerfully abandoned their children to nannies and governesses and enjoyed numerous delightful interludes with their lovers.'

'My dear Francis!'

'Will you kindly stop trying to undermine my authority by addressing me by my Christian name?'

'I'm sorry, but I was so appalled by your light-hearted attitude to such adulterous irresponsibility – '

'Good heavens, can't you see I was trying to signal my sympathy to you by making a joke about my own melancholy experience of family life? No, obviously you can't and I must apologize. I shouldn't have forgotten how sensitive you are on the subject of class ... But let's return to your marriage. You've admitted you were in a situation which would have driven me, if not you, to drink. How did you make life bearable for yourself?'

The rack creaked. Once more I found myself groping unsuccessfully for a strong response.

'Come along, Jonathan! Obviously you had to take drastic measures to preserve your sanity – '

'I volunteered for service at sea.'

'What a brilliant solution! But didn't the authorities try to tell you that a married chaplain should remain ashore with his family at the Naval base?'

'I talked them out of that. I said I'd been called to serve on board ship. I was very convincing.'

'And how did your wife feel about being abandoned?'

'She was no more abandoned than any other Naval wife! Anyway I made it up to her – whenever I came home our reunion was as good as a honeymoon.'

'But how did you get on at sea? There was little privacy and peace, surely, on board ship – '

'I had my own cabin. Once the door was closed I had the psychic space I needed and I was happy. That was when I finally faced the fact that I couldn't serve God properly as a married man, yet on the other hand – '

' – on the other hand you had a wife and two children and no doubt you still couldn't imagine giving up intimacy entirely. What an exceedingly difficult spiritual position! You led this divided life, you had no adequate spiritual direction, you must have become increasingly isolated – '

'But I'm a psychic! I was used to isolation, used to no one understanding, used to struggling unaided with my problems – '

'Nevertheless what a relief it must have been when she died!'

Silence fell after this ultimate turn of the screw. My psyche, jarred and jolted by the rack, flashed a warning to my brain that the strain was proving too much but before I could stop myself I was saying: 'It was terrible when she died. *Terrible*. If you think I was glad you couldn't be more wrong.'

'The dark side of bereavement lies in the guilt beneath the grief.'

'Why should I have felt guilty? She loved me, I did everything in my power to make her happy – '

'You're wonderfully convincing, Jonathan, and I can almost smell the red roses and hear the Strauss waltz, but unfortunately my sceptical streak means that I have a deep-rooted resistance to romantic fantasies. However I'm always willing to listen. Come back tomorrow and spin me another romantic fantasy about your chaste life as a widower.'

I stared at him. He stared back. I was acutely aware of my file bulging on the desk between us.

'Francis, I really can't see what relevance such a conversation can possibly have to my present predicament – '

'It's my business to see the relevance, not yours – and for heaven's sake stop calling me Francis! That's a privilege I'll allow you if you ever leave the Order but meanwhile I'm your superior and I don't want either of us to forget for one moment that I'm responsible for the care of your soul . . .'

XI

I dreamt about Hilda that night. In my dream she was committing suicide by hanging herself, but I was bound hand and foot, unable to save her. She was hanging herself on the gallows of the prison where I had worked as a chaplain, and as I watched the body twitching on the end of the rope I realized that I was lying in a pool of blood.

'You look a trifle pale,' said Francis when I returned to his room the following afternoon. 'I was sorry to see when I passed your door at three o'clock this morning that your light was on.'

'Why were you spying on me at three this morning?'

'Why should you automatically assume I was spying on you? What vanity! As it happens, I was summoned to the infirmary to attend to my poor little novice who hears voices. I'm afraid his place is in a hospital, not a monastery.'

'I'm sorry.'

'It was a salutary reminder that ninety-nine point nine percent of the people who hear voices and see visions are mentally ill. Now,' said Francis, having tested the rack and found it in good working order, 'let's return to the subject of your past. We'd established that your marriage was a nightmare – '

'It was not a nightmare! It simply had difficult aspects!'

'Were you faithful to her?'

'Of course I was faithful to her! How could I have gone on as a priest if I'd committed adultery?'

'Was she faithful to you?'

'Yes, she loved me.'

'Even after you ran away to sea? It sounds to me as if she was either mad or mesmerized. Were you abusing your psychic powers to keep her under control?'

'Certainly not, and if you hadn't known me during the most shameful period of my life it would never have occurred to you to ask such an obscene question! After my call to the priesthood no woman ever played Trilby to my Svengali – and anyway there was no need for me to play Svengali to ensure Betty's devotion. She loved me almost too much as it was.'

Francis at once made a note. I tried to read it but could only decipher the words 'unreciprocated love' and 'additional strain'.

I said: 'I think you've still got quite the wrong impression of my marriage.'

'Have I? Then before you start getting upset all over again let's now leave the subject of your marriage and examine your life as a widower.' Opening my file he turned to the page he had already marked. 'I'm going to read you another passage from James' notes,' he said. 'The dear old boy writes:

'"Today Jon made a full confession prior to his entry into our house tomorrow. I must admit I was privately shocked and saddened that he should have drifted so deeply into error, but I remain certain that life in the Order will solve this problem of his by preserving him from temptation, and my original opinion that he will make a good monk remains unchanged."' Francis closed the file and waited but when I remained silent he said not unkindly: 'Jonathan, I promise I shan't be censorious. You confessed these sins to James, he gave you absolution and from a spiritual point of view the matter's closed. I only raise the subject now because I want to see how far your difficulties as a widower contributed to your desire to be a monk.'

'Yes, Father.' I tried to pull myself together. 'I'm sorry,' I said. 'If I hesitate it's because I'm still ashamed, even now, that I failed to live as a priest should.'

'I can quite see how difficult it must have been for you. You were accustomed to an intense intimate relationship and you were in a state of spiritual weakness after years of a divided life . . . Did you never consider remarriage?'

'Never. I did try hard to avoid women and for most of the time I succeeded. But at the end . . . ' I fell silent again.

'Yes?' said Francis. 'What happened at the end?'

'I met this woman. It was 1923 but I didn't know when I met her that I was going to be able to enter the Order later in the year. I thought I was going to have to support Martin up at Cambridge. If I'd known he had no intention of going I might have resisted the temptation, but as it was . . . I felt I couldn't bear my unhappiness any longer.'

'But you'd had mistresses before 1923, surely?'

'I wouldn't call them mistresses. There were incidents during the War when I was on my own somewhere a long way from home. But Hilda

. . . That was quite different. She did voluntary work for a charity which aided discharged prisoners. I met her when I was calling at the home of a prisoner who'd just been freed and she was there too, visiting the wife and children . . . We were both immediately attracted. Chastity soon became quite impossible.'

'Did you ask her to marry you?'

'No, I told her from the beginning that I was only marking time until I could be a monk. But of course she never believed I'd go through with it.'

'How did you eventually extricate yourself?'

'I . . . No, I really can't describe the ghastliness of it all except to say that she threatened suicide and I nearly died of guilt. I hadn't hated myself so much since that poor girl died up at Cambridge.'

Francis printed: 'GUILT. HATES HIMSELF' on his sheet of foolscap and said without expression: 'Did she in fact commit suicide?'

'No.' I wiped the sweat from my forehead. 'She married someone else eventually.'

'And during this agonizing time did it not once occur to you, *not once*, that you might give up all thought of being a monk and marry this woman?'

'Oh no,' I said. 'The affair with Hilda confirmed what I already knew: that I couldn't stay in the world and remain a good priest. My only hope of fulfilling my vocation lay in entering a monastery.'

'Obviously your call was very strong but a satisfactory intimate relationship is no mean driving force either. I'd have thought – '

'Marriage was an impossible dream,' I said impatiently. 'I could never have borne the burden.'

Francis' pen paused in mid-sentence. 'Burden?'

'The burden of guilt that I'd married despite my knowledge that I was unsuited to married life.' Unable to look at him I glanced around the room until my gaze rested once more on the clock. The temptation to reduce my tension by projecting it in a stream of power from the psyche was very strong.

'But you've just admitted that you nearly died of guilt when you jilted her,' Francis was saying. 'Are you now implying – '

'Yes. The guilt would have been even worse if I'd married her. I chose the lesser of two evils.'

'How far were you able to set down the burden of all this guilt when you entered the Order?'

'The relief was instantaneous. I was finally at peace after years of torment.'

'How very odd! I wouldn't have thought that merely walking through the door of the Grantchester house would have made so much difference

– in fact surely your problems were only exacerbated when you wound up in such a mess as a postulant?'

'I agree I got in a mess and was miserable, but it was a different kind of mess and a different kind of misery. Grantchester was quite the wrong house for me, of course – but not, as I thought at the time in my arrogance, because it was spiritually slack. It wasn't, not then; James ran the place well enough in his own mild idiosyncratic way until old age made him lose his grip, but I was beyond being helped by a mild idiosyncratic rule. I needed the austerity of Ruydale, and Father Darcy realized that as soon as he met me.'

'So once you met Father Darcy –'

'I was happy.'

'Even when he followed that first meeting by flogging you in the London punishment cell?'

I stopped staring at the clock and swivelled to face him. 'Nobody enjoys being flogged!'

'No?' said Francis. 'I rather thought that according to modern psychology some people do.'

I finally lost patience with him. 'Can we forget the modern psychology for a moment and concentrate on the spiritual dimensions of what was going on? The flogging was necessary because I was so deeply sunk in pride that I was unable to learn humility and obedience in any other way – I was being forcibly turned around and redirected along the correct spiritual path. But once that had been done I was set free to realize my full ability to serve God at last – and *that's* why I can say with truth that an enduring happiness only began for me when I met Father Darcy.'

'And your happiness continued when he kicked you north to Ruydale, the toughest house in the Order – are you sure you don't enjoy suffering, Jonathan?'

'Is that another of the witty remarks which I'm supposed to find amusing? I can't tell you how irritated I'm becoming by your psycho-analytical poses – shouldn't you now pause to remind yourself that you're a priest and not a Harley Street quack? If you did you'd have no trouble understanding that the suffering I had to endure – *endure*, not enjoy – was a necessary part of my development into a good monk, and I endured it – *endured* it – because my call to be a good monk was so strong.'

'Yet now you have what is apparently an equally strong call to stop being a good monk – and why, Jonathan, *why*? Has your life at Grant-chester become too soft and easy for you? Do you think you'd suffer more if you went out into the world?'

'You're being deeply offensive. I absolutely deny –'

'Save your breath. Come back at four o'clock tomorrow and – hullo, the clock's stopped! Ah yes, of course – I forgot to wind it this morning.' Francis rose to his feet, moved to the fireplace and produced a key from a china vase on the mantelshelf. Then he looked back at me over his shoulder. 'What are you waiting for?' he demanded. 'You're dismissed.'

Retiring to the chapel I futilely tried to pray.

XII

I was now convinced that Francis was determined to reduce my call to a delusion by burying its spiritual dimensions beneath the rubble of a garbled psycho-analysis. I could see all too clearly the theory which he was developing. Deciding that I was a masochist who had finally exhausted the potential for suffering offered by the monastic life, he was toying with the idea that Father Darcy's death had been the mythical 'final trigger' which had sent me over the edge of sanity. Having suffered the delightful humiliation of being rejected by my mentor and the exquisite pain of failing to become the Abbot-General, I had realized that the Order now offered me nothing but an intolerably pain-free life at Grantchester, and unable to face a monastic future without my favourite sadist I was chafing to return to the world where with any luck I might acquire a wife who would beat me every night. How delicious! All I would have to do would be to buy a whip and a chain or two and then I could live happily ever after.

This atheistic vision of a maimed psyche so appalled me that I even wondered – and this was the final horror – if there could be a grain of truth in it. Surely if the theory were quite inapplicable I should be laughing at its absurdity? But my whole future was at stake. How could I laugh when the future I knew I had to have was now threatened with abortion? Indeed all thought of both present and future had suddenly become so agonizing that instinctively I took refuge in the remote past. Closing my eyes I reached up to clasp my mother's hand as we walked down the garden to find Chelsea, serene elegant Chelsea who washed her paws so fastidiously before the sitting-room fire on the long winter evenings when my father read his books and my mother sewed in silence and I sat listening to her thoughts.

'You and your cats!' said my father to my mother. 'In the old days you'd have been burnt as a witch!' And the high clear voice which had belonged to me long ago said in panic: 'They won't burn her now, will they? I don't want her dying and going away.'

My memory shifted. I felt Martin's small sticky hand in mine and heard him say: 'I don't want you going away any more.'

I said aloud in 1940: 'Martin – '

But then the light was switched off in my memory and stripping off my habit I went to bed and willed myself into unconsciousness.

XIII

'We've discussed your relationship with your wife,' said Francis, 'we've inspected your relationship with your mistress and now today we're going to examine your relationship with your children. What happened to them after your wife's death?'

'My mother-in-law took charge.'

'I detect a lack of enthusiasm. How did you tolerate her living in your home?'

'She didn't live there. She took the children into her own home and I moved to bachelor quarters on the Naval base. But I wasn't there much. I still spent most of my time at sea.'

'Did the children mind not living with you?'

'I told them that the quality of time fathers spent with their children was more important than the quantity.'

'Are you good with children?' said Francis idly, but I could feel his large sleek powerful psyche prowling around mine as he sought to induce a fatal relaxation. 'Are you one of those gifted adults who always know what to say to anyone under sixteen?'

'It depends on whether there's any psychic affinity.'

'And does such an affinity exist between you and your children?'

'No. I can't communicate with them without words as I used to communicate with my mother.'

'Disappointing for you. How you must have longed for a couple of little replicas of yourself instead of these two people whom you obviously found so alien!'

'You couldn't be more mistaken. I despise parents who long for replicas – I consider such a desire indicative of gross selfishness and an inflated self-esteem.'

'Aren't you reacting rather strongly? It's a very human trap for a parent to fall into, I've always thought, and it's certainly not an uncommon one ... However I won't press that point; we already know from Father Darcy's record that even if you didn't long for replicas you were nonetheless capable of finding your children a disappointment. But what about your grandchildren?' said Francis, sweeping on before I could argue further with him. 'Any affinity there? I notice you never mention them, but perhaps that's because you're so sensitive about your age that you dislike being reminded you're a grandfather.'

'Nonsense! My silence is because my grandchildren are strangers to me.

They were born after I entered the Order so I've seldom seen them.'

'What kind of a man is your son-in-law?'

'He's an outstandingly boring atheist who earns his living as an accountant in one of Starmouth's shipbuilding firms.'

'Tedious for you! If he's got to be an atheist he might at least have the grace to be an amusing one,' said Francis, and made a note which included the words 'strangers', 'antipathy' and 'disappointment'.

'Something tells me,' I said, 'that once again you're forming quite the wrong impression of my family life. Let me stress that I'm devoted to both my children and I've always tried to do my best for them.'

'Of course. You palmed them off on a woman you disliked and occasionally dropped in to see them whenever you weren't far away at sea.'

Once more I was slammed on the rack.

XIV

'So I wasn't mistaken,' I said as I clenched my fists to endure the pain. 'You have indeed formed quite the wrong impression of my family life. I wrote to my children frequently. When I was ashore I saw them as much as possible and when I left the Navy after the War I even undertook a very hard, difficult chaplaincy at Starmouth prison so that I could be near them during their adolescence. I cared deeply about their welfare, I –'

'Dear me, I seem to have drawn blood! What a sadist I am! But perhaps you only enjoyed sadism when it came from Father Darcy.'

'I most strongly deny – '

'Why did you really take on that hard difficult chaplaincy at the prison? I suppose that once the War was over and there was no chance of your being killed or maimed the Navy had nothing left to offer so you deliberately sought an environment where you could suffer vicariously with all the men condemned to be flogged or hanged!'

I said with great precision in my clearest voice: 'I'm deeply opposed to both corporal and capital punishment. I have never received a perverted sexual pleasure through either watching or receiving physical punishment. I have never either sought or welcomed flagellation.'

'You certainly gave me the impression you welcomed that flogging from Father Darcy. And if you're so deeply opposed to corporal punishment, how did you reconcile yourself to compulsory self-discipline as a novice?'

'Self-discipline! Nobody could hurt themselves with the kind of scourge the Order provides, and anyway even at Ruydale we often used to thump our beds to make the required sounds while the Master turned a blind eye – '

'I agree that for normal people self-discipline is little more than a symbolic act, but for a masochist entranced with punishment even a Fordite scourge could provide some interesting possibilities – '

'*I am not a masochist entranced with punishment!*'

'You certainly seem to be entranced with Martin who's giving you some heavy punishment at the moment! How did you really feel all those years ago when he kicked over the traces, cocked a snook at the Varsity and went off to daub himself with greasepaint?'

'I've already told you – '

'You've told me nothing! You mouthed a few platitudes, the sort of platitudes saintly fathers are expected to utter, but now I think it's time we heard the truth. How did you take this rejection by your son of you and your way of life?'

'He didn't reject me.'

'He has now! You've been a failure there, haven't you? You were a failure as a husband and a failure as a father – and while you were sleeping with your mistress you were a failure as a priest. No wonder you entered a monastery! After all those disasters the only way you could repair the damage to your self-esteem was to go through hell in order to be a success as a monk!'

Leaping to my feet I shouted: 'Damn you, that's a bloody lie!' Then I covered my face with my hands and somehow managed to say: 'I'm sorry, Father, that was unforgivable.'

'Vulgar behaviour – even blasphemous language – I can forgive,' said Francis, 'particularly when I was providing great provocation, but what I find hard to forgive is your persistent evasiveness. If you do have a genuine call instead of a mere emotional problem which could be solved with competent counselling, you'll want to be absolutely honest with me, and being honest in this context means giving frank answers to my questions about Martin.'

'Yes, of course. I'm sorry.'

'Very well, I accept your apology but if your repentance is genuine you'll now go away, pray that you may be granted a genuine humility which will prevent you lying to preserve your pride, and return tomorrow prepared to tell me all about that son of yours – and when I say all, Jonathan, I mean ALL, from Alpha to Omega.'

FIVE

'The silence of God has at all times been a great trial to mankind.'

W. R. INGE
Dean of St Paul's 1911–1934
Mysticism in Religion

I

I was in such distress that for a long time I could do nothing but pace up and down my cell. Francis was now behaving as if he suspected the quarrel with Martin had been the final trigger, and the most terrible aspect of this new development was that I myself, becoming increasingly aware of how deeply Martin had disturbed me, was beginning to wonder if he might not be connected with my vision despite all my previous doubts. However once I admitted the call was rooted in a psychological disturbance I remained convinced I would be doomed. Francis, ruthlessly setting aside any possibility of divine involvement, would speed ahead to a neat psychological conclusion and dispatch me to Ambrose for weeks of medical supervision; possibly I might even be ordered to resign as abbot. And all the time the chapel would be waiting for me in some corner of England which I would never find . . .

Or would it be waiting? My psyche froze as the demon of doubt finally encircled it. I remembered that I had received no further word from God either confirming my vision or clarifying it. I still had no idea what work I was being called to do.

Perhaps there was no chapel.

Perhaps I was deluded.

Closing my eyes with a shudder I knew I was in hell.

II

Hours later I fell asleep, and as I lost my grip on consciousness my life unfurled beyond finite time until past and present streamed side by side, interweaving and interchanging, while the future was the blank mirror waiting to reflect their final image. I dreamt I was studying the visions of Ezekiel and feeling frightened because my vision was so dull in comparison. Then Francis said as he removed my Bible: 'If your vision was genuine God would have ordered you to perform a symbolic act – remember Ezekiel!' But I answered: 'I performed my symbolic act. I entered the Order.' And I added to Father Darcy: 'I have to live in imitation of Christ. There's no other way I can live with myself and stay sane.'

Then Father Darcy took me to the punishment cell and on the wall hung the crucifix, the image of Christ crucified, Christ atoning, and I knew then, knew beyond any shadow of doubt, that for my children's sake all the suffering would have to be borne.

I said to my children: 'I'm doing it all for you!' but as I spoke I realized they had vanished and I was making a cross in the workshop at Ruydale. I worked and worked at my crucifix, that image of Christ crucified, Christ atoning, until at last Alfred the carpenter who had trained me said: 'You can put that aside now, lad. Martin no longer needs it. Just make a cross instead for the chapel in the woods.'

So I put aside my crucifix, image of Christ crucified, Christ atoning, and I began to make a different cross, a plain pure cross, an image of faith and hope – THE CROSS OF THE RESURRECTION – and then as I became one with the risen Christ, Christ redeemed, Christ liberated, I knew my long Good Friday was over at last and the sun was finally dawning on my long-awaited Easter Day.

III

I awoke in a daze of happiness which dissolved with lightning speed into confusion. I tried to remember Alfred's exact words. Had he really mentioned Martin? To my horror I realized the question could only be answered in the affirmative, and although I told myself the dream was a mere illogical aberration of the mind I knew the mention of Martin's name was significant. I tried to make further deductions but failed; I was too frightened of coming face to face with the fact that my call was a delusion. I did wonder how I was going to survive my next meeting with Francis, but soon I could no more think of Francis than I could think of Martin because I had suddenly realized I was feeling ill. I forced myself to attend prime and mass but as soon as the services were over I avoided breakfast and retired to my cell where I tried – futilely – to will myself to feel better. Five minutes later a note arrived which read: 'I have not given you permission to fast. Come to the refectory immediately.' With a great effort I reached the refectory, drank a cup of tea and swallowed a mouthful of bread but afterwards I knew I had no choice but to drag myself to the infirmary.

'This is just a physical manifestation of severe mental strain,' I said to Ambrose. 'Give me a couple of aspirin and I'll be well again by dinner-time.'

'I always enjoy your bold diagnoses, Father. Sit down, please, and I'll take your temperature.'

'It won't be more than ninety-nine.'

The thermometer registered a hundred and two.

'Obviously it's broken,' I said.

Ambrose smiled at me as if I were a wayward child who needed humouring and examined me for further symptoms but there were none. 'I doubt if you've got anything infectious,' he said at last, 'but take the corner bed away from the other patients.'

As I hauled myself from his office into the ward, a long light room with six beds flanking each side of a central aisle, I was aware of feeling very, very old indeed. This unnerved me, and as I removed my habit I started to worry about the damaged defences which had allowed my body to slide from the ease of good health into the dis-ease of physical impairment. I slid into bed. Ambrose gave me three aspirins, and after swallowing them I tried to stroke my psyche by recalling peaceful memories of the scenery at Ruydale. However I was too ill to concentrate on this exercise for long, and within minutes I had drifted into sleep.

When I awoke I knew it would be wiser to keep my eyes closed and the next moment I heard Francis muttering: 'It's entirely self-induced! He's trumped up this illness to avoid a distressing interview with me – in fact this is a typical example of a psychic controlling his body with his mind! What a shady, shoddy little parlour-trick!'

'With all due respect, Father, I'm convinced it's not a conscious willing of the mind. He was genuinely surprised to find he had a high fever.'

'You mustn't be too credulous, Ambrose. Don't let him manipulate you. These sort of people can be appallingly plausible. How are you going to treat him?'

'If the illness is psychosomatic, perhaps the laying-on of hands would help.'

'Absolutely not!' said Francis, keeping his voice low but allowing it to shudder with rage. 'I'm not pandering to his psychic tantrums by authorizing any charismatic healing which would enable him to claim a miraculous cure! You mark my words, Ambrose, that man can heal himself perfectly well if he wants to – give him orthodox medical treatment and stand absolutely no nonsense whatsoever!'

Francis stumped off. I could hear the slap of his boots on the linoleum, and the atmosphere, which had been swirling with turbulence, immediately became smooth. I opened my eyes, and when he saw I was awake Ambrose sat down at my side. Ambrose exuded a calm benevolent aura, just as a physician should; I felt my mind being enfolded by his sympathy.

'All set to stand no nonsense from me?' I murmured, and he smiled before saying: 'Father Abbot-General's very concerned about you.'

'Father Abbot-General!' I wanted to smile too but it seemed less effort to sigh instead. 'When I first met him up at Cambridge he was called Lord Francis Ingram. He had a greyhound which used to drink champagne. Nasty animal. I don't like dogs. Too much like dependent humans. But cats . . . ah, cats are quite different! One day, Ambrose, one day I'd so much like to tell someone about Whitby.'

'Ah, that was the cat up at Ruydale, wasn't it, the cat Wilfred mentioned in his letters . . . Father – '

'Call me Jon, Ambrose. I'm too ill to be Jonathan the Abbot at the moment.'

' – Jon – did you really raise that cat from the dead?'

'Careful, Ambrose. Superstition. Blasphemy. Shhh.'

'I suppose he was actually still alive – '

'That's what some people said about Our Lord in order to explain the Resurrection, but he did die. I've died too and now I've come here to wait for my own resurrection, but oh, how ill I feel! It's hard work being dead, and Whitby probably knew that. He didn't want to die – he had a great fighting spirit. Ah Whitby, Whitby, Whitby – what a cat you were, what a cat!'

Ambrose clasped my hand and released it. 'Try and sleep again, Jon. Try and rest your body and mind as much as possible.'

'I feel better already. A healing presence, a little conversation, someone calling me Jon . . . You must have good results with the laying-on of hands, Ambrose.'

'I can't channel power through my hands as Wilfred can – '

'That doesn't matter. The charism of healing doesn't always come in the form of power channelled through the hands. In your case the laying-on of hands would be a sacramental gesture symbolizing the healing action of your psyche as it enfolds another psyche in love and prayer.' I suddenly felt exhausted. As my eyes closed I murmured: 'Dear old Whitby, he was so pleased to be better,' and the next moment I saw Whitby, proud arrogant Whitby, stalking through the backyard at Ruydale with his tail pointed defiantly at the sky.

'May God bless you, Jon,' I heard Ambrose say from a long way away, 'and may he restore the strength you so badly need.'

I murmured an automatic 'Amen' and stooped to take Whitby in my arms.

IV

When I awoke again I heard someone calling: 'Ambrose! Emergency – a scalding in the kitchens,' and turning my head I saw Ambrose hurry away clutching the Gladstone bag in which he kept his first-aid equipment. I sat up, drank some water and glanced around the room. There were three other occupants, including a restless youth whom I had seen break his ankle while descending too rapidly to the crypt at the start of an air-raid. He looked bored enough to flout the rule of silence, and his restlessness created a succession of eddies in the atmosphere until I felt as irritated as if I had been trapped with a fly who persistently evaded the swatter.

I closed my eyes to ward off any illicit attempt he might make at conversation, but my psyche, raw and vulnerable, continued to be lacerated by the unpleasant emanations. I was only saved from losing my patience by the return of Ambrose, hurrying back into the ward with his Gladstone bag and making a rapid inspection of his patients as if he feared we might all have taken a turn for the worse in his absence.

'Awake again, Jon?'

'I think I've recovered.'

Ambrose set down his bag on the empty bed next to mine and produced a thermometer. 'It's most unlikely that you're wholly recovered,' he said, taking the instrument to the window and examining the mercury to make sure it was low in the glass, 'but let's see if you're right in thinking there's been an improvement.' And he turned aside from the window to place the thermometer in my mouth.

It was then that my perceptions tripped. I had just glanced at the Gladstone bag which was no more than six feet away from me, but the next moment I was seeing not the bag but the suitcase of my vision. All sound immediately ceased. I could see the triangular label clearly now, far more clearly than I had seen it in my vision, the label which showed a black and white ship floating above three wavy blue lines and six scarlet letters, the letters which spelt CUNARD. Then I saw another label, a label attached to the handle, a brown label fastened by string, but when I reached out to discover the name of the owner the entire suitcase vanished and the Gladstone bag was solid beneath my shaking hands.

I sank to my knees, squeezed my eyes shut and began to shudder from head to toe.

'Jon, it's all right – you're in the infirmary, you're quite safe, absolutely safe – ' His words made me realize I had conveyed an impression of fear but in fact all my fears had vanished. The shuddering ceased. As Ambrose helped me back into bed I tried to speak but he said at once: 'No, don't try to talk. You've had a shock. Take this extra blanket to keep you warm and I'll make you some tea.'

Across the room the young monk was boggling, but as I lay limply on the pillows I found his restless aura failed to irritate me. My psyche was infused with light. I closed my eyes but the light still shone in the darkness. I was at peace.

In the distance Ambrose said to someone: 'Tell Father Abbot-General I need to see him urgently,' but the words stirred no anxiety in me and later I never even flinched as the swirling tornado of a disturbed presence swept down the corridor into the infirmary. The tornado was deftly deflected by Ambrose into his office, and as my fellow-patients watched enrapt I slid out of bed, padded into the passage and noiselessly opened Ambrose's door an inch.

'. . . so whatever he saw he couldn't have seen for more than five seconds.'

'And your diagnosis?'

'Some sort of psychic experience. It couldn't be a hallucination unless his fever's got worse and he'd just said he felt better.'

I pushed open the door to reveal my presence.

Both men jumped. Then Francis exclaimed in fury: 'What the deuce to you think you're playing at, making an entrance like the demon-king in a pantomime?' and Ambrose said severely: 'Go back to bed at once and stop straining your heart by unnecessary exertion!'

I said to Francis: 'I saw the suitcase,' and walked out. Then I returned to bed and waited. After some minutes Ambrose appeared, bringing me the promised cup of tea, and took my temperature before I attempted to drink. The thermometer registered ninety-nine degrees.

'No hallucination,' I said satisfied. I began to drink the tea but it had been liberally sweetened to fortify me against the effects of shock and I was still grimacing in disgust when Ambrose said: 'Father Abbot-General wishes to talk to you in private and as your temperature's almost normal I'll allow you to get dressed and sit in my office. But you must finish that tea and you must wrap yourself in the extra blanket to ensure you keep warm.'

Downing the tea I pulled on my habit, swathed myself in the blanket and strode to the office where Francis, sitting in Ambrose's chair, was staring blankly at the blotter. It occurred to me that the sweet tea had been administered to the wrong man.

'If you think for one moment,' he said, rousing himself sufficiently to motion me to sit down, 'that you can convince me this call is genuine merely by producing a new parlour-trick – '

'The gifts of the Spirit can be recognized by their fruits. Gauge the effect this experience has had on me before you start accusing me of parlour-tricks.'

'You're being intolerably impertinent – how dare you lecture me about this new aberration!' said Francis, now overwhelmed by the most painful insecurity, and I saw my first task was to calm him down.

I tried to enfold his mind with my own, but such an enfolding is impossible without love and, as everyone knows, it is difficult to generate even the most modest fraternal concern for someone whom one has never liked. However I exerted the power of my will, and remembering what little I knew of his early days, I tried to approach him through a different psychological avenue.

I imagined him being brought up by some hired woman in his parents' vast mansion; I speculated that it had been his craving for affection as well as attention which had drawn him to a life of decadence; I thought of him enjoying every material comfort while his soul starved, and suddenly I was seeing him stumble across the Order, across different values and different people who would care for him in an entirely different way. Then I found I could easily picture him thriving at last in response to Father Darcy's powerful interest, and in a moment of enlightenment I realized that his bereavement when his mentor died must have run precisely parallel to my own.

At once I was conscious not only of sympathy but of empathy; I was seeing us for the first time not as rivals, but as the twin aspects of Father Darcy's complex personality, the mystical and the worldly, not in opposition but complementing each other, and then I understood at last why Father Darcy had taken such care to yoke us together, despite all our antipathy, in the years preceding his death.

I became aware that Francis was speaking. He had overcome his inner chaos sufficiently to say: 'Tell me exactly what happened,' and I found I could obey him calmly in a manner which could neither exasperate nor threaten him. 'It wasn't a vision,' I added when the moment came to comment on the experience. 'There were no physical symptoms preceding it, no dislocation of time and space. I believe it was what Julian of Norwich would have called a "showing".'

Francis finally managed to recapture his favourite defence, the debonair theatrical manner. 'You alarm me exceedingly! Can we keep Dame Julian out of this?'

'You'll understand my state of mind better if we bring her in. After her own "showings" she felt so happy, so confident, so convinced that all would be well – '

'Am I to deduce from these somewhat emotional utterances that you feel you've received a divine reassurance?'

'You can deduce that I now see my recent behaviour – all the lies and evasions, all the fears and anxieties – as demonstrating the most shameful lack of trust in God. I know now that all I have to do is have faith and trust that all will be well. If the vision's genuine I'll be led to a new life in God's service. If the vision's false you'll arrange for me to be cared for until I can continue to serve God in the Order. So my task here's not to worry about whether you can exercise the charism of discernment; my task is to trust God by trusting you because only by putting myself without reserve in your hands can God's will for me ever be conclusively revealed.'

In the silence which followed I sensed Francis' wordless thanksgiving but all he eventually said was: 'That sounds like promising approach. Am I then to assume – '

'Yes,' I said, 'I'm going to tell you everything at last. Everything from Alpha to Omega.'

V

'The truth's so painful,' I said, 'that over the years I've buried it by reconstructing my memories into a pattern which I could endure. You suspected this, of course, but I couldn't dispense with the defence this reconstruction offered; I had neither the courage nor the faith to do so.'

Francis' sleek powerful psyche, which always reminded me of a giant member of the cat family, was now entirely still and the stillness was mirrored in his motionless body. He had surmounted the acute strain generated by the burden of his responsibility, and having turned inward to dwell upon his own ordeal he was now turning outward to dwell with a new strength on mine.

I said: 'Everything I told you about my marriage was true, yet it was all false because I couldn't paint the past in the right colours.' As I groped for the right words I again ignored the rule which forbade a monk to stand while his superior was seated. I moved to the window. The dark events of 1940 were being enacted against the background of a brilliant summer, and instinctively I tried to fight my way through my own darkness by staring at the light sky beyond the rooftops.

'My marriage was hell,' I said. 'I hated my life as a husband. I was miserable, isolated, trapped with this woman who hadn't the faintest idea what my life was about. Sexual intimacy was the only compensation and even that in the end became a mockery underlining my loneliness. But the real nightmare was that this tragedy was all my fault. Betty was a nice girl in her own way and she tried hard to be a good wife. She really did love me – but I couldn't love her, not after the romantic passion was gone, and of course she came to realize that. People always know when they're not loved. She became angry, possessive, demanding – and the more demanding she became the more I withdrew from her. I couldn't help myself – not when my psychic space was being continually invaded and my whole inner life was cut to ribbons . . . If I hadn't gone away to sea the marriage couldn't have survived, but at sea I could recuperate until I had the strength to face another harrowing spell ashore – oh, what hell it was! And all the time I felt cut off from God by my failure to love as I should. I was in despair.'

I paused to calm myself. I examined the pattern of the roof-tops with care. I even counted the chimney-pots.

'When she finally died,' I said, 'the full horror of the tragedy dawned on me. She'd died after I'd psychologically abandoned her, and I'd abandoned her for no valid cause. She'd loved me; she'd committed no sin, but I'd made her suffer and suddenly as I saw the exact dimensions of my cruelty I felt unfit to live. That was when the crushing burden descended upon my psyche – I talked of the burden, didn't I? And I admitted the burden was guilt, but I only revealed a fraction of it, the guilt I felt when I jilted Hilda. My guilt was far deeper than I disclosed to you. It was a huge, crippling, back-breaking guilt, and I carried it with me during all those years I spent as a widower.

'At first,' I said after a rapid recount of the chimney-pots, 'I thought I saw how I could alleviate the guilt. I decided I'd do my best to love my children by being an exemplary father to them.

'But I couldn't.

'I should have applied to work ashore so that I could be at home with them – it was two years before the War so I didn't have to be at sea – but I couldn't face the thought of either my mother-in-law or a hired woman keeping house for me, destroying my psychic space – and worse still I knew I wouldn't be able to cope with the children, all the noise, all the mess, all the emotional demands – I couldn't do it, I just couldn't do it, I wanted to but it was beyond me, I'd have gone mad, broken down utterly – no, I felt it was quite impossible for me to be permanently ashore, but oh, how I despised myself, and oh, how guilty I felt! So I never alleviated the burden after all. What happened, in fact, was that I doubled it.

'My meetings with my children became so awkward; I tried hard to show them I cared and I did care, but ... I couldn't express my love adequately. The guilt crippled not only my power of expression but the love itself. Perhaps if the children had been more like me communication would have been easier, but Ruth, reminding me of Betty, only exacerbated my guilt, while Martin remained beyond my reach no matter how hard I tried to build an understanding between us. I did make an effort to share my life with him when he was an adolescent; I talked of the Church and my work and how happy I was in God's service, and there was a time when I thought he might become a priest – it was around the time of his confirmation – he was genuinely devout – I hoped ... even prayed ... which was stupid of me because I was just praying that my own selfish wish should be granted and not pausing to ask that God's will might be done. However I was still hoping that he might become a priest when he told me he wanted to be an actor – an *actor* – ' I could no longer continue.

'Yes,' said Francis. 'Yes. There's no need to explain how you felt.' And as he spoke I felt his psyche brush mine faintly in the dark.

I had to pause to focus my gaze on the view again. The sky beyond the chimney-pots was a radiant blue.

'I should have discouraged him,' I said. 'I should have insisted that he went up to Cambridge before making any decision about the future. But I didn't. And I wasn't being a noble understanding father. I was being a bad selfish one. I wanted to enter the Order so desperately that I put my needs before his welfare – I let him go into a notoriously amoral world so that I could have the life I wanted. How bad a father can a man be? I abandoned Martin – and I abandoned Ruth too; I let her marry a man I disliked because I wanted to get her off my hands and be free ... And so I failed my children, failed them as I'd failed my wife, and the burden of my guilt lay unredeemed.

'But by that time I'd worked out how I could finally exorcize the guilt. I knew I had to atone for what I'd done, atone for all my sins and my terrible failures. I had to live in imitation of Christ and suffer as he suffered on the cross – it was the only way, Francis, the only way, and I know that sounds as if I enjoy suffering but I didn't, I don't, I hated it, I hardly knew how to bear it, but I endured it because I knew it was the only hope I had of setting down that appalling burden which had been crushing me for so long.

'However there were two aspects of my call to the cloister, and unless I describe them both you won't understand the exact nature of the force which has kept me in the Order for all these years. The first and most obvious aspect involved this exorcism of the guilt by a spiritual purification. But the second aspect ... well, I hardly know how to put this, I feel so embarrassed, but as the years passed and my children flourished I came to believe that my atonement, my suffering, was somehow enabling them to live free of the shadow of my past sins. I came to think ... Francis, I know this sounds superstitious to the point of blasphemy, but I thought I'd succeeded in driving a bargain with God. I was desperately afraid my children's lives would go wrong because I'd been a bad father, so I told myself that so long as I remained a good monk God would repay me for my sacrifice by keeping my children safe. What pride, what intolerable arrogance to think that one can ever drive bargains with God! What a theological perversion ever to see the concept of atonement in those self-centred primitive terms – '

'Nevertheless it was still an attempt to raise up and reconcile all things in Christ. The form of the attempt might have been misconceived but the desire to atone was obviously genuine enough.' Francis' psyche, heavy and blunt yet trained to move with an elegant delicacy, encircled mine and supported it. Again his body mirrored the psychic action. Rising to his feet he crossed the room, guided me back to my chair and moved his own chair around the desk so that he could sit at my side.

'Last May,' I said when I could speak again, 'I was so pleased to see Martin on my birthday. He looked so happy too. I thought: how wonderful it is that he's doing so well! And I felt all my sacrifices had been worthwhile.

'Then he told me.

'Of course I can see now how brave it was of him, but I was so shattered I couldn't respond to that gesture of trust. Then in his pain he started making accusations, saying it was all my fault, saying I'd never been there when he needed me, saying everything which underlined my guilt until in the end I could bear it no longer. I told him to get out – my son – *Martin* – I rejected him absolutely, but as soon as I was alone I thought: how *could* I have treated him like that? And I hated myself. But then a very strange thing happened. Once the shock had faded I felt everything changing, as if the world was turning itself inside out. Instead of thinking: how deeply I've failed! and hating myself, I thought: how desperately hard I've tried to succeed! and I resented that Martin should be oblivious of all the suffering I'd endured for his sake. My anger was no longer turned inward upon myself; it had turned outward at last, and then as my self-hatred finally bgan to disintegrate I saw my superstitious bargain with God for what it was: superstition.

'The first aspect of the atonement represented by the monastic life had indeed been essential for me; I'd genuinely needed to assuage my guilt, purge myself of my sins and achieve the spiritual development which I could never have achieved in the world, but for me then to say to God: "I'll keep on atoning if you keep my children safe," was not only pathetic but futile. Ruth and Martin had gone their own way in the world and Martin at least hadn't been preserved from harm. The truth was I'd tried hard to be a good parent, I'd done my best, pitiful and inadequate though that was, and now there was nothing more I could do.' I hesitated, then heard myself whisper in imitation of Christ on the cross: 'It was finished.'

Silence fell, and this time Francis' psyche encircled mine not merely with efficiency but with compassion. Reaching out with his right hand he briefly covered my interlocked fingers.

At last I was able to say: 'Of course I can see now that I'm just emotionally disturbed. The meeting with Martin destroyed my need to atone and this triggered such an upheaval in my mind that I imagined I was being called to leave the Order. But in fact what was happening was that God, in his great mercy, had finally seen fit to relieve me of my self-hatred because he had realized that my call to serve him as a monk was so deeply entrenched that I no longer needed to be kept in the Order by a psychological compulsion. At the same time he had also seen fit to purge my call of the superstition which had become attached to it; indeed one could regard the whole experience as a further spiritual purification.' I paused. I was feeling calmer. Beyond the window the chimney-pots were bathed in a brilliant light.

'I'm sure now,' I said, 'that the vision was an allegory. I believe the ruined building behind the chapel represents my failures during my life in the world, and the chapel represents my life in the Order. The mysterious suitcase still represents change, but it's a change from a call underpinned by guilt to a call flowing from a psyche at peace. And the light at the end of my vision represents the confirmation of my call, just as Timothy said – the assurance that I'll be able to serve God as a monk even better than before now that I'm fully reconciled to the past.'

Francis slumped back in his chair but when I steeled myself to look at him I saw that although he was limp with exhaustion the expression in his eyes was friendly. Presently he even smiled.

'So that's how you finally see your situation, is it?' he said.

'Yes, Father.' As an afterthought I added: 'Please forgive me for calling you Francis just now when I was upset.'

But Francis, no longer intimidated but emanating an unmistakable air of confidence, merely waved this apology aside as if my offence were too trivial to be worth mentioning. 'You've no doubt you're right?' he persisted. 'No doubt at all?'

'No, Father. Not now.'

'Ah, Jonathan, Jonathan – ' Francis heaved a massive sigh ' – are you never to be cured of your intolerable arrogance?' And as I stared at him he added casually: 'Your new call is quite obviously genuine. You must leave the Order without delay.'

PART TWO

THE REALITY BEYOND THE VISION

'Rightly or wrongly (genuine mystics) are convinced that they have been in contact with objective reality, with the supreme spiritual Power behind the world of our surface consciousness. If they are right, this intuition must be a factor in what we believe about reality; it means that reality is spiritual.'

W. R. INGE
Dean of St Paul's 1911–1934
Mysticism in Religion

SIX

'(The mystics) are convinced that their communion with God is an authentic experience ... If a dozen honest men tell me that they have climbed the Matterhorn, it is reasonable to believe that the summit of that mountain is accessible, though I am not likely to get there myself.'

W. R. INGE
Dean of St Paul's 1911–1934
Mysticism in Religion

I

At first Francis refused to discuss his judgement and when I begged stupefied for an explanation he merely ordered me back to bed in the infirmary. Then he relented. Motioning me to remain seated he said: 'The turning-point was when I realized that I had to examine your original call to be a monk.'

'Yes, but – '

'Be quiet!' snapped Francis, revealing his exhaustion. 'If you want an explanation don't irritate me with ill-judged interruptions!'

I said at once: 'I'm very sorry. Please go on.'

Francis waited until he was calm before continuing: 'The point about your original call was that it was indisputably genuine. As you yourself said at the start of this conversation: the gifts of the Spirit can be recognized by their fruits – or, as a layman would say, the proof of the pudding's in the eating. You've become an outstanding monk, your skill as a spiritual director being acknowledged both inside and outside the Order. Clearly God called you to serve him in this way, and it seemed to me that if only I could discover how he had called you to start being a monk I'd be able to discern whether he was now calling you to stop being a monk; I suspected that this new call, if it was valid, would be a negative reflection of the old.'

Francis paused, grappling again with his exhaustion, but I took care not to distract him and at last he said: 'You had no vision calling you to be a monk, but contrary to what many laymen believe, calls from God aren't normally manifested by psychic or supernatural phenomena. Much more common are the cases where a man is put in a psychological vice and God proceds to tighten the screws. This is what happened to you. You had this tragic private life which went so disastrously wrong that you felt your only hope of survival was to serve God in the Order.

'It seemed logical to assume that if God called you to enter the Order by imprisoning you in a psychological vice, his first step, on calling you to leave, would be to loosen the screws and set you free. Your call to the Order, as you yourself pointed out, had two aspects. First, you wanted to set down the burden of your guilt, purge yourself of sin and achieve the spiritual development which you were unable to achieve in the world. And second, you thought you could drive a bargain with God to keep your children safe. The first aspect drove you into the Order; the second aspect kept you there. No matter how hard the life was you couldn't leave. You had to be a monk. No other option was open to you.

'However when you achieved that spiritual development which you could never have achieved outside the cloister, the role of the Order in your life became redundant. You were now fit to serve God in the world, and all that remained for God to do was to remove the various psychological fetters which were chaining you to the cloister.

'Father Darcy died, a death which liberated you from supervision by a mentor. You failed to become Abbot-General, a failure which represented the termination of any all-too-human ambition to reach the top of the Fordite tree. And finally, most vital of all, your so-called bargain with God was shown during your quarrel with Martin to have been an illusion.

'All these devastating blows rained down upon you within the space of a month, and while they were happening you were being goaded by the minor troubles, the recurring difficulty with your celibacy, the unfortunate birthday, the adverse effects of the War on your community and your work. It seems to me that you were being remorselessly manoeuvred into position to receive the knock-out blow with which Martin finally demolished your compulsion to remain in the Order.

'However you were a good monk. Out of sheer conscientiousness you were going to fight this systematic destruction of your old call, and so even after the knock-out blow had been delivered the new call had to be spelt out in a way you couldn't misunderstand: you were granted the vision.

'Now – ' Francis sighed as if he still found my vision a heavy cross to bear ' – it's impossible to say for certain exactly what was going on during this strange experience of yours, and the difficulty is exacerbated because you and I represent two quite different religious types. I'm not a mystic; I can only discern God through reason and logic. As far as philosophy goes I have the greatest respect for Platonic Idealism, but it's the respect of a man blind from birth for colours: when many good honest people tell me colours are beautiful I deem it reasonable to believe that this fact is true. Therefore as far as Neo-Platonic mysticism goes, I'm prepared to believe it's a symbolic expression of experiences which the mystic can recognize, but to me it's just a foreign language which I'll never master.

'I'm essentially a Pragmatist of the school of William James. I recognize the will to believe, acknowledge that it can have beneficial results and conclude that there's a form of religious truth here based on my subjective experience. To put it crudely, I'm a Christian because Christianity works for me; it enables me to live my life in a happy, productive, spiritually satisfying way. Intellectually I can recognize the absolute objective truths which lie beyond the Platonic veil of your own philosophical approach to God, but experientially that approach isn't mine. All I can say is that it works for you and therefore it's true for you. That's a truth I can deduce by using rational powers of observation, but when I'm obliged to deduce the meaning of a vision, an experience not grounded in logic, I find my intellectual powers quickly become no more use than a broken sword. "Spiritual is most rational," says that Cambridge Platonist Whichcote. Yes – but there comes a point in spiritual matters beyond which reason is unable to go.

'So having stressed my limitations in this field, let me now venture a very tentative opinin on this vision of yours. I don't think you saw the future. It strikes me as being much more like a dream than a concrete experience. I know the detail was very striking but detail can be striking in dreams too. Of course I'm not saying it *was* a dream, just that it was like a dream – not a glimpse of an actual happening and certainly not an allegory, which has always struck me as a contrived literary device requiring intellectual planning.

'I believe that many years ago you read about this chapel in a book, perhaps even saw photographs of it, and that the memory was retained by your subconscious mind. During the psychic earthquake you experienced in May, this memory was regurgitated and used as a medium for conveying the word of God. Now, I'm perfectly prepared to concede that one day you may actually come across this chapel – one must always allow in life for the one truly extraordinary coincidence – but I don't think it will have anything to do with your new call. To me, the pragmatist, the only thing of importance in your vision is the light at the end which imprinted the word of God on your mind; nothing else is relevant.

'When this call to leave the Order was imprinted on your mind, God completed, in my opinion, the necessary sequence of events: you were called to enter the Order, you achieved the required spiritual development, the psychological compulsion to remain was then destroyed and you were called to leave. In short, the whole sequence is all of a piece; the two calls are mirror-images of each other, and if your first call was genuine then this second call must be genuine too.'

As Francis sank into an exhausted silence I had the chance to speak, but now the words refused to come. Emotion mingled with my own exhaustion. I had to shield my eyes with my hand.

'You need food, drink and a great deal more rest,' said Francis abruptly, rousing himself. 'Go back to bed and we'll talk again tomorrow.'

But I was immobilized. I felt so old, so tired, so utterly overwhelmed not only by my recent battle but by the enormity of my unknown future that I even whispered: 'I don't want to leave the Order any more,' as if I were a spoilt child begging to be excused from the ordeal of being sent away from home to boarding school.

'Who cares what you want?' said Francis brutally. 'It's what God wants that's important. Stop snivelling and pull yourself together!'

I forgot the shame of my uncontrolled emotion. I exclaimed startled: 'You sound just like the old man!' and I added in disbelief: 'You're even beginning to look like him!'

'I suppose you'll be claiming next that you've seen his ghost – oh, for heaven's sake, Jonathan, go back to bed before you get up to any more convoluted psychic antics!' said Francis, and striding out of the room in a paroxysm of exasperation he banged the door violently behind him.

II

'I must apologize for that graceless exit,' said Francis when we met in his office the next morning. 'As you no doubt realized I temporarily succumbed to jealousy. I've never had a vision from God, nor, I dare say, am I ever likely to have one.'

I hardly needed to point out to him that God can communicate with man in numerous other ways. Nor did I need to tell him that the mystics are united in distrusting psychic experiences and usually treat them as either irrelevant or seriously misleading. The truth is that although psychic powers are a gift from God, like the power to express oneself through art, they are not by themselves any guarantee of either holiness or religious genius. In fact psychics, like artists, are usually conspicuously less than holy, subject as they are to any passing demonic force which can exploit their characteristically inflated pride and self-centredness.

However if the psychic powers can be harnessed by rigorous discipline and put to work in the service of God they can be used to supplement the charismatic power, that gift of the Spirit which God may bestow on anyone, psychic or otherwise. Francis knew very well that he was not excluded from hearing calls from God or from wielding charismatic power merely because he had no psychic gifts, but I sensed his statement represented more than a simple confession of jealousy. In an oblique way he was admitting an old anxiety about his spiritual limitations, an old dread that he might not live up to Father Darcy's high hopes for him, perhaps even a lifelong insecurity that he would be overlooked or judged second-rate unless he exerted his flair for calling attention to himself, and suddenly I recognized the isolation of the man of power who yearns for an equal in whom he can freely confide.

Making every effort to express sympathy without condescension I said: 'I'm sure your own call to enter the Order was in its own way just as powerful an experience as any vision granted to a psychic.'

'Possibly. But nevertheless I can't help feeling that to receive a vision of a beautiful chapel must be a more profound spiritual experience than to wake up hung-over in a strange bed one morning with the thought: if I don't become a monk I'll be dead within six months. The trouble with pragmatism,' said Francis dryly before I could comment, 'is that it has absolutely no glamour. How I've always envied you those "glamorous powers", Jonathan! When we were up at Cambridge, how *I* always longed to tell fortunes, conduct seances and hypnotize pretty girls into fulfilling my wildest dreams! And now, forty years later, I see to my shame and dismay that very little has changed. The envy's still there and it's there because I'm still hopelessly addicted to glamour. The old man did try to cure me, of course, but that was a case of the blind leading the blind – he was too addicted to glamour himself, the old rascal, to conduct the necessary purging effectively.'

'I'm surprised he even tried.'

'His efforts were certainly half-hearted. But at the end he said: "I should have sent you too to Ruydale instead of keeping you here like a pet poodle cocooned in vintage claret, visiting archbishops and vulgar chandeliers!" He knew he'd been too soft with me, but poor old boy, he was lonely at the end when all his favourite brothers started dying off, and he did suffer considerable pain from his arthritis. I could quite understand why he needed an amusing pet poodle to keep him company.'

'What an unjust description!'

'You think so? I wonder. I've got a weakness for luxury and a mind like a cash-box – how on earth have I ended up as a spiritual leader? And how on earth am I going to manage in future without my arch-rival stimulating me to do my spiritual best with the very limited talent at my disposal?'

I said briskly: 'I'll tell you exactly how you'll manage: you'll use the energy you've always wasted on our rivalry to rise to new heights in exercising the charism of leadership. The old man foresaw the exact dimensions of that charism, of course. He didn't choose a pet poodle to be the kind of leader the Order has to have. He chose the managing director with the financial brain, the organizing skills and the spiritual education which he himself had personally supervised. How obvious it all seems to me now! In fact I feel amazed that I could ever have resented his decision.'

'For a man who's just survived the rack you're being extraordinarily charitable – '

'No, not charitable. Honest.'

' – but now I must call an end to all this delectable fraternal flattery in order to discuss practical matters,' said Francis firmly. However he was much cheered, and conquering the melancholy which had prompted his unique confession he embarked on the task of bringing clarity to my clouded future.

III

'The Church authorities at Westminster tell me that they can't trace this chapel without knowing the name of the owner,' he said, 'so we have no proof that it exists, and in my opinion it would be the greatest possible mistake if on leaving the Order you sat around waiting for the chapel to materialize. On the contrary, your first task, it seems to me, is to set aside all thought of the chapel and try to work out exactly what you're being called to do.'

I could hardly deny that this was sensible advice so I had no difficulty in replying tactfully: 'Yes, Father.'

'One must never demote the faculty of reason in favour of a dubious mystical "schwärmerei",' said Francis severely, suspicious as always of my meekness and perhaps still wondering if I were envisaging a latter-day Star of Bethlehem to guide me on my way. 'You must approach your unknown future rationally – starting from now.'

Despite the fact that I had had experience of the sad task of assisting a monk to leave the cloister, I was surprised by the depth of my confusion when I found myself on the receiving end of an abbot's ministrations. I hated the talk of money, although I knew it was essential that I should have some means of support. I hated the thought of leaving my brethren, although I knew the departure from Grantchester would have to be faced, and I hated the prospect of making a plan for the immediate future although I did realize I could hardly emerge into the world with the mindless naïvety of a chicken hatching from an egg; I had to acquire – at the very least – a roof over my head, the prospect of hot meals and the services of someone who would do my laundry.

'. . . and you must buy some modern underclothes,' added Francis.

516

'Why?' I was becoming impatient with these worldly trivialities. 'Surely I can make do with what I have!'

'Do you want to be a laughing-stock to your laundress?'

Despite my impatience I could not help but be impressed by this all-embracing attention to detail. I had never told any of my departing monks to buy new underclothes.

'Now we must decide exactly where you're going to go,' said Francis, continuing to exercise his indefatigable talent for the practical. 'I always think that a departing monk should if possible spend his first few days in a normal home so that he can be reminded what life's like without people praying all over the place. Would your daughter have you to stay?'

But I had already decided to go to Ruth for a week. In a recent letter she had mentioned that my grandson would be visiting a schoolfriend in mid-August, but my grand-daughter would be at home and I liked the idea of discovering more about her. I wondered if I were being sentimental in assuming it would be easier to be a grandfather than a father.

'And where will you go for the next three weeks before you return to London to review your situation with me?' pursued Francis.

'I'd thought of Allington Court. I stayed there once before I entered the Order.'

Allington Court in Devon was the former home of a wealthy bishop who had bequeathed his estate to the Church of England under a trust which stipulated that his home should become a hotel offering inexpensive holidays to clerical families. The house boasted a remarkable library, several comfortable reception rooms and a chapel – though not a chapel built in the style of Inigo Jones. Nowadays the hotel was seldom patronized by clerical families with children, but clerical widows, retired priests and interested laymen arrived regularly, theological students came to recuperate from examinations and a variety of church-workers appeared in the hope of renewing their spiritual energy. The establishment was run by a warden, always a priest of distinction, and he employed two assistants who helped him to organize retreats, to respond to any requests for counsel and, on a more mundane level, to generate a sociable atmosphere.

I wrote to the Warden to ask if he could offer me accommodation at such short notice in August, but there was no difficulty; the war had depleted the ranks of his regular visitors. I also wrote to my daughter and received an ecstatic reply by return of post. Of course I could come to stay. I could stay for as long as I liked. She could hardly wait to see me. My news was so wonderful, so marvellous, so exciting. What did I like to eat? What did I drink? Did I want to meet anyone? Would I hate a party? Had I got anything to wear? (I thought of my underclothes.) Had I got any possessions at all? Would I like a book from Boots' Library? I was to tell her everything I wanted so that my every whim could be gratified.

After telling myself how fortunate I was to have such a devoted daughter I decided I found this flurry of questions curiously exhausting. With caution I wrote back to inform her that I would eat anything that was put in front of me and drink anything except spirits. Then I wrote even more cautiously that I would prefer not to meet strangers at this time since readjustment to the world would inevitably be difficult and I would need to channel all my gregarious inclinations into renewing my acquaintance with my family. I concluded by writing that if Boots had the latest detective story by Miss Agatha Christie I would be most interested to read it.

That night I went to bed depressed, although when I tried to analyse my feelings I could not decide whether I felt depressed because Ruth had reminded me of Betty, showering me with trivial questions, or because the reality of leaving the Order was at last impinging on my consciousness. However I allowed myself no respite from that particular reality; the next morning I embarked on the difficult task of writing the letters which would inform my friends in the world of the new turn my life had taken.

To Charles Ashworth alone I allowed myself to hint at the ordeal I had undergone. 'As you can imagine,' I wrote, 'I have been experiencing a most difficult time, but I trust that eventually, when I'm settled in my new life, we may meet and resume our friendship.' But even to Charles I wrote no word of my vision or of my utter ignorance about the nature of my new work.

With my letters completed I then reached the most arduous part of my severance from my old life: the parting from my brethren at Grantchester.

IV

Francis and I travelled to Grantchester in the height of luxury in the Abbot-General's Daimler, inexcusably purchased by Father Darcy to convey him on his annual visitations well before arthritis had confined him to a wheelchair. Our chauffeur was my friend Edward the master-carpenter who drove us at such a stately pace up the Great North Road that I thought we would take all day to reach our destination. I even told Francis frankly that we should have travelled by train but Francis, his weakness for glamour well to the fore, merely told me not to be such a spoilsport.

I will not record the scene in the chapter-house at Grantchester as my resignation was announced; the memory affects me too deeply even now. Later, after Francis had organized the election and installed my prior as the new abbot, there were various emotional moments as I took my leave.

David the beekeeper gave me a pot of our famous Grantchester honey. The novices proffered a hastily-written scroll of appreciation. My officers presented me with one of my favourite books from the library, *The Cloud of Unknowing*, and as I accepted it with gratitude I thought how appropriate it was that the title should so accurately reflect my current spiritual condition. I was much moved.

Eventually when all the farewells had been concluded in the chapter-house the new abbot escorted me to the front door. I was hoping he would restrict himself to a few formal phrases in order to lessen the awkwardness of the parting, but to my dismay he blurted out: 'If only we knew what you were going to do, Father! It would make your loss so much easier to accept!'

I could not speak. Not only was I paralysed by emotion but he had echoed my own sentiments with such precision that I could not have attempted to argue with him. However Francis exclaimed with a severity worthy of our mentor: 'If Jonathan can accept this new call from God with courage and dignity, Bernard, I really fail to see why you can't do likewise! This mawkish outburst can't be excused just because I've judged it unfitting at present to disclose further details of the call to you!'

Poor Bernard was crushed. He managed to say with the obedience of a good monk: 'Yes, Father,' but his grief remained as deep as my own.

In the Daimler Francis muttered: 'I know I was harsh, but it's no good allowing a new abbot to sink into sloppiness when his brethren are in an emotional state. He simply has to set a good example, keep a stiff upper lip – ' He broke off as he saw my expression. Then: 'Sorry,' he said. He sounded uncharacteristically abashed. 'It was harrowing, wasn't it? Poor Bernard. Poor brethren. Poor you.'

But I was sunk too deep in misery to reply.

V

In our final conversation which took place before I left the Order Francis said with the robust common sense which I had come to respect so profoundly: 'Jonathan, I know this is a difficult subject but I'm reluctant to close our talks without speaking my mind to you on the subject of women – and don't, I beg of you, now mutter some idiocy such as: "Oh, I'll be all right." I do accept that you've got the strongest desire to live as a priest should, but what I think may well happen is that once you're back in the world you'll soon be so busy wrestling with all manner of temptation that you'll be unable to concentrate on the vital task of listening for any further word from God about your call. Then once you're in such a debilitated spiritual state it's possible – not inevitable but possible – that you'll eventually start drifting into error.'

Here indeed was a harsh and painful reality. I said: 'You're tactfully reminding me that my last attempt to live a celibate life in the world ended in disaster.'

'Yes, but don't misunderstand. I'm not actively counselling you to marry; it may be that your new life in God's service will be so absorbing that celibacy becomes not only essential but easy. On the other hand neither am I actively counselling you to remain celibate; it may be that your new life will require the presence of a wife. But what I *am* strongly advising you to do is to keep an open mind on the subject of marriage.' He paused to choose his words with care before adding: 'Remember that you're a very different man now from that young priest who got into such a harrowing emotional mess. Remember that your marital problems arose not merely because at that time you were unsuited to marriage but because you'd made the mistake of marrying the wrong woman – and don't, whatever you do, automatically dismiss the possibility that somewhere in the world there may well be a woman who could enhance your life instead of diminishing it.'

Without hesitation I said: 'That's good advice. I'll do my best to be sensible.'

'That's not good enough.'

'I promise I'll pray that by the grace of God –.'

'That's better.'

' – I may be wise enough to make the right decisions and strong enough to live according to his will.'

'That's much better. Very well, you're ready to leave and tomorrow I'll release you from your vows.'

VI

The release from my vows took place before two witnesses, Ambrose and the Prior, in the privacy of the Abbot-General's office. The mercifully brief ceremony was set out in the constitution of the Order and Francis made no attempt to deviate from the text, but when I handed over my habit, that symbol of the way of life I was abandoning, I was overcome by such a profound sense of loss that I might not have known how to continue if we had not all been diverted at that moment by the chimes of noon ringing out in error to announce the half-hour.

'I must get that clock overhauled,' said Francis blandly when the ceremony had been completed. 'It's become much too temperamental lately.' And as the other two men left the room after wishing me well he handed me a large brown envelope. 'Here's the first instalment of your loan together with your identity card, ration book and the standard sheet of advice about the old age pension, how to sign on at the Labour Exchange and where you can go for help if you're destitute. There's also an additional sheet giving information about war-time conditions – I expect you've read about "Cooper's Snoopers" from the Ministry of Information and how the Local Defence Volunteers can ask you for your identity card, but you should also know that road signs and the names of railway stations are all being removed in order to confuse any invading Germans. I'd advise you to get hold of a map before the booksellers destroy their stocks.'

Again I was impressed by his attention to detail. Thanking him I stuffed the envelope in my pocket and groped for my suitcase.

'Not so fast!' drawled Francis, and he then gave me not only copies of the Bible, the Book of Common Prayer and the Fordite Missal but also Father Darcy's copy of *The Philosophy of Plotinus*.

The last offering touched me deeply. I had neither expected any memento of my mentor nor anticipated a gift which embraced the subject of mysticism. 'What a very liberal and courageous choice!' I said, ever mindful of Plotinus' dubious status as a pagen.

'The old man would have given you St Augustine's *Confessions*, of course,' said Francis, pleased by my response, 'but I can see I must fight the urge to turn myself into a replica of the old man.'

We left the house together, and as we crossed the courtyard to the main gate I was aware of the hot sunlight on the cobbles, the dull roar of the traffic beyond the wall and the glint of an aeroplane far above us in the cloudless sky.

'More trouble brewing,' said Francis, glancing up as he drew back the bolt on the gate. 'I don't know how much you've heard on the grapevine but the Luftwaffe have been making a big attack on the South-East during the last few days. However we seem to be holding our own.'

'Still our Finest Hour?' I said remembering one of Mr Churchill's felicitous phrases.

'Apparently.' He turned to face me and suddenly I realized that with the formal blessings all exchanged and the cenobitic rituals completed we were at last free to be ourselves. 'Make sure this is *your* finest hour,' he said bluntly, not as a superior preaching to his subordinate but as one man giving encouragement to another. 'Make sure *you* hold your own during all the inevitable assaults on your spiritual strength.' Then with a swift change of mood he exclaimed laughing: 'Something tells me we should now cut short this conversation before we both wind up as shattered as poor Bernard!' and I too somehow contrived to laugh as I clasped his outstretched hands in mine.

So all I said in the end was: 'Thank you, Francis,' and all he said was: 'Good luck, Jon.' Then the monastery gate swung wide, our hands slipped apart and tightening my grip on my suitcase I walked out at last into the world.

SEVEN

'The young have their own ideas, which are not ours. "The conversation of the young and old," says Dr Johnson again, "generally ends with contempt or pity on either side." '

W. R. INGE
Dean of St Paul's 1911–1934
A Pacifist in Trouble

I

Unlike the majority of monks who return to the world after many years of an enclosed existence, I had journeyed from time to time beyond the walls of my cloister and in consequence the shock of a permanent return was alleviated; there was no danger, for example, that I might be unnerved by the sight of a woman smoking a cigarette in public. Yet despite my persistent contact with the world the fact remained that I had lived apart from it and I knew I should expect to find my surroundings not only alien but possibly repellent. It was with wariness that I approached my visit to my daughter, and although I felt elated that I was free to respond to my new call I was at the same time conscious that disillusionment might lie no more than an undisciplined thought away.

Reaching Waterloo I boarded the train for the South-West and wondered how many changes I would see when I arrived at my destination. Ruth had lived all her life in Starmouth, where I had begun my ministry thirty-seven years ago, but although I knew the city well I had never liked it. Unlike the county town of Starbridge, which possesses great beauty and much historical interest, Starmouth is an ugly product of the Industrial Revolution, and as the train approached the city centre that morning I wondered how soon the shipyards would be pock-marked by bombing. Closing my Missal I said a brief prayer for all those who lived and worked near the docks.

The train entered the station. Thrusting my Missal back in my suitcase I abandoned my newspaper for the next occupant of the carriage, smoothed the creases from my unfamiliar trousers and adjusted my clerical collar. By the time the train halted I was ready to spring down on to the platform with a vigour which I hoped demonstrated courage as well as youth, but I knew this air of bravado was mere playacting; as always I was aware of the dread that I would fail to live up to Ruth's expectations of how an ideal father should behave.

I soon saw her. She came rushing forward, stumbling in her ridiculously high-heeled shoes, and then hesitated as if she were shy. Immediately I felt anguish that I should arouse such diffidence, and in an effort to sweep aside all constraint I dropped my suitcase and held out my arms.

'Daddy!' As she hurled herself against my chest I reflected, not for the first time, how odd it was to be called 'Daddy' when normally everyone under the sun addressed me as 'Father'. I could remember Betty and I arguing about how our children should address us. I had favoured 'Mama' and 'Papa' for infancy, 'Mother' and 'Father' when the children were able to pronounce 'th' without lisping, but Betty, to my horror, had shortened 'Mama' and 'Papa' to 'Ma' and 'Pa'; moreover when I had criticized these abbreviations as intolerably common she had called me a snob and burst into tears. After this stormy scene 'Mummy' and 'Daddy', then names which were becoming fashionable seemed the only possible compromise, but I had never liked being 'Daddy', and after Betty's death I had been tempted to ask my children to call me 'Father'. However my nerve had failed me. I had been too afraid they would interpret the request as a retreat into an unloving formality, so the name 'Daddy' had not only persisted but had even degenerated into 'Dad' (a vulgarity almost as bad as 'Pa') when Martin had entered adolescence.

All these memories flashed through my mind in seconds and by the time I gave Ruth the required paternal kiss I found I was thinking not of Betty but of my mentor. Ruth was the only woman I had been allowed to embrace during my years as a monk; Father Darcy had of course thought I should have no embraces with any member of the opposite sex, but since he had been unable to invent a justifiable excuse for depriving an innocent woman of the chance to show her natural affection for her father, the embraces which marked Ruth's visits had continued. Yet Father Darcy had been right in judging them undesirable. They had not only recalled memories of intimate moments with Betty but – far worse – stirred up complex feelings of guilt.

Ruth was one of those women who are almost beautiful but somehow only succeed in being pretty. She was taller than Betty and slimmer around the hips (Betty had been proud of her hour-glass figure) but she had the same small elegant waist and the same disconcertingly lavish bosom. Her dark hair was immaculately curled; I deduced she had recently emerged from a hairdresser's salon. She was wearing a blue coat and skirt, a spotted blue and white blouse and a matching blue hat but this smart assortment of clothes was ruined by the fact that she was also wearing lipstick, rouge and a very pervasive scent. I resent having an odour deliberately imposed on my sense of smell. I am also, I confess, quite unable to overcome the conviction shared by many men of my generation that the use of cosmetics other than powder is most improper for a respectable women.

'My dearest Ruth, how very fashionable and alluring you look!' The long compromise with the truth, in the name of what the world deems to be good manners, had begun.

'Darling Daddy, how lovely to see you in real clothes instead of that ghastly habit – and how excited you must be to return to the world at last after being cut off for so many years!'

'I wasn't in the least cut off!' I was trying not to take offence, since I knew she meant only to be affectionate, but I was unable to suppress an indignant protest.

'But you couldn't do any of the *real* things, could you, like going to the shops or listening to the wireless or chatting with the neighbours about the weather – '

'That's reality?'

'Oh Daddy, stop teasing me! I can't tell you how lovely it is to see you here – I was only saying this morning at breakfast . . . ' Ruth chattered away, just like Betty, just like the vast majority of people in the world, talking about everything but actually saying nothing. The constant talk was going to prove arduous, I could see that, but I knew I had to stop thinking like a monk; I had to make the effort to respond even to the most banal remarks without writing off the conversation as a tedious frivolity which trapped me in the world of appearances when I longed for the world of reality, the reality which lay beyond time and space and the puny perceptions of the five senses.

'What a smart motor car, Ruth! Is it new?'

'No, we got it last year – don't you remember me telling you about it?'

'Ah yes, so you did . . .' I had been listening with only half an ear at the time because I had been worrying about someone else's spiritual problem.

'Fortunately there's no difficulty at present in getting petrol – the allowance is quite generous – but Roger says rationing's bound to be severe eventually . . .'

Roger was my son-in-law. At forty-five he was too old for active service so Ruth was at least spared the constant anxiety which so many wives had to endure at that time. Dutifully I inquired after his health and was told that he was flourishing; the war had resulted in a promotion to a post of greater importance in his expanding firm of ship-builders, and as I murmured the necessary words of approbation Ruth began to talk with enthusiasm of the consequent increase in salary which had permitted her to purchase a new refrigerator.

Meanwhile we were driving through the streets of Starmouth and I was feeling exactly as if I had returned from the dead to inspect the haunts of my previous existence. A painful nostalgia, liberally laced with poignant memories of Betty, seared my psyche and temporarily diverted me from my alarm that I should be travelling in a motor driven by a woman. My alarm was exacerbated since Ruth was too excited to drive well, but eventually when we passed from the centre of the city into quieter districts, I was able to surmount both my nervousness and my nostalgia. I saw we had reached the former village of Hartley, now transformed into a select suburb where houses reposed in spacious gardens on either side of roads entitled 'The Bower', 'The Spinney' and 'The Mount' by authorities determined to breathe a 1930s' life into the concept of 'rus in urbe'. My daughter's home, I discovered, was distinguished by a wealth of half-timbering which was no doubt supposed to recall memories of Tudor architecture. I wondered what an Elizabethan would have thought of such a parody.

Inside everywhere was spotlessly clean and immaculately tidy. I wondered if Ruth had made a special effort to impress me or whether she really was a far more orderly housewife than her mother.

'I love housework,' she was saying, answering my unspoken question. 'Of course I have a daily – the neighbours would think it odd if I didn't – but I spend my whole time trying to think of things for her to do.' With pride she ushered me into the spare-room where a double-bed lay marooned on a spongy pink carpet. The counterpane was not only frilled but flounced. On the walls hung a series of pictures reminiscent of the sentimental daubs which so frequently adorn the lids of chocolate boxes. There were net curtains.

'What a beautiful vase of flowers!' I said, relieved to see at least one item I could admire, and immediately Ruth blurted out: 'Oh Daddy, you're not secretly hating everything, are you?'

'My dearest Ruth – ' I saw with foreboding that her eyes shone with tears.

'You're so silent – I never know what you're thinking – '

'I'm thinking how exceedingly lucky I am to have such a good daughter,' I said truthfully enough but somehow I only succeeded in sounding stilted and embarrassed. 'The house is most striking,' I said fervently in despair, 'and I'm sure I shall be very comfortable.' Giving her a kiss of gratitude I realized with relief that I had finally succeeded in behaving as she wanted me to behave, and seconds later my relief was expanding as I was left on my own to unpack.

Immediately I took down all the pictures and put them in the wardrobe. Then I hung up my other black suit, put away its clerical accompaniments and my change of underclothes in the chest of drawers and arranged my books on a shelf by the bed. The pot of honey I set aside to give to my grand-daughter. Having completed my unpacking I then read a psalm and prayed that I might be given the grace to overcome the guilt which so inhibited my relationship with my daughter, the guilt which stemmed from my past inadequacy as a parent and which so distorted my genuine affection for her that I found it impossible to express my feelings in a satisfactory way. Certainly I knew Ruth was never satisfied, just as I knew that her obsessive attention to me sprang not primarily from her innate warm-heartedness but from a deep-rooted subconscious fear that I had no love for her at all.

However my prayer for the grace to be the ideal parent was disjointed and, as I soon realized, ill-conceived, based on a self-centred desire to avoid the debilitating emotional scenes which would arise if Ruth found me inadequate. Rising from my knees in shame I tidied myself, visited an effete lavatory which even had a frothy piece of material covering the lid like a tea-cosy, and went reluctantly downstairs for luncheon.

II

Luncheon consisted of an excellent shepherd's-pie followed by cheese, and I began to feel more cheerful. Ruth and I were alone. Roger was at his office, my grandson was still on holiday with his schoolfriend and my grand-daughter had been dispatched to Roger's sister nearby.

'I wanted to have you to myself for the first couple of hours!' confessed Ruth, touching me impulsively as if to make sure I was not a mere figment of her imagination.

After luncheon I was given a tour of the house, but although I had wanted most particularly to see the children's rooms I found them disappointing. Colin, covering his walls with pictures of aeroplanes and motors, had revealed a passion for machinery not uncommon among boys of sixteen who never open books except when forced to do so at school, but the pictures reinforced my suspicion that I shared no interests with him. My grand-daughter's room indicated a fractionally wider outlook on life but its very femininity only emphasized the gulf which must always exist between the sexes; I noted an assortment of dolls, no doubt retained only for sentimental reasons now that Janet was twelve, a large picture of Princess Elizabeth and Princess Margaret Rose, and two shelves of storybooks bearing titles such as 'Mimsie in the Upper Fourth'. In neither room did I see a Bible, a prayer-book or even a volume of Biblical stories for children.

'Now I'll take you to the kitchen,' Ruth was saying. 'I've been saving it up till the last because I'm so proud of it. I'm longing to show you my new fridge!'

It was clear that the refrigerator interested her greatly and as she talked about it with animation I noticed that she finally became relaxed. I stood listening in courteous silence and thought how baffling the scene was. If she had said to me: 'I have this serious difficulty which is disrupting my spiritual life,' I would have known exactly what questions to ask. But to be told the virtues of a refrigerator and to be expected to make an intelligent comment was a trial indeed. I found the dialogue quite impossible to sustain.

I eventually contrived to escape from the kitchen by asking to see the garden, but when Ruth continued to chatter interminably about trivialities I began to feel very tired. However my spirits revived when my grand-daughter appeared at the back door and skipped down the path into my arms. We had not met for some months and I was disappointed to see that she was going through a plain stage. Her pale hair was scraped back from her face into pigtails and she wore a brace on her teeth, but her grey eyes sparkled and I thought for a moment that I had caught a glimpse of my mother although it was impossible to be sure.

We had just retired indoors when the telephone bell started to ring. At once I wondered if the call came from Martin but in the hall Ruth exclaimed: 'Pam, how lovely to hear you!' and began to talk about a forthcoming whist-drive in aid of the Red Cross. Hiding my disappointment I sat down at the kitchen table.

'Mummy's in an awful flap about your visit,' confided Janet impulsively as she sat down at my side. 'So's Daddy. They can't understand why you've left the Order when you were such a success in it.'

'But I could hardly have made it plainer in my letter that I've been called by God to work in the world again!'

'Have you really? Gosh, how interesting! Neither of them told me that. Did God speak to you from a cloud like in the Bible?'

'No, he entered my mind and arranged it in certain patterns.' It occurred to me that this was the first conversation I had ever had with my grand-daughter on her own and I hastened to make the most of Ruth's absence. 'Do you really enjoy your scripture lessons at school?' I said. 'When you told me at our last meeting about that ex-missionary teacher of yours I thought she sounded a bit of a bore. And what about your local vicar? I didn't ask you about him. Does he take a special interest in helping children of your age to take part in the life of the Church?'

The child became wary. 'I don't think so.'

'Think? Don't you know?'

She was immediately intimidated, and cursing myself for becoming too inquisitorial in my eagerness to discover more about her spiritual life I added swiftly: 'Of course I know your mother doesn't take you to church every Sunday but surely when you do go – ' I stopped. A bitter enlightenment had dawned. 'Don't you go to church at all nowadays?' I demanded. 'Not even at Christmas and Easter?'

The child was now tongue-tied with a guilty shame which, I knew, would later make her feel resentful and cross. I had made a mess of my first real conversation with a grandchild. In distress I groped for the words which would put matters right but before I could speak Ruth exclaimed angrily behind me: 'Really, Daddy, can't you talk about *anything* except religion? Can't you ask Janet about her friends and her hobbies instead of cross-questioning her about whether I'm being a good mother and taking her to church every Sunday?'

'My dear Ruth, I'm well aware that there are plenty of good mothers who have some difficulty which makes church-going impossible, and of course I quite understand how hard it is when a husband can't share his wife's spiritual life – '

'And now I suppose you're going to criticize me for marrying a man who isn't religious!'

'Ruth, is this really the wisest of conversations to conduct in your daughter's presence?'

The child saw an opportunity to channel all her confused resentment into an aggressive question. 'Mummy, why didn't you tell me that Grandad had had a call from God to leave the Order?'

'Oh, that's what he always says when he wants his own way!' cried Ruth, her insecurity rendering her quite unable to endure even the mildest disapproval from me, and in a storm of emotion which reminded me sickeningly of Betty she rushed out of the kitchen into the scullery and slammed the door violently behind her.

III

I stood up and at once the child said desperately: 'Please don't be cross with us because we don't go to church.'

I sat down again. Ruth could wallow in her tiresome tantrum; Ruth could wait. I saw clearly that to reassure the child was my first task, and taking her hand in mine I said: 'I certainly shan't love you less just because at present you're not a churchgoer. However . . .' I hesitated but was unable to resist adding: 'Churchgoing can be useful in helping one to approach the task of worshipping God. It provides a structure which makes the task easier – just as your teacher made the task of learning to write easier years ago when she gave you specially lined paper to help you form your letters.'

The child stared at me wide-eyed. Possibly no one had ever talked to her about worship before. In a home where a refrigerator was treated with reverence no doubt all the occupants would be seriously out of touch with reality, but although I enfolded her with my sympathy she remained unaware of it. To my acute disappointment she withdrew her hand and said in a voice which told me her earlier guilt had turned to anger, just as I had foreseen: 'Mummy's very upset and you don't care.'

'Of course I care,' I said, but my voice sounded much too austere and suddenly I saw myself as I must appear to her, a tall intimidating stranger, cool, aloof and baffling, the very reverse of the cosy old grandfathers who inhabited the best storybooks for children. I knew I had to project warmth in order to win her confidence, but I felt chilled by a sense of inadequacy. I could only add in a stiff voice: 'I'll talk to your mother. Don't be upset. I'll soon calm her down.'

'Mummy's very difficult to calm down when she's in a state. Daddy just gives up and goes off to play golf.'

'I don't play golf and I'm used to dealing with people who are upset.' I managed to smile at her. 'Sometimes I used to feel that being an abbot was like being the captain of a ship. I was forever steering my passengers and crew through troubled waters.'

I could see this description interested her and although she remained grave I sensed her resentment ebb. However she retorted severely: 'You wouldn't have been an ordinary captain – you'd have been a pirate, swinging a cutlass and shaking up everyone in sight.' And having described with a startling accuracy my mysterious talent for disruption, she slipped away out of the room before I could attempt a reply.

IV

I could postpone the moment no longer. Nerving myself to enter the scullery I found Ruth crying and took her in my arms.

'Oh Daddy, I didn't mean to be so rude but you made me feel so guilty that we don't go to church – '

I was acutely aware of her alien femininity, the lush loosely-corseted flesh, the pervasive odour of cosmetics, the unnaturally curled hair, the high voice and – most unnerving of all – the undisciplined emotion. How did one deal with such a creature? If she had been a disturbed relation of one of my monks I would have been kind but implacably austere, allowing no physical contact whatsoever; I knew exactly how an abbot should behave in such circumstances, but how a father should behave towards such a mysterious version of his own flesh and blood was a problem which quite defeated me. I suddenly found myself wishing the old useless wish that

Ruth could have resembled my mother, and the next moment in my memory I could see my mother, serene, silent and self-possessed, never making any exhausting emotional demands which could only fill me with a resentment born of guilty despair.

Carefully putting the precious memory aside I said to my daughter with all the kindness I could muster: 'Poor Ruth, I'm so sorry.' I was just wondering what I could possibly say next when I was saved by the ringing of the telephone bell, but although I again hoped the caller was Martin I again hoped in vain. Ruth began another conversation about the forthcoming whist-drive, and slipping past her I padded upstairs to my room.

I could not remember when I had last felt so overpowered by the need to be alone.

V

The next hurdle to be surmounted was the reunion with my son-in-law who had always abstained from visiting me in my cloister not, as he would have had me believe, because he could never manage to take sufficient time off from his work, but because he had a horror of an enclosed religious life; I suspected that even if he had found me the most delightful of fathers-in-law he would still have fought shy of visiting a monastery in order to pay his respects.

When he arrived home that night at half-past six his first act after the ritual of handshaking was to ask me what I wanted to drink. Possibly he had no idea what else to say to me. Equally possibly he could not face the reunion without a stiff dose of alcohol. Feeling sorry for him and realizing that I had to offer more than a meticulous politeness I requested a dry sherry in order to appear convivial. I have, I confess, never been attracted to alcoholic beverages as I dislike having the sharp edge of my psyche blunted, but as a Naval chaplain I had learnt the value of nursing a glass in order to repel any accusation of priggishness, and certainly I have never thought that a priest should feel under any obligation to be a teetotaller. Our Lord, after all, is indisputably on record as enjoying his wine at social gatherings.

My son-in-law was a bald man with an unremarkable countenance and when I saw how stout he had become I thought how lucky he was to have such a pretty wife. I hoped he appreciated his good fortune. However he paid scant attention to Ruth and aided by a very dark whisky-and-soda he began to talk in a boastful manner about his blossoming career. Since he had been at a public school, albeit a minor one, I thought he should have been trained to exhibit more modesty, but I realized that this childish desire to impress me sprang from his extreme nervousness. Clearly I needed to soothe him by making a friendly gesture, but it was not until he said to me after dinner: 'Can I offer you a glass of port, sir?' that I saw what form the friendly gesture should take.

'Roger,' I said, 'it was all very well for you to call me "sir" when you were a young man engaged to my daughter, but I feel it's high time we dispensed with such formality. Please call me Jon in future. And yes, I will have some port, although I'd prefer the measure to be a small one.'

We were alone by this time. Ruth and Janet were washing the dishes and although I had volunteered to help my offer had been received with a horror which I had forgotten would be inevitable. As a monk I had become so used to men performing all manner of domestic work that the traditional family practice of excluding males from the kitchen now seemed like an archaic custom, droll and not without charm but creating an artificial division between the sexes which could only foster the widespread delusion that the function of women was to wait on men hand and foot. I remembered one of my novices complaining at Ruydale: 'I want to be outdoors with the men – I don't want to be in the kitchen doing women's work!' and I remembered too my severe response: 'Men and women are of equal worth in the sight of God and all work, even the most menial task, becomes worthwhile when dedicated to his glory.' I wondered what my son-in-law would have thought of such a philosophy, but I could no more imagine Roger agreeing that men and women were of equal worth than I could imagine him washing dishes contentedly in the kitchen.

' . . . and may I ask,' Roger was saying, still not bold enough to address me as Jon despite the large amount of alcohol he had consumed, 'if you're about to land some important post in the Church of England?'

It would have been useless to explain that a priest should be uninterested in obtaining a position which the world deems important. Instead I said neutrally: 'My only plan at present is to adjust to the world as quickly as possible.'

'But you surely must have some idea of what you're going to do!'

'Apart from serving God, no. None at all.'

Roger was at once disturbed by my failure to behave like a normal person, and sensing the source of his anxiety I moved swiftly to soothe him. 'The Order has kindly granted me a loan to tide me over the next three months,' I said, 'so there's no danger that I'll starve – and certainly no danger that I'll be a financial drain upon you.'

'Well, of course if there's anything I can do to help . . .' His relief was almost palpable.

'It's extremely helpful that I'm able to spend my first week here, and I'm most grateful to you for your hospitality.'

No father-in-law could have behaved better. The last swirl of tension faded from the atmosphere as Roger was finally able to relax.

'Tell me,' I said before he could voice any insincere pleasure that I should be staying beneath his roof, 'have you heard anything from Martin?' This was a question which I had avoided asking Ruth because I had been too nervous of arousing her jealousy.

Roger's air of relaxation was abruptly dissipated. 'I'm afraid that's a difficult subject – ' He nerved himself to take the plunge ' – Jon. He turned up here two weeks ago, drank all my whisky and became pretty damned unpleasant when I refused to lend him money. I had to ask him to leave.'

At first I was surprised that Ruth had concealed this incident from me; her jealousy ensured that I usually heard promptly whenever Martin had been disagreeable, but then I realized that she had not wanted me thinking of Martin when for the first time for many years she had me all to herself.

'He's asked for money before, of course,' Roger was saying, 'but he never pays it back and this time I decided to put my foot down. I dare say you'll think me uncharitable, but – '

'Not at all. Charity isn't always synonymous with giving money. It may be better for Martin if he's taught that he can't continue to extract money from you on demand.'

Making the mistake of thinking I was entirely unsympathetic to my son, Roger said aggressively: 'Perhaps he'll now make more effort to get a job. Why can't he seek appropriate work like any other decent pacifist instead of loafing around as an out-of-work actor? In my opinion it's a pity he can't be press-ganged into the Army tomorrow – it would straighten out his drinking and make a man of him. I can't stand all this weak-kneed pacifist talk, and if you ask me I think Martin's decision to swim with the pacifist tide is just his immature way of showing off and calling attention to himself.'

I waited for five seconds until I had myself absolutely in control. Then I said in a voice which was devoid of emotion: 'Personally I'd rather Martin stood up for his beliefs by talking weak-kneed rubbish than compromised his integrity by talking strong-armed claptrap.'

Ruth, re-entering the room seconds later, found us sunk deep in a hostile silence. 'Coffee's ready!' she said brightly, trying to conceal her dismay, but I could only profess my need for an early night and escape once more to my room.

The next day I did not present myself in the dining-room until Roger had departed for his office. It was curious to be confronted by a cooked breakfast again. I was torn between finding the bacon and eggs repulsively rich and savouring such a nostalgic reminder of my youth.

Ruth was closeted with her 'daily' and Janet was playing with her friend next door, so in my solitude I was free to read the newspapers which had already been delivered to the house. Setting aside *The Daily Telegraph* I began my first inspection for seventeen years of that popular rag *The Daily Express*. Amazed, aghast and wholly absorbed by the bold headlines and even bolder photographs I marvelled at the violent, sex-obsessed, trivia-infested world I had been called to rejoin. This was indeed a world far removed from the decorous columns to which I had become accustomed. Guiltily I wondered what Father Darcy would have thought as I skimmed through the latest society divorce case and allowed my glance to linger on a picture of an exceedingly fetching actress, but I did not think of Father Darcy for long. I was too busy imagining the actress in one of the astoundingly brief modern bathing costumes which were displayed in an adjacent advertisement, and I was just wondering in alarm if I could be experiencing the onset of Monks' Madness when Ruth returned to the room.

'Now, Daddy, it's quite obvious you need a woman to take you in hand,' she said, sublimely unaware of the image which this normally innocuous phrase at once conjured up in my disordered imagination. 'I'm going to drive you to the shops. You simply must have some more clothes, and Roger and I have decided to give you a suit as a coming-out present.'

'How very kind,' I said, 'but the two suits I have at present are quite sufficient.'

'What utter nonsense! Daddy, you can't possibly go off to this hotel next week with no decent clothes – do come down to earth and be realistic for a moment! You must have a dressing-gown, pyjamas, slippers, some ties, a couple of ordinary shirts, some grey flannels and a sports jacket – and oh my goodness, I nearly forgot! Daddy, your *underclothes*! When we met outside the bathroom this morning – '

'I concede,' I said with dignity, 'that I need new underclothes, and of course if you and Roger truly wish to give me a suit it would be most ungracious of me to refuse to accept it, but the other items will have to wait. I can't possibly put you to such expense.'

'Yes, you can – we're not poor, and it's very important that you should get everything you need before they bring in clothes-rationing. Stop being so huffish and proud!'

Realizing that any further argument would only upset her I refrained from any mutinous comment, but I found Ruth demonstrating her love by well-meaning bossiness almost as exhausting as Ruth demonstrating her love by staging an emotional scene.

Half an hour later we motored to the centre of Starmouth, and there I was firmly led, like a small child dragooned by a nanny, to the gentlemen's tailors and outfitters' shop which I had patronized earlier in my life. There a surprise awaited me. I had expected merely to be measured for the suit, but it had already been bespoken. My measurements had been on file, Ruth had placed the order as soon as she had received word of my return to the world and the little tailor, who remembered me well, was now beaming as he offered me his latest sartorial masterpiece.

I said: 'It's navy blue,' and somehow succeeded in keeping the horror out of my voice.

'Isn't it lovely?' said Ruth pleased. 'So much nicer than dreary old black!'

The tailor said soothingly to me: 'The navy blue is very dark, sir, and perfectly seemly for a gentleman of your calling.'

Realizing I was on the brink of behaving badly I pulled myself together. 'I'm extremely pleased,' I said. 'This is a wonderful surprise. May I try it on?'

I was shown into a curtained alcove and abandoned with my new suit. The colour still looked unbearably frivolous and common but I told myself I had to stop thinking in such ascetic terms and that my snobbery was not only unattractive but in all probability out of date. Perhaps nowadays even aristocratic clergymen ran around in blue suits during their leisure hours. I held the material up to the light. The colour was indeed very dark. Perhaps at night or on a wet day it might be mistaken for black. That prospect seemed the best I could hope for.

Keeping my back to the looking-glass I slowly exchanged the old for the new, the sacred for the profane, but despite my antipathy I had to admit the suit felt a perfect fit. I allowed myself a moment of unedifying pride as I reflected how little my figure had altered in seventeen years, and then, fortified by my vanity, I nerved myself to face the glass.

I was appalled. A layman, smart and barely recognizable, confronted me. He looked like a successful actor playing the role of a celebrated politician – or possibly of a celebrated surgeon. Pride, arrogance and an aura of reckless ruthless individuality emanated from the reflection with a force which recalled all my most horrific memories. I felt I was glimpsing again the young undergraduate who had so unscrupulously used his gifts for his own aggrandisement, and this sinister exposure of the dark side of my personality made me yearn in panic for my black and white habit which, like some metaphysical corset, had encased my faults and concealed them behind the façade of a corporate identity.

'Does it fit?' Ruth was demanding, reminding me of Betty as she slashed my consciousness with the razor of her conversation. 'Can I come in?'

'I suppose so.' I disliked all this womanish bustling.

'I was sure you hadn't put on any weight, but even so I – DADDY! Darling, you look stunning, just like a film star! What a wonderful transformation!'

This was exactly the judgement I had no wish to hear. The last thing I wanted was to be transformed; that way lay danger, error and nightmare. 'It's a most generous gift, Ruth. Thank you very much,' I said with difficulty, but all the time I was longing for my pectoral cross and my abbot's ring.

'Daddy, is anything wrong?'

'No, I just feel odd dressed as a layman. I'll be fine once I'm back in my clerical suit.'

'But aren't you going to wear – '

'I'll save it for later.' I got rid of her, changed back into my familiar clothes and felt better, but when I emerged from the cubicle I found she had been rapidly buying a host of other items, shirts and ties to go with the new suit, the promised grey flannels and sports jacket, the pyjamas, dressing-gown, slippers – and even the underclothes.

'You need new shoes too,' she said. 'We'll leave everything here and just slip across the road to the shoe-shop – '

'Ruth, I'm quite sure you can't afford all this gross and unnecessary expenditure – '

'Now don't start being proud and huffish again!'

I gave up and allowed myself to be marched to the shoe-shop but as soon as we left I asked to be taken to the nearest church.

'Church!' She was much taken aback but after a moment's hesitation she said uneasily: 'I'll take you to the one nearest the house so that it'll be easy for you to walk home . . . Daddy, what is it? What's wrong?'

'Nothing. I just want to be in church for a bit, that's all. It feels so odd not to have been in church yet today.'

'I suppose you want to be alone. I can remember Mummy saying to Grandma: "In the end no matter what I do he always has to be alone."' And as I flinched she added in a rush: 'I'm sorry, I know talking about Mummy always upsets you. I'll shut up now and give you some peace.'

She left me at the church, a Victorian replica of the conventional Norman design, and drove away looking injured. I dragged myself inside. The interior was dusty and dark. Kneeling in a corner by a pillar I wrestled with my misery for a long time but eventually I sat back in the pew, took my Missal from my pocket and read the noon office. That soothed me, and afterwards I was at last able to concentrate on framing my personal prayers.

'What on earth have you been doing?' cried Ruth, opening the front door as I toiled up the drive in the middle of the afternoon. 'You've been gone for hours! I've been so worried – I thought you'd got lost, had an accident, suffered a heart attack – I even went down to the church to look for you but you weren't there – '

'I went for a walk. Then I found another church and – '

'Well, you might at least have telephoned to say you were missing lunch!' Once more she was deeply hurt. It was tempting to express my guilt and despair by shouting at her in exasperation but of course there could be no shouting, no scenes, no reaction other than a saintly contrition.

'I'm so sorry, how very thoughtless of me.'

'And now I suppose you'll say you want to be alone again!'

With a supreme effort I managed to say levelly: 'My dear, you mustn't take it as a personal insult. The truth is I'm just not used to the world yet and I need time to recuperate. Please try to understand and make allowances.'

Silently she stood aside to let me pass and awkwardly, feeling guiltier than ever, I slunk away up the stairs to my room.

VII

The depression began, stabbing deep deadening fingers into my psyche and casting a dark dragging shadow over my powers of reason. I knew that I was suffering from a reaction to the elation I had experienced when I had found myself free to respond to my new call; I knew I was emotionally dislocated, deprived of my cherished way of life; I knew I had to calm myself not only with prayer but with the knowledge that my distress would almost certainly pass, but I found prayer so difficult in that alien environment and the belief in my ultimate recovery was of small comfort. Meanwhile my psychic vitality was continually sapped by the unfamiliar noise of the world, from the meaningless conversation at mealtimes to the irritating stream of sound on the wireless. I began to feel increasingly debilitated and desperate.

However after three torturous days Sunday arrived and I had a chance to conquer my apathy by embracing the disciplined structure of corporate worship. I attended the early service of Holy Communion, which was tolerably well conducted, and later went to Matins and Evensong. Both sermons struck me as slipshod and unedifying. So did the music; the choir made much noise but sang flat. I felt saddened by the lack of men in the congregation and the predominance of elderly women. However at least I was participating in some form of familiar routine. It had a stabilizing influence on me, and as I walked home after Evensong I made up my mind to stop pining for my Grantchester chapel, for the voices of my brethren singing the office, for the ascetic atmosphere which I had found so conducive to a rich inner life. To recoil from the world was to fall into the trap of Dualism. No one could deny, in 1940, that evil was present in the world, but the world itself was good, a place to be loved and cherished, and it ill became a priest to regard the work of God with despair.

The next morning I found I had the will to battle against my melancholy, and although I was still tempted to incarcerate myself in my bedroom I left the house, took a motor-bus into the countryside and went for a long walk. Fields, hills, valleys, streams – all seemed radiantly beautiful in the summer light, and as I walked I felt the depression loosen its stranglehold on my mind. I was wearing one of my new shirts with my new grey flannels, and so for the first time in seventeen years I was able to enjoy hot weather without being burdened by heavy robes. I decided that there might after all be compensations for relinquishing the monastic life, and later when I stopped at a village inn for a pint of ale I sat peacefully in the small spare masculine saloon without once wishing myself back in the cloister.

When I returned to Ruth's house in the early evening I felt physically tired but mentally strong enough to surmount any emotional hurdle which my family might heave across my path – or so I thought. I did not ring the front doorbell. I sensed little Janet was waiting for me in the back garden so I strolled around the side of the house and pushed open the tradesmen's gate. However as I entered the garden I found that my intuition had been only partially correct. Someone was indeed waiting for me but that someone was not Janet.

It was Martin.

VIII

He was drunk, of course, but to my surprise I found this was a challenge I could meet without flinching. Women like Ruth might baffle me, but I was thoroughly experienced in dealing with men afflicted by Martin's problems, and no doubt the fact that I at last felt on familiar ground gave me additional strength. Having allowed myself three seconds to pray for the required pastoral skill I said with a smile: 'What a splendid surprise – I couldn't be more pleased to see you!' and firmly shook his hand.

This was evidently the right approach; as we sat down together on the garden-seat he offered me his hip-flask and said benignly: 'Have a swig.'

I recognized the olive-branch, and as I went through the motions of accepting the whisky I was careful to swallow to create the illusion that I had consumed a large mouthful. It was a technique I had perfected in the Navy.

'Sorry I didn't write,' he said in between gulping several large swigs of his own, 'but I couldn't face it.'

'The only thing that matters now is that you're here. When did you arrive?'

'An hour ago. Then Ruth and I had a screaming match and I was put out like a bloody cat that's made a mess, but at least Janet smuggled the whisky decanter to me so that I was able to refill my flask . . . No, don't ask me how I am! I know damn well you'll have guessed why I'm so conspicuously drowning my sorrows! So much for my dramatic declaration that I'd settled down and was as good as married – he walked out a week after I saw you and the last thing I heard of him was that he was living with a French chef. *A French chef!* Christ, how low can you get! I hate all those bloody pretentious messes which the Frogs push around their plates. Give me bangers-and-mash any day . . . Have another swig.'

'No, obviously you need the swig more than I do. I'm sorry you've been through such a rough time – '

'Balls! You're secretly cheering with relief, but if you think I'm going to react to this disaster by taking up with some frightful female – '

'Martin, I've spent many years of my life praying that you wouldn't take up with a female who was frightful.'

'Well, if you really want to know how I'm going to react to this disaster I'll tell you: I'm going to kick pacifism in the arse, bugger my way into the Army and bloody well get killed. That would solve all my problems nicely.'

I realized that this extravagant statement was an appeal for love and attention but nevertheless it is exceedingly upsetting when one's child expresses the wish to be killed. I felt my professional poise begin to slip. 'Martin – '

'I didn't really believe in all that pacifist rubbish anyway, not after Munich. I just put on an act because Bob was so keen on pacifism and I didn't want to be separated from him if we were called up.'

'But will you be accepted for the Army?'

'Don't be naïve, Dad! If they excluded from the Army all the men who'd ever committed buggery England would be entirely defenceless!'

'I was actually thinking of your age – '

'No, you bloody weren't! But perhaps you're hoping I'll change my mind yet again and become a monk – which reminds me, why on earth have you chucked it all up?'

'I told you in my last letter. I've had a call from God to serve him in the world again.'

'Yes, but for Christ's sake, what does that *mean*? What are you going to do? Oh God, I can't stand it when you do your Holy Mystic act – '

'I don't know yet what I'm going to do.'

'Then you must be crazy. You had that nice little nook at Grantchester, you were well-fed and well-housed with nothing to do all day except play the Holy Mystic, your favourite role, and yet you decide to chuck it all up in order to bugger around in this bloody awful old world again! It must be sex. There's no other explanation, but all I can say is that you'd better watch out. Don't turn into one of those nasty old men who get sentimental about girls of Janet's age – '

I stood up, crossed the lawn and began to contemplate the nearest flower-bed. No matter how healthy it was for him to vent his rage and misery, it was important that I controlled the conversation by demonstrating exactly how much offensive talk I would tolerate.

He came after me and tugged at my sleeve like a child begging for attention, the little boy who had never grown up. 'Dad – wait a minute – *Dad* – oh damn you, don't go all cold and silent – '

I swung round. 'When I want to look in a sewer, Martin, I'll pull up the cover of the nearest manhole. I've no intention of listening to such filthy conversation, and moreover I'm under absolutely no obligation to do so.'

'You bloody old prig!' yelled Martin and retreated to the garden-seat to seek solace in his hip-flask.

I waited till we were both calmer. Then I too returned to the garden-seat and said quietly: 'How can I help you?'

'You can't help me. You despise me.'

'How could I despise someone who's brave? You were brave to be an actor, brave to live your life as you felt you ought to live it, and above all you were brave to tell me about Bob – '

'I only did it to hurt you. I thought if I hurt you I'd make some sort of contact, get some sort of genuine reaction instead of this ghastly saintliness you project whenever you're playing the role of Father with a capital F – '

'Martin, this behaviour is unconstructive and it's induced by a surfeit of alcohol. Come into the house and I'll make you a sandwich.'

'I don't want a bloody sandwich!'

'Then what do you want, Martin?'

Without warning his bravado crumbled and his eyes filled with tears. 'I want you to tell me you don't mind me being the way I am. I want you to tell me it doesn't matter.'

'I can't tell you that,' I said, 'because it would be a lie. I do mind and it does matter, but that doesn't mean I no longer care about you – indeed it's because I care for you as much as ever that I want to do all I can to help. Look, I can see how much you've suffered, but suffering needn't be destructive. If you could only use it as a spur to begin a new life – '

'Oh my God, we're knee-deep in crucifixion and resurrection!' He struggled to his feet. '*I don't want your bloody religion!* All your bloody religion ever did for me was to give me a man who was more interested in being a bloody clergyman than a bloody father!' And as Ruth finally gave way to the temptation to erupt from the house in fury he blundered away through the tradesmen's gate without looking back.

EIGHT

'Religion, so far from being a disease, is essential to mental health, and if we may trust those who in other fields would be called experts in their subject, there is one thing of which they feel increasingly certain, and that is that in prayer and meditation they are actually in contact with a spiritual reality which is not a projection of their own thought and will.'

W. R. INGE
Dean of St Paul's 1911–1934
Lay Thoughts of a Dean

I

During the last part of my conversation with Martin I had been aware that Ruth was listening at the open scullery window so I was far from surprised when she decided to intervene. Nevertheless I was angry. I found her bright-eyed excitement unedifying and I was reminded of nursery scenes long ago when she had rejoiced at Martin's transgressions in the hope that she might consequently win extra favour.

'Poor darling Daddy – oh, how could he have said such horrible things to you, how could he!'

'He's intolerably unhappy.'

My response disappointed her; at once she became angry. 'I should have known you'd always stand up for him – even now he's a drunken pervert you're still busy pretending he's wonderful!'

So overwhelmed was I by my misery that I was unable to order her to be quiet. Retreating to my room I tried to pray, but I felt cut off from God and memories of my marriage, all hellish, screamed through my consciousness until my entire psyche was a dense ball of pain.

Half an hour later I was still groping for the will which would enable me to perform the simple task of changing for dinner when there was a mouselike tap on the door.

It was the child, her small face pale and grave. 'I'm sorry, Grandad. It was all my fault. I gave Uncle Martin the whisky and the whisky made him beastly.'

542

With unutterable relief I recognized a familiar situation: someone in distress had come to me for help and I had the opportunity to rise above my own pain by thinking of someone other than myself. Scooping her across the threshold I sat down with her on the edge of the bed. 'Uncle Martin had already decided to share his unhappiness with me,' I said, 'and the extra whisky merely made it easier for him to do so. You mustn't blame yourself. I know you wanted only to be kind.'

I was aware of her gratitude. She said confidentially: 'Mummy's livid with me because she says I made Uncle Martin drunk and Daddy's livid with me because he's just arrived home and found there's no whisky.'

'Both your parents are upset and not thinking clearly. It's only natural that you should feel hurt and cross, but in fact you're not the real source of their anger. They're angry with Martin for behaving badly, and although they may not realize it they're angry with me for being the pirate who boards their orderly ship and causes chaos.'

She was intrigued. 'But Grandad, how do you manage to cause such chaos? You're always so quiet and polite! Why is everyone reeling in all directions?'

I laughed. 'Perhaps I should offer myself to the Army as a secret weapon!'

'Gosh, what a ripping idea! You could knock out Hitler!'

'Exorcism would be more effective, I think.'

'Exorcism! I've read about that. But does it work?'

'Certainly. No demon can withstand the power of Christ.'

Far away in the hall Ruth called tensely: 'Dinner's ready!'

'Grandad.'

'Yes, Janet?'

'It's all real, isn't it? Religion, I mean.'

'Of course.'

'But why doesn't everyone understand that?'

'One of our limitations as human beings is that we find it exceedingly difficult to grasp reality – the ultimate reality which is spiritual.'

'Daddy thinks it's religion that's unreal. He thinks it's a sort of illness.'

'It's hard for people who operate on only five senses to perceive a reality which they can't hear, see, touch, taste or smell. However there's a vast mass of evidence which suggests that not only does this ultimate reality exist but that it can be perceived by man. For instance, Plato (who was a mystic) said that the fully real is fully knowable, and by that he meant – '

'*Dinner!*' shouted Ruth.

'What's a mystic?' said Janet.

'A mystic is someone who can perceive ultimate reality, the ground of our being, known variously as God or the Absolute or the One. Mysticism isn't confined to Christianity; it's the raw material of religion and exists independently of creeds and sects and religion in an organized form. However in my opinion a mystic should work within an organized church because he needs the discipline of a stable framework in order to remain spiritually healthy. It's a very regrettable fact of the spiritual life that a mystical approach to God is peculiarly subject to demonic influences.'

'I wish you taught us scripture at school,' said Janet. 'I know you're old but you still look nice and you talk about such interesting things.'

It was the kindest remark I had received for some time. I gave her a kiss and somehow found the strength to face dinner.

II

The sixth and penultimate day of my visit dawned at Starmouth. I had still not succeeded in sleeping through the night; old habits die hard, and when I awoke I read the office of matins. Later at half-past five I rose, shaved, dressed and read the office of prime before spending two hours in prayer and devotional reading. Every day I longed to receive the sacrament, but during the week there was no mass in Starmouth beyond the walls of the Roman Catholic Church. In my desperation I was tempted to attend mass there but I knew the inevitably voluptuous interior of the church and the stream of garbled Latin would distract me so much that the exercise could only be unedifying.

Ironically it was my time as a High-Church monk, not my career as a Broad-Church Naval chaplain, which had nurtured my antipathy towards the Church of Rome. The Anglo-Catholics' flirtation with ecumenism in the form of a reunion with Rome is a relatively recent development, and the Fordite Order, founded in the 1840s before Mr Ford's hero John Henry Newman had seceded to Rome, had remained true to the original spirit of the Oxford Movement when it re-established Catholicism as a powerful force within the Church of England. This famous 'ethos' had consisted in part of an outlook which saw Anglo-Catholicism as truer to the Early Church than the Catholicism of Rome which was judged to have been corrupted over the centuries. The Oxford Movement's later, more charitable view – that the true Catholic Church was tripartite, consisting of Anglo-Catholics, Roman Catholics and the Orthodoxy of Eastern Europe – was eventually accepted by the Fordites, but the anti-Roman bias lingered on and in fact the Fordites were still distinguished by the strong stress they laid on their separation from the Roman Orders. As a leading High-Churchman, Father Darcy had felt bound to encourage the reunion talks at Malines in the 1920s between the Anglo-Catholics and the Roman Catholics, but later in private he had told me he considered the entire exercise not only a waste of time but thoroughly undesirable. However this deep antipathy had probably been rooted in the fact that he considered his Order to be vastly superior to any of the Roman Orders and had hated to think that in the event of reunion he would have had to be servile to some foreigner called a pope who would almost certainly have regarded him with disdain.

My own feelings on the subject were as mixed as my mentor's. As a Christian I did my best to regard the authoritarian monolith of Rome with charity; as an Englishman I could not help but regard it with distaste, and as a mystic I could only regard it with horror. Profound religious truths are eternal; the man-made divisions of Christendom, trapped in time, are subject to corruption, and because of this no man-made institution should be allowed to interpose itself in a dictatorial fashion between the mystic and his God – indeed no man-made institution can effectively do so, and this, of course, explains why mysticism has so often been a running sore on the body politic of the Roman Church. No authoritarian regime likes the rebels who by circumventing its power cut it down to size.

Mystics, as I had told Janet, need the framework of organized religion, but when the organization can only offer a framework which insists on conformity at all costs then mysticism, if not crushed or driven underground, will flourish not because of the organization but in spite of it. The monastic life of the Fordites certainly had its authoritarian aspects, but the watchwords of the Church of England are liberty and tolerance, and certainly no one in the Order had tried to suppress or distort my spiritual gifts in the name of dogmatics. I had known then that although I was a Catholic I would remain an English Catholic and that the Church of Rome would always be alien to me.

So I abstained from attending mass at the local Roman Catholic church, but on the penultimate day of my visit to Starmouth I padded downstairs after reading Prime, stole a crust from the bread-bin in the larder, filched a drop of sherry from the drawing-room decanter and retired to my room to celebrate the Holy Communion. Afterwards I felt comforted, and it was in a strong tranquil frame of mind that I once more nerved myself to face the breakfast table.

'Daddy,' said Ruth purposefully as she delivered my eggs and bacon, 'I want to talk to you.'

My strength and tranquillity instantly evaporated. I had, of course, realized by this time that Ruth's devotion to housework and her new refrigerator could indicate the existence of a vacuum elsewhere in her life, and I had, of course, noticed that she and Roger talked only on the most facile of levels, but I had instinctively pulled down the shutters over my perceptive powers – and not because of my praiseworthy parental desire to avoid meddling in an adult daughter's private life. I had been driven by sheer cowardice buttressed by a strong sense of self-perservation; so debilitated did I feel by Martin's problems that I shied away from debilitating myself still further by embracing Ruth's.

'There's no need to look so alarmed,' she was saying with an exasperated affection. 'I just wanted to tell you about a lovely idea that I've had. Do you remember me mentioning last year that we thought of converting the space over the garage into a games-room? Well, we never actually got around to it, but why don't we now convert the space into a little flat for you? I know living "en famille" doesn't really suit you, but if you had a room of your own, quite separate from us, with your own bath and a little pantry-kitchen – well, you might come to visit us regularly, mightn't you, and later when you've retired . . . Well, Daddy, let's be realistic! You've got no private income and no prospect of any money when you retire except for the old age pension and some pittance from the Church, and I simply can't bear to think of you all alone and miserable in some sordid old people's home – '

'Isn't this fantasy a little premature?'

'Premature! How could it be? Daddy, you're sixty – *sixty years old* – '

'Quite.' I somehow managed to muzzle my rage.

' – and there might well come a time in the not-too-distant future when you'll need to be looked after, and as I like looking after people and as we do have the space over the garage – '

By a superhuman effort I mastered my temper and said in my gentlest voice: 'It's certainly not impossible that one day I might welcome such a generous and unselfish offer, but meanwhile I feel I've plenty of work to do before I can consider retirement and so it seems only sensible that I should continue to stay here "en famille" during my visits. I wouldn't want to put you to the expense of providing separate accommodation for me only to find that I was seldom able to use it.'

Her face crumpled.

'Ruth . . .' I was in despair. The memory of Betty encircled my psyche with a strangler's grip, and suddenly the guilt that I could not love her in the way she wished was more than I could bear. Pushing aside my untouched plate of eggs and bacon I stood up. 'Ruth, please – no more emotional scenes – '

'You hate it here – the visit's been a failure – '

'Nonsense!'

'Then why can't you accept my offer?'

'The real question is not why can't I accept your offer but why can't you accept my refusal.' Suppressing the urge to walk out I sank down again in my chair. That cost me so much energy that I barely had the strength left to say: 'The truth is that your distress here isn't rooted in my response to your offer. It lies in the fact that your children are growing up, Roger's absorbed in his own activities and you've begun to feel your family don't need you any more.'

But this glimpse of reality was much too painful for her to face, and at once she rushed sobbing from the room.

III

The fault was entirely mine; I had committed the error, unforgivable in an experienced counsellor, of confronting Ruth with a truth she was unable to digest, and I knew I had to give her time to resurrect her damaged defences. Accordingly I retired to the garden with my copy of *The Cloud of Unknowing* but I made no attempt to read it. I merely waited and after a while she came outside to join me.

'I'm sorry,' I said, standing up to meet her. 'Your offer was so good and kind and I feel almost criminally at fault for being unable to find the right words to refuse it. But you mustn't think I'm either ungrateful or uncaring.'

She struggled with her tears again but at last she said: 'I just wish I didn't find you so baffling. I don't understand a single thing you do – why you went into the monastery, why you've come out of it, why you've got to go off tomorrow into the blue when you could stay here with your family and be comfortable and loved and well looked after – '

'I think my monks at Grantchester felt much as you do and I can only tell you what I told them: I must do what I believe God requires of me. But how guilty I feel that you've never been able to express your bewilderment until now! I must try and make it easier for you to talk to me.'

'But I talk to you all the time!'

'I wasn't referring to the kind of conversation in which you tell me all about your new refrigerator. I was thinking of the kind of conversation in which you'd tell me your problems and I'd do my best to be helpful.'

'But I don't have any problems! I'm so lucky – I've got so much to be thankful for!'

'Yes, but – ' Automatically I fell back on a technique of which I was a master. Combining my practical experience with my psychic eye I picked a hidden subject, a subject which had hitherto remained unmentioned between us, and trailed it in front of her to lure her into self-revelation. 'But this is a frightening time, isn't it?' I said sympathetically and paused before adding the key words: 'Particularly for mothers of sons.'

At once she shuddered. 'If there's no invasion perhaps the war may last for years, and there's Colin, eighteen in two years' time – '

We were, as I believe they say in racing parlance, 'off and running', galloping away down the opening strait. I murmured: 'That's certainly a terrible prospect for you,' and waited, not unpleased by my skill, for the confession inevitably to unfold.

'I try to shut out the anxiety,' said Ruth, 'I try not to think about it, but I worry and worry and worry and Roger says I must stop, worrying does no good, I'm simply making myself ill, but it's easy for him to say that, he's got plenty of distractions, out all day at the office or at the golf club, and I've got nothing to divert myself with except cleaning, and I clean and I clean and I clean, but sometimes I feel I can't bear the strain, I love Colin so much – well, I love Janet too, of course, but she's been a bit peculiar lately, I suppose it's the onset of the awkward age and I've got to accept that she's not a little girl any more, but – oh, how I wish I had another baby! I always did want another but when we had our boy and our girl Roger said all right, that's it, that's all we can afford if we want to live comfortably in a nice home – although as things have turned out we could perfectly well have afforded one more, and now sometimes when I'm cleaning I find I'm thinking about it, the baby, I mean, the baby that never was, and I feel so sad and I start crying but that makes Roger so irritable and off he goes to the golf club and then I feel worse than ever, so sad and so alone, although of course I keep telling myself how lucky I am to have such a nice home and lots of smart clothes and the very latest refrigerator – '

'Why don't you go ahead and have it?'

'Have it? Have what?'

'The baby. You're only thirty-six. There's no problem now about money. What's stopping you? Would Roger object?'

'No, no, of course not!' she said at once, but when I saw her hands clench in her lap I knew the intimate side of their marriage had ceased. 'It's a lovely idea, certainly ... I'll have to think about it.' Giving me her brightest smile she rose to her feet. 'Well, I mustn't sit here gossiping about trivialities when I've got all the washing to do! If you'll excuse me, Daddy ...'

'Of course,' I said, and feeling profoundly distressed I watched her hurry away across the lawn.

IV

My first reaction to Ruth's pathos was the primitive one: I felt angry with the man who had made my daughter unhappy. But then I remembered those stern words: 'Judge not, that ye be not judged', and found myself asking whether Roger's failure to be an attentive husband was any worse than my own failure thirty-five years ago; when I had failed to make Betty happy I had regularly abandoned her for a far longer time than it took to play a round of golf.

Scraping together a professional detachment – a well-nigh impossible exercise in the circumstances – I tried to imagine why marital intimacy should have ceased. Late nights at the office and repeated absences at weekends did not necessarily indicate an adulterous husband; perhaps after years of over-indulgence in food and drink Roger had been plagued by recurring impotence until in humiliation he had abandoned sexual intercourse altogether. His absorption in his work and his golf could thus be seen not merely as a device to avoid his wife but as a method of blotting out his sense of failure.

I toyed with this plausible theory for some time. I liked it because it enabled me to regard Roger with compassion and to see Ruth as an innocent victim, but after a while it occurred to me to speculate how far the marriage had been dislocated by Roger's inclination to acquire inanimate possessions instead of additional children. Such behaviour by a husband could have a crippling psychological effect on the wife; I could well remember the sailor who had confided to me many years ago: 'As soon as my wife was told she couldn't have more children, padre, she lost interest in you-know-what.' However before I could dwell on this new theory another memory seeped into my mind. I saw a young priest whom I had counselled at Ruydale and heard him saying to me in despair: 'I've tried so hard, Father, but she absolutely hates it.' I could remember his wife too. He had brought her to see me once; I had told him I could not counsel a woman but I had thought it might help me to counsel him if I had some idea what kind of woman she was, and I could see her now, young and pretty, charming and delightful, a girl who had responded to my friendly enquiry about her parents by talking reverently, eyes glowing with hero-worship, about her father.

Standing up abruptly I began to walk around the garden. The top layer of my mind was still thinking of the poor young priest, one of my failures, someone I had been unable to help, but the next layer of my mind was contemplating my own guilt. By not loving my daughter adequately I had aroused in her an obsessive need for an attention which was paternal, not marital, and the need had destroyed the core of the marriage. Ruth's troubles were all my fault, I could see that now, just as I could see that Martin too was still suffering from my shameful failures as a father long ago.

Depression overwhelmed me again and sapped the last shreds of my spiritual strength. I wondered how Francis could ever have counselled me to keep an open mind on the subject of marriage, and as I sank down once more on the garden-seat I decided my mind had to be not open but resolutely closed. Remarriage was impossible. I was utterly unfit. A celibate life was the only answer, but how was celibacy going to be possible for me outside the walls of a monastery?

I knew myself too well not to experience another wave of despair at this point, and suddenly I was reviewing with a bleak clinical eye all my sexual responses to the world to which I had returned. They had ranged from the innocent pleasure of watching a pretty girl cross a road to the salacious stimulation of seeing scantily-clad women in newspaper photographs, from the harmless day-dreams of courting an ideal woman to the obsessive knowledge that it was now within my power to dress as a layman, take a 'bus into central Starmouth and commit fornication. In the cloister I could have confessed all the 'impure thoughts', poured out all my difficulties and somehow, with sympathetic counselling, won the battle for serenity and self-control. I would have been helped also by having my work to distract me, and in caring for others I would have been too busy to waste time agonizing over myself. But now I was alone, without work, without regular spiritual counselling, without, so far as I could see, any hope of a conventional happiness in the future. For one long moment, as my spirits hit rock-bottom, I doubted my ability to survive as a priest.

Then in my imagination Father Darcy exclaimed: 'Disgusting! What a weak, self-centred, cowardly, maudlin exhibition of ill-ordered, unedifying feelings! Pull yourself together this instant!' And my vision cleared. I saw that I could not be alone when God was with me; nor was I without work for I still had the task not only of worshipping him but of discerning what he required me to do. I was hardly deprived of spiritual counselling either, since Francis had promised to write to me regularly, and certainly I was not without hope of happiness in the future; I would be serving God, and without serving God no lasting happiness, conventional or otherwise, was possible.

Meanwhile I could wage war against despair by committing my anguish to paper and seeking advice.

I retired to my room to write to Francis.

V

My train to Devon departed from Starmouth at half-past nine the next morning, and Janet came with Ruth to the station to see me off. Disliking protracted goodbyes and fearful that Ruth might use the opportunity to stage yet another emotional scene I managed to part from them outside the ticket-office, but as I hurried on to the platform it was hard to avoid the conclusion that yet again I had wound up running away from my family.

My shame enveloped me all the way to the Devon border and manifested itself in the demon sloth; I was unable even to open my Bible. Then just as I was once more struggling to recall the saving image of my exorcist, I glanced up at the luggage-rack – and saw not my battered old suitcase but the elegant bag of my vision.

I leapt to my feet but it was already gone. I sank back, numb with shock, and some seconds passed before I realized that the Bible was now open in my hands. 'I have fought a good fight, I have finished my course, I have kept the faith . . .'

The famous words of St Paul instantly vanquished the demon, and with my courage renewed by the second 'showing' I travelled on into the unknown.

VI

I arrived at Allington Court shortly before luncheon and was warmly greeted by the Warden, Dr Sheen, who two years before had made a retreat under my direction at Grantchester. After a successful career as a schoolmaster he had suddenly decided in his mid-fifties that he was tired of teaching scripture to adolescent boys, and his retreat had taken place shortly before he had become Warden of Allington. I had had no doubt that the change had been right for him and occasionally after his departure from Grantchester I had pictured him ministering briskly, though perhaps a trifle too heartily, to his varied collection of guests.

I was shown to a large room overlooking the garden and possessing only one picture, a print of Massaccio's 'The Tribute Money'. As no women were depicted in it I decided it was insufficiently distracting to merit an incarceration in the wardrobe. I pressed the bed surreptitiously. The mattress was hard. Glancing around I noted a plain brown carpet and unobtrusive curtains. My spirits rose. I decided that this was a room in which I could feel at home.

'Now, sir,' said Dr Sheen, exuding the most worthy desire to put me at ease, 'don't be afraid that I'll pester you with questions about your new life – I've no intention of prying, and the only question I'd like to ask is how you'd care to be addressed now that you've left the Order. Obviously I shan't go around calling you "My Lord Abbot" – well, I never did, did I – but do you wish to be Father Darrow or just plain Mr Darrow nowadays?'

'I don't want to raise any hackles among your Low-Church guests. Let it be "Mr".'

Dr Sheen, mindful of the constant need to maintain harmony in his community, congratulated me on my charity in the face of possible bigotry.

It never occurred to him that my request might have arisen not from a saintly wish to avoid irritating others but from a selfish desire to obtain peace and quiet. Church-of-England priests who welcome being addressed as 'Father' too often wind up in debilitating debates about the value of the Oxford Movement, the evils of Popery and whether the use of incense is a valid aid to worship or merely a thoroughly nasty piece of un-English mumbo-jumbo. Anglo-Catholicism was capable of arousing strong passions among those who opposed it as a betrayal of Protestant values.

'I'd also be most grateful,' I added, 'if I could be allowed to blend in with your other guests as unobtrusively as possible. Of course there may well be people here who either know me or know of me, but I'm most anxious to avoid being treated with any fuss or fanfare.'

'My dear Darrow, I'm afraid my wife and I have already trumpeted your arrival to all our favourite guests! We were so excited at the thought of having you here, but don't worry, we've got a good bunch of people here at the moment and I'm sure they won't submit you to any tactless interrogation. I've already made sure you've been put at a civilized table – or do you want to sit by yourself at meal-times?'

I did, but I had already made up my mind that I must make an effort to be sociable in order to hasten my adjustment to the world. The dining-room at Allington, in common with the dining-rooms of ocean liners, had few single tables, and guests on their own were encouraged to share a table with others.

I had been considerably taken aback by Dr Sheen's carefree confession that he had already revealed my identity on such a sweeping scale, but I suppressed my exasperation by reflecting that my dreams of anonymity had always been unlikely to come true. Warily I went down to luncheon. In the dining-room the Warden's wife, hair firmly coiffed, front teeth well exposed, swept me to one of the central tables for six and introduced me to my fellow-guests as Mr Darrow. When the introduction had been completed I found myself in the company of a retired priest called Staples and his wife, a clerical widow called Mrs Digby, a professor of theology called Haydock and a most fetching American called Miss Tarantino who told me she had arrived at Oxford before the outbreak of war to do research and had decided to stay on; she gave no reason for this decision but I thought it not unlikely that she had been influenced by some romantic attachment, now defunct, which had resulted in her being stranded in a foreign country at such a crucial time. Enquiring about her research I learnt that she was writing a book about the influence of the Black Death on fourteenth-century religious thought. I would have asked more questions but at this point little Mrs Staples, wife of the retired priest, could no longer contain her curiosity.

'Dr Sheen's told us all about you, Mr Darrow!' she said, beaming at me with a disarming innocence. 'How very strange you must find it here after being locked up for so many years!'

'The Fordite monks aren't locked up, my dear,' said her husband hastily, 'and indeed Fordite abbots go all over the place. I believe the Abbot-General actually has a chauffeur-driven motor at his disposal.'

'Something tells me,' said the clerical widow Mrs Digby shrewdly as she noted my expression, 'that this particular abbot doesn't approve of chauffeur-driven motors for monks.'

I said in my firmest voice: 'I'm no longer an abbot. I'm just an ordinary clergyman of the Church of England now.'

'The last thing you could ever be, surely,' said the alluring Miss Tarantino with a flutter of her very long eyelashes, 'is just an ordinary clergyman, Mr Darrow.'

I nearly knocked over my glass of water.

Professor Haydock, exhibiting a remarkable imperviousness to both Miss Tarantino's allure and my confusion, demanded abruptly: 'Do you have a degree in theology?'

'Yes.'

'Perhaps you feel called to teach!' said ingenuous little Mrs Staples. 'I'm sure an abbot would know just how to keep order in the classroom. Or do you feel called to serve in some quite different field? Do tell us, Mr Darrow – I'm sure we're all fascinated to know what happens to monks when they go back into the world!'

A heavy silence enveloped us as the others wrestled with their embarrassment that Mrs Staples should be so sublimely tactless and I wrestled with my embarrassment that they should be embarrassed. However eventually Miss Tarantino saved the situation by drawling: 'What he's going to do is have a wonderful vacation sizing up exactly how much this wicked old world has to offer!' But just as I was relaxing with relief she gave me such a brilliant smile that I was again plunged into confusion.

Somehow I managed to restrain myself from bolting unfed from the room, but I was already wondering how I could survive for three weeks in such an atmosphere of gossip, curiosity and rampant carnal temptation.

VII

This state of horror, born of nervous anxiety and nurtured by the sheer novelty of lunching in unknown mixed company, was soon alleviated. I found that the Warden had not underestimated the essential good manners of my fellow-guests and eventually even Mrs Staples retreated into a conscientious discretion. Deciding that my panic had been both ridiculous and unnecessary I retired after luncheon to the library, which was as handsome as I remembered, and settled myself at one of the writing-tables.

On my arrival at Allington I had found a collection of letters waiting for me, and I now took the opportunity to read them at leisure. My correspondents included people to whom I gave spiritual direction; all regretted my departure from the Order and the majority asked if they could continue to consult me by post, but a small minority displayed their disturbed psyches by berating me for 'leaving them in the lurch' when they needed me most. I decided these gentlemen needed a prompt response.

I also received a number of letters from the monks, ranging from the most eminent to the most humble. Most of them wished me well and promised to pray for me, but there were a few monks who wrote not out of charity but in a self-righteous fury, claiming that I was 'letting the side down', 'throwing in the sponge' and 'dyed deep in apostasy'. One Yorkshire officer even raked up the Whitby affair and said he had always known I would come to an unedifying end. I mention these examples of antagonism because I may have given the impression, in describing my departure from Grantchester, that I was universally loved by my brethren, but the truth is that as a controversial figure I have always had my enemies and unfortunately monks are as liable as the rest of mankind to be invaded by the demons of envy and dislike.

The most important letter arrived on the morning after my arrival. In response to my unhappy communication from Starmouth Francis wrote: 'I'm inclined to think that in your despair you came to some highly questionable conclusions. I would regard the harrowing drama of the past week not as confirmation that you should never remarry but as a salutary reminded that you should never again attempt marriage to the wrong women for the wrong reasons. With regard to Martin and Ruth, I'd like to remind you of a remark you made to me once during a discussion of psycho-analytical theory. "I entirely disapprove," you said, "of the Freudian habit of blaming all a child's woes on its hapless parents." How wise you were! And how unfortunate that this wisdom should have been swept away by the hurricane of guilt which has temporarily reduced your rational faculties to rubble! In my opinion Ruth and Martin must be allowed to assume at least some of the responsibility for their errors and shortcomings – to deny them that responsibility in order to assume it all yourself is actually a perverse form of vanity. Besides, are you really such a complete failure as a father? Both your children seem to care deeply what you think of them, and if you were a complete failure they surely wouldn't give a fig for your opinion.'

This letter was a great comfort to me, and after reading it many times I embarked on a reply late that night in my room.

Again Francis answered by return of post. Knowing how busy he was I was impressed by this scrupulous attention to my welfare. After his opening paragraph in which he professed himself relieved that his earlier letter had provided a steadying influence he wrote: 'I'm delighted to hear that you're making the effort to be sociable at mealtimes. I know how difficult this must be for you, but I do wholly endorse your opinion that the effort should be made in order to accelerate your adjustment to the world.

'Don't be too frightened of the fetching American damsel. If she were what I believe is now called a "vamp" and what in our young day would have been called a "hussy", she would hardly have buried herself in a clerical playpen in Devon. The time to worry about the lady, I think, is when she invites you to her room to inspect her manuscript – or when you lure her to a secluded corner of the grounds in order to stop her watch. Meanwhile it's inevitable that you should find all women intensely interesting at present, particularly foreign women who appear to stand outside English conventions, and instead of fighting your interest in panic you might do better to accept it with a moderate amount of amusement. Remember that a reed which bends before the wind survives intact whereas an unyielding tree can be ignominiously uprooted.'

I spent much time pondering this excellent advice but I continued to find Miss Tarantino, who in fact was as well-behaved as she was charming, almost unbearably distracting. She had only to walk into the library and any serious attempt to read was destroyed. However within forty-eight hours of my arrival Miss Tarantino's effect on my equilibrium was less disturbing to me than the knowledge that I had become a centre of attention.

Unfortunately I have always tended to stand out in a crowd and this is not merely because I am six foot three and somewhat hard to overlook. At Allington people were primarily intrigued because I was an ex-monk, but even if my past had remained unknown to them I suspect I would still have attracted as much attention as a lighthouse in a desert. This mysterious aura, generated by my psychic powers under the pressure of mental stress, was part of what Father Darcy had called my 'infinite capacity for disruption', and the harder I tried to be unobtrusive the more readily every head would turn whenever I entered a room.

Finally the worst happened. Guests arrived who were incapable of either tact or discretion, and I was obliged to engage directly with their curiosity.

I had arrived at Allington Court on a Wednesday. On Saturday several guests departed and various newcomers took their place. At my table the retired priest Mr Staples and his ingenuous wife left after breakfast and at luncheon I found that their vacant chairs had been claimed by a middle-aged churchwarden called Braithwaite, a tiresome officious fellow who I had no doubt was a sore trial to his vicar, and by his wife, a woman who made Trollope's Mrs Proudie seem humility personified. As soon as they found out who I was they besieged me with questions. Why had I become a monk? What was the point of it? Didn't I think it wrong for an able-bodied man to be idle when he could be doing something socially useful? Didn't I think the monastic hatred of women was unhealthy? Didn't separation from women and the world lead to a grossly abnormal existence? How had I survived for seventeen years in such an environment? Significantly it occurred to neither of them to ask why I had left the Order; they merely leapt to the conclusion that I had at last come to my senses after a prolonged aberration.

When I was given a chance to reply to their bigoted, ignorant and ill-natured tirade I said with an iron courtesy: 'First, I became a monk because God called me to do so; argument would have been not only impertinent but irreverent. Second, the point of being a monk is primarily to obey the great commandment: "Thou shalt worship the Lord thy God with all thy heart and with all thy soul and with all thy might," so I most certainly wasn't idle. Also, in addition to worshipping God for several hours each day, I worked at various times as a domestic servant, a farmhand, a carpenter, a teacher, a counsellor and a managing director. I could even claim to have been "socially useful", since I helped various people in the world to overcome their problems, but even if I hadn't been "socially useful" why should that have invalidated my work for God? You can't define what God requires of us in terms of social utility, and indeed it's perfectly possible for work to be socially useful yet spiritually irrelevant. As for monastic mysogyny I can assure you that if monks do hate women they shouldn't, and indeed from my experience I believe that monks are more inclined than their brothers in the world to believe the great Christian proclamation that men and women are of equal value in God's sight. Does separation from women and the world lead to a grossly abnormal existence? It leads to a fundamentally different existence, certainly, but I suspect the people who would call it grossly abnormal are merely frightened of a non-conformity which calls their own so-called normality into question. You ask how I survived for seventeen years as a monk, and I'll tell you: I survived because I was happy and fulfilled, doing the work which I had been called by God to do, and because I was healthier in mind, body and spirit than I had ever been in my life before.'

'Well said, Darrow!' exclaimed Professor Haydock, who had clearly taken a dislike to the newcomers. Only the previous day he had been mooting the idea that monasticism had no place in the modern world.

'Well, I'm sure none of us would question your sincerity, Mr Darrow,' said Braithwaite, grudgingly retreating an inch from his entrenched position, but his wife had resolved to stand firm. 'I still say,' she declared, 'that it's not a natural life for a man.'

Professor Haydock said dryly: 'I rather doubt that it's theologically possible for God to call a man to an unnatural life. How would you define "natural", may I ask, madam?'

'Being natural,' said Mrs Braithwaite, bristling with hostility, 'means living with a wife and two children in a nice little house and going to church on Sundays – and if you'd ever done *that*, Mr Darrow,' she added, turning on me, 'we might find your defence of the monastic life more convincing.'

'My dear Mrs Braithwaite,' I said, 'before I became a monk I spent nine years of my life living with my wife and two children in a nice little house and going to church on Sundays.' Tossing aside my napkin I rose to my feet, murmured: 'I wish you all a pleasant afternoon,' and walked away.

'Game, set and match . . .' breathed Miss Tarantino enrapt, and I heard the Professor give his short caustic laugh.

Ten minutes later, feeling thoroughly disturbed, I sat down on the trunk of a fallen tree which lay by the lake on the far side of the grounds, and contemplated my latest failure to adjust satisfactorily to the world. I was well aware that I had behaved badly. I should have resisted the urge to make Mrs Braithwaite look ridiculous; I should have met her bigotry with a charitable silence – or at the very most with a quiet observation that I had once been a married man – and feeling not only ashamed of the anger which had impelled me to humiliate an ignorant and possibly unhappy woman, but also profoundly worried by my persistent sense of alienation from those around me, I decided to retire to my room to pray.

Retracing my footsteps I entered the house by the garden-door and walked down the corridor to the hall. No one was about. In the middle of the afternoon at Allington the guests were either reading, resting or outside enjoying the hot August weather. I was deep in thought as I endeavoured to recall a suitable text for meditation, and as I crossed the hall I might well have remained unaware of my surroundings if some mysterious antenna had not twitched in my psyche.

I stopped. I knew I could not go on without glancing around the hall. Slowly, very slowly, I turned my head towards the front door and there, far away by the door of the Warden's reception room, stood the beige suitcase with the dark brown corners.

I waited for it to vanish but it remained visible and – apparently – tangible. At once I thought I was hallucinating. I knew I was in a troubled, psychically unreliable state. If this vision was another 'showing', sent by God to strengthen my faith, why was the suitcase still visible? It should have been wiped from the retina of my mind within seconds, but there it remained, as solid and three-dimensional as any other object which existed in a temporal spatial world. My mouth was dry. Sliding my tongue around my lips I squeezed my eyes shut, took a deep breath and nerved myself to have another look.

The suitcase was still there. Moreover every other item in the hall looked wholly real. I saw no distortion of colour, no six naked women prancing on the carpet. My heart was now beating with unprecedented violence. Moving awkwardly, in the manner of a man wading upstream against a swift current, I reached out to touch the bannisters. They were solid. I edged forward just as the grandfather clock chimed three. Without doubt I was in finite time, and the suitcase, already substantial, became even more substantial as I edged closer. I could see the Cunard label clearly enough to realize that it was exactly as I had perceived it during my spasm of clairvoyance in the infirmary, and tied to the handle was the brown label which I knew would reveal the name of the owner.

Running the last six paces I sank down on one knee and grabbed the suitcase with both hands.

It was real. The expensive leather, a little scuffed in places but still in good condition, was sumptuously smooth beneath my fingers and as I caressed it I was suddenly overwhelmed by the knowledge that God should have finally brought his communication out of my psyche into the world of the five senses. For a second I was well-nigh paralysed with relief, wonder and above all an intense gratitude. Then just as I had pulled myself together sufficiently to grab the brown label to unlock the mystery of the owner's identity a cool voice demanded behind me: 'Can I help you?' and I knew the intuition I had voiced to Francis had been correct.

The owner was a woman.

NINE

'The mystic always finds it difficult, if not impossible, to describe what he has seen and felt. An experience recollected is not the same as an experience felt . . . If he wishes to make it available for other people, he must reconstruct and interpret and translate, as it were, into another language.'

W. R. INGE
Dean of St Paul's 1911–1934
Lay Thoughts of a Dean

I

I leapt to my feet. The woman had obviously just emerged from the Warden's reception room for the door was now ajar, but my absorption in the suitcase had been so deep that I had failed to hear either her approach or the distant voice of the Warden as he conducted a telephone conversation which, as I now realized, was still in progress.

I stared at her. If I had expected to see someone as alluring as Miss Tarantino – and of course I had – I had been doomed to disappointment. This woman was tall and somewhat stout. She wore a felt hat crammed down over short dark hair, hornrimmed spectacles, a coat and skirt of a severe shade of grey, a white blouse devoid of frills, thick brown stockings and a pair of heavy walking-shoes. I classed her as a forty-five-year-old spinster, probably a schoolmistress, possibly a missionary newly returned from organizing the natives in some obscure corner of the Empire. Then I noticed that her neck was unlined, her skin was fresh and her eyes were uncrinkled at the corners. Knocking fifteen years off her age I decided she was a business-woman, the private secretary of some gentleman who required a plain employee in order to allay the fears of a jealous wife. On the other hand the woman's voice, which was not merely well-bred but 'county', suggested I was confronting a lady of leisure. I was aware then of a mystery, a conundrum.

All these thoughts raced through my mind in seconds while simultaneously I tried to decide how I could explain my bizarre embrace of her suitcase. At last I said: 'I do beg your pardon but I thought I'd seen this bag somewhere before.' It takes a great deal to make me behave like an embarrassed schoolboy but I felt more gauche than I had felt for over forty years. I even wondered in horror if I were blushing. My face felt abnormally hot.

The Warden chose that moment to emerge from his room. 'So sorry to keep you waiting!' he said to the woman. 'It's amazing how often the telephone goes at the wrong moment – ah, I see you've just met Mr Darrow! Or are you perhaps already acquainted? No? Then let me introduce you: Mr Darrow – Miss Fielding; Miss Fielding – Mr Darrow.' He beamed at us, stooped to pick up the suitcase, winced at its weight and set it down again. 'One moment, Miss Fielding – I'll just summon Arthur,' he said, naming the burly yokel who was employed to flex his muscles when required, and bustled off towards the green baize door.

I said to Miss Fielding: 'How do you do,' and held out my hand.

'How do you do,' said Miss Fielding, clasping and dropping it without enthusiasm. Behind her glasses her eyes were a cold suspicious blue.

'Arthur! Arthur!' the Warden was calling in the mellow bass voice which resonated so impressively in the chapel during the daily prayers.

I said to the woman: 'If you'll excuse me – '

'Of course.' She turned aside as if she had completely lost interest.

I have no memory of the journey to my room. All I remember is slamming the door, slumping on the bed and shuddering with amazement as I asked myself if the key to my future could possibly lie in the hands of such an exceedingly unprepossessing young woman.

II

Since my arrival at Allington I had consistently avoided afternoon tea, a meal which I found both tedious and unnecessary, but that afternoon I was already loafing in the drawing-room as the waitress wheeled in the urn. The decision had been made to serve the meal on the terrace in order to take advantage of the fine weather, and I was just helping the Warden's wife to steer the trolley of crockery and cucumber sandwiches through the French windows when Dr Sheen himself crossed the lawn towards us.

Having cornered him I asked what connection his latest guest had with the Church, but to my disappointment he was vague.

'She comes from Starbridge where everyone seems to live in the shadow of the Cathedral,' he said, 'but otherwise I know of no reason why she should stay at a clerical establishment like Allington.'

'This is her first visit?'

'No, she's stayed here every August for the past five years, although of course I only met her when I took up my appointment in '38. However

I regret to say I know her no better now than when I first met her. She keeps herself very much to herself and I'm afraid she's dreadfully shy, poor girl.'

'She didn't strike me as shy. In fact I thought she was unusually self-confident,' I said, but the Warden had been diverted by a summons from his wife and at that point our conversation ended.

Accepting a cup of tea in the urn I waited for Miss Fielding to arrive but all that happened was that I was buttonholed by various guests with whom I had no wish to converse. Finally Miss Fielding made her appearance, but before I could detach myself from my group she had collected her tea, grabbed a sandwich and retreated to a seat on the far side of the lawn.

'That's Miss Fielding,' said the shrewd clerical widow Mrs Digby unexpectedly. 'She was here last year – a very strange woman, anti-social to the point of rudeness. Puzzling, I thought, because she's definitely a lady and one would expect her to behave with more grace.'

'Maybe she's shy,' said Miss Tarantino. 'I'm shy myself sometimes – it's so disabling.' She smiled up at me. 'Why are you so interested in the new arrival, Mr Darrow? You've been watching her ever since she came out of the house.'

'Anti-social people interest me,' I said vaguely, and beat a swift retreat to my room.

From my window I continued to observe Miss Fielding. When she returned her cup and saucer and headed back across the lawn towards the woods I padded downstairs again, slipped out of the garden-door and made an elaborate detour to avoid being seen by the people on the terrace. Then I plunged into the woods in pursuit of my quarry.

III

I failed to find her. The grounds were extensive and the woods prevented me from seeing more than a few yards in any direction. Reaching the falled tree by the lake for the second time that afternoon I wiped the sweat from my forehead, took off my jacket and told myself to calm down. Numerous opportunities to talk to Miss Fielding would undoubtedly arise in due course and meanwhile I was being given more time to consider my situation. I decided to write to Francis.

Yet again he replied by return of post. After the necessary paragraph in which he had marvelled at my clairvoyance he had written: 'But be careful. The temptation to jump to conclusions will be very strong, but it's possible that this bag has no connection with the chapel at all; you always said, remember, that it seemed superimposed on the chapel's reality.

'I'm relieved to hear that this mysterious woman is unattractive. That eliminates the risk of you being lured into some dangerous romantic fantasy, and personally I'm inclined to think that if she's of any real significance here, that significance will be revealed to you without any effort on your part. I'm not suggesting that you do nothing until Miss Fielding sidles up to you like an espionage agent and enquires "sotto voce" if you're interested in a chapel built in the style of Inigo Jones. Obviously you'll wish to converse with her in order to give the mystery a chance to unravel, but walk delicately, like Agag, and be prepared for the solution to be more obscure than you're at present inclined to suppose.'

I received this letter in the afternoon post on Monday. I had tried a couple of approaches to Miss Fielding on Sunday but had been rebuffed on each occasion; after matins I had said: 'What did you think of the sermon?' and she had replied: 'I ceased to listen after the first five minutes,' while during tea I had ventured to enquire: 'What are you reading?' and she had retorted: 'Shakespeare,' before reburying her nose in a battered volume of the Bard's complete works.

'I know why Mr Darrow's so intrigued by Miss Fielding,' said the shrewd Mrs Digby after Miss Tarantino had again commented on my interest in the newcomer. 'She's the only person here who doesn't pay the slightest attenion to him.'

That, as Shakespeare himself might have phrased it, was 'a palpable hit'. I began to wonder how far an affronted masculine vanity was exacerbating my curiosity and the speculation was not a pleasant one.

However when Miss Fielding appeared in chapel on Monday morning before breakfast my curiosity reached new heights and I forgot to worry about any unedifying masculine vanity. Holy Communion was celebrated only on Wednesdays and Sundays at Allington, but matins and evensong were recited daily and apart from one or two devout laymen it was the clergy who attended. I was most surprised when I entered the chapel and saw Miss Fielding already seated in a pew; I thought the Warden would have mentioned if she had been unusually devout in her religious observances for it would have explained her regular patronage of a hotel such as Allington. Choosing a pew across the aisle from her I was aware of her turning her head as I sat down. However her glance was brief and throughout the service she gave no further hint that she was aware of me.

After the blessing I remained kneeling for some minutes, not to pray but to avoid any vapid conversation, and it was only when I judged my solitude to be guaranteed that I rose to my feet to leave.

She was waiting in the porch.

'Is it my imagination,' she said, 'or are we bumping into each other abnormally often? I don't usually attend weekday matins but I found I

562

couldn't resist the urge to discover if it would lead to yet another encounter – and here we are.'

'But since you decided to lie in wait for me, wasn't an encounter inevitable?'

'Not at all. If you'd come out with the others you could have stalked by without a word. It's all very odd – or maybe it's simply that *you're* odd, Mr Darrow. I suppose you do realize that you're like a giant magnet? You enter a room and all the little pins start twinkling and twirling in your direction.' I laughed but before I could comment she was musing: 'First of all I thought people were fascinated merely because you're an ex-monk, but then I became more aware of that very peculiar atmosphere you exude – '

'Who told you I was an ex-monk?'

'Everyone from the Warden to the waitress.'

'How interesting,' I said at once. 'I was under the impression you talked neither to the Warden nor to the waitress nor to anyone else.'

'Then at least you now know I'm capable of speech.' Abruptly she turned away.

'Yes, but what I still don't know is why you're so keen to remain silent,' I said, following hard on her heels as she walked out. 'Do you have to talk a great deal in your profession with the result that on holiday you promptly sink into an exhausted silence?'

As she swung to face me I saw the astonishment in her eyes. 'What makes you think I have a profession?'

'Your self-confidence. You're not shy; you simply have no wish to be sociable. And you have an air of authority too which makes me think you're used to dealing with people on a business level. Ladies of leisure, who so often can define themselves only in relation to the men in their lives, tend to display more malleability and self-effacement when projecting their identity.'

'In other words you think I'm just a bossy old spinster unredeemed by any conventional feminine grace!'

'That's what you want me to think, isn't it? That's what you want everyone to think. But why are you going to such lengths to create an identity which I suspect is a grossly exaggerated distortion of your true self?'

She stared at me incredulously. Then turning her back on me a second time she fled back to the house as if pursued by the Furies.

IV

She succeeded in eluding me for some time after that, but on Wednesday morning we met, taking each other by surprise, in the remotest bay of the library, a corner at the far end of the gallery which flanked one side of the room. I was sitting on the window-seat with a copy of *Lux Mundi* in my hands and remembering how much Bishop Gore had influenced me in my youth. Miss Fielding, apparently also in search of seclusion before embarking on a nostalgic intellectual journey, entered the bay with her battered volume of Shakespeare's complete works and before she could recoil in dismay I said swiftly: 'Congratulations on finding the quietest spot in the house. May I offer you half my window-seat?'

'Thank you, but I'd be too afraid of twinkling and twirling like one of your magnetized pins.'

'What nonsense! Sit down and read your Shakespeare!'

'A bit bossy, aren't you?' said Miss Fielding, but she sat down. 'I can't remember any bossy abbots in Shakespeare's plays, but there are a couple of very wicked cardinals.'

'Beaufort in *Henry VI* and Wolsey in *Henry VIII*.'

As her eyes widened I knew the fish was hooked. Stealthily I began to reel in the line. 'My father was a schoolmaster,' I said smiling at her. 'His volume of Shakespeare's complete works was more precious to him than the Bible, and naturally some of his enthusiasm rubbed off on me.'

'But surely nowadays you only read religious books?'

'Not entirely. Last week I read a detective story by Miss Agatha Christie. I admired her grasp of the reality of evil but I'm afraid I found the plot improbable.'

'Life *is* improbable,' said Miss Fielding. 'It's improbable that you should have been so mesmerized by my bag when I arrived and it's even more improbable that you should have been prowling along in my wake ever since. Will I spoil your fun if I now ask you frankly what on earth's going on?'

Our voices had risen above the level of a murmur, and below us at one of the writing-tables someone hissed: 'Shhh!' Closing *Lux Mundi* I stood up. 'Come into the garden,' I whispered, 'and all will be revealed.'

'That sounds like a literary marriage between Agatha Christie and Lord Tennyson.'

Numerous heads swivelled to look at us as we left the library and to my surprise I noticed that Miss Fielding's cheeks had become pink. Perhaps the shyness did exist after all beneath the outer layer of self-confidence. Reminding myself of the danger of rushing to conclusions I said to her as we left the house: 'Let's sit on that seat on the far side of the lawn.'

'I'm not sure I want to bask in your peculiar limelight in full view of all the old dears on the terrace! I come to this place for a quiet life – '

'An unusual aspiration for a young woman.'

'What makes you think I'm so young?'

'Your neck's unlined. I doubt if you're thirty.'

'I'm thirty-two.'

'Then why on earth are you trying to look forty-five?'

'Why are you embarking on an interrogation? You're supposed to be answering questions, not asking them!'

'Getting impatient? As my superior said to me the other day: "Patience is one of the most difficult of all virtues and one which I think it would pay you to cultivate."'

'I shall hit you over the head with Shakespeare's complete works in a minute,' said Miss Fielding, and when I laughed she smiled at me.

Providing deep interest to all the guests languishing on the terrace we crossed the lawn and sat down a respectable two feet apart on the wooden seat.

'Now,' said Miss Fielding in the tone of one who is determined to stand no nonsense, 'about my bag – '

'I'd seen it before in a psychic experience.'

The inevitable silence fell. I waited for the equally inevitable amazement, scepticism, even fear – all those reactions which make the psychic shun the well-nigh impossible task of translating into words an experience which is ultimately beyond translation – but nothing happened. Miss Fielding meditated without expression on the statement which most people would have judged outrageous, and eventually said: 'I should have guessed you were psychic. For five years I've been coming here and everyone has accepted me at face value. Yet you take one look and see a mile farther than anyone else.' She hesitated before asking: 'In this psychic experience did you see me as well as the bag?'

'No.' I waited, but still no conventional reaction occurred. I was inflicted by no ill-judged questions, no banal comments, no torrent of feminine chatter. Miss Fielding's face was grave as she stared at the book in her hands but at last she raised her head and said abruptly: 'You don't want to tell me any more, do you? It's too private. But that's all right, I understand. I've got a great respect for other people's privacy because I value my own privacy so much.' And without giving me the chance to reply she rose to her feet and walked away across the lawn.

V

At luncheon I declined pudding, excused myself from my fellow-guests and lurked in the hall until Miss Fielding had abandoned her solitary table.

'At the risk of making a thorough nuisance of myself,' I said, waylaying her, 'may I ask when you can accompany me for another stroll in the grounds?'

'When? Not if? Here comes the bossy abbot again!'

'Before I was a bossy abbot I learnt how to be an obedient monk. Name the time and place and I'll be there.'

'Somehow I have trouble picturing you as meek and submissive – did you find life very difficult when you entered the Order?'

There was a long silence.

'Sorry,' said Miss Fielding rapidly at last. 'I didn't mean to give offence – '

'You haven't. I was merely surprised. Every layman I've ever met has always blithely assumed I took the monastic life in my stride.'

Silence fell again. Then Miss Fielding said abruptly: 'Let's meet by the lake. I hate all the old dears spying on us from the terrace.'

'Five o'clock by the fallen tree?'

She nodded and we went our separate ways.

VI

She arrived on time. That impressed me; women so often feel obliged to be late. She was wearing a floral-patterned dress which appeared to have been designed for a woman of fifty who had lost her figure, and I was wearing my clerical suit. I pictured us both looking irreproachably seemly as we seated ourselves well apart on the fallen tree, and I thought how odd it was that we should be linked by the far from seemly fact of my clairvoyance.

'I wanted to thank you for your extreme tact earlier,' I said. 'It would have been so easy for you to have made my confession an awkward one.'

'By showing scepticism? Or resorting to ridicule? No, I leave that to the scientists – the ones who can't bear to admit they don't know all the answers.'

I smiled. Then I said: 'It's not only the scientists who find clairvoyance disconcerting. It raises questions about the nature of time which baffle even the philosophers and theologians.'

'Does it?' said Miss Fielding intrigued, and I knew that once again the fish was hooked. As her defences relaxed I tightened my grip on her psyche.

'The crucial question,' I said, 'becomes this: how can one see the future unless there's a reality beyond what is colloquially described as reality – an ultimate reality in which all time is eternally present?'

'That's the sort of question which makes my head spin. But go on.'

I continued to smooth away her defences as I gently stroked her psyche. 'You remember, of course, that Plato said time was the moving image of eternity?'

'No, but never mind.'

This time we both smiled before I said: 'The key word is "moving". We live in a world of movement, of change, which is reflected in the words "past". "present" and "future", but beyond this world is another world to which we're inextricably linked but which we can only dimly perceive. This world is a kingdom of values, the absolute values of goodness, truth and beauty, and it's these unchanging values, present in our changing world of time and space, which reflect the other world, ultimate reality, which is beyond space and time.'

'It's hard to imagine something which can't be described in spatial and temporal terms.'

'That's exactly why any meaningful description of the other world really lies outside the scope of our vocabulary. For example, I call the time of this world "finite time" to distinguish it from the everlasting Now which is the only way we can conceive of eternity, but this terminology isn't wholly satisfactory because there are philosophers who argue that even our time is infinite. But that argument only stems from the fact that they can't imagine being at the edge of time with a blank wall instead of a future ahead. The truth is that if the universe is running down like a clock – '

'Stop!' said Miss Fielding. 'I can't cope with universes running down like clocks. Are you trying to say that when you're clairvoyant you step out of finite time into some form of eternity?'

'Perhaps one should phrase that more cautiously. All I know for certain is that I step out of time as we understand it where the past is always behind us and the future is still to come.'

Miss Fielding said suddenly: 'It must be like escaping from a prison. Isn't it strange how unaware people are of being locked up in time?'

'You find an unconscious awareness of this in the widespread longing to be immortal. Yet isn't it equally strange, when one remembers that we're also locked up in space, that no one seems to long to be ubiquitous?'

She laughed, and knowing she was now thoroughly relaxed I glided forward into my inquisition.

'Talking of eternity,' I said, 'I'm reminded of your home town of

Starbridge, the only city I know which possesses an Eternity Street. Do you worship at the Cathedral?'

Immediately her defences were resurrected; she displayed no hostility but I was aware of her extreme stillness. 'My aunt prefers worship at St Martin's-in-Cripplegate,' she said, naming the church in the centre of the city which had originally been erected for the benefit of the workmen building the Cathedral.

'You live with your aunt?'

'My parents are dead,' said Miss Fielding, looking at the lake, the trees, the sky but not at me. 'My aunt has a house in the section of the city called St Stephen's Fields. It's between Eternity Street and the river.'

'You work in the city?'

Her studied nonchalance disintegrated. 'What business is that of yours?'

'Absolutely none. Forgive me.'

We fell silent but gradually I became aware of her psyche, encased in an iron band but yearning to be free. As soon as I saw the iron band with my inner eye I visualized a file and pictured myself whittling the fetter apart.

'I work on a farm,' said Miss Fielding abruptly as the band snapped in two.

'Do you?' I said. 'I worked on a farm once. I was assigned to the cowman when I was a novice in Yorkshire, but I unconsciously projected so much antipathy towards the cows that the milk yield dropped and I had to be removed from the farmyard.'

She was amused and not unsympathetic. 'I'm not much good with farm animals either,' she said, and added after a hesitation: 'I work in the estate office.'

'I must confess I didn't quite see you as a land-girl – '

' – so you peeped into my mind and saw I was an administrator!'

'No, I can't read your mind like a book! If I could, I wouldn't be asking all these impertinent questions!'

'I think you're just asking the questions to confirm your psychic suspicions.'

'I have my psychic suspicions certainly – I can't help myself – but they could be dead wrong. If I were to make any deductions about you I'd base them on reason and experience before allowing my intuition free rein.'

She said sternly: 'And what are your deductions based on reason and experience?'

'I deduce that your aversion to normal social intercourse stems from the fact that at one time you trusted people far more than you do now – and paid a heavy price. I deduce that this deep wound in your psyche has remained unhealed with the result that you're periodically driven to play the kind of role you're playing here at Allington, a role which you can use as a shield to protect your true self.' I shrugged my shoulders to signal that I had no inclination either to criticize or to condemn. 'Neither of those deductions involved any psychic intuition whatsoever, of course. They're merely conclusions which any experienced counsellor might reach.'

'And what happens when you give your psychic intuition free rein?'

There was a pause while I debated what I had to lose by responding to the question and decided that I had everything to gain. 'I could be quite wrong,' I said, careful to maintain a casual tone of voice, 'but I think the traumatic incident in your past involved a massive loss and it was all connected with water. Perhaps someone close to you was drowned? Or perhaps someone you loved sailed away and never came back?'

As she stared I had a most uncomfortable memory of Francis warning me against exercising my psychic powers with a woman in a secluded corner of the grounds. 'I'm sorry,' I said rapidly, 'I'm behaving like a charlatan in a fortune-teller's booth on a seaside pier and I must stop at once. Let me now give you the rational explanation for those wild and no doubt inaccurate guesses: I saw the Cunard label on your suitcase. I've associated you with travel by water. I've now fused that association with the deduction that you've suffered in the past, and one of the most traumatic forms of suffering is bereavement. You see? There's really no psychic intuition going on at all. It's just the kind of mental sleight-of-hand which can be made to look so effective in a parlour-trick.'

For a long moment Miss Fielding was silent as she stared across the lake but at last she said: 'When I was twenty-six my fiancé broke off our engagement and sailed away on one of the transatlantic liners. My brother then took me on holiday to Cornwall to help me recover, and three days later he drowned while swimming in the sea.' She stood up, smoothing the creases from her dress. 'After that I knew my life had to change completely,' she said. 'The old life was burnt out and the new life had to begin.' She turned to face me and as I too rose to my feet I saw that her eyes were a clear tearless blue. 'That's what happens when someone becomes a monk, isn't it?' she said. 'They die to the old life and are born again in the new. There's some Greek word for it – '

'"Metanoia". Miss Fielding – '

'It's all right,' she said 'I don't mind you knowing because I'm sure you'll respect my confidence. But in future, Mr Darrow, could you somehow keep your psychic powers in check? My mind doesn't like being X-rayed with such horrible accuracy. It quite definitely doesn't like it at all.'

After that conversation I exerted my will-power, curbed my burgeoning curiosity and for two days made no attempt to seek another interview with her.

'. . . so you needn't worry,' I wrote as I concluded a long letter to Francis. 'I have the situation well in control and can say with perfect truth that I'm not in the least in love with Miss Fielding, who has no waist to speak of (I am exceedingly partial to waists) and is elsewhere too large when she should be small and too small when she should be large – not that I wish to be uncharitable, for she's obviously highly intelligent and sensitive, but my point is that since she's so lacking in conventional feminine allure I run no risk of making a fool of myself.'

I posted this most sensible letter on Friday morning but as soon as the envelope had dropped into the village pillar-box I realized I could no longer endure to keep Miss Fielding at arm's length and that afternoon I succeeded in luring her back to the lake.

'It seems almost indecent that we should be somewhere so peaceful at a time like this,' said Miss Fielding unexpectedly as we again settled ourselves on the fallen tree.

'That's a phenomenon of war – the non-combatant's guilt. But you shouldn't let it oppress you. Better to look upon our peaceful oasis here as a gift from God and give thanks for it.'

'I suppose that as you're a prayer-expert you can now automatically send off a perfectly-phrased prayer of thanksgiving. All I can do is mutter a fervent "thank you" and feel inarticulate.'

'A fervent "thank you" would be entirely admirable,' I said pleased, 'and you must never think for one moment that a trained religious necessarily prays more effectively than a devout layman. Prayer's the great leveller. Anyone can do it, and the only pity is that more people don't try.' By this time I was so consumed with curiosity about her spiritual life that I risked saying: 'Are you High-Church, Broad-Church or Low-Church?'

'I'm not at all sure what all those awful labels mean. If High-Church means the Anglo-Catholics and Low-Church means the Evangelical Protestants and Broad-Church means the vast majority of church-goers between the two extremes, then I suppose I'm Broad – I'm certainly a Protestant. I don't like anything which suggests the Reformation martyrs died in vain. I'm not saying all Anglo-Catholics should be burnt at the stake – well, that would be a bit tactless in present company, wouldn't it – but I don't like parsons calling themselves priests and Communion being called Mass, and personally I think the use of incense is a nasty piece of unEnglish mumbo-jumbo.'

'The glory of the Church of England,' I said at once, 'is that you and I, despite our very divergent views, can both belong to it.' But as I spoke I was thinking with delight: what a challenge! and wondering if I could convert her to my point of view.

Having reassured her that I was capable of conducting a normal conversation without oppressing her with my psychic peculiarities, I remained silent as we journeyed back from the lake, but when we reached the house I said: 'Mrs Digby leaves tomorrow afternoon and there'll be a spare place at my table. Will you join me for dinner?'

Without hesitation she answered: 'I'd rather not.'

'Very well.'

We entered the house.

'I'm sorry,' said Miss Fielding quickly after struggling with her conflicting emotions. 'That was abominably rude of me. Thank you for the invitation – in many ways I'd like to accept but nevertheless I'm going to ask you to excuse me.'

'Of course.'

'I seem to be making a complete fool of myself,' said Miss Fielding at last. 'Anyone would think you'd made an indecent proposal. Thank you, Mr Darrow, I accept the invitation and apologize for being so ungracious.'

I retired in triumph to my room.

VIII

'I understand the mysterious Miss Fielding will be joining us tonight,' said Miss Tarantino who was already seated at the table when I arrived in the dining-room on the following evening. Allington Court was by no means 'smart', but Miss Tarantino, sleek in dark red satin, exuded a glamour which was almost operatic. I was vaguely reminded of 'Carmen'.

'Miss Fielding will indeed be joining us,' I said, 'and I intend to pamper myself by sitting between the two of you and luxuriating in your combined feminine attention.' I had, it will be noticed, travelled a considerable way from the tense, wary ex-monk who had wanted to bolt from the dining-room ten days previously.

Miss Tarantino was prevented (perhaps fortunately) from replying by the arrival of the Braithwaites and the Professor. The Warden was already chafing to say grace, and I was just wondering if Miss Fielding's nerve had failed her when to my relief she entered the room. She was wearing another shapeless item from her dowager's wardrobe, a funereal black gown. I saw Miss Tarantino give it a look of pitying amazement although I sensed that the Braithwaites were more interested in the diamond necklace which Miss Fielding had slung around her neck. The diamonds had the effect of reducing Miss Tarantino's allure to a tinsel glitter and underlining the ugliness of Mrs Braithwaite's cultured pearls.

The meal proceeded uneventfully until the middle of the main course. Miss Fielding and I said little; Miss Tarantino and the Professor argued fitfully about Luther's view of the sacraments, and the Braithwaites talked in consequence about a handsome Lutheran church which they had inspected during a holiday in Germany in 1936. It was the mention of Germany which sealed the fate of the evening. The conversation drifted inexorably towards the war until we were discussing the prospect of increased rationing.

'Another thing we can expect to increase,' said Braithwaite, vigorously sawing his portion of chicken, 'is immorality.' He seemed to find the prospect stimulating.

'Oh don't, dear!' said his wife with a shudder. 'Every time I see those girls in uniform living like men I feel cold inside. A woman's place is in the home.'

Miss Fielding said: 'Are you implying that women are so lacking in moral backbone that they risk corruption the moment they step outside their front door?'

'It's a well-known fact,' said Braithwaite, using the phrase which in my experience so often heralds an old wives' tale, 'that once women stop being wives and mothers and start working alongside men there's an immediate decline in moral standards.'

'You mean,' said Miss Fielding, 'that if women are obliged to work alongside men there's a possibility that they may become as promiscuous as the men they meet – always assuming the men they meet are promiscuous. But the hole in your argument, Mr Braithwaite, is that promiscuity doesn't automatically follow the opportunity to be promiscuous. If immorality does increase as the result of the war it won't simply be because women are working alongside men. It'll be because both sexes are frightened to the point of instability in a time of great danger.'

Miss Tarantino said: 'Sure!' emphatically and the Professor grunted his acceptance of this rational contribution to the conversation, but Mrs Braithwaite was rigid with disapproval and Braithwaite himself clearly could not bear to be worsted in an argument with a woman. 'You talk with a great deal of authority, Miss Fielding,' he said harshly, 'but what do you really know about the ways of the world? Your argument might sound more convincing if it didn't come from an unmarried lady whose attitude to the opposite sex appears to be characterized by ignorance and dislike!'

I said: 'Braithwaite – ' at the same moment as the Professor exclaimed in disgust: 'Great Scott!' but Miss Fielding needed no one to defend her. She said strongly: 'The ignorance and dislike are all on your side, it seems!' You know nothing about me except for the fact that I'm not married, and your dislike is obviously because unlike most women I have the nerve to argue with you when you start slandering my sex!'

'There was no slander!' said Braithwaite, scarlet with rage. 'And I consider I'm justified in objecting to rude opinionated females who give spinsters a bad name!'

I leapt to my feet but so did Miss Fielding. Flinging down her napkin she said fiercely to Braithwaite: 'My God, you're a stupid man!' and stormed from the table.

All conversation in the dining-room ceased. I had a fleeting impression of the Warden's appalled face, but I ignored it and the next moment I was saying to Braithwaite in a voice calculated to travel the length of a sizeable church: 'As a gentleman your conduct was beyond the pale and as a churchwarden your conduct was beyond belief. Reflect on your behaviour. Examine your conscience. And I shall expect an apology to my guest within the hour.'

I made a superb exit, and it was only when I reached the hall that I allowed myself to pause. I could not remember when I had last felt so angry. Heading for the stairs I decided to pursue Miss Fielding all the way to her lair, but then I remembered that I did not know her room number, and as I paused again I was aware of the antenna twitching in my psyche.

I strode to the library and found her sitting on the secluded window-seat where she had interrupted my perusal of *Lux Mundi*. She had removed her glasses but as I sat down beside her she rammed them back on her nose as if they could hide all evidence of her tears.

I said: 'You were right. He's a very stupid man, and like so many stupid men he's pathetic, trying to bolster his self-esteem by telling himself that his gender makes him superior to fifty percent of the human race. But you're not stupid – and you're not pathetic either. You've got the brains and the courage to look back on that scene and see that it wasn't you but he who was so irretrievably diminished by it.'

While I spoke she took off her glasses again but by the time I had finished she had brushed the tears aside. Passing her my handkerchief I said: 'He's due to leave tomorrow so you won't have to endure his presence here much longer. In fact when tomorrow comes, breakfast in your room and then I'll take you out for the day.'

'If that's an offer made out of pity – '

'It's made out of admiration for your courage in standing up to that man, and how better could I demonstrate my admiration than by asking you to share my solitude?'

She could not speak, but when I took her hand in a gesture of comfort, her fingers closed trustfully on mine.

We completed our dinner in the privacy of the Warden's sitting-room after a subdued Braithwaite had proffered the required apology. Then the next morning the Warden drove us into the nearby town of Ashburton where, armed with a picnic-basket, we boarded the motor-bus which climbed up the winding country roads on to the high plateau of Dartmoor. We reached the church at Widecombe in time for matins, and by one o'clock we were sitting on a hillside overlooking the village as we embarked on our luncheon. The sun shone fitfully over the hills which ringed the valley, and below the outcrop of rocks which marked the summit of the nearest ridge a breeze ruffled the manes of the wild ponies.

After a prolonged silence in which we ate our sandwiches, sipped our tea and watched the shifting patterns of light playing on the vast expanse of heather around us I said suddenly: 'This reminds me of Ruydale. I lived there for fourteen years. It became home. Being transferred to Grantchester in '37 was a great wrench.'

'Is it usual for monks to be transferred?'

'No, it's rare – and my transfer was like a bolt from the blue. The wire arrived from the Abbot-General at ten o'clock one morning and by two I was on the train to London.'

She was appalled. 'But how horrible to be uprooted from your home so suddenly!'

I said nothing as I remembered how nearly my anger and misery had destroyed my will to obey orders without question. There had been no mention of Grantchester in Father Darcy's wire. I had thought I was being transferred to London so that I could be more accessible to the increasing number of clergymen who sought my spiritual direction.

'Why was there such a rush?' Miss Fielding was asking in bewilderment.

'The Abbot of Grantchester had just died and his death revealed urgent problems which required swift attention.' I had intended to say no more about the Order's private affairs but when she said: 'Was there a scandal?' I felt obliged to quash any melodramatic suspicions.

'From a monastic point of view it was scandalous,' I said, 'but I don't think a layman would have found the disorder particularly titillating. The main problem was that Abbot James had become very withdrawn during the last year of his life – it would be unfair, I think, to use the word senile – and all power had passed to the Prior whose previous heavy drinking then flowered into full-blown alcoholism. As a result discipline became disastrously lax and soon everyone, even the good men, spent too much time wallowing in sloth.'

Miss Fielding said with a most disarming sympathy: 'How on earth did you set everyone back on the rails?'

I was lured into further confidences. 'First of all I ordered everyone to clean themselves up; men get slovenly without either women to look after them or a discipline to keep them up to the mark. Then we all took part in cleaning the house from top to bottom; nobody can work well in a filthy environment.' I paused, remembering the odours of stale sweat, stale urine, stale food and the sight of thick grease, thick dust, thick grime. The details came back to me abruptly: the underclothes in holes at the garment inspection; the stained chamber-pots used as shaving-bowls to enable their owners to avoid 'the trough', the long narrow basin in the central wash-room where all monks but the abbot (who had his own basin in his cell) were obliged to shave; the sheet of noughts-and-crosses tucked under the hassock in the chapel to betray how at least two of the brethren had spent the time supposed to be devoted to worship; the dog-eared copy of *The News of the World* which lined the basket of the flea-bitten cat; the three-tiered cream cake brazenly sitting in the larder; the chocolate-box hidden behind the blackboard in the scriptorium, and – worst horror of all – the empty brandy bottles stacked high in the crypt.

'Then I changed the diet from a gourmet cuisine to predominantly vegetarian meals,' I heard myself say to Miss Fielding, 'restricted wine to feast-days and ordered that everyone, even the oldest monk, was to take some exercise every day. I'm afraid that at the start of my rule I was highly unpopular with the lazier members of the community.'

'I'm sure the good men were relieved to have a firm hand at the helm again.'

'The relief was mixed with resentment. They didn't like the Abbot-General's decision to bring in someone from outside to rule the community,' I said, and the next moment I was remembering my dibilitating sense of isolation, my homesickness for Ruydale, my struggles to avoid any self-centred expression of misery as I wrote the weekly report Father Darcy had demanded for the first six months of my tenure.

However the next moment I was diverted from these difficult memories when Miss Fielding asked with curiosity: 'What happened to the alcoholic Prior?'

'He was transferred permanently to London so that the demon drink could be exorcized by the Abbot-General.'

'A fate worse than death?' said Miss Fielding with a smile and I laughed before replying: 'Father Darcy was certainly formidable.'

'Darcy!'

'No relation to the famous Jesuit. Different spelling.'

'I was thinking of Jane Austen's hero.'

'Father Darcy was a hero to many of his monks but heaven only knows what Jane Austen would have thought of him.'

'Was he a hero to you?'

'No, he was my mentor. That meant our relationship had to be grounded in reality, not fantasy.'

'Well, I hope he gave you a pat on the back after you'd transformed the Grantchester house! How long did it take you to put everything right?'

So she had sensed I had no inclination to say more about my complex relationship with Father Darcy. With gratitude I answered readily: 'The worst difficulties were ironed out quickly enough but it took a least six months to reduce the minor irritations – the endless pettiness, the foolish squabbles, the incessant twittering in corners whenever the slackers thought their superior was out of earshot . . . The Fordites aren't Trappists and the rule of silence is never rigidly enforced, but gossiping is forbidden and personally I can't endure people twittering about nothing.'

Miss Fielding at once said: 'How difficult you must have found it to adjust to all the twittering at Allington!' and before I could stop myself I was confessing: 'To be honest I'm beginning to wonder if I've adjusted to Allington at all. I'm supposed to be giving serious consideration to my future, but so far I've found my attempts at meditation singularly unproductive.' However as soon as these words had been uttered I felt driven to exonerate Allington. 'The fault's mine, of course,' I said. 'I'm failing to make a satisfactory adjustment to normal society and that's why I persistently feel that I'm in the wrong place.'

'But maybe you *are* in the wrong place,' said Miss Fielding unexpectedly. 'I can see why you came here, but surely in your case a community like Allington can only seem a travesty of the type of community where you've learnt to feel at home? I almost wonder if you'd be better off in some remote rural guest-house where you'd be the only visitor.'

This struck me as a most perceptive observation. 'You may well be right,' I began, and then broke off as I suddenly realized which way the conversation was drifting. My heart seemed to beat a shade faster as I said with immense care: 'Miss Fielding, please don't take this amiss; I wouldn't like you to feel that I was engaged in some form of unwanted pursuit of you, but do you by any chance know of a remote spot in the Starbridge area where I might find the peace and quiet I need?'

There was a long silence. Miss Fielding was staring at the wild ponies grazing in the distance and she was still staring at them when she eventually said: 'I think I do know of a place which would suit you.'

I waited, not hurrying her, and at last she turned to face me. 'It's a manor house,' she said. 'It's at Starrington Magna, twelve miles from Starbridge.' Looking away from me again she began to trace a pattern on the grass with her finger. 'The owner lives there alone apart from the servants,' she said. 'It's a big house. You could be as secluded there as you wished, and there are twenty acres of walled grounds which are ideal for solitary strolls.'

Five seconds elapsed before I was able to say with a theatrical calmness: 'Can you tell me . . . is there a chapel in the grounds?'

Her eyes widened. 'Yes,' she said surprised, 'as a matter of fact there is.'

'And is there a ruined ivy-clad building behind it?'

I saw the colour fade from her face. 'The chantry,' she whispered. 'Yes.'

'And is the chapel Victorian but built in the style of Inigo Jones?'

By this time she was beyond speech. She was barely able to nod.

My voice said: 'Miss Fielding, forgive me for playing what must appear to be yet another psychic parlour-trick, but this place is of the greatest importance to me. Who's the owner of this manor house? I'd like to get in touch with him straight away.'

In the silence that followed, the world seemed entirely still; it was as if even the breeze had ceased to blow. But as Miss Fielding took off her glasses at last, like a soldier removing his camouflage after some complex battle, the truth hurled itself against my shattered mind and smashed awake my sleeping psyche.

'It's you, isn't it?' I could hardly speak. 'The chapel belongs to you.' And when, mesmerized by my emotion, she offered no denial I covered my face with my hands and silently thanked God for this great deliverance from the torment of my doubts.

TEN

'Our real self is not the captive of Space and Time.'

W. R. INGE
Dean of St Paul's 1911–1934
Mysticism in Religion

I

My emotion was so profound that I felt a need to be alone, and rising to my feet I crossed the heather to the stack of rocks which crowned the Tor. The wild ponies regarded me with mild interest but soon resumed their grazing. I looked back. Miss Fielding had been watching me but I saw her avert her gaze as if she wished to give me every privacy. Slowly I circled the rocks before retracing my steps through the heather.

When I reached her I began: 'Miss Fielding – ' but she interrupted me.

'My name's Anne Barton-Woods,' she said. 'Fielding is the name of my aunt who lives in Starbridge. I'm sorry I lied to you but I have such a horror of fortune-hunters that when I'm on holiday I find I can't relax unless I take on a false identity.' And as an afterthought she added: 'Of course you'll now think I'm a hopeless neurotic.'

Again I was aware that there was a taut fearful underside to the psyche which existed beneath the veneer of her self-confidence, and at once I said: 'I suggest we forget the word "neurotic", which is one of those fashionable modern words which are so frequently misused, and consider your situation from a calmer, more rational perspective. If you have a horror of fortune-hunters, how clever you are to retreat to an ecclesiastical backwater like Allington where any normal fortune-hunter would die of boredom within twenty-four hours! And how sensible to adopt a false identity so that no abnormal fortune-hunter, lurking among the clerical collars, can pursue you once you leave! This all sounds most closely reasoned to me.'

Miss Barton-Woods was sufficiently encouraged to say: 'I wish I could dispense with holidays altogether, but I find I need them. I work very hard running my estate.'

'No doubt you're wise to take an annual rest, but I do see that it must be an ordeal to spend two weeks among strangers.'

'Shakespeare helps,' said Miss Barton-Woods. 'After I arrive I always read *Henry V* – '

' "Once more into the breach – " '

'Exactly. Then later I read the light-hearted plays, *Twelfth Night, The Comedy of Errors* – '

'The plays in which a lost brother is found.'

She gasped but before she could speak I asked: 'How long have you been running your estate?'

'Since my brother died six years ago.' She hesitated, then added: 'The estate's been in the hands of my family since the Civil War – we were roundheads taking over from cavaliers – but now the family's died out and there's no one left except me. My aunt in Starbridge is on my mother's side of the family.' She began to clear up the debris of our picnic, and as she tilted her cup to spill the dregs of her tea on the ground the gesture seemed to emphasize the bleakness of her situation, drained as it was of family life. 'For a while I thought I would marry,' she said, 'but when I was engaged I found I wasn't much good at all that sort of thing – so you see, I don't just put on this mask to avoid the fortune-hunters. I put it on to keep all men at arm's length because I never want to get engaged again.'

'Of course. That makes perfect sense.'

She gave me a suspicious look. 'You're probably now thinking I'm just suffering from sour grapes because my fiancé broke off the engagement.'

'That would be Braithwaite's explanation, no doubt, but I'm not Braithwaite. My explanation would run like this: your broken engagement, combined with the loss of your brother, brought you profound suffering; you transcended that suffering by using it as a base on which to build a new life set in opposition to the old – a move, which made celibacy not only desirable, after the tragedy of your broken engagement, but essential to complete the process of "metanoia", the turning aside into the new life which would enable you to survive.'

She said simply: 'You're the only person who's ever understood,' and opening the picnic-basket she replaced the thermos as if she feared it might shatter in her hands. 'But I knew you'd understand,' she said, 'and that's why I'm willing for you to stay at the Manor. You won't be a nuisance and you won't mind me being – ' She bit back the word 'neurotic' ' – eccentric.'

'My dear Miss Barton-Woods,' I said, 'if you're still willing to offer me hospitality after my psychic parlour-trick just now I shall think you're the most courageous of women and you can be just as eccentric as you please! But now let me follow your confession about your identity with a far more bizarre confession of my own . . .'

I made no attempt to translate the spiritual quality of the vision into words, but this was not only because mere words could never have reflected satisfactorily that glimpse of ultimate reality as I journeyed beyond the borders of finite time. It was also because I was aware that my story was already so unusual that I shied away from any inadequate descriptions which might well have aroused her incredulity. Indeed so outrageous did my clairvoyance sound as I recited the bare facts that I feared she would inevitably judge me either mad or wicked or both, using my psychic powers to slither my way first into her confidence and then into her bank account.

'. . . and a light began to shine through the north window. As the light increased in power I knew it was the light of God. I then realized I was called to leave the Order,' I said colourlessly in the tone employed by the gentlemen reading the weather forecasts which I had heard on Ruth's wireless. I had been amazed when the announcers had droned on with such impressive lack of emotion about the numerous gales poised to ravage the North Sea.

Miss Barton-Woods was silent and inscrutable. I watched the breeze disturb her short dark hair which was shaped into a point at the nape of her neck. Her skin was lightly freckled; I noticed the small mole above the square line of her jaw, the shine on the tip of her wide nose, the dull unpainted red of her mouth. She looked no prettier without her glasses but there was a stronger impression of a striking individuality. I thought it not unlikely that she was one of those women who appear at their best not in youth, when their unusual looks preclude them from conforming to fashionable notions of beauty, but in middle-age when the unusual looks can be seen as 'distinguished' or even 'handsome'. Picking up the glasses I saw that the lenses were clear. The glasses had been part of the camouflage she had worn to protect herself, part of the degrading of the personality perhaps not so different from the degrading I myself had employed when to protect the privacy of my inner self I had referred to my vision as a parlour-trick.

At last I said abruptly: 'Do you believe me?' and she answered surprised: 'Of course.'

Greatly relieved I confessed: 'I was afraid you might think I was a confidence trickster.'

'That thought had, of course, occurred to me,' said Miss Barton-Woods, 'but the Warden knew you when you were at Grantchester so obviously you are who you say you are. I suppose it's just possible that you might now be sinking into iniquity, but I think if that were the case you'd have taken care to get the details of the chapel right.'

I forgot my fear of her distrust. 'What did I get wrong?'

'There's no wide space between the doors and the last pew; the pews do go all the way back. There's no plain altar-table with a wooden cross; the chapel's not deconsecrated but it hasn't been used since my grand-mother died, and my father, who wasn't a believer, gave the altar-table to a local church before selling the altar-furnishings at Sotheby's. As for the memorial tablet . . .' She hesitated before saying: 'That's really most odd. It does exist; it commemorates my uncle who was killed in the Boer War, but no one's placed lilies there since my grandmother died in 1919.'

'So the past was mixed up with the present and future. That happens sometimes.' I was so absorbed by these new facts that I barely noticed the astonished lift of her eyebrows.

At last she ventured awkwardly: 'This is all very – ' But she could not find the word which would have expressed the quality of her amazement and fascination. 'I suppose I should feel frightened,' she said, 'but I don't feel in any way endangered.' She groped for words again before concluding: 'It's because you're benign. There's no wickedness here for me to fear.'

'Father Darcy would have said that's because the vision came from God and not from the Devil.'

'In that case is it vulgar to say I feel exhilarated?'

'Certainly not! No one thought a spiritual exhilaration in the least vulgar until the religious philosophers of the Enlightenment made "enthusiasm" a dirty word.'

We smiled at each other before Miss Barton-Woods closed the picnic-basket and stood up. 'I'll leave tomorrow,' she said. 'Give me twenty-four hours so that I can talk to my housekeeper and have one of the spare rooms made habitable.'

I stared at her. 'But you can't possibly cut short your holiday!'

'Why not? I'm fed up with Allington and after last night I've got the perfect excuse to leave.'

'Yes, but – '

'If you take the noon train on Tuesday from Ashburton to Starbridge you can get the three-thirty train from Starbridge to Starrington Magna. I'll send my chauffeur to the station to meet you. You don't want to walk a mile with your baggage, and the village taxi's always breaking down.'

I almost baulked at the prospect of a chauffeur but managed to pull myself together 'How very kind,' I said. 'Thank you so much. But are you sure that my arrival won't cause awkwardness for you?'

'What kind of awkwardness?'

'Well . . .' I found myself floundering in the face of what I suspected was an aristocratic indifference to certain conventions. 'I was thinking of your neighbours,' I said. 'Might they not judge it a little unseemly if you were to grant hospitality to a man whom you've only just met?'

'Oh, good heavens!' exclaimed Miss Barton-Woods, confirming my suspicions. 'Surely it's only the lower classes who spend their lives worrying about what the neighbours might think!'

Old wounds broke open in my psyche. 'Possibly,' I said, 'but my background is very different from yours, Miss Barton-Woods, and I'm afraid you must make allowances for my tediously bourgeois anxiety.'

She looked stricken. Furious with myself both for upsetting her and for revealing my ineradicable sensitivity on the subject of class I said rapidly: 'I'm sorry. You were being refreshingly honest and I was being tiresomely inhibited.'

'No, I was being snobbish and you were quite right to reprove me for it. But don't worry about the neighbours,' said Miss Barton-Woods, resuming the casual confidence which can only be acquired from an upbringing in privileged surroundings. 'They wouldn't cut me unless I did something quite beyond the pale.'

'I think offering hospitality to a clairvoyant cleric might be construed as pressing the pale to its utmost limits.'

'We'll keep quiet about the clairvoyance and play up the clerical collar,' said Miss Barton-Woods smiling at me, but added in panic: 'Or are you trying to create an excuse for refusing my invitation?'

'Absolutely not!' I said with a robustness worthy of Francis. 'The very last thing I want to do is refuse! Thank you for displaying your hospitable inclinations so generously, Miss Barton-Woods. I can only confess I find your offer irresistible.'

III

Later on the motor-bus which took us back across the moor to Ashburton some confused impulse prompted me to say: 'I'm sorry I embarrassed you earlier by displaying the chip on my shoulder,' but she answered tranquilly: 'You weren't embarrassed by my chip – why should I be embarrassed by yours?'

'But to be over-sensitive about class is so tedious and commonplace – '

'A chip is never tedious or commonplace to its owner. It's always quite unique and utterly beastly. Fortunately I've never suffered from class prejudice, but I'm sure that if I had I wouldn't think a chip about class was tedious or commonplace at all.'

The motor-bus began to growl up a steep hill. When we reached the summit there was a brief pause as if the engine were gasping for breath, and at that moment my voice said: 'My mother was an orphanage girl who became a parlour-maid. When I was growing up I found that what the neighbours thought so often made the difference between happiness and misery.'

'Beastly old neighbours! I suppose they couldn't bear to think that your parents had not only married in defiance of the conventions but had actually had the nerve to live happily ever after.'

I smiled before saying: 'My parents were certainly devoted to each other.'

'I remember you saying your father was a schoolmaster. Did he teach at a public school?'

'Yes – but that was before he was married, of course. When he became engaged the headmaster suggested to him that my mother might find it difficult to fit in with the wives of the other masters in such a closed community, and so naturally my father resigned. After that he taught at the local grammar school for some years, but although that was a step down the educational ladder he never complained.'

'Beastly headmaster! Beastly public school! If you ask me, both your parents were well out of it. Did your mother manage to make many friends in her new life?'

'Good heavens, no! None of the neighbours would call. But she didn't mind. She'd got what she wanted.'

'And your father?'

'Oh, he never complained.'

'All the same – '

'They were happy enough. She had her household and her cats, he had his study and his books, and both of them were content in their isolation. *I* was the one who minded when the neighbour's children weren't allowed to play with me and the big boys tried to bully me at the local dames' school where I began my education.'

'Beastly, *beastly* children – '

'Fortunately I was big for my age and soon became more than a match for the bullies. Then eventually I went away to boarding school where no one knew my mother's background so I had no trouble living happily ever after.'

'Just like your parents . . . I'm glad your mother was happy in spite of the neighbours.'

'I suspect she wrote off their lack of charity as the price she had to pay for her security.' As soon as the word slipped out I knew I had made a mistake. I should have said 'romance' or 'happiness' but before I could attempt to gloss over the error Miss Barton-Woods commented sympathetically: 'I'm sure all orphans must long to feel secure in a nice home with someone they love,' and the next moment I heard myself saying: 'I remember her talking once about her favourite cat. "There sits Chelsea," she said, "washing her paws in front of the fire. She wouldn't be here if

583

she didn't love us, of course, but what she really loves is sitting in front of that fire on winter evenings and knowing she'll never be one of those alley-cats left outside to starve in the cold." She often used to express truths – truths which she could never have expressed directly – by talking about her cats. I remember – ' But I broke off. I had begun to wonder if old age had finally caught up with me by producing an urge to be garrulous in the company of sympathetic young women.

'Go on,' said Miss Barton-Woods, but I was silent, remembering the time over fifty years ago when Chelsea had given birth to four kittens, three of which had died. 'It's for the best,' my mother had said casually, mopping up my tears. 'If there are too many kittens the mother doesn't have enough love for them all and they're not brought up properly. Better to have one kitten who becomes a splendid cat than a bunch of nuisances who yowl around asking to be drowned.' And I had known then that she had never wanted another child after I was born. 'Of course her greatest sorrow,' my father had said after her death, 'was that she was unable to give me more children.' I could still recall the exact quality of my amazement as I had realized how imperfectly he had known her.

'I mustn't bore you with my past,' I heard my voice saying to Miss Barton-Woods, and at once she responded: 'There's no question of boredom but you mustn't think I want to pry. Why don't we sink into one of our restful silences?'

I smiled and said no more, but the atmosphere was neither awkward nor uncompanionable.

The motor-bus roared on towards Ashburton.

IV

'. . . but may I hasten to reassure you,' I wrote that night to Francis, 'that although I shall be staying beneath the same roof as an unchaperoned young woman I shall be in *no danger* of succumbing to Monks' Madness. Miss Barton-Woods is so much younger than I am that I can unhesitatingly think of her as a daughter, and even if she were older I would still be quite safe as I have *no inclination whatsoever* to respond to her in any carnal way. In short, I am in complete command of this situation.'

I reread this letter and decided that I had never sounded more sane. However the copious underlinings troubled me. I added: 'Forgive the emphatic style but I'm sure you're worried about me and I'm most anxious to allay your fears.' I almost continued: 'I know I myself would be worried if I were in your shoes,' but I thought better of it. I had quite enough to occupy my mind without trying to put myself into Francis' shoes.

Nevertheless I was unable to stop asking myself what he could possibly be thinking.

V

The next morning I said to the Warden: 'I've received an unexpected invitation from a friend who lives near Starbridge, so I regret to say I shall be leaving Allington earlier than I'd planned.'

To Miss Tarantino, who playfully accused me of plotting a secret elopement with the departing 'Miss Fielding', I said: 'So you've guessed my guilty secret!' and to Miss Barton-Woods herself I said as she left: 'I look forward immensely to tomorrow.' Then I retired to the chapel to meditate but I was so excited that I made a sad hash of my spiritual exercises.

The train reached Starbridge a quarter of an hour late on the following afternoon, but I still had five minutes in which to change platforms and pace up and down like a tiger at the zoo. Repeatedly during my pacings I stared at the spire of the Cathedral, soaring in the distance above the cluttered railway yard as if to symbolize my faith triumphing over my disordered doubts, but at last my view was interrupted by the arrival of the train to Starrington Magna.

The chauffeur was waiting when I arrived. His extreme age gave a venerable air to his peaked cap and gaiters, and infused his welcome with dignity. The motor was equally dignified; despite my ignorance on the subject of mechanized transport I did realize that I was about to complete my journey in a Rolls-Royce, and my automatic judgement was that it was a most unsuitable vehicle for a monk. But then I remembered that I was no longer a monk, and suddenly for the first time the full awareness of my liberation exploded in my consciousness. It was as if my psyche, long burdened with the strain of leaving the Order, had finally somersaulted free, and my depression now seemed not only remote but fantastic, a mental aberration which could not possibly be repeated.

We drove through a long village built in that pale golden stone which is quarried in the Starbridge area. Many of the houses had thatched roofs and were set beside a stream which for half a mile ran parallel with the road. There was no green but I glimpsed a Norman church tucked away down a lane, its steeple rising above the trees like the prow of a ship breasting the waves. I also noted two public houses and the usual assortment of shops including a post office where I could cash my weekly money order.

At the end of the village the road began to encircle the high brick wall of the estate and a minute later we were driving up the curling drive of the Manor. To my disappointment I saw it was not a beautiful house but its varied features, accumulated over the centuries, gave it a certain eccentric grace. It appeared well-kept but not smart; I realized I was moving into a quiet, casual, effortlessly well-bred world where smart country houses were considered the hallmark of the nouveaux riches, and for a moment I remembered my home long ago, the respectable little villa with the respectable little front garden where my mother had grown well-behaved flowers in order to impress the neighbours. I had never been allowed to play in the front garden. Only working-class children played so near the street, but I had been happy in the back garden where my mother moved dreamily in a bewitching silence among the undisciplined shrubs and the aromatic herbs and the wild lawn studded with daisies. I could see her long skirts trailing across the grass as she listened to her thoughts, and Chelsea was there too, sharpening her claws on the peach-tree in preparation for a new adventure, serene elegant Chelsea who savoured her security by the fire on dark winter evenings and was quite content with the one kitten who sat bright-eyed at her side.

The door of the motor was opening. Returning from the 1880s with a jolt I alighted just as the butler opened the front door.

He was very old, like the chauffeur, and had a mild innocent expression which reminded me of Timothy at Grantchester. I was given a civil welcome and ushered deferentially across the threshold before I was informed of the absence of my hostess. 'But she hopes to be back within the hour, sir,' he added after waiting for my murmur of regret, and began to lead the way upstairs.

I was taken to a large corner chamber with extensive views to the south and west. The furnishings were Victorian; my glance encountered a handsome brass bedstead, an elegant washstand and a vast but noble wardrobe. The carpet was probably beyond price but had faded into a distinction which rendered it mercifully unobtrusive. Noting the plain curtains and the war-time black-out blind with approval, I saw that the only picture in the room was an austere engraving of Starbridge Cathedral and at once I decided that this was one of those rare pictures which could not be automatically consigned to the wardrobe. Sighing with pleasure I became aware that the butler was asking me whether I required tea immediately.

'No, thank you.' All thought of food and drink seemed unbearably irrelevant. 'Can you please direct me to the chapel?'

The old man looked startled but led me to the south window and indicated the woods on the far side of the lawn. After pointing out the indentation among the line of the tree-tops and describing the dell he added: 'You'll find the path behind the summer-house, sir. You can't miss it.'

Immediately I was on my way.

VI

As soon as I joined that part of the path where my vision had begun I realized I was in the wrong time; at that moment my vision was not to be exactly reproduced. In the time in which I was now moving the sun was shining and the wood-pigeons were silent in the trees.

But the chapel was the same. I looked down upon it, just as I had in my vision, but this time I was so stunned to see it that I stopped dead. However the chapel remained, neither vanishing nor fading, no mere imprint on the retina of my psychic eye but a three-dimensional building accessible to the five senses, and hurrying on down the path I crossed the floor of the dell, bounded up the steps to the porch and flung wide the main door.

The pews stretched before me on either side of the central aisle and I saw the empty space below the east window where the altar should have stood. Then I found I could see no more. Slumping down on the nearest pew I covered my face with my hands and shuddered beneath the impact of the knowledge that three months ago I had journeyed through time and space in a manner which defied the known laws of physics.

After a while I became calm enough to notice the evidence of the chapel's disuse. The pews needed polishing. So did the brass memorial tablet. Cobwebs festooned the windows and dirt lay ingrained on the floor. There was also a pervasive musty smell, conjuring up images of long damp winters. The thought formed in my mind that I had to effect a restoration, but whether this was a mere emotional reaction from within or a faint call from without I had no idea.

I knelt to pray. At first I prayed in words, thanking God again for his guidance and asking that his will be fully revealed. Then I prayed in images: the classical architecture of the chapel, symbol of Beauty, one of Plato's three absolute values; the spire of the Cathedral at Starbridge, symbol of another absolute value, Truth; the cross on the summit of the spire, symbolic of Christ and of that third absolute value which Plato had called Goodness and which the Christians had exalted as Love. The images quickened. I saw Christ crucified, Christ resurrected, the old life giving way to the new, but then even the familiar images faded beneath the power of my desire to communicate with God, and I found myself praying in stillness, waiting upon the silence, my mind open, my senses in repose but alert for the slightest tremor of psychic movement.

Yet nothing stirred. No workless message formed in the blankness and in the end my concentration broke as my mind, overstrained, eased its way painfully back to a normal level of consciousness in the manner of an athlete slowing down from a fast sprint to a walking pace. My first reaction, not unnaturally, was to be disappointed; I had been so confident that once I reached the chapel I would receive a further revelation. My next reaction was to be baffled; here I was at the chapel and yet nothing was happening. My third reaction was to be cross; I had struggled through three exceedingly difficult months only to be kept in the dark when I could expect to be enlightened. However I then realized I was being preposterously arrogant, nagging God for another revelation like a spoilt child whining for a sweet, so my final reaction was to be ashamed. Father Darcy, as usual, would have been right.

With regret I resigned myself to the fact that the way forward was to remain hidden. But then, just as I was about to slide despondently back into the pew, I heard the click of the latch and knew that my hostess was entering the chapel.

VII

When she saw I was kneeling she immediately withdrew, and although I wanted to stop her the door closed before I could utter a word. At once I rose from my knees and strode outside.

She was waiting on the steps of the porch, and immediately I was startled because for the first time in our acquaintance she was wearing clothes which fitted her. I saw she had a waist – not a small waist and certainly not a wasp-waist, but nevertheless a waist. I also saw that the other attributes of her feminine figure were by no means as ill-proportioned as 'Miss Fielding's' wardrobe had led me to suppose. Of course she was still too stout and of course there was no possibility that I might find her sexually attractive, but I realized that it was not after all so surprising that she should have had a fiancé and I even felt it was not beyond the realms of possibility that one day she might have another.

My surprise gave way to a detached observation. Miss Barton-Woods was wearing a pale grey coat and skirt with a dark blue blouse and she looked, in a discreet way, the wealthy landowner that she was. Ruth would have dressed up such plain clothes with fussy costume-jewellery; Miss Barton-Woods wore a single cameo at the neck of her blouse. Ruth would have worn flimsy shoes with high heels; Miss Barton-Woods had exchanged 'Miss Fielding's' ugly walking shoes for a pair of brogues so elegant that I felt certain they had been hand-made. Ruth would have painted her face and dowsed herself with perfume; Miss Barton-Woods presented merely a powdered nose, a trace of pale lipstick and a faint fresh aroma which indicated that her uncurled hair had recently been washed.

I admired her good taste, applauded her lack of pretentiousness, and wished with a vague, guilty unhappiness that Ruth would refrain from concealing her natural advantages beneath such a vulgar layer of artificiality.

Meanwhile Miss Barton-Woods had succumbed to an unexpected bout of shyness. Immediately I gave her my warmest smile and held out my hand but when she could do no more than clasp it and mutter: 'Welcome to the Manor,' I realized I had quite failed to alleviate her discomfort. I wondered what I was doing wrong. As far as I was aware I was merely standing innocently in the sunshine, six foot three inches of faultless masculine propriety. However before I could inquire what the matter was she managed to reclaim her confident manner and ask in her most businesslike voice: 'Is the chapel as you saw it?'

'Apart from the differences you mentioned, yes.'

I could see that she too was moved by the thought of my vision being translated into the world of finite time, and sitting down abruptly on the top step of the porch she stared across the sward to the trees.

I sat down beside her. For a time we were silent but at last she decided that further comment was too difficult, particularly as I was offering her no encouragement and that a retreat into more mundane matters was required.

'I'm sorry I wasn't here when you arrived,' she said, 'but I suddenly decided I should slip down the road and take the cat to the vet. The trouble's only an ear-infection but it seemed better not to delay treatment when the poor creature was obviously in discomfort.'

A lark began to sing in the woods as I said: 'You didn't tell me you had a cat. What's his name?'

'William.'

'After Shakespeare, naturally,' I said smiling at her again, and to my relief I found she was now sufficiently relaxed to smile readily in return. 'What kind of a cat is he?'

'Just a tabby. But he's very clever.'

The lark was singing and singing. I heard myself say: 'I knew a tabby-cat once. He was very clever too.' And suddenly I realized that at long last I was going to talk about Whitby, proud arrogant Whitby, who had belonged to the community at Ruydale but who had obeyed no man's orders but mine.

VIII

'He was the house-cat up in Yorkshire,' I said. 'Soon after I arrived at Ruydale the old cat died and one of the local people gave us Whitby out of an unwanted litter. A new keeper was appointed to look after him, but

I soon realized the man had no idea how to bring up a kitten. Whitby quickly became wild and useless, but cats are kept for a utilitarian purpose in a monastery, just as they are on board ship; they're not kept to chase their tails while the mice eat all the food in the larder.

'Eventually I decided to report the keeper's mismanagement to the Abbot – an unorthodox move because a novice is supposed to take all problems to his Master, but I was afraid my Master would simply tell me to mind my own business. Mature well-educated novices are always a cross for a monastic nanny to bear – they're too ready to think they know everything – and I was well aware that my monastic nanny thought I was "a handful".

'So I went to the Abbot and told him the kitten was fast becoming a useless monster. Aidan immediately sent me back to the scriptorium, but because he was a good abbot, interested in even the most minor detail of his community, he investigated my complaint and the first thing he saw as he entered the kitchens was Whitby urinating in the flour-bin. Immediately the keeper was relieved of his responsibilities and I was assigned the task of training the monster.

'I was tough with him. I wasn't unkind – but I certainly wasn't sentimental either. It doesn't do to be sentimental about cats; the best ones don't respect you for it, but Whitby respected me and I understood him and before long he was a first-class cat, intelligent, efficient and resourceful. He soon decimated the rodent population. He used to leave the corpses piled up by the back door with the entrails of the ones he'd eaten arranged neatly on the mat. Once before he was fully trained he caught a bird but I rubbed his nose in the feathers and smacked him and he never did it again. Whitby learned fast. Ah, what a cat he was, what a cat!

'Our partnership lasted nearly six years. Then I was promoted from the carpenter's work-bench to the Master's desk in the scriptorium and Aiden said to me: "Since the novices will take all your time I'll appoint someone else to look after Whitby." Of course I couldn't argue. One can never argue when one's superior is laying down the law but I did say: "I don't think Whitby will care for the change at all." Then Aidan gave me a hard look and said: "Whitby's here to serve the community, Jonathan, not to dictate to it, and Whitby will have to learn to accept the change, just as you will."

'So that was that.

'But I hated to think of Whitby pining for my company and being fobbed off on a stupid new keeper who didn't understand him. I couldn't disobey orders, of course. That was out of the question, but as the days passed I thought I saw how I could demonstrate conclusively that Whitby was resisting Aidan's decision.

590

'When I'd entered the Order I'd been forbidden to make any conscious use of my psychic powers, not just because such powers can fuel one's pride to the point of spiritual unhealthiness but because any psychic manifestation can have a disastrous effect on an enclosed community by triggering an hysterical reaction. But now I thought: no one will ever know. And I began to manipulate Whitby with my mind.

'Animals are more open to unseen forces than humans, and often they seem far less deaf than humans to psychic communication. Certainly Whitby was far from being deaf; he was perfectly in tune with me, and when I projected orders with my mind he picked them up with an amazing consistency. Well, you can guess what happened. Gradually everyone began to notice that wherever I was Whitby would seek me out and leap purring into my lap. "Whitby's pining for Jonathan," people were soon saying, exactly as I'd planned, but the new keeper was so jealous that in his rage he accused me of sorcery.

'That made Aidan sit up. Sorcery's not a word which an abbot wants to hear in his monastery, and finally Aidan said to me: "I'm not sure what's going on. I'm not even sure I want to know what's going on. But whatever's going on must stop – and that's an order, Jonathan." He knew he couldn't prove I'd been using the powers, but he knew too that I wouldn't disobey a direct order. So I found I had to face the fact that I'd failed in my efforts to be re-appointed Whitby's keeper.

'But then it seemed Whitby genuinely began to pine.

'He became ill. I heard he was lacklustre, not eating, lying all day in his basket, and eventually a delegation arrived from the kitchens to beg me to intervene to save his life.

'Aidan was much exasperated but he told me to attempt a diagnosis, and as soon as I saw Whitby's bedraggled fur I knew what was wrong: he had a stoppage caused by a fur-ball. Whitby had unusually long hair for a tabby and he needed to be combed once a week to prevent him licking too many hairs into his stomach when he cleaned himself. The stupid new keeper hadn't combed him – probably out of a jealous spite towards me just because I'd stressed how important the combing was.

'I picked Whitby up and took him outside. The delegation tried to troop after me but I didn't want an audience so I told them to stay in the scullery. Carrying Whitby to the nearest patch of earth I dug a hole and sat him on it. Poor Whitby! He was too weak to dig a hole for himself. In fact he was barely conscious but I knew he recognized me because when I'd picked him up he'd started to purr.

'I stroked him for a while. It's important, before any attempt to heal, that the patient should be calm and relaxed. Then I prayed hard and pressed down my hands on him. I can't explain how the power is channelled, but when I laid my hands on Whitby he yelped and his fur stood on end and the next moment he was getting rid of everything, fur-ball and all, and we both knew he was cured.

'When he stopped mewing I picked him up, but Whitby didn't want to be carried now that he was well. Whitby had great pride. When he struggled I set him down again and seconds later we were entering the kitchens in triumph, I swaggering along like a master-magician who's just pulled off a magnificent trick and Whitby staggering along beside me with his eyes shining and his tail held high. The monks were absolutely agog. No magician could have wished for a better audience, and suddenly in my pride I was unable to resist "playing to the gallery", as they say in the theatre. I ordered: "Give him something to eat and drink!" – and from that moment we were all doomed. Do you recognize the order? After Our Lord had raised Jairus' daughter from the dead he advised that she be given food and drink, and of course every monk in the kitchens at Ruydale that night was instantly reminded of that miracle. A second later some fool was shouting: "Whitby's been raised from the dead!" and I was being treated as a wonder-worker. But I knew I'd gone beyond the pale and would have to try to redeem my mistake.

'I assured Aidan there had been no resurrection from the dead but I kept quiet about the charismatic healing. I said only that Whitby had cured himself while I'd been holding him, and Aidan, who's a wily old fox, decided to leave the necessary cross-examination to my confessor and thus seal up all the sordid details in the confessional. However his plan misfired. I was so gripped by the guilty urge to cover up what had happened that I remained silent on the subject when the time came for me to make my confession, and my confessor, although an excellent monk in many ways, was unfortunately no match for me once I felt compelled to manipulate him away from the subject of Whitby's miraculous cure.

'After I'd survived the confessional I thought I was safe. But in fact the real scandal of the Whitby affair was just about to begin.

'The word "miracle" was still reverberating around the house, and soon the community was divided into my allies, who called me a blessed healer, and my enemies, who called me a wicked sorcerer. Fanatical feelings were aroused on both sides, and soon the community was fully poised to go sliding down the slippery slope into hysteria.

'The more ignorant laymen often think that hysteria is endemic in a religious community – they even think hysteria's welcomed as a necessary adjunct to the mystical experience, but in fact the best mystics are all characterized by their rationality and their down-to-earth common sense. The sensational manifestations of an over-stimulated psyche are shunned or at best treated as a tiresome inconvenience by those who are experienced travellers along the spiritual way.

'The hysteria at Ruydale following the healing of Whitby began when a group of monks fell to their knees in the chapel and tried to kiss the hem of my habit as I passed by. At first I was so startled that I could only let them slobber over me, but just as I was making the effort to detach myself there was an outburt of speaking in tongues – a well-known charism but one which is peculiarly subject to demonic infiltration. At once I knew this was no gift from God. This was hysteria triggered by the Devil, and that was when I realized the situation was quite beyond my control. I turned to Aidan, but before he could act the unlatched door of the chapel creaked open and in walked Whitby. In my disturbed state I must have unwittingly sent out a distress-signal which he'd picked up, clever cat, and now there he was, prancing down the aisle to meet me.

'One of my enemies screamed: "It's his familiar!" and pandemonium broke loose, but at once Aidan acted. He snapped at me: "Remove the novices!" and as I left I heard him shouting orders to the other senior officers. In the end the hysterics were all either locked up or confined to the infirmary, but the whole place remained in chaos – and all because I'd disobeyed orders, used my powers and healed that innocent cat.

'The Abbot-General arrived three days later to mop up the mess.

'We needed him by that time. Aidan's a strong abbot but even Aidan felt he had to have help. A modern psycho-analyst would say we needed an exceptionally forceful personality to impose control upon all those dissociated minds, but Father Darcy didn't talk like a psycho-analyst. He talked about the Devil's presence, and he talked as one who *knew* the Devil existed, just as you and I can talk of Hitler and know we're discussing someone who's real. Father Darcy said: "We must trace the source of the demonic influence in order to exorcize it," and the spiritual purging of Ruydale began.

'He interviewed all the monks, beginning at the bottom and working his way to the top. Eventually I received my summons, and as soon as I walked into the room I knew that he knew. He'd ordered Aidan to be there as an observer, and I realized he wanted to teach him exactly how to deal with a high-ranking officer who had caused an entire community to go off the rails.

'For a while I tried to fob Father Darcy off with partial truths but I was wasting my time. He simply took my mind, psychic powers and all, washed it, scrubbed it and hung it up to dry. At the end of the interrogation I was in such a state that I could barely think straight but I remember being certain that he'd strip me of my office and possibly even transfer me to London so that he could keep an eye on me. I was in despair.

'However the situation was far more complex than I in my panic supposed. The truth was that Father Darcy didn't want my career to be ruined. He was convinced I could be a great asset to the Order and he remained determined that nothing, least of all a lot of nonsense over a cat, was going to demolish his plans for me. Yet obviously I deserved a severe punishment; it wouldn't be enough merely to dole out the mandatory punishment for disobedience and then send me back into action. What was needed at that point, as Father Darcy came to realize, was a masterstroke, an action which would teach me a lesson I'd never forget, complete the mass-exorcism of the community and ensure that the incident never happened again.

'That night when I was asleep Whitby was waylaid outside his favourite mouse-hole, taken to the water-butt and held under the water till he drowned. The next morning I was summoned to the Abbot's office but Aidan wasn't there. Father Darcy was alone and on the table in front of him was Whitby's corpse. Father Darcy just said: "I performed the execution but *you* were the one who killed that animal with your disobedience, your vanity and your utterly intolerable pride." Then he rang the bell and Aidan came in. Father Darcy pointed to the corpse and said: "Burn it in the furnace," and without a word Aidan picked up Whitby and took him away.

'I was sent to my cell to reflect on what had happened and at the end of the second hour Father Darcy came to me. He said: "You need to be healed, don't you?" and I broke down, spewing out all my grief and rage. I even said I couldn't go on as a monk. Father Darcy let me talk, but gradually I became aware of his silence stroking my psyche, soothing it, until at last the verbal haemorrhage stopped. Then he said a few sentences. There wasn't a single wasted word and although the words were firm, even severe, his voice was kind. While he was speaking I saw clearly that in order to keep my powers under control I had to live within the disciplined framework he offered me but although I tried to tell him that, I couldn't find the words. I could only kneel down in front of him, and when he laid his hands upon me in a formal sacramental gesture to complete the healing I knew I'd be able to go on in the Order. He knew it too, but afterwards all he said was: "Keep away from the next cat and never, never discuss this incident again."

'And I never have discussed it. Even now I never talk of Whitby. Indeed why should I? Who could possibly understand? He was just a cat who came to an untimely end. It happens all the time everywhere, so what's so remarkable about the incident and why should it matter now after all these years? I often ask myself those questions and tell myself the answers are no longer important, but then sometimes when I lie awake at night I think of him – proud arrogant Whitby, such a wild undisciplined kitten and yet such a first-class gifted cat – and it's as if he's reflecting my own career as a monk until suddenly *I'm* the one who's drowning in the water-butt and *I'm* the one who's burning in the furnace, and I grieve over his death as if it were my own.'

I stopped speaking.

I had not been looking at her during my long monologue. I had been watching the sunlight as it slanted through the trees, and when I stopped speaking I was too ashamed to face her. I saw I had been behaving in a most unbalanced manner, talking for minutes on end about a dead cat, and in horror I asked myself how I could possibly have been so stupid. No doubt she had long since regretted her offer of hospitality.

The silence which followed my monologue lasted ten seconds. Ten seconds can seem a very long time when one is inwardly writhing with humiliation, but at last my torment ended. She said unsteadily: 'How very dreadfully you must have suffered when he was killed and how very dreadfully you must have missed him since he died.'

Struck by the passion in her voice I turned to look at her, and it was then, as I recognized the profound understanding etched in every line of her face, that the scales fell from my eyes at last and I saw that she was beautiful.

ELEVEN

'Love is the great reality.'

W. R. INGE
Dean of St Paul's 1911–1934
Mysticism in Religion

I

'I've fallen in love,' I said eight days later to Francis.

'At the risk of infuriating you I must say that I'm not in the least surprised. Every time you wrote insisting that you found the lady unattractive I wondered how long you could possibly go on deceiving yourself.'

I had presented myself as planned at the Fordite headquarters at the conclusion of my first month in the world, and Francis had welcomed me not in his office, which was in the enclosed section of the house, but in the Abbot's Parlour, the room in which he received guests from outside the Order. It was so opulently furnished that I was reminded of the gaudy chambers of Brighton Pavilion. Francis, resplendent in his perfectly cut habit and bejewelled pectoral cross, looked quite at home there.

A young monk chose that moment to bring us some refreshment but as soon as he had departed I said: 'Of course I've fallen victim to Monks' Madness.'

'Do you take sugar in your tea?'

'You know perfectly well that I don't take sugar in my tea!'

'I thought you might have acquired a taste for it along with falling in love.'

'Francis – '

'Now Jon, you must calm down. You seem to be expecting me to show violent disapproval but at the moment I have insufficient information to show anything except a profound curiosity. Why don't you bring me up to date with what's been going on? Begin: "I arrived at Starrington Magna," and proceed from there.'

I talked in a disordered fashion for some minutes. Francis sipped his tea and looked inscrutable.

'Of course I can't possibly marry her,' I concluded in despair after I had reached the point where the scales had fallen from my eyes. 'Yet how can I endure it if I don't?'

'Let's set all speculation aside for the moment and stick to the questions which can be answered with hard facts. Have you been to bed with anyone yet?'

'No. And maybe – this is a terrible thing to say, but maybe this is exactly why I've lapsed into such insanity.'

'That doesn't necessarily follow at all; grand passions can strike the lechers and the chaste with equal ferocity. But don't let's make "a priori" assumptions. We haven't yet established either that you're insane or that you're in the grip of a grand passion. To what do you attribute your chastity?'

'Prayer.'

'Yes, yes, yes,' said Francis impatiently, very much the worldly priest. 'Of course you prayed and of course your prayers were important – obviously, since they've been answered – but we both know that the sexual drive of a man who's been celibate for a number of years is capable of grinding even the most cherished moral principles into the dust no matter how hard he prays for self-control. How do you explain your chastity in psychological terms?'

'I don't. It's all been a matter of luck. As soon as I met Miss Barton-Woods and realized she was the key to the mystery, sex – for once – took second place. Of course I was still plagued by impure thoughts – '

'Of course, but nevertheless I think you're being a little hard on yourself when you say your chastity's been a matter of luck. In the circumstances a month's self-control represents a considerable achievement, and I can't help thinking that if you were genuinely suffering from Monks' Madness you'd have bedded at least half a dozen women by this time. Now tell me this: why do you believe Miss Bartn-Woods is so unsuitable for you?'

'Francis, she's thirty-two. *Thirty-two!* I don't mind people whispering that I've sunk into an undignified dotage, but it would be so terrible for Miss Barton-Woods if her neighbours decided to cut her – '

'Why should they? They'd probably be delighted she'd at last got off the shelf, even if her rescuer did turn out to be a man twenty-eight years her senior. Contrary to what you seem to suppose, the real question here is not: what on earth will the neighbours think? But: what does Miss Barton-Woods think of you being sixty?'

'She doesn't know that I'm sixty.'

'My dear Jon – '

'I know, I know, but I just haven't yet found the opportunity to tell her – '

'Then create one fast! She'll feel deceived if you frolic around like a forty-year-old and then reveal, as you eventually must, that your children are in their mid-thirties. But let's leave the problem of age now and consider any other difficulties. What else makes this marriage undesirable?'

'The difference in class. I don't want to marry into the landed gentry and live in a big house littered with servants.'

'Jon, I'm well aware of your sensitivity on the subject of class, but are you really saying you'd have trouble facing the landed gentry in order to marry the woman you love?'

'I trust I'm gentleman enough to face anyone, prince or pauper, with equanimity whenever the need arises,' I said grandly, pride well to the fore, 'but I'm just pointing out how ill-suited I am by background, experience and inclination for that kind of life. And I couldn't talk about agriculture with Miss Barton-Woods, couldn't help her run the estate – '

'That would probably suit her very well. If she's been successfully running her estate for some years the last thing she'd want would be a husband who interfered. She's hardly a helpless little miss, is she?'

'No, she's a rich woman with a horror of fortune-hunters, and here I am, poor as a church-mouse – '

'Yes, but from her point of view all that matters is that you're obviously a man of integrity who wouldn't dream of marrying her for her money. However – ' Francis, who had been enjoying the challenge of demolishing my difficulties, now became more cautious. ' – don't misunderstand; I'm not saying the disparity in your financial and social positions is unimportant. Nor am I saying that the difference in age doesn't matter. All I'm saying is that these very real problems needn't be prohibitive. Is there, in fact, any difficulty which you regard as truly insurperable?'

'She's resolved to be celibate.'

'But surely she'll be willing to change her mind!'

'She may be psychologically incapable of changing it.'

'Ah, I see. What an alluring challenge for you!'

'I hope,' I said, trying not to sound annoyed, 'I don't see her merely as a challenge.'

'I don't believe you do, but nevertheless it might be salutary for you to be reminded that men who are successful with women are always fascinated by the ones who don't fall grovelling at their feet. However let's suppose that all inhibitions are overcome on both sides and that you marry Miss Barton-Woods. What makes you think you won't wake up one morning and find that she's "invading your psychic space", as you put it to me once?'

'She couldn't. She's too sensitive. She always knows when to be quiet and she never pesters me with unwelcome questions – and that's why I know beyond any doubt that I could be happy with her.'

'And would you remain happy when she was bearing your children?'

After a pause I said: 'If God should choose to bless the marriage with children I'd accept the situation and pray for the grace to be a good father.'

'That's the sort of pious remark,' said Francis, 'which I suspect has very little to do with the painful and complex reality to which it's supposed to correspond. Is this where we reach the one insuperable difficulty?'

'Certainly not! It's simply a bridge which I'm sure I'll be able to cross when I get to it.'

'Well, make sure you have your bridge-crossing ability developed well before the wedding. Presumably at some stage you intend to confide in her fully about your past?'

'Of course!'

'You greatly relieve my mind. So the crucial question at the moment, I think, becomes this: will Miss Barton-Woods help you or hinder you in the pursuit of your new call? Obviously it's no good if you marry a woman who's deeply entrenched in her family home and then find you've been called to be a missionary in China.'

I said in despair: 'I've received no enlightenment.'

'None? Are you sure?'

I stared at him. 'That sounds as if you disagree.'

'I can have no worthwhile opinion until you complete your account of your recent activities. So far we've only reached the point eight days ago when you made your long speech about the unfortunate Whitby and Miss Barton-Woods revealed herself as irresistible. What have you been doing since?'

Taking a deep breath I resumed my narrative.

II

'As soon as I realized I was in love,' I said, 'I knew I had to expend as much energy as possible elsewhere so that evening I asked Miss Barton-Woods if I could clean the chapel. She was horrified at the idea of a guest on his hands and knees with a scrubbing brush, but when I reminded her that as a monk I'd often done heavy cleaning and when I assured her that I'd enjoy making the chapel sparkle she reluctantly gave her consent.'

'You must be enthralling the servants. But don't let me interrupt you. There you were, scrubbing away in your clerical suit – '

'I bought a pair of dungarees. For a while I wondered if I might uncover serious structural decay beneath the grime, but the place seems to be in reasonable condition despite the years of disuse.' And I told him how Miss Barton-Woods' grandfather had quarrelled with the local vicar, who had been influenced by the Oxford Movement, and had built the chapel in order to avoid being subjected to 'Papist ritual' at the village church. 'He picked the site next to the ruined chantry,' I added, 'because he thought he'd be building on consecrated ground. The chantry, of course, was destroyed at the time of the Reformation.' I hesitated but eventually concluded: 'I can't help wondering if I'm to have a ministry centred on the chapel, a ministry which will require the removal of the back pews so that the chapel corresponds in every detail to my vision.'

Francis said briskly: 'That sounds most improbable. Although you may – *may* – have seen the future state of the chapel in your vision, that doesn't mean your own future necessarily has any connection with it. The chapel could be just another signpost along the way, like the bag.'

'Yes, but – '

'What are you going to do when you've exhausted the possibilities of your scrubbing-brush?'

'I thought I might build an altar-table.'

'And how long do you intend to go on inventing amusing little tasks for yourself at the Manor?'

'My dear Francis, please don't think I haven't been considering how I could occupy my time in a more appropriate manner for a priest! I was thinking that I might offer to help at the local church. The vicar's gone into the army, there's no curate and the services are at present being conducted by a decrepit, semi-blind retired canon who's anxious to be relieved of his responsibilities.'

'In that case I see no reason why you shouldn't help out on a voluntary basis for a couple of months while you wait for your call to unfold.'

'But what on earth am I going to do about Miss Barton-Woods?'

'I don't really have to spell out the most obvious advice, do I?'

I said reluctantly: 'You want me to leave the Manor.'

'Yes. Take a room in the village. I think it's important – even vital – that you should continue to see Miss Barton-Woods, but your bedrooms must be at least half a mile apart.'

'You think it's *vital* that I continue to see her?' I was astonished.

'Of course. In my opinion the key to your future lies not in the chapel but with Miss Barton-Woods, and the only reason why you've been unable to see that is because you've jumped to the guilty conclusion that your attraction to the lady is just a piece of elderly self-indulgence which can have nothing to do with God's purpose for you. But now think again. What's actually happened here? Almost as soon as you leave the Order this woman is thrust across your path with the result that you eventually reach the chapel. You then pray for a revelation – at which point Miss Barton-Woods reappears and some impulse drives you to break a ten-year silence on the subject of that murdered cat. And then you do have your revelation: you realize that you love this woman and want to marry her. Of course a cynic would explain all this by saying you're in an unstable state after years of celibacy, but in fact this explanation won't do because Miss Barton-Woods' remarkable arrival in your life and her connection with your vision are both facts which exist independently of your emotional state, stable or otherwise.'

'So what you're saying is – '

'I'm saying it's possible that this is a genuine call to matrimony. Of course I'm not suggesting God's called you back into the world solely in order that you should marry, but it does begin to look as if matrimony could well be an important element in a much larger call which at present we still can't perceive. However,' said Francis, smiling at me as he approached the most difficult part of his advice, 'the fact that you may be called to marry doesn't mean that you can sit back and leave it to God to preserve you miraculously from temptation while you await your journey to the altar. How far have you actually travelled with the lady? Have you allowed yourself, for example, a modest squeeze of the hand?'

I was so overwhelmed that he should be advancing the theory I had not dared believe that I could not immediately frame a coherent reply. However at last I was able to say: 'I've concealed my feelings. I was afraid that once I'd started to display them I wouldn't be able to stop.'

'Quite. How wise. Is she a virgin, do you think? I'm trying to gauge how likely she'd be to say no if your wisdom suddenly decided to expire.'

'I suspect there was a disastrous attempt at intimacy with the fiancé. If I'm right then the odds against her allowing herself to be seduced again would be high.'

'Good, but remove yourself from her house as soon as possible, I beg of you, Jon, and don't, whatever you do, propose to her in a rush of romantic enthusiasm before you know a great deal more about your future as a priest than you do at the moment. In fact I feel bound to say,' said Francis, looking me straight in the eyes, 'that in my opinion it's out of the question that you should marry either Miss Barton-Woods or indeed anyone else until you've been in the world for at least six months.'

It was the soundest possible advice. At once I answered: 'I wouldn't dream of marrying in haste!' but as Francis relaxed in relief I thought of Father Darcy turning my mind inside out, washing it, scrubbing it and hanging it up to dry. Father Darcy would have said: 'You're saying what you want me to hear but I hear the words you can't bring yourself to say.' And he would have talked of lust and pride and wilfulness, of the Devil striking at me through the Achilles' heel of my sexuality, until at last I would have confessed to him that I wanted to go to bed with Miss Barton-Woods that very night and that the possibility of a further five months of chastity was the beautiful dream of a monastic mind, a dream which had no hope of coming true.

I spent the night in one of the guest-rooms of the Fordite headquarters but the sober masculine atmosphere, which I had looked forward to sampling for a few hours, seemed so bleak in contrast to the glowing aura surrounding Starrington Magna that on the following morning I was relieved to depart. Francis, who perfectly understood that I could hardly wait to return to Miss Barton-Woods, remarked that at least he was spared the worry that I might be pining for the cloister.

'And how was London?' enquired Miss Barton-Woods when we met that evening; as usual she had been out all day at the estate-office. 'Did you see much evidence of the bombing?'

I described my fleeting visit to Westminster Abbey, where the great west window had been destroyed, and told her how the nocturnal air-raids murdered sleep. 'It's not just the bombs,' I said. 'It's the guns. My friend Father Ingram – who incidentally was looking just like one of Shakespeare's wicked cardinals – said that one got used to the noise after a while, but I suspect he was merely putting a brave face on what must be a tedious as well as a nerve-racking ordeal.' Exasperated by the tenacity of the RAF, Hitler had recently turned aside from his efforts to destroy the fighter bases in Kent and had unleashed his fury on the capital. But although hundreds of barges had been accumulated along the coasts across the Channel, although the tide had favoured the enemy, although the Home Guard had even been called to stand to arms, the long-awaited invasion had never come.

'Thank goodness you're safely back in Starrington!' Miss Barton-Woods was saying. 'But what happens next? Did Father Ingram approve of your plan to help out at the village church?'

'Yes, he did – and that means, I'm afraid – ' I allowed myself the luxury of a deep sigh ' – that I must leave the Manor. If I'm to work in Starrington in a pastoral capacity I must live in the village among my flock.'

'Ah yes, of course,' said Miss Barton-Woods without hesitation, but just as I was wondering in alarm if her alacrity indicated relief she stooped to pick up her tabby-cat and said: 'But what a pity you have to leave! William will miss you so much when you're gone.'

At once I said: 'I hope I'll still have the opportunity to see him regularly,' and I reached out to stroke William behind the ears.

As our chaperon purred loudly between us Miss Barton-Woods murmured: 'Call whenever you like.' But then she added, steering the conversation back on coarse as if she feared the atmosphere were becoming too impregnated with confusing possibilities: 'Are you sure you'll be allowed to work here? Supposing the Bishop thinks you could be more useful somewhere else in the diocese?'

I realized startled that this was a valid point. In my arrogance I had been so confident of getting my own way when I sought the episcopal permission to work in the village that it had never occurred to me that I should approach not only the Bishop but the Archdeacon with care. The Archdeacon in particular might be offended if an itinerant ex-monk invaded his territory and ignored him by dealing directly with his superior.

'I'm sure Dr Ottershaw will understand that as I'm still adjusting to the world I can at present only manage part-time work in a rural parish,' I said cautiously, 'but the Archdeacon, who would inevitably know this part of the diocese better than the Bishop, might well feel I could be of more use elsewhere.'

'Would it help if you met him?' said Miss Barton-Woods unexpectedly. 'I can easily arrange it. His name's Neville Aysgarth and his wife happens to be a friend of mine – I'm godmother to her latest baby.'

I said surprised: 'Aysgarth married late to a young wife?' My fascination must have been very obvious but Miss Barton-Woods answered tranquilly: 'No, he married in his twenties and he's still under forty.'

I was even more surprised. 'That's young to be an archdeacon! Is he a protégé of Dr Ottershaw?'

'Not Dr Ottershaw,' said Miss Barton-Woods. 'Dr Jardine – our famous fire-breathing bishop who had to retire in 1937 because of ill-health.'

'Ah.' At once I adjusted my mental image of Aysgarth. Since I had heard that Jardine and Ottershaw could hardly have been more dissimilar I deduced that their taste in protégés was unlikely to coincide.

'I met the Aysgarths through my aunt,' Miss Barton-Woods was saying. 'The Archdeaconry's attached to the benefice of St Martin's-in-Cripplegate so she's one of Aysgarth's flock.'

'Is he a local man? It's a Yorkshire name.'

'I think he was born in some town near Huddersfield, but he keeps very quiet about it. He's a self-made man – which may have been one of the reasons why Dr Jardine favoured him. Dr Jardine's a self-made man too, as you probably know.'

I did in fact know all about Dr Jardine, but it is not a priest's business to gossip about churchmen who are either famous or – as in Jardine's case – notorious, so although it would have been delightful to remain cosily 'à deux' with Miss Barton-Woods I terminated the conversation by standing up. At once Miss Barton-Woods exclaimed in alarm: 'Have I been repulsively snobbish again?' but I said firmly: 'It would be quite impossible for you to be repulsively anything,' and excused myself from her presence for five minutes.

Retreating to my room I retrieved the box in which the monks of the London workship had packed my cross, and swiftly rejoined her downstairs. 'This is something I made before I left the Order,' I said, 'so it belonged to the monks, but Father Ingram today insisted that I should offer it to you as a gift for the chapel.' And setting down the box I removed the lid to reveal the glowing oak within.

Miss Barton-Woods was overwhelmed. 'Is it the same as – '

'Yes.'

'It's beautiful.' She lifted the cross and was surprised by its weight. 'How very satisfying it must be to have the skill to make something so beautiful,' she said. 'Thank you, Mr Darrow. Thank you very much.' And still clasping the cross she smiled radiantly at me.

The desire was almost annihilating. How I succeeded in excusing myself from her presence in order to change for dinner I shall never know.

IV

I shall refrain from describing my mental and physical reactions as my carnal urges, exacerbated by years of celibacy, ploughed remorselessly through every particle of my being. As Francis had pointed out, never do moral convictions seem so insubstantial as when a man is invaded by a powerful sexual desire. Suffice it to say that after a sleepless night I took a cold bath, rejected the possibility of eating breakfast and walked to the post-office to inquire about accommodation in the village. By this time I suspected that Miss Barton-Woods' visitor who talked like a gentleman and scrubbed floors like a skivvy was the talk of the parish, and my suspicions were confirmed when the post-mistress, a stout plain eminently respectable married woman, did not refer me to the nearest guest-house but offered me her own spare room with all the satisfaction of someone bringing off a 'coup' guaranteed to stun the neighbours.

The room was not large but it was clean, and as it faced the garden at the rear instead of the high street at the front I judged it would be tolerably quiet. I made arrangements which encompassed the provision of breakfast and an evening meal. Then I retired to the chapel to pray.

V

As soon as I moved to my new lodgings that evening I missed my large light airy room at the Manor. I also missed not only the house itself but the grounds – the flowers, the lawns, the woods, the dell, the chapel, the chantry – and above all I missed Miss Barton-Woods. This moping was quite uncalled for since I had an open invitation to visit the Manor whenever I pleased, but nonetheless I regret to record that I gave way to the urge to behave like a lovesick swain and I moped. Trailing around the village after dinner I wound up loafing morbidly in the churchyard among the tombstones. A priest has no business speculating on how much longer he has to live; his duty is to get on with the task of serving God, not to sink himself in self-centred introspection. But that evening I contemplated the tombstones and reflected that as I was no longer a young man I might well drop dead before I had been to bed with Miss Barton-Woods. The thought was intolerable. A feverish urgency ungulfed me. I did not like to enter the church when I was in the grip of thoughts so unbecoming to a priest, but I sat down on the stone bench in the porch and for the first time began to grapple ruthlessly with the future.

It did not take me long to confront the fact that I had to marry Miss Barton-Woods immediately and that 'immediately' could by no remote stretch of the imagination be construed to mean 'after six months in the world'. That decision promptly brought me face to face with a most unpalatable fact: a man who is both unemployed and living on borrowed money is not in a position to marry. No consolation lay in the knowledge that Miss Barton-Woods had enough money for both of us. Even the idea that I might be 'kept' by a rich woman made me shudder in horror, and besides, I was already haunted by the recurring fear that Miss Barton-Woods might decide I was a sponger and refuse to marry me.

Abruptly I tossed aside the notion that I should engage in unpaid part-time pastoral work as I waited for my call to unfold. I needed to be employed. I needed to be employed immediately. And I needed to be employed on my future wife's doorstep in the parish of Starrington Magna.

Rising to my feet I opened the ancient oak door and stepped into the church. For a long moment I stood gazing at the altar but unfortunately my thoughts were very far from spiritual. I was wondering where the parish stood in the financial structure of the diocese and how difficult it would be to dredge up enough money for a curacy.

It occurred to me that these were questions an archdeacon could answer, and sitting down in the nearest pew I began to plot my conquest of young Neville Aysgarth.

VI

I met Aysgarth a week later at a luncheon-party given by Miss Barton-Woods. I had expected to find a man of obvious ability, perhaps someone who would reflect the wit and worldliness of his benefactor Dr Jardine, but when I first saw Aysgarth I could detect no remarkable qualities in him.

He was short, no more than five foot seven, and somewhat ill-proportioned, his shoulders too broad for the rest of his frame; it occurred to me that he needed to be half a stone heavier to create a more fetching effect. He had waving brown hair, a high handsome forehead, blue eyes set deep, a Roman nose and a thin straight brutal mouth. It was an odd face, a face of conflict, a face which even I, experienced as I was at summing up people, found it difficult to judge with confidence. I had an impression of an iron will juxtaposed with a shy, sensitive, possibly even a deeply emotional nature, and these seemed explosive attributes for a priest. In fact the more clearly I sensed that he had the determination which is essential to achieve worldly success, the more acutely I wondered, as a director of souls, about the quality of his spiritual life. It occurred to me that the sensitive side of his nature – if indeed it existed – would need to be carefully nurtured to save it from being trampled underfoot by the other, less desirable features of his personality.

His wife, on the other hand, was clearly a much less complex character, a dark pretty woman who preferred to talk of her home and children, as so many wives do, but who was also capable of discussing an eclectic collection of books with Miss Barton-Woods. Aysgarth was evidently adored. Her conversation was littered with sentences which began: 'Neville thinks . . .' or 'Neville feels . . .' or 'Neville says . . .', and her adoration made me take a more respectful second look at the Archdeacon who by achieving a happy marriage had succeeded where I had failed.

The other guests at the luncheon-party consisted of another young woman in her thirties, Mrs Wetherall who was the wife of Starrington Magna's absent vicar, and three people of my own generation, a couple called Maitland who owned the second largest property in the parish, and Miss Barton-Woods' solicitor from Starbridge, a gentleman called Musgrave. The latter at first regarded me with a wariness which suggested he feared I might be a fortune-hunter, but after an exquisitely veiled cross-examination over the pre-luncheon sherry he decided, to our joint relief, that I was an acceptable acquaintance for his client.

The Maitlands too had regarded me with a certain bemusement when I had first entered the drawing-room, but this startled response could no doubt be attributed to the fact that I had decided to wear not my clerical uniform but my new lounge-suit. My vanity had of course preserved the memory of Ruth saying that the suit made me look like a film-star, and I regret to record that I had now given in to the dubious desire to 'make a splash', surprising the other guests who had probably expected a desiccated old man in a dog-collar, and dazzling (so I hoped) Miss Barton-Woods who had never before seen this secret sartorial weapon in my armoury. I did dimly remember how I had earlier hated the suit so much that I had longed for my monk's habit but that eccentric behaviour now seemed part of a very remote past.

When the ladies withdrew at the close of the meal Colonel Maitland was put in charge of the decanter but Aysgarth and I, declining both port and cigars, wandered away from the table towards the nearest open window. As Maitland and Musgrave began to debate how much longer the Luftwaffe could continue to bomb London every night I said to the Archdeacon: 'I think I find smoking the most difficult habit to tolerate now that I've left the cloister.'

Aysgarth murmured a sympathetic response but I wondered if he himself smoked in private like my friend Charles Ashworth. The younger generation of churchmen seemed to have fewer scruples about 'lighting up' once their clerical collars had been discarded than the priests of my age.

Opening the window wider I remarked idly: 'What a pleasant parish this is! But since it's so extensive I'm surprised Mr Wetherall was obliged to manage without a curate.'

'It's the usual story,' said Aysgarth with a shrug of his shoulders to indicate resignation at the passing of the old order. 'Changing economic conditions have resulted in the vicar being barely able to keep himself, let alone a curate.'

'But I understand this parish is in the Bishop's gift. Can't the endowment be improved by prising open the diocesan coffers without trying to tap the funds of the Church Commissioners or Queen Anne's Bounty?'

'I'm sure Dr Ottershaw would feel that in war-time there were more urgent demands on the diocesan coffers.'

'Quite. But – ' I decided to lay my cards on the table ' – it had occurred to me that I might contribute to the war-effort on the Home Front by taking care of this parish while the Vicar's in the Army. Of course I'd prefer to work on a purely voluntary basis but unfortunately I do need some form of stipend.'

Aysgarth's expression immediately became so inscrutable that I felt uneasy. 'I'm sure, sir,' he said, 'that Dr Ottershaw could find work for you which was a great deal more commensurate with your distinguished career in the Order.'

Impatience elbowed my uneasiness aside. 'My dear Archdeacon, since Our Lord was content to wash the feet of his disciples without wondering whether or not it was commensurate with his career as a teacher, surely it would ill become even the most distinguished priest to turn up his nose at serving God in a country parish?'

'I take your point, sir,' said Aysgarth politely, refusing to be intimidated, 'but I put it to you that we nonetheless have a duty to serve God to the best of our ability, not to squander that ability in work which is unsuited to us.'

I found myself becoming increasingly annoyed. 'You think I'm unsuited to work in a country parish?'

'That's not for me to judge. I'm only fit to judge whether in view of the war-time shortage of clergymen it's essential for this parish to have a parson, and in my opinion – '

'Supposing I were to tell you that I'd been led to this place by God? Would you continue to close your mind to the possibility that I might have been called to serve here?'

I expected Aysgarth to capitulate at this point. It is hardly easy for a young archdeacon to stand his ground when a distinguished ex-abbot starts talking forcefully about God, but Aysgarth's obstinate mouth only hardened and I felt his will confronting my psyche with the strength of a steel wall.

'If you feel called to serve in this parish, sir,' he said in a voice devoid of emotion, 'then of course you must discuss your position with Dr Ottershaw. But I can't help thinking that if you really want to do some worthwhile war-work you'll acknowledge that the Home Front extends beyond the boundaries of Miss Barton-Woods' estate.'

So he had noticed Miss Barton-Woods' expresion when she had seen me in my new lounge suit. Cursing the vanity which had betrayed me I simultaneously marvelled at his nerve in administering the rebuke. I had been a Fordite abbot, the equal in rank (so it was usually held) of a bishop. Within the Church there was even a school of thought which held that an abbot was superior to a bishop. Yet here was this young archdeacon not only lecturing me about war-work but even daring to imply that my humble aspiration to be a country curate might be rooted in an aspiration which had nothing to do with humility at all! In my rage I almost felt that his perspicacity was more intolerable than his insolence. I was seething.

'May I suggest,' I said in my coldest voice, 'that you think a little less about the worldly power you wield as an archdeacon and a little more about the spiritual needs of the untended souls in your archdeaconry?'

'And may I suggest,' said Aysgarth instantly, 'that you think a little less of your own needs and a little more about the needs of our war-time Church?'

In the deep silence which followed I suddenly realized I had not only involved myself in a most unedifying skirmish but had made a potentially dangerous enemy. Shame mingled with consternation and bred incredulity as I tried to work out how I could have allowed my pride to lead me so far astray, but I decided that a full analysis of the disaster could wait. My immediate task was to patch up the damage.

'This conversation does neither of us any credit,' I said tersely, 'and I must apologize for raising such an obviously difficult subject. It was hardly my intention to sabotage what I'd hoped would be a cordial relationship.'

'I've certainly no wish for our relationship to be other than cordial,' said Aysgarth with a primness which I found quite repulsive, 'but I'm not one of your monks, Mr Darrow, and you shouldn't expect me to humour you with unquestioning obedience.'

I felt not only as if he had spat on my olive-branch but as if he had had the impertinence to flagellate me with it. Before I could stop myself I said: 'I assure you, Archdeacon, that if you'd been one of my monks this conversation would have taken a very much more Christian course.' And turning my back on him I rejoined Musgrave and Maitland at the dining-table.

VII

'What on earth was going on between you and Aysgarth?' said Miss Barton-Woods when I was at last alone with her in the drawing-room. 'Mr Musgrave told me the clerical fur was flying "sotto voce" by the window and brotherly love appeared to be conspicuous by its absence!'

I achieved a casual laugh. 'I'm afraid Aysgarth and I made a very clumsy attempt to explore each other's personalities,' I said, 'but no doubt we'll become more adroit in time. I must say, I'm surprised he didn't volunteer to be an army chaplain. He's obviously the sort of priest who enjoys a fight.'

'Isn't the age-limit between twenty-eight and thirty-eight? I think he must be a fraction too old. Philip Wetherall's forty, but he had a military uncle who pulled strings for him as soon as war was declared.'

'The Church has the final word in recommending a man as suitable.' I thought of Charles Ashworth who was now also forty; he had had to slip around the official age-limit, but Charles, a former protégé of Archbishop Lang, had friends in high places.

'In that case I suppose Dr Ottershaw decided that Wetherall could be spared and Aysgarth couldn't,' Miss Barton-Woods was speculating. 'After all, an archdeacon's more important than a country vicar . . . I say, I'm awfully sorry if you found Aysgarth heavy going! I've heard he's occasionally a bit stiff with men – some form of social insecurity, perhaps – but I assure you he can be charming, especially with women.'

'Ah!' I said, wondering if I were now detecting a resemblance between Aysgarth and his benefactor Dr Jardine other than a breathtaking capacity for insolence.

'Of course he's always the soul of propriety,' said Miss Barton-Woods hastily. 'He's devoted to his wife. But sometimes I suspect that beneath that rather prim exterior there lurks a secret hankering for wine, women and song. He adored the dinner-parties at the palace when Dr Jardine was bishop – and Dr Jardine, of course, was famous for his titled ladyfriends and his vintage port.'

'At the risk of sounding insufferably priggish I feel bound to say that an interest in titled ladies and vintage port is best left to laymen.'

Miss Barton-Woods laughed. 'You weren't one of Dr Jardine's admirers?'

'I'm afraid not.'

'Aysgarth hero-worships him, although I don't think they see much of each other now that Jardine's retired to Oxford. They think alike on clerical matters – Aysgarth always supported Jardine against the Archbishop of Canterbury and the High-Church party.'

'Yes, I sensed his antipathy to Anglo-Catholicism when he persistently refused to address me as "Father", referred to priests as parsons and displayed an open contempt for monks.'

'Heavens, how boorish!' exclaimed Miss Barton-Woods, and in her annoyance she turned a most becoming shade of pink. 'I *am* sorry!'

'It's hardly your fault that internecine strife is common between the different wings of the Church!' I retorted, making her laugh again, and the conversation turned to other matters but the memory of my clash with Aysgarth continued to make me feel uncomfortable. It was not the kind of prelude I wanted to my new career in the diocese of Starbridge.

VIII

Miss Barton-Woods had evidently been intrigued by the fact that Aysgarth and I represented different wings of the Church, for when we next met she said tentatively: 'I must admit I find it hard to connect you with Anglo-Catholicism – I'd have thought you'd favour a more austere approach, just as Aysgarth does.'

'I'm austere in my private worship, but public worship is quite a different matter.' I hesitated, not wanting to bore her with a religious polemic, but when I saw she was genuinely interested I said: 'A rich liturgical tradition can play a vital part in providing symbols for truths which can't easily be expressed. In my opinion ritual can make complex truths more accessible – and particularly to people who lack the education to receive truth in the form of complex word-structures. Hence the effectiveness of the Anglo-Catholic slum-priests.'

'But have you always been an Anglo-Catholic?'

'No.' I thought of my father, an agnostic who could only tolerate Sunday worship when it came in the form of an intelligent sermon and the minimum of ritual. Then I remembered my mother, a deeply religious and spiritually gifted woman who had had little interest in organized religion. 'My parents went to church as a concession to middle-class respectability,' I said, 'but they always attended matins, never Communion. As a child I found church-going very boring. I did become more interested in worship when I was introduced to Holy Communion at the time of my confirmation but the ethos of my public school was protestant evangelical and I just couldn't connect this expression of religion with my private "gnosis", the knowledge which I sensed in every fibre of my being but which I couldn't express verbally. It was only when I went up to Cambridge, where there was a variety of churches to choose from, that I discovered Anglo-Catholicism and saw at last how my private "gnosis" could achieve a full, meaningful public expression.'

'Were the Fordites in Cambridgeshire then?'

'They'd just opened the Grantchester house. I used to visit them regularly, and soon I was enrapt by the whole Anglo-Catholic ethos. My hero was Charles Gore – '

'Bishop Gore? He was very important and famous, wasn't he?'

'He was one of the greatest religious leaders of the Church in this century. It was Gore who adapted the Anglo-Catholicism of the Oxford Movement to a more modern era when he enabled it to meet and master biblical criticism, Gore who encouraged young Anglo-Catholic priests to work among the poor, Gore who founded a brotherhood of celibate priests, Gore who seemed, when I was a young man, to have his finger on the pulse of an up-to-date dynamic version of Christianity, Gore who laid the foundations of the twentieth-century Anglo-Catholic tide which is sweeping through the Church of England – ' I had run out of breath. I broke off, recovered myself and laughed. 'But I must stop at once! What a sermon! Forgive me, I'm afraid preaching is a terrible clerical vice.'

'I like good preaching,' said Miss Barton-Woods generously, 'and I've no objection to hearing more about Anglo-Catholicism.'

'But you still doubt that I could convert you!'

'On the contrary, I'm sure you could convert me to anything if you put your mind to it!' she said amused, and I knew I should leave at once before I lost all control and started converting us both to the pleasures of fornication.

It was on the next morning that I received my letter from the Bishop of Starbridge. I had written to him directly after the luncheon-party. I can write very clever letters when I choose and this letter had been exceptionally clever. I had not mentioned Aysgarth.

In his reply Dr Ottershaw declared how delighted he was to hear from me and how he quite understood why I had not presented my compliments to him earlier; naturally I had needed time to adjust to the world after my years in the cloister, and how very wise I was to stay in such a quiet beautiful spot while I was engaged in laying the foundations of my new life. However he would deem it a great honour if I would 'dine and sleep' at the episcopal palace as soon as I felt prepared to venture forth from my rural retreat. 'My wife and I are simple people,' concluded the Bishop modestly, 'so you need not fear being inundated by a tidal wave of worldliness as soon as you cross our threshold. Moreover war-time austerities have forced us to close both wings of the palace and manage with only a few servants, so lavish hospitality, I fear, is very much a thing of the past. Nevertheless I trust we can offer you a quiet, comfortable and possibly not unstimulating evening should you wish to visit us.'

On receipt of this letter I obtained Miss Barton-Woods' permission to use her telephone and rang the Bishop up. Dr Ottershaw was delighted. He sounded exactly like the benevolent holy man which all prelates should be but so few are. I guessed him to be seventy, silver-haired and stout, and when I met him a couple of days later at his episcopal palace I found my guess had not been inaccurate.

I dined at Starbridge on Saturday night. On Sunday I attended the morning services in the Cathedral, but by tea-time I had returned to Starrington Magna and at five o'clock I was walking up the Manor's drive to call on Miss Barton-Woods.

IX

I found her reclining on the drawing-room sofa as she browsed through the unread corners of the Sunday newspapers. Her long legs, clad in the sheerest of silk stockings, were coiled in a manner which displayed her slim ankles to perfection. I belong to a generation which was brought up to regard the occasional flash of a feminine ankle as erotic, and at that moment I found the sight of those two elegant ankles, so generously displayed, almost overpoweringly alluring. She had discarded her shoes in order to put her feet up, and now for the first time I could feast my eyes on her toes which sloped from the inner to the outer edges of her feet with remarkable symmetry. She was wearing a dark blue afternoon frock with a severe cut which emphasized the generous lines of her bosom, flattered her waist and offered tantalizingly veiled vistas of her hips. Her dark hair again emanated its aromatic newly-washed aura of purity, and her skin, radiating that quality which the florid poets call 'the bloom of youth', was worthy of a Shakespearean sonnet. Indeed so banal did any speech not written in blank verse seem at that moment that I had great difficulty in making my opening remark. It was: 'I hope I'm not interrupting.'

'Of course not!' She tossed *The News of the World* casually on to the floor. Miss Barton-Woods ordered all the papers on Sunday. I thought it was magnificently extravagant of her and showed a broad charitable interest in human nature, even the human nature reported so pruriently in the paper she had just discarded. My eye caught the headline: RUNAWAY VICAR: NEW SCANDAL: CHAMBERMAID TELLS ALL.

William was purring around my ankles and I stooped to pick him up. He was not a handsome cat but he had that subtle air of distinction which intelligence always confers.

'I'm glad to report,' I said in response to her eager inquiry, 'that Dr Ottershaw was really most obliging. He saw no difficulty about opening the diocesan coffers, and suggested that I begin work in mid-October as soon as the inevitable bureaucratic details have been sorted out.'

Miss Barton-Woods' pleasure was delectable to behold. 'Wonderful!' she exclaimed. 'So you'll be running the parish until Philip Wetherall comes home from the war!'

'Precisely. Miss Barton-Woods – ' I set down William as carefully as if he were made of bone-china ' – now that I'm no longer a penniless ex-monk but a priest with a respectable stipend, I hope you won't think it too great an impertinence if I tell you how very much I want you to be my wife. Will you marry me?'

She never hesitated. She said simply: 'I thought you'd never ask!' and the next moment we were in each other's arms.

TWELVE

'The psychical man, for St Paul, is the self of our normal experience . . . He may rise to the spiritual man, or he may sink to the carnal man, or, as most of us do, he may fluctuate uneasily between the two.'

W. R. INGE
Dean of St Paul's 1911–1934
Mysticism in Religion

I

There followed an interlude chacterized by fragmented conversation, unfettered exuberance and a succession of embraces so stimulating that I felt no more than thirty-five. My fiancée certainly could have passed for eighteen, but eventually proved sophisticated enough to suggest we might cool our ardour with champagne.

'. . . oh, and Mr Darrow and I are getting married, Portman,' said Anne as an afterthought after giving the order.

The ancient butler, who had been padding away towards the door, stopped dead, revolved slowly to face us and beamed from ear to ear. 'That's very pleasing news, I'm sure, madam,' he said with verve. 'May I offer you my congratulations, sir, and express the wish that you and Miss Barton-Woods will be very happy?'

'Thank you, Portman.' My secret uneasiness with servants meant that I was relieved as well as touched by his sincerity.

When Anne and I eventually drank to the future I was delighted to be reminded that champagne, a beverage which I have rarely encountered during the course of my ministry, tastes very much more intriguing than dry sherry.

'When can we get married?' I said emboldened by my first sip. 'I hope you'll agree that the only possible answer to that question is "soon".'

'As soon as possible,' said Anne, having taken three gulps in rapid succession. With a shudder she added: 'I must tell you everything now. His name was Hugo. We had a long engagement. A huge wedding had been planned at the village church.'

'In that case I'll get a special licence and we can be married at the end of the month. I suggest a plain ceremony at the chapel in front of a handful of close friends.'

Suddenly she began to weep. 'I was putting on my wedding-dress when the letter arrived. It was vile – everything was vile – a cruel horrible nightmare – '

As I took her in my arms I said: 'There's no need to say any more.'

'Oh, but there is!' As she raised her tearstained face to mine I saw the painful honesty in her eyes. 'There's one thing I simply must tell you before we go any further. He – I – ' But the words refused to come. Breaking down she clung to me again and I waited, stroking her hair until she was calmer. Then I said: 'Since he was a fortune-hunter I've no doubt he did everything possible beforehand to get you into his power and secure his future. So of course he would have done his best to break down a door which should never have been opened.'

'So you guessed.' But she was no longer upset; she was only relieved that I could accept the sad truth without expressing either censure or distaste. 'Oh, if only I could describe how *polluted* I felt afterwards when I realized how little I meant to him – '

'Someone you loved breached your trust and treated you with contempt. Naturally you felt polluted – the very centre of your psyche had been laid waste. But from his point of view, what went wrong? Why didn't he go through with it?'

'With my consent he had a meeting with my solicitors before the wedding in order to discuss money, and Mr Musgrave told him that much of my capital's tied up in trust. I hadn't mentioned that; I hadn't thought it mattered. Huge said he had a large private income of his own . . . But he hadn't. He didn't mention money in the letter he wrote me, of course – it was Mr Musgrave who told me later how shattered Hugo had been at the meeting. The letter just said – ' But again she was unable to go on.

'If he had the kind of maimed stunted psyche I suspect he had,' I said, 'he would have made some disparaging remark about the way you demonstrated your love for him, and declared that you could never have made him happy – and of course he would have been right; that kind of deformed psyche is always impossible to please and no woman would ever have satisfied him. Clearly it was he, not you, who failed in the intimate relationship, but by slandering you in such a wicked way he was able to hide from his own inadequacies and run off like a coward to leave you bearing the burden of his failure.' And as she stared, astounded by this radical re-interpretation of her past, I added in my most authoritative voice: 'It's plain he had a hatred of women and you should on no account think ill of yourself just because an emotional cripple made a cruel remark designed to boost his self-esteem.'

Her gratitude was so overwhelming that it was some time before she could speak but at last she whispered obscurely: 'Do you mind?'

'I mind that you suffered. I mind that any man could treat a woman so badly. But I don't mind about you not being a virgin. Love's too important to mar with quibbles about physical technicalities, and as for the moral aspect of the tragedy your repentance is so obviously genuine that no priest would hesitate to grant you absolution.'

She said: 'I love you so much I can hardly bear it,' and struggled again with her tears.

'Bear it,' I said, 'and have another glass of champagne.'

That made her smile, and we sipped in companionable silence until I had summoned the courage to say: 'There's a lot I too must tell you about the past.'

'I hope I shan't feel as intimidated by your first wife as Mrs de Winter felt by Rebecca.'

An interval followed while the reference to Miss Du Maurier's novel had to be explained to the ignorant ex-monk but at last I was sufficiently enlightened to exclaim: 'What a distressing example of marital mis-understanding! Why couldn't he have told the new wife straight away that he'd been so unhappy?'

'I suppose it was guilt – and the fear that she'd be horrified by what he'd done.'

'Ah.' I paused before saying sternly: 'You're on no account to visualize Betty as a goddess on a pedestal!' and after another pause I added: 'Of course I'll tell you all about my marriage one day.'

To my great relief Anne said: 'I'm more interested in Ruth than in Betty – after all, Ruth's the one I'll eventually have to meet. Has she been married long? I suppose if you've got no grandchildren that must mean – '

'I do have grandchildren. Ruth has a son called Colin and a daughter called Janet.'

The inevitable question followed: 'How old are they?'

'Growing up fast.' For several agonizing seconds I wrestled with pride, vanity, shame and sheer fright before I forced myself to add: 'Ruth herself is thirty-six now.'

'*Thirty-six?*' exclaimed Anne amazed.

'Thirty-six.' I drained my glass of champagne. 'I'm afraid – very much afraid – that I'm probably a little older than you suspected. I married at twenty-three Ruth was born a year later. So as far as my age is concerned . . . well, it seems quite fantastic – indeed sometimes – well, fairly often – I can hardly believe it, but in actual fact – well, the truth is – '

'You're sixty. How distinguished! I wouldn't have you a day younger. More champagne?'

Now it was my turn to be overcome with gratitude. Speechless with relief I turned my back on old age and once more pulled her into my arms.

II

Twenty-four hours later I was still wreathed in euphoria but I felt sufficiently composed to communicate with those concerned for my welfare. Deciding to tackle Francis first I wrote:

'You will be aghast to learn that I have proposed to Miss Barton-Woods and we are to be married on October the first. You will also be startled, if not aghast, to learn that I've decided to work here full-time as a curate, and I'm glad to report that when I volunteered my services to the Bishop of Starbridge he couldn't have been more willing to produce a stipend. Let me hasten to add that I'm sure I haven't been called back into the world solely to be a country priest; my true call will no doubt unfold in due course but while I wait it seems better that I should be fully occupied.

'Don't be too cross with me, my dear Francis, because knowing myself as I do I'm convinced that an early marriage is the best safeguard against the error to which I'm particularly prone. Moreover since I have no doubt now that you were right and that I'm being called not only to marry but to marry this particular woman, I see no point in prolonging my celibacy for a day longer than necessary.'

'Allowing myself to relax after the ordeal of informing my spiritual director that I proposed to toss his advice to the winds, I then penned a request to Charles Ashworth. Charles was now stationed with his regiment less than forty miles away on Starbury Plain, and I hoped that he might obtain leave not only to attend my wedding but to conduct it. Anne did not care for the retired canon who had been taking the essential services since the Vicar's departure, and having heard me talk of Charles she was anxious to meet him. There were other priests whom I might have asked to conduct the ceremony, but Charles had a special place in my affections; I often felt that the crisis which I had helped him surmount in 1937 had indissolubly linked us together. He had been the first priest who had sought my help after my arrival in Grantchester, and the absorbing complexity of his case had helped relieve the acute stress which had burdened me as I had struggled to bring my lax community to order.

Having written a long affectionate letter to Charles with ease I was then confronted with the ordeal of breaking the news to my children. My heart was already sinking at the prospect of either of them attending the wedding; I found it all too easy to imagine a nightmare in which Martin arrived drunk while Ruth staged some emotional scene, and I knew I wanted no reminders of my first marriage as I embarked on my second. Could any paternal attitude have been more unworthy of a Christian priest? I thought not, and in a paroxysm of guilt I began the required letter to my daughter. Eventually I produced a communication which read:

'My dearest Ruth: You will be greatly surprised to hear that I am to be married to someone I met at Allington Court. Her name is Anne Barton-Woods. The wedding will be on October the first in the family chapel of the manor house where she lives here at Starrington Magna, and I do hope that you, Roger and the children will be able to attend. I have just been appointed curate of this parish while the Vicar's absent in the Army, so my new life is rapidly taking shape. As for Miss Barton-Woods, she is a woman of your own generation, a fact which encourages me to hope that in due course you will become friends. Meanwhile I send you my love and blessing, and in assuring you that you're always in my prayers I remain your devoted father, J.D.'

I sent a copy of this letter, amended where appropriate, to Martin and tried to suppress the hope that neither he nor Ruth would find the invitation irresistible.

The first response to all this arduous letter-writing came in the form of a wire which read: DELIGHTED BY YOUR NEWS FLATTERED BY YOUR REQUEST HONOURED TO ACCEPT EAGER TO SEE YOU MANY CONGRATULATIONS CHARLES.

In contrast to this happy communication Ruth wrote: 'Darling Daddy, I have just received your rather worrying letter. Of course I wish you every happiness but I can't help wondering if you're being wise in rushing into marriage with a girl half your age whom you've only known for a few weeks. It's none of my business and I wouldn't dream of criticizing you, but it does all seem a little undignified, and I do feel it's my duty as your daughter to point out that there are plenty of people less loyal to you than I am who will make some very snide remarks behind your back. In fact speaking as one who loves you I feel bound to say that in my opinion a man of your age should approach marriage with the greatest caution – if indeed he should approach it at all. Yours in deepest love and concern, RUTH. P.S. Thank you for the invitation to the wedding, but in the circumstances I think it would be less awkward for Miss Barton-Woods if we didn't accept. I'm sure she wouldn't want to be reminded on her wedding-day that she's marrying a grandparent who's old enough to be her father.'

I wondered if Martin would write a letter which was equally unspeakable, but to my relief he failed to reply.

However Francis was hardly the man to abandon me to my fate without comment. He took longer to respond than Ruth but I knew the delay arose because he had been praying and meditating on the problems I had posed him. Finally he wrote: 'My dear Jon: Did I really expect you to wait until you had been in the world for six months? Probably not. But I felt I had to set you a goal, even if it proved to be a goal which you chose to repudiate. You would not have respected me, I think, if I had murmured indulgently: "Yes, yes – marry the lady tomorrow!" and you would not respect me now if I were to respond to your news by writing: "Bless you, my friend – run off and live happily ever after!" But before I start making you uncomfortable, let me congratulate you on abandoning your earlier conviction that you should live the rest of your life as a celibate. I myself have always been convinced that despite your sad past you should live in the world as a married man, and therefore I'm delighted that you've coaxed an apparently sympathetic, compatible woman to promise to accompany you to the altar.

'My main anxiety – and this is where I start to make you uncomfortable – is not that you're rushing to the altar in such haste. I think you're being precipitate, certainly, but after all you're a man of considerable experience and you should be granted at least some liberty to act with an incisiveness which in a young man would deserve the description "hot-headed folly". No, my main anxiety is that you may be busy glossing over all the difficulties which inevitably surround your situation. I'm just an ignorant old bachelor, of course, but I seem to remember hearing somewhere that a honeymoon can be a time of profound disillusionment if either partner has failed to be as honest as the rules of the game require.

'Let me complete your discomfort by asking you a series of questions: (1) Have you talked frankly to your fiancée about why your marriage went so wrong that you felt you could never marry again? (2) Have you explained why the subject of parenthood is peculiarly painful to you? (3) Have you even discussed the subject of parenthood? (4) Have you made any attempt to describe Ruth and Martin in terms which bear at least a passing resemblance to reality? (5) Have you talked to your fiancée in detail about your spiritual needs so that she has a true idea of the amount of time you devote daily to prayer, meditation and devotional reading? (6) Have you warned her that in order to satisfy your spiritual needs you're obliged to spend much time being what the world deems unsociable? (7) Have you discussed the contribution she might make to your work in the parish? (8) Will she in fact be able to give you the support you need when she's busy running her estate? (9) How are you going to resolve the conflict arising from the fact that you belong to different wings of the Church of England? (10) Have you had a frank converstaion with her about money? (11) Have you had a conversation with her, frank or otherwise, about marital intimacy, a matter which could create grave difficulties if the emotional damage proves hard to heal? (12) Have you in truth paused long enough to imagine what this marriage will really be like, or are you at present only capable of imagining how charming Miss Barton-Woods will look in her night-gown? (13) –

'But no. Twelve awkward questions are quite enough, and meanwhile I trust I've made my point: when one's in love one's instinct is to present oneself in the best possible light, but I can't counsel you too strongly to present yourself "warts and all" to Miss Barton-Woods at the earliest opportunity. But perhaps you've already done so. In which case I humbly beg your pardon and offer you my sincere congratulations.

'There's a great deal I could say to you about your sinister acquisition of the curacy, but I'd prefer to explore the spiritual dimensions of this when we meet – and I trust we can meet soon. You will, of course, be as keenly aware as I am that there's much you need to discuss before the wedding, so I beg you to write by return to suggest a date for your visit. Meanwhile . . .' And he concluded with the formal reference to prayers and blessings before signing himself my devoted friend and brother in Christ.

I could not help thinking that this letter was a masterly example of how to conceal rampant disapproval beneath a diplomatic expression of trenchant common sense. Indeed it took me some hours to rouse myself from my admiration but at last I composed a reply which read:

'My dear Francis: As usual you've given me excellent advice and I must thank you for it. I must also thank you for your support of my decision to marry. In the circumstances I regard this as very generous.

'I find your reference to the curacy somewhat strange. I hardly think the spiritual dimensions of its acquisition are so pregnant with menace that I need to be hauled immediately to London! In fact it's extremely difficult for me to get away at present as there's so much to do before the wedding, and indeed I may be obliged to postpone my next visit to you until after the honeymoon. However please don't think I intend to approach my wedding in a murky spiritual state; Starwater Abbey's no more than fifteen miles from here, and I shall see Cyril soon to make my confession.

'May I thank you again for your letter and repeat how much I value your advice.'

I did not expect a swift reply, but Francis, meticulous as ever in his pastoral care, wrote back promptly: 'My dear Jon: So be it! But may I leave you with two more questions to consider during your very limited spare time? (1) What was your exact motive for seeking this curacy, and (2) precisely how did you obtain it? The second question is the interesting one, of course; I fear the answer to the first is painfully obvious. As a churchman experienced in financial matters I can only regard your success in coaxing the Bishop to produce a stipend out of thin air as miraculous – in fact I'd have been less surprised if you'd told me that he'd produced six white rabbits out of his lawn-sleeves! Of course we all know that dear old Ottershaw, like our own late Abbot James, finds it almost impossible to say no to anyone, but nevertheless I can't help thinking that this latest triumph of yours puts even stopping watches in the shade. My dear Jon, beware of those "glamorous powers"! Once you start twisting bishops around your little finger you stand at the top of a very slippery slope indeed, so step back from the brink, I beg of you, by reminding yourself of the truth no priest can afford to forget: we're here to serve God, not ourselves.'

I sat thinking about this letter for a long time. Then I wrote to Abbot Cyril to suggest a date when I could visit Starwater to make my confession.

III

'I'm rather worried about all these Anglo-Catholic habits of yours,' confessed Anne when I told her of my decision to visit Starwater, and in a rush she added: 'Are you secretly cross because I don't want to go to confession too?'

'Good heavens, no! Anyway, you've made your confession – to me. And even if you hadn't you have a perfect right, as a member of the Church of England, to abstain from confession to a priest.'

'Yes, but since you're always doing it – '

'My case is quite different from yours. I've spent many years living in an environment where a weekly confession was built into the structure of my spiritual life, and in returning to the world I'm certain to have problems which could lead to spiritual debility unless they're regularly aired with someone skilled in giving advice.'

I paused. We were in the chapel some hours after I had received Francis' second letter. I had been working on the new altar-table, and Anne, arriving home from the estate-office, had walked through the grounds to exchange news with me before I returned to the village for my evening meal. We were now sitting hand in hand in the front pew.

'Anne, talking of confessions – ' I stopped, took a deep breath and began again. 'Talking of confessions I really must tell you all about Betty and my children,' I said with commendable determination, but then found to my horror that I was unable to continue. This ordeal was much worse than merely confessing my age, and as Anne waited, the model of patience and tact, I realized that part of my difficulty lay in the fact that I could not discuss Betty frankly without referring to the one subject on which Anne was so painfully sensitive; it would hardly be good for either her morale or my honeymoon prospects if I were now to reveal that her predecessor's 'forte' had been sexual intercourse.

In panic I scraped together a few pale platitudes. 'It was a typical romance of youth,' I said. 'I was attracted by her looks but in fact we were utterly mismatched and made each other very miserable. I did my best to be a good husband – ' The terrible half-truths ran on and on ' – but life was difficult. One of the reasons why it was difficult was because – ' I reached for the whole truth but knew it was going to slither through my hands; I was too afraid she might think me an Anglo-Catholic fanatic ' – was because I need a certain amount of time alone for prayer and meditation and devotional reading, and Betty could neither understand nor accept that.' I hesitated, knowing I should specify the amount of time I needed, but the next moment my voice was saying: 'However the situation was eased when I felt called to serve at sea.' I told myself I really could not let the lie about a call pass. But I did. I was too frightened of being judged a deserting husband who had walked out on his loving wife.

'Once I was no longer at home all the time we got on much better,' said my voice with despicable glibness. 'It was a case of "absence makes the heart grow fonder". However nothing could change the fact that the marriage produced tensions which interfered with my spiritual life, and when Betty died I knew I could serve God best as an unmarried man. I wanted to be a monk straight away but of course I had to stay in the world to provide for my children.' Too late I corrected myself by saying: 'To care for my children.' Sweat prickled the nape of my neck. I dared not look at her. 'However when they were grown up and going their own way in the world – ' I told myself I really could not gloss over my difficult years as a widower. But I did. I was terrified that she might recoil when she heard how I had not only failed to live as a priest should but had even jilted the woman who loved me. ' – when my children no longer needed me, I joined the Fordites. For years I remained convinced that I should be celibate, but recently when I was called to leave the Order I realized that my marital unhappiness had arisen not because I was unsuited to marriage but because I'd married the wrong woman when I was too young to know better.'

I told myself I could go no further, but in my imagination Father Darcy was looking at me with contempt and at last my pride came to my rescue. I really could not allow myself to be such a coward. Making a mighty effort I said: 'That's not much of a confession. The truth's far darker than that. I was haunted by guilt that I couldn't love Betty as she loved me and I conceived of becoming a monk as a form of atonement. Later I did fall in love but I rejected the woman by entering the Order. I've done appalling things, Anne. I hurt my wife. I hurt my – ' Balking at the word 'mistress' I grabbed a term which in my youth had been capable of an innocent meaning ' – my lover. And of course I hurt my – ' But at that point cowardice reclaimed me. My courage was exhausted and I could not utter the word 'children'.

In the silence which followed, Anne's fingers intertwined comfortingly with mine and I felt so grateful for her silent sympathy that a few shreds of my courage rose phoenic-like from the ashes. Remembering Francis' letter I resolved to embark on a realistic description of Ruth and Martin.

'Of course my difficulties have affected my children,' I said in a resolute voice, the voice of a man determined to tell the truth, the whole truth and nothing but the truth, 'and they've been through certain awkward times. But I couldn't wish for a more devoted son and daughter and I really am tremendously proud of them. I know Ruth's being silly about the wedding, but she's only acting out of a misguided concern for my welfare. And I know Martin should have replied to my letter by now, but I can only conclude that for some reason he hasn't received it. Martin always replies to my letters – and replies very amusingly too, I might add. He's got an excellent sense of humour, and women always seem to find him very attractive and charming.'

I stopped speaking, and gradually as the silence lengthened I became aware that I was staring at Anne's engagement ring, a Victorian circle of gold set with garnets, which I had bought at a small jeweller's shop in Starbridge. The ring was so pretty that I had not felt ashamed that it was cheap, and at the time of the purchase I had thought the garnets symbolized the fire of love. Now I was aware only that they were the colour of blood. I felt as if I were suffering some profound haemorrhage.

'Darling!' said Anne warmly, and suddenly the garnets flashed past my eyes as she slipped her arms around my neck. 'How lucky your children are to have a father who obviously cares so much for them!'

Shame nearly annihilated me. 'Anne, I really can't let you believe . . . you really must understand that I . . . I mean, I can't possibly let this conversation end without stressing my terrible faults and weaknesses – '

'Silly man, I don't expect you to be a saint!'

'But I have such crippling peculiarities – '

'My dear Jon, if I'd wanted to marry the dead-norm of English manhood, would I have looked twice at anyone who'd just spent seventeen years being a monk?'

'But maybe you'd be a great deal happier with the dead-norm of English manhood – '

'Absolutely not! It was a man claiming to be the dead-norm of English manhood who jilted me! Now stop agonizing about yourself in this morbid fashion and come up to the house for a drink before you sail back to your doting post-mistress – I think you need a very stiff sherry to set you back on the rails of optimism . . .'

IV

That night I reflected for a long time on this harrowing conversation with Anne but eventually I told myself it was neither possible nor desirable to attain an absolute honesty in a single interview. There was too much emotional constraint on my side and too much emotional vulnerability on hers. To subject her to a single prolonged and inevitably turgid confession of my failures would only upset her, and it seemed to me that I had a moral duty not to strain her love by wallowing self-indulgently in guilt. 'Stop agonizing about yourself in this morbid fashion,' she had said, and I was neither so stupid nor so insensitive that I could not detect her antipathy. Women, I knew, did not like self-indulgent wallowing. It filled them with impatience and contempt.

'Thank God your father's not the complaining sort,' said my mother in my memory. 'I can't abide men who moan and groan.'

'You won't believe this,' said my father to me lightly, years after her death, 'but because I was so much older than your mother I was always haunted by the dread that she might find me an elderly bore. Silly of me, wasn't it? Of course she was as devoted to me as I was to her, I can see that now, but I always guarded my tongue to ensure we never exchanged a cross word – with the result that despite the differences in our age and rank we were able to live happily ever after, as of course you remember.'

I shuddered suddenly, then cast the memory aside, but that night I dreamt that William the tabby-cat had disappeared, abandoning those who loved him to a hell of loneliness and desolation, and my mother was saying severely: 'You've no one to blame but yourself. You shouldn't have moaned and groaned about your past like that,' while my father said urgently: 'Guard your tongue. Never exchange a cross word. Never complain.'

I awoke sweating in the dark.

After a long while I repeated to myself that I would, of course, tell Anne everything; it was unthinkable that I should even consider not telling her everything; but I would not tell her everything just yet. The revelations had to be made little by little at carefully judged intervals, and meanwhile a long healing silence seemed called for.

Drifting back into sleep I found to my relief that William was purring peacefully in my arms.

V

The next morning I forced myself to reread Francis' letter in order to confirm that I had addressed myself to all of the many problems he had listed.

I had dealt with question (1), my unhappiness with Betty. The subject of parenthood, which had occupied questions (2), (3) and (4), would have to wait. I examined question (5). Had I talked to my fiancée in detail about my spiritual needs? No, but I had made it plain that I required time to satisfy them and Anne had appeared to accept this without complaint; after all, unlike Betty she had her work to occupy her and would not expect my undivided attention twenty-four hours a day. Had I warned her that my spiritual needs often made me unsociable? No, but that was of no consequence since Anne was hardly a social butterfly, cramming her calendar with frivolous engagements. Had we discussed the contribution she might make to my work in the parish? No, but I had already decided that the nature of her contribution should be given time to evolve; I had no wish to burden her immediately with parish matters when her war-work was so important. Nevertheless, in answer to question (8), I felt confident that she would eventually support me to the best of her ability, just as a good wife should.

How was I going to resolve the conflict arising from the fact that we belonged to different wings of the Church? There was no conflict. She was willing to learn about Anglo-Catholicism and eventually I would educate her to share my point of view.

Had I had a frank discussion with her about money? No, but what was there to say? She would manage her money and I would manage mine and naturally I would not dream of interfering in her financial affairs. Had I had a conversation with her about intimacy? Yes, and further conversation would at this stage be inappropriate. Any sexual problems could be sorted out on the honeymoon. Had I paused long enough to imagine what this marriage would really be like or was I at present only capable of imagining how charming Anne would look in her nightgown? How impertinent! But Francis had merely been trying to needle me into confronting the difficulties, and now that I had indeed confronted them this final question did not require a serious answer.

Deciding that I had made a tolerable, if not entirely perfect, response to my spiritual director's interrogation, I happily began to count the hours which separated me from my first glimpse of Anne's nightgown.

VI

On the afternoon before the wedding all four Ashworths arrived, accompanied by the children's nanny. Realizing how much I wanted to see Charles Anne had insisted that they be invited to dine and sleep at the Manor, and when I reminded her that such an offer would compel us to abandon the tradition that the bride and groom should not meet on the night before the wedding she displayed an admirable contempt for superstition. So the matter was settled, much to my delight, and I began to look forward to the luxury of a long talk with Charles.

When I saw him again I felt I was being granted a new insight into the misguided but all-too-human weakness which had led Father Darcy to keep Francis by his side in London. How delightful it was to have a friend twenty years one's junior who so exactly fulfilled one's specifications of the ideal son! Charles had his faults; as his spiritual director I knew that better than anyone, but he was an able priest, a loyal husband and a devoted father – all the things Martin would never be – and there were times when I was tempted to jettison the detachment which made me so successful as a counsellor and manifest a paternal affection. But that would have been unforgivable. It was my detachment which made me valuable to Charles as he wrestled with his problems; he needed a spiritual director, not a father, and besides I was quite astute enough to see that my paternal impulse was primarily selfish, springing not from an altruistic desire to benefit Charles but from an urge to compensate myself for the agony of Martin's shortcomings.

All those thoughts passed through my mind as we greeted the Ashworths and showed them into the drawing-room, but at last I roused myself sufficiently to hear Charles say to Anne: 'I can't tell you how grateful I am for your invitation! It's hard to brave a hotel with two children under three, and although Lyle suggested leaving the boys behind in Cambridge with Nanny I hated the thought of missing them when I had leave.' He added that although he had considered the idea that they might all stay with a local acquaintance of his, a doctor who lived in the village of Starvale St James, the doctor's wife was unfortunately not the most hospitable of women.

'Is that Dr Romaine?' said Anne interested. 'I've never met him but one of my friends is always saying how wonderful he is with mothers and babies.' And as the inevitable comments followed about what a small world it was I saw Charles had put her at ease. One of Charles' gifts – a very useful one for a clergyman – was his ability to be immediately and effortlessly charming to people from all walks of life.

Later I took Charles down to the chapel and after he had expressed the most gratifying admiration we settled down in one of the pews for our talk. I had no wish to compromise my detachment by disclosing too much personal information, but of course I had to tell him how I had met Anne, particularly when he pressed me for details. However I somehow restrained myself from talking about my vision. My role in Charles' life was not to burden him with my spiritual problems – nor to enthral him with my spiritual challenges – but to help him along his own spiritual way.

'I realize now how much I've missed our regular meetings at

Grantchester,' he said after we had discussed his problems. 'And what a relief it is to find you still as rational and serene as ever despite all the turmoil you must have gone through! In fact one of the things I most admire about you, Father, is that you never seem to have any serious difficulties – or if you do you apparently always have the strength and wisdom to overcome them without effort.'

'My dear Charles!' I shall never cease to be amazed by how imperfectly we are known even by those closest to us. 'You're very flattering, but I hardly think Father Ingram would recognize me from that description!'

'That's the new Abbot-General, isn't it? I hear he's a Cambridge man – did he read theology?'

'No, French novels and Oscar Wilde,' I said, making him laugh, and began to talk about Francis' rise to monastic power from such remarkably inauspicious beginnings.

To my delight the dinner-party that evening proved a most happy occasion apart from one incident which revealed a tension which no doubt the Ashworths would have preferred to conceal. Halfway through the last course the elder boy pitter-pattered into the room in search of entertainment and both his parents gave exclamations of dismay.

'Why aren't you asleep?' demanded Lyle, but the little boy, ignoring her, ran straight to Charles and scrambled up on to his knees.

'He says he feels sick.'

'He's always saying that. It's his new ploy to get attention. Come along, Charley – back to bed – '

'No!' cried the child, and hid his face in Charles' jacket.

Lyle, whose normal manner was one of cool confidence, suddenly became ruffled. 'Stop being so naughty this instant! There's Michael upstairs, fast asleep, good as gold – '

As the child screamed with rage Charles exclaimed: 'Stop throwing Michael's name in his face! Can't you see he hates it?'

'Well, I hate him misbahaving! He plays up to you, Charles – he knows perfectly well you're as soft as butter with him – '

'Who's as soft as butter with Michael?'

I stood up to terminate this disturbingly abrasive exchange, and moving over to the child I began to stroke his hair.

He looked at me in surprise. Unlike Michael, who was the kind of infant guaranteed to excite much admiration, Charley was a plain child who was probably unused to special attention from strangers. His sullen mouth hinted at a termperamental nature but his eyes, bright now with unshed tears, reflected his intelligence and I could sense his little thoughts flashing anxiously hither and thither as he tried to understand what I wanted. Very gently I enfolded his mind with my own, and a second later he was stretching out his arms towards me.

'Well!' said Lyle, sufficiently astonished to forget her tension. 'I've never seen him respond to a stranger like that before!'

I picked the child up and he relaxed against my chest with a sigh. Stroking his hair again I was acutely aware of Anne's enrapt admiration and I was also acutely aware that I enjoyed it.

'You're going to sleep now, Charley,' I said. 'You're tired, very tired, so tired that your eyelids feel heavy.'

His eyelids promptly drooped over his pale brown eyes. His thumb rose to his mouth. He was at peace.

'Well!' said Lyle again, matching Anne's admiration. 'That's the kind of magic I wish I could bottle and take home!'

She came with me upstairs to put him to bed, and when we had tiptoed from the room she said: 'Thanks – that was amazing.' For a moment I thought she had no intention of saying anything else but then she blurted out: 'I'm sorry I got so irritated but I feel under frightful strain at the moment.'

I assured her in my most neutral voice that there was no need for her to apologize, but with a sinking heart I realized she was unable to resist the urge to confide.

'I'm just no good without Charles,' she said. 'I get so depressed, so afraid – and don't tell me I'm just one woman among thousands with husbands in the Army and that we all have to make sacrifices in war-time; that sort of platitude does no good at all.'

'Then what exactly do you want me to tell you, Lyle?'

She stopped at the top of the stairs. 'Tell me it's not all some ghastly punishment.'

'It's not all some ghastly punishment. War-time life is simply a difficult challenge which you must surmount as best you can. Don't you have any friends in Cambridge?'

'They're all *his* friends, and anyway all the nice men are away and all the women are absolute cats – '

'Then if you have no friends to offer support, you must turn to your family. I know you have no family of your own, but Charles has parents to whom he's devoted – why don't you take a house near them in Epsom?'

'Charles doesn't know this, but his mother and I can't stand each other.'

'Why doesn't Charles know? Why haven't you discussed such an unfortunate problem with him?'

'I'm afraid of him being upset. I'm afraid he'll stop loving me. If Charles stopped loving me I think I'd kill myself – I'd feel so worthless, so contemptible, so – '

'There's no need to resort to talk of suicide – I can hear what you're trying to say. You need someone who'll blot out those feelings of worthlessness by making you feel cherished and special.'

'But there's no one.' The tears started to fall. 'No one, I swear it. No one except Charles.'

I regarded her in silence as she found a handkerchief and dabbed her eyes daintily. Then I said: 'The real solution is to exorcize that guilt which is giving you these unbearable feelings of worthlessness. You should go to seek help from Dame Veronica again.'

'I can't. She dislikes me.' More tears fell. '*You're* the only one who can help because you're magic and you always know all the answers.'

I sighed, partly because she was exasperating me, partly because I felt sorry for Charles being burdened with such a troubled wife and partly because I did feel a genuine compassion for her in her misery. Abruptly I said: 'You need a sympathetic older man who'll offer you a platonic paternal friendship. Try Dr Romaine. He'd do anything for Charles.' And without giving her time to reply I strode away downstairs to the dining-room.

At the end of the meal when the ladies had retired Charles said to me: 'I'm sorry Lyle and I clashed over Charley like that, but as I warned you earlier at the chapel she's under great strain. What a pity it is that she and my mother don't get on! I'd feel much happier if Lyle could take a house in Epsom.'

'I quite see it's the most difficult problem.'

'To tell you the truth – and I didn't mention this earlier because I don't see how it can ever come to pass – I think the perfect solution would be for her to take a house near Starvale St James She likes Alan, and – '

' – and Dr Romaine would be so pleased to look after her for you! What a splendid idea!'

'Yes, but you can imagine the difficulties – my parents would be angry – they'd feel slighted – there'd be jealousy, sulks, barbed remarks – '

I could endure his torment no longer, and taking a deep breath I prepared to plunge through his confusion to rescue him. 'Charles,' I said firmly, 'your first duty is to your wife. Your parents must come second, and if they start to make a fuss you must be tough with them. I know how hard it is for you to be tough with your parents, but you should take the line that while you're fighting for your country you need their unqualified support. That's the kind of language your father at least will understand.'

Charles actually sagged in his chair with relief. 'You're right, of course,' he said. 'I can see you're right. Yes, that's the line to take.' He began to look cheered. 'I'll write to Alan tomorrow.'

'Before you do that, follow the advice I gave you earlier at the chapel and have an honest conversation with Lyle about your mother. I can't stress to you how important it is that a husband and wife should feel able to confide in each other on even the most difficult subjects.'

Immediately Father Darcy's voice exclaimed in my imagination:

'"Physician, heal thyself!"' but I pretended not to hear. Once again Charles had miraculously diverted me from my own problems, and besides . . .

I hardly wanted to think of Father Darcy on the night before my wedding.

VII

After the Ashworths had retired to bed Anne came outside to see me off. 'I like Charles,' she said. 'I feel he's got great integrity underneath that glossy exterior, but I'm not so sure about Lyle. I think she could be a bit of a siren.'

This astute remark prompted me to wonder how my body had ever judged Lyle worthy of an automatic sexual response. How disturbed I must have been! As I now compared Lyle's small slim figure with Anne's generous, even queenly curves, I felt as if I were comparing a common garden sparrow with a golden eagle.

'. . . and what a way you have with children!' Anne was exclaiming. 'You were amazing with that little boy!'

I opened my mouth to reply: 'It was a parlour-trick. I did it to impress you,' but the words which emerged were: 'When I stroked him he reminded me of a cat.'

'Funny little boy, what a pity he's so plain – but oh Jon, that baby! Isn't he adorable? I looked at him and thought . . . wondered . . .' She hesitated, but by the time I said: 'Yes,' she was already adding in a rush: 'It's strange because I've never been particularly maternal. Perhaps I felt I didn't dare be maternal so long as I was unmarried – but now . . . Oh Jon, I do so hope – '

'Of course you do,' I said, and a second later my tongue was dutifully wrapping itself around the words she wanted to hear. 'So do I.'

A prolonged embrace took place during which my mind was entirely occupied with picturing the consummation of our marriage. When I next spoke I only said: 'You're not worried about tomorrow night, are you?' and she answered with a touching simplicity: 'No, because you'll make everything come right.'

For a brief moment I thought of Whitby, purring in absolute trust as he waited to be healed. Then the curtain came down over my memory, and giving Anne one last kiss I walked away down the drive to the village.

VIII

I had resolved to hold a service of Holy Communion the next morning, but I had asked Charles if he would be the celebrant in order that Anne and I might kneel together at the altar-rail. The three of us met at the chapel at eight. Lyle, to my relief, had chosen not to attend, although whether this was because she had no desire to communicate or because she was sensitive enough to realize that I wanted to be on my own with Anne before a priest at such a special time, I could not determine.

Charles performed his part with an unpretentious dignity which impressed me; I had never before seen him going about his work. Outside the sun was shining, and within the walls of the chapel I could sense in the extreme stillness the underlying unity of all things.

We were married at noon. In her desire that the occasion should be as unlike her ruined wedding-day as possible Anne had wanted the minimum of witnesses, so the majority of her acquaintances had been excluded. However her aunt Miss Fielding came and so did the neighbouring Maitlands who had known Anne all her life. Mr Musgrave the solicitor and Mr Dawson, who helped Anne run the estate, completed the bride's guest-list. I had not heard from Martin and did not expect him to appear, so in the absence of my family I issued a handful of invitations to members of the local church. I invited Mrs Wetherall, the wife of the absent vicar; I also invited the Bishop and his wife, although they were unable to attend, and finally I invited the Aysgarths. I felt Aysgarth could hardly trample on a second proffered olive-branch, and when he accepted my invitation with civility I hoped that my peacemaking efforts would bear fruit in future.

There were also a number of other onlookers at the wedding; in accordance with Anne's wishes the indoor servants and the two gardeners trooped into the back pews with their spouses and offspring.

I wore my clerical suit. Anne, shying away from any costume which resembled a wedding-gown, wore a bright blue frock. Colonel Maitland gave the bride away and Charles conducted the service as admirably as he had celebrated mass. Although Anne had rejected most of the music traditionally associated with weddings, Mrs Maitland played the piano (transferred from the house to replace the defunct organ) as we all sang the Twenty-Third Psalm, and at that point the simplicity of the ceremony moved me. I was reminded of the services I had conducted in the Navy during the War when the well-worn phrases of the Prayer-Book, recited in an unorthdox environment, had acquired a fresh meaning.

Finally the moment came, and glancing up at the north window I thought of the light I had seen in my vision. Then I put the ring on Anne's finger and became, after twenty-eight turbulent years as a widower, once more a married man.

PART THREE

THE FALSE LIGHT

'We must beware of what the "Theologia Germanica" calls the false light. "The Devil hath his contemplatives as God hath his . . ." '

' "If a man seeks the good life for any reason outside itself," says Plotinus, "it is not the good life that he seeks." '

W. R. INGE
Dean of St Paul's 1911–1934
Mysticism in Religion

THIRTEEN

'Next, faith-healing is very much entangled with sacerdotal magic; and as no suggestion is more potent than that which is reinforced by religion, some of the most striking cures which have been reported are connected with alleged miraculous powers.'

W. R. INGE
Dean of St Paul's 1911–1934
Lay Thoughts of a Dean

I

We gave our guests as lavish a luncheon as war-time austerities permitted, and departed from the Manor at three o'clock when the chauffeur drove us to Starbridge. I was determined not to travel far on the first night. I entirely disapprove of couples who begin their marriage drained by weeks of increasing tension, debilitated by gluttony at the reception and demolished by a long journey in the opening hours of the honeymoon.

I had booked a room with an adjoining bathroom at the Crusader, the most comfortable hotel in Starbridge. I still had no money of my own, but when I had recently opened a bank account in the city the bank manager had had no trouble persuading himself that he should be obliging to a priest who gave the Bishop's name as a reference. Anne had offered to contribute to the cost of the honeymoon but I had refused. Years of bringing up a family on a modest clerical stipend had taught me how to make a little money go a long way, and although I deemed it essential to spend lavishly on the all-important first night I had made more modest arrangements for the remainder of the honeymoon.

As soon as we had been shown to our luxurious chamber I took Anne in my arms, kissed her and said: 'I don't want to wait a moment longer.'

She seemed to find this statement eminently reasonable.

We went to bed.

II

At the risk of sounding calculating I must confess that I had spent much time plotting the opening manoeuvres of my honeymoon, and I had come to the practical if unromantic conclusion that my first task was to attend not to Anne's nerves but to my own. To put the matter bluntly, one cannot rescue the maiden in distress unless one's rescue equipment is in working order, and although the evidence suggested that advancing years and a celibate life had not resulted in a fatal atrophy I was still haunted by the knowledge that I was a sixty-year-old man who had not been intimate with a woman for seventeen years. Impotence, that dread state, is so often born not in the body but in the mind, and my mind, chaotic with passion and anxiety as soon as the blind was drawn, was at that moment hardly an example of masterly self-control.

I tried to concentrate on essential matters. I let her keep on her petticoat, first because she made no move to take it off and second because I thought she might be more inclined to relax behind some camouflage; her nakedness was a non-essential delight which could be saved for later. I myself took off all my clothes but that was for utilitarian purposes. I wanted nothing to obstruct my movements or mar my concentration.

It was essential, I considered, that we should be in a sensual environment so I was relieved to discover that the double-bed was wickedly soft while the linen sheets were voluptuously smooth. So far so good. It was also good that Anne was willing – shy, anxious but willing; I had been afraid of a last-minute panic. I wondered whether I should murmur something soothing in order to encourage the willingness and damp down the anxiety, but I was too afraid that words could only be banal in such circumstances so I remained silent.

As I began to kiss her I became aware that I was sweating. That worried me. Honest sweat has its place in the human condition but that place is not, I fear, between the sumptuous sheets of a double-bed on the first night of a honeymoon. I started to wonder feverishly about strokes and heart attacks, but managed to convince myself that hypochrondria, like Anne's nakedness, was merely a non-essential refinement which could be saved for later.

By this time I had obtained the only physical reaction which was of any importance but before I could savour my relief I found myself plunged into the anxiety that I might be incompetent. The anxiety was heightened by the fact that I was now confronting the difficulty of consummating the marriage without causing pain; Anne's virginity might be non-existent but I was sure her bad memories were doubling by the second. I tried to stroke her soothingly but the next moment I realized I was dicing with disaster by attempting a postponement, and after seventeen years of celibacy I was in no position to dice with anything. I pressed on. My psyche was reeling as if it were punch-drunk. Emotion roared through my body like a tidal wave.

To my relief Anne continued to cling to me but she was so tense that I knew I must be hurting her. Deeply troubled I paused, trying to decide how I might best help her relax, but when she moved, unnerved by my stillness and wanting, I knew, only to please me by an active response, the moment came and the wave broke. I had been inside her for no more than a dozen seconds.

I kissed her, rolled on to my back, stared up at the ceiling, thanked God that the marriage was at least consummated, and realized I was exhausted. I would have felt happy but I was too worried about Anne. Rolling over towards her again I gathered her in my arms and told her how much she was loved.

She said in a small voice: 'But I wasn't much good, was I?'

'Don't steal my lines – and don't talk as if you're a performing seal at a circus! We're here to love each other, not to bring an audience cheering to its feet.'

She smiled. Using my last particle of strength I smiled back, kissed her again and sank like a stone into oblivion.

III

I awoke when the scars on my back began to tingle. For one confused moment I thought I was back in the London punishment cell, and shouting: 'No!' at the top of my voice I sat bolt upright in bed.

Anne, who had been caressing the scars with her forefinger, gasped in fright and at once I pulled her into my arms. Then I waited for her to ask about the scars. Betty would have asked. Hilda would have asked. Every other woman I had ever known except my mother would have asked, but Anne was silent and suddenly my good fortune overwhelmed me. I had waited sixty years for the right woman and finally I had found her. It seemed almost too good to be true. Perhaps it was indeed too good to be true. Perhaps it would all end in disaster. Perhaps –

'Anne, don't leave me.'

'Don't *what*?' Anne was justifiably astounded by this idiocy, but although I struggled to pull myself together I could only tighten my clasp and remain silent.

'Silly man!' said Anne at last, wisely deciding to gloss over my insanity by adopting a brisk practical manner. 'What an extraordinary thing to say!' And when she stroked my hair to soothe me I belatedly remembered that I was supposed to be soothing her.

Propping myself on one elbow I said firmly: 'Don't worry about anything. What happened just now was a mere handshake. The real dialogue has yet to begin, but there's no rush. We'll let it develop at its own pace.'

I saw her relax. No threatening demands were being made; our marital relationship would evolve steadily; there was plenty of time.

'I'll be all right in the end, won't I?' she said, touching in her vulnerability.

'We'll both be all right,' I said with all the confidence at my command, and when she smiled at me in relief I felt sure I could ring down the curtain on her past as successfully as I had rung down the curtain on my own.

IV

After this bout of arrogance had lured me into underestimating the problem some time elapsed before I realized that Anne's liberation from her past was going to prove more difficult than I had anticipated. Perhaps I was too busy weaving my new experience into the fabric of my life; I found myself thinking often of the Order, of the difficult days which had resulted in spiritual growth, and I felt glad that I could still recall my years as a monk without any sense of time wasted. My monastic experience had made me the man I was and that man was the man Anne loved. I wondered if she would have loved the unhappy priest who had jilted Hilda, and thought not.

I remembered my past with Betty too and wondered if the scars on my psyche would be finally cauterized by my new marriage or whether they would always remain, like the scars on my back, to remind me of past suffering. However such speculation was difficult, reminding me that I had not been honest with Anne about my children, and soon I gave way to the urge to consign all thought of my first marriage to the very back of my mind.

On the morning after our wedding we departed by train for Dorset where we were received at our small, modest but not uncomfortable inn (recommended by Charles) with a very civil hospitality. To our pleasure we found that our room faced across the low cliffs to the sea and was marred only by the presence on one wall of a sentimental canine portrait which, much to Anne's amusement, I immediately incarcerated in the wardrobe. Despite the existence of indoor plumbing I did suffer a pang of anxiety that Anne might find the inn too primitive, but to my relief she insisted that the simplicity delighted her.

The October weather was dry, enabling us to take long walks along the cliffs above the shingle beach, and the sight of the sea affected me deeply; I forgot the horror of the Battle of Jutland and thought only of the good times I had enjoyed in the Navy when the sea had represented freedom and the chance to draw closer to God. I began to talk in more detail to Anne about my years in the Navy, and when I told her I had decided to be a sailor at the age of eight after my mother had taken me on an excursion to the seaside, she began to talk not only about her own mother, whom she had already described in loving detail, but about her adored dead brother as well. Then gradually as she talked a third figure began to permeate the conversation until suddenly I saw that here at last stood my true adversary as I struggled to sever Anne from her unhappy past. The fiancé had certainly been a disaster for her, but the seeds of his destructive behaviour had fallen on ground well-cultivated to receive them. Beyond the fiancé, beyond the broken engagement, lurked the household idol called DADDY whose influence lingered on malignly so many years after his death.

That was when I realized that healing Anne was going to be more difficult than I had anticipated. The straightforward ravages of the fiancé could be erased by a sustained diet of patience and gentleness, but the subtle sinister crippling wrought by DADDY was far more difficult to obliterate, and as the picture emerged of an arrogant autocrat who had given her such a poor sense of her own worth as a woman a terrible truth began to crawl out of the darkest corner of my mind into the light. I realized that DADDY was not unfamiliar to me; in fact he was a man I knew all too well.

'Daddy did love me,' said Anne, 'but he loved my brother better because Gerald was the boy and more like him than I was. I tried so hard to please him, but no matter how hard I tried I never felt I was succeeding and that made me feel so sad and upset. It was as if he never saw *me* at all – he just saw a girl who wasn't the sort of child he wanted, and then I'd feel so humiliated, so second-rate, such a failure. Of course he pretended I was wonderful, but I knew it was just a pretence; it was as if he couldn't accept me as I was so he had to pretend I was someone quite different, and looking back I can see he made the same mistake with Gerald when he set him up on a pedestal and idolized him . . .

'I'm glad Gerald wasn't younger than I was. If he'd been younger I'd have hated him for being the favourite, but as he was five years my senior I grew up hero-worshipping him and the hero-worship elbowed all jealousy aside. It took me a long time to see how flawed he was. He was so athletic, so good-looking, so charming – and I was so plain, so shy, so hopeless at games and so useless with animals that I couldn't even learn to ride properly. Poor Daddy! I was such a disappointment to him. No wonder he preferred Gerald . . .

'The situation got even worse when I was an adolescent. It was so awful when Mummy died – well, I don't have to tell *you*, do I, what hell it is to lose one's mother when one's fourteen – but it was awful for me in all sorts of stupid ways which used to depress me so dreadfully and make me feel more inferior than ever. For instance, there was no one to advise me about clothes and I'm sure I always looked a fright and I never knew how to endure parties. Coming out was a nightmare – ugh! How I hated it! Poor Daddy was quite mortified by my lack of social success, and I felt so miserable because I knew I was letting him down.

'Gerald was a great social success, but although his girlfriends thought he was a story-book hero, all glamour and courage, he wasn't. He wasn't like that at all. Underneath the glamour he was frightened, frightened of not being the sort of man Daddy wanted him to be, frightened of being a failure and a disappointment . . .

'I thought he'd be better once Daddy was dead – I thought we'd both be better – but I was wrong. We still felt guilty, I because I hadn't been the kind of daughter Daddy had wanted and Gerald because he knew he couldn't live up to this idealized image which Daddy had created. So we both tried in different ways to escape from our guilt. I fell in love with Hugo; I think I knew from the start that there was something off-colour about the romance, but I just thought how pleased Daddy would have been that I'd got off the shelf. Then Gerald tried to escape by abandoning the estate and leading a wild life in London. He got in a mess in the end, of course – some woman or other, and I knew he was drinking too much – and when my engagement was broken off he was relieved to have a good excuse to turn his back on his problems in order to take me on holiday.

'When he was drowned I – no, I never thought it was suicide and the verdict was accidental death, but sometimes I think it was as if he subconsciously preferred death to life. That's a terrible thing to say, isn't it? But I think that sometimes the truth is very terrible and there's nothing one can do but stare it straight in the face in order to master it and go on.

'And I did go on after Gerald's death. The estate was in the red and I knew I had to save it because it was all I had left, but after a while I became aware that I wasn't acting through self-interest or even on account of a pious family feeling. I was saving the estate in order to show Daddy that I wasn't the second-rate creature he'd always thought I was; I was saving it to show him that in the end it was the despised daughter, not the idolized son, who was following so successfully in his footsteps. Isn't that odd? I was behaving as if he were still alive to see me, and sometimes I feel almost as if he *can* see me, although I don't truly believe he's a disembodied spirit perpetually looking over my shoulder . . . Jon, what does happen to the dead? What do heaven and hell really mean? What do you think really goes on?'

Overcoming my revulsion towards the appalling DADDY who might so easily have been described by Ruth. I slipped with relief into the role of priest and began to talk confidently about the hereafter.

V

'It's exceedingly difficult to talk intelligibly about life after death,' I said, 'because we're so pitifully limited by being trapped in time and space, but if you keep firmly in mind the fact that we're really incapable of thinking in anything but spatial and temporal terms you'll see that heaven and hell are spatial symbols while eternal life is a temporal symbol. All religious language is symbolic in that it attempts to bridge the gap between the describable and the inexpressible, but that doesn't mean it's untrue. Quite the reverse. Just as poetry and myth can sometimes express truth better than prose or scientific aphorisms, so religious language can convey truth by symbols. The symbols point the way to reality, and reality is a kingdom of values. Insofar as we partake of the three absolute values – truth, goodness and beauty – we can never die because those values are eternal. Plotinus, who was probably the greatest religious philosopher who ever lived – and a pagan, incidentally – said: "Nothing that really *is* can ever perish." '

'Yes, I see. Or I think I see. But – '

'You're wondering if we survive as individuals after death. Christianity says we do. On the other hand the Indian mystics claim that we don't; we merely become absorbed in the Absolute. However Plotinus holds that although there's a merging with other spirits individuality is retained; each soul is an individual as a face or a body. So the question then becomes: what is the relation of this "soul" to the "I" of personality? Or in other words, who is it who survives after death? Is it the ego, the demanding self of our daily lives whom we know all too well? Or is the real self not the ego at all but the spiritual presence which we share with all other human beings, the ennobled self which often prompts men to sacrifice their lives for others and share the burden of another's suffering? It's worth remembering, I think, that in classical times there was no word corresponding to our own "personality" and that the cult of the individual, glorifying the ego, is a fairly modern phenomenon. I suspect that the doctrine of survival which has come down to us means not the survival of the ego but the survival of the true self, the spiritual self, which after death joins other spirits in everlasting life – although everlasting life, of course, being outside finite time, is quite beyond our power to imagine.' I smiled at her. 'But you're thinking I still haven't answered your question about whether your father can see you following in his footsteps.'

'Yes, you have – he's not in space and he's not in time so it's ridiculous for me to picture him hovering on a cloud and watching me through a pair of binoculars!'

I laughed before saying: 'Nevertheless it's possible that your father's essence, his spiritual self, can penetrate finite time and enfold your psyche in that eternal value, love. If it's possible then your outward behaviour would reflect his love, like a mirror, and you'd be at peace, but what seems to have happened here is that his spiritual self is blocked from communicating with you because his ego is lingering on in your consciousness in the form of sad difficult memories. That often happens when someone dies leaving unhealed wounds and unresolved conflicts. The dead ego leaves a stain on the psyche which has to be wiped clean.' I was careful not to use the word 'exorcism' with all its dubious and discredited connotations.

By this time several days of the honeymoon had elapsed and intimacy had become easier for her. As practice made me more adroit I was at least able to ensure she felt no acute discomfort, but her response remained maimed, reflecting the damage in her psyche, and soon I realized that her fear lay not in the possibility that I might hurt her but in the belief that she would disappoint me, just as she had disappointed DADDY, by failing to display an unflawed femininity. She seemed to be telling herself – unconsciously, of course – that if she refused to compete in this particular race she would run no risk of the ignominious failure she feared so much, and this psychological withdrawal manifested itself in a refusal to let me touch her where it mattered most.

As our honeymoon entered its second week I became more determined than ever to set matters right but I knew I had to employ some radical new strategy. Although I was doing my best to demonstrate in a multitude of ways that I found her very far from being second-rate it seemed she could never quite believe that my attitude did not spring merely from a desire to be kind. The hallmark of psychological damage is irrationality.

One wet afternoon when we were in bed together she said suddenly: 'Do you promise me you're not secretly wishing I were thin like all the first-rate women?' and when I retorted: 'What's so first-rate about being thin? I like my women to be women, not effeminate boys!' she laughed. This pleased me. Laughter in bed represented progress. As a priest I am certainly in favour of treating the intimate side of marriage with a proper reverence, but I would argue with any puritan who insists that laughter has no place in the bedroom. Sexual intercourse should be a pleasure, not a penance, and laughter can lead to that vital relaxation without which the deepest pleasure can remain unobtainable.

I said: 'I like to hear you laugh!' and when she kissed me I saw with my inner eye a psyche which was ready to be healed.

In my memory Father Darcy began to drone that I should exercise the charism of healing only with men and only when they became emotionally disturbed during the course of spiritual counselling, but I ceased to listen. Father Darcy had merely regarded women as a man on a diet might regard a box of chocolates: pretty to look at, delicious to taste but quite irrelevant to sensible nourishment, and certainly he had never known what it was like to be in bed with a wife who was so painfully longing to express her love in the fullest possible way.

However Father Darcy's training was less easy to slough off than his views on my suitability for the ministry of healing, and automatically I found myself struggling to perceive my motives. I knew I wanted to heal Anne for her own sake so that she could be completely happy in the physical expression of our marriage, but beyond this truth were other less edifying truths, and lurking in their dark shadow was my old enemy, the demon pride. The demon was making me unwilling to accept that I could not wholly satisfy my wife; he was demanding incontrovertible evidence of sexual success in order to blot out my fear of old age, and he was whispering that after seventeen years of celibacy I was entitled to the best possible marital pleasure in compensation.

Yet although I could perceive the demon's machinations so clearly I told myself that Anne's need remained genuine, no matter how murky my motives were, and the next moment I had begun to pray.

I prayed in words, although the silence in the room remained unbroken, and offering my powers to God I prayed that he might use me as a channel for his Holy Spirit. In an attempt to override all my unsavoury motives by an expression of selflessness I also prayed: let thy will, not mine, be done. But the prayer was a mere formality, no better than the magic incantation of the sorcerer, and the next moment it was *my* will which drove me to take Anne in my arms, *my* will which determined that I should now have what I wanted and *my* will which egged me on to embrace the solution I could no longer withstand.

VI

Having taken Anne in my arms I said to her: 'I'd like to try an experiment, but don't be intimidated; if it doesn't work it'll be my fault, not yours.'

Despite my reassurance she immediately became nervous. 'What sort of experiment?'

'An exercise in telepathy. Now – ' I moved until I was astride her in such a manner that I could place my hands comfortably on her breasts ' – don't protest that you're incapable of it! Imagine that I've switched on a wireless. All you've got to do is listen as I slowly turn up the volume knob – and listening will be easier if you now close your eyes and think of William.'

'*William?* My cat?'

'I wasn't aware that you knew anyone else called William.'

Anne laughed, and as she thought of the safe, comforting image of her cat I was conscious of her muscles relaxing. Some seconds passed. Then I found I could distinguish her psyche clearly enough to reflect it in my mind as a visual symbol; I saw it as a bright ball with a clouded patch deep in the centre. I was unable to see William but that was because she did not know how to project the image. As an experiment I projected the image of Whitby but there was no response. I was still too far away. Moving to the edge of the bright ball I began to press into it towards the central darkness.

'Imagine William washing his paws.'

'I was! How clever of you!'

I thought this success was probably a coincidence; I was still unable to see William. 'Is he in a basket?' I said, thinking of Whitby.

'No, William hates baskets. He's sitting on his special blanket in my room. No, wait a minute, it's not William at all! His hair's too long. I'm sorry, my mind's wandering, I must have been thinking of your description of Whitby – '

'You're doing splendidly. Now imagine that the voice on the wireless is becoming audible and that it's finally possible for you to hear the message.' As I pressed on through the brightness I was aware of a change in the visual image; I now saw a patch of rapids on a swift-flowing river, and I was swimming steadily upstream towards the white water.

'I'm afraid I'm no good at this at all,' said Anne. 'I can't hear a thing.'

'Say the first word that comes into your head.'

'Love.'

'Good. Now keep listening, listen to the voice, listen, listen, listen . . .' I had reached the rapids and there ahead of me in the centre of the white water lay the black rock which had to be crushed. I fought my way on.

'Trust,' said Anne suddenly. 'Hope. Faith.'

The rapids died. The black rock lay unprotected before me and at once I began to draw my hands down over her breasts. Anne gasped, Whitby yelped and as the vertical line of time was fractured, past and present streamed side by side into the future.

'*Jon, your hands –* '

'Don't be frightened, just look at me, Anne, look and keep looking – ' As I touched the rock the image of the river dissolved so that I found myself confronting the darkness at the centre of her psyche. The final visual image flashed in my mind; I saw the darkness as a cancer, and a second later my mind was stretching to encircle it.

'Jon –'

'Don't speak, just listen, *listen*, LISTEN –'

But Anne no longer needed to listen. She had heard the message of love which lay far beyond the power of mere words to express, and in a moment of direct communication her psyche lay open before mine. The cancer was encircled. For one long moment I focused my entire psychic strength on it. Then as she herself placed my hand on her body the darkness exploded, her love expanded unhindered at last, and seconds later she was sobbing in my arms.

VII

Just as Whitby had expelled the furball and all the matter which had been poisoning him, so Anne now expelled her anguish and pain on the subject of the opposite sex. She said she had hated her fiancé for calling her a sexual cripple. She had hated him for letting her down so cruelly. Men had always let her down, never asking her to dance, never taking any genuine interest in her, never realizing she was just as much a human being as the girls who had the luck to be pretty. Sometimes she had even hated Gerald for treating her like an overgrown puppy; she had hated him because he had had access to the worlds which were closed to her, the worlds of freedom and independence where young men could chase the opposite sex and have a good time and escape from the clutches of DADDY.

'I hated Daddy too sometimes,' said Anne. 'He wouldn't let me do anything or go anywhere. I wanted to go up to Oxford, but he said higher education was pointless for women. I wanted to go to London and get a job but he said that was common and no girl of my class should consider it. All he wanted me to do was be a social success and get married and when I failed it was awful – *awful* – I hated him just as much as I hated myself – but then I felt worse than ever, so guilty, because of course I did love him very much and he was so often perfectly sweet to me –' She broke off, unable to continue, but I picked up my counsellor's cue with the ease born of long practice and said firmly: 'You didn't want someone being perfectly sweet. You wanted someone to understand the hell you were going through.'

'But he couldn't help not understanding! It was just the way he was made!'

'My dear, no one should excuse their faults by saying smugly: "I'm so sorry but this is just the way I was made." '

'Well, he never actually did say that, but –'

'If he didn't you certainly shouldn't. I'm quite willing to believe your father was a remarkable and delightful man in many ways, but you should never forget that he was also human enough to make mistakes – and some of those mistakes may well have been so serious that you have every right to be angry with him.'

'But that makes me feel so guilty – '

'Why? God made you as a unique individual in his own image. You wanted to be that individual and your father stopped you. This was not only a bad mistake; it was also morally wrong. You have a right to be angry, but you mustn't turn the anger in on yourself because that only compounds the damage which has already been done. You must turn the anger outwards. Hate him for hurting you! Be angry with him for rejecting your true self! And then when all that anger and hatred have been spent you'll be able to think: poor Daddy, never realizing what a first-class daughter he had – poor Daddy, cut off from so much love and happiness by his lack of understanding – poor Daddy, how very, very sad! And when you see, as you will, that he was the loser while you've gone on to win the life you were denied, your old anger will dissolve, your new compassion will expand to take its place and then at long last forgiveness will become possible.'

She was silent for a long time but eventually she said: 'He must have been very unhappy. People always are, aren't they, when they can't face reality? He must have known Gerald was no good. He must have known I'd be better off up at Oxford. But he couldn't cope with the knowledge. Mummy would have helped him cope. She was a very sensible, down-to-earth person and she wouldn't have let him retreat into this fantasy world where Gerald was the faultless heir apparent and I was the conventional heiress – she'd have helped him to put aside his dreams and face up to the way things really were, but without her he just didn't have the courage to do that. In fact,' said Anne, speaking more rapidly as her insight deepened, 'I can see now he must have been a frightened sort of person underneath that confident exterior. Insecure. Perhaps even a little weak. Isn't that strange? Maybe Gerald was far more like him than I ever realized . . . How eerie it is to think that families can spend years under the same roof yet know each other so imperfectly!'

'Eerie, but not unusual.'

Another long silence elapsed. Then Anne said simply: 'Poor Daddy. I suppose it was all a sort of tragedy, wasn't it?'

I took her in my arms to celebrate her first steps along the road to recovery.

VIII

Later Anne said: 'I feel as if I've climbed Mount Everest!' but I could only respond: 'I'm wondering if I've sunk into a bottomless pit.'

Anne looked astonished. 'What on earth do you mean?'

I sighed and began to tell her how I had abused my powers during my days as an undergraduate up at Cambridge.

IX

'I can quite see why you got into trouble when you were too young to know better,' said Anne, exercising great charity after I had completed my confession, 'but now that you're so wise and good why shouldn't you heal people if you want to?'

'Because I'm capable of being unwise and very bad.'

'Oh, rubbish!' said Anne robustly. 'You're setting yourself impossibly high standards!'

'Healing demands high standards. Father Darcy was always convinced I was temperamentally unsuited to any healing ministry which extended beyond the counselling of men.'

She was baffled. 'But why?'

'The humility required for such a ministry is so great that it really has to be inborn. I'm not naturally a humble person – I can attain humility, but I have to work hard to achieve it. My natural inclination is to be proud and arrogant.'

'But why does healing require this great humility?'

'Because healing is really an exercise in power, and as everyone knows, all power corrupts. The humble man will be in a better position to withstand corruption because he doesn't find power attractive, but the proud arrogant man is vulnerable because power provides the most delectable fodder for his hungry ego.'

'But if you have the gift of healing,' persisted Anne, 'isn't it wrong not to use it?'

'Strictly speaking there *is* no gift of healing – all healing comes from God. A ministry of healing begins when an individual feels called to offer himself as a channel for the healing power of the Holy Spirit. The power comes from without, not from within.'

'But surely you must have some inborn gift! What about the way you can make your hands tingle?'

'That's an interesting physical phenomenon but by itself it accomplishes nothing. You don't have to make your hands tingle in order to be a healer.'

'Let's get this straight,' said Anne in her most businesslike voice: 'What exactly did you do just now?'

'I used my gifts as a psychic to perceive what was going on in your mind. Then I prayed for the charismatic power, the gift from God, to excise the blight from your psyche. This power was granted but the healing was accomplished not merely by the laying-on of hands but by the use of various hypnotic techniques and – most important – by the listening and counselling afterwards. Throughout the whole process the psychic power was used merely as a tool to buttress the charismatic power, and that's strictly orthodox, strictly as it should be.'

'But if you followed the rule-book so conscientiously,' said Anne mystified, 'and the result was so successful, why are you so ambivalent?'

'Father Darcy said – '

'Yes, I know he said you were unsuited for a ministry of healing, but this wasn't a ministry, it was just one isolated act and I can't see any harm in it!'

'Father Darcy said I was never to heal women. If he'd ever dreamt that I'd again try to heal a woman under sexual circumstances, he'd have had apoplexy.'

'But this was quite different from – '

'Yes. But it was a dangerous thing to do. Father Darcy said healing would always be dangerous for me. He wanted me to teach – that's a charism too, of course, and Father Darcy thought I was ideally suited to keep order, command my pupils' attention and cram knowledge into their heads with the maximum of efficiency. He said a touch of arrogance never did any harm in the classroom.'

'But did you want to teach?'

'Not in the least, no, but I wanted to be a good monk so that meant I had to obey orders to the best of my ability. As a matter of fact I was a highly successful Master of Novices – nearly all my men went on to become priests. Father Darcy said – '

'Jon,' said Anne, 'have you any idea – any idea at all – how often you mention this man? And have you any idea – any idea at all – what a monster you make him seem?'

'He *was* a monster. I detested him all the while I was admiring him.'

'How thoroughly creepy and peculiar!'

My psyche flinched. I said carefully in a voice devoid of emotion: 'You speak, of course, from ignorance, so let me try to explain the relationship in terms you can understand. We were two mountaineers roped together and he was showing me the way up the mountain. That meant that the essence of our relationship consisted of neither love nor hate but trust. I trusted him to lead me to the top and he trusted in my ability to follow him there. As men we disliked each other but as psychics we found each other fascinating and as monks we were obliged to love each other as brothers.'

'I've never heard anything quite so convoluted in all my life! Was he responsible for those scars on your back?'

'Yes, but – '

'What a sadistic brute! I simply don't understand how you could have borne to go on obeying him – he beat you up, forced you to do work you didn't want to do, *murdered your cat* – '

'He saved me.' I used my harshest voice and saw her recoil. 'He taught me how to live with myself. He showed me how to survive. Perhaps you think it's fun to be a psychic but it's not. It can be terrifying beyond belief. One spends most of one's time feeling either cut off from the rest of humanity or else invaded, battered and laid waste by forces beyond one's control. A lot of psychics either go mad or go to the Devil, but Father Darcy saved me from either of those fates – he made me the sane healthy man you love today. What if he did beat me? What if he did kill that cat? Those were mere pinpricks compared with what I might have suffered if I hadn't met him! If you're drowning in the sea and someone comes along with a lifeboat you don't care if he drags you aboard by your hair and slaps your face to revive you – oh no, quite the reverse! As soon as you're conscious you just go down on your knees and thank God that the lifeboat turned up in time!'

I stopped speaking. I was shaking. I opened my mouth again to apologize for shouting at her, but it was she who spoke first. She said in a small voice: 'I'm terribly sorry. I didn't realize. Please forgive me for being so stupid and not understanding.'

I groped for her hand and held it. Eventually I was able to say: 'The fault's mine. I never explained my spiritual history. Anne, there's so much I haven't told you – '

'Well, at least I understand now about Father Darcy.'

'Then you'll understand why I feel so ambivalent about the healing.'

'Yes, but *I* don't feel ambivalent!' said Anne. 'I think the healing was utterly wonderful and I want to make mad passionate love to you until we both pass out with exhaustion!'

Father Darcy's memory immediately receded. Indeed for the first time in seventeen years it occurred to me that I could survive remarkably well without him.

X

However next morning Father Darcy had returned to his habitual corner of my memory and I became convinced that I was drifting into a most dubious spiritual state. Deciding that I should seek solitude in order to apply myself to some rigorous spiritual exercises I wondered how to sever myself tactfully from Anne, but the problem was solved when she revealed she had encountered the onset of her monthly indisposition. With a clear conscience I left her to rest at the inn.

After walking some way into the hills I found a church set half a mile from an isolated hamlet and decided that I had reached the ideal place in which to smooth a bedraggled psyche. In fact by that time I could barely wait to sink myself in the austerities of meditation, prayer and 'lectio divina', and the hours passed in a healing silence as I read my Missal, studied passages from *The Cloud of Unknowing* and prayed with all the concentration at my command.

After praying for Anne I prayed, as I did daily, that I might receive further enlightenment about my new call, and when I paused at last I found my mind dwelling idly on the ministry of healing. Was it possible that I now had the wisdom, the maturity and the spiritual strength to triumph consistently over my innate pride and thus attain the continuous humility which such a ministry required? Almost certainly not, and Father Darcy would have said the Devil had put this question into my mind. Nevertheless it was an interesting question. I saw no harm in allowing it to interest me, but of course I could hardly deduce I had received a call to be a healer just because my wife had been enrapt by a healing which would have given Father Darcy apoplexy.

'Stop whining that you've never felt called to teach!' said Father Darcy in my memory. 'I want more priests at Ruydale. This house has been all brawn and no brains for too long.'

The years continued to roll back and the next moment my father was saying: 'If you want to be a clergyman I couldn't be more pleased – such a fine respectable profession – and of course you could still teach eventually, couldn't you? With your ability you could have a most successful career at any of the leading Church-of-England public schools . . .'

My memory somersaulted away from him into my childhood until I heard myself say to my mother during our excursion to the seaside at Brighton: 'I want to be a sailor when I grow up.'

'I see you on a big ship,' said my mother, gazing out to sea, 'a grey ship with guns on it. But I don't think you're a sailor.'

'Then what am I?'

'You're yourself, living in harmony with the universe,' said my mother, much as she might have said: 'Tomorrow we'll have mutton chops for dinner,' and added: 'That's good. Most people don't.'

'How will I know if I'm living in harmony with the universe?'

'You'll feel that your profession fits you as snugly as a bespoke suit from a very expensive tailor.'

I recollected myself. My mind had wandered, and as I hauled it back from its travels I seemed to hear my mother wondering if the ill-fitting healer's clothes I had worn up at Cambridge had at long last been transformed into a bespoke suit from Savile Row. My mother would have been deeply interested in any career as a healer. But what would my father have thought? He would have seen a call to heal in professional medical terms, of course; in his view anyone practising medicine other than a qualified doctor was a quack. But in his own way he would have supported me. 'If you want to be a doctor I couldn't be more pleased – such a fine respectable profession – and you could still teach eventually, couldn't you? With your ability you could have a most successful career at any of the great London teaching hospitals . . .'

Again I recollected myself, this time with a shudder. What my parents would have thought of a call to heal was irrelevant. All that mattered was what God thought, and God was still silent, his opinion shrouded in a darkness which remained impenetrable.

Closing my Missal I set off on the return journey to the inn.

XI

Anne ran out to meet me as I approached the house, and to my alarm I saw she was thoroughly overwrought.

'Darling – ' I held out my arms and she hurtled into them ' – what is it? What's the matter?'

I sensed her relief receding as her anger gained the upper hand. 'Where have you been?' she demanded in an unnerving echo of Ruth. 'You've been gone for hours and hours! What on earth happened?'

'Nothing! I've just been praying, reading and meditating.'

She stared at me. 'All this time?'

I suddenly realized my premarital reticence was about to catch up with me yet again. 'I'm sorry,' I said rapidly. 'I see now I should have warned you – '

'Yes, you damn well should!' stormed Anne. 'How could you have been so thoroughly selfish and insensitive! Didn't you think of me at all?'

'Oh yes! I spent a long time praying for you – '

'I didn't mean that!' shouted Anne, and then stammering: 'I thought you were dead,' she collapsed sobbing against my chest.

'Obviously I've been very much at fault,' I said as we attained the sanctuary of our room.

'But you silly man, why didn't you tell me you liked lots of time for prayer and meditation?'

'I did tell you. When I was trying to explain about Betty, I – '

'You did drop a vague hint, yes, but you gave me no idea what you really meant. Now let's get this straight,' said Anne, drying her eyes and taking refuge in her most businesslike manner. 'How much time do you need and when do you need it?'

'Darling, you mustn't let it worry you – I'm prepared to compromise – I do realize that now I'm no longer in a monastery I can't expect to – '

'*How much and when?*'

'Well, I like to get up at five-thirty and pray, read and meditate for two hours before breakfast – '

'Why on earth didn't you say so? And why haven't you been doing this since the start of the honeymoon?'

I did not like to say I had needed the extra sleep after making love to her so frequently. That would have reminded her of my age. 'Well, it was awkward – sharing a room – I didn't want to be a bore or a nuisance – '

'Now look here,' said Anne, 'I don't know why you felt you couldn't talk to me about this but I can't have you not being honest and tying us both up in some fantastic knot. You must take as much time for prayer and meditation as you need each day and I promise I shan't complain – I shall only complain if you starve yourself of solitude for my sake and then disappear into the blue for eight hours in order to make up for lost time.'

'My darling Anne, I can't apologize enough – '

'Did you think I wouldn't understand about your need for solitude? But why? I like to spend time on my own too!'

'Do you? Truthfully?'

'Of course! After all, I've been on my own for six years; do you think I haven't learnt how to be happy with my own company?'

After a pause I said: 'Betty never learnt.'

'But I'm not Betty, am I?'

I merely embraced her, and as I did so the evening sunlight began to slant through the window into the room. In the distance the sea was a calm soothing blue.

Suddenly Anne whispered: 'Do you want to? You can if you like,' but when she saw my astonished expression she was overcome with confusion. 'Some men don't care about the curse, I know,' I heard her mumble, and I knew the oaf of a fiancé had been wreaking havoc here too, trampling on her needs in order to satisfy his own. 'But obviously if you find the idea repulsive – '

'It's not a question of repulsion; God made us as we are, bodily functions and all, but I do feel some private acts of the body aren't suitable for sharing, and my respect for privacy is such that I've always believed a man has a duty not to intrude on a woman at such times,' I said, but although this speech reflected my feelings honestly enough, only some of my feelings were being revealed. I had been brought up amidst the peculiarly Victorian ethos which dictated that decent middle-class women, particularly the women of one's own family, should be set upon metaphorical pedestals, treated with reverence and protected from any sordid fact of life which might soil their carefully nurtured purity. When I had finally escaped from the monastic atmosphere of my public school and the extreme propriety of my home I had been amazed to discover that women from other classes behaved as if this ethos had nothing to do with the facts of life and even regarded their middle-class sisters with pity. Betty in particular had had great fun puncturing any prim notions of femininity which remained to me after three years up at Cambridge, and part of her fun had derived from periodically seducing me during those times when any middle-class woman would have had the refined sensibility to withdraw into a self-imposed purdah. Thus Anne was now, without knowing it, seeking an intimacy which aroused both inhibiting memories of my middle-class upbringing and unsavoury memories of Betty's perverse exercise in power.

But there were other reasons why I had no desire for intimacy at that moment. The first was that after achieving intense spiritual satisfaction from an ascetic retreat I was reluctant to conclude the day by plunging into sensuality; such behaviour would have resembled following a glass of pure spring water with a slice of cream-cake. And the second reason why I wanted to abstain from intimacy was because I needed to; I had spent ten days living at a sexual pace more suitable for a man half my age, and the dread of impotence, never far from the surface of my mind, prompted an awareness that I should husband my resources more carefully.

'I'm sorry,' Anne was saying in a rush. 'You obviously think I'm behaving like a female sex maniac.'

'Nonsense!' I said firmly. 'A healthy desire for marital intimacy is entirely right and proper!'

'Even for a clergyman's wife?'

'Especially for a clergyman's wife. People entirely misunderstand Christianity when they think it's against sex. It's against the abuse of sex, which is quite different,' I said, but as I spoke I was experiencing a revelation and it was not a pleasant one. I saw that by healing her I might have wrecked some hidden equilibrium which would have kept our relationship finely tuned not now, when I was an active sixty, but later when I was an ageing septuagenarian. However that glimpse of the future was too disturbing to contemplate, and at once I scrabbled to scrub it from my mind.

'Let's go to bed.'

'But you said – '

'Never mind what I said. I want you. If you want me – '

Victorian inhibitions, Betty's memory, ascetic inclinations and the dread of impotence – all were swept aside. I only knew I had a young wife who had to be satisfied; I only knew I had to fight with all my power to keep old age at bay.

XIII

Afterwards, when Anne had slipped away for a quick bath before dinner, I crawled off the bed and limped to the basin to wash. Both my legs were aching, a pulled muscle was throbbing in my back and I felt stupefied by tiredness. Old age leered at me from the glass above the basin, and shuddering I looked away.

Anne eventually returned to the room. She seemed so young, so fresh, so brimful of vitality that I felt as if someone had plunged a knife into my psyche, and at once intense fear overwhelmed me again. As she wandered past I grabbed her so abruptly that she gasped, imprisoned her in the tightest of embraces and whispered: 'Don't leave me.'

'Jon!' She was shocked as well as astonished, and as I slackened my grip she reached up to cradle my face between her hands. 'That's the second time you've said that. Why on earth should you think – '

'I'm so old. Supposing I have a stroke and become a vegetable. Supposing I can't make love to you any more. Supposing you get tired of me, turn to someone else, go away, never come back – '

Anne said violently: 'I should never do such dreadful things. I shall always love you, even if you wind up a vegetable. Please stop being so silly this instant.' She sounded shattered.

At once I struggled to pull myself together. To have an elderly husband was bad enough; to have a silly elderly husband would be intolerable. 'I'm sorry,' said my voice, 'what an un-Christian panic! Of course I must face the future with hope and faith, not sink into an ignominious despair.' The crucial word here was 'ignominious'. My pride had come to my rescue when hope and faith had failed.

'Dearest Jon,' said Anne kissing me, 'you don't have to apologize – I suppose we all have our irrational fears, even people like you who seem so wonderfully well balanced, but I must say I do find it unnerving when you become so peculiar. It's as if you stop being the man I love and become someone else altogether.'

There was a deep silence as I digested this speech and she tranquilly began to brush her hair. I saw so clearly then that in order to maintain her love I had to protect her from my irrational peculiarities. I had to be the kind of husband she wanted me to be: youthful, strong, sane, wise, authoritative, confident, fearless, sexually accomplished – and bewitchingly endowed with all manner of glamorous powers.

I began to think again of a ministry of healing.

FOURTEEN

'(There exists) in the English Church an intense repugnance against the priestcraft of the Roman hierarchy.'

W. R. INGE
Dean of St Paul's 1911–1934
Outspoken Essays

I

Three days later we returned to Starrington Magna and the regular arrival of the newspapers which we had tried to avoid on our honeymoon. However even in the depths of Dorset without either a wireless or a newspaper we had heard that the battering of London had been continuing night after night: one hundred thousand books had been destroyed in the University College Library and a bomb, crashing through the roof of St Paul's, had destroyed the High Altar. 'Our ordeal continues,' wrote Francis. 'Just as we were congratulating ourselves on having survived the threat of a summer invasion, Anti-Christ plunges us into hell again with his "Donner-und-Blitzen" tactics.' And suddenly I saw that I had been so busy congratulating myself on finding not only the chapel of my vision but the woman of my dreams that I had overlooked the fact that a new and possibly more demanding phase of my return to the world was just about to begin.

My most immediate difficulty was that although I had to think of the Manor as my home I was still gripped by the desire to shun the main reception rooms as much as possible in order to avoid the servants. However I did realize I could hardly conduct my married life while hiding in corners, and it occurred to me that if I were to acquire at least one room where no servant would ever go, the knowledge that I had a bolt-hole would give me the necessary mental stamina to survive the intrusions of the servants elsewhere. Reluctantly I broached the subject with Anne, but she was very sympathetic and suggested that I might like to annex the large dressing-room next door to our bedchamber. This pleased me but trouble surfaced when I began to strip the room naked by hauling out all the wardrobes and tallboys. Apparently this ugly clutter had belonged to

DADDY and when Anne wanted to know why I was unable to be satisfied with the furniture of a country gentleman I felt exactly like the parlour-maid's son that I was.

'I'll choose another room,' I said. 'Perhaps I should be banished to an attic? Then you wouldn't have to worry about me not behaving like a country gentleman.'

'Oh, shut up – stop being so prickly and proud!' cried Anne, much upset, and at once I panicked, apologized profusely and said it would be an honour to live with Mr Barton-Woods' venerable wardrobes and tallboys.

'Now don't start being dishonest!' said Anne, becoming crosser than ever. 'Why say it would be an honour when you've made it quite clear it would be a thundering bore? Chuck everything out and for goodness' sake make yourself thoroughly at home!'

When the bolt-hole was bare I imported a small chest of drawers from one of the spare-rooms and constructed a cupboard between the chimney-piece and the window so that I would have no need of a wardrobe. In the attics I found a table and chair, both broken, but they were easily mended and when I placed them by the window I thought they looked well. I put up a couple of shelves in the hope of increasing my book collection (I had already ordered the new edition of St Augustine's *De Civitate Dei*) and built myself a small plain oratory in a corner. Before this refurbishment I had cast out the carpet and curtains and painted the room white; the blackout blind provided all the covering the window needed, and the revarnished floorboards were quite handsome enough to render any rug superfluous.

'Funny man!' said Anne when she was finally allowed to inspect the alterations. 'You've created a monk's cell! But never mind – here's something which will soften the austerity,' and she gave me the engraving of Starbridge Cathedral which I had admired when I had boarded in her spare-room.

This gesture was without doubt both kind and generous, but I had been dreaming of a room where there would be no pictures to distract me and although I admired the engraving I found I was still reluctant to abandon my dreams. Having accepted the gift with fulsome gratitude I hid the picture in the cupboard as soon as Anne had left the room. Later, of course, she found out. Our consequent altercation could hardly be described as a row but it was definitely a tiff and afterwards I regret to record that I sulked. However eventually I remembered that I was a married man who should be prepared to compromise, not an abbot with a licence to do as he pleased, so before I went to bed that night I hung the engraving over the fireplace. I always think St Paul's admonition: 'Let not the sun go down on thy wrath,' should be permanently inscribed on the memories of all married couples.

I had barely succeeded in working myself into a position where I could regard at least a small corner of the Manor as 'home' when the next problem loomed on the horizon: I had to revise my view that it was quite unnecessary for me to know anything about Anne's money. I had already made it clear that I did not want to take a penny of it for my own needs, that I wished to contribute, albeit in a modest way, to the cost of running the household, and that she was to continue to manage her financial affairs as if I did not exist, but in fact, as I now discovered, I had been insensitive. Anne wanted to share her money with me; she saw the sharing as a gesture of loving trust, and when I had repudiated it so peremptorily she had felt hurt. As soon as I realized my mistake I changed course. I agreed to be briefed on her financial affairs, but I still could not bring myself to accept her offer of a joint bank account and when she tried to give me an absurdly large sum of money I was quite unable to conceal my horror of being 'kept'.

'You're being thoroughly pig-headed and proud again!' exclaimed Anne exasperated. 'You know perfectly well you need some extra cash at the moment – take the money, pay off the loan from the Order and for goodness' sake buy some more clothes before the government starts to ration them! Daddy ordered all his clothes from a Starbridge tailor who used to work in Savile Row.'

The word DADDY was like a red rag to a bull. Knowing I was being difficult but finding I was quite unable to stop myself I said obstinately: 'Savile Row's not my sort of place. Unnecessary extravagance. I'll find a cheap tailor elsewhere.'

'I don't want my husband dressed in cheap clothes!' exploded Anne, and at once the chasm of class yawned between us again but this time it was she who made the effort to bridge it. Controlling her temper she said with a sympathy I hardly deserved: 'Darling, don't think I don't understand what you're going through – I know how hard it must be for you to adjust to your new life and believe me, I spend a lot of time worrying in case you're secretly miserable.'

That made me pull myself together with unprecedented speed. The last thing I wanted was to be such a tiresome burden to her that she spent her time worrying about me. 'I'm fine!' I said firmly. 'In fact I'm even beginning to feel comfortable with the servants.' But I knew this statement still bore more resemblance to wishful thinking than to reality.

My extreme sensitivity on the subject of servants arose not merely because of my mother's background, although of course the fact that she had been a servant inevitably precluded me from adopting the comfortable upper-class assumption that servants were a race apart who welcomed being treated with an authority devoid of inhibitions. My own inhibitions, which I knew I now had to overcome, also arose from the fact that I had not been brought up in a house well-populated with servants. Priding herself on her housekeeping skills, my mother had preferred to do her own cooking, shopping, dusting, polishing and sweeping; a succession of raw young girls had been employed to shift coal, help with the laundry and toil over the heavy cleaning, but since these creatures had been mainly confined to the scullery I had seldom encountered them. Certainly I had never had to give them orders.

When I had married, Betty had dealt with the inevitable female who had to be employed as the maid-of-all-work, and again my contact with the servant had been minimal. It was true that years later as an abbot I had been waited on hand and foot by numerous monks performing the work of servants, but since we had all been brothers, all doing our different work for God and for the community, my inhibitions had not been aroused. However my position at Starrington Manor was very different from my position at Grantchester, and I found it hard not to feel that a walk through the house was a walk through enemy territory where a housemaid lay waiting to ambush me around every corner. Ridiculous though I knew my inhibitions were, they still contrived to make me feel debilitatingly ill at ease in the early weeks of my marriage, but in fact the servants were very kind, possibly because they had soon realized I had no intention of meddling in their routine, possibly because I treated them with consideration and never rang bells unnecessarily. When I sensed I had won their approval I did venture to hope that I would adjust to them in the end, just as I would eventually adjust to the fact that I should from time to time accept money gracefully from my rich wife, but the next obstacle in my path certainly seemed as if it might defy all my attempts to adjust to it. I found myself becoming increasingly troubled by Anne's social life.

I had already realized that Anne had a wide circle of acquaintances in the county but I had not imagined that she would have to see them so often. Doubtless I had been misled by my memories of the unsociable 'Miss Fielding' at Allington, and I was surprised when she showed a pronounced inclination to be gregarious.

I am a sociable person in the sense that I find people interesting and am more than willing to devote myself to their spiritual needs, but I have a horror of vacuous conversation conducted amidst a surfeit of food and drink. Moreover after I had embarked on my curacy I found I was too tired in the evenings to regard dinner-parties as other than a senseless ordeal. I had been willing to be paraded at the estate office; indeed I had enjoyed my tour of the Home Farm. I had also been willing to be paraded before Anne's acquaintancs; it seemed only polite that we should offer them hospitality to make amends for their exclusion from the wedding. But a life-time of regular parading would have been unendurably tedious. 'I'm not suggesting we should give up our social activities entirely,' I said, trying hard to be tactful, 'but in future I must restrict myself to the engagements which are essential to my position as curate. And talking of my curacy – ' I hesitated but felt impelled by the seriousness of the matter to continue ' – have you thought yet about how you might best help me in the parish? I know I said I was willing to let your role evolve, but perhaps the time's come for you to give the evolution a helping hand. If you spent a little less time being a social butterfly and a little more time considering matters which are truly important – '

'How dare you call me a social butterfly!' cried Anne. 'You know perfectly well I prefer to be curled up with a good book instead of talking to some old bore about hunting, shooting and fishing, but these are people I've known all my life and I can't cut them altogether just because I've married a clergyman! Some social obligations simply have to be honoured; it's a question of being polite and kind and decent – and if you can't see that, I think you're being thoroughly unChristian!'

Eventually we sorted ourselves out. I said that of course she must honour her social obligations and of course it was wrong of me to make additional demands on her time when she was already burdened with her vital war-work on the estate and of course it would be sufficient if she did no parish work at all but merely came to church on Sundays. Anne said that of course she would do parish work and of course she would cut down ruthlessly on our social engagements and of course she understood my point of view. 'I'm sorry I lost my temper,' she added, 'but I couldn't bear it when you started behaving like a Victorian autocrat bringing up a child bride.'

I apologized again before saying tentatively: 'I'm afraid I do tend to be very single-minded about my work, but I feel so deeply that when one's working for God every other activity is potentially a pointless distraction.'

In the silence that followed I realized that at last Anne was seeing me not through a romantic haze but in the cold clear light of reality, not as an alluring ex-monk but as a fanatical priest who thought nothing of carving up his wife's social life and dictating to her about how she should organize her spare time.

I panicked. 'My darling Anne, you mustn't think I don't fight hard against fanaticism – of course balance and moderation are always essential in a religious life – '

'It's all right,' said Anne abruptly. 'I love you as you are, fanaticism and all, but I can see now that I've underestimated the importance of this curacy. I've been thinking of it as a hobby for you while you waited for your call to unfold. I didn't realize you'd take it so seriously.'

'All work for God should be taken seriously.'

'Of course. I've been stupid.' Impulsively she gave me a kiss. 'I'm sure you'll make a huge success of the parish!' she exclaimed with her warmest smile. 'I shall feel so proud of you!'

And that was the moment when I knew I could never burden her with my rapidly expanding problems as the curate of Starrington Magna.

II

However before my problems as a parish priest could unfold in their full magnitude I was busy repairing the rift with my children. On my return from the honeymoon I wrote again to Martin and this time, to my profound relief, my communication bore fruit. I received a letter which read:

'Dear Dad: Just collected your last two screeds – my old cow of a landlady hadn't forwarded them. Cngratulations on the bride. That's fast work for an ex-monk. In fact that's fast work for anyone. But presumably at sixty one feels there's no time to lose, and why the hell shouldn't you have some fun while you still can? If that bitch Ruth is behaving as if you ought to be censored by the Lord Chamberlain, take no bloody notice. MARTIN. P.S. Despite my advancing years I got into the Army, first by persecuting the military father of an old school-friend (long live the old school tie) and second by persuading the army medical men in a triumph of acting that I'd never had a homosexual thought or too much to drink in my life. So now I'm busy learning how to kill people and I hope you're pleased. P.P.S. New address enclosed but please don't write unless you can produce a letter which doesn't read as if it's come hot from the pen of a religous maniac.'

I wrote the required careful reply, urging him to visit me as soon as he had leave, but no further word came. However at least I was able to assure Anne that I had been correct in assuming Martin's failure to attend the wedding was the result of ignorance, not ill-will. I could also tell her with pride that he was anxious to fight Hitler, but my pride was shadowed by the dread that in his desire to convince me of his masculinity he had picked a role he would never be able to sustain.

To distract myself from worrying about him I turned my attention to Ruth and wrote:

'I have been thinking so much of the difficulties which are keeping us apart, and I wonder if it would ease matters if you made your first visit to Starrington without the family? Much as I would like to see Roger and the children I feel the need to give you my undivided attention.'

At this point I paused, remembering how DADDY, that repulsive specimen of masculine arrogance, had caused Anne so much unhappiness by treating her as if she were second-rate, and the next moment my guilt was driving me to add:

'Please think of this invitation from my point of view as well as your own. I'm so anxious to show you off to Anne! You're my only daughter and *most important to me*. It's not enough for me to tell Anne how proud I am of you. I want her to see for herself how smart and attractive you are.'

A week later Ruth and I were travelling from the station to the Manor in Anne's Rolls-Royce.

III

Ruth was looking exceedingly fetching in her over-dressed way but I knew she was nervous. Her nervousness unfortunately took the form of a manner refined to the point of caricature, but I told myself to suppress all critical thoughts and be grateful that she was on her best behaviour.

Anne was nervous too, and her nervousness took the form of abrupt remarks; I was reminded of 'Miss Fielding' at Allington. However she tried hard to make Ruth feel welcome and when she asked to see photographs of the children I could sense her guest becoming more relaxed.

Ruth appeared to admire the house, but to my annoyance I saw her testing the drawing-room mantelshelf for dust while Anne was looking the other way. Mindful of Ruth's interest in domestic matters I suggested that Anne might show her the kitchens, but Ruth at once became absurdly grand and declined. However after luncheon I made the right move and bore her off to the chapel, not merely because I wanted her to see it but because I knew she would welcome the chance to have me to herself. As she was wearing high-heeled shoes a walk through the woods posed difficulties, but fortunately Anne was able to lend her a pair of Wellington boots.

'Well, it's a lovely place, I must say,' said Ruth, glancing back at the house as we crossed the lawn, 'but isn't it funny that someone of her class could be content for her home to be so shabby and old-fashioned? I'd get a new three-piece suite for that sitting-room *and* I'd do something about the plumbing! That Victorian lavatory in the downstairs cloakroom is really very peculiar.'

'Stop worrying about the lavatory and enjoy these beautiful woods.'

'Yes, it's a nice garden, isn't it, and of course she's nice too, I can see that, although since she's got money I'm surprised she's not smarter. What a pity she doesn't do something about her hair! Still never mind, the only important thing is that she's nice, although I must say you seem rather like a fish out of water in these "county" surroundings. I shouldn't have thought it suited you in the least – a little flat over our garage would have been much more to your taste, but I do see that it'll be nice for you to have a young companion in your old age.'

'Look to your left,' I said, 'and you'll see the chapel.'

'Oh yes, how sweet. Of course the age difference doesn't matter now when you're an active sixty and she hasn't the dress-sense to look as young as she should, but in ten years' time – '

My patience snapped. I rounded on her. 'Ruth – ' I began, but I won the battle for self-control. All I said in the end was: 'My dear, I do beg you not to be jealous.'

'Jealous! What an obscene thing to say!'

I suddenly felt I could not bear her to enter the chapel. The thought of her polluting its serenity with her troubled psyche was repugnant to me. Still struggling not to lose my temper I said: 'I'm sorry. Obviously I should make allowances for your profound unhappiness.'

'I'm not unhappy!'

'I think you are – indeed how can you not be unhappy when you're cut off from God and adrift in such an unreal world?' I knew this was quite the wrong thing to say but as my patience finally expired I could conceal my true feelings no longer. 'I can't tell you what a grief it is to me that you've stopped going to church and that your children are being brought up in an utterly secular environment – '

'Oh Daddy, please! *Please!*'

'I know it must be very difficult being married to an atheist who can think of nothing but unrealities such as possessions, but I feel so strongly that if only you could renew your links with the Church – '

'It wouldn't be any use. I'm just not a religious sort of person, and anyway in the end I came to feel that God wasn't interested in me, didn't care – '

'How can you say that when he's conferred such blessings on you? Of course I'm aware that there are difficulties; life's never perfect, but by the grace of God even the most intractable problems can be – '

'Oh, for God's sake shut up about bloody religion and stop criticizing me the whole damned time! You've got the sort of daughter you want now – although heaven only knows what you see in her – so why don't you just leave me alone?'

The scene ground remorselessly on into disaster.

IV

'You both looked very white around the gills when you returned from your walk,' said Anne after the chauffeur had borne Ruth away in the Rolls. 'Was there some ghastly scene at the chapel?'

'No,' I said, mindful that the scene had taken place in the woods.

'What did she think of the chapel?'

'Her exact word was "sweet".'

'What an extraordinary adjective to choose!' Anne said astonished but decided to press the matter no further. Instead she asked: 'What did she think of me?'

'She said how nice you were.'

'What a relief!'

There was a small but deadly pause as we both wondered what to say next. In the end I heard myself remark abruptly: 'I dare say you were surprised by how common she was.'

Anne's expression changed. I was acutely aware of her wondering how she could be kind without forfeiting her honesty, but to my relief she decided that to be honest was to be kind. 'Well,' she said, 'to be absolutely frank, yes, I was.'

'Betty was the daughter of a man who kept a tobacconist's shop,' I said colourlessly, once more cursing the premarital reticence which had been regularly tripping me up, just as Francis had prophesied, ever since my journey to the altar. 'Her mother was a cheap vulgar silly woman and when she took charge of the children some of that cheap vulgar silliness inevitably rubbed off on Ruth. Martin escaped, of course; he went away to school.' I hesitated but forced myself to add: 'I'm sorry I didn't tell you all that earlier.'

'Are you?' said Anne. 'How curious. It's comparatively unimportant. What's much more important is that Martin's a homosexual alcoholic, and I'm very sorry indeed that you didn't see fit to tell me that earlier.'

Here indeed was the day of reckoning for my premarital reticence. I felt as if all the breath had been battered from my body. 'Ruth told you? She actually told you?'

'Well, of course she told me! She wanted to see how married we were and how far you'd confided in me, so as soon as you went to the lavatory after lunch – '

'But how dare she!' Panic and guilt were conveniently submerged beneath my rage. 'How dare she behave like a spiteful little girl and humiliate you like that!'

'Don't be a damned fool!' said Anne in fury. 'Do you think I let her get the better of me? Of course I said I knew everything there was to know about Martin!'

There was a long silence. Finally I found I had to sit down.

'It makes me wonder what else you haven't told me,' said Anne, her voice shaking. 'I thought we trusted each other. I feel very hurt. I'm sorry, I'm trying hard to be forgiving, but – '

'Oh Anne, Anne – '

' – but it's pretty damn difficult. I felt so upset,' said Anne on the verge of tears. 'That horrid glossy manicured bitch hating me behind her ghastly façade of refinement – why didn't you warn me she was like that? The least you could have done was warn me, but no, you went on painting this utterly false picture of a charming housewife who disapproved of your quick marriage out of a saintly concern for your welfare! I was absolutely unprepared for her sheer vulgar awfulness, and then when she tried to trap me about Martin – oh, it was vile, *vile* – I hated every minute of her visit and I never want to see her again!'

She rushed out of the room. The door banged. In despair I covered my face with my hands.

V

'My darling Anne, forgive me – I didn't mean to put you in such a humiliating position – '

'Well, you did. Look, I didn't mean to be so beastly about Ruth – she's probably not as bad as all that and I don't mind trying to be nice to her for your sake, but Jon, I just don't understand why you couldn't confide in me.'

We were sitting on the edge of our bed. I was leaning forward with my elbows on my knees and clasping my hands so tightly that they ached. Anne was bolt upright, her fingers clutching the folds of the counterpane so hard that her knuckles shone white. At last with a great effort I managed to say: 'My children show me in such an appalling light and I didn't want you to see me in any light which was appalling.'

Anne stared. 'That sounds as if you've tied yourself up in a most fantastic knot again. Why do you keep doing this? Why are you so frightened of being honest with me?'

'I have a horror of wearying you with my private burdens. I'm afraid of you losing patience, finding me an elderly bore – '

'Oh good heavens, I do believe you're worrying about being a deserted vegetable again! Now stop being so silly and let's sort this out. Why do you think your children show you in an appalling light?'

Very slowly I began to paint my painful portrait of the past.

VI

Some time later Anne said: 'Plenty of people have to endure far less paternal attention than you gave your children, and most of them have no trouble turning out well. I think Ruth and Martin were very lucky to have a conscientious father who did his best for them in difficult circumstances, and if they now turn out to have ghastly problems why shouldn't they accept at least some of the blame?'

'That's a question Francis has asked. But letting them assume some of the responsibility for their fate does nothing to erase my guilt about my own share of the responsibility.'

'But are you sure this guilt isn't misplaced? If you ask me, all that's really going on here is that you happened to father two children with whom you've no particular affinity – with the result that you can't dote on them quite as much as they'd like.'

'That's a comforting theory because it exonerates me from blame, but – '

' – you can't believe in it. All right, supposing your guilt was justified; why is it still crucifying you? Didn't you atone for your guilt when you became a monk?'

'I went through the motions of atonement, certainly, but it was all based on the false premise of that superstitious bargain with God. I still can't feel that I'm forgiven for my sins.'

'Well, I'm no theologian,' said Anne, 'but I thought that if one demonstrated a true repentance – '

'I always feel in my heart that my repentance isn't true. I always feel that if I were in the same position as I was in thirty-six years ago I'd commit the same sins all over again because I'm incapable of being anything but an inadequate parent.'

'But Jon, what about when *we* have a baby? You surely don't think – '

'Oh no, no, no!' I said rapidly, cursing myself for the fatal indiscretion. 'Any child of yours would be quite different! My guilt about Ruth and Martin is all bound up with my guilt about Betty.'

'But it must be such a crippling burden! If only you could feel you were forgiven – '

'Every time I see Ruth and Martin I always know the forgiveness has been withheld. I can't describe to you the sheer awfulness of the scenes which go on.'

'Poor darling, but never mind,' said Anne kissing me. 'I'm sure that next time you'll be a huge success as a father – I've every confidence in you.'

Before I could stop myself I was praying that we might remain childless.

VII

This reaction shocked me so much, contrary as it was not only to a fundamental aim of Christian marriage but to Anne's hopes of happiness, that instead of celebrating mass by myself the next morning in the chapel I confessed the sin before God, set myself a penance and spent an additional hour in spiritual exercises. I should, of course, have journeyed to Starwater to make my confession to Cyril – Father Darcy would certainly have thought this a more profound exercise in humility – but I told myself I was too busy grappling with parish matters; by that time I was very much aware that my major problem, the problem which overshadowed all others, was my ministry as a country priest.

Starrington Magna was a large village and the parish boundaries included not only the hamlet of Starrington Parva but an area of scattered farms and smallholdings. Altogether I had the care of some two thousand souls of whom about a hundred were Methodists who gathered weekly in a hall near the station. I was told there were no Roman Catholics in the parish, and this fact was declaimed in the manner of a virtuous housewife announcing that her home was free of mice. Of those who belonged to the Church of England, a minority never went to church and a majority entered it only for christenings, weddings and funerals but a respectable number turned up at Christmas and Easter. Allowing for the decline in regular church-going I thought the number of weekly worshippers was more than merely respectable, although of course I immediately found myself wondering how this loyal band of supporters could be increased. All this useful information about the parish had been recorded by Mr Wetherall himself in an account which he had written for the benefit of those who had the care of his flock in his absence; he had also set out details of the various social clubs and the areas of the parish which required special visiting.

I had realized at once that transport presented a problem for I could hardly go visiting the poor in Anne's chauffeur-driven motor, and although I was prepared to walk everywhere, long journeys on foot are time-consuming. As I had always worked in small areas I had never encountered this problem before, but fortunately Mrs Wetherall, foreseeing my predicament, offered me her husband's bicycle and I soon accustomed myself to riding it. It had proved a pleasant surprise to discover how greatly the machines had improved in comfort and safety since my youth in the 1890s.

Mr Wetherall had relied very much on his bicycle. He had been active among the rural poor in the remote areas of his parish, and his work in listening, helping and consoling had borne fruit; the congregation consisted not merely of the comfortable middle-classes but of the humbler families as well. Obviously he had been an admirable pastor, and I found that thanks to his hard work I had inherited a parish which had been only minimally debilitated by eight months of caretaking.

From one point of view this was an asset, but from another it was a disadvantage. Mr Wetherall had been popular. With his memory now glorified by his war service the villagers tended to see him as a paragon with the result that I was continually being confronted with such fatal phrases as: 'The vicar said . . . the vicar believed . . . the vicar did things *this* way.' I could not even remove the most repulsive vase of dried flowers from a secluded alcove without a chorus of females telling me: 'The vicar wanted the flowers to stay there because they came from old Mrs Lacy who was so kind to him,' and soon I realized that there existed an influential clique who believed any change whatsoever would be nothing short of stabbing Mr Wetherall in the back. Of the two churchwardens one was Anne's friend Colonel Maitland who was anxious to be accommodating to me, but the other was a formidable bore called Pitkin, the local chemist, who talked as if he and Mr Wetherall had run the parish unaided. I immediately realized that Mr Wetherall, a man twenty years younger than this power-mad churchwarden, had allowed himself to be bullied far too often, and I saw that one of my first tasks was to teach Mr Pitkin that his bullying days were over.

However a more serious problem lay neither with the potent memory of Mr Wetherall nor with the troublesome male members of the congregation but with the females. As I have already made clear, I was unaccustomed to dealing with women on a pastoral level, but it is a notorious fact of parish life that middle-aged and elderly women form the nucleus of the congregation, representing the brigade of churchworkers whom no clergyman can do without. I had to adjust to my brigade and adjust quickly, but I found it a strain which took a heavy toll on my spiritual stamina.

The women were mostly good women in their own way but soon I encountered bickering, backchat, gossip and a general level of pettiness sufficient to irritate any man beyond endurance. The problem was compounded, I am sorry to record, by the fact that as the male in the centre of their band I became an object of intense interest verging on obsession, and soon they were all vying in a most unedifying fashion for my favour.

It is easy to laugh at this problem, but the Whitby affair had taught me that situations which start by being mildly amusing can quickly become dangerously bizarre. I knew I had to dampen the ardour of my ladies' hero-worship but because of my inexperience as a pastor of women I was uncertain how this could be achieved. Being hero-worshipped by men is quite different; one can be firm to the point of brutality yet still put everything right by giving a brief smile at the end of the reproof. The result is that the men respect one's toughness, know they have to pull themselves together yet know too that they remain unrejected. When I tried this approach with one of the women she merely dissolved into tears. I was both horrified and baffled. What was I to do? What had Mr Wetherall done? But Mr Wetherall was the same age as Charles and the prevalent feminine attitude to him had clearly been maternal. I was a man of their own generation and their attitude was predatory. It made no difference that I was married. They all appeared to like Anne, and besides probably none of them wanted me in any straightforward carnal way. They only desired endless carnal titillation from my presence. The situation was most perturbing, and the most perturbing part of all was that the more inpeccably I behaved the worse the situation became. Impeccability evidently inflamed them. I began to suspect that short of transforming myself into a cross-eyed midget I was to have no escape from this absurd and potentially unhealthy situation.

I can never quite understand why women find me attractive, but since there is consistent evidence that they do I have been obliged to accept the attraction as a fact. And of course this fact is highly gratifying to my pride. (Small wonder that Father Darcy thought my ministry should be only to men.) But once pride is cast aside and the female attitude viewed dispassionately the root of the attraction remains embedded in mystery. I am not in the least handsome in any conventional sense of the word. I have a bony angular face which often looks positively ugly when I shave it in the harsh light of early morning. I also have a pallor which in a woman could be described as 'interesting' but which in a man can only appear sinister. Apart from my unusual height the most striking detail of my appearance is that my hair and eyes are a matching shade of grey but this is a recent development, and when I was a young man with mouse-coloured hair and pale eyes framed by spectacles I could only judge myself very plain indeed. However even in those days plenty of women appeared to disagree with me. I can only conclude that in some mysterious way my attraction lies in the powers, those 'glamorous powers', which have so consistently embroiled me in trouble. Women sense them and respond. 'You have such an unusual presence,' a girl had said to me once, and another had added: 'That air of authority's so striking.' When I was in the cloister I had assumed that my grey hair would provide me with a new respectability, countering the unsuitable raciness exuded by the powers, but now I realized in dismay that instead I had acquired a touch of distinction which only enhanced my appeal to the opposite sex. The result was that I was probably less suited than I had ever been in my life to work in a pastoral capacity among women.

Even if I had been single I would have had no desire to misbehave with any of my attentive females, all of whom I found effortlessly resistible, and we were certainly a long way from an outbreak of hysteria at matins, but the atmosphere of simmering sexuality was an intolerable distraction and very bad for everyone's spiritual health. Women should come to church to worship God, not to ogle the priest. The priest should feel free to move without constraint among his flock, not smitten with the urge to groan when trapped in the vestry by a purposeful admirer.

I used the vestry as an office; I considered it my duty to be as accessible as possible to those who needed me, and my humbler parishioners might well have thought twice before knocking on the door of the Manor, but I was so often pestered by women who wanted to chat about nothing that I soon wound up well-nigh demented with exasperation. Most of my day seemed to be wasted on trivialities. I had little scope for my talents, and the work often appeared not only dull but unrewarding. I had struck an edifying pose to Aysgarth when I had insisted that the former Abbot of Grantchester should not be too proud to serve as a rural priest, but Aysgarth's argument that I had a duty to find a post commensurate with my abilities in order to serve God best had in fact been the sounder spiritual position. Deprived of the opportunity to exercise my special skill, the counselling of churchmen in varying degrees of distress, and unable to make use of my special experience, acquired at Ruydale, the training of men for the priesthood, I found that my psyche was quickly invaded by boredom, frustration and restlessness.

My alienation from my new work was exacerbated by the fact that I still felt spiritually disorientated. Carefully I set aside a portion of each day for prayer and meditation, but I missed the framework of the monastic office and ever since my return to the world I had been depressed by the turgid level of worship in the churches. After seventeen years in a monastery, where worship is regarded as of the first importance, I could not help but be appalled by the poor singing, the lacklustre responses and the general air of genteel ennui. Possibly I was being too critical; probably I was setting an impossibly high standard for laymen; but the fact remained that my dissatisfaction increased my irritation with the curacy I had so unscrupulously managed to obtain.

Once or twice I started a frank letter to Francis but I tore my efforts up and sent a bland report instead. I was too proud to acknowledge the truth we both knew: that I had taken on the curacy for the wrong reasons. In addition although I was now paying the price for my self-aggrandisement I was too proud to admit the cost was proving more expensive than I had anticipated. I did see Cyril at Starwater every two weeks to make my confession but Cyril, though a formidable priest in many ways, had neither Father Darcy's uncanny power of intuiting concealed truths nor the worldly scepticism combined with hard logic which made Francis so difficult to deceive. In other words, I found I could manipulate Cyril. However at least I was not too proud to recognize that this was a most unsatisfactory state of affairs, and finally I tried to face up to the mess by praying for the grace to improve my situation in the way which would prove most pleasing to God. It then occurred to me that instead of secretly moaning that the members of my flock were driving me mad with their trivial problems, banal activities and limp attitude to worship, I had to serve them with a verve which would rouse the entire parish from its languid mediocrity.

I had already dusted down the organist and shaken up the choirboys; the former had been playing at a funereal pace in keys which favoured alto-tenors, and the latter had become accustomed to stuffing themselves with sweets during the sermon. (The retired canon who had been taking the services had been too blind to see this disgusting exhibition of juvenile greed.) I now cultivated the organist by encouraging him to venture deeper into the rich pastures of English Church music, and I took a similar winning interest in the choirboys; I singled them out for special attention when I visited the village school once a week to take the obligatory scripture classes. The choirboys' mothers also benefited from my benign attention with the result that all the little surplices were washed and starched, all the little heads possessed clean, parted hair and all the little feet were clad in shining shoes.

As I had proved at Grantchester, clean people in a clean environment perform their work better, and having polished the choirboys to a high lustre I turned my attention to the church by engaging a new cleaning woman whom I judged would wage war on dirt with a zeal worthy of Ruth. I then organized my brigade of ladies into a flurry of flower-arranging and sent the altar-cloth to the cleaners.

More innovations followed. I changed the disagreeable brand of communion wine despite howls of protest from the communicants who possessed a sweet tooth. Chopping verses ruthlessly from psalms and hymns I tried to make the conventional services brighter and brisker; it is a fallacy, as both the Low-Church and the High-Church parties have proved in their very different ways, that reverent worship can only be recognized by its dreary pace and somnolent content. Then I reduced the time of the sermon. It is a characteristic of Anglo-Catholic worship that less emphasis is placed on the sermon than on the liturgy, and rather than declaiming for half an hour in true Protestant fashion I offered my congregation between ten and fifteen minutes of simple but I hoped not insignificant discourse. I am not one of those flamboyant oratorical preachers such as Dr Jardine, the former Bishop of Starbridge, but nevertheless in my own austere way I have always been able to make an incisive impression on an audience. Preaching too is a charism, of course, and like all charisms it can be subject to abuse but I was very careful, as I strove to rouse the parish from its apathy, not to give way to the temptation to resort to the shadier methods of evangelism.

I knew from the beginning that it would be unwise for me to introduce a form of worship which reflected my High-Church inclinations into a parish where antipathy to Catholicism ran high, but when I embarked on my effort to stimulate my congregation I found I could not accept that the only Anglo-Catholic touch I was allowed to make was the reduced length of the sermon. Cautiously I introduced a few candles, and when no one objected I stealthily planted more. Still no one objected, and step by step I then began to incorporate further rich touches of Anglo-Catholic symbolism into my services. I took care to explain each innovation so that no one could accuse me of staging a mere pretty pageant, and for a while I thought I was encountering a miraculous conversion on all fronts to my belief that colourful ritual can aid devotion by making complex religious truths more accessible, but gradually rumours reached me of rebellion.

In the beginning no one made any pointed remarks except my bossy churchwarden Mr Pitkin who asked if it were true that I intended to install a statue of the Virgin and order my congregation to worship it. 'The worship of statues constitutes idolatry, Mr Pitkin,' I said austerely, 'and besides, although St Mary must be regarded by us with the greatest reverence, worship should be confined to the Trinity.' I added to reassure him: 'This is the English, not the Roman Church!' and he retired satisfied, but I then made a fatal mistake. The following Sunday I announced during Matins that I intended to set aside a certain time each week for the hearing of confessions.

My purpose in making this move was not simply to gratify my longing to return to my work as a confessor; I still conducted a certain amount of spiritual direction by correspondence with men I had counselled as a monk so I was far from being wholly frustrated in this field. However I hoped that my gesture in offering myself as a confessor to my community might identify those who were in deep need of spiritual help yet had so far been too shy to come forward. Carefully I explained to the congregation that confession to a priest was not compulsory within the Church of England, but the very word 'confession' reeks of Popery to a certain type of Protestant, and I found I had opened the floodgates to a tidal wave of complaints about my 'Romish' practices.

In vain I insisted that the Anglo-Catholics did not recognize the Pope's jurisdiction and that the English Catholic Church had all the advantages of the Church of Rome (the heritage of the Early Church, the rich liturgical tradition, the distinctive spirituality) and none of the disadvantages (the accretion of superstition and myth, the chaotic history of the Papacy, the despotic power of a leader who purported to be infallible). To my protestant congregation only the word 'Catholic' was audible, and the fact that the Anglo-Catholics were within the Church of England merely provoked the response: 'What can the Church be coming to?'

I was accused of genuflection as if it were adultery, of facing east at the crucial point of the mass as if I were a Moslem praying to Mecca, of making the sign of the cross with the frequency of a magician performing a conjuring trick and of retaining my hold on the chalice as if I feared one of my communicants might run off with it. All my attempts at explanation – and naturally I was quite prepared to justify these alien practices – were brushed aside as the complaints thundered on. I had littered the church with 'nasty Papist candles'. I had a thoroughly objectionable habit of referring to the service of Holy Communion as mass. (It was true that after seventeen years with the Fordites I did sometimes let slip the word 'mass' in public, but in fact the habits of one's early years die hard and I usually had no trouble remembering to say 'communion' instead.) Then I was accused not only of reserving the sacrament; I was even accused of plotting to import a pyx, but fortunately I could deny this latter charge with a clear conscience since I had had the sense to realize that to introduce perpetual reservation at that stage would certainly have been to push my Anglo-Catholic luck too far. However I insisted that I would continue to reserve the sacrament for the sick, and my enemies, maddened by my firmness, roared back into the attack by accusing me of smuggling incense into the vestry; I had indeed planned to introduce incense into the services at Advent and had even gone so far as to order a censer, but when I saw that no one appeared able to pronounce the word 'incense' without a shudder my nerve failed and I protested that the incense was only for use in the village schools' nativity play.

In the midst of all this nonsense my confession-hour was overrun by my brigade of ladies, who saw it as a legitimate opportunity to talk to me alone, and the whole worthy experiment dissolved into futility.

I felt so enraged, so frustrated and so dibilitated by these unedifying events that I actually sat down to pen a full confession to Francis, but the letter was never written.

The military police informed me that Martin had unsuccessfully attempted to commit suicide.

VIII

The suicide attempt had been half-hearted, no more than a cry for help from an actor unable to sustain his role, but in the military hospital the extent of his alcoholism was discovered and he remained a patient there for some weeks before his inevitable discharge from the Army. Of course

I visited him but since we still seemed to be incapable of meeting without upsetting each other the psychiatrist in charge of his case deemed it wiser that I should temporarily keep my distance. I consoled myself with the thought that at least my son was being cared for in a safe place, but I was made very miserable by the incident and for a while all my other problems seemed trivial in comparison.

Anne was kindness itself to me throughout this agonizing time but I remained haunted by the anxiety that I might try her patience too far; I was sure the last thing she wanted was to see me crucified by the legacy of my first marriage, and I was also afraid that in my distress I might betray my horror of begetting more children who might grow up profoundly unhappy. Accordingly I drew a veil over my suffering to protect her from it and renewed my efforts never to weary her with any self-centred display of grief.

I did write a brief letter about Martin to Francis who replied with sympathy and urged me to visit him, but when out of a reluctance to discuss my other problems I declined to leave the parish at that time, I suspected Anne was relieved. London was still under heavy attack, and the Archbishop, bombed out of Lambeth Palace, had even withdrawn to Canterbury; I could not help but think critically of him for his retreat from the capital in such a time of crisis, but Dr Lang was an old man now and perhaps it ill became me to criticize him when I myself was safe in the country. As all the reports made clear, London had become a nightmare, and soon the nightmare was extended when the Luftwaffe at last turned aside to bomb the provincial cities. In mid-November the great cathedral at Coventry was smashed to rubble, but no bomb could destroy the spirit that dwelt there. Immediately a cross was fashioned from the scorched beams and a month later the Christmas service was broadcast to the nation from the ruins.

Meanwhile the citizens of Starbridge were anxiously eyeing their famous spire but Starbridge, unlike Coventry, was not an industrial centre and its cathedral remained intact, a symbol of the indestructible miraculously persisting in a world where destruction had become a way of life. I have always thought that one of the most demonic aspects of war is the way in which evil comes to be accepted as normal to such an extent that it is even woven into the mundane pattern of daily existence. I travelled around the parish with my regulation gas-mask and soon found I could sling it in my bicycle-basket with no more emotion than I expended in putting on my hat. I talked to the Home Guard, a jolly, friendly bunch of men, and found it easy to forget they had been licensed to commit murder. I spoke to air-raid wardens who enforced the black-out and never boggled at the possibility that a stray bomb could blow us all to smithereens. I embarked on a campaign to raise money for the victims of Coventry but soon ceased to be horrified by the revolting fact that these innocent civilians had been maimed by men deliberately pulling levers in machines travelling far above the earth. Insanity and normality went hand in hand, and as I approached the familiar Christmas festivities I saw my own private world reflecting the war in microcosm again, my dark stark problems flowing with a sinister invisibility alongside my comforting Christian routine.

With the help of Anne and the village schoolmistresses I staged a magnificent nativity play. A well-attended carol service, designed to cater to Protestant taste, followed the next day, and on Christmas Eve I decided I had earned the right to celebrate a midnight mass in the best Anglo-Catholic tradition. My devoted ladies, all of whom had become Anglo-Catholics, praised me fulsomely afterwards, but the wretch Pitkin was outraged and before the end of the year I had a visit from the Rural Dean, a round rubicund gentleman who supervised six parishes in my corner of the diocese and whom I found prowling around the altar one morning as if he were sniffing for incense. I gave him luncheon at the Manor, plied him liberally with vintage port and expected to hear no more from the authorities, but in the new year Aysgarth wrote to request an interview, and with a sinking heart I realized – too late – that my talent for disruption had landed me in the sort of trouble which any priest in his right mind would have been at pains to avoid.

IX

I received Aysgarth in the vestry. A small paraffin heater alleviated the chill in the room, but apart from this one touch of luxury my surroundings were impressively spartan. If Aysgarth had expected to see me languishing in luxurious vestments amidst a cloud of incense, he had been doomed to disappointment.

'I'm sorry to trouble you like this,' he said civilly when we were both seated. 'After the Rural Dean reported that in his opinion the fuss was a storm in a teacup I was going to do no more than write you a letter, but since the Bishop himself has now received a complaint he's suggested that it might be helpful if we had an informal talk.' He paused before adding blandly: 'When a new clergyman takes charge of a parish it's important to iron out any initial difficulty as quickly as possible.'

'I'm trying hard, I assure you, Archdeacon, to iron out my initial difficulty, but unfortunately Mr Pitkin doesn't take kindly to being ironed.'

Receiving this good-natured comment with a repellent absence of humour Aysgarth said stiffly: 'I'm sorry to hear you've fallen out with Mr Pitkin. It pays a parson to keep on good terms with his churchwardens.'

I was well aware of this obvious fact of clerical life and I disliked being treated as a parish novice by a man who was young enough to be my son. Abruptly I demanded: 'What's the exact charge against me?'

'It's said that you deviate frequently from the rubric.'

'But everyone knows the rubric isn't strictly enforced nowadays!'

'Nevertheless it represents the rules governing worship in the Church, and if you deviate from orthodox practice your opponents have a legitimate grievance against you. For example, I'm told that you present the chalice to the lips of the communicants instead of "into their hands" as the rubric orders – '

'Would you like me to see the Bishop to reassure him that I've no intention of going over to Rome?'

Of course he hated being reminded that I had the Bishop under my thumb. I saw his hard mouth tighten but he kept his temper and merely continued to list the charges against me. One or two, like the example he had already cited, were justified. The rest were a tribute to Pitkin's anti-papist paranoia.

'I can't urge you too strongly to stick to the rubric in future,' concluded Aysgarth at last despite my vigorous defence of my rights as a Catholic within the Church of England, 'and I'd also urge you to make your peace with the hostile minority by soft-pedalling the Anglo-Catholic touches for the time being. In a rural parish like this it's vital to acknowledge the strong conservative bias in your congregation by making changes slowly. Of course I'm willing to allow for the fact that you've no previous experience in a rural parish, but – '

'Thank you, Archdeacon, but there's no need for you to sweeten your reproof with a coating of sugar. I trust,' I said, inwardly seething with rage, 'that I'm capable of acknowledging my errors with a proper spirit of humility. I'm sorry you've been troubled by this matter. I shall do my best to see you're not troubled again.'

That terminated the conversation but I could see I had once more annoyed Aysgarth by adopting a tone which would have been better suited to admonishing recalcitrant monks. I wished then that I had been less inflamed with angry pride but the damage had been done and I knew I had wound up enemies again.

My career as a parish priest seemed to be going from bad to worse.

I felt deeply depressed.

X

After Aysgarth had departed I wanted only to return home to seek solace in the chapel but instead I had to face a bunch of my ladies who arrived five minutes later for a committee meeting. We were due to discuss the arrangements for an evening of entertainment in the church hall to raise money for wounded airmen, but as usual at such committee meetings the conversation continually soared off at irrelevant tangents as my ladies fell increasingly in love with the sound of their own voices. I squeezed a couple of decisions out of them with a ruthlessness which I fear they enjoyed and then terminated the proceedings by announcing my obligation to visit the alms-houses.

The women drifted away, still gossiping, and I was just preparing to follow them when I heard a loud groan resounding in the nave. Hurrying from the vestry I found the new cleaner, Mrs Purvis, doubled up over her mop and pail halfway down the central aisle. My ladies, clucking in sympathy, were anxious to help but the sufferer could only gasp that there was nothing they could do.

I strode down the aisle, the ranks parted and poor Mrs Purvis, quite immobilized by pain, at once turned scarlet with embarrassment.

'It's my lumbago, Vicar.' (I was often granted this title as a courtesy.) 'I mean no disrespect but I can't move. I'm ever so sorry.'

I felt as if someone had injected me with a drug which delivered instantaneous amnesia. I forgot the humiliating interview with Aysgarth, my unhappiness in my ministry and my misery over Martin. I was aware only that I was being offered the most alluring of challenges and beyond the challenge I sensed an admiring audience was already poised to restore my self-esteem.

'Where exactly is the pain, Mrs Purvis?' Kneeling beside her I put a reassuring hand on her arm.

'Low down in my back, sir – oooh, it's ever so awful, worse than childbirth – '

I touched her at the base of her spine. 'Here?'

'That's it – oooh! I can't get up, truly I can't – '

'Never mind about getting up for the moment. Just keep in a position which gives you the least pain.'

'I feel ever such a silly – '

'Never mind about that either. Just concentrate on getting into the best position . . . That's it. Now try to relax as far as you possibly can. Relax your arms first . . . and let the relaxation spread up your arms to your neck . . . and slowly, very slowly, inch by inch down your back . . . Good . . . And breathe calmly . . . deeply . . . Excellent! Now Mrs Purvis, I want you to concentrate very hard on that part of your body where the pain is and picture the pain as a big red glass ball which you want me to smash. Close your eyes and you'll be able to picture it better . . . Can you see it?'

'Oooh yes, sir – a beautiful red glass ball with air bubbles in it – '

'That's your pain. Concentrate very hard on it, very, very hard, so hard that your mind aches – and now picture me raising a hammer to smash the glass to pieces. Are you concentrating? Concentrating hard – as hard as you possibly can? Good. Now picture me raising the hammer. I'm going to count to five and when I say SMASH the ball's going to shatter. Ready?' I prayed silently. 'One . . . Two . . . Three . . .' I increased the intensity of the prayer '. . . Four . . . Five – SMASH!'

'Oooh!' gasped Mrs Purvis.

'Oooh!' gasped my ladies as I grasped Mrs Purvis' shoulder with one hand and pressed hard on the base of her spine with the other.

'Oooh!' gasped Mrs Purvis again, shocked into straightening her back. 'That felt ever so funny, Vicar!'

'But you can move now.'

Mrs Purvis was stupefied. 'So I can!' She turned her body gingerly from side to side. 'Well, I never!' She was enrapt. Her honest country-woman's face was aglow with gratitude. 'That's a miracle, that is!'

I made no comment but merely helped her to her feet before advising her to go home and rest.

'Yes, sir – thank you, sir – oh, just wait till I tell all my neighbours! Doctor can never do a thing for my lumbago, never, nothing he gives me for it ever does any good at all!'

I looked at my ladies. They were as breathless and shining-eyed as the monks who had witnessed the recovery of Whitby. Finally someone said in a hushed voice: 'It *was* a miracle, wasn't it, Father?' and at once I answered: 'Nonsense! Pain can often disappear spontaneously if the sufferer is relaxed and confident,' but even as I spoke I could see that none of them believed me.

I shuddered at the memory of Father Darcy, but the terrible truth was, as I knew all too well, that for the first time since I had embarked on my curacy I felt genuinely happy as a country priest.

FIFTEEN

'The line between a quack and a scientific healer is not always easy to draw.'

W. R. INGE
Dean of St Paul's 1911–1934
A Pacifist in Trouble

I

'Might this be a sign about your new call?' was Anne's immediate reaction that evening to the tale of Mrs Purvis.

'Not necessarily.'

Anne remained fascinated but I sensed her thoughts moving more cautiously. '*Was* it a miracle?'

'Good heavens, no! Of course there's a perfectly rational explanation. Mrs Purvis was deeply embarrassed that she should have been caught in such a ridiculous position, and the pain would have been aggravated by her excessive tension. As soon as I had helped her to relax, the pain eased sufficiently to enable me to terminate the spasm by using a mild form of hypnosis. I need hardly add that I haven't cured her of the lumbago – she'll get another spasm sooner or later. All I did was alleviate the symptoms of a particularly unpleasant attack.'

Anne said after careful consideration: 'I don't see anything wrong with that.'

'There's certainly nothing wrong "per se" in alleviating Mrs Purvis' pain. The complications are going to set in when other people ask me to cure their aches and pains.'

'Well, if the prospect troubles you – and it obviously does – why don't you go to Francis and ask his advice?'

'It's so hard to find the time to go to London.'

'Surely you could find the time if you wanted to! I think it would do you good to unburden yourself to Francis about Martin and Pitkin and – oh good heavens, I nearly forgot to ask! What happened when Neville Aysgarth called on you today?'

I gave her a colourless account of the unpleasant scene in the vestry and she exclaimed angrily: 'Of course Aysgarth follows his mentor Dr Jardine who never had any sympathy with the Anglo-Catholics!'

I forced myself to say: 'In a very real sense our conversation wasn't about Anglo-Catholicism. It was about my inexperience as a parish priest.' With a superhuman effort I managed to add: 'He had a point. I've probably introduced too many changes too quickly.'

Seeing that Aysgarth had upset me Anne became angrier than ever. 'But think of all you've achieved! You're electrified the parish!'

'Yes – like a bolt of lightning which splits a tree in two,' I said, but unfortunately this reply, intended as a light remark, emerged as a bitter comment and at once I was furious with myself. It would never do to bore her by moaning about my lot. 'Isn't it an irony,' I remarked, trying to dismiss the jubject with good humour, 'that the English, who pride themselves on maintaining the most elaborate ceremonial in so many areas of public life, have this extraordinary mass-antipathy to any elaborate ceremonial in religion?'

Anne laughed but said with an unexpected earnestness: 'Darling, I can see how depressed you are by all this bigotry, and I really do wish you'd cheer yourself up by slipping up to London for a couple of days' undiluted Anglo-Catholicism – '

'That sounds as if you want to have a holiday from me.'

'Oh you silly man, don't talk such nonsense!'

'I'm not complaining about my work – please don't think I'm complaining – '

'I know you're not and sometimes I worry about that too. I don't think it's good for you to bottle everything up and pretend that everything in the garden's lovely – '

'Everything in the garden *is* lovely,' I said firmly. 'I just have one or two little difficulties at the moment, that's all.'

But although Anne made no effort to argue further with me I suspected that I had only partially alleviated her concern.

II

That night I was unable to consummate my marriage. It was not the first time such a failure had occurred after a long hard day's labour in the parish, but now in my depression I felt doubly humiliated, doubly angry and – worst of all – doubly frightened about the future.

'Don't say anything,' I muttered to Anne, although she had given no indication that she was about to speak, and then before I could stop myself I was sliding into the most shameful tantrum. 'How I hate being sixty!' I burst out. 'I hate it, hate it, hate it!' But immediately I despised myself for being too exhausted to suppress the urge to complain.

After a while Anne said: 'Am I allowed to speak now?'

'Yes, but don't tell me not to mind about being sixty.' I was so miserable that I sounded like a thoroughly irascible old man.

Anne said gently: 'I was going to remind you of our honeymoon. Do you remember when you said: "Don't talk as if you're a performing seal in a circus"?'

'Maybe one day you'll decide you'd be better off with a performing seal.'

'Oh, for heaven's sake, Jon!' Understandably she lost patience. 'Stop being so damn ridiculous!'

Fear grabbed me by the throat and settled there in a lump. Burying my face in her breasts I tried to apologize but no words came. I was quite unable to speak.

'Silly man!' said Anne, somehow recapturing her patience and even lovingly stroking my hair. 'What's one night? As if it mattered!'

But it mattered to me.

I lay awake worrying in the dark.

III

Two days later at Matins every pew was occupied and afterwards a long queue of people formed to shake my hand as if they wanted to sample my 'magic touch'. A beaming Mrs Purvis announced: 'I told everyone how your hands gave off those funny electric shocks, Vicar!' and her husband, who was clearly enjoying his wife's new fame, declared admiringly: 'Reckon we've got a magician for a parson!' I did say austerely that the practice of magic would hardly have been a fitting occupation for a priest, but nobody was listening. My parishioners were too busy asking me to call on aged relatives housebound by rheumatism, arthritis, lumbago, sciatica and a host of other debilitating complaints, and although I was careful to refer to the doctor anyone who had not received a professional diagnosis, I promised to call on the chronic cases which could no longer be helped by orthodox medicine.

I regret to say I found this deep interest in me immensely stimulating, and that afternoon when I should have been praying quietly in preparation for Evensong I was in such good spirits that I retired to bed with my wife and made amends in no uncertain fashion for my failure two days earlier.

'Thank goodness you got over that depression!' said Anne afterwards. 'But after all the hordes in church this morning it's small wonder that you're in a good mood. Don't you think it's obvious now that you're being called to the ministry of healing?'

I knew the correct reply was: 'I must continue to pray for guidance,' but when I saw the passionate enthusiasm in her eyes the words were never spoken. I could only bask in the warmth of her unstinted admiration and eventually I found myself reflecting that it did indeed seem as if my new call had begun to unfold.

IV

I could do little for the housebound old people although they all seemed determined to believe that I had relieved their pain to some degree. I suspected that they derived comfort principally from the fact that someone in authority was prepared to listen sympathetically to their troubles, but by this time the village was more than ready to believe their parson had miraculous powers and I was just wondering how I should deal with the continuing stream of requests for help when I received a visit from the local doctor.

Dr Garrison was a man in his fifties with a bluff hearty manner and a resolute atheism courteously expressed. At our first meeting he had said: 'I wish you well, Darrow, and if there's anything I can do for you let me know, but I'm afraid you won't see me in church because I'm a practical down-to-earth fellow who hasn't time for theories which can't be scientifically proved.' In other words he acknowledged only five senses and was determined to justify this limitation by embracing logical positivism. However plenty of excellent people are logical positives, and since he had tried in his own way to give me a friendly welcome to the parish I had seen no reason to dislike him.

'Well, I won't beat about the bush,' he said, bustling into the vestry and flinging himself down in the visitor's chair. 'What's all this I hear about faith-healing? I wouldn't have thought a man of your distinction would dabble in quackery, Darrow!'

'You thought correctly.'

Garrison at once became irritated, and beyond the irritation I sensed his fear of matters which defied conventional explanations. 'Then perhaps you'd be good enough to explain the incident with Mrs Purvis,' he said abruptly. 'How did you remove the symptoms of her lumbago?'

'I offered myself to God as a channel for the healing power of the Holy Spirit.'

He went scarlet. 'Don't joke about this, please. It's a serious matter.'

'I don't joke about God. I'm a priest.'

'You may be a clergyman – why do you have to use a damn Papish word like "priest"? – but you're behaving like a witch-doctor! Don't you know that removing symptoms by hypnosis can lead to a serious illness remaining undiagnosed?'

'You diagnosed the lumbago in this case. I would never attempt to help anyone who hadn't first consulted a doctor, nor would I ever attempt to help anyone solely by using hypnotic techniques. The charism of healing can't be reduced to a parlour-trick.'

'No? It looks damnably like a parlour-trick to me!'

'Dr Garrison,' I said, 'you may choose to confine yourself within the narrow boundaries of medical science, but I fail to see why those you can't help should be similarly confined.'

He was incensed. 'That's a highly offensive remark!'

'Not half so offensive as your accusation that a gift from God is a man-made trick. Now may I suggest we conduct the conversation in a calmer, more rational manner? I'm not trying to steal your patients. I'm simply offering comfort to sick people by praying that the Holy Spirit will use me to ease their dis-ease, and if you're the sensible down-to-earth fellow you're always claiming to be you'll now ask yourself why we shouldn't work in harmony.'

'I'm not lending my support to any goings-on which reek of superstitious quackery, and if I find you're wreaking havoc among my patients I'll bloody well lodge a complaint with your Bishop!'

'Why are you so upset, Garrison? What is it you're really afraid of here?'

'*Afraid?* Damn you, I'm not afraid of anything!'

'Then may I suggest you stop behaving as the Church behaved when the scientists first suggested the world wasn't quite so flat as everyone had always thought it was?'

He stormed out and slammed the door.

V

'Silly old duffer!' said Anne that evening.

'He did indeed behave very stupidly, but I should have resisted the temptation to put him in his place.'

'Nonsense!' said Anne. 'It'll do him good! He's become much too bossy, and I've a good mind to transfer my allegiance to Charles' friend Dr Romaine in Starvale St James.'

This certainly was a development I had not anticipated, and my instinctive response was one of alarm. Dr Romaine 'had a past', as we used to say so euphemistically in the 1890s, and although he had been living a life of flawless respectability with his third wife for some years I could not help but feel lukewarm about the prospect of him attending an attractive young woman of thirty-two who also – and here, of course, lay the rub –

happened to be my wife. However since all my information about Romaine had come from confidential talks with Charles, I was unable to explain my feelings to Anne and had to content myself with remarking: 'Romaine's in his late sixties. Wouldn't you prefer a younger man?'

'No,' said Anne, responding in a way I might have predicted if I had been less absorbed in thoughts of Romaine's 'past'. 'I like doctors to be fatherly.'

'I'm sure Garrison will start behaving sensibly once he calms down –'

'I doubt that very much,' said Anne frankly, and her doubt was soon justified. When my offer of peaceful co-existence was spurned a second time I decided I should leave him to wrestle alone with his secret insecurity, and at that point Anne, exasperated by Garrison's pigheadedness, called on Dr Romaine.

As I well knew from my conversations with Charles, Romaine was a man of considerable charm and guile. The result of the interview did not surprise me but I did not like to think of Anne being charmed and beguiled by a member of my own generation, and it cost me a great effort to retain a benign expression as she embarked on her paean of praise.

'He was absolutely delightful!' she exclaimed. 'We talked for ages – he'd heard all about you from Charles, of course, and almost before I knew what was happening I was telling him about the healing. Darling, he was fascinated! He told me some amazing stories of healers in the East – apparently he lived for years in Hong-Kong, and his second wife was a Chinese Christian who firmly convinced him that all healing came from God –'

That was the moment when I bowed to the inevitable and acknowledged that Dr Romaine, clever Dr Romaine, had acquired another devoted patient. However I feared the rift with Garrison would become impossible to heal now that my wife had abandoned him, and my gloom increased the next day when I heard he had been invited to dine with Pitkin. The thought of a Pitkin-Garrison axis was most depressing.

By this time I was so frequently interrupted by parishioners in search of healing that it was becoming difficult for me to work in the vestry, and I was just toying with the idea that I might hold a special service in order to satisfy all the sick simultaneously when something happened which deflected me abruptly from any thought of my new calling.

Anne, returning from a second visit to Dr Romaine, announced that she was having a baby.

There had been physical indications that conception had occurred but I had dismissed them as mere passing phenomena which were of no significance. I knew that part of Anne's interest in Romaine might have stemmed from his reputation an as obstetrician, but I had chosen not to dwell on this aspect of his practice. The truth was that by this time I had successfully hypnotized myself into believing I was sterile – once a man turned sixty surely fertility if not potency abruptly declined? – and fortified by this new-found faith I had regularly dismissed as impossible any hint that I might still be capable of begetting a second family. With this pathetic defence now brutally shattered, I found myself confronted by a truth I was unable to endure. Mechanically I tried to tell myself that God had seen fit to bless my marriage in the best possible way, but I found this statement represented a platitude which was beyond my power to believe. I could only reflect with horror that having bestowed on me the great blessing of a loving wife God had now decided to crush us both by imposing a burden I was quite unfit to bear.

I panicked. My guilt about the past, laced now with a terror of the future, produced a lethal despair. I felt rebellious towards God – a disastrous state of mind for a priest – and my rebellion cut me off from him. Hell is being cut off from God. I was in torment.

But of course I could disclose no hint of this torment to Anne.

'How very exciting!' I said as soon as she broke the news, and before my face could betray me I drew her into my arms for an embrace.

'Now look here,' said Anne, giving me a jolt by disengaging herself and adopting her sternest voice, 'it's going to be all right. You'll still have your peace and privacy – you won't be drowned this time beneath a tidal wave of disorder – and the baby will quite definitely be a good thing. It'll keep you young in outlook and soften the awfulness of being over sixty.'

'My dear Anne, you're preaching to the converted! I'm absolutely delighted by the news, and it gives me the very greatest pleasure to see you so happy.'

I retired to my cell. Prayer was impossible. I could only sit on my wooden chair and wrestle with the demon despair. My psyche was writhing like a flogged snake. I tried to stroke it with various meditation techniques but when it became more contorted than ever I began to be afraid of uncontrolled bursts of kinetic energy. I tried to expel the energy by willing my pencil to fall off the table, but nothing happened. I was unable to channel the energy effectively, and rising to my feet I decided to go to Starwater to talk to Cyril.

But then I sat down again. What could a man who had never been a husband and father know of the terrible conflicts which were now grinding my psyche towards dementia? I thought how I enjoyed and needed marital intimacy yet often found it a physical strain and an emotional burden which interfered with my inner life; I thought how I wanted to give Anne a child yet recoiled from all thought of fatherhood; I thought how my great longing for solitude was juxtaposed with my deep fear of losing Anne's companionship. How could I even begin to explain these tortuous paradoxes to either Cyril or Francis? No childless celibate, no matter how sophisticated, could possibly understand. Indeed so bizarre did the paradoxes seem that I began to doubt that anyone on earth was capable of understanding them. It was at this point that I automatically turned back to God, and overwhelmed by the compulsion to bridge the abyss which separated us I decided to retreat to the chapel to make another desperate attempt at prayer.

But I never reached the chapel. In the garden the mild March sunshine was so pleasant that I sat down on one of the wooden seats by the lawn and sought to soothe my psyche by watching the daffodils nod tranquilly in the breeze. How long I sat there I have no idea, but just as I was trying to summon the energy to resume my journey the daffodils began to change.

I watched them turn a brilliant yellow as the surrounding grass glittered into emerald green, and all the while part of my brain was denying what was happening, declaring that this vision was arriving too soon after the last one to be genuine. As if to confirm my scepticism, the vision failed to develop. I found myself still sitting in the garden, still inhabiting my body, and at last the landscape reverted to its normal colouring. Having concluded that the alteration in my visual perception had been a freak generated by my beleaguered psyche I then received a great shock. I saw that not only had the daffodils faded but the trees were in full leaf.

I gasped but before I could leap to my feet I became aware that I was no longer alone. The hair prickled at the nape of my neck but this sensation was experienced by the Jon of March 1941 because the other Jon, the Jon of the summer day around me, was tranquil. It was as if I were having an impaired vision with the result that I was in two times at once, neither of which seemed wholly real.

Very slowly I turned my head to the left.

A little boy was watching me. He was about ten yards away. He had fair hair, which I knew would darken later, and grave grey eyes set deep in a small serious face. Recalling a photograph taken when I was four years old I realized I was looking at my past self. I was sure of this because I could talk to him without words and I knew that at that moment he was longing for an invitation to sit beside me on the garden-seat. I signalled that I wanted his company, and as he understood he smiled serenely, reminding me of my mother. Obviously my psychic faculties had become addled because I was mixing up the past and present in the most chaotic way imaginable, seeing myself as a child in Anne's garden while telling myself all the time in the March of 1941 that my powers had gone beserk.

Then I became aware of a detail which stupefied me. The little boy was wearing dungarees and a pullover. I was just thinking dazed that I had projected my past self into modern times when I was further shattered by the revelation that the little boy was a stranger. Far away on the terrace I heard an unknown woman's voice call: 'Nicholas! Nicholas!' and as the child turned his head in response the darkness began to creep across my vision from the left.

I cried urgently: 'Nicholas – don't go!' but I was in 1941 and he could not hear me. He ran off across the lawn but although I leapt to my feet in pursuit the darkness blotted him out, the dizziness overcame me and sinking back on the seat I covered my eyes with my hands.

VII

When I opened my eyes the daffodils were nodding in the breeze and I was once more pinned firmly in time. I found I was in a profoundly emotional state. My hands were shaking. My cheeks were wet with tears. My voice was whispering: 'Nicholas ... Nicholas ...' and suddenly I knew all would be well. I thought: 'All shall be well and all manner of things shall be well ...' And as the famous words of Julian of Norwich rang triumphantly in my mind I knew I had received another 'showing'. God in his infinite mercy had taken pity on me in my torment and had given me this assurance that I could go forward into the future with confidence. All would be well with the child, who had beyond doubt been revealed as the sort of son I had always wanted. All would be well with my marriage. All would be well with my ministry of healing. I felt as if a huge burden had been lifted from my psyche, and in a burst of joyous energy I rushed to the chapel to give thanks for yet another great deliverance from the demon of despair.

VIII

When I returned to the house I recorded the vision and placed the account in an envelope which I sealed with wax. I was strongly tempted to tell Anne that I had seen our future son, but I had long since made it a rule that I should never discuss my visions with anyone who could be closely affected by them. There are many futures and not all of them come true, as I knew well enough from my previous psychic experiences. It was bad enough that I myself should occasionally wind up waiting for something which never happened; to impose such a burden on someone else, particularly someone I loved, would have been the height of irresponsibility.

It was only when the sealed envelope was safely tucked away in my cupboard that it occurred to me to wonder why I had chosen the name Nicholas for my new son. I liked the name but there were others I liked better. I could only conclude that it was Anne's favourite name and I had generously allowed her to have her own way.

That evening I was unable to resist saying to her: 'What shall we call the baby if it's a boy?'

'Gerald after my brother,' said Anne promptly, 'and Jonathan after you.'

Automatically I said: 'I don't like my name.' I was so taken aback that I was even tactless enough to add: 'I don't like the name Gerald either.'

'All right, what about Richard, Robert or Nigel?'

I was silent, trying to make sense of all these irrelevant suggestions, and the next moment Anne was exclaiming: 'Why are we assuming it'll be a boy? Maybe it'll be a girl! I like the names Susan, Margaret, Penelope – ' She paused expectantly, but still I was silent. 'Come on, Jon! What are your favourite names?'

'Florence. Beatrice. Enid.'

Anne laughed. 'But no little girls are called Florence, Beatrice and Enid any more!'

'Aren't they?' I said vaguely, forgetting my bewilderment in the relief of seeing her so happy. Smiling back at her impulsively I clasped her hand in mine and added with regret: 'No, I suppose they're not.'

'Darling!' said Anne, tactfully avoiding any further comment on my old-fashioned Victorian taste. 'I can't tell you what a relief it is to me that you're quite obviously in the best of spirits! It sounds silly, I know, but I had this terrible feeling that the baby would tie you up into one of your knots and I wouldn't be able to unravel you.'

We laughed together at this absurd possibility. Then I said jubilantly: ' "All shall be well and all manner of things shall be well!" ' but nevertheless as I spoke I again felt baffled that we should be so far from naming our future son after the perfect child who had visited me that afternoon.

IX

As I had anticipated, Dr Romaine had advised Anne to abstain from marital intimacy until the most common time for miscarriages had passed, so without consulting her I set up a camp-bed in my cell; I had thought it obvious that if one is obliged to be chaste one should at least take the elementary precaution of sleeping alone, but to my dismay Anne was most upset and accused me of being 'monstrously insensitive'. At once I explained that my withdrawal would have been unnecessary if I had not still felt her to be intensely desirable, and when she saw my action had not sprung from sexual antipathy she calmed down, but afterwards I was angry with myself for not handling the matter with more tact.

I missed the intimacy, but I had to admit to myself that the solitary nights in my cell were exquisitely refreshing. Every night I would stay up late reading and meditating, sleep soundly for six hours and rise at five-thirty for prayer. Anne never woke before seven-thirty and as the pregnancy advanced she liked to be in bed each evening by ten. This meant that I had nine and a half hours entirely to myself, and my psyche, secretly undernourished after a diet of reduced solitude, began to thrive again. I found I had more energy for my work, and as this new energy developed, so my healing skills began to flourish.

I achieved a success which was even more dramatic than Mrs Purvis' recovery: a child who had been immobilized for months after an attack of infantile paralysis was able to rise from his wheelchair and walk three steps. Word of the healing spread swiftly not only through the parish but through the surrounding villages, and soon a reporter from *The Starbridge Weekly News* was knocking on the vestry door. I declined to grant an interview on the grounds that it would be most unfitting for a priest to connive at publicity, but the reporter, undaunted, discovered several loquacious villagers who were only too ready to exaggerate my achievements. Less than twenty-four hours before my first service of healing I found myself confronting the highly unedifying front-page headline:

MIRACLES IN STARRINGTON:
EX-MONK'S MARVELS MESMERIZE ALL.

I had thought and prayed a great deal about whether I should hold a service of healing. Certainly I judged it would meet the needs of the vast majority of those who called at the 'surgery' which I now held twice a week at the vestry; these callers were far from being seriously ill but nevertheless they craved comfort for their minor ailments, and I was tempted to think that if I dealt with these lesser cases 'en masse' I would have more time to devote to the chronic sick. These incurables needed my individual attention as I sought to improve the quality of their lives by renewing their spiritual strength, but although I did not think they were likely to be greatly helped by being treated 'en masse' I saw no reason why they should not derive at least some benefit from a service of healing.

I also favoured holding a service because I felt such a gesture would place the healing firmly in a respectable Christian setting. By this time Dr Garrison was not the only person muttering about quackery, and I was aware of a growing desire to defend myself in the most dignified manner available against my enemies' uncharitable slanders.

However I knew I had to approach my task with care, and I realized that my first responsibility was to reduce the risk of any over-emotional behaviour by making the service as plain as possible; this was most definitely not the time to indulge in a riot of Anglo-Catholic ritual. Accordingly I drew up a service which included an opening hymn, a short address in which I exploded any misconceptions about the ministry of healing, an appropriate reading from the New Testament, three spoken prayers and a period of silent prayer. After this interval those wishing to be healed would assemble before the chancel where I could begin the laying-on of hands. I considered anointing but rejected it. I was too afraid my audience would associate the practice with Popery and I wanted no hostile feelings impeding the flow of the charism. Following the laying-on of hands we would sing a second hymn and then I would give a blessing to conclude the service.

These proceedings seemed harmless enough, but I knew I would still have to exercise great vigilance in order to beat back any demonic infiltration. Before I had entered the Order I had out of curiosity attended two services of healing in London and both in their different ways had appalled me. The first service, performed by a renegade priest, had been a spectacle centred on the glorifying of his own personality; the Devil had been hard at work there, cultivating the demon pride and calling forth an idolatrous response. The second service, performed by an individual who was clearly motivated by good intentions, had plunged into chaos because of his lack of authority; unable to control his congregation he had soon been presiding over a gathering where tears, groans, even shrieks were mingled with regular shouts of 'Hallelujah!'. Fortunately he had achieved no striking cures. If he had, the congregation would no doubt have tottered the last inch over the brink into the abyss of hysteria and some deluded victim would have insisted that the congregation was being visited by the Spirit.

From these descriptions it will be clear why the hierarchy of the Church of England tended to regard the public exercise of the charism of healing with a singular lack of enthusiasm, and having planned my service I knew my next step was to win my superior's approval. Accordingly, curcumventing Aysgarth, I made a special journey to the Cathedral Close at Starbridge in order to call on the Bishop.

Dr Ottershaw, once more displaying his endearing willingness to be wound, so to speak, around my little finger, confided that he had always been greatly interested in the charism of healing and declared that as

I was such a distinguished churchman he was sure that any service I conducted would be a model of propriety. He even mused what a pity it was that a prior engagement prevented him from attending the service himself.

I returned in triumph to Starrington.

Fortified by the Bishop's approval I then wrote to Aysgarth to inform him of my plan and received a chilly letter of acknowledgment. He told me that although he would not presume to criticize a plan which had had an episcopal blessing he nevertheless feared that my scheme would only divide the parish more deeply than ever. Did I really feel that it was in the best interests of the Church to quarrel with such a pillar of the community as Dr Garrison? Mr Pitkin had said I was even giving interviews to journalists; surely such a move could only result in a publicity which would attract the wrong people to my service? In short, despite the Bishop's charitable response, should I not consider altering my course in order to pursue a policy of reconciliation with those who were so deeply opposed to this extension of my ministry?

After sparing a growl for the pest Pitkin who had so grossly misrepresented me, I was driven to the reluctant conclusion that Aysgarth had been right to worry about unseemly publicity. The headlines of *The Starbridge Weekly News* had certainly been unnerving, but at that stage I felt it was too late to cancel the service. Too many sick people would have been disappointed, and in addition I remained convinced that the service represented the logical next step as I advanced along the road of my new call.

On the appointed day I rose early in order to celebrate mass by myself in the chapel. Then I fasted, prayed and meditated in absolute seclusion until two o'clock when I walked on my own to the village church. In the interests of austerity I was tempted to wear an unadorned black cassock, but I reluctantly concluded that this would make me look striking in a way which might stimulate quite the wrong response among the ladies, so on reaching the vestry I donned my white surplice in the hope that it would exude a suitably asexual aura.

Emerging from the vestry I noted that the pest Pitkin was conspicuous by his absence, but Colonel Maitland and his team of sidesmen were directing the assembling hordes into the pews with unruffled efficiency. My heart sank when I spotted four men emanating the insatiable curiosity of journalists, but I refused Maitland's suggestion that they should be asked to leave. Possibly these men were religious. Possibly as the result of the service they might become religious. Certainly they were entitled to charitable treatment, and I thought they should be given at least the chance to behave with decorum.

Anxious to be self-effacing in such special circumstances, Anne was sitting halfway down the nave instead of in her usual front pew, and beside her, I noticed with a disagreeable shock, were the Aysgarths. I had not expected Aysgarth to attend and I disliked the thought of him being present. My resolve to conduct a dignified service hardened; retreating once more to the vestry I said my final prayers and then, taking my courage in both hands, embarked on my new adventure.

X

Afterwards I was so exhausted that it was impossible for me to talk to anyone, but I had anticipated this extreme debility after such a massive outpouring of my powers, and Anne had ensured that the motor was waiting beyond the back wall of the churchyard.

'Darling, you were utterly wonderful!' she exclaimed shining-eyed as I collapsed beside her in the back seat, but although I was immediately aware of a blissful security I was too exhausted to do more than grunt in gratitude. As soon as we arrived home I hauled myself upstairs to my cell, sank on to my camp-bed and slept for fourteen hours. The ban on intimacy had by this time been lifted, but I had kept the camp-bed in my cell to ensure chastity on the nights before I attempted any concentrated sessions of healing at my twice-weekly 'surgery'. The rock-bottom truth about sexual intercourse, a truth which it is becoming increasingly fashionable to forget, is that no matter how delightful the experience it only wastes energy which could be more profitably spent elsewhere.

However I had now had fourteen hours' sleep, my exertions as a healer lay for the moment behind me and I felt as exuberant as the most incorrigible hedonist. Waking promptly at half-past five I invaded the kitchens, and in the absence of the servants who never began work before six I made a great mess assembling an enormous breakfast for myself. Then much stimulated by this rare descent into gluttony I bounded back upstairs, bathed, shaved and slid naked into bed with Anne. I was feeling as frisky as a kitten and could hardly wait to prove that the humiliating weaknesses of old age were still a million light years away.

'You were such a success yesterday!' sighed Anne when she finally had the chance to speak. 'I was so proud of you!'

For ten seconds I luxuriated in the warmth of her approval. Then I remembered her companions at the service. 'What did Aysgarth think?' I said with reluctance.

'It's hard to know what he thinks when he puts on his poker-face, but I'm sure he was impressed by your integrity – in fact I don't see how even your worst enemies could find fault with you this time!'

'Rest assured that they'll try,' I said dryly, and sure enough a day later I received a letter from Aysgarth in which he invited me to Star-bridge for a 'frank and friendly' discussion of my ministry at Starrington Magna.

XI

'It is my earnest wish,' said Aysgarth with a pompous air which made me suspect he was nervous, 'that this interview be conducted in a Christian spirit, Mr Darrow, without the animosity which has characterized too many of our previous conversations.'

'Such an aspiration strikes me as being entirely admirable,' I said with a mannered politeness worthy of a character in Jane Austen's novels, 'and I assure you I shall do my best to see that it's fulfilled.' But as I spoke I was remembering Whitby, humouring a mouse by letting it think it could dictate the terms of the battle and then moving in with his paw for the big pounce.

We were seated in Aysgarth's study at his vicarage, a rambling townhouse adjacent to the church of St Martin's-in-Cripplegate. The study, cosy and bookish, exuded an atmosphere of intellectual polish which pleased me despite the fact that the room was the antithesis of my uncluttered cell at the Manor. I was interested and not a little perturbed to see that Aysgarth's taste in reading was dangerously eclectic; below the works of theology, below the classics of English literature, below the tomes of history and biography, lurked a range of modern novels whose spiritual value was reputed to be questionable. I confess that even I, who had argued so fervently to Father Darcy that priests should not be too narrow in their reading, could only boggle at the sight of a volume with D. H. LAWRENCE inscribed boldly on the spine. Aysgarth was not a monk and there was in fact no reason why he should not read widely to extend his knowledge of human nature, but I really did think that a man who was not only a priest but an archdeacon should take the trouble to encase the work of a writer like Lawrence in discreet brown paper before consigning it to a shelf in his library. However no doubt Aysgarth, being a member of the younger generation, would have judged this reaction to be a typical example of Victorian hypocrisy. I shall only add that there are times when I think 'Victorian hypocrisy', the younger generation's label for an attitude which values tact, discretion and good taste above boorishness, boastfulness and vulgarity, has been greatly maligned.

Since the books occupied most of the walls there were no paintings in the room, but the mantelshelf was adorned with framed photographs of his pretty, radiant wife and his bright-eyed, good-looking children. This flaunting of a successful family life irritated me, but I told myself all jealousy should be ruthlessly suppressed. I made a new resolution to be well-behaved.

Meanwhile Aysgarth, prim and proper in his archidiaconal uniform, was looking as if he had never heard of D. H. Lawrence, and this impression of a double-image, of a man with racy tastes living alongside a man who was the soul of propriety, intrigued me deeply. To some extent we all have our double-images, our public and private selves, but there are cases when the split between the two can widen into such an abyss that an intolerable strain is put on the psyche. I had encountered such cases during my work as a director of souls, and since all the men afflicted had wound up in a state of spiritual debility I now wondered anew about Aysgarth's inner life. However I was uncomfortably aware that such critical speculation ill-became a priest who had shied away from his own spiritual director for some months while making only the most perfunctory confessions to the Abbot of Starwater.

'I was most interested in the service of healing,' Aysgarth was saying as I recalled my wandering attention, 'and I congratulate you on maintaining control of the congregation in such a charged emotional atmosphere.'

I at once said: 'Hysteria's actually very rare.'

'Is it? In circumstances such as this when the clergyman attempts to assume extraordinary power over the congregation and stimulate the most primitive emotions? I had heard otherwise. However,' said Aysgarth, giving me no chance to comment, 'let's not dwell on the dangers you were skilful enough to avoid. How successful was the service in terms of healing?'

'Most of the sufferers have claimed improvement, but in some cases – particularly the ones involving sight and hearing – it's still too early to look for marked results.'

'You've had success with cases involving sight and hearing?'

'Certainly, but that's an area where healers are often effective.'

'Dr Garrison,' said Aysgarth, speaking with great care, 'has ventured the opinion that your successes are achieved entirely by a hypnosis which eventually wears off, leaving the sufferer's condition unchanged.'

'Balls.'

Aysgarth looked as shocked as if I had uttered a blasphemy and I began to feel exasperated. 'Come, come, Archdeacon!' I said smiling at him. 'There are no ladies present, and you can't tell me they don't use words like that up in Yorkshire!'

Aysgarth said with an insufferable priggishness: 'I think a clergyman has a duty to avoid vulgar language even when there are no ladies present.'

This of course was true but I was deeply annoyed that my attempt to lessen the stiffness of the atmosphere by injecting a casual masculine informality had been so ruthlessly rebuffed. Then I realized with fury that he had outmanoeuvred me. The word had not shocked him in the least but by pretending that it had he had seized the chance to tilt the balance of power in his favour by administering a justifiable rebuke.

I tried to tilt the balance back. 'May I suggest we dispense with the debate on clerical etiquette and stick to the subject under discussion? Let me state as firmly as possible that I'm not a quack performing tricks with hypnosis. I'm a priest offering myself to God as a channel for – '

'Do you deny you use hypnosis?'

I spared a second to reflect that this young man was wasted in the Church; he should have been sporting a barrister's wig and battering witnesses in a court of law.

'No,' I said, trying to remain unruffled but aware that I was not entirely succeeding, 'I don't deny I use hypnotic techniques occasionally as a tool, just as a surgeon would use a scalpel, but I tend to confine these techniques to situations where the patient is distraught. Certainly at the service of healing I made no use of hypnosis at all.'

'What about the hypnotic power with which you controlled the congregation?'

'There was no hypnotic power. I was merely exercising the charism of leadership.'

'You're saying the charism of leadership never involved hypnosis?'

'I'm saying the gift of leadership bestowed by God doesn't need hypnosis! It's the gift of leadership bestowed by the Devil that runs amok with hypnotic power – compare Hitler with Churchill!'

'You don't have to tell me that the gifts of the Spirit can be recognized by their fruits, sir, but since you admitted using hypnosis as a tool when you exercised the charism of healing I thought you might also regard it as a tool when you exercised the charism of leadership.'

He was relentlessly driving me into a corner and I knew I had to punch my way out. 'Let's get this straight,' I said. 'Are you accusing me of abusing my powers? Because if you are, I'd like to assure you that I would never under any circumstances sink to manipulating people for shady purposes.'

'No?' said Aysgarth blandly. 'You seem to have been doing rather nicely with the Bishop.'

I sprang to my feet. So did he. He was very pale and I sensed he was frightened of me, but I sensed too that he was determined not to let his fear stop him from speaking his mind and doing what he conceived to be his duty. I respected him for this admirable display of courage. But I was seething. I did not like this jumped-up pipsqueak of an Archdeacon casting aspersions on my ministry of healing; I particularly disliked this jumped-up pipsqueak of an Archdeacon implying that I, the famous spiritual director, was not as spiritually healthy as I should be, and I loathed this jumped-up pipsqueak of an Archdeacon spotting the chink in my armour and moving in ruthlessly for the kill. I felt as Whitby would have felt if the mouse had stood up on its hind-legs and smartly bashed him on the nose.

'Enough of this skirmishing,' I said tersely at last. 'No more beating about the bush. I take it you hated the service.'

'Yes, I thought it was thoroughly dangerous and should never have taken place, but in fact that's not the main issue at stake here. The main issue is that the service was just one more example of how you've torn that parish apart by your – I'm sorry but I must say this – by your arrogant, reckless and thoroughly insensitive behaviour. Please don't delude yourself that no one objected to this service except Pitkin and Garrison. There were many others who strongly resented their parish church being used to give a spurious air of respectability to practices which are generally held to be dubious in the extreme.'

He stopped speaking. There was a silence while I mentally reeled under the impact of such monstrous insolence but at last I was sufficiently recovered to say in my coolest voice: 'Aren't you exceeding your authority? An archdeacon may be "The Bishop's Eye" but only the Bishop himself should deal with disciplinary matters. I'm not obliged to listen to your offensive lectures, Aysgarth, and I strongly object to being judged on the biased information provided by my enemies!'

'You shouldn't have enemies,' said Aysgarth, cutting me down to size yet again with his ruthless forensic skill. 'You pass judgement on yourself merely by using the word. As for Dr Ottershaw I shall now go to him and say that in my opinion an episcopal intervention is required. I regret that I've given you offence but I quite understand that you're far too proud to accept any criticism from a mere archdeacon.'

I was so unused to being trounced in debate that for a moment I could only flounder speechlessly again, but then the instinct for survival asserted itself and I realized that the last thing I wanted was to be hauled before the Bishop. Anne would be upset and Anne had to be protected at all costs from any incident which showed me in an unattractive light. With a vast effort I pulled myself together.

'I'm sorry,' I said in the special meek voice of the monk who concedes his recalcitrance. 'I wouldn't like you to trouble the Bishop when I can see so plainly that I've been in error, giving way to anger and making this difficult interview so very much more unpleasant for you than it should have been. Let me now try to make your task easier by asking for your advice. I can't give up the healing; I believe it to be a call from God. But what can I do to stop it exacerbating the divisions in the community?'

Aysgarth said without hesitation: 'Don't use the parish church for the healing in future – in fact try to keep the healing ministry as separate as possible from your parish duties. Is it possible, do you think, that you could confine all future healing to some quiet corner of the Manor?'

And then I knew I was face to face at last with the chapel of my vision.

SIXTEEN

I have long been interested in the claims of spiritual healers,
about which I am perhaps unduly sceptical.

W. R. INGE
Dean of St Paul's 1911–1934
A Pacifist in Trouble

I

So enrapt was I by the fact that the chapel was now poised to move to the
centre of my ministry that I found myself capable of penning my first
frank letter to Francis for some months.

'I confess I've found my life as a country priest difficult,' I wrote, 'and
no doubt this was only to be expected, since I took on the curacy for the
wrong reasons (yes, I admit it – better late than never!), but I'm happy to
report that at last events appear to be moving in a more promising
direction.' And having given a detailed account of my new ministry I
described the service of healing with an enthusiasm which I was careful
to temper with modesty.

'Unfortunately,' I continued, my pen travelling with increasing fluency
over the paper, 'the Archdeacon now informs me that the bigoted minority
who have consistently opposed my efforts to improve the spiritual life of
this parish have been protesting about my use of the church for what they
are pleased to call quackery, and it's now been suggested to me by Aysgarth
himself that I should confine my healing to "a quiet corner of the Manor".
Could there be a clearer indication that I'm called to use the chapel? I
think not. I also see at last why the back pews must be removed: we'll be
obliged to create extra space for the wheelchairs. So bearing all these things
in mind I have no doubt now that this ministry of healing represents a
true call from God, and this confidence will give me the patience to tolerate
the ill-natured opposition. I admit I find the dissension in the parish
tedious, but of course I see now that the parish is only of secondary
importance here.

'You will be wondering about my marriage so let me report that we're
very happy with no problems whatsoever. No doubt you'll want to know

what form Anne's parish work has finally taken, and I can tell you with pride that despite the heavy demands on her time made by her war-work on the estate she has provided notable assistance at a number of special events held to raise money for charity. Certainly she gives me constant moral support and I couldn't wish for a better wife. Indeed I've quite overcome my fear that I'd be miserable as a married man – and I'm delighted to tell you that I've also quite overcome my fear of fatherhood. Anne is expecting a child in September.

'I confess I could not immediately overcome this latter fear, but finally after a time of considerable torment a miracle happened. Francis, I'm not a man who uses such language lightly, but in my opinion this incident was a gift from God. I experienced another "showing", and after that I was aware only of the kind of joy and comfort received by Julian of Norwich. I don't have to remind you of the quotation.'

Having described the vision of Nicholas I added: 'I feel God wouldn't have been so generous to me if I'd been on the wrong road, and that's why I believe this showing was not only a promise that I'm to have the sort of son I've always wanted but also a confirmation of my call to the ministry of healing. It's hard to describe how I felt afterwards, but it reminded me of how I feel when people ask me to heal them: all my problems fall away and none of my difficulties seem to matter any more. Isn't it wonderful that by the grace of God I can cast aside my self-centred preoccupations in order to serve others? I really believe that in this new ministry I shall both do good and find the most unique fulfilment at last.'

I reread the letter carefully but could find no fault with it, and greatly relieved to have renewed an honest correspondence with my spiritual director I waited in pleasant anticipation for a benign and laudatory reply.

II

'My dear Jon,' wrote Francis by return, 'how very pleased I am that you have at last felt able to write to me at length. Of course you've been much in my thoughts during this silence, and now that we're in touch again I have the satisfaction of knowing that at least one of my prayers has been answered.

'First of all may I congratulate you on your impending fatherhood and say that I'm extremely glad that you've been able to welcome the prospect. Your description of the new "showing" is certainly intriguing. Have you discussed it with Cyril? You will remember how adamant Father Darcy was that you should report any psychic experience immediately to your spiritual director and/or confessor so that the experience can be properly analysed. I'm not suggesting that this latest vision is a demonic delusion

– your peace and joy afterwards are certainly more compatible with divine intervention – but it's always possible that such an experience isn't quite as you think it is and is in fact conveying a message which you've entirely failed to read.

'I hesitate to conduct an analysis from a distance but I'd like to put two questions to you. (1) Did this child look *exactly* as you did according to the photograph taken when you were four? (Forget the difference in clothes.) I know a remarkable likeness can exist between fathers and sons, but an exact replica must be extremely rare, perhaps even impossible. (2) Who was the woman calling Nicholas from the terrace? Are you quite sure this voice was unknown to you? You're treating this experience as a glimpse of the future but in fact it could equally well be a bizarre distortion of the present and past.

'I trust I'm not impertinent enough to discuss your marriage with you until I know a great deal more about it than the euphoric picture you painted in your letter. Suffice it to say that I'm delighted that you've been rendered so charmingly uxorious. I must confess, however, to a twinge of anxiety about your wife who seems to be trying to be all things to all men: a farmer dedicated to producing more food for a nation at war, a wife dedicated to producing the ideal marital partner for a harassed country priest, and a woman dedicated to producing an infant. Dare I ask if you've actually had a frank conversation with her about the emotional, mental and physical stresses of her life at present? No, I daren't! Let me turn instead to your ministry of healing, a subject on which, unlike matrimony, I'm rather more qualified to speak candidly.

'Of course I'm deeply interested by the turn your life has now taken, but I'm also deeply perturbed. I need not mention Father Darcy in this context; his opinion on your suitability for such a ministry is unlikely to have been forgotten by you, although you may well feel entitled to dismiss his opinion as irrelevant now that you believe you're responding to a call from God. However I feel bound to remind you that such a ministry poses great problems for those who undertake it, and as it's vital that you should be in first-class spiritual health in order to perform such work successfully, I urge you to see Cyril *at least* once a week to make your confession and discuss any difficulties which may arise. I'd also like you to come up to town for a couple of days to see me. I've no wish to cast any aspersion on Cyril, who's certainly more than capable of giving you the proper direction, but there's so much about you that Cyril doesn't know and something tells me – am I being excessively cynical? – that you haven't been too busy enlightening him.

'There's more I could say but I shall hold my fire. I could ask, for instance, how the parish is going to fare now that you've dismissed it as being of only secondary importance. I could also ask whether the miraculous feeling of release from your problems, a phenomenon which you say accompanies your work as a healer, could not better be described as a psychological escape from reality. However I shan't ask either of those tiresome questions, my dear Jon, because I'm sure I've already irritated you quite beyond endurance, so all I shall now do is conclude this letter by begging you to let me know by return when I'm to have the pleasure of seeing you again.'

This letter did indeed make me feel exceedingly irritated, and it occurred to me to wonder if Francis were jealous – subconsciously, of course – of my young wife and my new career in the world. Even a man who thrived on the cenobitic life was never immune from the desire to embrace the worldly blessings he had renounced, and deciding that Francis was being influenced by feelings which his jealous nature could not quite control I wrote severely but not (I hoped) unkindly:

'My dear Francis, I thank you for your letter but regret that I'm unable to accept your invitation. Much as I would like to see you I'm reluctant to leave Anne on her own at this time.

'With regard to my new ministry, let me hasten to assure you that I'm well aware of the problems; I'm neither ignorant nor a fool. A very heavy responsibility has certainly been placed upon me, but since I have no doubt whatsoever that the call is genuine I believe that by the grace of God I shall be granted the strength and wisdom to respond in the right way. The latest "showing", as I tried with apparent lack of success to explain, indicates that I can proceed into the future with confidence; I was unmistakably assured that all would be well. The fact that I'm being driven to use the chapel for my ministry – even driven to remove the back pews – also leaves me in no doubt that my call is unfolding in accordance with my vision.

'What heavy weather you've made of the showing! The child was certainly very like me, but how can I say whether or not he was a replica? I had to compare this little boy with my memory of a sepia photograph which I haven't seen for many years. You're implying, I know, that he was not my future son but a mirror-image drummed up out of my subconscious mind, but although I myself thought this at first I was convinced by the end of my vision that I was mistaken. If he were indeed my past self, why didn't the woman call him Jon? You're implying, of course, when you ask who the woman was, that at some time in the past I heard a woman call out: "Nicholas! Nicholas!" and that my memory has now tossed up this forgotten incident to complete my delusion. However a far more simple explanation is that the woman was the child's nurse; Anne is already talking of engaging a nanny for the baby.

'As you say you don't intend to ask the questions which you nonetheless posed in your last paragraph, I really fail to see why I should answer them.

But of course I must assure you that I shan't neglect my parish duties. Your suggestion that I'm in reality serving myself (by running away from my problems) instead of serving God (by responding to a genuine call) is worthy of Father Darcy at his most malign and I believe my most effective response is to preserve a dignified silence. I deeply regret that you should take such a suspicious, cynical view of my current activities.'

Francis wrote in return: 'My dear Jon, I'm extremely sorry if I've given you offence. Remember that I write only with your spiritual welfare in mind and remember too that a morbid sensitively to criticism is often a symptom of an unhealthily rampant pride.

'Taking my courage in both hands I'll now point out a couple of distortions in your logic. (1) I see no evidence in your showing that the reassurance "all will be well" extends beyond your family life. If the showing be genuine it certainly has nothing to do with your ministry of healing and cannot be regarded as setting the seal of approval on it. (2) You mention the removal of the back pews as if this too were a confirmation of your call, but in fact all the removal proves is the remarkable degree of clairvoyance you achieved when you saw the interior of the chapel in your vision. You may now indeed feel you have a cogent reason for removing the pews, but this has no bearing whatsoever on whether or not your call is valid. You're like someone who sets a table and says: "Now that the table's laid I've proved that dinner's about to be served!" But in fact the larder's empty and no one's on duty in the kitchen.

'I can't stress too strongly how careful you must be not to jump to convenient conclusions. Why have you really undertaken this ministry of healing? It may well be a call from God, but until you're completely honest with yourself about your motives true discernment can only be displaced by wishful thinking, a self-deceiving frame of mind which will clog your psyche as you seek to open it to receive the Holy Spirit. Go and see Cyril, open your heart to him and let him help you put your current life under the necessary microscope.

'If you're still reading this letter I shall now deliver my parting thrust which I've saved to the end in the hope that it'll ring the vital alarm bell resoundingly in your ears: REMEMBER WHITBY!'

I laughed. Then I exclaimed: 'What a blow below the belt!' and tearing up the letter I tossed the fragments abruptly into the wastepaper basket.

III

'Have you heard from Francis yet?' said Anne who knew I had finally written to him at length.

'Yes.'

'What does he think of the healing?'

'He said he was deeply interested by the turn my life has taken.'

'You mean he approved?'

I was silent.

'Jon, I do wish you'd confide in me! I've got this nasty feeling that you're busy tying yourself into a knot again – '

'Nonsense!'

'Is it? If you think I can't see that Francis has upset you in some way – '

'He merely reminded me of the difficulties attached to my new work and advised me to discuss the situation with Cyril.'

'Thank God. When are you going to Starwater?'

I was somewhat taken aback by this excessive display of relief but I told myself allowances should be made for the emotional moods of pregnant women. 'If you can spare the motor I'll go this afternoon,' I said soothingly, 'but my dearest, you really must try not to worry so much about me! If there's one thing I know beyond any shadow of doubt it's that all will eventually be well . . .'

IV

'I must confess to anger,' I said to Cyril five hours later. 'I was furious with the Archdeacon and furious with Francis.' And I told him not only about the interview with Aysgarth but about Francis' epistolary counselling.

Cyril was small and wiry with a curiously military presence; I always felt he ought to be sporting a moustache and wearing a khaki uniform. Twenty years of managing the boys' school at Starwater Abbey had made him brisk, bossy and a trifle too hearty. I found myself missing Aidan's subtle understatements and wily silences in the confessional at Ruydale.

'If you're so confident about the validity of this call,' said Cyril, 'why are you getting so rattled?'

'Am I getting rattled?' I said smiling at him.

'Well, aren't you? No beating about the bush! Two people express disapproval, one in the world and one out of it, and immediately you're on fire with indignation! Why don't you just say compassionately: "Poor chaps! They don't understand!" All this anger suggests something being covered up. You know your Shakespeare: One must be suspicious of people who protest too much!'

'Yes, Headmaster!' I said, smiling at him.

'You're fencing with me, Jon,' said Cyril severely. 'Come along, roll up your sleeves and work harder.'

I worked harder, which meant that I still fenced with him but disguised it. Cyril began to shift in his chair. His bushy eyebrows twitched. The Fordites use no confessional box, as the Roman Catholics do, and confessor and penitent sit facing each other across a table in a small plain room with an oratory in one corner. The difficulties are discussed first. Then the penitent makes the formal confession on his knees before the cross. Cyril and I were still facing each other across the table.

'I see no sign that you repent of this anger,' said Cyril at last. 'How do you expect me to absolve you?'

'How can you say you see no sign of repentance when I've had the insight to realize that my anger stems from injured pride in the face of justifiable criticism? I always repent of my pride!'

'Yes, yes, yes, don't we all, but what's really going on here, Jon? Since we seem to be going round and round the mulberry bush and getting nowhere, I suggest we now approach the problem from a different angle. Suppose you suddenly realized your new call was a delusion; what would you do next?'

'Continue with the curacy, pray for enlightenment and wait.'

'Yes, but supposing the war ends, the vicar returns and you're out of a job. What then?'

'I'd have to find other work. I couldn't just sit back and live on my wife's money.'

'Why not? Maybe God's provided you with a rich wife so that you can concentrate on your work as a spiritual director without having to worry about where the next penny's coming from!'

I stared at him. 'But I've had no hint from God that I'm to continue with my work as a spiritual director beyond maintaining my correspondence with those I used to counsel.'

'My dear Jon,' said Cyril, 'you're so busy being too proud to live on your wife's money that you wouldn't see a hint from God even if it were written in the sky in letters of fire! Now let's try and view this situation without pride – and without any preconceived opinions. If this call to heal is in fact a delusion, what would be the most likely work that God would wish you to do?'

'Spiritual direction. But – '

'Very well, supposing God allows for your weakness and realizes that you'd die of shame rather than be supported entirely by your wife. What would be the next most likely work he'd call you to do, work which would earn you a salary?'

After a pause I said: 'Teaching.'

'Exactly!' said Cyril, pleased. 'Now supposing, just for the sake of argument, I were to tell you that I'm having a tough time here at present as so many of the lay teachers have left to serve in the war, and supposing I were to offer you a job. Would you construe that as a call from God?'

'No, I'd construe it as a call from you.'

'I agree it wouldn't be suitable for you to come back to work among the Fordites – too disturbing both for you and for us – but there are other educational institutions in desperate need of teachers at the moment. The Theological College at Starbridge, for instance – '

'I'm not called to teach, Cyril.'

'But you did wonders at Ruydale!'

I said nothing.

Suddenly Cyril said: 'Why do you feel you're not called to teach?'

I still said nothing. If I were once to admit I disliked the idea of teaching Cyril would say that I was putting my self-centred inclinations before the possible will of God.

'Do you know what I think?' said Cyril at last. 'I think all this – the compulsion to heal, the reluctance to teach – is in reality a gigantic rebellion against your father.'

The silence was absolute. I had stopped breathing. Perhaps Cyril had too. We stared at each other for a long moment before Cyril added as an afterthought: 'Your spiritual father, I mean. Father Cuthbert. Father Darcy, as you always insist on calling him – correctly now, I suppose, since you've left the Order.'

I said the first words which entered my head. They were: 'Francis and I always thought Cuthbert was such an absurdly inappropriate name for him.' I had started breathing again.

'I can't think why! St Cuthbert,' said Cyril, unable to resist the temptation to play the pedegogue, 'was a most remarkable man, tough as old boots, who lived a Christian life of great power and acquired a band of followers so devoted that they even took his bones with them when the community had to flee from the Norsemen. And you're carrying your Cuthbert's bone with you, aren't you, Jon – except that they're not bones, they're memories. He forbade you to heal; he wanted you to teach, and now that he's dead and you've left the Order you're suffering from a compulsion to rebel against him, just as some of my pupils rebel against me when they leave school and start sowing their wild oats.'

There was a pause. Cyril looked at me expectantly and at last I said: 'You could be right.'

Cyril looked relieved, as if an exceptionally dense pupil had finally comprehended the solution to a simple problem. 'What you've got to do, Jon, is to sort out all these convoluted feelings of yours about Father Cuthbert, and then I'm sure the way ahead will become clear.'

'Yes,' I said. 'Yes, I'm sure you're right.' I assumed a humble, thoughtful, chastened expression, the expression of a man who understood his errors sufficiently to profess a valid repentance of his anger and pride.

'The truth is,' said Cyril, 'that in your heart you feel guilty that you're defying Father Cuthbert on the subject of healing, and this is why you reacted so strongly when you received criticism. You don't want to admit the guilt and you're too proud to concede the call could be mistaken. The road to repentance lies in summoning sufficient humility to reconsider your situation from a completely unbiased perspective.'

'Yes, I understand. I'll try.'

The penitent had professed a genuine repentance. Cyril was satisfied. Absolution was now inevitable. 'Of course I'm not suggesting you don't need a lot more help here,' he said, 'and certainly I'm willing enough to try to give it to you, but ideally, I think, you should make a retreat under the direction of Father Abbot-General who's so much better acquainted with you than I am.'

'Unfortunately it's impossible for me to leave my wife at present.'

'What a pity! Yes, I suppose it is.' For a moment Cyril looked cross that I should be inconvenienced by such a distracting object as a pregnant wife but then he recollected himself sufficiently to say: 'In that case you must come back and see me as soon as possible – in fact now that we've identified the source of your difficulties we should meet every week.'

'I'd like nothing better, but there's a growing problem of obtaining petrol for the motor, and – '

'Leap on a train!' said Cyril briskly, as if he were addressing a slothful prefect. 'Why not? You're surely not so old that you have to be carted everywhere in that delightful Rolls-Royce!'

'No, of course not, but the train journey is really most awkward – '

'Tolerate it. What's a little awkwardness once a week when your spiritual health is at stake?'

To keep him happy I smiled and pretended that I fully accepted his advice.

V

When I arrived home I retired to my cell, knelt at the oratory and in protestant fashion confessed my sins directly to God. I knew very well that my Anglo-Catholic confession before a priest had gone so seriously adrift that I could consider it a nullity. Cyril was the wrong confessor for me. I thought how Aidan, that wily old fox, would have said: 'You were silent for a long time. There's something you'd like to tell me, perhaps, about that silence.' And Francis would have said: 'You're being wonderfully meek and contrite, but why is it that I always feel suspicious when you start behaving like a model monk?' And Father Darcy would have said as usual: 'You're saying the words you want me to hear but I hear the words you can't bring yourself to say.' Yet Cyril, springing energetically from conclusion to conclusion with the zest of a mountain-goat leaping from crag to crag, had been too enchanted by his admirably plausible theory to realize he should have looked deeper and listened harder in order to extricate me from my difficulties.

However I felt it was unfair to condemn Cyril for a failure which sprang primarily from my inability to be honest with him, and in an effort to demonstrate my repentance I rose from my knees, sat down at the table and tried to approach my current situation with humility. There was, of course, no possibility that I might give up the healing – how could I when I knew beyond all doubt that my call was genuine? – but since I had embarked on such a difficult, dangerous ministry I might be wise to seek advice from someone who was far more experienced in the art of healing than I was.

This struck me as a pleasingly humble acknowledgment of my fallibility, and accordingly I wrote to Wilfred, the infirmarian at Ruydale, explained how I had been approaching my work as a healer and asked him not only for helpful hints but for stern criticism of any errors. This exercise in humility certainly soothed my conscience, and I then found I could face Francis' suggestion that the showing of Nicholas had been a delusion drummed up by my subsconscious mind to allay my fear of parenthood.

Deciding that my most sensible course was to refresh my memory of the photograph I wrote to Ruth, to whom I had given all the family memorabilia when I had entered the Order, and asked her to send me the appropriate album. Fearful of tiresome questions I merely mentioned that I wanted to show Anne a photograph of my parents. My correspondence with Ruth had been sporadic since her disastrous visit to the Manor, and although we had formally patched up the quarrel I had made no effort to invite her to Starrington again.

I was still waiting to hear from Wilfred when the album arrived, and to my surprise I found I could hardly bring myself to open it; the thought of seeing my parents again aroused such powerful emotions, but eventually I managed to confront the picture taken on their wedding day. My father, tall, trim and bespectacled, looked dignified, decent and dull. My mother, her slender figure discreetly veiled in elaborate draperies, looked elegant, enigmatic and alluring. They were standing very close together but not touching each other at any point. Abruptly I turned the page and saw my mother holding an undistinguished bundle in a christening robe. She looked as if her thoughts were far away but she was holding the bundle with authority. More studio portraits followed – taken in the days before my father acquired his camera – and at last I found myself confronting the photograph I remembered, the picture of myself at the age of four.

I stared, trying to decide if Nicholas had been a hallucinatory mirror-image, but I was quite unable to make up my mind. The difference in clothes was distracting. Encased in a formal black suit with a frilly shirt I might have inhabited a different planet from the little boy in the dungarees, yet the eyes were the same and the bone structure was certainly similar. The hair should have been different but my mother had kept mine unfashionably short. I did think I appeared tougher than the child in my vision, but perhaps the unfamiliar camera had stimulated me to display the pugnacious side of my nature.

Later when I showed the album to Anne she was much intrigued. 'You look like both your parents,' she said. 'How strange! I somehow got the impression you took entirely after your mother.' And after studying the photographs again she remarked: 'He's got a sad face. Was he happy as a schoolmaster?'

'Very. He had a gift for teaching.'

'But you told me he was quiet and scholarly. Teachers like that often have trouble keeping order.'

'Not my father. He had a commanding presence – that's something which doesn't come over in the photographs – and when he was before an audience he projected complete confidence and authority.'

'You saw him in action? I assumed that as you hadn't attended the grammar school where he taught – '

'He used to lecture sometimes at the Working Men's Institute and he would take me with him if he thought the subject would be of interest. I was always enthralled. So was everyone else in the room. His gift was very remarkable.'

'How sad that he didn't have a brilliant career at a leading public school!'

'He never complained.' Abruptly closing both the album and the conversation I retired to my cell again to meditate on Nicholas; now that my attempt to distinguish him as a person other than my four-year-old self had neither succeeded nor failed I felt more confused than ever, and after rereading Francis' letter I directed my attention towards the unknown woman whom I had assumed to be Nicholas' nurse. Was I in fact entirely certain that I had not heard that voice before? Groping in my memory for a Nicholas whose mother I might have encountered long ago I suddenly remembered the Nicholas who had lived three houses away on our sedate little street. We had met at Sunday school but he had been forbidden to play with the son of a parlourmaid, and on the one occasion when I had wandered into his garden to look for him, his mother, a very grand female who bedecked herself with lavish hats, had dismissed me so brutally that I had run home in tears.

I grimaced at the memory, rejected it as irrelevant and decided my careful re-examination of the showing should cease. In the absence of any evidence to the contrary I felt I could assume Nicholas was my future son, and I was still savouring my relief that I had repelled Francis' unpleasant insinuations when Wilfred's letter arrived from Ruydale.

VI

Wilfred suggested tactfully that I was making various mistakes and his first concern was that I was being too indiscriminating.

'You can't heal everyone,' he wrote firmly. 'Nor should you try to. You're not a miracle-worker. You're an ordinary man with a special supply of energy but this energy isn't inexhaustible and to squander it on all and sundry is unwise. You must be discerning. Learn how to say no, not only to those who suffer from a "malade imaginaire" (and I fear they are legion) but also to those who are attracted to you as a source of "magic" which may succeed when doctors fail. You are quite right to refer everyone first to the doctor; this is good. But do not, whatever you do, succumb to the temptation to try to outdo the doctor by taking on every case he can't help. Accept that some cases really are beyond help. Learn to spot them and by all means offer sympathy, but don't waste your special energy when it could be put to more effective use elsewhere.

Now let me turn to the subject of services of healing. I'm opposed to such services for several reasons: (a) The Devil can so easily slip into the front pew and cause disruption. (b) A bunch of sick people tends to emanate a melancholy aura which impedes the healing process. (c) The healthy members of the congregation are often present solely in the hope of seeing a miracle, and the aura they emanate is thus essentially negative, creating quite the wrong psychic currents in the atmosphere. (d) The healer tends to exhaust himself before the end and this means that the last people he treats derive no benefit. This exhaustion is also bad for the healer physically, mentally, emotionally and psychically. *Never overstrain your powers*. If you do, you won't have the strength to fight the Devil.

'This is how I suggest you should conduct your ministry: heal in small groups of no more than four patients but enlist the support of as many of their friends and relations as you can. This means that when you conduct the healing every person present will be there because he genuinely cares about at least one of the sick and is busy praying for his recovery. You'll have eliminated the seekers after vicarious thrills and the psychic atmosphere will be pure. Moreover you'll be in no danger of running out of energy and overstraining yourself, so your powers should be more effective.

'The procedure should be as follows: (a) See the patient in a preliminary interview. (b) See him again with all the truly sympathetic supporters he can muster and explain to them how they should pray in order to be of maximum assistance. (c) Form a separate prayer-group whose business it is to pray for the sick. This will give you extra support. (d) Hold the brief private service in the chapel when you feel everyone is ready. (e) During the service perform the laying-on of hands as before but in future administer unction as well. Oil has a very soothing effect and is not, as you seem to think, a mere sacramental gesture. If anyone objects to it as Roman Catholic ritual unfit for Protestants say: "Rubbish!" very firmly. Anointing goes back far beyond the founding of the Roman Church, as of course you know.

'The above procedure is no good in emergencies, I admit, but then emergencies should always be referred to a doctor. Concentrate on the cases of chronic illness where you may well alleviate distress and thus induce remissions. Concentrate on the non-chronic but lengthy illnesses where the patent's recovery can be quickened by your power. But don't look for miracles. Never keep a tally of successes. Never make the patient feel he's to blame if the healing is ineffective. Never regard a death as a personal insult from God. (I'm sure you wouldn't but healers do sometimes get unhealthily overwrought about their failures.) If you do find yourself getting emotionally overstrained, *stop all healing at once* and seek spiritual direction. An overstrained psyche, burdened with undisciplined emotion, can be a very snug little nest for the Devil, so make sure your psyche is fit and rested. You should take the Holy Sacrament every day and make confession twice a week, but of course you're not in the Order now and such a regime may well not be possible. Nevertheless you should follow it as closely as you can and pray constantly. This all sounds very arduous, I know, but God can't use a channel which isn't kept clear for the passage of his Holy Spirit.' And after giving me his blessing and promising to pray for me Wilfred added in a startling postscript:

'I think it would be best, while you're adjusting to your new ministry, to avoid all exorcisms. They take a great deal of psychic energy and may debilitate you too much at this stage. Refer all requests to your bishop who doubtless had an exorcist at his disposal. I mention this subject because the ministries of healing and deliverance go hand in hand, and you may already have had requests to purge houses of unpleasant auras. This is a fairly simple procedure and a little prayer and holy water will usually do the trick (I never recommend celebrating the Eucharist unless a ghost has actually been seen) but nevertheless I think you should abstain even from simple exorcisms at the moment. Certainly avoid all exorcisms of people. Fortunately this type of possession is rare these days as such a large proportion of the population is baptized, but such cases can be *very dangerous* and exorcism should never be attempted without at least three strong men in attendance to give physical protection.

'Forgive me if you already know all this. Perhaps you do. The late Father Abbot-General was the most gifted exorcist, of course, and may well have given you instruction. Certainly he and I had many interesting conversations on the subject during his visits to Ruydale. I miss him. He was a great man. The new Father Abbot-General is also a most gifted man, I saw that when he made his first visitation here last year, but his gifts are of a different order.'

This communication interested me deeply, and because Wilfred had accepted my call without question I showed his letter to Anne as evidence of support from someone within the Order. However this move proved to be a mistake since Anne was horrified by Wilfred's laconic references to the Devil. It is very difficult for a well-educated modern person to believe that the demonic force in our imperfect world does not cease to exist merely because a sophisticated civilization has judged the Devil to be an unfashionable symbol. Even intelligent people are more influenced by fashion than they realize, and I sometimes think that it is only in the cloister, where every effort is made to exclude the ebb and flow of ephemeral fashions, that the fundamental forces of darkness and light can be clearly perceived.

'Are you going to follow his advice and give up the large services of healing?' demanded Anne.

'I must give one more because I've promised so many people that I would, but I can see the advantage of healing in small groups,' I said, and indeed as soon as I tried implementing Wilfred's suggestions I found that his advice had been sound.

As the summer advanced I became so absorbed with this new approach to my ministry that I postponed the second large service of healing. The biggest advantage of a postponement was that it kept my ecclesiastical opponents quiet, for now that I was healing people so discreetly in my quiet corner of the Manor Aysgarth had decided not to recommend an episcopal reproof; at the same time Cyril could be more easily manoeuvred to the conclusion that I was engaged in easing my way out of a mistaken ministry, and Francis, regularly dosed with the descriptions I sent him of my life as a dutiful parish priest, could be coaxed to believe the healing was an increasingly minor activity, undertaken solely to alleviate the lot of the chronic sick.

I did indeed try to be a dutiful parish priest, but I was very mindful that Wilfred had urged me to conserve my energies and soon I was reducing my parish work to a minimum. The reduction gave me a twinge of guilt but I countered it by reflecting that since I had done too much too soon to introduce my parishioners to more fruitful forms of worship a touch of benign neglect would now do them no harm and might even help them to adjust to my less extreme innovations. Since Aysgarth had advised me to keep to the rubric I had eliminated some of my Catholic touches but I found I could still practise a muted version of Anglo-Catholicism.

It is one of the ironies of history that the Church of England emerged from the Reformation with Protestant Articles of Religion and a Catholic Prayer-Book, and although my opponents might still grumble I had a perfect right to make the most Catholic use I could of the Book of Common Prayer.

I am uncertain even now, with the wisdom of hindsight, when my psyche began to slip into a serious dis-ease. Some would argue that it began when I tore up the last letter from Francis and manipulated the crucial confession to Cyril, but although I was without doubt gravely at fault I was still sufficiently aware of my errors to make my gesture of humility and seek advice from Wilfred. Indeed since my skill as a healer improved, thanks to Wilfred's counselling, my psyche must have been in tolerable working order for some time afterwards, but I can see now that my spiritual health was steadily degenerating. I was like a consumptive who, ruddy-cheeked and bright-eyed, looks the picture of health all the time the shadow is darkening across his lung, and like the consumptive I was in a position where any additional strain on powers already weakened could only accelerate my deterioration.

I suspect this acceleration began in June when I had to say goodbye to Charles. I had been seeing him regularly since my marriage but now his regiment was on the move and rumoured to be heading either for North Africa or the Far East. As soon as I heard this news I found myself tormented by the memory of my vision of the prison-camp, and when he came to see me for the last time before his departure I hardly knew how to conceal my dread.

At first he talked of his family. His wife and children had been installed in a rented house on the outskirts of Starvale St James where Dr Romaine, clever Dr Romaine, continued to charm and beguile his way into Lyle's confidence. 'Awful old villain!' said Charles, who was very fond of his elderly friend. 'But I have absolute faith in his ability to look after her – and of course it's also a relief to know that you and Anne are so near.' He then began to talk about his sons. There were various worries associated with the older one whose volatile temperament made him difficult to manage. 'He needs a great deal of loving attention and Lyle is somehow inhibited about giving it to him . . .' I listened and thought how often a tragic streak ran through even the happiest of families.

'How far have you confided in Dr Romaine?' I said at last.

'I said nothing for a long time. Then when I learnt I was going overseas I did tell him, but of course he'd already guessed. He thinks Lyle's secretly paralysed by guilt that she should have produced such a difficult child.'

This struck me as a shrewd judgement. 'If that's true,' I said, 'then you may find she'll be able to cope with Charley much better in your absence.

She won't have to exhaust herself by worrying that you secretly find him a bore.'

'But I've told her and told her – '

'Obviously your assurances aren't quite ringing true, and the most likely reason why this is happening is because you're not, in fact, telling the exact truth. After all, let's be honest; difficult children can indeed be a bore, so instead of protesting nobly to Lyle that you love him no matter what he does, might it not help her to relax if you were to say instead: "Yes, he's a thorough nuisance sometimes, but never mind, I'm still absolutely committed to his welfare." '

'I don't like to complain – '

'People make a great mistake when they never complain,' said my professional persona, the accomplished spiritual director. 'Whatever they gain by patience they lose in honesty. Conversations begin to ring false. Suspicions are aroused. Resentments multiply. Relationships are poisoned. I always look askance at a man who makes a virtue of never complaining no matter how great the provocation to do so.'

'I agree martyrs can be thoroughly tiresome, but I'm just so afraid that if I complain Lyle will immediately conclude I don't love her and sink fathoms deep into depression.' He sighed before adding: 'Sometimes I ask myself if I regret marrying her but I know at heart I don't. She presents an endlessly alluring challenge. A good simple woman would have bored me in no time.'

I smiled but said nothing and there followed a long silence which I gradually realized he did not know how to break. At last I said: 'The time's come to talk of you, Charles. We've discussed your worries about your family; now tell me your worries about yourself.' And as he responded with relief to my invitation to unburden himself of his darkest fears I found myself slipping back twenty-five years to my days as a Naval chaplain before the great battle of Jutland.

'I hate to admit it – well, I wouldn't admit it to anyone except you, but . . .'

I listened to him confessing his fear of death.

'. . . and I feel so ashamed. When I think of all those Christians bravely facing the lions – '

I recognized my cue and interposed effortlessly: 'Do you honestly think the martyrs felt no fear as they marched into the amphitheatre? After all, it's only human to be nervous at the prospect of an unpleasant journey into the unknown, even if one has absolute confidence in the reality of one's final destination. And besides, why shouldn't you feel fear at the prospect of leaving Lyle a widow and your children fatherless? If you felt no fear I'd be exceedingly worried about you!' And I talked on, soothing him yet encouraging him to face his fears until the moment when he exclaimed: 'How I admire your indestructible serenity – I can't tell you what confidence you give me!' Then I had to suppress a shudder of relief that I had managed to conceal my dread from him. I heard myself promise to pray daily for his welfare, and later when I had given him my blessing he said simply: 'I'm ready for anything now.'

We parted. I felt annihilated. After a while I was unable to stop myself trying to peer into the future but the fear closed my psychic eye, all possible futures were reflected in a blank mirror and I remained in a terrifying ignorance. Then it occurred to me that enlightenment might have been even more terrifying and that God was being merciful by keeping the mirror blank. In panic I retreated to the chapel, but my psyche was so lacerated by distress that I was incapable of achieving the quality of prayer needed to master such a profound anxiety. Instinctively I turned back to my work to keep my fear at bay, and it was then, when my spirits were at their lowest ebb, that I allowed myself to go too far with that proven panacea for all my troubles, my all-absorbing ministry of healing.

VII

The next day I had a visit from one of the farm labourers on Anne's estate, a man in his forties called John Higgins who lived with his wife and children in a tied-cottage and came to church every week. A simple soul, he had once told me that my services were as good as a visit to 'the pictures', and knowing he had intended this dubious remark as a compliment I was well pleased; it confirmed my belief that Anglo-Catholic ritual is more successful in communicating religious truths to the working-classes than the staid Protestant services patronized by the well-to-do. I took an interest in Higgins, and when I learnt that he had been neither confirmed nor even baptized I offered to give him instruction so that he could be formally received into the Church, but the word 'instruction' intimidated Higgins, who was almost illiterate, and I was still trying to persude him that membership of the Church did not depend on either one's education or one's mental ability.

On the morning of his visit I had been praying in the chapel, and it was when I left that I found him waiting patiently, cap in hand, on the steps of the porch.

'Pardon me for trespassing, sir,' he said. 'I did call several times at the church vestry but you were never there so finally I got desperate and came looking for you.'

I suppressed the guilt that one of my parishioners should have had such difficulty in finding me, and doing my best to put him at ease I took him into the chapel. 'Well, Higgins,' I said as we sat down together in the nearest pew, 'how may I help you?'

He twisted his cap and looked deeply embarrassed. I recognized an honest man in confusion, but beyond this elementary deduction which required no psychic skill whatever I was in ignorance.

'How's your wife?' I hazarded, offering a question which could pave the way to a discussion of marital difficulty.

'Very well, thank you, sir, but I haven't come about her. I've come about Him.'

'Him?'

'Him who follows me about and gives me orders.' More cap-twisting followed but finally he blurted out: 'He's not a real person, he's a Thing in my head. He wants me to murder the cows and I'm afraid to go to work in case he forces me to obey him.'

I made the diagnosis: paranoid schizophrenia. Aloud I said: 'Does this person – this presence in your head – talk in words?'

'Yes, sir. He says: "Take the scythe and cut the throats of the cows."'

'How often has he done this?'

'Twice. I told him to go away each time and he did. But I'm afraid that one day he'll come back and won't go away when I tell him to.'

'Exactly what words did you use when you ordered him off?'

'I said – excuse the language, sir – I said: "For Christ's sake, fuck off, you bloody bugger."'

I noted that Christ had been invoked, albeit with a blasphemous irreverence, but all I said was: 'Had you been drinking?'

'I don't drink, sir. My father died of it and my mother made us all take the pledge.'

'I see.' I paused to consider the situation.

'Can you lay your hands on me, sir, and make me strong enough to keep him out?' said the poor man with a touching faith which was very hard to withstand but I answered as kindly as I could: 'I'd have to be sure that was the best way of dealing with the problem, Higgins, and I can't be sure until you've taken medical advice. Do you have the money for the doctor?' I added, for by this time I was accustomed to people who regarded me as a cheap alternative to Dr Garrison, but Higgins said with admirable dignity that the money would be found.

I wondered what Garrison would make of the case, and the next day I was just debating whether I should call at Higgins' cottage when Anne returned greatly perturbed from the Home Farm. She had by this time reduced the number of hours she spent in the estate office, but she still liked to look in every day to talk to the agent. 'What do you think's happened?' she exclaimed as soon as we met in the drawing-room. 'Garrison's packed off Higgins the cowman to the lunatic asylum at

Starbridge! Sane, stolid, respectable Higgins! I feel utterly shattered – do you suppose Garrison's finally gone off his head?'

'Much as I'd like to say yes I'm afraid the answer's almost certainly no,' I said reluctantly, and without disclosing any details of the case, I told her that Higgins had visited me in a disturbed state of mind. 'He certainly wasn't mad when I spoke to him,' I added, 'but possibly I caught him in a lucid interval. I did wonder if he was possessed, but there were no outward signs of possession and the most likely diagnosis is some form of schizophrenia.'

Anne blanched. 'But what's the difference? I thought possession was just the old-fashioned way of saying someone was mad!'

'In the old days when little was known about mental illness there was undoubtedly much confusion, but now it's easier to see possession is quite distinct; for example, mental illness usually has an incapacitating effect on the sufferer, while the person who's possessed remains capable of holding a job supporting a family and leading an ostensibly normal life. He's also sane enough to realize that he's being periodically invaded by an alien presence and he desperately wants to rid himself of the invader. Many victims of mental illness, on the other hand, have trouble admitting there's anything wrong with them.'

'But have you ever actually met someone you thought was possessed?'

'Good heavens, yes!' I said surprised. 'Cases of possession haven't ceased to exist just because doctors like Garrison fail to recognize them! I sought permission to perform exorcisms when I was a prison chaplain but the governor turned the request down and the victims were all transferred to hospitals for the criminally insane. However I dare say it was just as well my request wasn't granted. I actually knew very little about exorcisms before I met Father Darcy, and ignorance can be dangerous when you deal with the Devil.'

'How absolutely *foul*,' said Anne vehemently, and to my consternation I saw she was profoundly upset. 'Jon, I don't want you to have anything to do with Higgins' illness.'

'But my dearest Anne, I've already said that Higgins showed none of the outward signs of possession – '

'What are they?'

Belatedly I decided that this was the most unsuitable conversation for a pregnant woman. 'That's not important,' I said firmly. 'All that matters is that I don't think Higgins needs to be exorcized.'

That night Anne had a nightmare. 'It's all this beastly talk of the Devil,' she said, shuddering in my arms. 'I'd never thought twice about the Devil until you turned up with all your talk of charismatic corruption and demonic infiltration and religious hysteria and drowned cats and sinister exorcisms and brutal old monks – '

'Anne, Anne – '

'All right! All right! I know I must calm down, but I hate all this talk of the Devil, *hate it* – that letter from Wilfred was thoroughly creepy and beastly – '

I was astounded as well as shocked. 'But it was a model of down- to-earth common sense!'

'If you think that, you're mad. Or maybe I'm mad. I don't know, I don't know anything any more except that you've become much too peculiar – '

'Peculiar!' I was horrified.

'You were all right before you took up the healing – you were unusual and eccentric, I know, but you were normally unusual and eccentric and I felt I could cope. But now I'm absolutely out of my depth and I've got an awful feeling something ghastly's going to happen and oh God, if only there was someone I could turn to but I can't think of anyone who could possibly understand – '

Although I was profoundly distressed I knew how important it was that I should remain calm so I made no attempt to argue. I merely held her close, stroked her hair and repeated soothingly, using a mild hypnotic technique, that I had no intention of embarking on a ministry of deliverance. This reassurance comforted her, but when I had at last succeeded in coaxing her back to sleep I lay awake worrying for some time. Anne was not normally the sort of woman who tottered on the brink of hysteria, and I was driven to wonder if she had been overtaxing her strength as her pregnancy advanced. Perhaps now was the moment when she should retire completely from her work at the estate-office. I toyed with the idea of seeking Dr Romaine's advice, but as always I felt lukewarm towards this medical cynosure of so many admiring feminine eyes. I had not yet met him. I had been too busy shunning the social occasions where we might have encountered each other, and Starvale St James, although nearer than Starwater Abbey, was still too far away to be visited quickly by bicycle.

However the next morning I found to my relief that Dr Romaine's advice was not needed; Anne had even recovered sufficiently to be ashamed of her irrational outburst.

'I didn't mean what I said about the healing having a malign effect on you,' she said. 'After all, how could it? A call from God can only be benign.'

'But if you're worried and unhappy – '

'I'm not! Pregnancy just makes me fanciful and silly sometimes, that's all. So long as you're happy in your work then I'm happy too.'

A great load rolled off my mind and I found myself saying impulsively: 'I won't hold another large service of healing after this next one in July, and I'll take on fewer small groups. Then you won't have to worry about me overstraining myself.'

Anne looked relieved but said: 'Do you really have to hold this service?'

'I don't see how I can cancel it – I've already postponed it once and disappointed numerous people.'

'Can't you write and ask Francis if he thinks it's advisable to go ahead?'

'Well, I intend to write to him, certainly, but I'm rather busy at the moment and –'

'Quite,' said Anne flatly, and turned away.

I suffered a sharp pang of anxiety. 'I'll discuss the service with Cyril, of course –'

'Cyril doesn't have your respect as Francis does.'

'Well, I concede there may be an element of truth in that, but nonetheless he's a very competent priest and –'

Anne suddenly seemed to lose interest in the conversation. 'I'm being neurotic and stupid again, aren't I?' she exclaimed as if she were exasperated with herself. 'For heaven's sake don't take any notice of me!' And having given me an affectionate kiss she added: 'Don't worry, I do understand how busy you are and I quite accept that you haven't the time at present to write to Francis.'

Some days later I was just reflecting in relief that Anne's moodiness had been entirely conquered when an event occurred which made me fear its revival: Higgins was discharged from the mental hospital. The doctors had been unable to find anything wrong with him.

VIII

Without telling Anne I called at Higgins' cottage and sat drinking tea with him in the front parlour.

'The hospital doctor said that after a rest I'd be as good as new,' said Higgins placidly, 'and I am.'

'Why did he say you needed a rest from work?'

'Not from work, sir. From Her.'

I wondered confused if the presence had changed sex. 'Her?'

'Mrs Higgins, sir. My wife.'

'Ah.' I remained puzzled. 'You didn't tell me there was a difficulty with your wife.'

'No more there is, sir. She nags a bit, but I'm used to that. Her nagging's just water off a duck's back to me.'

'Then why did the doctor think –'

'He was mad, sir, like all the poor souls in that place. He said that though I *think* I don't care about the nagging, deep down inside me I do, and when I want to kill the cows what I really want is to kill my wife.'

'Ah.'

'I did right not to tell Doctor what I thought of his idea, didn't I, sir? It wouldn't have been polite. But of course the truth is it's not *me* that wants to kill any living creature. It's Him.'

'Did he visit you in hospital?'

'No, sir, not once. Maybe he's gone for good now.'

'Let's hope so.' I talked to him for a little longer but he did indeed seem the picture of bucolic health and his placid sensible manner was very reassuring.

When I next saw Anne I said as casually as possible: 'It seems Higgins had a mild nervous breakdown brought on by a marital difficulty.'

'Martial difficulty?' said Anne astonished. 'But they always seem so tranquil and well suited!' However before I could attempt a comment she added: 'Well, I suppose a lot of couples manage to cover up their troubles – thank goodness there's an explanation for his peculiar behaviour.'

I thought no more of Higgins. I was too busy organizing the service of healing, and as the appointed hour in July drew closer I became entirely absorbed in my preparations. Then on the very day of the service disaster struck. At ten o'clock that morning Anne's land-agent telephoned from the Home Farm to say that Higgins had butchered a cow, barricaded himself in the barn with a scythe and was bellowing that I alone had the power to deliver him from his nightmare.

SEVENTEEN

'(Christ) unquestionably taught that unclean spirits, no less
than the Holy Spirit, may make their abode within us.'

W. R. INGE
Dean of St Paul's 1911–1934
Christian Ethics and Modern Problems

I

Luckily Anne was out, paying one of her regular visits to Dr Romaine,
so I did not have to endure another emotional outburst on the subject
of exorcism. Responding at once to the urgency of the call I mounted
my bicycle and arrived five minutes later at the Home Farm to find
that a large crowd had gathered outside the barn. The land-agent
greeted me with the news that the village constable had already telephoned for reinforcements. Meanwhile the crowd of yokels, eyeing me
with excitement, were all agog at the possibility of a supernatural
intervention.

I dealt with this unedifying aura by telling them to keep well back.
Then moving confidently in order to conceal my considerable trepidation
I announced myself at the door of the barn and promised Higgins that I
would perform the laying-on of hands, just as he had originally requested,
if he would abandon his scythe and come out.

The door creaked open an inch. When he saw I was alone the inch
widened to a foot. He was still holding the scythe and his clothes were
covered with blood. He looked frightened but sane.

'I'm not coming out,' he said. 'They'll overpower me. You must come
in.'

'Very well, but you must put the scythe outside the door – and I can't
come in alone. I must have three people with me to pray while I perform
the laying-on of hands.'

'You promise they won't overpower me and tie me up?'

'Once you're delivered from this spirit who's tormenting you there'll
be no need to tie you up.'

He considered the situation. I still saw no signs of possession. Finally he opened the door wider, dropped the scythe in the yard and said: 'Come in.'

A gasp rippled through the crowd as the scythe flashed in the light. Beckoning three of the burliest labourers I said to Dawson the land-agent: 'Keep everyone out, even the police.' Then after instructing my bodyguards I led the way into the building.

This particular barn was used for housing farm vehicles and when I entered I saw that Higgins had retreated to a position behind the wheel of a tractor. However he made no attempt to retreat further, and I was just concluding in relief that I had once more encountered the sufferer during a lucid interval when the nape of my neck prickled I stopped dead, and suddenly I saw all the signs Father Darcy had described, the hidden look in the eyes, the tightening of the muscles at the side of the jaw and the abrupt unnecessary movements which were now manifested as the man sat down, drew up his knees in a foetal position, uncoiled himself again and finally leant back against the tractor. Sane stolid simple Higgins had vanished. Another presence occupied the shattered psyche. Automatically my hand reached for my pectoral cross.

Until that moment I had merely felt nervous but now I felt very frightened indeed. In preparation for the afternoon's service I had been spending hours in fasting and prayer, and my psyche, honed by this rigorous discipline, was at its most receptive with the result that my confrontation with this demonic force formed the spiritual equivalent of being struck in the stomach with a battering ram. I had taken care to bring a small crucifix with me. Still holding my pectoral cross with my left hand I produced the crucifix from my pocket. The man flinched. Holding out the crucifix I ordered: 'Repeat after me: Jesus Christ is Lord.'

He tried to obey. Sweat stood out on his forehead. Then the fiend grabbed him again and as his fingers curled into his hands like claws – another symptom – he rushed forward shouting that he would tear my eyes out. Immediately my three bodyguards leapt to the rescue, but with the abnormal strength of the possessed he tossed them aside and rushed at me again. I shall never know how I stood my ground but I shoved the crucifix at the maniac and shouted: 'In the name of JESUS CHRIST, depart from this man, you demon of violence, and trouble him no more!' Just in time I remembered that the spirit not only had to be named but directed elsewhere to avoid all risk of it merely moving from one body in the barn to another. 'In the name of JESUS CHRIST,' I shouted again, 'depart and possess the body of a cow fifty miles away!' My choice of a cow indicated my extreme fright; as I confronted the shell of the cowman it was the only animal I could remember, and it is a curious, even astonishing fact that this bizarre command, far from sounding a note of bathos as any sane civilized person would expect, rang out with the lethal power of a bullet from a shotgun. Higgins had stopped dead in his tracks as soon as I had invoked the name of Christ, but now he was blasted backwards and the next moment he had slumped unconscious to the ground.

The evil miasma vanished from the atmosphere as abruptly as if someone had heaved it from the barn. For a second I thought I too would lose consciousness, but as the atmosphere lightened the dizziness ebbed. My three companions were shivering as if they were shell-shocked. At last I managed to say to them: 'Thank you. You can leave now. Tell everyone to remain outside.'

I prayed by the inert body until Higgins awoke ten minutes later. His first words were: 'He's gone.' Tears of relief sprang to his eyes. 'He won't come back now, will he?' he said. 'He'll never come back again.'

I asked him to say: 'Jesus Christ is Lord,' and when he uttered the words without difficulty I offered him the crucifix which he now had no trouble clasping. Before I laid my hands on him we prayed together, thanking God for the deliverance. Higgins cried soundlessly all the time and afterwards when I gave him my handkerchief he could only sob pathetically: 'What's to become of me?' but unfortunately there was no easy answer to that question; I foresaw another visit to the mental hospital as the authorities went through the motions of closing the stable door after the horse had bolted, but at least I could promise that my wife would bring no charges against him for the slaughter of the cow.

'Poor Buttercup,' said Higgins, shedding fresh tears. 'She had such a lovely nature. Oh God, oh God, how terrible to think I killed her!'

I thought of my responsibility for Whitby's murder, and somehow found the strength to comfort him.

II

When I returned home it was noon and I had exactly three hours to rebuild my strength before the service. The hours of fasting now combined with a delayed shock to render me disordered, even panic-stricken, as I realized how far I was from being prepared for the arduous afternoon ahead, and when Anne waylaid me in the hall I wanted only to escape from her.

'I've just got back and heard the news,' she said distressed. 'Dawson phoned. Jon, how *could* you have been so utterly reckless and foolish! If you'd been killed by that maniac – '

'But I wasn't.'

'No, and weren't you lucky! It just seems so appallingly irresponsible, tackling a lunatic when you were armed only with a crucifix, and anyway you promised me, you absolutely promised you wouldn't have anything to do with exorcisms – '

'How could I have ignored Higgins' cry for help when he was in such appalling torment? Look, Anne, I'm sorry but we'll have to talk about this later – I can't stop now.' I spoke more sharply than I should have done but the increasing pressure on my lacerated psyche was fast becoming intolerable. However I had made a fatal mistake. The last shreds of Anne's patience deserted her as anger destroyed her self-control.

'Talk later?' she exclaimed. 'You won't talk later! You'll sidestep any honest conversation as usual, but has it never occurred to you that I'm beginning to feel bloody well abandoned? I've tried and tried to be a good wife to you, never complaining about all the parish work even though I'm often worn out with the farm; I've stood by you in all your troubles, never offering one word of reproach when you alienate half the village, never uttering a word of complaint when you offend my friends by refusing to accept their invitations, never betraying a hint of what I really feel about this awful alien ritual which completely distorts all our cherished services – '

'Anne!' I was so dumbfounded, so wholly appalled that I could do no more than whisper her name.

' – never criticizing you as you go charging along hell-bent on getting what you want the whole damn time, but now I'm not standing any more of this monstrously selfish behaviour – it's time I told you how horribly unhappy you're making me! You seem to believe that so long as you can satisfy me in bed you can treat me like a doormat, but all I can say is that if you think you can go on trampling me underfoot like this you've made a very big mistake. I need some respect, consideration and – yes, damn it – LOVE, and I absolutely refuse to let you get away with treating me as I can now see you must have treated Betty!' And as I remained transfixed with horror she rushed away from me across the hall.

It took me several seconds to recover sufficiently to blunder after her. She had collapsed sobbing on the drawing-room sofa but when I tried to put my arms around her she pushed me aside. 'Go away.'

'But Anne, we must talk, we absolutely must – I insist – '

'There you go again. Always what *you* want the whole time – you're so arrogant, so self-centred – '

'But – '

'GO AWAY!' shouted Anne, and dashed out of the room. I tore after her but I was slow off the mark again and this time the door was locked as she took refuge in the library. 'We'll talk later,' I heard her say in a muffled voice, 'after you've given your dazzling performance as the Wonder-Worker. Now just go away and leave me alone.'

I was silenced. For one long moment I stared stricken at the closed door. Then I turned aside and crept away.

<h2 style="text-align:center">III</h2>

Words flickered in my consciousness, useless inadequate words reflecting my agonized state of mind, and the words were: pregnant, irrational, emotional, didn't mean it, couldn't mean it, just an overwrought mistake, she'll take every word back when she's calmer.

These words sustained me until I reached my cell. Then the over-powering sincerity of Anne's tirade blasted aside this feeble defence and annihilated my remaining strength so that for some time I could only sit numbly in a chair. Prayer was impossible, meditation quite beyond my power. All I could do was concentrate on recovering the will to move.

At length I managed to creep back downstairs. Anne had evidently recovered; I could hear her talking to someone in the drawing-room and I wondered who the visitor was but I supposed the police might have arrived to talk to her about the cow. I had already made my statement to them and as I was in no mood to make another I took refuge in the dining-room. To my surprise I saw the table was set for two. That was odd. I had given instructions that I would need no food until after the service. Dismissing the extra place as a servant's vagary I moved to the sideboard, sniffed the decanters to identify the brandy and poured a hefty measure into a tumbler. I disliked brandy but I felt in desperate need of medicine to restore my equilibrium.

Having consumed the brandy as quickly as I could I then found I had no idea what to do with the glass. I could hardly leave it on the sideboard. What would the servants think? I shuddered, but the brandy was giving me a new energy and moving swiftly from the room, the glass still in my hand, I escaped into the garden.

Halfway to the chapel I felt dizzy and knew the brandy had been a mistake. I sat down to wait until I felt better, and as I leant against a tree-trunk I thought how beautiful the sunlight was as it slanted through the beeck-leaves. I remembered teaching my novices about nature-mysticism. 'Excellent!' Father Darcy had exclaimed after eavesdropping in the scriptorium for half an hour during one of his annual visitations. 'Now admit it, Jonathan – isn't imparting knowledge to an enrapt audience more satisfying that healing constipated cats?' And although I had wanted to hit him for this mocking reference to Whitby I had been unable to resist a smile as I savoured such unprecedented approval.

Poor Whitby.

REMEMBER WHITBY, Francis had written, and I was remembering him, murdered martyred Whitby, lying stiff as a board on the abbot's desk while Father Darcy pointed his finger at me and said: '*You* killed that animal with your disobedience, your vanity and your utterly intolerable pride.'

I suddenly realized that I had to cancel the service. Father Darcy would be so angry if I held it. I shuddered, reminding myself that he was dead, but somehow his memory seemed to be hardening in my mind and feeding upon my psyche as it sought the strength to project itself upon the ether ... But such a projection would have been a mere parlour-trick. Father Darcy was at peace, with God. I could hardly expect to be aware of him as a disturbed discarnate presence, and any ghost I succeeded in conjuring up would only have been a manifestation of my disordered psyche.

'I never recommend celebrating the Eucharist,' Wilfred had written, 'unless a ghost has actually been seen.'

'That letter from Wilfred was thoroughly creepy and beastly ...'

As Anne's voice echoed in my memory the brandy glass slipped from my hand and shattered on a stone. The sound had the same effect as the click of a hypnotist's fingers as he awoke his subject from a trance, and struggling to my feet I kicked the fragments of glass into the undergrowth before I stumbled on down the path into the dell.

The chapel faced me at last, and suddenly as its serene atmosphere enfolded me I felt I could not possibly cancel the service. For the sake of the sick I had to cast all doubts aside.

In the chapel I knelt to pray but my mind was blank. Then slowly, very slowly, my battered spyche was bathed in a subtle alluring light until I could see the words of a prayer. It was inscribed on my consciousness in the most beautiful lettering and it read: grant me a spectacular cure today so that I can believe my call is right; grant me a spectacular cure so that I can feel young and vital and successful, dazzling not only my wife but the world with my magnificent glamorous powers.

A second later I was recoiling in horror; I had recognized the Devil's presence in this travesty of a prayer, and automatically I grabbed my pectoral cross to beat him out of my psyche. Indeed so appalled was I by this spiritual deviation that it was some time before I could whisper to God: 'Help me. give me the strength I must have in order to comfort these sick people.' But then I thought of Anne accusing me of being concerned only with my own wants and I realized that even this prayer was hopelessly self-centred. In despair I retreated to the vestry to change into my cassock and surplice.

When I had dressed I tried to pray for others. I prayed for Anne, whom I had wounded so deeply, and as soon as I remembered her I thought of the baby. I recalled my showing, its joyous aftermath, my absolute conviction that I was on the right road and that all would eventually be well.

The showing had sustained me in the past and now I knew it sustained me still. So long as I could believe in that showing I would survive, and rising from my knees at last with my faith restored I found I had sufficient strength to face the service.

IV

The congregation approached the chapel by passing through one of the side-gates in the wall which encircled the grounds and proceeding for some two hundred yards along a track into the dell. By a quarter to three the chapel was packed and Colonel Maitland's sidesmen were being obliged to turn people away. However I gave permission for a number to stand at the back beyond the five patients in wheelchairs, and although the Colonel expressed doubts about the wisdom of packing people into this confined space I pointed out that if anyone should be overcome by claustrophobia the exit was conveniently close.

'The point is they're blocking the exit for the rest of the congregation,' said Colonel Maitland, but unwilling to be distracted further by trivial details I dismissed him so that I could be alone again in the vestry. I had not ventured out of it to inspect the congregation because I was afraid Anne might have decided not to attend, and by then I felt it was vital that I did not risk becoming further distressed.

Three o'clock arrived. Colonel Maitland informed me that all was ready, and after a brief final prayer I moved from the vestry to the altar.

When I faced the congregation the first thing I saw was the hat in the fourth row.

It was a large hat eleborately bedecked with artificial flowers and it was being worn by one of my ladies, a widow named Mrs Hetherington. But I barely saw Mrs Hetherington. I was too busy staring at her hat, so like the hats worn long ago by our neighbour Mrs Simmonds who had refused to let her child play with the son of a parlourmaid. But once little Nicholas had slipped out of the house when his mother was looking the other way; he had seen me passing down the road and he had wanted to say hullo to me, just as he always did at Sunday school. I could see him now in my memory, a small thin boy with red air, and in my memory too I could hear his mother calling: 'Nicholas! Nicholas!' as she realized he was missing.

The showing shattered.

I knew then that I had gone horrifyingly astray, and as I stood paralysed with shock before the hushed congregation I felt the Devil himself gently stroke the hair at the nape of my neck.

The temperature in the chapel started to fall.

I stared around, wondering why no one was shivering. I felt deathly cold, and it was only with the greatest difficulty that I managed to speak. I said: 'There's an enemy among us.' I did not think before I spoke. The sentence arrived fully formed on my tongue. I had to let the Devil know that I was fully aware of his presence.

The congregation gaped, and when I realized in confusion that they had not understood I heard myself say to them loudly: 'The forces of darkness are waging their eternal battle against the forces of light.'

Still they stared, and shuddering with the cold I began to move forward to the first row of pews. 'The forces of darkness,' I said, speaking very distinctly, 'are trying to destroy me.'

A gasp finally rippled through the congregation, and at once it seemed as if the rows of faces were transformed into wooden blocks, dry and inanimate, waiting for the spark which would set them ablaze.

Meanwhile my glance was raking each row for the source of the evil which threatened me. I had realized that the Devil was no longer a climate, chilling the chapel. He had become incarnate, hiding from me behind a human mask, but I knew I dared not let him elude me. I had to hunt him down and force him into the open where he could be confronted, overpowered and vanquished.

'Stand up, Satan!' I shouted suddenly. 'Stand up and show yourself!'

A second later I saw Anne's face, white with terror, but before I could yell at her to escape, the man beside her slowly rose to his feet and at once all trace of the rational world dissolved.

The man was Father Darcy.

V

I gasped.

Then I tried to back away but something seemed to have happened to my legs; they were so heavy that I could hardly move them. I wanted to rub my eyes but my arms had become heavy too, so heavy that I could no longer raise my hands, and all I could do was stare at the figure in the Fordite habit. I knew I could not be seeing Father Darcy yet at the same time I knew it was Father Darcy I was seeing. Panic overwhelmed me. Dragging my arm upwards I scrabbled for my pectoral cross but found that in my disordered state I had forgotten to put the cross on again after donning my cassock.

My panic increased. I tried to say: 'In the name of JESUS CHRIST . . .' but my tongue seemed to have disconnected itself with my brain so that I was unable to repel this manifestation of the Devil with the exorcist's most powerful weapon. Finally fear drove out the shock which had been inhibiting my movements. Backing away I bumped into the altar and swung round to grab the wooden cross but I had forgotten its weight and the next moment it had slipped through my shaking hands. I bent to retrieve it; immediately it assumed the weight of lead and became impossible to shift. Unnerved by this malign displacement of the laws of physics I tried to say: 'Jesus is Lord,' and when nothing happened blind terror overwhelmed me for I had realized that *I* had become the Devil incarnate. The evil lay not among the congregation but in me. Having made a mockery of God's will by following my self-centred deluded desires I had laid myself open to demonic infiltration and now the Devil himself had stepped forward to annex my soul.

This appalling truth flashed through my mind in a single second but I could not pause to dwell on it. There was no time. Looking back over my shoulder I saw Father Darcy not as the Devil incarnate but as God's servant the exorcist. He was as fit and active as he had been when we had first met, and all the jewels glittered in his well-remembered pectoral cross as he moved silently, eerily, purposefully up the aisle to annihilate me.

I whispered: 'Keep away!' and edged around the altar-table, but I knew I would be powerless against him. In desperation I shouted: 'No one must touch me! I'm the Devil – I'll kill anyone who touches me!' and at once the naked flame blazed in the tinder-box as someone screamed in terror.

Hysteria erupted. Screams, shouts, yells, cries, howls – we were all plunged straight into hell. A chaotic stampede broke out as everyone plunged towards the exit, but although I was aware of the noise increasing as the hideous wave of violence struck the packed crowd at the back of the chapel I found I could not watch what was happening. I was mesmerized by Father Darcy. Oblivious of the pandemonium behind him he had reached the altar and was now facing me across the table. I sensed the power of his will as his concentration deepened, and when his psyche wrapped itself around mine I felt disorientated because it was not as I remembered it. Father Darcy's psyche had been muscular and powerful but subtle and sinuous. This new psyche was muscular and powerful but blunt and abrasive. Realizing he was trying to disguise himself I thought: how clever! But I knew I had to let him know I was not deceived. Raising my voice above the chaotic noise I shouted: 'I know who you are! You think you can destroy me just as you destroyed Whitby, but I'm going to put you back in your coffin, I'm going to burn you to ashes, I'm going to –'

Father Darcy suddenly moved with a speed which terminated my power of speech. He stooped. He grabbed the oak cross. He slammed it down on the table between us. Then he cried with a force which knocked the breath from my lungs: 'In the name of JESUS CHRIST, I command thee, Satan, to depart from this man to a distant savage and never return!'

All the power drained from my body.

I lost consciousness.

VI

When I awoke I thought I was in the London punishment cell. Then I recognized the bare walls of the chapel's vestry. I was lying on the floor with an object which felt like a pillow beneath my head but which turned out to be my surplice, folded and bunched to make me comfortable. I was still wearing my cassock.

As I stirred, a chair scraped on the floor behind me and someone dressed as the Abbot-General of the Fordite monks quickly knelt at my side.

'Francis! Oh my God – ' The return of memory and the return of sanity were equally horrifying.

'Here,' said Francis, shoving his bejewelled cross into my hands, 'hold this. You're all right.'

I grabbed the cross, gabbled: 'Jesus is Lord!' and collapsed back on the surplice, but fear soon elbowed my relief aside. 'Francis, don't let them take me away – don't let them put me in an asylum – '

'No one's taking you anywhere. Calm down.'

But I was in a frenzy. 'Where's Anne?'

'She's not here at the moment.'

'Has she left me?'

'Of course not!' Francis sounded scandalized.

'Francis, promise – swear – she hasn't left me – '

'I promise. Swearing's quite unnecessary.'

'But Francis, Anne doesn't love me any more – '

'Nonsense! It's because she loved you that I'm here. She wrote to me.'

This was very difficult to digest. 'She wrote to you? Anne? But what on earth did she say?'

'What do you think? She said you needed help and she was desperately worried about you.'

I said dazed: 'You must have been the guest at luncheon. I saw the extra place laid in the dining-room but I never dreamed – '

'Cyril had also written to me, of course – he even sent me a blood-curdling cutting from *The Starbridge Weekly News*, and we'd just decided that one of us should intervene when I received the appeal from your wife and realized the intervention had to come from me.'

I struggled for words but since I was now inundated with a shame which saturated the length, breadth and depth of my being, speech was quite impossible. I could only cover my face with my hands, abandon the last vestige of my pride and shudder with the most profound humiliation.

'There, there!' said Francis kindly in the manner of a nanny who had rescued a wilful child from a somewhat tiresome nursery prank. 'It's not the end of the world! You took a wrong turn and wound up making a fool of yourself, that's all, but that's not an unusual thing to happen. Thousands of men wind up making fools of themselves every day but they soon recover and bounce back.'

Anger restored my power of speech. 'What a frivolous way to talk!' I exclaimed outraged. 'How dare you toss aside a case of demonic possession so lightly!'

'There was no demonic possesion.'

I stared. Then I managed to stammer: 'But I couldn't say "Jesus is Lord" – I couldn't hold the cross – '

'My dear Jon, you were merely a magnificent example of someone self-hypnotized by guilt!'

I found myself becoming outraged again. 'But if you didn't think I was possessed, why the deuce did you exorcize me?'

'Because I happen to have at least a rudimentary understanding of psychology. As soon as you revealed that you thought I was Father Darcy I realized that the only way to deal with you was to behave as you expected – and wanted – the old man to behave.'

'But the exorcism was so successful . . .' For the second time outrage was displaced by confusion.

'There was no exorcism,' said Francis patiently. 'How could there be when there was no possession? I simply defused your mental disturbance by a psychological trick. In fact this whole episode can be explained perfectly adequately in rational terms without resorting to the super-natural.' He stood up. 'Come into the chapel so that we can both sit down in comfort, and I'll do my best to help you understand what was really going on.'

But I shrank back. 'Not the chapel. I can't go in there, can't face it . . . How long was I unconscious?'

'Less than a minute at first. But then you opened your eyes, announced: "I must sleep now," and passed out for another three quarters of an hour. You'd obviously remembered that after an exorcism the person delivered always sleeps.'

'I don't recall – '

'No, probably not. Well, if you won't go into the chapel, come and sit on the steps of the porch. A little fresh air certainly won't do you any harm.'

I followed him unsteadily outside. The sun was still shining radiantly through the beech-leaves. I felt battered, defeated, old.

'I know you'd much rather see yourself as a hero wrestling with the Devil instead of as an elderly priest floundering into an unholy mess,' said

Francis, speaking frankly but not unkindly as we sat down on the steps, 'but I'm afraid this is the moment when you must cast aside illusion and face reality. Now let's start by considering how you've arrived in your present unfortunate state. First and most obvious of all, you've been under strain for some time with your divided parish, your demanding ministry and your unresolved private problems. Then during the past twelve hours you've been fasting, a precedure which in adverse circumstances can lead to physical debility. Have the circumstances been adverse? They have. You endured a horrific scene this morning when you overpowered a madman by mesmerizing him into docility – '

'I exorcized him.'

'Quite. But you must have realized by this time that I'm unable to utter the word "exorcism" without a shudder of distaste – it's my own personal act of rebellion against our mentor. Why don't we just say you dealt with the cowman? You then had a row with your wife – '

'How do you know?'

'She told me. And that row, I venture to suggest, was the last straw. By the time the service began your psyche needed the kind of control you were far too exhausted to provide, so is it any wonder that when you saw a man dressed as the Abbot-General you should start to hallucinate? Father Darcy always forbade you to exercise the charism of healing. I suspect that subconsciously you felt guilty all along that you were disobeying him, and because this guilt was never alleviated by an honest discussion with a spiritual director it was allowed to accumulate until eventually, in your severely weakened state, it broke into your conscious mind with disastrous results: the shock of the hallucination caused your psyche to reel around in panic and regurgitate the memory of this morning's nightmare.'

After a long while I was able to say: 'There was a trigger which sent me over the edge,' and I told him how the showing had shattered.

Francis said simply: 'I'm very sorry. But of course I couldn't help wondering if your psyche had cleverly devised a way in which you could live with your problems without facing up to them.'

'He seemed so real,' I said. 'I was genuinely looking forward to him.' To my shame my eyes filled with tears.

'You need food and drink,' said Francis briskly, rising to his feet. 'Come along, I'll take you back to the house in the motor.'

I felt older and more battered than ever. 'Motor?' I said blankly. 'What motor?'

'*The* motor,' said Francis, and when he had succeeded in steering me down the track to the road beyond the wall I found not only Father Darcy's cherished Daimler but my friend Edward the master-carpenter who was sitting patiently behind the wheel.

We embarked on our short journey around the perimeter of the grounds but it was some minutes before the Daimler, swaying along at its customary stately pace, turned through the main gates of the Manor. Portman opened the front dor before the motor had halted. I dared not look him in the eye for fear of what stories he had heard, but Francis said with his aristocrat's ease as we entered the hall: 'I trust you received the message.'

'Yes, sir. The sandwiches are in the drawing-room.'

'Good. You can bring the tea now. Come along, Jon.'

After I had been piloted to the drawing-room sofa I heard myself say anxiously: 'Where's Anne?'

'She's not here at the moment.' Once more Francis sat down at my side.

'But where is she?'

'She's gone to Starbridge with the Aysgarths.'

'*Aysgarth was at the service?*' I nearly lost consciousness again. Then I said confused: 'But why has Anne gone to Starbridge?'

'I'll explain later. Start eating those sandwiches, please,' ordered Francis, and when out of habit I obeyed him he embarked on a long fluent monologue. At first I found it difficult to concentrate on what he was saying but gradually I became aware that he was casting a sympathetic eye on my troubles in order to encourage me to beat back any incipient feelings of despair. I was duly grateful but after a while my gratitude was blurred by bewilderment as I realize he was repeating himself, albeit in a most elegant and skilful way, over and over again. What did this mean? Was there perhaps a hidden reason for this interminable but stylish monologue? I tried to think coherently enough to answer these questions but was promptly distracted as he offered me yet another sandwich.

'Francis – '

'Well, yes, as I was saying . . .' He was off again, weaving his mysterious verbal patterns, and again my concentration ebbed and flowed as I grappled with my bewilderment. Isolated sentences caught my attention; isolated phrases surfaced and faded away. I felt as if I were listening to a wireless which possessed an erratic volume knob. '. . . so this doesn't mean that your original call to leave the Order was a delusion. I'm quite certain God has work for you to do in the world . . . equally certain the final revelation of his will is still to come . . . easy to see why you went astray . . . ministry centred on the chapel, everything seemed to fit . . . tempting to see the chapel as a stone siren luring you to disaster, but in fact it wasn't the chapel propelling you along, was it? Later we must discuss your motives, but meanwhile perhaps it's better to see the chapel as neutral, like money, something which can be used for good or for bad . . . But let's forget the bad for the moment, let's dwell on the positive side . . . did a lot of good among the sick . . . genuine desire to serve God mixed up with your other motives . . . still humble enough to seek advice from

Wilfred . . . picture by no means completely black . . . mistake to use the disaster as an excuse to wallow in guilt and self-pity . . .' On and on Francis continued in this soothing vein until I heard him say to the butler who had returned with more tea: 'Thank you, Portman – and fetch the brandy decanter and one glass, please.'

'No brandy for me,' I said with a shudder, but Francis merely confirmed the order before he tried to embark on another ramble through the pastures of sympathy and consolation.

However at this point I interrupted him by asking the qustion which had been bothering me for some time. 'Why are you stuffing me with food and drink like this?'

'Because I want you to regain your strength as quickly as possible and since you're not interested in food and drink I know you've got to be force-fed. Do you remember Father Darcy saying – ' And he launched into a reminiscence which lasted until Portman returned with the brandy decanter, the soda siphon and a tumbler.

'Francis, I really don't want – '

'Nonsense, of course you do. Brandy's a splendid restorative.'

'Yes, but – ' I waited till Portman had left the room ' – I had a brandy before I went down to the chapel and it nearly finished me off altogether. I don't see how I can possibly face alcohol for a second time today.'

'Try a little will-power.'

Since it seemed less trouble to give in than to protest I began to sip the brandy. In fact by this time I was feeling considerably stronger. Francis' utter sanity was very bracing.

'That's better,' said Francis when my glass was empty. 'Now we'll go upstairs. When I told your wife I wanted to wear my habit for the service, she kindly allowed me to change out of my clerical suit in a room which she referred to as your cell. I'll just change back now into my suit and you can shed that cassock. Then Edward will drive us to Starbridge.'

I stared at him. 'To Starbridge?' Dimly I realized I was about to grasp the scene's hidden dimension, and at that same moment the fear scythed through my psyche as I saw the darkness falling across the future. All I could manage to say was: 'Something's happened.'

'Yes, there was a crush in the chapel when everyone panicked.' Francis spoke calmly but with increasing speed. 'Several people were knocked over and one of them was your wife, but very fortunately her doctor was among the congregation and when he said she should go to Starbridge Hospital the Aysgarths volunteered to drive her there. I wasn't aware of all this at the time, of course. I was too busy dealing with you, but later a gentleman called Maitland came to the vestry while you were still asleep and – '

Terror finally untied my tongue. '*Why the hell didn't you tell me this straight away?*'

'*Because you were in no fit state to be told!* Of course I had to keep you here while I built up your strength – I couldn't have let you tear off to the hospital after an unbroken fast, paranoid hallucinations and a complete physical collapse!'

'But if Anne's dying – '

'My dear Jon, it's not even certain that she's miscarrying – she may be quite all right. She's only gone to the hospital because the doctor thought it best to take no chances.'

But I was already visualizing unutterable horrors, and without further delay I blundered from the room.

VII

The Aysgarths and the Maitlands were in the hospital waiting-room. It was very hard for me to face them, particularly as I could sense their embarrassment mingling with their anxiety, but to my relief Francis took control of the situation. He said: 'How kind of you all to wait, but after Jon's very public ordeal in the chapel he would prefer this ordeal to be entirely private. Would you care to give me your telephone numbers? Then I can keep you informed of Mrs Darrow's progress.' Francis was hard to withstand when he was wielding authority with such ruthless tact; even Colonel Maitland hesitated for no more than three seconds before offering his telephone number and departing. Aysgarth, handing Francis his card, paused long enough to say to me: 'I'm sorry. This is terrible for you. Please don't doubt that you have my sympathy,' but the next moment he too was gone and I was alone with Francis and half a dozen strangers in that large room with the cream-coloured walls and the battered wooden chairs and the floor covered with olive-green linoleum which had cracked at the seams.

'I said to Francis: 'I'm sure you now want to withdraw to Starwater. All these hours in the world must be very tedious for you and I'd be selfish if I claimed your company a moment longer.'

'My dear Jon,' said Francis, 'I'd be a poor sort of priest if I scuttled back to the cloister when a brother was in such desperate need.'

I was still struggling to frame a grateful reply when a large figure in a white coat ambled into the waiting-room, spotted the two men in clerical suits and padded swiftly in our direction. At once I recognized him from Charles' descriptions, and as he held out his hand I said before he could introduce himself: 'You're Alan Romaine.'

It is always curious to meet a person about whom one had heard so much for so long. I was at once aware that I knew him well yet at the same time had never grasped the essence of his personality. I recognized the stoutness of his tall frame, the shrewdness in his bright eyes, the way he moved gracefully, lightly, like an elderly cat accustomed to prowling all manner of alleys with insouciance. But his psyche, scarred with past pain and emanating a profound intuitive sympathy, was new to me. I had thought of Romaine as a failed doctor, prevented by his past mistakes from rising to the top of the medical tree in London. Now I realized that God, by cutting him off from the worldly success which would have inevitably destroyed someone of his sensual temperament, had in fact saved him so that his gift for healing had been able to develop to the full. I thought how in my arrogance I had judged him harshly, and I was ashamed.

Absorbed by these thoughts I at first forgot Francis' information that Romaine had witnessed my breakdown at the chapel, but even when I remembered I felt no embarrassment. Possibly this was because by then I could think of nothing except Anne's crisis, but possibly too it was because Romaine, unlike the Maitlands and the Aysgarths, showed no embarrassment himself. As a healer he was far too busy being concerned for my welfare.

'I'm sorry we should meet under such difficult circumstances,' he was saying, 'and I'm even sorrier to have to tell you that your wife's miscarrying. Let me say straight away that I don't anticipate unusual complications and I expect her to come through safely, but of course it's not a good situation and I'm afraid it'll be some time yet before it's over.'

His quiet authority was so reassuring that for the first time I allowed myself to believe that Anne might survive. I heard myself saying urgently: 'Can I see her?'

'You could. But whether you should is a different matter. You're quite understandably very upset and it's important that she should be surrounded now by people who are very calm, people she doesn't have to worry about.'

I saw the good sense of this. 'I don't want her to worry about me. I'll wait here,' I said, but as soon as the words had been spoken I was plunged into terror again. My voice said: 'I've got to be told if she's dying. Supposing she died and I wasn't there?' I suddenly found I had to sit down. Sweat was trickling down my forehead and my heart was hammering in my chest.

Romaine said at once: 'Of course you'd be summoned if things went wrong.'

'You're just saying that to calm me down. You don't really mean it. You'd forget all about me and then only remember when it was too late.' I was losing control of myself. In desperation I turned to Francis. 'I can't find any more words. You tell him. Make it absolutely clear that *I've got to be there when she dies.*'

Francis immediately stepped forward. 'My name's Ingram,' he said to Romaine. 'I'll look after him. I'm sure you want to get back to your patient.'

But Romaine sat down beside me; Romaine took my hand in his as if we were old, old friends, and Romaine said to me in the gentlest possible voice: 'You've lost someone before in tragic circumstances, haven't you? And you've never forgiven the person who failed to summon you to her bedside when she was dying.'

There was a silence broken only by the visitors murmuring on the far side of the room. I was dimly aware that Francis was transfixed as if he had received some electrifying revelation, but my eyes could see only Romaine. I said: 'So long as you understand, that's all right. I'll wait down here.'

Francis said to Romaine: 'Is there a place where I can sit quietly with him and drink some tea?'

'Go down to the end of the hall, turn right and keep going.' Releasing my hand he stood up and patted me on the shoulder. 'You'll be constantly on my mind,' he said, 'and I give you my word that no matter what happens I shan't forget.'

Francis led me to the hospital canteen, an even larger, drearier cream-painted room where we drank strong tea out of squat white cups at a secluded table. For a while he waited for me to talk but I was too absorbed in my anxiety, and eventually when he realized that I had failed to grasp the magnitude of my revelation he said: 'It's curious, isn't it, how often we think we know the truth about a person and then suddenly we make a discovery which puts all the familiar facts in a different light. I remember you said to me once that exploring a personality is like peeling an onion. You have to strip off layer after layer of skin before you finally reach the core.'

I nodded but I was still thinking only of Anne.

'I always did think it was strange,' said Francis, 'that a young man from your very respectable background should have sampled such a variety of women so speedily once he had escaped from both his home and his boarding-school, but now for the first time I believe I understand what was happening. You weren't just flailing around in an unsuccessful attempt to find a woman who matched up to your mother, were you? You were trying to work out how you could relate to the opposite sex without laying yourself open to pain. Hence the brevity of your affairs; you knew you had to leave your girls before they could leave you.'

It began to dawn on me that he was saying something important. My worry about Anne was temporarily displaced.

'And of course I see your marriage in quite a different light now,' I heard Francis say. 'You didn't just marry for sexual reasons. It was all far more complicated than that. You married a woman you didn't love because you knew that if she left you, you wouldn't care enough to suffer as you'd suffered once before.'

Instinctively I clung to the last layer of the onion-skin. It was a reaction I had seen so often in those I had counselled. The thought of an unhealed wound being exposed to the cold air of truth is very threatening to a disturbed psyche.

'I don't understand you,' I said, but he only answered: 'I should have guessed earlier. Almost your first words when you awoke this afternoon were: "Has she left me?" You're afraid that any woman you love will abandon you, and it was this irrational fear which lured you into cutting such a dash with your powers. You felt you had to keep your wife spellbound in order to ensure she didn't go away.'

I said: 'When I was healing none of my fears mattered any more.' Then I said: 'I'm so old and she's so young,' and rubbed my eyes. Finally I whispered: 'I'm a dull sort of person really, not sociable in the accepted sense, absorbed in my work, obsessed by ideas which are unfashionable among the younger generation. Anne didn't know me when she married me. She just saw me as a mysterious, alluring ex-monk. I was so afraid she wouldn't want me any more if she found out I was just a dull difficult tiresome old man. That's why I had to go on being mysterious and alluring. That's why I took up the healing. It was so glamorous. I dazzled her. She loved it.'

'At first, perhaps, but later? Why do you think she turned to me for help? Because she saw you not as an alluring ex-monk nor – heavens above, what unprecedented humility! – as a dull, difficult, tiresome old man but as a much-loved husband whom she intends to stand by "till death do you part".'

'Yes, but . . . one never quite knows. Someone may say: "I shall never leave you," and yet – '

'But she didn't mean to leave you, did she?' said Francis, and I knew we were no longer talking about Anne. 'She didn't desert you voluntarily.'

'No, but all that mattered was that she wasn't there. The pain was indescribable. There was no one else who understood, you see; no one else with whom I could communicate on a psychic level.'

'I quite see it would have been a devastating bereavement.' Francis allowed a pause to develop before adding: 'You must have felt angry later.'

'Eventually, yes.' I thought carefully, viewing the extreme past from my remote position in the present, and was relieved when I felt no emotion. Emotion might have detached the last layer of the onion-skin. 'I wanted to blame someone for the catastrophe,' I said, 'but don't misunderstand – I didn't wind up hating my mother and turning against all women. After all, as you pointed out, she didn't leave me voluntarily. And I couldn't wind up hating God either; even at the age of fourteen I was too much aware of his reality to believe he was just a cross old tyrant with a cruel streak, and in fact it was my awareness of God's reality which enabled me to survive that terrible time. I knew he understood me even if no one else did, and eventually I came to accept that the suffering was his way of making me the man he wanted me to become.'

'So if you couldn't be angry with God,' said Francis, 'and you couldn't be angry with your mother – '

'It was all very awkward,' I said as if we were discussing some embarrassing breach of social etiquette. My psyche was still clinging fearfully to the last layer of onion-skin. 'I wasn't allowed to be angry with anyone else. Nobody ever got angry in our house, you see. Nobody ever complained.'

'Ah!' said Francis. 'So I got it wrong. This story isn't about your mother after all.'

And then at last after its long imprisonment in the darkest corner of my psyche my father's memory, complex and multi-faceted, began to move steadily forward into the light.

VIII

'My father's name was Jonathan Darrow,' I said, and as I spoke I knew Francis' understanding was generating the trust which would finally enable me to let go of the truth. 'My mother called me Jon to distinguish me from him, but my father always called me by my full name. Jonathan. I hated it. It wasn't me. It wasn't me at all. It was him.

'My father wanted a replica. He wanted another Jonathan Darrow, just like him, to live the life he'd never managed to lead. That makes him sound like a monster, but he wasn't. He was . . . But how can I describe him? I realized just now when I met Romaine how hard it is to convey the essence of a personality in words. I told Anne my father was a good man with a gift for teaching, and that was true. I told you that he was quiet and scholarly and a little afraid of me when I was grown up, and that was true too. Yet those descriptions convey the impression that he was essentially a nonentity, and he wasn't. Not my father. He wasn't a nonentity at all.

'He was a *proud* man. That was the essence of his personality. He was very, very proud, far too proud to admit he'd made a mess of his life with that socially disastrous marriage which had blighted his career as a schoolmaster. My father never complained not because he wanted to be saintly but because he wanted everyone to believe he had no regrets. His pride was such that even the most genuine compassion would have been intolerable to him.

'So there he was, good, kind and decent, never complaining, but as I grew up I realized that underneath all this sweetness and light there was a powerful, intimidating personality. It was his other self, his true self, the self that came alive whenever he taught. I was very much afraid of this hidden self when I was a child; all the pent-up emotion, the dense invisible ball of anger and frustration, generated a frightening psychic aura, and I lived in terror of displeasing him. Whenever he was displeased with me the kind gentle mask would slip to reveal the fierce stranger beneath, but as I grew up I realized that the way to keep the mask permanently in place was to be the replica, the son who would live his life over again for him and wind up the headmaster of a famous public school.

'At first it wasn't too difficult to be a replica. It simply meant getting good reports at school and taking a precocious interest in Shakespeare. Then the going got harder. He recognized the psychic affinity I shared with my mother and started to worry about me being "odd". For years she and I concealed my developing psychic gifts from him, but shortly before she died I had my first vision and then no concealment was possible.

'The mask slipped. He was outraged. First of all he thought I was lying. Then he thought I was going mad and it took a Harley Street specialist to convince him that there was nothing wrong with me. But all the time my mother and I knew that the real problem, the problem that bothered him most of all, was that I wasn't behaving like a replica. He worked himself into a frenzy, and I became so distressed by his inability to accept me as I was that my mother finally turned on him. "Why should you assume everyone else is as limited as you are?" she said. "You yourself may be obliged to wear spectacles, but you're hardly so stupid as to believe this means everyone has defective sight!" It was the only time I ever heard her speak harshly to him, and of course he was much too proud to answer back. He simply preserved a dignified silence, and with my psychic eye I saw him nailing the mask back in place. Later he just said: "This incident is never to be referred to again and we'll treat Jonathan's aberration as if it had never happened."

'I might have been seriously disturbed by this hostile attitude to my developing psychic powers, especially as I was at such a vulnerable age, but fortunately my mother was there to put everything right. She said to me: "You mustn't be frightened by the vision. It's part of nature and nature is in the mind of God. The vision was God's thought, flashing in your soul." Then she found a faith-healer who gave me lessons in controlling my psychic energy, but we never told my father about him because my father wouldn't have understood.

'After we found the faith-healer I said to my mother: "I'm finding it more and more difficult to be Jonathan, but I can't tell Father because he'd be so disappointed." Of course she understood exactly what I meant.

She said firmly: "You must be yourself. How else can you fulfil God's purpose for you?" And then to my great relief she added: "When the right moment comes, I'll deal with your father." I was so grateful that I exclaimed: "What would I do without you?" and she answered with a smile: "You'll never have to do without me. I'll always be here."

'She died a month later. It was typhoid. I was away at school. Typhoid's a long illness and in her case the crisis didn't come until the third week. My father had ample time to send for me but he never did. He said he hadn't been able to believe she'd die. Then he said he hadn't wanted to upset me. Then he said he was sorry, he realized he'd make a mistake. I looked at him. I could only hate him and wish he were the one who had died – but then I hated myself for thinking such an evil thought, and the guilt made me more miserable than ever.

'My father didn't understand how miserable I was, how desolate, how absolutely alone. He just said: "You're being very brave, old chap. I'm so proud of you." And I said sweetly: "You're being very brave too, Father" – but all the time I was shouting in my head: "You don't care she's dead! You don't care that I'm in hell!" and I hated him more deeply than ever. My poor father! Of course he cared in his own way, but I was too young then to understand that and I felt quite cut off from him.

'Later we repaired the relationship. He was so good, so kind, so decent, always writing to me so regularly when I was at school, always coming to see me whenever he could, always looking after me so conscientiously whenever I was home for the holidays. How could I have gone on hating someone who was such a model father? I couldn't have lived with my guilt – and indeed I began to think that my one hope of keeping the guilt at bay lay in playing the model son. So we went on living this fiction that I was growing up into a replica, but finally the day arrived when I had to confess I wanted to read theology, not English, up at Cambridge.

'Francis, I can't describe to you how frightened I was of telling him! I worried myself into a frenzy, I hardly slept for nights on end – but in fact he took the news wonderfully well. He still couldn't accept that I didn't want to teach, of course. He merely saw me teaching theology instead of English literature, and even later when I broke the news that I wanted to be ordained he still couldn't accept that I wanted to be a priest doing pastoral work, not an academic clergyman teaching in a Church-of-England public school.

'However when I was ordained I was finally obliged to tell him that I'd made up my mind not to teach. What a terrible moment that was! I was waiting for him to discard his mask and roar with rage at last – in fact I was almost looking forward to it because I thought we could then have an honest conversation, but Francis, he kept that mask in place. I'll never know how he did it. He was so kind, so decent, so full of enthusiasm and admiration – ugh! How unreal it all was! I wanted to hit him, but of course I didn't; I smiled and shook his hand and said how grateful I was to him for understanding . . . and so it went on.

'Later when I was in my mid-twenties he remarried. That was when I realized that the boot was on the other foot at last and he was the one who was frightened. He hardly knew how to break the news, but Francis, you can't imagine how good and kind and decent I was, how magnificently Christian! I gave the performance of my life and I gave it because I was my father's son and I knew that this was how one had to behave when one was upset, yet all the time I was being so saintly I wanted to shout: "You bastard, how dare you be so disloyal to my mother's memory!" But of course I said nothing and soon he had married this plump frothy little widow, someone from his own class at last, and he was so happy that I hated visiting them, hated it, but I did visit them, I visited them regularly, had to, no choice, because I knew that was my Christian duty.

'I wondered if he was still hoping for a little replica but none arrived and perhaps now that he was so much happier he lost interest in the idea of living vicariously through a son. But I always knew I'd disappointed him by not being a replica, and I never forgave him for . . . for what? For refusing to accept me as I was? For trying to relive his life through me and thus putting me under an intolerable psychological strain? For failing to send for me when my mother was dying? For turning his back on her memory years later? Why can't I forgive him and exactly what is it I can't forgive?

'Sometimes I think it's the lack of honesty which I find so unforgivable, and then I blame that pride which drove him into such a destructive dissimulation. But sometimes too I think I can't forgive him because I know, in my heart of hearts, that he came to regret marrying my mother and I'm sure this would have made her unhappy. Outwardly they seemed a contented couple, but who really knows what goes on in any marriage? I could so often sense the emotion swirling around him like a tornado and now when I look back I can see how he must have felt. After all, he'd given up his most precious ambitions to marry this woman – and what was the result? My mother was an excellent housekeeper and made him very comfortable, but when all was said and done she was still the cat that walked by herself. Marrying her must have been like grasping shining water and seeing every drop slip through one's fingers. I know he always said he loved her, but how can I be sure he meant it? Of course he'd say he loved her! His pride wouldn't have permitted him to say anything else.

'Naturally he wanted me to marry well. I've often wondered if the main reason why I married Betty was to hit back at him – to be able to say: "You wanted a replica. Well, here I am, marrying a working-class girl out of lust, just as you did! Aren't you pleased and proud?" He was always immaculately civil to Betty but my marriage must have been a horrible disappointment to him – which of course was exactly what I had in mind. I *wanted* to disappoint him. Teach? Good God, no, never! The idea of being a schoolmaster revolted me. That was what *he* wanted and he bloody well had to be disappointed. I felt that if I disappointed him I'd make him angry and if I made him angry the mask would slip and if the mask slipped I'd have the chance to communicate with him, *with him*, my real father, the true self he kept locked up, but no, he wouldn't share himself with me, he didn't love me enough because I wasn't a replica, and so everything was cheating, everything was lies, everything was false, *false*, FALSE from beginning to end.'

I stopped speaking and gave a violent shudder. Around us in the sparsely populated canteen the low murmur of voices droned on in my ears and I could hear the clink of cups as they were collected on a trolley nearby, but these were only background sounds, unimportant, and only the silence which followed my monologue was meaningful. I felt numb. My psyche lay limp, stripped naked. There was a large hole where years of hidden grief had been gouged out, and gradually I became aware of Francis' own psyche padding around the gaping hole as delicately as a velvet-pawed cat and patting it gently at the edges to staunch the flow of blood. When he said: 'Now at last I see what has to be done,' I sensed the presence of the Spirit and knew that by the grace of God I would eventually be healed. Despite all my charismatic power and my psychic gifts, despite all my confidence and my pride in my ability to heal others, I had always been quite unable to heal myself.

I felt as if God had reached out with a long scythe and slashed my arrogance to shreds.

It was a moment of the profoundest humility.

IX

At nine o'clock that night Anne was delivered of a son. Romaine came to tell me the news minutes afterwards. 'She's all right,' he said, 'and I see no reason why she shouldn't continue to be all right, but I'm afraid the news isn't so good about the baby.'

I was so overpowered by relief that Anne should be alive that I failed to comprehend the last part of the sentence.

'I'm afraid he's very premature,' said Romaine.

I grappled first with the pronoun, then with the present tense but could register neither. 'Of course it's dead,' I said, 'but I'd expected that.'

'No, he's alive.'

This information was very difficult to grasp. For months I had been expecting Nicholas and although this illusion had shattered I had had no time to develop a new mental image of the infant. Moreover Anne's miscarriage had led me to assume that no new image was necessary. I began to struggle with the idea that somewhere in the hospital was a small being quite unknown to me for whom I was now responsible.

Francis was saying to Romaine: 'We'd better not delay the christening.'

'The hospital chaplain's been sent for.'

I roused myself. This was a detail I could understand. I myself had been a chaplain accustomed to spiritual emergencies. Firmly I said: 'I'll christen it.' Then I remembered the infant was a boy. 'Christen him,' I corrected and tried to imagine a son who was neither Nicholas nor Martin. The mystery of this unknown person began to intrigue me. I allowed myself to picture his future.

'I think that might be too much for you, Jon,' Francis said as my imagination conjured up a fair-haired choirboy in a spotless surplice. 'Why not leave it to the chaplain? I'm sure he'll be very competent.'

'I'd be competent too!' I protested, but I was beginning to feel confused, aware that I had one foot on the shore of reality and one foot in the boat of illusion while the water widened inexorably between the two. Uncertainly I added: 'All the same, perhaps you're right and I should leave it to the chaplain. The baby's not real to me yet.'

'Let me take you upstairs,' said Romaine as if he not only understood my confusion but wanted to help me grasp reality. 'I'm sure you want to see both the baby and your wife.'

I saw Anne first. She looked real, even surprisingly normal, deep in sleep after her anaesthetic, and I was reassured by her peaceful breathing. Then I was shown the infant, a little bundle of skin and bones in a blanket.

'Are you sure he's alive?' I said amazed to Romaine.

'Yes.'

'But surely he must be dying!'

'Yes.'

'Ah, I thought so,' I said, but in fact I had no idea what I had been thinking. 'I see,' I added, but my psychic eye was confronting only the blankness of a future which would never happen. I felt increasingly distressed that he had no reality for me beyond the idealized dreams concocted by my imagination.

The chaplain arrived, an elderly man who spoke in a whisper, and on Romaine's recommendation the baby was christened not in the distant chapel but in the empty side-ward next to Anne's room. Remembering Anne's wishes I chose the name Gerald. The baby never cried, not even on the application of the water. I still had difficulty in believing that he was not already dead.

'Of course I must stay here till he dies,' I said afterwards to Francis, 'and of course you must now set off for Starwater.'

'Even if you told me you wanted to be alone with him I'd simply wait in the motor.'

'I doubt if there'll be long to wait,' said Romaine before I could attempt to argue, and minutes later the beby's condition began to deteriorate.

I saw myself as if from a great distance as I stood up and I heard my voice as if from a long way away as I said: 'He's almost there.' I knew the moment had come because the walls of finite time had become fluid and now as I watched they curved to form the mouth of the tunnel. There were gates but they were open and as I saw the great darkness which marked the start of the journey I knew at once I had to tell him there was no need to be afraid. 'God is love,' I said, 'and love is stronger than death,' but of course I was attempting to reach him with words, impotent inexact useless words, words which he had never had time to learn, and I knew that communication must lie elsewhere. Picking him up I held his minute hand firmly with my thumb and forefinger to tell him he was not alone, and suddenly I felt the flash of psychic recognition as the departing soul, perfectly formed, utterly individual, brushed mine lightly, gratefully, lovingly in the dark.

I cried: 'He's alive!' For love is the great reality, and in that moment, the moment of death, he became real to me at last. Then the gates of finite time closed soundlessly after him as he began his journey through the darkness to the bright light at the end of the tunnel, and the moment I was alone I found myself finally face to face with the full horror of what had happened.

I laid the infant on the empty bed of the side-ward, and suddenly I stood not in the hospital at Starbridge but in the Abbot's room at Ruydale. I was facing Father Darcy across Whitby's corpse and Father Darcy was saying: '*You* killed that animal with your disobedience, your vanity and your utterly intolerable pride.'

I turned to Francis. I said as my son's lifeless body lay between us: 'I killed him,' and the next moment I had broken down completely beneath the weight of an unendurable grief.

PART FOUR

THE LIGHT FROM THE NORTH

'The mystical experience seems to those who have it to transport them out of time and place and separate individuality. This, of course, brings us at once among the most formidable philosophical problems. Those mystics who are also philosophers generally hold that neither space nor time is ultimately real.'

W. R. INGE
Dean of St Paul's 1911–1934
Lay Thoughts of a Dean

'If we believe that the world of time and space, which necessarily supplies the forms under which we picture reality, and the language in which we express our thoughts, is an image or reflection of the real or spiritual world, we must recognize that, except when we are concerned with the absolute values, and even then when we try to interpret them to ourselves, we cannot dispense with symbols.'

W. R. INGE
Dean of St Paul's 1911–1934
Mysticism in Religion

EIGHTEEN

'Truth is one of the absolute values, and those who seek it must follow the gleam, humbly but confidently.'

W. R. INGE
Dean of St Paul's 1911–1934
Mysticism in Religion

I

Everyone was very kind – Romaine, the sister on duty, even the chaplain who talked in such an irritating whisper – but they all seemed so far away, like figures glimpsed through the wrong end of a telescope, and Francis was the only one who was near. When someone in a white coat offered me two pills I said: 'I never take drugs,' but Francis exclaimed: 'Why are you turning up your nose at conventional medicine? What arrogance!' and this language, so harsh yet so familiar, was the only language I could still understand. I took the pills. Francis bore me off to Starwater. I had expected to be housed in the guest-wing but Cyril took me to a little room off the infirmary where a very large monk offered me an evil-smelling concoction of herbs. I said: 'Where's Wilfred?' but I was confused by the drugs and wanted only to sleep.

I slept for ten hours and when I awoke I found Francis was once more at my side.

'I'm staying on here for a few days,' he said after I had remembered where I was and what had happened. 'Cyril has some difficult war-time problems concerning the school and I need to study them carefully so that I can help him reach the right solutions. I suggest you stay on too until your wife comes out of hospital. It's very important that you should be properly looked after.'

'But I must see Anne!'

'Edward will drive you to the hospital every day while I'm here, and after I return to London Cyril will arrange for one of the local people to provide the necessary transport.'

'But Francis, you don't understand the difficulties of travelling at present – non-essential journeys are discouraged – '

'But of course it's essential that you should see your wife every day!'

'Yes, but what I'm saying is that you'll never be able to get the necessary petrol coupons – '

'Nonsense, these things can always be arranged,' said Francis with a superb nonchalance. 'Whenever I want extra coupons I simply ring up a most charming gentleman in Whitehall.'

I boggled and then bowed to the inevitable.

II

My first visit to Anne was very difficult. During the opening minute I was incoherent and the words of remorse were repeated in a feverish fashion until it dawned on me that Anne was much more concerned about my health than my guilt. Then I realized that I was much more concerned about her own health than about my self-centred need to indulge in an expression of penitence. Having at last sorted ourselves out and agreed we were both on the road to recovery it was then Anne's turn to display remorse. She said in a small voice: 'Can you ever forgive me for writing to Francis behind your back?'

'Don't be ridiculous – it was the wisest thing you could possibly have done!'

'I was very nervous before he arrived,' said Anne, 'because you said he looked like one of Shakespeare's wicked cardinals. How could you have misled me like that? He's not in the least like Beaufort or Wolsey – he's more like an avuncular Prospero! Anyway before I knew where I was I'd dissolved into tears and told him everything – I didn't mean to, I kept thinking how angry you'd be, but he was so kind and understanding that I just couldn't help myself. He held my hand and gave me the most beautiful handkerchief to cry into and – '

'This all sounds most improper!' I said, and when we laughed I felt we had passed a small but significant milestone along the road to recovery. Realizing that we were now strong enough to discuss our loss I said gently: 'Have you seen the baby yet?'

'No. I don't think I can. I don't think I could bear it. So long as I don't see him he's not quite real and I can beat back the pain, but if he were to become real – '

'He *was* real.' I told her about my psychic experience at the moment of death, and when she began to cry I said: 'Grief's nothing to be afraid of. Nor is it something to be swept under a rug and forgotten. Your grief is a symbol of your love for him, and why should you want to lock up your love like some monster which must never see the light of day?' I let her weep for a little longer before I added: 'If you never see him then we can share him only through my memories, and in the long run will that really be good enough for you?'

She shook her head, but still she wept.

'I think that in days to come you'll want a memory which belongs to both of us,' I said, but she was barely listening. Drying her eyes at last she whispered: 'He mustn't feel that I'm rejecting him. He mustn't feel unloved,' and then I knew she had already embraced his reality.

Leaning forward I rang the bell for the nurse.

III

Later when she was holding him she said: 'Are you aware of his spirit now?'

'No, he's too far away. It's only older people who have the psychic strength to imprint themselves on the atmosphere for a few days after death.'

We were silent for a time before she said unsteadily: 'Dr Romaine said I might have miscarried anyway. Seven months is a very common time for miscarriages and the cause isn't always known.'

'He told me that too when I broke down and blamed myself for what had happened.'

Anne said fiercely: 'You mustn't blame yourself. That makes it seem as if this were all a punishment, but I refuse to believe God kills babies to punish people.'

'That would indeed be a very primitive view of God and not at all compatible with the teachings in the New Testament.'

'Then why –' The ancient question was again hammering on the door of mystery, the great mystery of the imperfect world, the great mystery of a Creator who would permit the impermissible, the great mystery of human suffering. 'Why did Gerald have to die?' said Anne. 'Why did this have to happen? What's the point of putting him in the world only to take him away again?'

Recognizing the call of a soul drowning in the sea of mystery I set off at once to the rescue in the lifeboat of mysticism. 'Those hard painful questions only seem unanswerable,' I said, 'because you're viewing them from the wrong position: you're in the world and looking out. But now step outside the world and look in. The first thing you'll notice is that it's a world of change. There's this huge dynamic force, life, which is constantly banging against the walls of time and space as it contracts, expands and develops. Now step closer and you'll see that this continual change can't be represented by a vertical line, only by a circle. Half the circle is dark and half is light. The dark side of change is suffering, the light side is growth, development, flowering, and the dark and the light follow each other endlessly in the great cycle of birth, death and resurrection. Now this means that the light and the dark sides of the circle aren't merely related to each other; they're interdependent, and this interdependence means that without suffering there can be no growth, no development, no flowering. Without suffering, in fact, there would be no life as we know it; we'd all be wooden images, utterly static, in a world where nothing ever happened and where God's love would fall on barren soil.'

'That's all very well, but – '

'Now step back and look at the world from yet another angle. Look at it as an idea in the mind of God, a brilliant dynamic idea which we ourselves can't fully grasp except that its dynamism ties us to the change we can't escape. But beyond the idea, beyond the mind of God, is God himself, the unchanging perfection of ultimate reality. In other words, this cage we live in, this prison of time and space, isn't ultimately real. Gerald may have slipped out of the cage ahead of us, but that doesn't mean he's ceased to exist. As part of the ultimate reality his existence is reflected back into the world of time and space in the form of the absolute values, the values which can never die, and the value in which we can most clearly see him reflected is love.'

'Yes, but – '

'Love transcends suffering, and it's love that gives Gerald's life meaning. What we have to do is to weave our love for him into the fabric of our marriage so that our love for each other becomes richer, stronger and more complex. The truth is the wheel of change is still turning – and beyond the suffering the new growth, the new development and the new flowering are all waiting to begin. What we have to do now to make Gerald's life meaningful is to scramble up on to the back of the darkness and then use it as a springboard to leap into the light.'

I paused for breath but I had not spoken in vain. Amidst the profusion of symbols which I had thrown out to her in the manner of a sailor heaving a succession of life-belts to a drowning man, one had been gratefully clutched and embraced.

'I like the idea of our love weaving Gerald into the fabric of our marriage,' she said. 'I can see our marriage as a Persion carpet, very unusual and interesting, and he'll be a small beautiful pattern which recurs in unexpected places.'

I relaxed. Then I said to conclude my rescue as I hauled the victim into the lifeboat: 'You see how important his reality is for us? Plotinus the pagan summed it all up in that single famous sentence: "Nothing that really *is* can ever perish" – or as St Bernard wrote from a Christian viewpoint: "Love is the great reality." And for both of them, Christian and pagan, that great reality is eternal.'

Anne was crying again, hugging the baby tightly, but when I stopped speaking she dashed away her tears, kissed him and pulled the little blanket over his face. 'I'm glad we've both seen him,' she said. 'It'll make it easier to weave him into the fabric. I feel better now.'

Leaning forward I took her in my arms.

IV

Gerald was buried three days later next to Anne's brother in the churchyard at Starrington Magna, and I conducted the service myself. I sensed this shocked some people who felt I should be bowed down by grief or even bowed down by shame after my very public spiritual collapse, but I had done my grieving, and since I was still a priest I saw no reason why I should crawl into a corner like a defrocked villain when my son required burial. I also felt that conducting the funeral would be an act of love, similar to the holding of the infant's hand as he approached death, and since I knew his individuality would remain distinct as his soul merged with others in the stream of eternity, I could not regard the funeral as a gloomy acknowledgement of his extinction. As Plotinus wrote, at death the actors merely change their masks.

Since I had announced the time of the funeral to only a handful of people, I was not required to drum up the courage to face a crowd. Anne was still recovering in hospital, but the Maitlands came with the land-agent and his wife, and Aysgarth's wife surprised me by travelling all the way from Starbridge to attend the service. But my biggest surprise came when Romaine slipped belatedly into a back pew, and as I allowed him a moment's prayer before I began the service I remembered Charles telling me that Romaine was a churchwarden in his parish of Starvale St James.

Afterwards I said to him: 'How very good of you to come,' but he only answered: 'It's hard when a child is lost.'

On an impulse I invited him back to the Manor where I had planned to spend the day before returning to resume my convalescence at Starwater. The invitation astonished me for I had thought I wanted to be alone, but when we sat down together in the drawing-room, I with my small glass of sherry, he with his cigarette and his whisky, I wondered if I had been instinctively seeking a healing presence. I found he had a soothing effect on me; he was calm and relaxed and seemed quite untroubled by my long silences.

'Does Father Ingram's absence mean he's gone home?' he inquired idly after a while.

'No, he's still at Starwater but I wouldn't let him come to the funeral. Monks in an enclosed order shouldn't be required to leave their cloister unless it's absolutely necessary.'

'I rather thought Father Ingram was taking absolute necessity in his stride! Incidentally, how does he get the petrol for that fantastic machine of his?'

'I think it's probably wiser not to ask.'

Romaine laughed but said nothing else and suddenly I realized that his silence was the silence adopted by doctors and priests when they want to encourage confessions, the sympathetic, deeply intuitive silence of the listener who signals that he has all the time in the world to hear whatever needs to be said. Then I realized that there were indeed questions which I wanted to ask a medical man with a wide experience of the world, but even though my pride had been so severely chastened there were some fears which I was still reluctant to air.

In confusion I said tentatively: 'I'm glad you're here.'

At once Romaine recognized that I wanted to communicate with him. 'How are you feeling?' he said casually. 'You look better than I thought you would, but after so much distress I dare say you still feel considerably shaken.'

With relief I grasped the chance he was offering me to be honest. 'Well, to tell the truth,' I said, 'I do feel much older than usual.'

'Disturbing.'

'Very.'

'Worried about staying in good working order?'

As soon as I heard this peculiarly apt phrase I realized that no detailed explanations would be required; he had already guessed the cause of my anxiety. Gratefully I said: 'I'm not too keen on being over sixty. In fact sometimes I feel thoroughly depressed about it.'

'Very natural,' said Romaine comfortably, puffing away at his cigarette. 'When I turned sixty I was so depressed I nearly ordered my coffin.'

'Really?' I was deeply interested.

'Ate, drank and smoked too much. Couldn't even cheer myself up in bed any more.'

'Really! But how did you –'

'My wife took me in hand. Put me on a diet, rationed my cigarettes, locked up the drink and packed me off to the golf club twice a week for exercise. Wonderful! Within six months I was a new man.'

'Ah! So now –'

' – so now my wife makes sure I stay that way. But you don't need a fierce wife to keep you in order, do you? You're naturally strong-minded.'

'Well, I don't smoke, certainly, and I'm not much of a drinker and I take a fair amount of exercise on my bicycle –'

'My dear fellow, you're an example to us all! Keep going along those lines and I assure you that you stand an excellent chance of ticking over briskly for some time to come.'

This was very encouraging but I still had trouble regarding the future with unvarnished optimism. 'Nevertheless,' I said, 'I can't help worrying about Anne. If I get really old – '

'But she'll keep you young! Regular practice and moderate habits – that's the secret once you're past sixty.'

'Even so I suppose one can't expect to go on for ever.'

'Why not?' said Romaine. 'I certainly intend to! I plan to die in bed after a glass of champagne in a haze of post-coital bliss.'

It was impossible not to laugh and impossible too that my next words should be other than: 'I'm glad we finally met.' I felt infinitely cheered.

'You must come and see me,' said Romaine, 'and I don't mean merely for a physical examination, although I'd be happy to look you over if that would set your mind at rest. Drop in for a social visit one day soon and I'll dig out another glass like that thimble you've got in your hand and pour you the required soupçon of dry sherry.'

'That's most kind of you,' I said, not sure how far he spoke out of compassion and how far out of a genuine desire to be friendly, 'but I know doctors always lead such busy lives.'

'Not when they get to sixty-nine. I've got a new young partner who can hardly wait to put me out to grass so I have to take a lot of time off in order to keep him happy. Wonderful! I just see the patients I like and leave all the tiresome ones to him.'

'Well, I suppose that must be rather pleasant – '

'Pleasant? It's sheer bliss! In fact I can't tell you how much I'm enjoying life now that I'm within gasping distance of seventy – how absurd to think I spent my sixtieth birthday wallowing in depression! The truth is I'm back in the mainstream of life now that I have a family to look after. I teach Charley card-tricks, I read stories to Michael, I hold Lyle's hand when she tells me how awful life is without Charles – oh, it's all such fun, I feel positively reborn! So the message is never despair, you see, no matter how old you are, because you never know what delights may be waiting for you around the next corner – but of course that's a message you must have preached a thousand times over, isn't it? Silly of me – and how impertinent too to lecture a clergyman on the Christian message of hope! Do forgive me for being so thoroughly "louche"!'

But I looked at him, that battered old doctor with his nicotine-stained fingers, and knew I was hearing the voice of the Spirit. A psychic impression formed of the intricate patterns we all made as we wove in and out of each other's lives, but all I said was: 'It was the message I needed to hear,' and I thanked him.

'You will visit me, won't you?' said Romaine as we parted, and I knew now he spoke out of friendship. 'Perhaps we could even play chess together. My wife keeps a strict eye on all my friends and past-times, but I'm sure she'd be tickled pink if I started playing chess with a clergyman.'

It occurred to me that this was the first friend I had made since leaving the Order, and I began to wonder if a more comfortable phase in my long difficult adjustment to the world was finally about to begin.

V

'How is your wife adjusting to the idea that you might want – even need – to accept some responsibility for this death?' said Francis that evening when I had returned to Starwater.

'So far I've only skirted that aspect of the tragedy with her because at first it was clear she wasn't ready to face it. Her initial reaction was to avoid blaming me by blaming God.'

'Railing against the mystery of suffering?'

'Precisely. It's a very common response to bereavement, of course.'

Francis sighed 'This is one of those times when I'm very conscious of the fact that I've never worked as a priest in the world. What on earth does one say to a bereaved mother who rails against the mystery of suffering?'

'Well, of course each bereaved mother is different, and provided that the priest is emanating a genuine sympathy some women may prefer the sentimental approach, but I'm always reluctant to respond to the death of a child with some banality such as: "Don't worry, he's safe with Jesus." The mother doesn't want the child to be safe with Jesus; she wants him to be safe with her. In my opinion it's best to confront the mystery of suffering as just that – a mystery – and then try to illuminate it by the use of mystical symbols. The sufferer may only understand one word in ten, but at least she knows the priest is talking about matters which he's studied deeply and at least she knows he's treating her suffering with the utmost seriousness. If the priest can then set the suffering in the context of the absolute values and somehow relate it to the redemptive and creative power of love – '

'This is obviously the voice of a pastoral miracle-worker. I'd still be stammering: "Don't worry, he's safe with Jesus." '

'No, you wouldn't! You'd be unleashing that peculiarly theatrical charm of yours as you held the sufferer's hand and offered her your best handkerchief to cry into!'

'Ah, so your wife's been revealing my rusty pastoral skills with the opposite sex!'

'I thought they sounded rather well-oiled. Anyway, to return to the subject under discussion – '

'Yes, how successful has your mystical approach been with Mrs Darrow?'

'I think we've made a little progress; she's accepted the idea that the suffering can be used creatively to strengthen our marriage, but of course the loss is very difficult for her and there's still anger beneath the grief. It would be better if she could acknowledge the anger by directing it against me for holding the service, but she won't and now that she's no longer blaming God there's a real danger that she'll turn the anger in on herself and lapse into a profound melancholy.'

Francis looked concerned but did not immediately reply; I sensed he was pausing to consider the situation. 'I agree it might well be better for her if you took some of the blame for the disaster,' he said at last, 'but do you in fact feel you're to blame? It would be wrong to manifest a synthetic guilt.'

'Well, of course I'm to blame!'

'What about Romaine's suggestion that the tragedy might have happened anyway?'

'Romaine was right to remind me that we never know all the circumstances of a tragedy, I said, 'and from there one can certainly argue that all the judgements should be left to God who alone knows exactly what happened, but personally I find it very difficult to believe the miscarriage wasn't caused by the events in the chapel – the events for which I must assume full responsibility.'

Francis ventured no opinion of his own but merely asked: 'You see the tragedy as a punishment?'

'Yes, I do – I allowed my pride to cut me off from God with the result that I'm now grieving for a lost child and consumed with misery that I should have brought such suffering on my wife. That's a punishment. But the punishment didn't come from God. It came from my wrong actions.'

I saw Francis make the counsellor's decision that this verdict was worth underlining. 'In other words, you're saying that we create our own punishments when we cut ourselves off from God, just as we create our own repentance when we try to understand our errors sufficiently to renounce them and turn back to him.'

'Yes, but how can that best be explained to Anne? If I could only show her that guilt, like suffering, can be used constructively to redeem a tragedy and rebuild a life, then perhaps she wouldn't fight shy of expressing her anger and the process of healing would be unimpeded . . . But these are difficult concepts to grasp when one's distracted by grief.'

Francis said cautiously: 'Mightn't this be a case where actions speak louder than words? If you let her know you accept some degree of responsibility for the death and then go on to rebuild your life in the most positive way possible, you'll be spelling out your message in unmistakable terms. And if that's so – '

'If that's so then my most immediate task is to get on with rebuilding my life – which at present means sorting out all my private problems not only to ensure such a disaster never happens again but to ensure my ears are wide open to receive the real call from God which is still to come.'

'Precisely.'

There was a silence while I groped my way forward through my confused emotions but at last I managed to say: 'Thanks to our recent conversations I do feel I've travelled a long way towards sorting out my private problems.'

'Hm.'

Immediately I experienced a pang of alarm. 'You don't agree?'

'I think our conversations – particularly the one which included your long confession in the canteen – have certainly helped you to take a major step forward. The problems have now been identified. But have they been resolved? I think not.'

I automatically opened my mouth to argue with him but he allowed me no chance to speak. 'There seem to be two major problems which are closely but not inextricably linked,' he said 'The first is your mother's death and the second is your father's life. The first I regard with optimism; I believe that with your wife's help you'll finally be able to master this irrational terror that every woman you love is going to leave you. But the second problem is much more complex and intractable. It's a question of forgiving your father, isn't it? And to be quite frank I don't think you're anywhere near a genuine forgiveness at present.'

I was both astonished and appalled. 'But I told you in my confession – or at least I implied – surely you didn't think I was entirely without the understanding necessary to generate forgiveness?'

' "Why can't I forgive him?" you said in the canteen – '

'That was really a rhetorical question. I then went on to analyse the situation and I made it clear that I could at last regard him sympathetically. Don't you remember me saying how difficult it must have been for him to be married to a woman who was so detached?'

'Yes, but I suggest to you that this sympathy is purely intellectual. At an emotional level you're still angry and bitter, unable to sympathize with him at all.'

'That's not true!' I was deeply upset.

'Isn't it?' I saw the scepticism join forces with logic again in that combination which made Francis such a hard man to deceive. Leaning forward across the table he said abruptly: 'Supposing I were to say to you as Father Darcy once said: "Jonathan, you must teach." '

I recoiled.

'You see?' said Francis. 'You haven't forgiven him. You're still paying him back for trying to make you into a replica.' He stood up. 'Go to bed and think about it,' he said, not unkindly, 'and we'll talk again tomorrow.'

VI

The next morning we went for a walk together by the lake in the grounds of the Abbey. The school term had recently ended and the boys had dispersed, leaving Horatio Ford's country mansion shadowed and still. I thought of the teaching monks sinking back with relief into the enclosed section of the house and savouring the prospect of eight weeks' peace as they renewed their spiritual strength. Teaching was hard work. I could remember not only my bouts of mental exhaustion at Ruydale but my father relaxing quietly with his books as he recuperated from his day at the grammar school.

'Well?' said Francis as we sat down on a seat overlooking the lake.

With extreme reluctance I forced myself to confess: 'You were right. I'm still angry. There's been no forgiveness.'

'Congratulations! If you can acknowledge that, then you've taken another major step forward.'

'The only trouble is that I don't see where to go next. I feel as if I'm now confronting a brick wall.'

But for Francis the way ahead was clear. 'You need to discover a genuine sympathy for your father in order to discard this synthetic pity you've created,' he said. 'If you could set aside the distorting effect your anger must inevitably produce and reconstruct his memory accurately, you might stumble across something which would help you to identify yourself with him.'

'I think not. The estrangement ran too deep.'

Francis remained patient. 'You say that because your anger's creating a distortion as usual, but just try to suspend your anger for a moment and cast your mind back to the days before the anger began. Surely you don't deny love existed once between you?'

'He killed my love for him by not loving me as I was. He was only capable of loving the replica.'

'That reply seems to indicate you're incapable of suspending your anger,' said Francis, still immaculately patient. 'Very well, let's tackle the anger directly and try to explode it with logic. Now consider for a moment: aren't you painting this picture in somewhat crude dark primary colours? And wouldn't you come closer to reality if you stroked in a few subtle pastel shades? After all, what actually happened all those years ago? Your father had a dream: he wanted you to follow him in his profession. A lot of fathers have this dream. It's very common. Inevitably there's disappointment if the cherished dream fails to come true, but in most cases the dreamer picks up the pieces and goes on – as indeed your father tried to do in the only way he knew, by never complaining, by putting up a brave front. If he hadn't loved you – loved *you*, not the replica – would he have bothered to go to all that trouble? Of course not! He'd have turned his back on you and refused to speak to you again. Obviously he loved you in his own way but for some reason he couldn't express that love in a manner which you would have found acceptable. Perhaps you reminded him too much of your mother and his relationship with her was so convoluted that it inhibited his ability to communicate his feelings to you. Perhaps he was paralysed by guilt that he'd failed to summon you to her deathbed and this effectively prevented him from revealing his emotions. Perhaps he was terrified he'd failed you by behaving so unsympathetically about your visions. Perhaps . . . But there are any number of explanations. All I'm trying to point out is that his desire for a replica doesn't necessarily mean that he didn't also love you as you were. It's a failure of logic to believe here that paternal love and paternal ambition can only be mutually exclusive.'

'You can invoke the deity of logic as ardently as you please, Francis, but the fact remains that you're merely speculating. You never met my father. You've no idea what he was really like – '

'But have you any more idea than I have? You've just admitted the estrangement ran very deep – '

'Of course I know what he was really like! Didn't I live under the same roof as him for years and years?'

'That's no guarantee of intimate knowledge, particularly if the parties are hopelessly estranged!'

'I don't deny the estrangement, but if you think I didn't know him inside out – '

'Prove it. Sum him up in a single sentence.'

'He was a failure.'

'A failure?'

'He failed me, he failed my mother, he failed himself. A wasted life. Pathetic.'

In the silence which followed I suddenly became aware that Francis was engaged in a fierce struggle to control his temper. On the one hand he was telling himself sternly that a clever well-trained monk, acting as a counsellor, should never lose his grip on his self-control, but on the other hand he was mentally shouting that I deserved a punch on the jaw. So startled was I by this cerebral battle which flashed before my psychic eye that for one long moment I could only stare at him speechlessly. Then I managed to say a feeble 'Francis?' in an effort to express my bewilderment.

'Oh, don't mind me!' said Francis. 'You just took my breath away, that's all, but don't worry, you have that effect on me sometimes, it's not unprecedented, and fortunately it only takes me a few seconds to recover.'

'I didn't mean to sound uncharitable – '

'Oh, splendid! I'm so glad!'

'Now listen to me, Francis – '

'No, you listen to me! That flash of arrogance was quite intolerable and I absolutely refuse to let you get away with it. By what standards are you judging that man? I hardly think they can be described as Christian! Your father stood by your mother; he stood by you; he accepted his lot – and day by day, all through his working life, he served God by exercising his gift for teaching. Thousands of boys must have benefited from his skill and had their lives enriched – how dare you call him a failure!'

I shouted: 'But what about all the pain I suffered when he rejected me?' Then I said violently: 'He failed me. He couldn't accept me as I was. He failed me.' And without waiting for a reply I walked away, stumbling the few yards downhill to the shore of the lake.

An interval followed as Francis allowed us both time to compose ourselves. I stared at the limpid water beneath the light sky and struggled to master my misery. In an effort to turn aside from self-pity I thought of Francis, now almost certainly battling with his own distress as he reflected on the ruined interview, and resolved not to hold his harsh words against him. All councellors, even the most successful, have their disastrous sessions when for some reason they are unable to maintain their emotional detachment, and suddenly I was recalling with painful clarity my failure to help Martin when we had met in Ruth's garden shortly after my departure from the Order.

The pebbles crunched behind me on the little shingle beach. Francis' voice said: 'Sorry. My fault. What a mess,' but as I turned to face him I answered: 'It's all right.'

'That's very kind of you to say so, but I don't see how it can be. I lost my temper, behaved like an overbearing counsel for the prosecution and even tried to force-feed you ideas which you're at present psychologically unable to accept! How on earth could I have made such appalling mistakes?'

At once I said: 'Because my case means a great deal to you. Because the ordeal we both endured when you had to examine my call to leave the Order has bound us together in such a way that you feel deeply involved with my new career. Because you're so anxious to help me overcome my troubles that you couldn't resist trying to wind up the case in double-quick time before you're obliged to return to London. Now do you understand why I said: "It's all right"? The mess arose not because you didn't care but because you cared too much, and besides . . . the mess was hardly all your fault.' I sighed as I offered him my hand in reconciliation. 'I'm sorry too. Obviously I need much more help.'

Francis gratefully clasped my hand. 'The trouble is that since you're beyond the reach of logic I'm not sure which approach to adopt next. I wonder what the old man would have done? I suppose he'd have wiped your mind clean by some esoteric exercise of his will and then claimed to have exorcized you. Ugh – how repulsive!' And he shuddered.

'You're only repulsed because you're mentally defining exorcism in the modern sense and associating it with witchcraft and quackery. But exorcism in the classical sense could be just as respectable as psychiatry. After all, what are the two facts about Christ which no one but a fool would dispute? He was a healer and an exorcist in the best possible sense of both terms.'

'True, but – '

'Father Darcy wasn't Christ but he certainly wasn't a witch-doctor either, and I'm sure that in the present situation he would have adopted a traditional mystical approach, employing the ancient symbol of the battle between the forces of darkness and the forces of light: he would have called on God for help and then embarked on the task of ejecting the demon which was burdening my psyche.'

Francis was unable to resist another shudder. 'You mean he'd have peeled away all your defences in order to expose the raw psyche to the light of truth. What a dangerous game to play!'

'For a quack, yes. But not for the gifted exorcist who always knows exactly what he's doing.'

'Well, I agree you need to see your father in the light of truth, but if you think I'm going to resort to exorcism – '

'No, obviously you can't do that, not because you're incapable of healing me but because you couldn't heal me by a process in which you've no faith.'

Francis meditated on this before saying tentatively: 'I suppose it's a question of how the healer turns on the light. I'm still groping for the switch to turn the light on by hand but the old man would have turned it on by sheer will-power.'

'The old man would have claimed he never turned on anything.'

'Yes, I'm sorry my metaphor was too secular. Of course he would have said the light was the light of God bestowed by grace, not a source of power which he could flick on and off at will.'

'Precisely. He would have seen the light as a miraculous gift which inevitably triggers a major revelation in the psyche.'

'Like the light in your vision,' said Francis, 'the mysterious light from the north.' Restlessly he stooped, picked up a pebble and threw it in such a way that it skipped across the surface of the water. 'And that reminds me – ' He straightened his back ' – did you ever read the magazine *Country Life* in 1931?'

I was considerably startled. 'What an extraordinary question! Why?'

'Your wife tells me that there was an article in it then about Starrington Manor, complete with photographs of the chapel both inside and out. I just wondered if perhaps during one of those unusual trips to London from Ruydale after the Whitby affair you found a discarded copy of *Country Life* on the train and – '

'My dear Francis!'

' – and received, as it were, a preview of your vision – '

'You appal me!'

'Of course I'm not accusing you of lying – obviously you've forgotten you read the article and the memory was retained only in your subconscious mind – but it would explain the extraordinary degree of clairvoyance you achieved in your vision. Now I'm willing to concede,' said Francis generously, 'that every story should be allowed one big coincidence, and in this case the coincidence would be your meeting with Miss Barton-Woods, as she then was, at Allington, but as far as your vision's concerned – '

I decided to terminate this sad spectacle of an intelligent man struggling in the toils of his earthbound logic. 'Your trouble, Francis,' I said kindly, 'is that you're an incorrigible sceptic. I shall preserve a dignified silence which I hope will be even more effective than an equally dignified denial.'

'A little healthy scepticism never did an honest psychic any harm! However,' said Francis, becoming serious again much to my relief, 'I shall respect your dignified silence and merely conclude this somewhat unfortunate session by urging you to have faith in the future and be patient. Despite your recent disaster and your continuing difficulties I'm still convinced that light will shine from the north for you in the end . . .'

VII

'Francis visited me on his way home to London,' said Anne on the following day when I called again at the hospital. 'He brought me those gorgeous flowers over there from the garden at Starwater. Wasn't that nice of him? We talked a bit about the baby – and about you too, of course. He was very interesting. He said I must be sure to speak my mind to you about various things because otherwise you'd be continually imagining I was thinking thoughts I wasn't really thinking at all.'

I said dryly: 'I'm afraid Francis is incorrigibly sceptical about my psychic powers.'

'Oh no, I'm sure he believes in them, but he has such a refreshingly down-to-earth approach! "Don't rely on Jon to read your mind accurately," he said, "because for every genuine psychic insight he receives he makes two wild guesses which have no relation to reality." '

'That's quite the wrong percentage! Good heavens, what a slander – '

'So I said: "That's a relief because I don't want to be married to a miracle-man – I'd much rather be married to an ordinary human being who sometimes gets things wrong and stumbles into messes, just as we all do now and then." That pleased Francis very much. He said: "I thought so! Now make sure you tell him that." So here I am, telling you.'

'What did he say about the baby?'

'He said I mustn't be afraid to be angry or to show you that I was angry; anger was all part of the process of grief which had to be worked through. However I told him I didn't feel angry any more, I'd got over it because I felt Gerald's life would have meaning, woven into the fabric of our marriage. Then Francis said a very peculiar thing. He said that nevertheless you might need a bit of anger; he said that if I were angry with you, you could regard it as part of a penance and use it to come to terms with your guilt. "Well, I'm sorry," I said, "but I can't display anger where none exists, and no matter what you say I think it would be more helpful if I displayed love, not anger." Then Francis laughed and said how lucky you were to be married to me. He really is the most charming man.'

'Hm.' I had my own views about Francis' charm but I decided to keep them to myself. Anne belonged to the other sex. They saw men differently there.

However I was grateful to Francis for extracting from Anne important facts which might have taken me a long time to uncover, and on my journey back to Starwater I mentally composed him a letter of thanks. Meanwhile, as I discovered when I reached the Abbey, an equally important letter had arrived for me in the afternoon post: the Bishop had written, expressing with exquisite simplicity his sorrow that I should have suffered such a time of anxiety and grief. The service of healing was never mentioned, and in a paroxysm of guilt I immediately wrote back offering my resignation. By that time Aysgarth had recalled the retired canon to conduct the Sunday services while I recovered from my disasters, so my life as the curate of Starrington Magna had already moved into abeyance, but I thought that the least I could do in response to Dr Ottershaw's most Christian charity was to spare him the ordeal of sacking me.

But instead of accepting my resignation with relief Dr Ottershaw invited me to the palace to discuss the future, and on the day before Anne's discharge from hospital I found myself journeying to Starbridge to see him.

Freed from the rigours of being wound around my little finger the Bishop delivered an unexpectedly detached judgement. I saw then that I had underestimated him; he was at the mercy neither of Aysgarth, who would obviously be opposing the continuation of my curacy, or of the Pitkin faction, who after the required amnesty following the death of the infant would now also be campaigning for my removal. He was quite capable of steering a sensible course of his own.

'I think I should abstain from any decision for six months,' he said, 'while you recuperate and receive regular direction from Father Ingram. It strikes me that what you need most of all at present is a breathing space – in fact I've always wondered if you were denying yourself the proper amount of time to settle down in the world after your long absence. Leaving the cloister's such a big step, isn't it, and in retrospect I confess I feel guilty that I allowed you to take on that curacy before, perhaps, you were ready for it. Yes,' said Dr Ottershaw, setting me an admirable example in humility, 'there's no doubt I should share a large part of the responsibility for your present difficulties.' And as he referred so tactfully to my spiritual breakdown I saw with a clear eye how erratically I had rocketed from one life to another without giving myself sufficient time to adjust to the world I had rejoined.

Much chastened I returned not to Starwater Abbey but to the Manor in order to resume my life at Starrington.

VIII

The next morning I arose even earlier than usual and faced a task which I had been steadily postponing: my return to the scene of the catastrophe. I felt strongly that I had to perform a ritual purification, a symbolic act which would surmount my repulsion and heal the raw wound which memory was keeping open in my psyche.

It took a great effort of will to open the door but once I had crossed the threshold my tension eased. The chapel had been cleaned and tidied; the defilement was not visible to the eye, and although the atmosphere was clogged with an intangible grime I was confident that I had the power to cleanse it; I felt as if I were confronting an unwashed window and reminding myself that beneath the dirt the glass would still be clear.

I set to work. First I prayed. Then I filled a bowl from the tap in the vestry, blessed the water and used it in making the sign of the cross on every row of pews. I also made the sign on all the doors. Once this ritual had been accomplished I celebrated mass. I knew no ghost had been seen; Father Darcy's image had merely been a projection of my disordered mind, but I thought Wilfred would have sanctioned a sacramental gesture to complete not the exorcism of the chapel but the neutralizing of a painful memory.

The sun began to shine through the east window, and when I returned to the chapel after washing the chalice in the vestry I found that the atmosphere was once more pellucid and serene. Sinking down in the nearest pew I thanked God and savoured the peace.

Later when I had returned to the house I headed on an impulse to the conservatory and cut some of the lilies which Anne's grandmother had favoured long ago. Her handsome glass vase was still in the flower-room, and soon I was setting it in its old place beneath the brass memorial tablet. I thought I would take Anne to the chapel that afternoon so that she too might conquer her natural aversion to the scene of the catastrophe, and I hoped that the lilies, symbol of beauty, would help her to see that the chapel was no longer polluted.

Once again I returned to the house. Then as soon as I had breakfasted I summoned the motor and set off to Starbridge to bring Anne home from the hospital.

IX

'Jon, there are more things which Francis said I should tell you,' said Anne as we sat hand in hand in the front pew during our visit to the chapel that afternoon. 'I thought I wouldn't be able to just yet but the chapel's so soothing and you're so serene again that I no longer feel frightened.'

'*Frightened?*' I was appalled. 'But my dear Anne, what on earth do you mean?'

'Didn't you guess? That awful outburst of mine just before the service didn't spring from anger but from terror. I thought the reason why you were neglecting me to sink yourself so fanatically in the healing was because you were secretaly miserable and dissatisfied.'

'With the curacy, you mean? Well, I must confess – '

'No, not just with the curacy. With everything. I was absolutely tormented by the dread that you were bored to tears in quiet dull little Starrington Magna and had come to regret your hasty marriage.'

'Regret my – I'm sorry, obviously I've misheard you. Did you actually say – '

'That's why I encouraged you to take up the healing,' said Anne, rushing on. 'I wasn't easy in my mind about it but I could see it kept you busy and happy and compensated you for being such a big fish in such a small pond. I thought that so long as you were happy being a healer you wouldn't get tired of me and go away.'

'Go away? *Me*? But – '

'That's why I didn't speak up to you about all the Anglo-Catholic business – I knew you were making a mistake by introducing those changes so quickly, but I didn't dare say anything because I was afraid of making you upset. I thought: so long as he's happy, worshipping in the way he wants, he'll be able to overlook the fact that I haven't followed the example of his devoted ladies and become a fervant Anglo-Catholic – '

'But I don't want a wife who switches to Anglo-Catholicism for all the wrong reasons!'

'Yes, but I was so afraid you might be secretly regretting your marriage to someone you couldn't convert – '

'I could never regret our marriage. I don't care whether you're Low-Church, Broad-Church or High-Church. All that matters is that we belong to One Church, *The* Church, Our Church, the English Church – '

'Darling!' said Anne, kissing m. 'But you do see, don't you, why I felt I couldn't be honest? I was so terrified that you'd become dissatisfied.'

'But my dearest Anne, I spent my whole time fearing that *you* might become dissatisfied! I was so worried about being old, so anxious that I wouldn't be able to satisfy you in bed – '

'*You* were anxious about that? But Jon, I tortured myself with the terror that *I* wouldn't satisfy *you*!'

'I must be imagining this conversation,' I said. 'I'm hallucinating.'

'I used to think to myself: it's all right now I'm young but supposing he gets tired of me when I'm middle-aged? That's why I got so upset when you set up the camp-bed in your cell as soon as I was pregnant. I thought you were already tired of me and were glad to have an excuse for a separate bedroom.'

'My darling Anne, I . . .' Words temporarily failed me. However at last I managed to say in my firmest voice: 'I shall never get tired of you, no matter how middle-aged you become. How on earth did we sink into this absolutely appalling muddle?'

'Francis said that since I'd had the painful experience of Hugo and you'd had the painful experience of Betty it was inevitably going to take the two of us much longer to learn to trust each other than it would take the average couple.'

I had a vivid memory of Francis saying: 'Of course I'm just an ignorant old bachelor . . .' and I felt humbled. Here indeed was a case where the onlooker had seen most of the game.

I could only exclaim stupefied: 'But this is unforgivable of me! I was so absorbed in my own fears that I completely forgot about your adverse experience with your fiancé – I just assumed that once the sexual difficulty had been overcome all would automatically be well, but how could I have ignored the possibility that not all the psychological scars would be healed?'

'We both have our scars. But all that matters now is that we're not hiding them from each other.' She kissed me again before adding in her briskest, most businesslike voice: 'Jon, there's one thing more I simply must say and it's about bed and it's this: sex is very nice but if it results in us perpetually worrying ourselves into a frenzy about whether we're satisfying each other then it's soon going to become very awful. Please try not to worry about me too much. As far as I'm concerned love's more important than sex, and there you'll always satisfy me, even if you wind up bald, bedridden and toothless. You see, to be quite frank – ' She took a deep breath ' – I like you being old. I could never trust any man of my own age again, but an older man . . . Well, the older you get the more secure I shall feel. The last thing I'd ever want is a young husband. I'd never have a moment's peace of mind.'

And then for the first time since my mother's death I found I could love without fear of the future.

X

Later that afternoon when Anne was resting I retired to my cell, removed from the album the best photograph of my mother and propped it up on the mantelshelf. I found I could look at her without pain; it was as if I could at last see her death in perspective. Now it seemed so obvious that the unhealed bereavement, damaging my trust of the opposite sex, had been one of the factors which had driven me into the fatal marriage with a woman I had not loved, the marriage which in turn was to drive me towards those seventeen years of celibacy in the Order. I could see clearly too the power of my Maker, that ultimate force, as he had quite literally created me, casting me into the crucible of suffering so that I could be moulded into the man he wanted me to become. Out of the pain had come the growth and the development; after the darkness had come the light. And as I saw my life illuminated by these mystical symbols I could look at my mother's photograph and think: yes, it was a terrible bereavement. But I lived through it, I endured it and now at last I know I've survived.

'How lucky you were to have the perfect mother for fourteen years!' Francis had said during one of our healing conversations as he had shifted the emphasis from the pain I had suffered to the love I had enjoyed. 'But what would it really have been like if she'd lived? Could you ever have looked seriously for a wife with this remarkable woman always hovering in the background? Even the most heterosexual of men can have problems with remarkable mothers, particularly if the remarkable mother falls into the notorious maternal trap of being too possessive, and although your mother might have been perfect for you when you were a child, would she in fact have been quite so perfect later? Even if you'd managed to detach yourself for long enough to reach the altar, how would she have got on with your wife? These are difficult questions, and perhaps it's just as well that you've never been obliged to answer them.'

Remembering these disturbing questions which it had never occurred to me to ask during all the decades of my long bereavement, I wondered for the first time what my mother would have thought of Anne but they were so far apart in time that it was hard to picture them together. My mother would have been eighty-four if she had lived. I tried to imagine her as an old woman, perhaps a little querulous and demanding, not in good health, maybe even verging on senility, and I shuddered. My mother would have hated old age. She would have wanted me to remember her as she was in the prime of life, bewitching in her silence as she glided across the daisy-studded lawn and idly stooped to stroke her cat by the peach-tree. Then remembering Chelsea I found I knew exactly what my mother would have thought of Anne. I could hear her saying as she picked up William: 'This is a most intelligent, interesting little creature, not only sensitive but sensible too – a good companion, always loyal and affectionate and never a yowling nuisance. Chelsea was always very partial to tabby-cats.'

I smiled, left the photograph on the mantelshelf and strolled downstairs into the garden.

The weather had changed. The sky was now heavy with unbroken cloud and the sultry air hinted that a storm was approaching. Halfway across the lawn I almost turned back to fetch an umbrella but in the end I decided not to bother; the humid heat was conducive to laziness. Drifting on across the lawn I entered the woods, which were verdant with the summer foliage, and wandered in the dim green light down the path which led to the chapel.

I was thinking of nothing in particular. I had already decided that concentrated thought should wait until I reached the chapel so I strolled on like a somnambulist, my mind restfully inactive as I listened to the distant call of a wood-pigeon. I had just become irritated by his persistence when I glanced below me into the dell and realized in a single electrifying second that I was finally duplicating the walk I had taken in my vision.

I never stopped. On I moved, my brain blank with shock until at last, scarcely able to breathe in case some wrong movement should shatter this bizarre replication in time, I crossed the floor of the dell. As I walked I glanced to the right but although the suitcase stood beneath the trees

I saw it only in my memory, and on reaching the porch I ran up the steps without a backward glance.

The latch clicked. The right-hand door swung wide, and there before me was the chapel of my vision, the wide space at the back where the pews had been removed, the wooden cross on the plain altar-table, the lilies which I had placed that morning beneath the brass tablet. For one long moment I stood staring at them all. Then closing the door I crossed the open space and began to move down the aisle.

No light shone through the north window.

At the front pew I stopped and waited. Sweat trickled down my temple; I had to make an effort to breathe evenly. Then I told myself that the light in the vision had been symbolic. Had I really expected a light to shine from the north? Yes. How unrealistic! I now had to stop thinking like befuddled romantic and behave like an intelligent priest. Reminding myself that the hallmark of genuine mysticism is a practical no-nonsense outlook, I knelt in the front pew, closed my eyes and applied myself with a workmanlike efficiency to the task of communicating with God.

To liberate the full power of my psyche I had to phase out all distractions; it was as if my mind were a brilliantly illuminated house and I were engaged in moving from room to room to extinguish every lamp. Only in the darkness, as I knew from past experience, would I have the light to see with the eye of the soul.

The process of darkening took some time and required an intense concentration which I found almost impossible to sustain because of my spiritual debility. I was like an athlete who had fallen out of training, but I prayed for grace and persisted. More time passed, although in such states of altered consciousness time tends to fragment into a succession of timeless moments. I prayed again for grace but that was my last prayer in words. The river of consciousness became darker and deeper. I tried to see but my psychic eye was still myopic; closing it again I waited in the dark. God was there, but it was the God of the Neo-Platonists, the God of the Pseudo-Dionysius, the God of John Scotus, above everything, beyond everything, indefinable because any definition would only render him finite. I knew him by his absence and by his very absence he was there.

Then I felt his warmth. It was like the sun coming up over the horizon, but although the warmth was very bright it was a brightness which no eye could perceive so I still saw only darkness. The warmth was as paradoxical as the brightness, bracing not enervating, clear and pure as ice in the radiant heat. Yet even as I saw the image of ice I recognized the warmth of life and in the heart of that life was the flame of love. God was here too, not the God of the Neo-Platonists but the God of Julian of Norwich and Walter Hylton and the unknown author of *The Cloud of Unknowing*, the God of the joyful English mystics, personal, loving, immanent, real.

I opened my eye again, the psychic eye, and in the warmth I was able to relax without consciousness of the self. I could see clearly then; I saw all kinds of people, both the people who had sought my spiritual direction when I had been a monk and the people whom I had yet to meet. I saw not their faces but their psychic entities; they formed a continuous strand so that I knew my work in the world would be similar to the work which I had undertaken as a monk, but the exact nature and context of that work remained hidden from me. I was aware that all the burdens and constraints of my monastic life had been rolled away so that I could concentrate on my work with a new freedom; I was aware that so much past sorrow had been smoothed away, slotted into place at last in the jig-saw of my life, but immediately I saw the image of the jig-saw I realized one piece was still missing and that this piece was somehow blocking the light of the revelation. I could only grasp the knowledge that I had been sent back into the world to be neither a parish priest nor an unqualified doctor but to reflect Father Darcy's training on some broad stage which at present lay beyond my power to define. Contrary to what I had always supposed, the end of my monastic career did not mark a complete break with the past; in a very real sense there was no new life beginning, only the old one continuing, but now God had responded to my deepest needs by giving me the right wife so that with both body and soul in harmony at last I could reach the height of those powers which I had long since dedicated to his service.

I had a sudden awareness of God's generosity, and the next moment I was overwhelmed by the boundless and indescribable nature of the divine love. I opened my eyes – my physical eyes – and for a split second the psychic and material visions collided so that my oak cross on the altar vibrated with light. I saw Christ crucified, Christ redeemed – and at that moment it was imprinted on my mind that I was finally liberated from all my past guilt. The tide of forgiveness was too strong; no anguish and self-hatred could face it and survive.

I heard Julian of Norwich call across the centuries: 'He is love!' and the darkness blazed with fire. I could not look at the light pouring through the north window but I knew it was there and as I stretched out my hands towards it I felt the brilliant darkness enfold my psyche. For one radiant second my fingertips touched eternity, and then as I slipped back through the levels of consciousness into the prison of time and space I knew that the missing piece of the jig-saw lay with Martin and that I had to write to him without delay.

NINETEEN

'The mystics all speak the same language. But there is
something singularly impressive in reading (Plotinus') testimony, vibrating with restrained emotion, not in some ascetic
of the cloister, but in one of the great thinkers of all time, a
Greek and a loyal disciple of Plato, the last deep organ-voice
in that long series of lovers of wisdom, which begins with the
cosmic speculations of the Ionians, and ends, as we have seen,
in a profoundly religious philosophy . . .'

W. R. INGE
Dean of St Paul's 1911–1934
Mysticism in Religion

I

I am unsure how long I remained in the chapel while I recovered from
the immediate effects of such a profound experience, but as soon as I was
strong enough to put one foot in front of the other I struggled back to the
house.

On reaching my cell I sank down at the table and picked up my pen to
embark on the vital letter. 'My dear Martin,' I wrote and stopped. I had
belatedly realized I had no idea what I was supposed to say. Had I really
thought that God would write the letter for me as soon as I held my pen
over a blank sheet of paper? I was behaving like a befuddled romantic
again. Conscientiously I roused my intellect and began to frame in my
mind the conventional enquiries about Martin's health and activities, but
almost at once I realized that conventional enquiries were now irrelevant;
they had been no more than meaningless platitudes offered by a father
bowed down by guilt. Again I was overwhelmed by the tide of forgiveness
I had experienced in the chapel and suddenly I saw what I had to write.
Instead of cowering behind the wall which my guilt had built around me
and shooting polite arrows of inquiry over the ramparts I had to abandon
my bow and arrow and walk out of my refuge to meet him.

Without further hesitation I wrote: 'I've recently wound up in the most
humiliating mess: I had a spiritual breakdown before a large congregation

when I thought I was possessed by the Devil. I'm better now but Anne had a miscarriage as the result of this catastrophe and the baby was born prematurely, dying within an hour. We called him Gerald. I should have written to you and Ruth but I was in such an agonized state of mind that I didn't. I'm sorry. The notice did go in *The Times* but I don't suppose either of you saw it. Anne is home now and I'd so much like you to meet her. Please come and see us. I feel very old and battered at the moment and I need you to cheer me up with some of your amusing theatrical stories. Yours, etc, J.D.'

This letter, so painfully honest, so utterly unlike any letter which I had ever written to either of my children, seemed so strange to me as I reread it that I even wondered if I had finally lost my mind. But I knew the letter had to be sent. Cramming it in an envelope I printed the address in capital letters to make sure there was no misdirection, slapped on the stamp and bicycled straight to the village to drop the letter safely in the pillar-box.

II

'Dear Dad,' wrote Martin by return of post, 'you poor old sod! I do sympathize – making a balls-up before an audience is the actor's permanent nightmare. I remember I was playing Jack Worthing once in *The Importance of Being Earnest* when Lady Bracknell went over the top. You've no idea how powerful that line about the handbag can sound when screeched out with the volume of four express trains about to dive into a particularly nasty tunnel. We had to carry the poor thing off the stage in the end, but six months later, believe it or not, she was hamming it up in some ghastly farce and saying she felt positively reborn – so the whole story had a happy ending.

'I shall arrive on Saturday at lunchtime unless I hear from you to say this doesn't suit. Please lock up all drink and offer me fizzy lemonade very firmly. Yours, MARTIN. P.S. Sorry the new little Darrow was so short-lived. You don't have much luck with your replicas, do you?'

I stared at this sentence for a long, long time. Then I wrote a brief line to say how much I was looking forward to seeing him.

III

'It's good to escape into the country for a few hours,' said Martin. 'London's hell at the moment. Maybe I should chuck up my dreary clerical job, abandon all my efforts to get into ENSA or the BBC and volunteer to work on the land, but the trouble is I'm most definitely not the bucolic type. And talking of farming that reminds me: what a secretive old devil you've been about your farmer-wife! I thought you'd married some upper-class nitwit who was incapable of reading anything but *The Tatler*! Why didn't you tell me you were married to this charming business-woman who possesses not only the entire works of Noel Coward but a cat called William after Shakespeare?'

'I'm afraid I haven't been very good at communicating vital information to you, Martin – '

'Well, never mind, better late than never . . . My God, what's that down there? It looks like Inigo Jones' pipe-dream of the Eighth Wonder of the World!'

I showed him around the chapel and was pleased by the genuine admiration which lay beneath his actor's hyperbole. 'I love beautiful things,' he said 'The world's so foul and ugly but a glimpse of something beautiful makes one forget for a moment how bloody awful life is.'

I cleared my throat. 'That sounds as if you've succumbed to the Manichean heresy, but it's a mistake, in fact, to see the world as – '

'Oh my God, he's going to play the Priest with a capital P! Don't do it, Dad, don't do it! I can't stand it when you start playing your favourite roles. I like you so much better as you are now with all the greasepaint stripped off by your experience of going over the top as a miracle-worker – I feel I'm seeing your true self at last. You're *such an actor*, Dad! In fact sometimes when I see you acting I wonder if against all the odds I did wind up after all as that replica you always wanted.'

From the moment I had read the postscript of his letter I had known this moment would arrive. I was aware of the urge to retreat, take cover, hide, even bury my head in the sand and pretend I had not heard him, but I conquered the temptation to be a coward; I stood my ground. I heard myself say: 'I've been thinking about that a lot lately. I must have made life very difficult for you when you were growing up. Perhaps now's the moment when you should finally tell me exactly how difficult it was.'

And then at last I knew I no longer saw my father in the dark glass of estrangement but with blinding clarity, face to face.

IV

'I'm not sure when I first realized I was meant to be a replica,' said Martin, 'but I remember the sheer awfulness of my panic. I thought: I can't possibly grow up because once I'm grown up he'll discover I'm not a replica. And I couldn't bear the thought of disappointing you. I mean, there you were, always so good, so kind, so decent, never complaining no matter how naughty Ruth and I were – and you were such a hero too, fighting in the

War, winning that medal at Jutland . . . what an act to follow! I remember lying awake at night and shuddering at the terrible task which lay ahead of me.

'At first it wasn't too difficult to be a replica; I just worked hard at school and took a precocious interest in religion. Then gradually it dawned on me that you wanted me to be not just any priest but the sort of priest who would go right to the top of the Church-of-England tree – it dawned on me that I was supposed to live your life again for you without making the mistakes you made when you married a woman of the wrong class and wound up in a dead-end chaplaincy. *My* life (so you thought) was going to be quite different. I was going to marry well and glide effortlessly upwards from vicar to canon to archdeacon to dean to bishop, redeeming your past and keeping you perpetually drenched in paternal pride. What a dream! But I knew it hadn't a hope of coming true. God knows what I think about religion – I'm still too mixed up about it all to know – but I've never deluded myself that I could succeed as a churchman. I'd have died of boredom while I was still a curate – it just wasn't "me" at all. But you didn't want to know "me", did you? I wasn't allowed to be "me". I was only allowed to be the replica. My God, I used to feel so angry and miserable, trapped in the cage you'd created for me and worrying myself to death about where it would all end . . .

'Then when I was eighteen the end came and I told you I was going to be an actor – but lo and behold! I dropped the bomb and there was no explosion. No shouts of horror, no shrieks of rage – only a saintly resignation. In fact you were so kind, so good, so sympathetic, so understanding, so noble and so heroic that you bloody nearly killed me with guilt! But after I'd recovered from my relief that I'd survived I began to feel angry. At first I didn't know why. Then I realized it was because none of the emotions you were projecting were real. You *hated* me being an actor! You *hated* me not going into the Church! And most of all you *hated* me smashing your cherished dream that I'd be a replica! Oh, if only you could have shouted: "You silly little bastard, how dare you do this to me!" Then we could at least have had an honest conversation, but no, our relationship had been dishonest for years and that scene just put the final nail in the coffin of our dishonesty. After that no matter how often I yelled at you all I got was this mask of saintly resignation studded with Christian platitudes.

'After I had my breakdown I said to the psychiatrist: "The most ghastly thing about my father is that *he never complains*. He just smiles and says whatever I do he still loves me, but can't he see that's all rubbish? Can't he see that if he really loved me he wouldn't wall himself off from me with all this acting? Can't he see that he's absolutely destroying me by maintaining this relationship which is false from beginning to end?"

'The psychiatrist was a maddening old bird who often pretended to be stupid in order to needle me into talking. He put on his stupid look and said: "But why can't you believe your father when he says he loves you whatever you do?" I told him you couldn't love any son who wasn't a replica, but he just said: "Why should the fact that he wanted a replica mean he didn't also love you as you were?" God, how he irritated me! I said: "My father rejected my true self by wanting a replica. If you reject something you don't love it," but the stupid man couldn't accept that. "If he's rejected you," he said, "why didn't he wash his hands of you as soon as you told him you were going to be an actor?" "Because he's an actor himself!" I shouted. "And he felt he had to put on this fantastic act for me!" And do you know what this madman said next? "What an exhausting thing to do!" he said. "If he cared nothing for your true self, why should he go to all that trouble?"

'Well, of course one can't argue with doctors who think they know everything so I said: "Okay, perhaps he does care about me in his own peculiar way, but he shouldn't have wanted me to be a replica." I thought that if I made that concession the conversation would come to an end, but no, back came the madman with the question: "Why do you think he wanted a replica? If you understood this desire better perhaps you wouldn't be so angry with him." "I understand it perfectly," I said coldly, and trotted out my theory that you secretly wanted to compensate yourself for the career you never had. Then the moron exclaimed, pretending to be enlightened: "Ah! So what you're saying is that your father is a deeply frustrated and unhappy man! How sad! Why don't you stop being angry with him and feel sorry for him instead?" Silly old fool! Of course I then told him in no uncertain terms that you'd always been happy as a lark ever since your ordination – except when Mother died and your happy marriage came to an end.

'At that point the madman pretended to be puzzled. "Funny!" he said. "If your father was so happy, why should he have wanted a replica? I don't think your theory can be correct. There must be some other reason. Is your father perhaps very proud and arrogant, the sort of man who desires a replica of himself to fuel his self-esteem?" That made me laugh. "You couldn't be more wrong!" I told him. "My father has very simple modest tastes, he's devoted his whole life to helping others and he couldn't possibly be described as proud and arrogant!" And do you know what the madman said next? He said: "Well, if he doesn't want a replica because he's miserable and he doesn't want a replica because he's proud, why on earth should he want one at all? I'm beginning to think that he's both miserable *and* proud but you've never realized it. How well do you really know your father? Is it possible that you've never really known him at all?"

' "Of course I bloody well know my father!" I shouted, finally losing patience. "He's the war-hero, the crusader, the brilliant priest, the devoted husband and parent!" "Now isn't that interesting!" said the madman. "I'd formed the impression from you earlier that he was an actor, a religious fanatic and the very opposite of a family man – in fact I was reminded of Kipling's cat that always preferred to walk by himself."

'Well, of course he was deliberately twisting what I'd said earlier in order to make me think more deeply about you, and although I was so exasperated that I stormed out of his office I did in fact begin to ponder later on your resemblance to Kipling's cat . . .

'You really do prefer to walk by yourself, don't you? Or are times changing now that you're again stalking along with the right companion at last? I wonder. I can't forget that Kipling also wrote about the leopard who couldn't change his spots, and I suppose you'll always tend to be aloof, but I shan't mind that so long as you stop this interminable purring at all the wrong moments and hiss occasionally like any normal feline . . . Funny the way you always had with cats. I'll never forget that tigerish masterpiece you introduced me to up in Yorkshire, the one who almost talked to you – and think of Pussy-Boots long ago in Starmouth! he used to shiver in ecstasy whenever you entered the room. I remember Mother saying how spooky that was . . . Incidentally, talking of Mother . . . Dad, I know you were devoted to her, but did she ever drive you crazy occasionally? I mean, I can see how luscious she was, brimming with vitality and S.A., and of course I adored her, but somehow every time Ruth drives me mad with her tempestuous stupidity I look at her and remember Mother and wonder if your devotion ever got a little frayed at the edges . . .'

Very slowly, often faltering in my quest for the right words, I embarked on the task of introducing myself to the son who had known me only as a stranger.

V

That evening after Martin had gone I opened the album and took out the photograph of my parents on their wedding day. My father no longer looked dignified, decent and dull. He looked dignified, decent and dedicated. I could see the dedication clearly now, the dedication to a son who baffled him, the dedication to a wife whose spirit had eluded him, the dedication to the career which had gone in the wrong direction, the dedication to the present which meant that no word of regret could ever be uttered about the past. I felt I knew at last how much all that dedication must have cost him, and suddenly in the light of my new knowledge I saw his refusal to complain not as hypocrisy but as heroism. I realized how lonely he must have been, isolated by his marriage, struggling to come to terms with his broken dreams, eking out whatever happiness he could find with his mysterious wife and son while all the time he poured his whole soul into his teaching, the one part of his life where he could escape from his troubles and express his true self.

Propping the photograph on the mantelshelf alongside the photograph of my mother I continued to stare at both my parents as they stood so close together without touching each other at any point. I felt as if I were inspecting their marriage from a perspective which I had never dreamed could exist, and I realized then that although they had loved each other enough to try hard to make the marriage a success they had remained fundamentally mismatched. No doubt my mother's death had been a release to my father, just as Betty's death had been a release to me, and no doubt he too had had to wrestle with the complex aftermath of guilt and grief which had followed his bereavement. As this insight dawned on me I remembered again how I had felt in the chapel when Martin had opened my eyes and unstopped my ears; I felt I was seeing my father not as the alien stranger but as my mirror-image, my other self.

I knew now why Francis had become so angry with me by the lake at Starwater. What right had I to judge my father when I had not only never known him but had committed all the same errors, cutting myself off from my own son in my unhappiness and laying upon him a psychological burden which had crushed his spirit? Martin had been more vulnerable than I had been in childhood and adolescence; the damage had been greater there. Yet I had had the insufferable arrogance to judge my father a failure! I wondered how I could have been so blind for so long, and it was then that I realized how profoundly my mother's death had dislocated our relationship. If she had lived she would have acted as a bridge between us, but her death had sealed us off for ever in our private worlds. In my need to blame someone for the disaster I had tried to exorcize my grief by projecting the unbearable anger on to my father, yet despite my efforts the exorcism had failed; the anger had been projected but the wound had remained unhealed until the day of Gerald's birth and death when Francis had exposed the sore to begin the process of healing.

I could now see how the healing was evolving. Having accepted my mother's death at last, having come to believe myself secure with Anne, I had been ready to hear what Martin had had to say and the last piece of the jig-saw had finally fallen into place in my psyche. The light from the north had been the light of revelation but the revelation had not, as I had always blithely supposed, been of my new call. The revelation had been of myself, of the dark corners of my soul, and now that this psychological landscape had been illuminated I was at last able to perceive the call which had always existed but which I had always been too maimed to hear.

Instinctively I wished my father were alive so that I could beg his forgiveness for my part of the estrangement, for the eyes which had failed to see and the ears which had failed to hear, but I knew I was already forgiven. The light in the chapel had bleached my psyche clean and now, as I remembered that intersection of eternity with finite time, I knew that my father had returned to my life not as a malign memory but as a benign presence. In that world of values which represented the eternal reality, the quality which I had recognized as his dedication was reflected back at me as love, and in the light of that love I could see the way ahead fully revealed.

I sat down to write to Francis.

VI

When Francis received my letter he telephoned me. My first reaction was to be shocked that I should be offered spiritual direction through the medium of such an unpleasant modern instrument. Then I realized I was glad to have the chance to talk to him.

'I shall put all this in writing so that you have the chance to meditate on it properly,' he said, displaying a reassuring self-consciousness about his latest effort to bring the Order into the twentieth century, 'but I thought I should warn you immediately not to rush into any impulsive action while you're still in a euphoric state following this extraordinary catharsis. Remember your position. You're a curate subject to the authority of your bishop who has wisely advised you to take six months off work so that you can rebuild your spiritual strength. Your duty to God at the moment is to get fit, not to rush off to the nearest educational institution and say: "Here I am!" '

'But I feel so much stronger now! I'm sure I don't need six months to – '

'You need it. And remember that patience is the most difficult of all virtues but one which it would undoubtedly pay you to – '

'What an unsatisfactory instrument the telephone is!' I exclaimed. 'Are you smiling or have you become genuinely pompous?'

Francis laughed, said neatly: 'Of course I assumed you could see me as well as hear me,' and hung up the receiver before he could hear my exasperated laugh in reply.

Cyril had offered me the weekly guidance of his best counsellor, a younger man than myself but one who I soon realized was greatly gifted as a director of souls, and helped not only by this new acquaintance but also by Francis' regular letters I worked hard to regain my spiritual health. Later I made a week's retreat in London. I was saddened to see that a bomb had damaged the chapel, but the monks were already busy with the repairs. Meanwhile the war had entered a new phase. Hitler had attacked Russia, that graveyard of European dictatorial dreams, and I thought the tide would now turn for England, just as the tide had now turned in my own personal battle to find peace in a hazardous world.

In November as I studied the war news I suddenly said to Anne: 'The Japanese are going to sink a lot of American ships in the Pacific and the United States will enter the war.' But after Pearl Harbor I said to her: 'For heaven's sake don't tell anyone I prophesied the attack or I'll be tempted to start a new career as a miracle-man!' I was very mindful of the danger in which I stood as I struggled to recover my spiritual health, but I had already made much progress and when at Christmas Anne lapsed into a depression at last I was able to use my new strength to help her overcome her grief 'I was so sure I didn't feel angry,' she said in the new year. 'I didn't want to be angry at all.' But bereavement can take many unwelcome forms and often, as I knew all too well, cannot be mastered by a simple act of the will.

When Anne was better I then nerved myself to make a long-postponed visit to Ruth. I fully expected emotional scenes to erupt as usual as soon as I set foot in her house, but to my astonishment the atmosphere remained tranquil; it was as if some vital ingredient had disappeared from our explosive relationship, and when Ruth said marvelling: 'You're different. Everything seems much calmer now,' I realized what havoc had been wrought by my disturbed psyche, writhing beneath the burden of my guilt. Ruth even said: 'I'm glad you married if it's made you happier. People get difficult when they're unhappy – I know that better than anyone,' and the next moment she was telling me that Roger had recently ended a long affair with his secretary.

'. . . and she treated him so badly that he was shattered enough to suggest we should make a fresh start. At first I was proud and said no, but then I started thinking about what I really wanted – '

I expressed admiration by telling her she was being exceptionally courageous, and at once the warmth of my sincerity had a radical effect: Ruth was at last able to relax in my presence.

'I'm sorry I was so awful when I visited the Manor,' she said in a rush. 'I expect you thought it was because I minded her being a lady. I thought your choice of someone upper-class was an indirect criticism of me for not being quite ... although I've tried so hard to better myself, truly I have – I even took elocution lessons once and I've read dozens of books on etiquette and I always try so hard to dress in the very best of taste – '

'My dearest Ruth!' I felt so shattered by this further evidence of my past blindness that I was at first unable to respond to her pathetic confession, but when she even whispered: 'I always thought you might love me better if I was a lady,' sheer horror enabled me to find my tongue. 'Ruth,' I said, 'I married Anne not because of her class but in spite of it. I was the son of one working-class woman and the husband of another. The only question here is not whether you're a good enough daughter for me but whether I'm a good enough father for you, and I can only conclude, when I review my gross insensitivity towards you over the years, that I'm not. I seem to have been a quite unforgivably stupid and useless parent.'

I might have wallowed in guilt for much longer but Ruth – fortunately, perhaps, for our emotional equilibrium – decided I was joking. I was called a silly-billy, given a kiss and patted on the head as if I were a naughty old duffer for whom allowances had to be perpetually made. Then she manifested her forgiveness in a more acceptable fashion by suggesting that she should visit the Manor again, this time with the children, during the Easter holidays.

I felt like a guilty man pardoned after a magnificent display of clemency, and feeling greatly chastened I travelled back to Starrington.

It was on the day after my return home that I journeyed to Starbridge in response to a summons from the Bishop. Dr Ottershaw, welcoming me with his customary courtesy, soon said how delighted he was to see me looking so well after my six months' recuperation, and at once, somehow contriving to conceal my excitement, I declared myself ready to undertake whatever work he saw fit to assign to me.

'Well, I've been thinking and praying about this, of course,' said Dr Ottershaw, 'and I've finally decided – after considerable deliberation – because of course there are many pros and cons – and indeed one can easily get into a state where one can't see the woods from the trees – or sift the wheat from the chaff – but I've finally decided,' said Dr Ottershaw, rescuing himself from this labyrinthine sentence, 'that it would be best if you resumed your duties as curate.'

There was a silence. This was not what I had expected. I was aware of my heart sinking.

'Unless, of course,' said Dr Ottershaw, ever courteous, 'you have some very pressing reason to persist with your resignation.'

I somehow resisted the urge to wind him around my little finger. 'It must be absolutely as you wish, Bishop. If I hesitate, it's because I'm so acutely aware of all my past mistakes.'

'Well, that's just it,' said Dr Ottershaw, seizing the chance to explain his decision. 'You're like a man who's fallen off a horse and the best possible thing to do. after such a disaster, as any equestrian will tell you, is to get back on again as soon as you're fit to do so. In fact the way I see the situation is this: you're going to have to live in that parish, and as things stand you're living with the unhealed wound of all that dissension. So I feel I must give you the chance, for your own sake as well as for the sake of the parish, to attempt a ministry of reconciliation. Why don't you have a shot at it and we'll review the position in a further six months?'

'Very well, Bishop,' I said, meek as a model monk, but I was bitterly disappointed and this time it was I who resorted to the telephone to talk to Francis.

VIII

'Ottershaw's reached a difficult decision after much prayer,' said Francis. 'Who are you to say he's mad as a hatter? What arrogance! Do I really have to remind you that we're called to serve, not to run around whining: "I want, I want, I want," like some detestable spoilt child? Pull yourself together, stop thinking selfishly and start reuniting that parish which you've successfully split from end to end – and don't you dare try to tell me that's beyond the scope of your infamous glamorous powers!'

I rang off and slunk away.

IX

The resumption of my curacy was, I think, one of the most difficult tasks I have ever faced in my career as a priest, but once I had vowed to be flexible and unobtrusive instead of intractable and flamboyant I found that after the first agonizing Sunday my ordeal was not as humiliating as I had feared. Drawing on my experience in the Navy when war-time conditions had often demanded a flexible approach to worship, I re-examined my task with as much detachment as I could muster and faced the fact that this particular flock in this particular corner of England at this particular time could best be spiritually nourished by being allowed to graze in their cherished conventional pastures. In times of great stress people need rituals which are familiar, and the parishioners of Starrington Magna, conservative by nature after generations of living peacefully in such a pleasant well-ordered corner of the world, had earned the right to draw strength from their traditions at this crucial moment in England's history.

I could never have sunk into the bibliolatry of the Low-Church tradition; that would have been quite alien to my spiritual inclinations, but I thought I could descend to the moderate Protestant pastures from my Anglo-Catholic peaks without intolerably compromising my ideals. Those who grazed in those pastures formed the backbone of the Church of England. Professional churchmen might divide themselves into Evangelicals and Anglo-Catholics and engage in internecine strife but most laymen were uninterested in the finer points of theology and merely wanted to worship God without fuss. It was my task to nurture this simple, entirely admirable ambition, not to distort it, thwart it or even snuff it out by pigheadedly imposing my liturgical tastes on theirs. Setting aside my Anglo-Catholic touches with a selfish reluctance but with a Christian resignation, I resumed my career at Starrington not as the village priest but as the local parson, and my reward came some weeks later when I overheard one formerly hostile lady say to another: 'I think even dear Mr Wetherall would have approved of that service if he had been here.'

I had many requests for healing but I referred them to the Guild of St Raphael, the body which had been set up some years before to deal with all aspects of this ministry. I also had requests for exorcism but I referred these to the Bishop. It remained of great interest to the community that the unfortunate Higgins had completely recovered from his aberration; Dr Garrison continued to bluster that Higgins had killed the cow as a substitute for his wife during a psychotic episode brought on by family problems, but naturally I had the good sense to offer no comment.

Easter arrived. Martin came to see me again, and soon afterwards Ruth made her promised visit with the children. My grandson asked numerous intelligent questions about the Home Farm tractor, my grand-daughter insisted on sketching the chapel and Ruth herself was charmed by the Manor's electrical carpet-sweeper, an instrument which was referred to as a 'Hoover'. At one point I opened my mouth to declare that such modern material items were quite unimportant, but I realized just in time that such a remark would brand me as a priggish narrow-minded old codger. Instead I said how right it was that we should all occasionally pause to admire the mechanical marvels of the age.

'There's nothing more tiresome,' Romaine had said to me not long before, 'than an elderly bore who looks down his nose at today's way of life. One of my friends said to me the other day: "If only we could turn the clock back to the halcyon days of the nineteenth century!" And I said: "Oh yes – child prostitution, public hangings and women dying 'en masse' in childbirth. wonderful!" That shut him up pretty quickly, I can tell you.'

I enjoyed seeing Romaine for our weekly games of chess not only because he amused me but because he had regular news of Charles who was now in North Africa. Charles also wrote to me, but tended to confine himself to spiritual matters; Romaine offered more diverse news. One day in that spring of 1942 he showed me a letter in which Charles had written: 'Now that you know Darrow better perhaps you won't be surprised when I tell you that he's the reason why I can face the future with confidence. When I last saw him he was so serene, so absolutely untouched by any profound anxiety, that I knew I was going to be all right. I felt that he must have received some psychic foreknowledge that we would meet again; if he'd had any premonition of disaster he couldn't possibly have maintained that remarkable serenity of his.'

I read the letter. I looked at Romaine. I heard his unspoken question, and at once I saw that Charles' mistaken belief would protect him no matter what ordeals lay ahead. Quite unwittingly, by the grace of God who had covered my terror with tranquillity, I had ensured that Charles had the psychological strength to cling to life in circumstances where other men would die. I said to Romaine: 'He'll be all right.'

'Well, one never really knows, does one?' said Romaine, tucking the precious letter carefully away in his breast-pocket again. 'And the Middle East is hardly a garden-party nowadays.'

I said no more. It would have been wrong to behave like an infallible prophet, but I remembered how I had predicted the attack on Pearl Harbor with such accuracy and suddenly I knew with the absolute certainty of a successful psychic that Hitler's General Rommel would never take Tobruk.

I was still savouring this reassuring foreknowledge when my life as a curate came abruptly to an end. An ecclesiastical plough in the form of Dr Ottershaw plucked me from my monotonous parish furrow and once more I found myself travelling to Starbridge.

X

'My dear fellow!' said Dr Ottershaw. 'I had absolutely no idea! Do forgive me – what could you have thought? If I'd only known – I do so reproach myself – I said to my wife: "How could I have got in such a muddle?" and she said: "All too easily," which was so true but I confess I felt more mortified than ever. I do hope I'm not going senile.'

I was by this time accustomed to Dr Ottershaw's elliptical conversation when he was flustered. I said mildly: 'Do you feel you've offended me in some way, Bishop? I assure you I've been quite unaware of it.'

'Dear me, what a relief! You see, I had no idea – *no idea* – what had happened at Ruydale. I thought you'd been the Prior! How could I have made such a mistake? I remember when you first came here to dinner I asked you about your career as a monk and I could have sworn you said you were the Prior – although perhaps you only said: "I could go no higher," meaning that the Abbot was bound to be succeeded eventually by a fellow-Yorkshireman – '

A ray of light dawned. Still adopting my mildest voice I said: 'Please don't worry about it, Bishop. It's not important.'

'But my dear fellow, that's just it – it's vital! I've been informed not only that you were the Master of Novices but that a high proportion of your men went on to become priests! Well, of course as soon as I heard that I telephoned Cyril Watson at Starwater Abbey and he said that in the opinion of the late Abbot-General you were one of the most gifted teachers in the Order. "Why didn't you tell me before?" I cried and he said astonished: "But I assumed you already knew!" Well! I nearly had apoplexy but when I'd recovered I saw at once that God Moves in Mysterious Ways and that no doubt this delay has been All For The Best.' Dr Ottershaw enunciated the crucial words in such a way that I knew he had mentally assigned them capital letters.

'Yes, of course,' I murmured, not entirely sure what proposition I was confirming. 'Of course.'

'If I'd known then what I know now,' said Dr Ottershaw, rushing on, 'I might have been tempted to throw your parish to the winds and scoop you over here straight away, but that wouldn't have been right. I had to give you the chance to pour oil on the troubled waters.' He sighed happily before adding: 'You will come, won't you?'

'Come where, Bishop?'

'Oh good heavens, I've omitted the crucial explanation! I really must be going senile, but perhaps I'm simply dazed by my unexpected good luck. My dear fellow, haven't you heard about our crisis at the Theological College here in the Close?'

'As a matter of fact Father Watson did mention – '

'As the result of the war the shortage of teachers has become so acute that the Principal's now saying he'll have to close the College unless he has at least one more experienced priest who can not only shoulder the burden of teaching but also assist with the spiritual direction – '

'Spiritual direction!'

'Yes, just up your street, isn't it, but of course I didn't know you had the right teaching experience. Quite obviously you're heaven-sent! I must arrange an interview with the Principal at once.'

By this time my curiosity had triumphed over my elation. 'Before you do that, Bishop,' I said swiftly as he reached for the telephone, 'may I ask who eventually told you that I'd been the Master of Novices at Ruydale?' I knew Francis was more than capable of intervening on my behalf, but I had expected no intervention until I had served the full six months allocated to my ministry of reconciliation at Starrington.

'It was the most remarkable coincidence,' said Dr Ottershaw cosily, forgetting the telephone and settling down to gossip. 'My predecessor Dr Jardine is visiting Starbridge at present and staying with the Aysgarths. Jardine always took a keen interest in the Theological College when he was Bishop so naturally he asked how it was faring and when Aysgarth told him about the crisis he said: "The solution's sitting right here in your diocese," and began to talk of your achievements at Ruydale. Oh, he knew all about you! Apparently he'd been obliged to search for a spiritual director once for a young clerical acquaintance of his who was in deep trouble, and you were recommended to him by – '

'Yes, I remember the case. So Dr Jardine's back in Starbridge! I wonder why.'

'He's been busy looking up some of the official papers relating to his episcopate – did you know he was writing his memoirs? They say the Archbishop – no, Lord Lang we must call him, mustn't we, now that he's retired with a peerage – they say Lord Lang can hardly sleep a wink at night for fear of what the book may contain! Jardine, as I'm sure you remember, had a very singular approach to the truth.'

'Very singular.'

'Not that I wish to criticize him in any way,' said Dr Ottershaw hastily, 'and really how fortunate it is that he should have turned up in Starbridge at the exact moment when I needed his help! But I'm jumping the gun – here I am, talking as if I've already captured you and I haven't even given you the chance to decline the offer! How arrogant of me! But I do hope you don't feel God has other plans for you.'

'Now that I've had the chance to pour oil on the Starrington waters I hope I can make some contribution, no matter how small, to the welfare of the Theological College,' I said with a humility which would have satisfied even Father Darcy's exacting standards. 'I'm happy to serve wherever you think I'm needed, Bishop.'

'Splendid!' said Dr Ottershaw. 'What a load off my mind! You must see the Principal without delay.' And expelling a vast sigh of relief he once more reached happily for the telephone.

XI

Two hours later after my interview with the Principal I walked from the Cathedral Close to the church of St Martin's-in-Cripplegate and knocked on the door of the vicarage nearby.

'I've just been offered a post at the Theological College,' I said as I entered Aysgarth's study, 'and since I hear the offer stemmed from information provided by your guest I thought I'd call to thank him. I also called to say, of course, that I hope you and I will find it easier to be civil to each other now that I'm not busy turning an exemplary parish into an archdeacon's nightmare.'

Aysgarth gave the shy smile which was so much at odds with his brutal mouth. He said: 'You'll have noticed that I've had no complaints since you resumed your curacy. But I'm glad you've finally accepted work commensurate with your gifts.' He turned aside adding: 'I'll call Dr Jardine,' but the summons proved unnecessary. The next moment the door opened and in walked the former Bishop of Starbridge, flaunting his premature retirement by wearing an immaculately cut grey lounge-suit, a daring tie, an elegant fob-watch and – horror of horrors – a carnation in his buttonhole.

It would of course be possible to write a long description of such a celebrated controversial figure as Dr Alexander Jardine, but I shall leave his daring Modernist views to the theologians, his nouveau-riche episcopal extravagances to the social historians, his combative fiery personality to the psychologists, his personal attractions to the ladies and his career as a priest to God. My own brief description of his apparel, so monstrously inappropriate even for a retired churchman, will, I trust, convey both the essence of his debonair attitude to life and my own opinion of a priest who feels called to court all the publicity which unfortunately the press are only too happy to provide.

'So we meet again!' he exclaimed as if we were in the habit of bumping into each other, but in fact I had only met him once before. After he had retired from his bishopric in 1937 he had come to Grantchester to seek advice about his future from someone who by chance knew rather more about him than most people did, but since he was the kind of man who seeks advice but seldom takes it our meeting had hardly been fruitful. During our interview I had done my best to overcome my antipathy sufficiently to treat him with charity; nevertheless when I heard no more from him afterwards I had assumed my charity had failed to ring true, and the news that morning of his benign intervention on my behalf had come as a considerable surprise to me.

'Well!' said Jardine, as I reflected on Dr Ottershaw's reminder that sometimes God did indeed move in mysterious ways. 'Do we shake hands?'

'I can't imagine why not.'

'No? Back in 1937 I received the distinct impression that you disapproved of me!'

I saw then that my disapproval had rankled with him and that his present intervention represented a desire to prove to me that he was not such a bad fellow after all. I regarded this as an indication of a disturbed psyche. We should not spend our time worrying obsessively about what others may think of us; this shows an unhealthy preoccupation with the self.

'If I gave you the impression of disapproval,' I said, 'then I must take the blame for the unsatisfactory nature of our meeting. I'm glad to see you well, Jardine, and I'm greatly in your debt for enlightening Dr Ottershaw about my career at Ruydale.'

'That old scatterbrain! I assure you that if *I'd* still been occupying the palace you wouldn't have been left to moulder for months in a rural backwater!'

Seeing my expression as I mentally reeled in the face of such bumptious discourtesy to Dr Ottershaw, Aysgarth said in a rapid attempt to change the subject: 'Have you heard that Dr Jardine's writing his memoirs?'

'Yes,' I said, 'I understand that's the reason for his visit to Starbridge.' I turned to Jardine. 'Or are the memoirs merely providing an excuse to look up old friends?'

'Now why should you make me feel as if even looking up old friends is a sin? What a very formidable fellow you are when you radiate that chilling austerity!' said Jardine lightly, and added amused: 'You should warm up a little by writing your own memoirs – I'm sure they'd make fascinating reading!'

'On the contrary,' I said, 'you know as well as I do that when one's a priest all the best stories can never be told.' I turned to take my leave of Aysgarth but Jardine remained determined to engage me in conversation, and suddenly beneath the mask of levity I sensed the complex restless priest who was lonely enough to resent my lack of warmth. With a sinking heart I realized that I had to make a new effort to be charitable, and reminding myself of Jardine's recent important intervention in my life I began to wonder if God had propelled me into this meeting for some special purpose. As far as I could see I had merely called at the vicarage of my own free will in order to be polite.

'Before you rush off,' Jardine was saying, 'you must let me congratulate you belatedly on your marriage. A wife whom I'm told is charming and intelligent as well as good and devout is indeed one of the ultimate prizes . . . Have you ever talked to Father Darrow, Neville, about your quest for the ultimate prizes?'

Aysgarth at once said: 'No,' and looked wary, but his mentor ignored this hint that the subject should not be pursued. 'Neville grew up in adverse circumstances,' he explained to me, 'and in order to inspire himself into surmounting them he saw life as a quest for prizes – not just the commonplace prizes which were available to people from more comfortable backgrounds, but the ultimate prizes – the common prizes glorified. What this means in practical terms, of course, is that Neville's always chasing perfection.'

Aysgarth cleared his throat. 'Before Mr Darrow reminds me that perfection is unattainable in this world, may I make it clear that I'm not a monster of worldly ambition? My one desire is to serve God to the best of my ability – '

' – and what's wrong with worldly ambition if it helps you fulfil that exceedingly laudable aim? For example, you're surely not ashamed of your Balliol scholarship which led you into a world where you could at last approach Christianity intellectually!'

'Well, I do agree, certainly, that the ultimate prize of a place at Oxford represents worldly ambition in its most acceptable form, but I'm sure Mr Darrow's thinking – '

'Darrow's wound up with the perfect wife, the perfect home and the perfect new career – all ultimate prizes – so don't start imagining that he's too holy to know what ambition means! Why, I'll wager that at this very moment he's savouring his prospects at the Theological College and calculating his chances of becoming the principal!'

Aysgarth looked so acutely embarrassed that I decided it was time to ride to his rescue. 'Come now, Jardine!' I said in the voice of an abbot addressing a boisterous monk who was continually smitten by the urge to show off. 'You're just being provocative because you want to puncture what you've mistakenly diagnosed as hypocrisy on Aysgarth's part and priggishness on mine. In actual fact Aysgarth's very properly modifying your cavalier attitude to worldly ambition, and my expression of amazement which no doubt greeted your remarks springs not from priggishness but from concern. Surely a priest of your eminence should be declaring that true perfection lies only in the absolute values and that the ultimate prize for any soul can only be union with God?'

I had thought that this shaft would put the Bishop firmly in his place but I was mistaken. 'My dear Darrow,' he said exasperated, 'have you entirely lost your sense of humour? I sincerely hope you didn't leave it behind with your habit when you left the cloister!'

'I haven't lost my sense of humour – I've merely retained my good taste. Good-day to you both and God bless you,' I said in a tone which would have silenced even the most recalcitrant monk, and strode from the room without looking back.

XII

On the train to Starrington I conceded that I had responded too severely to Jardine's remarks and regretted that I had not been more patient with a man who was obviously unhappy. His bitter comment about my wife, home and new career indicated jealousy; his jibe about my ambition to run the Theological College suggested that his desire for my approval had declined into a resentful dislike when that approval had failed to appear.

I had never thought Jardine spiritually gifted. Now, with his career cut short and his time devoted to the dubious art of autobiography, a form of writing in which both honesty and humility are famous for their absence, he seemed to be drifting deeper into a spiritual dead-end.

Remembering my speculation that God might have propelled me into the interview I wondered if I were supposed to assist Jardine in some way, but I remained convinced that he was beyond my help, particularly now that our antipathy had hardened. Then I wondered if I were supposed to help Aysgarth; I was in fact deeply concerned that a young priest of such promise should have such a questionable mentor, but I could hardly offer my services as a counsellor unless I were invited to do so, and it seemed highly unlikely that Aysgarth, mindful of our past antagonism, would ever turn to me for help.

I thought of him, clever efficient Aysgarth, running his private and public lives with such conspicuous success, and I wondered what went on in his head when he talked to God. However one of the commonest errors a counsellor can make is to assume everyone is secretly writhing beneath the weight of intractable problems. Perhaps Aysgarth was one of those fortunate people who sail through life without encountering any major difficulties. Perhaps after surmounting his troubled background his path through life had been enviably smooth.

I might have continued to speculate for some time in this idle and unprofitable fashion, but I was too excited about my new career to ponder on Aysgarth for long. When I arrived home I found that Anne was out, visiting Romaine to discover whether she had succeeded in embarking on a second pregnancy, so I hurried straight to my cell to write to Francis. By this time my room was a cell no more; it had become a study, a silent witness to my final adjustment to the world. I had possessions. The room now boasted four shelves of books, a modern lamp, an easy-chair with a footstool (had I finally come to terms with old age?) and a pretty water-colour of the chapel which my grand-daughter had painted from the sketch drawn on her Easter visit. On the shelf above the fireplace stood the photographs of my family, including my grandson in his new Naval uniform. I felt very pleased that Colin had chosen to serve in the Navy; I thought it would give us something to talk about at last. For a second I prayed, as I did every day, for his safety, but then I turned aside from all thoughts of the war and fingered the plain wooden frame which I had made to hold the photograph of my parents on their wedding-day.

I pictured my father's reaction to my appointment. 'The Theological College at Starbridge? Very distinguished! And how suited to your gifts – what scope for a rewarding career!' he would have said with genuine pleasure, and as his words echoed in my imagination I found myself wondering if I would indeed wind up running the Theological College.

But of course that sort of idle thought, reeking of worldly ambition, came straight from the Devil and had to be ruthlessly suppressed. My task was to serve God, not to serve myself by pursuing the road to self-aggrandizement, and suddenly I was thinking of Aysgarth again, Aysgarth and his ultimate prizes.

It occurred to me then that God in his subtle way had propelled me into that interview at the vicarage not so that I could help either Jardine or Aysgarth (how arrogant that I should have automatically assumed I was being called in to play the wonder-worker!) but so that I should be prompted to meditate deeply, before I began my new career in the world, on the nature of ambition and its often ambivalent fruits. Of course one should regard any expression of ambition with suspicion, even if it appeared not to be centred on the self, but had I perhaps defined ambition's ultimate prize too narrowly when I had declared it could only consist of the soul's union with God? perhaps Jardine had not after all been so wildly astray in taking a broader view and Aysgarth's chase for the prizes should not be automatically condemned. If perfection lay in the absolute values, that bridge between our world and ultimate reality, then perfection could be grasped by embracing those absolute values and trying to incorporate them into one's daily life. Naturally one's success would be limited, since the human race could never fully achieve perfection on this earth, but the absolute values could indeed be seen as ultimate prizes, something for man to aim at, a target for his innate acquisitive streak, a symbol luring him to stretch upwards to a better life when he might otherwise sink downwards into an animal existence which was unworthy of his unique power of reason and self-awareness.

I saw then in a moment of revelation that I too had gone chasing the prizes, the ultimate prizes of Truth, Beauty and Love, and now at last my quest had borne recognizable fruit: I had grasped the Truth about my past, an achievement which had set me free to serve God in a new way; I had found the chapel, that symbol of Beauty, which would forever stand at the centre of my life, and I had in Anne received the Love that made me whole and would eventually transform me, so I hoped, into a better man.

As I thought of those absolute values which reflected the spiritual world I suddenly saw them as Plotinus would have seen them, overflowing from the fountainhead past tier after tier of existence, the waters of ultimate reality bathing the world in light. Then I thought how the Christians had adapted Platonism, centring the absolute values in the person of Christ and the presence of the Holy Spirit which poured forth through the world into the minds and hearts of men. Why had not Plotinus become a Christian? I had often asked myself that question but Plotinus had left no answer. Perhaps he had disliked the organization of the Early Church;

mystics are notoriously antipathetic to organizations. Or perhaps he had merely felt that Christianity was a bastard religion, half-Hellenic, half-Semitic, just another syncretistic approach to the One, an approach which could only fall short of the glories of Greek philosophy. Or perhaps he had even felt that to be Christian in those days was to limit oneself to one sect, a prospect which would not have interested him as he strove to address all mankind. 'The mystical faculty,' Plotinus had declared encouragingly, 'is one which all possess but few use.' Could he conceivably have felt that those who used it could dispense with organized religion and that organized religion itself was only an aid to enlightenment for those whose mystical faculty would have remained otherwise undeveloped? This was the age-old trap which had ensnared so many mystics, but it was hard to imagine Plotinus, described by his disciple Porphyry as a man of great goodness and humility, ever being arrogant enough to divorce his mysticism from a formal religious context. Plotinus had been a deeply religious philosopher, and in his formal Hellenism mysticism and religion were inextricably entwined.

As I had discovered in my younger days, a mystic who dispenses with a religious framework lays himself open to corruption. But on the other hand a religious who tries to discard mysticism lays a dead hand on his spiritual life. Mysticism is the raw material of religion, as I had once said to Janet; without raw materials building is impossible, and without a structure designed by architects raw materials remain raw materials. However although the raw materials of mysticism can be found world-wide as they permeate all the great religions, the architecture which springs from them is as varied as the human race itself. The mystics may all speak the same language but the language has many dialects, and for me, if not for Plotinus, there was one voice which spoke that langue more finely than any other, the voice of Christ as re-created by the Fourth Evangelist in one of the greatest mystical tracts ever written, the voice of St John proclaiming the eternal values of ultimate reality as he unveiled the great mystery of the Incarnation.

I was still meditating on the Fourth Gospel and thinking what a model of clarity it was when compared with Plotinus' obscure, tortuous prose when Anne returned home with good news from Romaine.

'The baby's coming for Christmas!' she said kissing me. 'Alan said he hoped it wouldn't disrupt Matins!' And without giving me time to respond she asked me what had happened in Starbridge.'

Sensing her fear that I might still be lukewarm about fatherhood I took care to reassure her by postponing a full account of my own news and returning at once to the subject of the baby. 'Now that I've got over my arrogant, self-centred desire for a replica by conquering my past unhappiness,' I declared, 'I shall look forward to this infant's arrival in the hope that we'll have a daughter who'll take after you. Then I'm sure I shall find parenthood very pleasant.'

Anne was sufficiently relieved to exclaim generously: 'I think a replica of you would be rather fun!'

'Oh no, it wouldn't!' I said with a shudder. 'In fact I can see now what hell it would be to have a son who was as proud, arrogant, wilful and obstinate as I am – what would happen to my dreams of a peaceful old age? Life would be one long battle!'

'Nonsense!' said Anne firmly. 'Anyway we can't have a girl because I've just had the most brilliant idea for a boy's name. Darling, as the baby will always be able to claim he was brought by the reindeer instead of by the boring old stork, why don't we call him after Father Christmas?'

'*Father Christmas?*'

'St Nicholas!' said Anne happily, enrapt by her cleverness. 'Don't you think that's the perfect solution?'

Utterly speechless I pulled her into my arms and wondered when I had last felt so ambivalent.

AUTHOR'S NOTE

The character of Jon Darrow is fictitious.

Darrow's religious thought is derived from the writings of WILLIAM RALPH INGE (1860–1954), one of the leading intellectuals in the Church of England in the late nineteenth and early twentieth century. Educated at Eton and at King's College, Cambridge, where he obtained a first in classics, he then taught at Eton before being ordained in 1888. Following his ordination he became a fellow of Hertford College, Oxford, where Idealist philosophy was in the ascendant, and it was there that he turned from pure scholarship towards metaphysics.

In 1895 he began to read the work of Plotinus, first of the philosophers now called Neophatonists, and his encounter with Neoplatonism led him to make a special study of Christian Mysticism, the subject of his famous Bampton Lectures in 1899. Inge played a leading role in the twentieth-century revival of interest in mysticism. He believed that this human experience of the presence of God provided as indestructible religious truth which the current attacks on the institutional churches and the authority of the Bible could not touch; in his view the mystical experience of God, vouched for in a smiliar manner amidst different religions at different times and in different places, represented a timeless witness to a reality which was not subject to passing fashions in theological or philosophical thought. Inge saw reality as the spiritual world, a kingdom of values which he equated with the Platonic doctrine of Ideas. When accused of being more of a Platonist than a Christian his response was that in his opinion the Christian doctrine of the Incarnation perfected and completed the philosophical system of his much-admired Plotinus.

Inge was a successful, though strikingly individual churchman; using modern terminology one could say that although he operated 'within the system' he was not 'an organization man'. In 1904 his great friend HERBERT HENSLEY HENSON, then Rector of St Margaret's Westminster and later to be Bishop of Durham, offered him the living of All Saints, Ennismore Gardens, and in accepting the offer Inge at last moved from Oxford to the capital (and from bachelorhood to matrimony). However in 1907 he returned to academic life; he became Lady Margaret Professor of Divinity at Cambridge where he remained until 1911. At that point he received his famous preferment: he was appointed Dean of St Paul's Cathedral, a post he held for twenty-three years. After his retirement he continued his writing, both scholarly and journalistic, and the fruits of a lifetime's study of mysticism were displayed in his last book, *Mysticism in Religion*, published when he was eighty-eight.

Inge was brought up in the High-Church tradition but gradually he detached himself not only from the Anglo-Catholics but from the Evangelicals, the two powerful opposing wings of the Church. He claimed to represent a third party within the Church; he saw his 'religion of the spirit' as not only embodying the highest wisdom of the past but offering a profound spiritual relevance to the past but offering a profound spiritual relevance to the world of today and tomorrow. In *The Platonic Tradition In English Religious Thought* he wrote: 'My contention is that besides the combative Catholic and Protestant elements in the Churches, there has always been a third element, with very honourable traditions, which came to life again at the Renaissance, but really reaches back to the Greek fathers, to St Paul and St John, and further back still. The characteristics of this type of Christianity are – a spiritual religion based on a firm belief in absolute and eternal values as the most real things in the universe – a confidence that these values are knowable by man – a belief that they can nevertheless be known only by whole-hearted consecration of the intellect, will and affections to the great quest – an entirely open mind towards the discoveries of science – a reverent and receptive attitude to the beauty, sublimity and wisdom of the creation, as a revelation of the mind and character of the Creator – a complete indifference to the current valuations of the worldling.' It is this religion of the spirit which I have tried to reflect in the character of Jon Darrow.

Glamorous Powers is the second of a series of novels about the Church of England in the twentieth century. The first novel, *Glittering Images* was narrated by Charles Ashworth and set in 1937. The third novel, *Ultimate Prizes*, will focus on Neville Aysgarth after the war.